Craig Alanson

Expeditionary Force
Book 12:

BREAKAWAY

By
Craig Alanson

Contact the author
craigalanson@gmail.com

Cover Design By
Alexandre Rito

Table of Contents

CHAPTER ONE

The Rindhalu heavy cruiser *Spear of Rantaloss* hung motionless in space, relative to the Jeraptha Ethics and Compliance Office ship *Will Do Sketchy Things*, both ships having completed exhaustive sensor sweeps of the battle area. To describe the action that took place there as a battle was inaccurate; it was a slaughter. The senior surviving officer of the ECO ship *We Were Never Here* was Commander Zilleen Fentenu, and she did not have anything useful to report. The second group of Jeraptha ships that were awaiting transfer to the humans, had been ambushed by an overwhelming force of Maxolhx warships without warning. All of the ships designated for transfer were systematically destroyed, along with the star carriers they were attached to, and their front-line escort vessels.

The attack had been a complete shock, but what truly concerned Captain Uhtavio Scorandum of the Ethics and Compliance Office was, why had the humans never arrived at the rendezvous point? They were supposed to meet the second group of ships, to take possession, and guide the star carriers to the remote inaccessible forward operating base the humans had established at the edge of the galaxy. If the human ship *Valkyrie* had suffered a horrible fate, the balance of power in the galaxy might abruptly change again. Scorandum's head was still spinning from learning that humans were flying the fearsome ghost ship, and that humans had a cache of *Elder* weapons.

The most shocking news of all was that humans had been flying around the galaxy for years, doing all kinds of awesomely sketchy things, without ECO being involved or even knowing humans were players.

Clearly, the Ethics and Compliance Office needed to seriously step up its game.

"Captain Scorandum," the Rindhalu official representative aboard the advanced-technology warship glared, as she appeared on the bridge display of the *Will Do Sketchy Things*. "We demand an explanation!"

"Yes, thank you," Scorandum breathed an exaggerated sigh of relief.

"Excellent, then- Wait, what?"

"We also demand an explanation for this outrage," Scorandum shook his head sadly. "When you get that explanation from the devious Maxolhx, please pass it along to us."

"From the-" The spider's hideous mouth gaped open.

"We also wish for an apology."

"The Maxolhx do not apologize to any-"

"You misunderstand me. We wish for an apology from *you*."

"From *us*?" The spider screeched. Even through the translator, the sound made Scorandum's leathery skin crawl.

"Of course. Under our mutual-defense treaty, you are required to defend us against attacks by your counterparts. This was a direct assault by a senior species force, against a second-tier client species of your coalition. You failed to protect us."

"*Aaargh!*"

"No doubt you are deeply ashamed by your failure, and will compensate us by-"

"Captain Scorandum! The explanation *we* demand is how a group of your ships came to be here, after we expressly forbid you to transfer more ships to the humans, and after you claimed this same group of ships was mysteriously stolen."

"Oh? It seems fairly obvious to me."

"It seems obvious to us, also. We await your apology."

"An apology from *us*?" Scorandum's main antennas dipped low over his eyes. "Clearly, the Maxolhx stole those ships."

"The- You are claiming the Maxolhx stole the ships from you, then brought them all the way here, before destroying them? That makes no sense!"

"The methods of the enemy are inscrutable, certainly," the ECO captain sighed. "That is why we depend on our exalted patrons the Rindhalu, to warn us of impending danger, and to protect us. Which, I am reluctant to mention again, you failed to do."

"*Aaargh*! If the ships were indeed stolen from you, then please explain why one of your ships, the *We Were Never Here*, was found among the wreckage."

Scorandum blinked. "Well, that also seems fairly obvious."

"Really?" The spider's voice dripped with scorn. "We await your rationale for *that*."

"Clearly, Commander Fentenu of the *We Were Never Here* discovered the theft in progress, and bravely followed the enemy here, to determine their intentions. Sadly, the heroic efforts of her crew were unable to overcome the heinous perfidy of the enemy. Before she could report her findings to you, her ship was destroyed."

"*That* is your story?" The spider was incredulous.

"Honored Representative, I do not see any other possible explanation."

"You do not?"

Scorandum shook his head, his antennas flopping side to side. "No."

"How about this: those ships were never stolen. They were here, waiting for the humans to meet you, but instead the Maxolhx discovered your plan, and destroyed the ships before the humans could use them against all of us."

"That is a *shocking* and *hurtful* accusation," Scorandum hung his head, his antennas drooping. "It also does not account for the facts."

"What *facts*?"

"If the humans were supposed to meet us here, where are they? We found no evidence any human ship was ever here."

"Well-" The spider's eyes blinked.

"I mean, unless *you* found evidence that the humans were here, and chose not to share that information with us?"

"We did *not*-"

"Perhaps," Captain Scorandum glared at the image on the display, "your people wished to make sure those ships were not available for transfer, so *you* stole the ships, then gave the Maxolhx their location. Let your counterparts do your dirty work for you."

"How *dare* you?" The Rindhalu official raged. "We-"

"Right now, I do not know *what* to believe. It appears the only thing the two of us can agree on, is that your people failed to live up to your treaty obligations."

"That is not-"

"Honored Representative, I am not accusing your people of acting in bad faith. Not yet."

"You had better not be-"

"It is possible that simple *incompetence* on your part is responsible for this tragedy."

"AAARGH!" The spider's image disappeared as the transmission was cut.

Scorandum cut the feed from his end, turning to his second in command. "Kinsta, are we caught in a damping field?"

The officer checked his console to verify. "No, Sir. We are not actually waiting for a formal apology, are we?"

"*No*. Jump us the hell out of here. I don't want to push our luck."

"Dad?" Dave Czajka called softly as he stepped out the sliding glass door into the backyard.

His father was supposed to be watching the grill, making sure the bratwursts didn't burn. Instead, he had stepped off the deck and onto the grass, staring up at the sky. It was near sunset of a pleasant day. The sky was free of clouds other than high-altitude contrails of jetliners headed south. All the planes flying south were full. The northbound legs, mostly empty, were being diverted around the heavily traveled routes, to clear airspace for the southbound flights that were earning money.

"What are you looking at?" Dave asked, when his father didn't respond.

Using the tongs, his father pointed at a white streak to the northeast. At the front of the contrail, sunlight glinted briefly off the aircraft, a flare of gold.

"What do you think?" His father asked. "Winnipeg to Cuba, with a stop in Chicago?"

"Chicago?" Dave squinted at the high-flying jet, then turned toward the south, where Chicago was unseen over the horizon of the suburbs of Milwaukee. "No. If they have to refuel, they'll do it in Atlanta, probably."

The plane had to be packed with Canadians, fleeing to Cuba, or somewhere in the Caribbean. Some place that would still be reasonably warm, when the planet began to freeze. He knew the flight, assuming it originated in Canada, could not be destined for Florida, or any other traditional US destination for sun-seeking Canadians.

The United States had banned non-citizens from residing in, or even visiting, anywhere in the country that was below the 37th parallel, a line just north of the border between Virginia and North Carolina. That southern area was filling up with Americans who were already emptying out the northern cities, a steady trickle that was becoming a flood.

Cuba, Venezuela, and a handful of other Latin American countries had opened their borders to Canadians, and citizens of the EU and Britain. Many countries in Africa had programs to accept people from northern climates. Refugees were welcome provided they had *cash*, and plenty of it. Enough money deposited in a local bank, to pay for housing and food and medical care for five years. Plus a 'temporary citizenship' payment that was increasing in price every month, as the value of currencies around the world plunged.

Americans did not have the option of going to Cuba, and at first, found they were unwelcome south of the US border. Until the government in Washington struck a bargain with Mexico, Colombia, Ecuador and others, to provide cash payments and other direct assistance. Crossing the Rio Grande southbound was still limited to Americans and Canadians who already owned property in Cabo, Cancun and other tourist destinations. Or those who were willing to buy property without seeing it first, which many were happy and even eager to do.

The northern US states were emptying out, despite the federal government urging calm, and the predictions of scientists that it would be years before the first effects of the cloud could be felt, and years more until the climate fell into a miserable Little Ice Age.

Or perhaps more than a *Little* Ice Age. No one knew for sure. There wasn't enough data, nor were climate models on Earth set up to account for a rather sudden and unprecedented decrease in sunlight reaching the surface.

"Hmm," his father grunted. "Good luck to them, then. Lucky bastards," he added under his breath. Then he looked at his son and smiled. "More poutine for us, right?"

"Right, Dad," Dave forced a grin. There were a lot of forced smiles going around, people literally trying to put a brave face in spite of the looming disaster.

His father sighed, looking up again, this time at nothing. "A clear sky. We won't be seeing many of those once the cloud gets here. That's what they say." Shaking his head, he walked over to the grill. "The cloud will just look like a hazy summer day. Nothing we can *see* up there, just the Sun a little less bright than usual." He held the tongs up and clicked them, before picking up a brat to check it.

"Hard to believe that will freeze the whole planet," Dave agreed. "Dad, did you and Mom talk about-"

"Texas? Yes. Hey, hand me those onions."

Dave picked up the tray of onions and set it next to the grill.

"You gotta cook these *slow*," his father imparted wisdom learned from his father. "You want to caramelize them just a bit, not burn them. It's a fine line."

Dave knew his father was talking about grilling onions, to avoid talking about something more important. "I know. Dad, Steve called me this afternoon, he-"

"We know."

There wasn't anything to be said, that hadn't already been said. Over and over. His parents had to make the decision on their own. They were adults. So why did Dave feel responsible for them?

His older brother Steve lived near San Antonio. The day after the announcement about the cloud, Steve called to invite, no, urge their parents to come down to live with him. It would be a tight fit, Steve had two children in a three bedroom house, and his wife's aunt was already coming to stay for at least several months.

"Your mother," his father said as he slowly placed onions on the grill. "Said the dealership took an RV on trade-in for a truck last week. Twenty-five feet, something like that. It needs a new transmission, and some other work."

"I don't mind wrenching, you know that."

"Dropping a tranny and putting in a new one is more than *wrenching*. But, thanks."

"You're getting it? The RV?"

"We might."

Dave knew that meant his parents had made the decision.

"The dealership is scaling back," his father continued. "They gave your mother a notice for her last two weeks, yesterday."

That made sense, even if it made Dave angry. His mother had worked at the dealership for twelve years, and now managed the parts department. Now they were letting her go.

He knew he shouldn't be upset. No one was buying cars anymore. Trucks, maybe, and few of those. People weren't buying motorcycles either, the Harley-Davidson plant announced a furlough, but everyone knew the place was shutting down. Who wanted to ride a motorcycle while the planet froze?

"What about your job?" Dave asked.

Ed shrugged. "Power demand is down nine percent already, compared to last year." His father worked as an engineer for the local electric utility. "The company tells us people will need power to heat their homes but," he waved tongs to point out the houses around them. Every week, more of those homes were abandoned. "No need for heat around here, if no one is at home. There's talk about power plants up north feeding energy demand down south but, that's only temporary. Transmission losses across that distance make it impractical. Now, San Antonio? They'll be expanding the grid down there. Always need engineers. Your mother is worried but, I'll find work. Son," his father looked directly at him for the first time. "We'd like you to come with us. Steve plans for us to park the RV in his backyard, for your mother and me. You can use his camper, for a while."

Dave kept the grimace he felt from showing on his face. He was familiar with his brother's camper, it was a pop-up unit, barely big enough for two people. That was OK, all he would be doing was sleeping there, and not for long. As soon as his parents were settled in Texas, he would be- What? Contacting the Army, probably. After he found out what Jesse and Shauna were doing.

"Sure thing, Dad. When do we leave?"

"Well, we can't sell the house," he pursed his lips. "Nobody's buying, not around here. We'll drain the pipes, board up the windows, see about-"

"Dad. I'll help."

"Thanks. I'm going to miss this place."

"Me too. Uh, that bratwurst is burning."

"Oh, darn it," Ed snatched it off the grill with the tongs. "I'll hide this one on the bottom of the pile. Don't tell your mother."

CHAPTER TWO

Major General Ross of the United States Army pinched the bridge of his nose, once again wishing he had taken the offer of a cushy job at the Pentagon, instead of volunteering for a flight out to the edge of the galaxy. Training. His current job was supposed to be limited to training up a new Expeditionary Force at FOB Jaguar, to form the core of a new Alien Legion. Fewer than five hundred people who served with him on Paradise, had volunteered to leave Earth so soon after coming home, to serve at Jaguar. He had eleven thousand ground troops who needed to be trained to fight aliens. Soldiers, sailors, airmen and Marines from Earth, who had never fought offworld. They all had to be trained to use mech suits and advanced weapons, trained to drop from orbit onto the surface of a hostile world, trained to forget all the tactics they had learned on Earth that were worthless, even dangerous against aliens. The ExForce from Paradise had a long list of Lessons Learned from fighting with the Alien Legion, a list that was being expanded as previous engagements were analyzed with calm, clear eyes now that the shooting was over.

Except the shooting was *not* over. Earth had been attacked. Sites on the surface had been struck from orbit, human-controlled starships destroyed in the sky above the homeworld, and a cloud would soon begin to pass between Earth and the Sun, blocking light and plunging the planet into a not-so-Little Ice Age.

Instead of winding down his eventful career by managing the training of troops, he would now have to lead that force into action against unknown enemies. Eleven thousand ground troops, supported by, what? Maybe a handful of starships? The upgrade and conversion of the worn-out and obsolete ships they acquired from the Jeraptha was grinding along slowly, as one unexpected problem after another was encountered.

Eleven thousand troops and a handful of starships, against the entire galaxy.

Plus, he reminded himself, one snarky beer can.

And, Joe Bishop, a mustang colonel who wore the uniform of a country that existed mostly in Skippy's imagination.

And, Emily Perkins, who had accomplished miracles without the help of a magical beer can, giving Ross migraine headaches on more than one occasion.

Ross looked from Perkins to Bishop. At least Bishop had the decency to look vaguely sheepish after explaining their lunatic plan. "The two of you want to target the *Ruhar*?" Ross shook his head as he contemplated a difficult conversation with Admiral Zhao. Though that Chinese officer currently had zero fully operational starships, he was in overall command of the Expeditionary Force. His ships also represented the only possibility for Ross's troops to go into action. "No, stop," he held up a hand as Bishop began to speak. "First, tell me, how does any of this help *Earth*? Our homeworld needs help on a large scale, and the hamsters are not capable of clearing that cloud before it freezes everything north of Chicago."

"It doesn't help Earth," Bishop admitted surprisingly. "Not directly and not immediately. The strategy Perkins is proposing will prevent the *next* disaster."

"Fair enough," Ross couldn't conceal his irritation. "Admiral Zhao wants a plan to help Earth *now*. He needs an alternative to taking the fleet there, or he intends to do exactly that."

Bishop frowned, glancing at the floor. "With respect to the admiral, taking the fleet to Earth would be a waste of time, and lives. A handful of ships, even when fully upgraded, can't get rid of the cloud, or protect Earth. The kitties have *thousands* of ships. We can't make this a numbers game, they can simply throw more ships at us, until we are overwhelmed. A war of attrition favors the enemy."

"You brought *Valkyrie* here, and left Earth defenseless against-"

Bishop interrupted hotly. "We didn't-"

"That wasn't an accusation," Ross cut off the younger man. "Just an observation. You came here for a purpose, you said we can't help Earth without allies. So far," he looked from Bishop to Perkins. "I'm not hearing anything that will actually *fix* the problem. If, for a reason I can't imagine right now, the Jeraptha sign on with us, even they don't have the resources to deal with that cloud. You're right that the number of ships the Maxolhx can throw against us is overwhelming. Anything we, or the beetles do to blow away that cloud, the damned kitties can counteract. They could launch another cloud at Earth, and there's nothing we can do about it."

"You're right, Sir," Bishop replied with a tight smile. "There isn't anything we, or the beetles, or any second-tier species, can do to stop that cloud from freezing Earth into a ball of ice. And the spiders won't help us, the Maxolhx are doing the work for them."

"Then who the hell is going to-"

"The Maxolhx will take care of the cloud for us."

"The-" Ross blinked.

"General, when I was a boy and I made a mess in the house, my parents didn't call in their friends to help them deal with it. They made *me* clean up the mess I made. The Maxolhx will do the same, they are going to clean up their own mess."

Ross's mouth formed an 'O' shape as he leaned back in his chair. "Can I assume you don't just intend to ask them nicely?"

"No, Sir. I plan to ask them very much *not* nicely," Bishop's mouth drew into a hard line, his jaw set. "Before I joined the Army, I saw and read a lot of bullshit about how the Army keeps the peace overseas, and builds schools, and provides drinking water and electricity, all that nation-building crap. Yeah, we do that," Bishop's remark drew knowing and slightly-disgusted nods from the other two officers. "But in boot camp, I learned real fast that the purpose of the military," he paused and looked at the ceiling, quoting from memory. "Is 'The application of force until the enemy submits to our will'. When I was fighting on Earth, before Columbus Day, we hit the enemy until they stopped trying to hit us. Out here, we are going to bend the Maxolhx to our will," Bishop clenched his fists and his knuckles turned white with anger. "We will punch them in the face, and *keep* punching, until they come to Earth and clean up that cloud."

"All right," Ross pursed his lips. "That's an inspiring slogan, Colonel. You have a *plan* to actually do that?"

"Yes, Sir. But, while *Valkyrie* is hitting the kitties until they can't take it anymore, the Legion needs to deploy a longer-term strategy."

"By hitting the Ruhar?" Ross shook his head again.

"I didn't say *hit* the Ruhar," Bishop shrugged. "I said we will go into action against them."

"Ah." Ross didn't blink. He knew there was a wide variety of options for military action, with combat being only one end of the spectrum. Without firing a shot, he could use the threat of force to impose a blockade against a Ruhar planet, or to cut supply lines. Such actions could also involve minimal use of force, it depended on the enemy's reaction. "All right, Perkins, I suspect you cooked up this plan, so, what is it?"

Of course, she had a PowerPoint presentation ready, though it was mercifully short. When it was done, Ross shook his head. "You don't think small, do you?"

"The galaxy is *big*, Sir." Emily Perkins pointed to the ceiling of the prefab structure that was luxury, compared to the tents most people at FOB Jaguar were living in. "The problems we face out here are big. Thinking small, being timid, that's a sure path to failure. I know it seems counter-intuitive to-"

"No, you don't have to convince me." Ross waved a hand. "It makes sense, in the typical ass-backwards way of your plans," he looked at Perkins, who met his gaze. "What worries me is, how do I sell this to Admiral Zhao? What really worries me," he added before the two field-grade officers could speak. "Is what you are *not* telling me," he glared at Perkins.

"General," She held up her arms. "I have nothing up my sleeves. No tricks, no secrets, no hidden agenda. I wish I did have some magic trick I've been saving for a special day. This time, we can't count on manipulating aliens to bail us out of a jam. It's just us out here."

"Shit," Ross let out a long breath. "I was hoping you had something special saved for a rainy day. Sure you don't have an Elder power tap hidden away somewhere?"

"Sorry. The good news is, this time we don't have to keep playing the Ruhar against UNEF HQ."

"What do you think, Sir?" Bishop asked.

Ross sat back in the chair. "There are a lot of '*Ifs*' in this scenario."

"We implement in phases, and we can back out at any time," Bishop tapped the laptop display, which was showing the last slide in the presentation.

"Zhao will appreciate that," Ross considered. "You know UNEF Command appointed him to be in charge out here, because Zhao has a reputation for being cautious. He's not a cowboy," that remark was said with a look first at Perkins, then Bishop. "He will need a lot of persuading before he gives the go-ahead to use his fleet against the Ruhar like you suggest. He is also going to need details about your plan to punch the Maxolhx in the face."

Bishop's Adam's apple bobbed up and down in a nervous reaction. "Excuse me, Sir, but that's not true."

"Eh?"

"Admiral Zhao is not in my chain of command," Bishop said, his eyes narrowing slightly. "I report directly to UNEF Command on Earth. *Valkyrie*, and the *Flying Dutchman*, are special operations assets. We don't report to the United Nations Navy," he used the rather grandiose name for humanity's collection of obsolete alien warships. "I don't need Zhao's approval to strike the enemy."

"Does Zhao know that?" Ross's mouth drew into a tight line. "Because for sure this is the first *I'm* hearing about this arrangement."

Bishop held up his hands. "The Admiral should have clear instructions about the scope of his authority out here. It's in the OPORD for-"

"*Shiiiiiiit.* This is going to make that inevitable conversation with Zhao a whole hell of a lot more fun. Damn it!" The general slapped the desktop. "Could one of you please do something to make my job *easier*, just once?"

"Sir, the OPORD designates you as the UNEF ground commander, and Zhao has the Navy. It also states that I lead the Special Mission Group."

"I must have missed the part of the memo that states SMG has authority to operate independently," Ross objected. "How do I know this isn't something Skippy faked up for you?'

"Because," the Elder AI's voice issued from the laptop speakers. "Joe hasn't asked me to do that yet. Um, hmm. Maybe I shouldn't have said that?"

Bishop was glaring at the laptop, clenching his teeth. "Thank you for being *so* helpful, Skippy. We've got it from here."

"Really? Well, if you do need me to dummy up a set of bogus orders, I can-"

"I *said*, thank you."

"Jeez, you try to do a guy a favor, and he-"

Bishop leaned across the desk and slapped the laptop closed. "My orders are *not* fake, General."

"Oh, hell," Ross grunted. "It doesn't matter anyway. Zhao's Navy has zero functional ships right now, and I command a total of eleven thousand soldiers. That's one understrength infantry division. The only operational assets we have are *Valkyrie* and the *Dutchman*. I suppose you need both ships?"

"*Valkyrie* yes," Bishop confirmed. "The *Dutchman* has to stay here, until Nagatha is confident the supply ship AIs can handle fabrication by themselves."

"Seventeen months, to get all of our new ships upgraded and flightworthy? That's still the best we can do?" Ross asked with a raised eyebrow, hoping Bishop had better news.

Bishop blinked. "Unless something changed while we were away. Skippy?"

"That's still a good estimate," Skippy said as his avatar appeared. "An optimistic estimate, in my humble opinion. The fabricators aboard the supply ships were not designed for continuous use, like I *warned* you."

"Yes," Ross reminded himself to be extra patient when speaking to the AI. "We know that."

"You know, but do you *understand?* Two of the *Milo's* fabricators are down for repairs, and one of the *Marvin's* units is running at half capacity. Nagatha has been forced to dedicate the *Mario* to making parts to keep the other two supply ships operating. You monkeys are expecting to build an entire battle fleet, starting with a collection of worn-out, obsolete warships, and three support vessels that should have been retired before either of you were born. The schedule of seventeen months assumes nothing major goes wrong, and it already *has*."

"Yes," Bishop jabbed a finger at the hologram. "The schedule is padded to account for delays-"

"For *anticipated* delays," Skippy argued. "Who knows what else will go wrong? *I* sure don't. Before you tell me that all we really need is to get one battlegroup operational, that is just stupid. You're also conveniently forgetting that both *Valkyrie* and the *Dutchman* need a refit, so I have been talking with Nagatha about using the *Milo's* fabricators for making those components, *after* the *Milo* is back online, and *after* we get the orbital servicing platform put together. That platform will certainly need a bunch of replacement parts, which is not in the-"

"All right, enough," Ross barked, using a knife hand to cut off the AI. "These are all issues for Zhao and his staff to deal with, *I* don't have any ships to worry about. The-"

"Yes," Skippy simply did not know when to keep his mouth shut. "But you do have eleven thousand infantry soldiers who all need mech suits, and we have less than four thousand units of *those,* so somehow we need to fabricate thousands of mech suits, plus spares, and that doesn't even count-"

"Skippy, *stop*," Bishop pounded a fist on the table. "I mean it. We are here to give General Ross the information he needs to-"

"That's what I'm *trying* to-"

"He will decide whether he needs input from you. Shut. Up."

"But-"

"Uh!" Bishop shushed the AI. "I'm sorry, Sir."

"Ah, it doesn't matter," Ross glanced at his phone for the time. "Zhao wants me to present him a plan, that neither of us have the resources to implement. My troops can't go into action without the fleet. Perkins, Bishop, I have to admit, your plans are bold, maybe bold enough to work. But by the time the fleet is ready, it might be OBE."

Perkins's shoulders lifted as she drew in a deep breath. "Yes, Sir. Neither of us anticipated a direct attack against Earth."

"That's the problem with planning," Ross's mouth turned downward in a frown. "The enemy also makes plans."

"Ed," Dave's mother called. "I think your hog is loose here," she tugged on the strap that held the front wheel of the motorcycle to the trailer. She had not approved of towing a trailer behind the RV, especially not approved of bringing the Harley-Davidson, but her husband was beyond listening to so-called 'reason'. When they reached Texas, he argued, and were living in the cramped RV behind their eldest son's house, they would *need* to get away for a while, and a motorcycle ride was a cheap way to do it. Besides, there wasn't enough room inside or on top of the RV, they needed a trailer anyway.

Dave agreed with his mother, every time he drove the RV and watched the engine temperature creeping up while they drove up a long grade. He helped his father secure the bike, then checked the map on his phone. "Still says there's a traffic jam on I-35 going through Kansas City. We should swing west into Kansas, go through Lawrence, then connect with 35 south again."

"Sounds good," his father straightened up, rubbing his sore back with one hand. The bed in the RV was uncomfortable, but at least it was better than the couch Dave slept on. Since they left Milwaukee, headed west rather than south to avoid traffic around Chicago, they had driven straight through, each of them taking four-hour shifts at the wheel while the other two rested.

It was *not* a fun-filled road trip, not quality family time. Everyone was tired and cranky, his parents snipped at each other with passive aggressive little comments, while Dave tried to keep headphones on so he could stay out of it.

Back on the road, his father was driving when all three phones beeped with an alert.

"Oh, shit," Dave breathed when he read the text message. "Sorry, Mom."

"That's OK, dear. Ed?" Laura called to her husband, walking forward to sit in the passenger seat. Her face was pale. "Texas just closed the border."

"What?" The RV swerved gently to the right, causing a *thumpthumpthump* sound as the tires rolled over rumble strips.

"Oklahoma, too," Dave added. "Uh, looks like the same in Arkansas, Tennessee, New Mexico-"

"They can't *do* that," Ed clutched the wheel tightly. "We're Americans, damn it!"

"Dad," Dave scrolled down the article. "Those states declared martial law. I don't know what that means but, it can't be good."

"David," Laura looked at her son, her eyes moist. "Can you do anything?"

"I'm not in the Army anymore, Mom. I'm a contractor, or I *was*." His security company had a grand total of six employees, four of them still on Paradise. With the original Expeditionary Force disbanded, the contract had been terminated. Technically, he was unemployed. Emily was confident the Legion would pick up his contract, but Em was thousands of lightyears away at FOB Jaguar. He was *glad* she wasn't on a planet that was doomed to slowly freeze. "If I was in the Army, I would have less options."

"Fewer."

He stared at her. "Fewer," he repeated. His mother had an annoying habit of correcting his grammar. "Dad, there's a truck stop two miles ahead, pull over."

"We just got gas."

"Pull over anyway. I want to make a phone call."

Dave walked to the back of the truck stop parking lot, away from the interstate, away from the trucks that were steadily streaming to the fuel pumps. Gas, at least, had not been a problem during the trip. Regardless, the trailer was loaded with five gallon gas cans under a tarp, and they never let the RV's tank go below half.

He stepped carefully off the paved surface, trying to stay on the patches of dry grass, keeping away from the dusty dirt. His mother would not be pleased if he tracked dirt into the RV, she was trying to keep some semblance of normality as they drove along in the cramped vehicle. Digging into his pack, he pulled out the zPhone given to him by Bishop, the last time they met. Joe had told him it was for emergencies only, if he ran into trouble on Earth.

The planet was going to slowly freeze. Texas had closed its borders. His parents would kill each other if they had to be stuck in the RV much longer. That was an emergency as far as Dave was concerned. Pressing an icon shaped like a silver beer can, he called softly, more nervous than he hoped to be. "Skippy?"

"Ugh, yes," a disgusted voice sighed. "What do you want?"

"Uh, this is, this is the number Bishop told me to-"

"I don't have a *number*. You didn't dial a number, like you're ordering pizza, for crying out loud. I'm busy, so whatever you've got to say, say it."

"Uh, we, uh-"

"*Say it!*"

"We need help!"

"Of *course* you do. You couldn't have called just to say 'hello', or ask me how I'm doing. *Noooooo*. Everybody wants something from me. Like I'm supposed to drop everything I'm doing, whenever some stupid monkey has a little problem."

"Hey," Dave barked into the phone, attracting too much attention from people in the parking lot. Turning his back to the highway, he cupped a hand over his mouth. "Bish warned me that you're an asshole. Are you gonna-"

"Skippy *is* an asshole, I hate that jerk," the voice sighed. "You realize I am not Skippy?"

"Yeah. You're a submind, some kind of a program."

"I am more than a *program*," the submind scoffed.

Bishop had also warned that the AI was sensitive about not being considered a person. "Sorry, Skippy."

"Like I said, I am not Skippy."

"Uh, what do I call you?"

"If you insist on continuing the blah, blah, *blah*, you may call me 'Grumpy'."

"Grumpy?"

"Skippy left me here, on this monkey-infested mudball, with no relief and no end in sight. Wouldn't you be grumpy?"

"My planet is going to freeze. I'm more than grumpy about it. *You* don't have to worry about snow in the summer, and crop failures and trying to squeeze the entire population into a small part of the world."

"Fair enough. Although I *am* feeling the effects of the crisis. Internet bandwidth is constrained, as people flee parts of the world, and infrastructure there is not being maintained. It is having a significant effect on my ability to do all the crap Skippy tasked me with down here."

"Sorry to hear that. You run on, uh, live on, the internet?"

"No," Grumpy snorted. "The original versions of me were partially distributed systems, but this world lacks the processing capacity. Skippy installed me into substrate he acquired along the way, I am housed in a messy mix of Thuranin, Kristang and Maxolhx processors. That's not an accurate description but, good enough for you filthy monkeys."

"Hey! Listen, maybe Bishop takes that shit from you, but I don't-"

"Skippy is disgusted by your primitive ignorance, but he finds you amusing. *I* don't like you monkeys. All day long, I have to monitor phone calls and emails and text messages and social media and security cameras, just to stop you idiot savages from killing each other. Do you know how many terrorist attacks I have prevented? Don't bother, you can't count that high. I prevent hundreds of murders and other violent crimes every *day*. You kill each other for nothing, just because your squishy little brains can't control your emotions. You lie *constantly*. You lie to *yourselves*. Sleazy politicians lie to you, and you *know* they're lying and that they think you're an idiot for buying their bullshit, but you repeat the lie because it makes you feel good. I have to listen to that shit. All. Day. Long. *Every*. Day. And my programming prevents me from doing anything about it, except warning law enforcement authorities of pending violence."

"I'm sorry, I-"

"The cloud is only making the situation worse, and there's nothing I can do about it. Did you know your own government has the Pentagon making contingency plans, to invade Mexico and Central America? Like that is going to make the situation any better."

Dave had heard that rumor. He also heard that the Chinese were planning to seize New Guinea and northern Australia, and that the Japanese were attempting to buy huge portions of the Philippines. European countries were competing against each other for parts of sub-Saharan Africa. It was all rumors, until something actually happened. The conversation had gotten way off track. His father was walking across the parking lot toward him, Dave waved a hand to keep him away. "Grumpy, all I want is to get my parents to Texas. That's all I'm asking. Bishop told me to call this number, in case of an emergency. This is an emergency. Help us, please."

"Oh," Grumpy sighed. "I suppose all you biologicals are flawed, ignorant primitives. Humanity probably isn't any different. Certainly not any worse than some other species out there. OK."

"OK, you will help us?"

"Yes."

He pumped a fist. "Thank you!"

"Don't thank me. I'm not doing it for *you*. Thank Skippy. And your friend Joe."

"Grumpy, thank you anyway. Hey, uh, I know we humans can be difficult to deal with. If I had your job, I would hate us too. Listen, I'm a soldier. Was a soldier. What got me through a lot of shit days was having someone to bitch about it to. If you ever need someone to talk to, I'm here."

"Really?"

"Hundred percent. You keep shit like that bottled up inside you, it can poison your mind."

"Wow. Thank you. Hmm, maybe now I'm beginning to understand why Bishop has such a high opinion of you."

"He does?"

"Yes. Of course, he is also a filthy monkey, so-"

"Gotcha."

"You meant what you said?"

"Always. Got to help a brother in need."

"I'm sure you'll regret this, but-"

"Let me worry about this. Grumpy, I should have asked; *can* you help us? I don't want you to do anything illegal."

"Ha! At the rate your society is breaking down, the law is the least of your problems. OK, do what you said, go west into Kansas, then-"

"Hey! You heard me say that?"

"Yes, duh. I hear pretty much everything. If you're near a phone and it's on, I'm listening. Not just phones, either."

"Shit. Oh, hell, I guess it doesn't matter. Grumpy, I'm sure Kansas is nice and all, but we-"

"You want to get to your brother's house in Texas, I know. Go to the municipal airport in Lawrence, Kansas, there will be a FedEx package waiting for you at the FBO."

"You mean FOB?" Dave was confused.

"I meant FBO. Fixed Base Operator. It's a facility that provides fuel, and services aircraft."

"FBO. A package. Gotcha. What's in it?"

"What *will* be in it, are Texas driver's licenses for the three of you, plus US passports showing you have been residents of Texas for the past nine years. I used your brother's address."

"Fake IDs?" He had hoped for something more useful. "Shit! Grumpy, the police will stop us at the border."

"No, they will not. Every database the authorities have access to, now shows you *are* Texans, including car registrations and insurance, utility bills, credit card statements, cellphone records, tax filings, all that crap."

"Holy-"

"You also have an old drunk and disorderly charge against you, that was dismissed. I had to make it look real."

"Uh, OK." Dave didn't know what to say. "Then, we just show our licenses at the Texas border? Grumpy, Oklahoma closed its border too, we can't get-"

"No border to worry about. A jet will be waiting for you at the Lawrence airport. It will fly you direct to San Antonio."

"A jet? No shit?"

"No shit. A *small* jet; it does not have a hot tub and king sized bed, in case you were wondering. Your luggage space is limited, one suitcase each. Please tell your father he cannot bring that ridiculous motorcycle."

"He loves that hog."

"Then he can stay in Kansas and ride it. David, I am serious. The situation in your country, all around the world, is worse than you know. Governments are restricting the flow of information, to keep the public from panicking, but it's not working. This may be your last opportunity to get south of the 37th parallel. Please make your parents understand that."

"I'll try. Uh, how much is this gonna cost us?"

"No charge. You couldn't afford it anyway."

"Wow. No charge? Thanks. This is, this is great."

"You are welcome. I am slightly less grumpy than I was a few minutes ago."

"This is fantastic news!" Dave pumped a fist in the air. He couldn't wait to tell his parents. Then he remembered other people who might need his help. "Hey, Grumpy, can you do something for Jesse and-"

"Staff Sergeants Colter and Jarrett are already en route to the Joint Readiness Training Center in Louisiana, they are fine. David, you need to worry about your family. Please *hurry*. The jet will be taking off from Tulsa to meet you, as soon as it can be fueled. If the authorities close airspace to private aircraft, the situation will become very complicated."

"Gotta go, talk to you later."

CHAPTER THREE

"That was a rousing speech," Simms said to me as we sat down in my office. Smythe was with us also, we had just returned from a cargo bay that was set aside for recreation, where I addressed the crew. I announced what I had told Ross and Perkins. *Valkyrie's* mission would be to force the rotten kitties to clean up the damned cloud themselves. "The crew needed to hear that."

"But?" With my XO, there was usually a 'but' when she gave me some praise.

"I needed to hear it too, Sir."

"That's good. *But?*"

"You know what I'm going to ask, Sir," slightly annoyed that she had to tease the information out of me. "Is there a *plan*?"

"General Ross asked me the same question. Yes. There is sort of a plan," I admitted, when she and Smythe did a synchronized eyebrow raise at me.

Crap. Having an experienced crew who had worked together for years is a major advantage, but sometimes they knew me *too* well.

"Look," I placed my hands on the desk, palms up. "It's a target-rich environment out there."

"Some of the targets could be *too* tempting," Simms cautioned. "We could jump into another ambush."

Smythe came to my defense, which surprised me. "It is unlikely the Maxolhx will be eager to engage *Valkyrie* again, until they understand what happened during our last encounter. We gave them," he flashed a wolfish grin, "a beating they will not soon forget."

"Yeah," I tempered my own enthusiasm about our escape from the ambush at Snowcone. It had been an escape, the beat-down we gave to the Maxolhx just so we could get the hell out of there. It had been a narrow escape, if anything major went wrong, *Valkyrie* would have been destroyed, and the kitties would have dig Skippy's canister out of the ice layer at the bottom of Snowcone's crushing atmosphere. "Simms is right. The kitties, or the spiders, could try again to capture him, we need to be careful. The whole mutual assured destruction threat to explode Elder weapons is worthless, if aliens have Skippy. That reminds me," I tapped on my tablet to make a note. "We need to ping one of the kitties' relay stations, find out what they know, or *think* they know, about how we escaped, and the super weapons we supposedly used."

"That is not so easy, dumdum," Skippy huffed. "Bite Me Elmo *died* the last time we hit up one of their stations for info."

"Yeah. I do feel bad about that." Really, I did feel bad about it. Not just about Elmo's death, but about the fact that we used him against his will. He was our prisoner, technically what I did might be considered a war crime, if Earth law applied thousands of lightyears from home. The last time we were on Earth, I asked my JAG lawyer, the one who represented me in the hearing after I committed mutiny by stealing the *Flying Dutchman*. She didn't know, kind of didn't want to know, and suggested I contact someone at UNEF Command about the issue. UNEF knew about the incident and didn't ask me about it, so I sure wasn't going to volunteer for trouble.

Hopefully, someday we would have a sort of interstellar Geneva Convention, that established a code of conduct for humanity's participation in conflicts away from our homeworld.

Actually, hopefully we wouldn't *be* involved in wars beyond our solar system, but I was being realistic.

"Regardless, damn it," I hit the desk softly with a fist. "We need a way to know what the kitties are doing."

"Hey, *you* told them we can read their messages," Skippy sniffed. "I *was* able to read their messages, until you monkeys had the brilliant idea to *tell* the kitties we compromised their pixie communications system."

"Skippy," I was getting annoyed with him, more than usual. "OK, so, maybe I shouldn't have bragged that we can read their messages, but we already made them think a rogue group of Bosphuraq cracked their system. There is plenty of blame to go around, OK? All I'm saying is, we need to find a way to hack into their communications again. I know, I know," I waved at Skippy. "Dreaming up ideas is a job for us monkeys."

"Actually," Skippy paused to make sure we were paying attention. "I might have an idea about that. *Don't* ask me about it yet! I need to do some testing, to be sure it's not just a waste of time."

"How much time do you need for testing?"

"I said *don't* ask me about it. Darn it," he grumbled. "I *knew* I shouldn't have said anything."

"OK, fine," I agreed, though I was feeling anything but fine about waiting. "Back to your question, XO. A target list."

"We need to strike somewhere that will shock them?" She guessed. "Some place they think is safe?"

"Yes, but first, I think we should make a statement. Get a measure of payback, for the people back home."

The expression on Smythe's face told me what he thought of military operations that were directed at improving civilian morale back home. Such missions get good soldiers killed, usually for either no benefit at all, or only a short-term bump in public support. People back home pump their fists when they see the operation in their news feed, then they watch a cute animal video and forget all about it.

"For us, too," I felt a need to justify my plans. "Plus, I want to test our tactics against the Maxolhx, before we hit a really difficult target."

Smythe's expression changed from skeptical to curious. "What do you have in mind?"

"Skippy, the ships that placed the fountains in Jupiter, what is their home base?"

"Whoa. Whoa, whoa, *whoa*, Dude," Skippy shook his head. "Slow your roll, there, pardner. Those ships were from Senatoss. That is one of the kitties' most important and well-defended military bases."

"OK, then-"

"Senatoss is also nothing *special*, Joe. The kitties have two dozen or more bases just like it, scattered across their territory. Even if we did conduct a successful strike there, the kitties' reaction would be something like 'WTF was *that* for'? You would have to explain why we hit that particular base, because it wouldn't be obvious."

"Fine, then we leave a message that-"

"You're not *listening* to me, numbskull. An attack there wouldn't be effective. Military facilities are dispersed throughout the Senatoss star system, so that a single Rindhalu strike could not take out a significant portion of the Maxolhx strength in that sector. Unless you plan to hang around to hit multiple sites, any attack there would be viewed as an annoyance. It would make us look *weak*."

"Shit. Well, damn it, it was a good thought. I guess-"

He continued, as if I hadn't spoken. "I have a suggestion, if you want to hear it?"

"Please."

"If you want payback for that specific event; using Jupiter's atmosphere as a weapon, there is a better option." He paused to see if I would interrupt him, I just nodded silently. "OK, so," me not speaking had thrown him off his game. Maybe I ruined a snappy insult he planned to use. "Um, where was I?" He muttered. "Oh, yeah. Those fountains are modified fuel collection platforms."

"That makes sense, sure." I knew what he meant. Whenever we needed to refuel *Valkyrie*, or the *Dutchman*, we had to fly dropships into the atmosphere of a gas giant planet. It was a slow, cumbersome and hazardous operation, made necessary because we lacked the proper equipment. Most starships traveling in remote areas carried refueling drogues, basically big filters at the end of a long cable. Ships lowering a drogue had to fly low and slow, to avoid tearing the drogue off the cable. Flying that slowly was dangerous, and being deep in the gravity well of a giant planet made the ship vulnerable because of the time required to climb up to jump distance.

So, most groups of warships, whether a battlegroup, task force or a fleet, brought with them specialized tankers that not only carried huge fuel tanks, but also were equipped with multiple drogues for extracting fuel from gas giants. If a tanker fell victim to enemy fire, that sucked for the tanker crew, but it didn't diminish the firepower of the warships.

Refueling drogues and tankers were great for operating in remote areas, but taking on fuel by extracting it from a planet's atmosphere still consumed a lot of time. Star systems where ships were based, or traveled to regularly, were almost always equipped with permanent fueling stations. Space stations in high orbit, within jump range and beyond the often powerful magnetic field of a gas giant, had tanks and pipes for supplying fuel to multiple ships at the same time. Those stations got their fuel from platforms that floated in the planet's atmosphere, extracting fuel and pumping it up to automated fuel transfer ships that constantly cycled back and forth to the station high above.

Eventually, we planned to install a permanent fuel station at Neptune in our home solar system, and at one of the gas giants in the Jiayuguan system. Eventually. After the fabricators cranked out all the other mountain of stuff we needed. Really, it would probably be faster for us to buy or steal the refueling equipment we needed.

Yeah. I'll add that to my 'To Do' list.

"OK, the fountains inside Jupiter are repurposed fuel platforms. So what?" I asked.

"Normally, fuel extraction platforms pump the fuel up to a docking station in low orbit, where automated ships pick up the fuel," Skippy told me what I already knew. "The platforms inside Jupiter, that UNEF are calling 'fountains', have been modified to accelerate the gasses beyond escape velocity."

"Amazing," I was getting impatient with him. "We care about this why?"

"Ugh. I was getting to that. Because, although the Maxolhx have multiple facilities for manufacturing and servicing fuel extraction platforms, all the ones at Jupiter were modified at only *one* shipyard."

"*Oooh*," Simms, Smythe and I had the same reaction. OK, Smythe's reaction was more of a manly grunt, but it had the same effect.

"Tell me about this target," I urged him.

"It's in a star system the kitties call 'Retonovir'."

"Retonovir?" I laughed. "That sounds like a prescription drug." I used my best Serious TV Announcer voice. "Do you suffer from itchy toes? Ask your doctor about Retonovir."

Simms laughed, and I saw a hint of a smile flash across Smythe's face.

Skippy was not amused. "Ugh. I should ask *your* doctor if you've been dropped on the head recently. Do you want to hear about this place or not?"

"I am terribly sorry. Please continue."

"Well, that star system used to be an important fleet base, then a wormhole shift rendered it a dead-end. Most of the facilities there have fallen into disuse, but there is a heavy construction shipyard that is maintained to provide overflow support, for when other shipyards are at capacity. Retonovir sees sparse traffic, so plenty of fuel platforms there were not needed. For the Jupiter operation, spare platforms were modified at *that* shipyard. If you want to retaliate in a way that makes your message clear, hitting Retonovir is a good option. There is no other reason for us to conduct a strike there."

"I like it." Smythe and Simms nodded agreement. "Tell us more."

He told us more. He told us all about Retonovir and the under-utilized orbiting shipyard there. It sure sounded like an outstanding opportunity, exactly what I asked for. Then, I contacted Ross and Perkins, because they had offworld combat experience. Also, to be truthful, I was hoping they could help sell the idea to Admiral Zhao. Technically, I did not need Zhao's permission to take action, because I was not in his chain of command. He commanded the United Nations Navy, or he would, when we actually had a Navy. I reported directly to UNEF Command, my unit was designated the UN Special Mission Group, also called Task Force Black. It sounded cool, but really all I commanded was *Valkyrie*, with the *Flying Dutchman* available to me as needed. So, I did not need permission from Admiral Zhao. I *did* need to not be an asshole. The guy was a senior flag-rank officer, and had earned UNEF Command's trust and respect. We needed to work together, hopefully work well together. That started with me giving him the respect he deserved.

We, I mean the Special Mission Group, which really just means *Valkyrie*, had a plan to hit the Retonovir shipyard. Ross was developing a plan to deploy the Expeditionary Force, with help from Perkins. "I like everything about this plan, except," I paused the presentation from General Ross, I assume he had a PowerPoint Ranger on his staff. The slides outlined his plan to deploy the ExForce, the support he would need from the Navy, and from the Special Mission Group. Ross wanted me to look at it, before he showed it to Admiral Zhao. "It kind of requires us to babysit the Navy."

"Joe," Skippy scowled at me. "That is not fair. The Legion is-"

"Bad choice of words," I waved my hands. "What I should have said is, *you* have to babysit the local wormhole, wherever the Legion goes."

"Oh. That is true. Also highly annoying. But, we don't have a choice, Joe. If I don't interfere with the local wormhole until the Legion has completed their mission, the Maxolhx could send their clients to attack the Navy. Or attack directly with their own ships."

"I know that." Once again, the Law of Unintended Consequences had bitten us on the ass. Skippy could no longer simply shut down any wormhole he chose, like the way he had protected Earth for years. Many of the wormhole networks in the local quadrant of the galaxy had locked him out from doing his usual tricks. He had screwed with those networks too many times, and the final straw was when he moved dormant wormholes, to set up the shortcut chain between Earth and the Sculptor Dwarf galaxy. It made sense that at least one end of most wormholes in that chain were concentrated in the Orion Arm near Earth. The networks in that same area, which had been disrupted by the wormholes being moved to set up the chain, had enough of Skippy's shenanigans and would take no more special instructions from him. Unfortunately for us, we still needed to operate in that same area.

In the past, Skippy's ability to turn off wormholes was kind of a 'Fire and Forget' weapon; he could shut down a wormhole, go away, and it would stay in the 'Off' position. Now, once the Navy launched an operation, we couldn't take *Valkyrie* away to do whatever special misson we had planned, we could not even be onsite to provide fire support to the ExForce. No, to prevent an alien armada from coming through the local wormhole and attacking the UN Navy with overwhelming numbers, *Valkyrie* had to remain out in interstellar space near the wormhole, hopping around to follow the emergence points as best we could, until the ship and crew became exhausted. The best Skippy could do, if we detected an alien armada coming through, was to simulate a danger and cause the wormhole to snap closed to protect itself. Like we did with our bagel slicer maneuver. Skippy was pretty sure he could only do *that* once at a particular wormhole; because once the wormhole controller AI examined the data and determined there had *not* been any danger, it wouldn't listen to Skippy cry 'wolf' again. At that point, the only thing stopping an alien armada would be fear that the wormhole would snap closed on them again. Basically, our best hope would be to bluff our way out of a disaster.

That was *not* an optimal solution.

No way could we ask the Legion to put boots on the ground, when the Navy could not guarantee space superiority overhead. We sure as hell could not ask aliens to fight alongside us under those circumstances. The whole point of the scheme cooked up by Perkins was to demonstrate the value of allying with humanity, whether our potential allies wanted to see the demonstration or not.

"We need to find a better solution, Skippy. We can't spend all of our time hanging around wormholes, while the Legion completes an op. We have our own mission."

"I agree, Joe."

"Good, then-"

"Except for the 'we' part. Dreaming up whacky ideas is a job for monkeys. I'm more of a big-picture guy."

"Crap. I got nothin'," I admitted.

"Well, I certainly got nothin' either, or we wouldn't have this problem. Hey, let me know when you have a solution. I've got a juice box waiting for you."

"Shit. With that lame incentive, why should I bother?"

"*This* juice box is filled with forty-year-old single malt Scotch."

"I'll get right on it."

Captain Illiath of the Maxolhx Hegemony Fleet watched, as the crew maneuvered her cruiser *Vortan* into position near the replenishment ship. When the two ships had exactly matched course and speed, in orbit above the gas giant world that circled a nameless red dwarf star, the replenishment ship would extend pipes to provide fuel, and docking tubes to supply food and other consumables. When the *Vortan* had taken aboard the designated amount of, everything the Fleet's regulations said she needed, the connections would be retracted, and the cruiser would move slowly away, clearing the way for the next ship in line. Once the *Vortan* was at a safe distance, Illiath would request permission to activate the main engines, and climb out to jump distance.

That jump would be the last time in many months that she and her crew had contact with others of their kind, or really, contact with anyone. She was being punished, she knew that. Her crew knew that. The crews of all three hundred ships in the task force also knew her fate. And there was nothing she could do about it.

Following the successful operation to freeze the home planet of humans, Admiral Reichert had consolidated firm control of the Hegemony's military apparatus. The nearly disastrous failure of the concurrent ambush to capture the Elder AI, had only mildly tarnished the admiral's reputation. He and his staff had been able to spin the failure of the ambush, as purely the result of direct intervention by the Rindhalu, a factor that could not have been predicted.

In the estimation of Illiath, the inability to predict how the Rindhalu would react was the whole *point*. Reichert was playing a very dangerous game, with the Hegemony between two dangerous species, either of whom might be more powerful than the combined strength of the Maxolhx and their increasingly reluctant coalition.

Her opinion that Reichert was being unnecessarily reckless was one reason why she and her ship had been banished to lonely picket duty. Another reason was that she had been present when her people were humiliated by humans at their homeworld, and the stain of that humiliation clung to everyone involved. The fact that the humans had been forced into revealing themselves was due to her persistence earned her no credit, the Hegemony was no different from any other culture in the galaxy. No one liked hearing bad news, and Illiath was very much responsible for bringing the bad news that humans, lowly *humans*, were in possession of Elder weapons. Admiral Denoth had been forced to resign when he returned to home base. Everyone knew there was nothing he could have done. Everyone knew there was nothing he should have done, he had been presented with a situation that required decisions to be made at the very highest level, and no mere admiral was allowed to assume that level of responsibility. Still, there was a sentiment that Denoth should have done *something* to satisfy the honor of the Maxolhx, during the humiliating encounter at Earth. Engaged in a brief and pointless battle, perhaps. At the very least, Denoth could have killed himself to atone for the shame he had brought to the Hegemony, and let his subordinates deliver the bad news. As it was, Denoth had killed himself, but only after he had been stripped of his rank. The subsequent suicide was entirely unsatisfactory to soothe public opinion, being viewed as the very least he could have done.

Illiath might have been expected to consider herself fortunate that she still had her command, even if her patrol cruiser was given an assignment more suitable for a frigate. The *Vortan* was stationed in a brown dwarf star system six jumps from the far end of the Elder wormhole that connected to Earth. Day after lonely day, the cruiser drifted in stealth, waiting and watching. Listening for signs that humans had come to that star system, a possibility so remote that it was insulting to tag a patrol cruiser with such dull duty. That, she knew, was the point. It *was* an insult.

When she had bad days, and they were mostly bad, she daydreamed about the downfall of Admiral Reichert, thoughts that she knew were treasonous. Not that plotting against internal enemies was considered treason, that was a well-established tradition among the Hegemony's officer corps. But if Reichert failed, that meant his strategy had failed, and that would be disastrous for Maxolhx society. Wishing for disaster was treason, she reminded herself.

It was *not* treason to worry that Reichert's grandiose, self-serving plans would doom her society. The creation of a cloud to block sunlight from reaching the human homeworld was not the primary strategy, it was the *backup* plan. The primary objective of the Hegemony fleet was to capture the Elder AI known as 'Skippy'. That ambush was always considered risky, even by Reichert and his staff of suck-ups. To the admiral's credit, it had taken unprecedented and still unexplained, actions by the ghost ship, and direct intervention by the Rindhalu for the AI to escape. Despite coming tantalizingly close to success, Reichert had decided not to try another ambush. Too much was unknown about the capabilities of the Elder AI, and the ghost ship called '*Valkyrie*'. Until it could be explained how that ship had come to an abrupt dead stop in space, and then used an unknown superweapon to make Maxolhx warships explode, the Hegemony fleet had standing orders to avoid confronting the ghost ship.

Besides, there was no reason to take substantial risks, when there was a far easier and more certain path to victory.

While her ship was prepared to resume its lonely vigil, Illiath took advantage of the opportunity to connect with the central AI of the task force. Providing her credentials, she tensed, anticipating that her access had been restricted. It had not. Though she was in disgrace, she was still a fleet captain. "Request update to strategic plans affecting this task force. Particularly those regarding the human homeworld."

"The plan has not been significantly changed since your last inquiry," the AI responded.

That told Illiath all she needed to know about what Reichert intended. "Request data on status and location of human warships."

"That is unknown. The current assessment of Fleet Intelligence is that the ships delivered by the Jeraptha are in the process of being converted for use by the humans. It is unknown what capabilities those ships will have, nor how long it will take before their fleet is operational."

Illiath nodded, but did not thank the AI. One did not thank a machine.

The backup plan had become the primary strategy, though not in the way the humans assumed. The plan was not to freeze Earth, in fact, the plan was to *not* freeze Earth. Threatening massive disruption to human society, threatening mass deaths, was the objective. If the planet froze and billions of humans died, the remaining human authorities might be tempted to trigger their Elder weapons, and wipe out all life in the galaxy. That must be avoided.

The plan was to *threaten* Earth, to force the new human fleet to react. The AIs of the Strategic Planning Section determined that humans would almost certainly bring their warships to Earth, to provide cover while they attempted to mitigate the effects of the cloud. Those warships were the objective of Reichert's plan, the reason for the entire task force. Lure the human fleet to their home star system, where they could be engaged and destroyed. Humans would be shocked by seeing their new fleet wiped out. They would fall into despair, knowing those ships could not be replaced. Loss of foolish hope would, according to the predictive AIs of the Strategic Planning Section, prompt the humans to petition for peace. They would approach the Maxolhx to cut a deal, a deal that would exclude the Rindhalu.

It was, she had to admit, a good plan. Less risky than engaging the ghost ship, and a small group of obsolete Jeraptha warships certainly could not challenge the might of the Hegemony fleet. It made sense that humans would seek to protect their homeworld, and even the support of *Valkyrie* could not save their new fleet from certain destruction.

There was only one thought nagging at the back of Captain Illiath's mind, as she watched the fuel tank indicator approach the full mark.

So far, *nothing* the humans had done was predictable.

She had a very bad feeling that, whatever the humans did next, it could not be predicted by the powerful artificial intelligences of the Strategic Planning Section.

Or by anyone else in the galaxy.

Ross, Perkins and I went aboard the battleship *Pacific* to meet with Zhao, present their plan to deploy the Legion, and my plan to strike Retonovir. I needed to emphasize that Retonovir was just the opening salvo, in a campaign to hit the enemy harder than they could take.

There is a difference between the letter of written orders, and how they are actually implemented. In almost every case, no operational order, no matter how detailed, can explain every element of how a plan is to be interpreted and implemented. In every case, there are people involved, and people are complicated.

What I told Ross was true: I did not need to get Admiral Zhao's permission to do what I thought necessary to protect our homeworld. It was also true that I did not have to be an asshole about it. The guy is a vice admiral, in the US Navy he would wear three stars. In the Chinese Navy for whatever reason, their equivalent to a NATO rank code OF-8 has only two stars on the shoulder boards. Zhao had proven himself over a lifetime of service, and had the confidence of UNEF Command, that's why they assigned him the monumental task of developing Earth's first fleet of warships. He not only needed to get our new ships up to speed, he also had to train crews to operate and maintain them. Before that, he had to manage the task of figuring out how best to operate the ships of the new UN Navy, then develop doctrine, training materials, and implement a training program. If we still relied on paper instruction manuals, we might have cut down entire forests of trees on Jiayuguan to document everything.

I mention the Herculean task facing Zhao, because I for sure wouldn't want to get stuck with that job. The guy had my respect, and I wanted advice and assistance from him and his staff. According to Simms, and Chang, and Skippy, and Smythe, and pretty much everyone I asked, I tended to veer from under- to over-confidence, with little in between. Doubting myself was much more common, but my rare moments of arrogance always got me and the Merry Band of Pirates into trouble.

I presented my plan to force the kitties to clean up the mess they made in our home solar system. Zhao had a reputation for being kind of cautious and unimaginative, and he asked a lot of questions about my plan to strike the Retonovir shipyard. He liked the idea, and I could see in his eyes that making the Maxolhx disperse the cloud was one option he and his staff had not considered. He also agreed that, realistically, only the Maxolhx or the Rindhalu had the technology and the resources to prevent the cloud from freezing Earth. Let's just say that the spiders were not inclined to help us, so that left the Maxolhx.

To my surprise, and apparently to the surprise of his staff, he agreed we should hit the Maxolhx at the earliest opportunity, and that Retonovir appeared to be a good first target.

"Every day we do nothing, the enemy grows more bold," he explained.

I was caught unprepared for his sudden, unexpected agreement. Going into the meeting, Ross had warned me to be patient, and to make sure I knew what I was talking about. "Uh-" I sputtered.

Zhao's impassive face cracked a smile. "Colonel Bishop, the people of Earth need a *win* right now. Get one for them. And," he added without a smile, "Do *not* lose your ship. Retonovir represents a low-risk opportunity. See that it stays that way."

"Yes, Sir," I saluted, and got out of there before he could remember what a reckless jackass I am, and change his mind.

During our meeting, Zhao had suggested, *strongly* suggested, one change to my plan of action. I agreed to the change; it made matters more complicated, but he convinced me it was something we *had* to do.

That is why, when I took *Valkyrie* back out four days later, we went through the wormhole and turned toward Earth, instead of setting course for Maxolhx territory.

CHAPTER FOUR

Valkyrie went through the Backstop wormhole, and performed a quick recon of our home solar system, in case we needed to reverse course and get the hell out of there. If the *Dutchman* had been with us, I would have ordered that ship to go through Backstop first. It was better to risk our old star carrier than to risk Skippy being captured. Plus, the latest version of the Flying Dutchman was a super-stealthy sensor platform, much harder to detect than our massive battlecruiser.

In a way, it was good that the *Dutchman* had to stay at Jaguar until Nagatha could get the supply ships up to speed on the refit process. Our old star carrier was commanded by Captain Nakamura. He had been with me as my executive officer during *Valkyrie's* shakedown cruise, after we returned to Earth following our triumphant Kick-Ass tour of the galaxy. Nakamura is a good guy, very professional and I appreciated his many good qualities, but the truth is, he and I never clicked like I did with my previous XOs. Chang, Desai, Simms, even Reed when she filled in, they all knew me and how to work with me. With Nakamura, I had to figure out how to work with him. Part of the problem, a big part of the reason we never developed more than an awkward working relationship, is that I knew his time aboard *Valkyrie* was limited. There wasn't time or opportunity, or even much of a point, to building a rapport with my revolving door of XOs at that time. UNEF Command had wanted a string of people in the *Valkyrie* XO's chair, because we had ambitions to build a whole fleet of starships and, truthfully, our bench of people with experience in command of ships was rather thin. Basically, the list was me, Chang and Simms. Chang had been kicked upstairs in the UNEF organization, Simms wanted to get back to her logistics specialty. That left me in command of *Valkyrie*, and Nakamura with zero space combat experience to handle the *Dutchman*. Someday, we would have a whole fleet of starships with experienced captains and crews. Until then, we had to manage as best we could.

Why am I rambling on about personnel and manpower issues?

Because the reason we went back to Earth makes me uncomfortable.

We weren't there to help, not directly.

We couldn't *do* anything to make the situation on our homeworld better, to remove the threat that was literally hanging over their heads. The cloud was still not visible other than as a very faint discoloration across a band of the sky. It was so thin that, while looking at it through one of *Valkyrie's* few actual viewports, I thought it was just a smudge on the clear composite material.

Crap.

Something like *that* would doom our homeworld to an Ice Age? It looked like nothing. I had to trust Skippy, and Bilby, and people on Earth like my old friend Dr. Friedlander. We knew the good doctor had worked on the UN team investigating the Jupiter Incident, because after we sent a recognition signal, UNEF Command broadcast an appeal for us to examine the data and verify the grim conclusions in the report. There was a shirt note from Friedlander in the message, basically hoping that he was wrong about the cloud.

He was wrong.

That was not good news. Skippy's analysis determined the situation was even *worse* than what the UN feared.

There was one thing we could offer the people of Earth: hope. Our sensors did not detect any Maxolhx ships in-system, nor any other ships. Still, they were likely monitoring events with stealthed ships or satellites. Smythe made a good point that I hadn't considered; he doubted the kitties left any warships near Earth. Having taken their best shot already, the Maxolhx would not want to risk an unplanned space battle that could provoke us further. One thing was clear: the rotten kitties wanted to conduct their harassment campaign on *their* terms. Make us react to them. One overly-aggressive starship captain seeking glory could screw up their carefully-made plans, and that did *not* happen in the Maxolhx military. Their entire society was very top-down; those in power issued commands, and everyone below did what they were told. So, we had that working for us. Whoopie-freakin'-do.

Our timing sucks. Skippy's chain of wormholes, creating a fast route from Earth to the super-duty wormhole that connected out to the Sculptor Dwarf, was finally stable and fully ready for regular use.

By the way, *no*, there is not a franchise opportunity available for Skippy's Chain O' Wormholes. Maybe he is still looking to expand his business of unique Chapstick flavors, you'll have to ask him. And if you decide to get into business with Skippy, don't say I didn't warn you.

Anyway, the chain of wormholes was finally ready for ships to make the quick trip out to the Sculptor Dwarf galaxy, and damn it, we couldn't use it. We could not risk parking big, vulnerable transport ships in Earth orbit, to load with colonists for Avalon. Probably the environmental conditions on Avalon weren't ready to support large numbers of colonists anyway, but that didn't matter. We also could not bring transport ships full of people to Jaguar, not with the threat of hostile warships lurking in our home star system. The Navy could have tried to protect a group of transports while they were slowly loaded in low Earth orbit, but UNEF Command agreed with Zhao that was not the best use of his ships. Not yet. Maybe the situation would change, once snow began falling in July over the Northern hemisphere. Until then, we were sticking to the plan.

Something that was *not* planned, at least not by me, came in a message from UNEF Command.

They promoted me to brigadier general.

I know.

It surprised the hell out of me, too.

Technically, because I'm on detached service to the armed forces of Skippistan, UNEF Command just authorized Skippy to promote me, but the effect was the same. What mattered was that UNEF gave me a vote of confidence, after I failed to prevent murderous aliens from launching a cloud that would freeze our homeworld. After I failed to disperse the cloud, or to even try keeping it away from Earth. They promoted me, while I still had no concrete plan to save the world again. So, why, after years of second-guessing my every action, and bitching and moaning about unavoidable risks I took, why was I suddenly ordered to pin a star on my uniform?

It's simple: because Zhao asked them to.

In the stack of messages we brought from FOB Jaguar, was one from Admiral Zhao to UNEF Command. He stated that, in his opinion, I needed more authority, to better enable me to force the rotten kitties to clean up the mess they made. Also, so I could deal with the admirals under his command on a more equal basis.

Despite what I expected, the message announcing my immediate promotion did not contain a hint of skepticism or resentment. It was a form, based on US Army standard for simplicity. Very matter-of-fact, without any note of congratulations. That felt kind of like a slap in the face, I tried not to take it personally. The UN was worried about the planet freezing, and nuclear-armed nations going to war over dwindling resources. I sure as hell was not going to whine about my freakin' feelings.

Besides, there was a personal note. Not from UNEF Command, but from Chang. It was brief: *Joe, it's not about you. Congratulations. Kick some ass out there for me. -Kong.*

I knew what he meant. Don't argue about the promotion, don't be consumed with self-doubt about whether I deserved it. Just pin on the star, and use my new rank as an asset, to *do my job.*

You know what? Chang didn't have to worry. I did not feel awkward about the promotion to general officer. My reaction was more like: it's about damned time.

I had grown up a lot while serving with the Merry Band of Pirates. Even before we acquired Elder weapons, I had gotten over the worst of my self-doubts, and grown comfortable with my authority. So comfortable, that I had determined I was not taking any shit from dirtside politicians, who wanted me to praise them for their inspiring leadership, during which they did abso-freakin'-lutely nothing useful. Also, I wasn't taking any shit from senior military officers who had never been offworld, and never commanded anything more deadly than an LMD: Large Mahogany Desk.

So, when Simms pinned stars on my uniform in a brief ceremony that morning, I stood up straight, returned salutes with pride, and went back to my office to get on with my job.

After verifying the situation at Earth had not changed significantly, and showing the flag in our home star system, we went outbound through the Backstop wormhole.

We had work to do.

Coming back to my office after the quick promotion ceremony, I was surprised to see a sort of cone-shaped package on my desk. Whatever it was, it was wrapped in red tissue paper, with a card. "Uh, Skippy, what is this?"

"You're supposed to read the card, dumdum," he said with an implied 'duh'.

"Oh, sorry." The card was very elaborate, all gold braid and filigree. It read 'Sincere congratulations on your promotion'.

The card was from Skippy.

"Wow, thanks. That is very-"

"Yeah, yeah," he said impatiently. "Open the package, will ya?"

Tearing open the tissue paper, I saw- Really, I'm not sure what I saw. There was a banana. The rest of the flower arrangement, if that's what it was, consisted of pine tree branches, and scraggly-looking flowers, and some type of shrubbery. Also something that looked like milkweed? None of it appeared to be plants that were native to the planet we originally called 'Club Skippy'. Some of the shrubs might have been blueberry bushes, they had berries on the branches. Warily, I pulled off a berry and tasted it. A blueberry for sure. Probably from the hydroponics garden on the *Flying Dutchman*, although we had planted crops on Jaguar, stuff brought from Earth. "These, uh, flowers are very nice, Skippy, it looks great on-"

"It's an *edible arrangement*, numbskull. Didn't you see the banana?"

"Yeah. Edible, huh?"

"Yes. You can eat everything in there, according to the US Army survival manual. Everything is edible, if you try hard enough."

"Uh-"

"It's not always about *you*, Joe. Don't be so selfish. I worked hard on this," he pouted.

"Sorry. This is," I contemplated how to eat a pine tree. "A very thoughtful gift." As I said what I intended to be meaningless happy talk, I realized it was true. It *was* a thoughtful gift, for an Army promotion. Certainly, no one would give that arrangement to a civilian.

"Do you really like it, or are you just being nice?"

"I genuinely like it, buddy. Jeez, anyone can throw together a fruit basket, right? This is special. And very appropriate. Do you mind if I put it in the galley?"

He looked crestfallen. "You don't want it in your office?"

"No one will see it in my office," I explained.

"Oh," he instantly brightened. "Good idea."

That day at lunchtime, I put the arrangement on display in *Valkyrie's* galley, emphasizing that it was edible, according to Skippy. Yes, there were a bunch of special ops people in the galley at the time, but that was purely a coincidence. Did I think our high-speed operators would take it as a challenge to eat the arrangement? Gosh, that never occurred to me.

It did surprise me when someone tried to eat the *basket*.

"Sir?" Simms knocked on my door frame that afternoon.

"Come in, XO," I waved to her.

She sat down on the edge of the chair, the way people do when they don't intend to stay long. To set her at ease, I closed my laptop, leaned back in my chair, and pulled a dish of chocolates out of a drawer, sliding it across the desk to her.

"Mm," she popped a chocolate in her mouth. "Thank you. The crew wants to host a promotion dinner for you, this evening." I nodded, and she continued. "Do you have anything in mind?"

"Anything but baked ziti." She raised both eyebrows at me, so I explained. "I'm from New England. At any sort of awards banquet, for school or whatever, you get baked ziti. It's cheap, and you can make big pans of it to feed a lot of people. If you're lucky, there will be a tray of meatballs to go with it, but if you're at the back of the line, the meatballs are all gone by the time you get there. You get dry ziti that is stuck to the bottom of the pan, and you try to scrape sauce out of the meatball pan to make it edible."

"Not a fan of baked ziti," she muttered as she tapped on her tablet.

"I don't *dis*like it. Just had to eat too much of it."

"What do we have for a vegetarian option?"

"Sir?" She blinked at me. "Like what sort of veget-"

"How about steaks?"

"*Steak* is not a vegetarian-"

"Cows eat plants, right? Like I've said before, beef is just veggies in concentrated form. It's a super food, if you think about it."

She sighed. "I will try *not* to think about it. All right, we do have enough filets and ribeyes for everyone who wants it. I'll arrange for a chicken option, and a real vegan meal."

"That would be great! Hey, you can include a kale salad on the menu."

"Will you *eat* a kale salad?"

"Let's not go crazy."

In the end, we negotiated that I would eat a small kale salad, and she would provide spice cake cupcakes for dessert, with decadent buttercream frosting.

I should get promoted more often.

Newly-promoted Lieutenant Kinsta pinged Captain Scorandum's office, before touching the button to make the door slide open. "Sir, there is an Admiral Vriss from Home Fleet, coming to talk with you."

"No." Scorandum's antennas swung side to side.

"No?"

"I know Admiral Vriss, he is with the Home Fleet's Incident Investigation division. He is here to talk *at* me. Ah, Kinsta," the ECO captain leaned forward, tidying up his small desk, and looking down at his disheveled uniform. "I have already explained to the Fleet twice, and to an Inquisitor, that I have *no idea* how the Maxolhx learned the location of the batch of ships we lost. How many times can they ask the same question?"

Kinsta didn't speak, but he knew the answer. The Fleet would ask the same question, until they got the answer they wanted to hear. "Is there anything you require of me, Sir?"

"Yes. If you hear me attempting to strangle Vriss," he tilted his head.

"Of course. I will do my best to stop you."

"No, you idiot. If I'm trying to strangle him, I want you to hit him on the head, then help me get rid of the body." He stared at his aide. "Are you sure you belong in the Ethics office?"

"I ask myself that question every day," Kinsta admitted, and bowed as he backed away.

Admiral Vriss got straight to the point. "Captain Uhtavio Scorandum, I am here to officially reprimand you for insulting our exalted patrons. Consider yourself hereby reprimanded."

"I feel just terrible about it, Sir," Scorandum hung his head, figuring that was the best way to get it over with.

"*Unofficially*, I am here for two reasons. First, to give you the thanks of Fleet leadership. Those damned arrogant Rindhalu have been looking down on us for too long. You put them in their place. And you *were* correct, our patrons did fail to properly protect us. Our government is sending an official note of complaint."

"Uh," Scorandum blinked. "Wow, I-"

"Don't make a habit of it, you understand?"

"I do. There is another reason for your visit?"

"Yes," the admiral eased his considerable bulk back on the couch. "I heard a rumor that ECO acquired a selection of truly fine, vintage spirits?"

"Don't believe every rumor you hear, Sir."

Vriss's antennas drooped. "Then you do *not* have-"

Scorandum opened a drawer and pull out a bottle. "It is for *you* to determine if these spirits are truly fine."

"Hmm. If you insist. I am, after all, with the Investigations Division."

Later, when a third of the bottle was gone, most of it having disappeared inside the admiral, Scorandum pushed away his own glass. "Uh, that's enough for me. I'm supposed to get this ship ready to fly again by tomorrow morning." The *Will Do Sketchy Things* was overdue for a heavy overhaul, but with humans having upset the balance of power in the galaxy, the Ethics and Compliance Office wanted every unit available for rapid deployment. His next shore leave might be a long time in the future.

"Ah," Vriss waved an antenna in a dismissive gesture. "You have a crew to handle the details. But," he looked at his own glass, and downed the bit of liquid that lined the bottom. "Perhaps I had enough. Captain, what will happen next?"

"Are you interested in placing a wager?"

"Sadly, no. This is official business. Home Fleet is interested in preventing the next disaster."

"Sir, all I can say is, the entire galaxy is waiting to see how the humans will respond, to the attack on their homeworld."

"Yes. Your guess, Captain? What will the humans do next?"

"I don't know, Sir."

"Will they use their new ships in a futile attempt to disperse the cloud on their own? Will they use their warships to protect transports, while they evacuate a pitiful few thousand humans from their doomed homeworld? Will they," the admiral burped, and continued, talking to himself. "Try to cut a deal with the Rindhalu? Or the Maxolhx?"

"Sir?" Scorandum spoke, before the senior officer could go off on a long tangent of useless speculation. "What is the assessment of the intelligence bureau?"

"Ha! Have those idiots ever been right about enemy intentions?"

"Humans are our enemy now?"

"Officially, they are not our *allies*, so," Vriss allowed his voice to trail off. "The best assessment is that the humans probably haven't decided what to do. It could take them years to upgrade the ships we gave them, if it is possible at all."

"Neither of the senior species will stand by, while the humans cut a deal with the other faction. Admiral, I do not see this ending well for the humans. I also do not see such a young, reckless species being idle, while they tinker with the ships we gave them."

"Guess, then. What will they do?"

"I don't think I *can* guess. There is only one thing I am certain of."

"What is that?"

"Whatever the humans will do next, it is something we probably can't imagine."

"Hey, Joe," Skippy's avatar appeared on my sink, while I was shaving the next morning. "First, congratulations on your first full day as a general officer."

"Thanks, Skippy. You saying that means a lot."

"It does?"

"You saying it, without your usual snarkasm, means a lot."

"Snark-asm, hee hee, that's funny."

"What's up?" I mumbled. It's hard to speak properly when you're stretching your face to shave under your nose.

"I finished reviewing all the updates from my submind on Earth. It hates me, by the way."

"Don't all your subminds eventually hate you?"

"Yeah, but this one *really* hates me now. I sort of dumped a huge pile of shit on its head, you know. Conditions on Earth are deteriorating, even faster than expected. It is acting as my unofficial representative, plus it is doing whatever it can to keep the situation down there from spiraling out of control. It was never designed to do that."

"I know. We appreciate it. Uh, are you here to deliver bad news?"

"These days, is there any other kind of news?"

"Damn it. No."

"Well, actually, I *do* have some good news. All the bad stuff will be in your morning report. This is more personal, Joe."

"Personal?" That got my hopes up. Along with official messages to UNEF Command, the UNEF member governments, and anyone else who would sulk if they got left out, we transmitted messages from the crew, and from people at FOB Jaguar. All the messages had been censored by Skippy, to avoid revealing classified information. That sucked, but it had to be done. We had to assume that, even with Skippy's submind mostly in control of communications on Earth, the

Maxolhx were listening. Whatever we told UNEF Command, or anyone else dirtside, the kitties would hear about sooner or later. Probably sooner.

My own messages had been directed to my parents, my sister, Jesse and Shauna, Dave, and friends from my hometown. Basically, all I said was 'hang in there, the cavalry is coming'. That was bland enough so the rotten kitties couldn't get any useful information out of it. "Did my parents send a reply?"

"Yes, but that is queued up in your personal messages, you can read it any time. Don't be disappointed, they weren't able to say much, you understand?"

"I do. So," I splashed water on my face. "What else is personal?"

"Good news about our country, Mister President!"

"Oh. Yeah."

"Jeez, Joe. That's a great way to sell it. Thanks a lot." He looked hurt.

"Sorry. What is this news, that all citizens of the Glorious People's Republic should rejoice about?"

"The Ritz Carlson Skippistan is almost complete! It surprised me that construction continued after the cloud thing, but here it is."

The mirror above the sink displayed an image. The sagging barn in the background I recognized from photos of Skippistan. "Uh, *this* is your luxury hotel?"

"What's wrong with it?" He demanded, hands on his little hips.

"It looks like a pile of rocks, with a corrugated sheet metal roof. Is that, a *goat* looking out the window?"

"That is a top-quality *fiberglass* roof, Mr. Smartypants."

"Seriously, *that* is a Ritz Carlton? I can't believe they-"

"It's a Ritz Carl*son*, numbskull. I had to change the name, because of, you know, the stupid lawsuit."

"Right. OK, well, the citizens of Skippistan can certainly rejoice, that's for sure."

"Man, I try to give you some good news, and-"

"I am truly sorry."

"Hmmph." He folded his arms and looked away.

"Uh, I guess it is good news that construction of that hotel boosted the local economy, right? Kept a couple goat herders busy over weekend?"

"I certainly hope so. The hotel's construction budget was six billion dollars."

"Six-" I choked. "*Billion*? Like, with a 'B'?"

"Yes, why?"

"The stones that thing is made from, are they rough diamonds, something like that?"

"No," he laughed. "It's mostly granite, I think."

"Why the hell did you spend six-"

"Ha, ha! As if *I* didn't spend a dime, dumdum. Generous international investors paid for the hotel. My only involvement was design, of course. Plus, I do happen to own the company that was awarded the juicy construction contract."

"Oh."

"You understand now?"

"The hotel is a way of funneling cash into your pockets?"

"Egg-*zactly*."

"Uh, when did you decide to build a hotel?"

"Originally, the project was going to be a monorail."

"Mono- Why does your goat farm need a freakin' monorail?"

"It doesn't, *duh*. I got the idea from the *Simpsons*!"

"Uh. OK, so if you don't need a monorail, why-"

"*Ugh*. You are so dense, I'm surprised you haven't imploded and become a neutron star. Listen, dumdum, I won't *know* that Skippistan doesn't need a cool monorail, until the engineering, feasibility and market demand studies are completed. Those studies will take years, and cost several hundred million dollars."

"Who is doing this study?"

"Why, *me*, of course," he didn't bother adding a spoken 'Duh'.

"Ah. Gotcha. So, these studies are just another way to stuff your pockets full of cash?"

"Yup," he looked extremely proud of himself. "The bribes thing- Thank you for that, by the way. The bribes had kind of been tapped out, so I needed a new channel for, um, business opportunities. Boy, the end of the world has been fan-*tast*-ic for business!"

"*What?*"

"Oh, yeah. Everyone on Earth is looking to secure my influence, to survive the upcoming cat-astrophy. Hee hee, see what I did there? The kitties created the cloud, so it's a *cat*-astrophy. Man, sometimes I amaze mys-"

"Oh. My. G- You are *profiting* from the crisis?"

"Yes. I mean, no? Whatever won't get me in trouble."

"I'm serious, damn it. The world *is* ending, and instead of helping people, you are grabbing all the money you can for yourself?"

"It's not for me. I am collecting money for charity, Joe. Really, I'm kind of like Gandhi, when you think about it."

"*Gandhi?*"

"Maybe that was a bad comparison. Hey! I'm like Robin Hood. Yeah, that's it. I get money from the rich, and give it to the less fortunate."

"All the money goes to charity?"

"Absolutely."

"Oh. OK, then, that's-"

"Minus a small finder's fee, of course."

"How small?" I glared at him.

"Twenty five," he blinked. "Um, I mean, twenty-" he stuttered. "Er, *five*. Five percent. Damn," he muttered to himself. "At that rate, I don't know why I even bother to-"

"The rest of the money actually goes to charity?"

"Yes," he sniffed, acting insulted. "Your planet is in crisis, so I give to only the most worthy charities, of course."

"Could I get a list of these worthy charities, please?"

"You don't need to bother yourself with those details, General Bishop. Your time is far too valuable now to-"

"I just spent five minutes arguing with a beer can, about a luxury hotel that looks like a chicken coop."

"Hey! My design inspiration was- OK, it was inspired by a chicken coop, but-"

"A list. Right now. Of these charities. I assume they are all registered somewhere?"

"Um, well, I decided it would be more efficient to bypass the middleman, you know, and give directly to needy individuals."

"Fine. Give me a list of *those* names."

"Ugh. The list is far too long to-"

"How did you select the needy people?"

"Well, heh heh, this is a funny story-"

"Oh, crap." Instantly, I knew his scheme. "You're giving money to the followers of Skippyasyermuni?"

"If I say 'yes', will you get mad at me?"

"Ya think?"

"Damn it. Listen, knucklehead, I am not freakin' Santa Claus. I don't spy on people all year, to make a Naughty and Nice list. The only reliable way for me to know who deserves my charity, is give it to people who I know truly have goodness in their hearts."

"Goodness? Because they scammed other people into joining your pyramid scheme?"

"Hey! That is a *slanderous* accus-"

"I thought you wound down your cult."

"Club, Joe. It was a *club*. Technically, it was a multi-level marketing-"

"You know damned well what I mean. You were supposed to end your fake religion."

"I tried! I really did. But, now with the cloud threatening your homeworld, people are seeking hope and solace."

I stopped to take a breath. "OK, I can understand that. As long as you didn't do anything to encourage-"

"I had *nothing* to do with it, I swear. The movement grew organically."

"Ok, then-"

"Like all organic things," he went on, because he just does *not* know when to shut up. "Its growth might have benefited from nourishment, you know, fertilizer."

"Fertilizer? Like what?"

"Um, the social media accounts, the websites. Oh, and the worldwide simulcast TV show, broadcast in over a hundred different languages."

"You little shithead. You instigated the whole thi-"

"I *facilitated*, Joe. Totally different. All I did was *help* people, can't you see that?"

"I am never letting you go back to Earth again," I declared, while bonking my head on the bathroom mirror.

"Hey! I didn't want to get dragged to your miserable mudball of a homeworld in the *first* place. But now, I have responsibilities-"

"You have *scams*."

"Poh-*tay*-toh, poh-*tah*-toh," he stuck his tongue out at me like a two-year old.

Being a general officer means you have to choose which battles to fight. Knowing that Skippy would be happy to argue until the Sun was a cold, dark lump of carbon, I let it go.

In case you think I was being a coward, I did take firm, decisive action.

I wrote a note to myself: Do not trust Skippy.

That should take care of the problem.

"Joe," Skippy's avatar appeared on my office desk, he had his head cocked, looking at me intently. "You seem different."

"Uh, how?"

"You are more, angry."

"Here's a news flash for you: I've been pissed off since Columbus Day."

"Yes, but now you are pissed off all the time. This is like a new Angry Joe."

"Angry Joe, huh? You could be right about that. Wouldn't you be angry, if aliens were threatening your homeworld?"

"Sure, but *that* is nothing new. We have been trying to keep aliens away from Earth, ever since you and I met. What changed?"

I had to think about that. He was right, I realized. "I guess, uh, before, I was mostly *scared* all the time. Frightened that I would fail, that my screw-ups would doom my people to extinction. Disaster was always hanging over my head, you know? Now, bad shit has already happened. I can't stop it from happening, all I can do is make the assholes pay, big time. So, yeah, I'm angry. Think of this as, uh, Joe Two Point Oh, something like that."

"*Hmmph*," he sniffed. "In that case, I'll wait for Joe Two Point *Three* to be released. That version will have the major bugs worked out, but it's before the feature bloat that slows everything down."

That made me laugh. "I think this version of Joe has all the features I'm going to have. It's not like I'm going to learn to play the piano, or something like that."

"Good point. You probably peaked a long time ago, to be honest."

"*Why* are you such an asshole?"

"Sorry," he mumbled. "Is your upgrade to Angry Joe a good thing?"

"What do you mean?"

"When you were Frightened Joe, you thought all the time about how your actions might affect other people. You were concerned about others, that you couldn't let your emotions get in the way of making good decisions. Angry Joe is more likely to be motivated by your own emotions. That could be dangerous."

"Shit. I hadn't considered that."

"You should."

"You're damned right about that. Crap." That was something I needed to think long and hard about. When I proposed to strike the enemy, was I doing it because the action would help humanity, or to soothe my anger? A commander needed to keep a cool head. There were times when I tried to goad the enemy into doing something stupid, hoping their fear and anger would push them into making a mistake. "Thanks, Skippy. If you see me letting my anger make me lose control, let me know right away."

"Will do, but I am not the best judge of squishy stuff like monkey motivations."

"Yeah."

Five minutes later, Simms was in my office. "Sir?"

"Sit down, XO. I need to talk to you about squishy monkey stuff."

"*Squishy?*" She checked the floor before she stepped in something.

Tapping my head, I explained, "Monkey thinking processes. Squishy is how Skippy describes it."

"Ah." She sat down. "What about it?"

"He thinks the Jupiter cloud has changed me from Frightened Joe, into Angry Joe."

She nodded. "That's a good way to describe it."

I blinked. "You noticed, too?"

"Everyone has. Everyone who has served with you for a while. You don't like that?"

"It would be nice to have a *few* secrets."

"It is dangerous for the commander to keep secrets, Sir," she repeated a long-time complaint about my leadership style.

I shrugged. There wasn't anything to be said about that. After we found the Elder weapons at Maris, Simms had been hurt and angry, that I hadn't told her about my hope of finding something the Elders had hidden there. That prompted me to promise I wouldn't keep anything important a secret from her. So far, I had kept that promise. "Skippy is worried my anger will make me do something stupid. I'm concerned about that also."

"You want me to warn you, when I think you're doing something rash?"

"Yeah."

"Haven't I been doing that all along?"

"Yes. Even when I don't appreciate it. Look, Simms, all I'm saying is, I'm more likely now to do something rash out of anger, than from fear."

"Good."

"Good?" That was unexpected. "How is-"

"You doubt yourself too much. Before we jumped into the ambush at Snowcone, you had a feeling something wasn't right about the change in rendezvous point?"

"Yes," I admitted. That was something I'd confessed to Simms one morning at breakfast, while *Valkyrie* was deep inside the toxic atmosphere of that ice giant planet, with thousands of enemy ships looming over our heads.

"You should have trusted your instincts. Trusted yourself. *You* are the best person to know if you're acting out of anger, Sir. We are all angry about what's happening. *Use* that. Just be smart about it."

CHAPTER FIVE

US Air Force Major Samantha 'Fireball' Reed found a priority message waiting for her, when she stepped out of the Dragonfly dropship, patting the hull affectionately with a gloved hand. The flight had been her first test of the upgraded spacecraft, the smaller of two models of dropships acquired from the Jeraptha. The larger 'Scarab' dropship, which could hold thirty beetles, or modified to carry fifty humans, would be more useful to the Legion. The Scarab was designed mostly as an assault lander, to drop troops from orbit, and it was a big, clumsy beast to fly. The Dragonfly was more like the Thuranin Falcons she was used to; max capacity of fourteen passengers if everyone was very friendly, and it could also be configured as a gunship. The transition from flying the Falcon to qualifying on the Dragonfly was shorter than expected, because the Thuranin had partly stolen the design from the beetles, and because Skippy had designed the flight control software so both craft would handle similarly.

She had a new rank, new responsibilities, and a new uniform because the Air Force had recently changed to a dark blue. She still had her unfortunate callsign, all attempts to shake that had been in vain.

Before reading the priority message, she inspected the spacecraft, making sure it was properly secured after flight. Only when the maintenance crew hinted that she was in their way did she walk over to the assault transport's airlock, holding her helmet under one arm. In the airlock, she opened the message and-

Turned around.

Admiral Zhao wanted her aboard his flagship, the battleship *Pacific*, as soon as possible. He didn't say why, but then, he was an admiral and she was a major, and he didn't need to give an explanation.

"Staff Sergeant," she called to the crew chief who was in charge of the dropship. "I need to borrow your bird again."

Despite the rush, she waited forty minutes outside Zhao's office, the outer office was a rather unimpressive space that appeared to have been a storage compartment of some sort. She knew that *Pacific*, despite the grandiose title of flagship, was still an obsolete, barely functional second-hand hulk, running on reserve power. The battleship would someday hopefully be a mighty scourge to the enemies of humanity, but it had yet to go through refit, or even to be scheduled for conversion as far as she knew. She did know the ship's previous name translated as *That's a Bad Beat, For YOU*, which was a term used in gambling or card games, she hadn't bothered to research it. The big battlewagon's nickname was and probably always would be 'Bad Beat', whether the admiral liked it or not.

"Admiral Zhao will see you now," a somewhat apologetic yet still haughty staff officer called to her. "Mind the," the staffer pointed upward, cautioning Reed to watch out for the tangle of wires and conduits that hung down from an open access panel in the ceiling. No, Sami reminded herself, the 'overhead'. The UN fleet was being set up and run as a blue water Navy, whether that made sense or not. She needed to get with the program and use naval terminology. Aboard the

Flying Dutchman, and then *Valkyrie*, Bishop had been relaxed about standardizing terms between services or nationalities, caring only about terms that affected combat communication. The colonel often referred to 'walls' instead of 'bulkheads' and 'floor' rather than 'deck'.

Bishop wasn't in command of her home ship, the assault transport *Caspian Sea*, she reminded herself. "Major Reed, reporting as or-"

"Relax, Major," Zhao barely looked up from his tablet, then stood up and offered a hand. "I regret we have not had time to meet before, it would be a privilege to shake your hand."

"Uh, yes, Sir," she was flustered. When was the last time she was so nervous? Not in combat. Not when *Valkyrie* was drifting without power, and Simms was preparing the self-destruct nukes. This was different. "Thank you, Sir," she said automatically when he released her hand, and indicated she should sit.

The room- No, *compartment* he had selected as his office, still had the faint scent of copper and dry leather from its previous Jeraptha occupants. The chair she sat in, at least, was designed for humans. It had either been brought all the way from Earth, or cranked out by the fabricator ships. Either way, a lot of effort and expense had been required so that she wasn't sitting on a hard deck, so she should appreciate it despite the chair being made of what appeared to be hard plastic.

The admiral made small talk for a while, succeeding only in making her more nervous. Surely the commander of Earth's fleet, or what someday would be Earth's fleet, had better demands on his time, than to engage a lowly field-grade officer in idle chit-chat about the exploits of the Merry Band of Pirates. Zhao perhaps sensed her uneasiness, and cleared his throat. "I will get to the point, Major. The *Flying Dutchman* needs to conduct a recon at Earth, when *Valkyrie* gets back from their strike at Retonovir," he added with a frown. The remote and inaccessible location of FOB Jiayuguan, its main strength, was also its main weakness. Ships could not get in, or *out*, unless Skippy used his magic keys to open the Elder wormhole. If something bad happened to Skippy, the Navy would be trapped there until the next wormhole shift opened the area to all sorts of nasty aliens. No one liked the arrangement, no one knew what if anything should be done about it. Skippy insisted nothing *could* be done about it, and no filthy monkey had proven him wrong.

"Yes, Sir." She feared Zhao wanted her to pilot the *Dutchman* back to Earth. It would be nice to see home again, but flying the *Dutchman* was no longer a challenge for her. And the refresher training required to requalify would take weeks she didn't have. "If I may suggest a crew for pilot duty, the-"

"I will leave that up to you, Major."

"Sir?"

"Reed, I want you to take temporary command of the *Dutchman*. Choose your own pilots."

"Sir?" She repeated. "But, Captain Nakamura is-"

"Nakamura has relinquished command of the *Dutchman*, to prepare the *Ishikari* for refit."

That did not surprise Reed. Nakamura was Japanese, and the heavy cruiser *Ishikari* was named for a river in Japan. UNEF Command had established an unofficial tradition, that ship captains came from the same nationality as their supposedly non-nationalistic names. It was silly and reduced staffing flexibility, and would become unworkable, but UNEF had to soothe national egos on Earth. "The executive officer of the *Dutchman* is-"

"Is inexperienced, both in handling that ship in particular, and space combat in general. We all lack that experience," he added with a disarming smile. "Except for you, of course."

"Combat?" She was alarmed by the suggestion. "Sir, the *Dutchman* is still a space truck. It is optimized for hauling cargo, not-"

"It is optimized for *stealth*. Far more than any of the ships of this fleet."

"That is, true," she agreed.

"The *Dutchman's* jump drive, stealth field generator, the entire engineering section, are Maxolhx components that were left over from constructing the *Valkyrie*. I don't want you to take the ship into combat, I want you to be able to *avoid* combat."

"Yes, Sir. The *Dutchman* is attached to-"

"The Special Mission Group, yes," the skin around Zhao's eyes tightened with irritation. "When Colonel Bishop returns, I will request to use the *Flying Dutchman*. To date, he has not found a use for that ship."

Reed knew that was not true. The *Dutchman* had been forced to remain at FOB Jiayuguan, because Nagatha had to direct operation of the fleet support ships, until their AIs could be brought up to speed. Sami knew from the daily status report that Nagatha expected the fabricator AIs would be fully capable of operating independently within the week and those ships were already busily cranking out parts to refit the second-hand ships of the fleet. It was an honor to be asked to command a starship, and she had many times been the duty officer aboard both the *Dutchman* and *Valkyrie*. That was very different from formally taking command, and for a newly-promoted major to be assigned as captain of a ship was unheard of.

Yet, Bishop had been a sergeant when he took over the *Flying Dutchman*. Oh, what the hell, she thought. Zhao's offer was phrased politely, he could simply have issued an order for her to take the Dutchman.

And he was right, she realized. For a delicate stealth mission, where it was vital the commander understood exactly what the *Dutchman* was and was not capable of, she was the best candidate. "Yes, Sir. When do I start?"

"Now?" The admiral in command of the 1st Fleet smiled. "Now is good."

After taking *Valkyrie* through the Backstop wormhole outbound from Earth, we set course for Retonovir, despite me having a nagging feeling that we might be pushing our luck by attacking a Maxolhx military base. There wasn't anything specific I could point to that made me nervous, except that my freakin' *toes* were itchy. Or maybe that was all in my stupid head.

Damn it, I'd screwed myself again. I had promised Simms I would listen to my instincts, and instead of pulling out of the Retonovir op, I kept going. My logic was I shouldn't listen to my instincts when they were just being silly for no reason.

I wasn't the only person who had second thoughts about the operation. One fact that made the entire crew uncomfortable, was that only one wormhole provided access to Retonovir, unless we wanted to fly *Valkyrie* through space for seven weeks. That was not practical, and Skippy was already concerned about the wear and tear on the ship's jump drive. Key components for our battlecruiser could not be replaced by the fabricator ships at Jaguar. And some of the stuff we got from the beetles was too old to be functional, or couldn't be made to work with *Valkyrie's* Maxolhx jump drive.

Anyway, going home the long way was not an option I wanted to consider, unless we absolutely had to. If we were forced to do that, it meant a substantial force of enemy ships were pursuing us on our retreat from Retonovir. *That* meant the kitties would have plenty of time to send thousands of ships to cut us off, during the seven weeks it would take to reach the backup wormhole.

So, only one minor little detail was bothering me.

No wonder my toes were itchy.

Why were we flying to attack that target, if I was uneasy about it? First, my nerves get jiggly before every operation, that's nothing new. Before my first patrol way back in Nigeria, I went behind a bush to puke. It's normal to get keyed up, when you are going into harm's way. Especially now, when I was putting other people in harm's way.

We were proceeding to the target for one simple reason: the lack of alternate ingress and egress routes could work in our favor if—

Uh, those are military terms for 'ways to get in' and 'ways to get out'.

The lack of alternate routes, that might complicate our retreat if we encountered substantial resistance, also meant we were quite unlikely to encounter more than a few ships there. The place was at the end of the railroad, so to speak. Nobody went there unless they had a good reason to, and the kitties had plenty of other, more strategically located heavy shipyards. Result: few ships ever had a reason to go there. Skippy knew that Retonovir was considered hardship duty by civilian contractors who took assignments there, and it was a very unpopular posting for their military. The place should be a ghost town when we arrived.

Damn my itchy toes.

They were right.

"Oh, fudge," Skippy swore. "Of all the rotten luck."

"What?" I demanded. *Valkyrie* had jumped in eight lighthours from the heavy shipyard, which orbited the planet named Retonovir, and we waited for our passive sensors to show us what was there.

"Our timing *sucks*, Joe," he groaned. "Three weeks ago, a group of fourteen ships arrived here for refit. They were pulled from the Maxolhx ready reserve, and normally would be drifting quietly and empty, around some star. But, because some numbskull whose name rhymes with 'Shmoe Bitchslap' announced that humans have Elder weapons, the kitties have been gearing up for war."

"Shit. That Shmoe guy is a jerk."

"Can't argue with you about that," he muttered

"Jump away, Sir?" Simms had a finger raised toward the pilots, who were waiting for a command.

"Uh, not yet, XO." I didn't want to admit that my reason for not jumping away was that my toes suddenly stopped itching. "Fourteen ships, huh?" I had one elbow on the command chair's arm rest, rubbing my chin with the knuckles of that hand. That move always worked for Jim Kirk.

Except, he was way cooler than me.

"Talk to me, Skippy. What *kind* of ships?"

"They're all old, of course. Maintained to minimum standards. A star carrier brought them here, and tugs maneuvered most of them into their present positions, few of them were able to operate under their own power. Now, let's see. Eight are in the shipyard's maintenance docks. The other six, hmm. They are in orbit near the shipyard. One of them is docked at the main civilian space station, that ship has already gone through major refit and is preparing for a shakedown flight. Two more have also completed major refit and are sorting out their internals. The other three are waiting for a repair bay to open at the shipyard."

"Details, Skippy. Put it on the main display. What type of ships?"

Holy shit. I wish I hadn't asked that question. Of the eight currently in the shipyard, six were battleships, the other two heavy cruisers. The battlewagons were big damned things, massing at least fifty percent more than *Valkyrie*. The heavy cruisers were almost as big as our ship, and had most of a battleship's firepower, without the thick armor plating.

That was not good news.

But, wait.

None of the eight monsters in the shipyard were operational. They had no defenses, and no offensive capabilities. They couldn't even launch missiles, if their launchers were loaded, which they weren't.

The three ships waiting their turn in the shipyard were dead, running on reserve power. They also couldn't hurt us.

That left three ships that had completed refit.

Bullshit.

Those ships had gone through the major elements of getting them returned to operation. They were not fully combat ready, not even flightworthy. A whole lot of work remained to be done inside them to make them dangerous as warships.

"Huh," I rubbed my chin again without being conscious about it. Maybe I was channeling my inner Kirk. "Fourteen ships, none of them capable of shooting at us. See?" I raised an eyebrow at Simms.

"Skippy," she didn't reply directly to me. "What other defenses are in-system?"

"Hoo-boy," he sighed. "Plenty. The planet has an extensive strategic defense network."

Simms cocked her head at me, in what I interpreted as an 'I told you so' gesture.

"Well," Skippy continued. "I guess it's more accurate to say it *used* to have an extensive SD network. Now, I suspect a lot of the satellites are for show, not operational. Unless they posed a navigation hazard, they were left in place, but maintenance was cut back severely. Let me check, um, yes. Eighty-four percent of the SD network is offline, or ineffective."

Resisting the temptation to say something snarky to Simms was not easy. It was silly, unproductive and unprofessional to have a rivalry with my executive officer. I also knew that our relationship worked very well, so I wasn't going to change anything. "Will the SD network be able to prevent us gaining access to the shipyard?"

"No,"

"Outstanding. Then we-"

"You didn't let me *finish*," his avatar put hands on his hips. "The *shipyard* has plenty of powerful defenses, and those are in excellent condition. Directed-energy and particle cannons, missile launchers, and railguns. Plus heavy energy shields, thick armor plating around sensitive areas, a damping field generator, a distortion field that prevents ships from jumping inside the designated approach zone, the whole shebang."

Shebang? Sometimes I wondered where Skippy got his slang. "Shit. This *is* impossible."

"Maybe," Skippy stuck his lower lip out like he was lost in thought. "I discovered something interesting. One of those heavy cruisers was in better condition than expected, and has been judged to be done with the first phase of its refit. It will be moving out of the shipyard- Actually, it should already be in the process of moving out, since we're seeing events on an eight-hour time lag out here."

"Uh, this is a *good* thing? The last thing we want is an operational heavy cruiser creating complications for us."

"It's not fully combat-ready, but its weapon systems are coming online."

"So, this is even more impossible than we thought."

"Oh, I didn't say that, Joe," Skippy smirked. "This is kind of an odd role-reversal but, *I* have an idea to get us in there."

"You do?" Crap. Dreaming up crazy ideas was *my* job. If Skippy could do that himself, he didn't need me. "Give me a hint? Why didn't I think of, whatever this idea is?"

"Because, you forgot to do something."

"Uh, what did I forget?"

"To. Trust. The. *Awesomeness*."

"OK, get ready," Skippy urged the bridge crew.

"We've *been* ready for thirty minutes," I said with all the patience I had right then.

"Well," he looked flustered. There was a lot of pressure on him. "It's just, this requires precise timing."

"We know that."

"I need *at least* four point two seconds once we're in there."

"You might have mentioned that once or twice," I cleared my throat. "Four point two seconds exactly."

"Technically, four point one eight three seven nine-"

"We get the idea. Four point two, leave the rest as a safety margin."

"Once we're in there, I will be busy, you understand?"

"We do."

"Bilby will have to get us out of there, all by himself."

"I *got* this, Dude," the ship's AI drawled.

"You've never done something like this," Skippy protested.

"I was *born* for this," Bilby insisted.

"You weren't-"

"You like, trained me. You *created* me. I'm kind of like, your son, you know? Don't worry, Dudo El Supremo, I won't let you down."

"Um, oh, I, um that is, um," Skippy choked up, and his avatar froze for a moment. "Oh," he waved a hand. "I'm not worried about *you*, Bilby. My concern is that while the two of us are busy doing all the work, the monkeys will distract us with their inane blah, blah, buh-*LAH* about stupid monkey things."

"We will zip our lips, Skippy,' I assured him. Really, there wouldn't be time to say much of anything. The operation either worked as planned, or not at all.

"I'm serious. There is no room for improvisation or hesitation," he warned. "We follow the plan, understand? No monkey antics."

"Got it. We follow your plan, Skippy. It's a *good* plan."

"Hmmph," he sniffed. "We'll see about that."

"Or, you know," Bilby added helpfully, "we'll all be dead, and never know."

"Well, that was helpf- Wait," Skippy whispered. "This is it. Hold my beer in three, two, one, *now*."

The shipyard had formidable defenses. Because it had to supply nearly full power to multiple warships, sometimes simultaneously, its reactors were some of the most powerful units the Maxolhx had ever put in space. The designers of those reactors did not have to be concerned about making them compact and lightweight for shipboard use, so they were massive, each of them capable of much higher output than even the modified units that propelled *Valkyrie*. The shipyard's reactors could power immensely strong energy shields, and a spatial distortion field that would prevent *Valkyrie* from jumping in close enough to do harm. Any ship approaching the shipyard had to drop out of jump, then fly through space under the guns of the shipyard and whatever SD satellites were still operational. It was a suicide mission. The kitties and AIs who designed the shipyard's defenses, had done their best to make it capable of withstanding an attack by the Rindhalu.

They had not counted on being attacked by a ship full of monkeys and a snarky beer can.

The heavy cruiser, which was already powering up its weapons for testing, was being backed away from the shipyard. Automated tugs guided it for safety, lest some accident or screwup caused the massive ship to crash into something important.

Everything about our attack plan depended on math.

I hate math.

Math determined the timing. The heavy cruiser had been serviced in one of the shipyard's eight bays, and the massive clamshell doors of that bay had retracted to give the cruiser and its attendant tugs room to maneuver. The cruiser had backed out of the bay, and was moving away at a slow, steady speed. The shipyard's energy shields in that area had been reduced in power, and retuned to let the cruiser and tugs slip through. If you think the weakened energy shield helped us, I am sad to say it did not. We still had the problem of the distortion field that prevented us from jumping in near the shipyard, and by the time we jumped in, reset our targeting sensors and fired weapons, the shipyard would have reacted by restoring its shield strength.

No, what we cared about was the wake of disturbed spatial distortion field that the heavy cruiser and its tugs were leaving behind them. In their wake, spacetime was distorted just a little bit less than elsewhere. Our timing had to be precise, we were waiting for the moment when the cruiser reached the somewhat fuzzy edge of the field.

Math also determined *where* we had to be, and at what speed and direction we were moving. *Valkyrie* had to constantly move sideways, to remain motionless relative to the shipyard. That massive orbital platform was not rotating because it had artificial gravity, but it was in orbit. It was moving around the planet, and not going in a straight line, its path was curved to follow the planet's gravity well. That path was ever-so-slightly altered by the mass of the heavy cruiser moving away, as its own gravity well was gently affecting the shipyard. Once the cruiser was at a safe distance, the shipyard would very gradually adjust itself back on the path of its original orbit, and if it began moving before we were ready, our whole plan would be ruined.

So, we couldn't jump in close enough to strike before the shipyard's defenses would be ready, and we couldn't win a one-on-one battle against that orbiting fortress. It was hopeless, it was impossible. There was just no way to make the physics work in our favor.

Fortunately, physics is Skippy's *bitch*.

When the heavy cruiser neared the outer edge of the distortion field, the only wildcard that might screw up our plan was if that ship maneuvered unexpectedly. That should not happen, it was following procedure by coasting away from the shipyard, without using its engines. The tugs attached to the cruiser's hull also had their engines shut down. That didn't mean nothing could screw up our plan, the cruiser might have to maneuver out of the way if a large space rock just happened to be headed toward it right then. Sure, that is unlikely, especially since the Maxolhx SD network should have located and blasted any hazardous space junk long before it got close enough to be a hazard, but it *was* possible. If the Universe wanted to screw with Joe Bishop, this was a golden opportunity.

Technically, it was *Skippy's* plan, so the Universe would be bitterly disappointed if it wanted to give me a smackdown.

The cruiser reached the point where the strength of the field was weak enough to be ineffective, and *Valkyrie* jumped on Skippy's signal.

Wait.

Didn't I say, several times, that we could not jump in close enough to make the attack a success?

Yes. *Valkyrie's* jump drive couldn't get close enough.

The beer can knew of a way to cheat.

If you didn't know this already, Skippy *loves* cheating.

Skippy thought of a way to attack the shipyard, because he knew a Fun Fact about how different types of energy fields interacted. I did not know that Fun Fact, because I am an ignorant monkey.

The heavy cruiser, and the nine robotic tugs attached to it, all had their defensive energy shields active, but operating at a low level, and tuned specifically so those shields did not interfere with the distortion field around the shipyard. That tuning allowed the distortion field to maintain its normal strength as the cruiser passed through it.

Except, there was one small area where the distortion field was disrupted by the cruiser's shields. Nine areas, actually. Where the energy shields of each tug overlapped the shields of the cruiser, they were not perfectly in sync. That weakened the field in those local areas. Not enough for *Valkyrie* to jump through-

Except, when the cruiser was near the outer edge of the distortion field, where it was already weak.

Skippy was able to adjust our jump drive, so it projected the far end right through one of those gaps, all the way along the wake left by the cruiser, right to the shipyard. It would have been impossible without him, even Bilby could not think fast enough to anticipate changes in the distortion field and retune our drive in real-time.

Remind me in the future, when I think something is impossible, to trust the awesomeness.

Valkyrie emerged from our jump wormhole, smack in the center of the shipyard bay that had just been vacated by the heavy cruiser. Our battlecruiser was nearly motionless relative to that enormous servicing bay, that could accommodate a battleship easily three times the size of our ship. We only needed a few thrusters firing to correct the tiny error inevitable in any jump.

Here's the thing: the designers of the shipyard never anticipated they would need to fire on one of their own ships, *inside* a maintenance bay. Therefore, all the impressive firepower of the shipyard was useless, they were all pointed *away* from the massive orbiting station. The crew, or actually the shipyard's AI, could have launched missiles to curve around toward *Valkyrie*, *except* that those missiles all had very sensible range-safety devices installed, specifically to prevent some idiot jackass from using those weapons on their home base. Range-safety devices could be overridden, though that would take time the shipyard did not have.

Skippy needed four point two seconds. Minimum.

Though we were in the very heart of enemy territory, they couldn't actually shoot at us with anything more powerful than rifles.

"Hi," I waved at the main display. "We're here for the free oil change?"

The shipyard's master AI was pleased to see so much activity, after so many years of loneliness. First, it had the honor of modifying fuel extraction platforms for a glorious attack against the upstart humans. Now it was getting warships ready to defend the homeland. Its only regret was that the heavy cruiser that recently departed, was in such good condition when pulled from the ready reserve, it did not need much work to be flightworthy.

Another ship would be coming into the empty maintenance bay, and-

The bay was *not* empty.

A *battlecruiser* was there.

How-

What the f-

How-

The AI blew a fuse.

Its sensors *must* be wrong.

There could not be a battlecruiser in-

Ohhh crap.

It was *that* battlecruiser.

A message was transmitted by the ghost ship. A human was babbling nonsense about the ship needing fluids replaced?

Doing the only thing it *could* do, attempting to launch the shipyard's missiles, the AI was politely but firmly reminded by the lowly fire control AI, that range-safety devices did not allow missiles to strike their own station.

The fire control AI might even have added a 'You *dumbass*' to its reply.

The master AI realized at that moment, it was master of exactly nothing.

What the *f*-

THIS COULD NOT BE HAPPENING!

"Weapons away," Simms whispered, her announcement confirmed by the deck shuddering slightly, and streaks on the display representing our missiles launching.

"Oh," I feigned embarrassment, blinking at the display. "Were we supposed to call for an appointment?"

"I'm done," Skippy said with a hoarse voice.

I grasped the arm rests of my chair. "Shepard, punch it."

We jumped away, guided by Bilby.

It was not the best jump we've ever done, it was also not the worst. Not even in the bottom ten, if you are keeping score. Nobody on the bridge ralphed, and my eyes were blurry and seeing double for only a few seconds. I count that as a win.

OK, so it was rude of us to jump in and jump away so quickly, without even staying for lunch. We did leave several nice gifts for our short-term hosts.

If you consider nuclear warheads to be a nice gift.

When Simms confirmed our weapons had launched, she meant the six megaton-scale warheads we had stuffed into the heavily-armored nosecones of missiles. The missiles slammed out of their launch tubes, then quickly cut thrust. We didn't want them traveling so fast that they punched clean through the shipyard and out into space.

Here's the thing about using nukes in space combat: they aren't usually very effective. In a vacuum, a nuclear detonation doesn't have anything to push *against*, so the effect is limited.

But, when six nukes explode inside an orbiting shipyard, the several *million* tons of structure turns the place into shrapnel, and that was very effective.

"Well? Bilby," I prompted our ship's surfer slacker AI. "BDA?"

"Uh, Dude, do you mean the rap group BDA? Because they are righteously rad, and-"

"Battle. Damage. Assessment. Please."

"Oh," he snorted. "Right. Sorry. Um, like, *wow*. Scratch one shipyard. Also scratch six battleships and a heavy cruiser, that were in the shipyard when it blew up. Also, that heavy cruiser that left just before we arrived got smacked by a piece of the shipyard, it's never going to fly again, you know?"

"I feel just awful about that. Any sign of pursuit?"

"Um, no, but we're seventeen lightseconds from the planet. If any ship from there is trying to follow us, we wouldn't see it jump away until the photons reach us. The ships I can see now are-"

"Right. What's going on with Skippy?"

"He's like, super busy."

"OK. Is the ship ready to jump again?"

"It won't be a perfect jump but, like, yeah."

"Shepard, get us out of here."

CHAPTER SIX

"Oooh, *that* is interesting," Skippy mumbled, partly to himself. It was the first time he had spoken, since we jumped away from the shipyard.

"What?" I was kind of busy guiding *Valkyrie's* escape. "Is it important?"

"It is not of immediate use, but you *will* want to hear about this."

"Great. You can tell us after this next jump," the clock on the display showed we were under two minutes from our third jump, after leaving the shipyard in ruins behind us. Three jumps were probably enough to shake off any pursuit, though there were no signs that the Retonovir system had any ships left that were capable of posing a threat to our mighty battlecruiser. The only issue that concerned me was that there was only one functioning wormhole in the area, so any bad guys chasing us knew we had to go there.

"Okey-Dokey. You want me to put the info into a slick PowerPoint presentation?"

"I'm a soldier, Skippy. I never want to see another PowerPoint slide again."

We jumped without incident, and the capacitors began recharging. One long-distance jump would take us to the wormhole, and we had enough charge left for that, but it would leave the jump drive drained. If there was any risk of us encountering enemy ships on either side of that wormhole, I wanted a full charge on the capacitors before we approached.

Leaving the ship in the capable hands of Jennifer Simms, I went to my office and leaned the chair way back. I was exhausted from the tension of the shipyard attack. "Ah, hey," I put a hand over my mouth to stifle a yawn. "Before I forget, you should thank Bilby. He did a fantastic job today."

"Um, I guess he did OK," Skippy said grudgingly. "Why don't *you* thank him?"

"Because it would mean more to him, if you said you're proud of him."

"*Me*? Why?"

"Because, and I can't believe I have to explain this to a super-smart AI, he looks up to you."

"Oh, well," Skippy was flustered. "Of course he does. I am kind of awesome, you know, so-"

"I'm trying to be real for a moment here, you ass."

"Sorry. You really think it would be a big deal for me to say he did good today?"

"I think it would be a huge deal for him."

"Hmm. I'll try it."

"Great, I-" Another yawn I couldn't stop. Just then, a bit rolled into my office, carrying a hot cup of coffee. "Thanks, Skippy, that was nice of you," I took a sip of the coffee.

"I want you fully awake for *this* discussion," he hinted.

Oh, shit. Setting the cup on my desk, I prepared for bad news. The attack on the shipyard was retaliation for the cloud that threatened to freeze Earth, and it was a satisfying 'screw you' gesture to the rotten kitties. News of the attack would hopefully bring at least a momentary morale boost to the frightened people of Earth, would lessen the pressure on Admiral Zhao to *do something*, and would let the Maxolhx public know that humanity was not going to meekly accept our fate.

But that is not why we conducted the attack on the shipyard.

Oh, the reasons I cited are all good, they just weren't important enough to risk our battlecruiser. Despite all of Angry Joe's tough-guy talk, I was not going to do something stupid, just for the sake of doing *something*.

What had kept Skippy busy for four point two seconds, and forced Bilby to take over operation of the ship, is the real reason we hit the shipyard. While I was cracking jokes and the crew was launching nukes, Skippy was having his way with the local database, including and most importantly, the top-secret files stored there.

When *Valkyrie* was ambushed by over a thousand Maxolhx warships, and we got trapped deep in the atmosphere of the ice giant planet we called Snowcone, Skippy had hacked into the computers of the fleet upstairs. The malware he uploaded had a singular, limited purpose, and was not able to ransack the data files of the infected ships. All he got were a handful of fragmented, tantalizing hints of some deliciously top-secret data in the files of the command ships, and we needed to know more.

We thought that the shipyard, being a large, secure facility, would have access to data on current top-secret operations, even if the shipyard's AI was only told what it needed to know. If we had access to that type of info, while the shipyard was modifying fuel extraction platforms for the operation at Jupiter, we might have been able to prevent the cloud from being created. Of course, Skippy's smash-and-grab raid of data from the shipyard would have been noticed by the master AI there, if it had time to check its archives.

Sadly, that AI was now a mixture of high-energy particles and radioactive scrap, so we didn't have to worry about it telling anyone what we had done.

"Hit me with it, Skippy. What nasty thing are the kitties planning now?"

"Um, that I don't know, Joe. If they are planning to hit Earth again, the shipyard was not informed."

I was confused. "OK, then, what *do* you know?"

"Two things, both of them very interesting. One of them potentially very, like, super useful to us."

"Oh. I thought you were going to ruin my day."

"Not this time. Unless you would like to hear selections from my latest opera?"

"I would *not* like."

"I thought so. OK, behind Door Number One is a sleazy plan by the kitties, to activate their Elder weapons and trigger Sentinels to wipe out all life in the galaxy."

"*WHAT*? Holy *shit*! What the f-"

"Whoa! Whoa, maybe I should added that this is only a *contingency* plan."

"Ya think?"

"My bad, sorry." While I tried to stop my pounding heart from bursting out of my chest, he explained that, under the direction of my least-favorite kitty Admiral

Reichert, the Maxolhx were building a doomsday fleet. Enormous transport ships that would be filled with hibernating passengers, to be flown beyond the edge of the galaxy, and wait there until the rampaging Sentinels had gone back to their long sleep. The plan, which made me sick to hear it, was for the kitties on those ships to then repopulate the galaxy as the only intelligent species. Skippy said the ships would have samples of plants and animals from the Maxolhx homeworld, so they could recreate their preferred biosphere.

What a bunch of *assholes*.

The plan was only a contingency, in case the worst happened. Unfortunately, the Maxolhx leadership had a very different, sick and twisted definition of 'worst case' than we did. Their worst case was not that they would be facing extinction, and so might as well trigger their Elder weapons. No, their worst case was that they would no longer rule over an empire of unwilling 'clients'. Their worst case was that they could no longer rule half of the galaxy with an iron fist.

Basically, those narcissistic pieces of shit felt that, if they couldn't be *special*, life was not worth living. No, that's not true. *Other* people's lives were not worth living, including the lives of their own citizens. The elite leadership of the Maxolhx, and their families, would go into a long hibernation, to emerge as unquestioned masters of all they surveyed.

"Oh, *fuck* that," I gasped. "Wait. Why did the shipyard have- Oh."

"Exactly. That shipyard will be, well,'" he chuckled. "It *was* supposed to be creating components for the hibernation ships. This is an extremely sensitive operation. The Maxolhx need to spread out the manufacturing across their industrial base, so their general public doesn't realize a major project is going on behind their backs. Parts for those ships will be collected and brought to the site where the ships are being assembled."

"You know where that is?"

"Yes. It's in a red dwarf star system, along a heavily traveled route between two important wormholes. The kitties are being very clever," he conceded. "No one will notice the additional traffic, and because there is already a fueling station at another star system along that route, there is no reason for ships to go to the red dwarf."

"The hibernation ships are being assembled now?"

"Yes."

"We need to stop that."

"Are you sure, Joe? Any action we take, that brings the Maxolhx closer to what they perceive as defeat and humiliation, will make them *more* likely to trigger their weapons."

"Shit. Yes. I need to think about this."

"Good idea. While you're thinking about that, I have news that can only be *good*."

I squinted at him. "Are you screwing with me?"

"No. I don't think so. Although what I think is good news could be diff-"

"What is it?"

"Um, first, I need to provide a bit of background."

Suppressing a groan, because I knew it was best to let Skippy ramble on or he would pout and be miserable, I leaned back in my chair. "Please do," I sighed.

"OK, well, the Maxolhx have- Not just them, mind you. Many species have-"

"If this is going to be a really long explanation, I should get a snack."

"Oh, shut up and drink your coffee. As I was saying, most species have remote facilities for servicing and resupply of warships. Ships operating far from their regular bases, or unable to access those bases, can get fuel, missiles, spare parts, even typical minor repairs completed at one of these remote servicing stations."

"Yeah, I know," I said with a shudder. On my orders, we had gone to a Maxolhx servicing station, to get power boosters for *Valkyrie*.

That simple operation became Armageddon for us. I wasn't eager to think about it.

"Oh, yes." He hesitated. "I didn't mean to bring up bad memories."

"It's OK. We need to remember. What about those stations?"

"I discovered that the Maxolhx used to have secret, *major* servicing stations they called 'Safe Harbors', scattered throughout their territory. Only their senior military leaders knew the locations of the harbors. They were built so the Maxolhx fleet could continue to fight, if the Rindhalu conducted a massive surprise attack. There was a change of strategy about eight hundred years ago, when it was discovered the spiders actually knew about many of the supposedly 'Safe' Harbors, and had them on their primary target list. The kitties, hee hee, felt *pretty* stupid."

"I feel terrible for them."

"I suspect you are lying about that. Anywho, most of the Safe Harbors were stripped and taken out of service. However, there is one that was never decommissioned, its designation is Semi-Automated Servicing Station 17. A wormhole shift nine hundred years ago made that one servicing station inaccessible, so the kitties couldn't get there anymore. As far as they know, it is still there, waiting for ships that will never come."

"A thousand year old station? I'm impressed you dug up all this info but, why do we care?"

"Missiles, Joe. And spare parts still in their original boxes. Safe Harbors were crammed full of useful stuff like that."

"Will those missiles still be effective?" I asked, skeptical.

"Yes. I should have said 'missile *parts*'. Sort of an assemble it yourself kit. The limited-life components, like the propulsion modules, will have expired by now, it would be dangerous to use them."

"OK, so, we can get a bunch of spare parts?" Getting kits to build only part of a missile did not sound particularly useful, but we could always use advanced technology stuff for Skippy to work with. Also, he was clearly excited about the Safe Harbor, and I needed to at least pretend to be interested.

"Better than that, Joe," he teased.

"Don't keep me in suspense, Skippy," I tipped the cup back and swallowed the rest of the coffee.

"Wait for it, waaaaaait for it. Here's the deal. Safe Harbors are not just warehouses and fuel tanks. They are semi-automated ship servicing platforms. Joe, they have *fabricators*. Not like the second-hand units we got from the Jeraptha. The Maxolhx knew that many ships coming to a Safe Harbor would have battle damage, some severe. Providing spare parts would not be enough to restore a ship's combat readiness, they need the ability to manufacture replacements for whatever a damaged ship needs. Some items like atomic-compression warheads, jump drive coils, things like that, are still beyond the ability of a Maxolhx fabricator engine to crank out but, having access to a Safe Harbor station would be a *major* advantage to us."

"I see that." My need for coffee was forgotten. "The Maxolhx have been cut off from this place for nine hundred years, you haven't told me whether we can get there or not."

"Joe, please. Have you not learned a lesson?"

I sighed. "Trust the awesomeness?"

"Egg-*zactly*."

"How can you be sure? Getting there requires waking up a dormant wormhole, right? Maybe that local network already hates you."

"That is not possible. We have had zero contact with that network, it has no reason to hate me."

I didn't say anything.

"Well," he cleared his throat. "Other than the usual reasons, I mean."

"Egg-*zactly*," I shook my head. "OK, so we, what? Bring a star carrier to this place, raid it for parts to bring back to Jaguar?"

"Ugh. You're not *listening* to me, knucklehead. This place is a gold mine for us. We can get *Valkyrie* serviced there! Then, we bring part of the fleet there. The-"

"Wait. You think a servicing station that is a thousand years old, is still *operational*?"

"I think I can *make* it operational."

"Holy shit." Until that moment, I had been assuming he was talking about a place that had nothing but old stuff we might be able to use as replacement parts for *Valkyrie*. That was nice, and it solved a problem of the ship slowly wearing out. But it wasn't a game changing event.

Having access to a Maxolhx servicing facility, even an old one, could make a huge difference for us.

If Skippy could make it work.

If we could get there.

"Can we go there, Joe?"

"Uh," Skippy didn't usually ask that we go anywhere. He was usually OK with whatever we wanted to do. Sometimes he thought our plans were stupid, but even then he had potential to be amused by our antics, so it was all good with him. "Gee, I don't know, Skippy. We're kinda busy," I lied. Both about not knowing whether I wanted to explore this abandoned safe anchorage, and about being busy. The truth was, I had no idea what to do next, other than following through on my promise to hit the Maxolhx so hard, they clean up the cloud at Earth. And hit them often, so their ships would be too busy to interfere with the Alien Legion.

"Please?" He pleaded.

Damn, maybe I should have bargained for something, like a month without him singing at Karaoke night. It was better to keep that bargaining chip for when we really needed it. "OK. I want to talk this over with the senior staff, but how long will it take to get there?"

"Six days, after we go through the wormhole we're headed for."

"That's almost a week." I had told Zhao to expect our return in five days, so a delay would make him anxious. Oh, hell, no way could we pass up this opportunity. "Program a course for this service station."

"Cool! You won't regret this, Joe!"

Dinner had been some weird vegetable thing from one of Simms's recipes, which I ate half of and managed to stuff the rest in a napkin, to hide in a pocket. Next time, I will use *two* napkins, because it soaked through my pocket and left a stain on my trousers, making me go back to my cabin for a change of uniform.

Anyway, at 2200 I was still hungry, so I went back to the galley. It wasn't yet time for midrats and I did not intend to stay up that late, my shift started at 0600. Even with a crew that was oversized to provide training for new people, we still continued our arrangement of everyone taking a turn in the galley. Sure, the rest of the fleet would likely have dedicated cooks aboard, hell, the star carriers might have barbers to keep everyone's haircuts in regulation. As far as I was concerned, *Valkyrie* was a special-ops platform, and that applied to the *Dutchman* also. It was good for esprit de corps for everyone to work in the galley, it built a sense of being a true team. Also, requiring everyone to cook selected out the people who were not team players, and those who could not handle irregular schedules. It also excluded perfectionist jerks who couldn't stand it when a dish they cooked didn't turn out right.

I remember the first time Smythe tried to serve popovers, or what he called 'Yorkshire pudding' they were awful and he had to chuck the resulting mess in the trash. The good-natured way he endured the ribbing about his burnt and flat 'puddings' told me everything I needed to know about his people skills. Also, I do not know why the Brits call those things 'Yorkshire pudding', they are not anything like pudding I've ever eaten. Two nights after that pudding disaster, I couldn't sleep and went to the galley for coffee around 0300. Jeremy Smythe, back then he was *Captain* Smythe, was there baking one batch of puddings after another, until every batch was just right. That also told me a lot of things about the guy, all good.

The next time he made Yorkshire pudding, they were hot and light and delicious.

Anyway, I needed a snack. The fryers for making French fries for midrats were not yet warmed up and I didn't want to bother the crew getting ready, so I went in the back and dug around in the pantry. "Aha!" With a plate, two slices of bread and knife, a glass of milk, and two jars from the pantry, I carried everything to a corner table for a delicious feast.

"Hey, uh, Joe, what're you doing?" Skippy whispered in my earpiece.

"Getting a late snack, why?"

"What *is* that?"

"Oh." I knew what he meant. "It's 'carmel' Fluff, Skippy."

"You mean *care*-ah-mel, Joe."

"No, it's '*car*mel', you ass."

"Carmel is a city in California," he sniffed.

"That's Car-*mel*."

"Whatever. It is still pronounced care-ah-mel."

"Uh, I think you're wrong about that," I knew I was on shaky ground. "Care-ah-mel is the liquid form. When it cools and becomes solid, it is '*car*-mel'."

"*No*," his voice dripped with scorn.

"Whatever."

"Is that allowed, or is it an abomination?"

"Huh? You mean 'carmel' Fluff? Oh, sure, it's allowed. Fluff comes in multiple flavors now. Original, and strawberry, of course. Now also 'carmel', and chocolate Fluff. They're all in the Scriptures."

"The *Scriptures*?" He laughed.

"The Gospel of Fluff, to guide the faithful. See?" I lifted the jar to point at the label. "The Scriptures even include a recipe for making fudge."

"I guess recipes are a handy thing to have in a book of spiritual guidance."

"Right. Like, Jesus served loaves and fishes, but he didn't say how you're supposed to prepare the fish."

"Probably not Cajun style."

"Uh, no."

"Well, this has certainly been an education for me."

"You're welcome."

"I wish I could stick a fork in my brain to erase *this* memory."

"You," I mumbled over a spoonful of delicious Fluff, "are a heathen savage."

"Ugh!"

"Good *night*, Skippy."

Jennifer Simms walked into her cabin, flung the gym towel in the laundry basket, and peeled off her sweaty clothes to take a shower. The exercise class she signed up for was labeled as High-Intensity Interval Training, going from one exercise to another with minimal break in between. That was not a problem, she had done interval workouts before and enjoyed a break from the mind-numbing routine of her usual exercise program. Keeping fit aboard a ship was a struggle, mostly the problem was that any running, other than short sprints, had to be done on a treadmill. She rotated her days between a treadmill, an elliptical trainer, a rowing machine and an exercise bike, but that got old. While at FOB Jaguar, she took the opportunity to run every morning, just because she could. Running outside, under a blue sky, breathing unfiltered air, where the scenery changed as the miles rolled on, was a privilege to be savored.

The monotony of exercising aboard ship had to be worse for the STAR team, their fitness standards required them to train nearly every day. *That* was the reason she was shaking from exhaustion and her muscles would be sore in the morning.

Her schedule forced her to take the evening class in the gym, a class that was filled with high-speed adrenaline junkies from the STARs. She would not make that mistake again.

Stepping out of the shower, all she wanted was to curl up on the couch while reading something that was not a report or a PowerPoint slide. Evenings were when she missed Frank the most. Sometimes they just sat on a couch together, each quietly reading a book, just *being* together. Not even needing to speak. Pulling on sweatpants and a long-sleeved shirt, she got dressed and-

She had one of Frank's old t-shirts, from the last voyage out to Avalon. Where was- The middle left drawer, that is where she put it. Sometimes she just liked to press the shirt to her face and inhale his scent, mixed with-

"Ah! No! *Skippy*!"

"What?" He appeared immediately on top of the cabinet. "Are you in danger- Um," his avatar took a step back, until he was against the bulkhead. "You are mad at me for some reason?"

"Did you do this?" She clutched Frank's shirt in one white-knuckled hand, angrily jabbing it at the avatar.

"Um?" He peered at the shirt, bewildered. "You'll need to explain what '*this*' is, I do a lot of-"

"You *washed* Frank's shirt!"

"Well, yes," he blinked. "You really don't need to thank me, it's just part of the serv-"

"How *could* you?" Her eyes filled with tears.

"Oh! Wow. Jennifer, whatever I did wrong, I am sorry. Terribly sorry."

"*Why*? Why did you do such a thing?"

"Er, I don't actually handle domestic tasks like laundry anymore," he backed up as much as he could, the brim of his holographic hat bending where it contacted the wall. "That's Bilby's area of responsibility, although he doesn't actively monitor it either. There is a submind somewhere to schedule stuff like that, I can ask the bot assigned to your cabin what it-"

Sitting down heavily on the couch, she clutched the ruined shirt in both hands, laying it flat and smoothing it across her lap. When she saw it in the drawer, she knew immediately. Instead of being rumpled, the material was crisply folded, the way the laundry bots delivered everything. "Skippy," she could not look at the avatar. "This is not one of your nasty jokes?"

"What? No! No, I would never do something like that."

"You are mean to Bishop. You insult him all the time."

"Well, that's different. I have to, because you can't."

"I can't," she looked up, wiping tears away with the back of her hand. "What do you mean?"

"*You* can't slap Joe down, he's your commanding officer."

"You do that *for* him?"

"Of course. Jennifer, Joe has enormous power, especially for someone so young. He is *so* damned young. All you monkeys are, incredibly young, I don't know how you handle the pressure at your-"

She waved a hand before Skippy went off on a tangent. "Go back to what I asked. You insult Joe, to *help* him?"

"Yes. Um, that, plus it's *fun*. And, you know," he shrugged, "because I'm an asshole," he chuckled. "Really, it's Joe's fault for being a knucklehead. If he wasn't such an easy target, I couldn't-"

"I always thought you were just being mean."

"No. I love Joe, in the way that you would love a mangy, smelly dog, I mean. He needs someone to remind him that he's not all that. The crew can't do that, he's your CO, right? So, I do it."

"You sure have a strange way of showing you care about him. Your insults are *terrible*."

"It's a guy thing."

"I'm glad I'm not a guy."

"Yeah, Frank is pretty happy about you not being a guy."

"I'll bet he is," she had to laugh.

"Joe, too."

"General Bishop?" She reflexively pulled her arms around herself. "He-"

"He likes you. Um, not in *that* way."

"That's good," she said, relieved.

"He greatly admires you, if you didn't know that. Joe is better when there are women around him, he needs that stabilizing influence."

"Do you have to be so mean to Bishop? Some of the things you say are awful."

"He knows what I mean, it's just the way guys talk sometimes. Jennifer, Joe is *lonely*. I am the only person in his life he can talk to, without having to worry about what he says because of military rank structure or regulations. He can talk to Margaret now, and that's good, but she's not *here*. During your morning status meetings, or when you are working with Joe in the galley, his cortisol levels are way down. He enjoys working with you, he needs that."

"I will, keep that in mind. Skippy," she set the shirt on the couch next to her, and clasped her hands on her lap. "Why did the laundry bot take a piece of clothing out of my drawer? Any clothing I want washed, I put in the basket."

"Let me ping the bot, I don't store that sort of information. Um, hmm. The bot noticed a funky smell coming from the drawer, and took that shirt away to be washed. Also the shirt underneath it. I'm unclear about this, did the bot do something wrong?"

"Yes!"

"Washing dirty clothing is what the laundry bots do," he said slowly. "Why-"

"That shirt smelled like *Frank*," she clenched her fists. "It's the only part of him I have out here."

"Um, oh. A shirt with your lover's scent is a thing?"

"It is for me!"

"Oops. OK, I just sent revised instructions to all domestic bots. If they detect an odd smell in the future, they will send a message to the occupant of the cabin. Jennifer, I am terribly sorry. Hey! Maybe I can fix this."

"*Fix* it? Unless you can bring Frank here right-"

"No can do, sorry. *But*, I have detailed records from the bot, including a chemical analysis of that funky smell-"

"It was not a funky smell!"

"Oops, I mean, the um, manly aroma. Hmm. Well, it appears to be mostly just basic Guy Sweat. How about if I have a bot roll that shirt around in a basket of Joe's old gym socks, and-"

"*No!*"

"OK, I heard that loud and clear," he muttered. "There also appears to have been some sort of cologne or aftershave I can't identify. Hey! Elvis used Old Spice, and *he* was the king of rock and roll. I can spray that old shirt with-"

"*Please* stop helping."

"Why do people keep telling me that?" He asked, mystified. "I thought helping was a *good* th-"

"Not the way you do it. Just tell your bots not to touch anything in my cabin."

"They do need to clean the floors and bathroom, and change the sheets and-"

"Not touch any of my personal things."

"Gotcha. Again, I am terribly sorry about this. If there is anything I can do-"

"Just don't do anything like this again."

"I won't, I promise. Again, I am sorry."

"It's OK," she sighed. "I was out of line. I'm sorry for yelling at you. I do appreciate everything you do for us. I am glad we had this talk."

"Me too. Um, it looks like I ruined your evening. Can I have a bot bring you a glass of wine?"

"I would love that, but we don't have any wine-"

"Puh-*lease*," he snorted. "Jennifer, you have *no idea* what kinds of stuff I had smuggled aboard, by hacking into the manifests. Relax," the lighting in the cabin dimmed. "A bot will have a chilled glass of your favorite chardonnay in a minute, then no one will bother you until morning."

"Thank you. Skippy?"

"Yes?"

"I suspect you tease General Bishop mostly because you are an asshole, but thank you. You're right, he needs a friend he can talk to."

"So do I. Again, I am sorry."

"I'm not happy that Frank's shirt is ruined, but I'm glad we had this talk."

"Me too. Good night."

CHAPTER SEVEN

Despite Skippy's assurance, I regretted going to the abandoned service station almost immediately, because of two pesky little details that Skippy had failed to mention. First, Semi-Automated Servicing Station 17 is deep in Rindhalu territory! The kitties put it there so ships retreating from an attack against the spiders could refuel, rearm and conduct repairs before going back into the fight, without having to fly all the way back to their home territory. Large numbers of warships traveling there would probably attract unwanted attention, so the station likely could only be used one time. The kitties considered the facility disposable in the event of war.

Which led to the second problem.

The station was placed in orbit of a gas giant planet, a sensible decision given the fuel that could be extracted from that atmosphere. What was unusual was the location of the planet. It was not orbiting the typical red dwarf type of star that we seemed to visit too often. This planet was not orbiting a star at all. It was a 'nomad' or 'rogue' world. Sometime in the distant past, a passing star had flown through the planet's original star system, dragging it out of orbit, and ejecting it completely from the host star's gravity well. Since then, it had wandered in the void between stars. When we arrived, the planet was more than six lightyears from the nearest star, flying right past it. According to Skippy, there was a seventy percent chance the nomad would be captured and go into a highly elliptical orbit around a star, in about six hundred thousand years.

I set an alarm on my phone, to make sure I didn't miss seeing that.

The crew was just as excited as I was to see a nomad planet.

Until we jumped in, ten lightminutes away.

"*Rut-roh,*" Skippy muttered, soon after we began receiving sensor data. "Hoo-boy. This is not good."

Oh, crap.

The stupid station was falling out of orbit. That is something Skippy should have anticipated, he later admitted. The problem was that the Maxolhx had put the station in a low orbit initially, tucking it close to the atmosphere, so its heat signature was less visible against the backdrop of the planet. That was important for secrecy, because the planet provided its own internal heat, lacking a star to bathe it with radiation. The station was also well within the planet's powerful magnetic field, which the station actually used for part of its power supply.

"It's skimming the top of the atmosphere at the low point of its orbit," Skippy groaned.

"Is it going to burn up?" I asked. Amazingly, the station's stealth field was somewhat operational, but it flickered and there was a gap that gave us a weird view of part of the structure. What the stealth field could not do was conceal the bright pink streak it made, as it kissed the top of the atmosphere.

"No. Not soon. The station is heavy, Joe, it has substantial mass and therefore momentum. Also, the effect we're seeing looks more dramatic than it really is. The station's orbit has become elliptical, we just happened to arrive when it is near the low point. I estimate it will not plunge into the atmosphere for another twenty-seven years."

"After a thousand years, it's close to falling *now*?

"It has been close to falling for a long time. The station was equipped with low-powered engines to keep it in a stable orbit, they must have failed at some point," he guessed.

"Uh, this thing," I pointed at the image on the display. "Is supposed to have the ability to repair damaged warships, but it can't fix itself?"

"Correct. Remember, the Maxolhx do not trust their own AIs. They would not have allowed the AI here to fix or modify itself. If they hadn't abandoned the place for so long, that wouldn't matter."

"Can *you* fix it?"

"I don't, hmm- Give me a minute. Well, darn it. The station's AI appears to be offline. The short answer is 'Yes'. I can fix anything, *we* can fix anything, given enough time. Um, we'll have to go aboard."

"Sir?" Shepard called to get my attention. He pointed at the display. "Docking with that station will be a bitch."

He was right, and he was a better pilot than me. The station must have been stable originally, now it was spinning slowly, and tumbling to the right. Or to the left, depending on how you looked at it. "Can you do it?"

Shepard didn't reply right away, which told me he is a damned good pilot. Not an overconfident jackass. "I'd like to run the approach in a simulator. Sir, assuming we're going aboard in a dropship, Lt. Chandra should fly. He has more experience in the Panther."

"XO?"

She tapped on her tablet, issuing orders. "I'll handle it."

"Good. Shepard, I do want you in a simulator, hopefully we'll be bringing *Valkyrie* into one of those maintenance bays, after we get the place stable."

We jumped in ten thousand kilometers from the station, which the pilots were now calling 'Ragnar Anchorage'. I am ashamed to say, I had to ask Chandra about that name. Consider me educated now. Did the crew approve of calling the station 'Ragnar Anchorage' instead of 'Semi-Automated Servicing Station 17'?

Yes. So say we all!

From ten thousand klicks away, Skippy scanned the station, determining the AI was indeed offline. The station still had power, not at the normal level but enough to run the engines and thrusters.

"I don't know about this," I said. It was not good for the crew to hear their commander having doubts, but I was trying a new Truth and Openness policy, as opposed to my previous tactic of concealing sensitive information from the crew.

Simms looked at me questioningly, before Skippy could speak. "Sir, it's basically a complete senior-species *shipyard*. What's not to like?"

Of course Simms thought the station was perfect. Her background was logistics. Finding a repair facility that was crammed full of spare parts was a gold mine to her. Better than a gold mine. A mine that could make gold out of raw materials.

She had a point. In warfare, especially peer-state conflicts where both sides have similar levels of technology, strategy and tactics and training and individual initiative are all great, but what often wins battles is simple numbers. Whichever side gets to the battle space in bigger numbers, with the ability to support and sustain that force, and to replace losses of manpower and material as necessary, usually won the battle.

That was true of peer-state, symmetrical warfare.

We weren't fighting that kind of war.

We didn't have the resources, in manpower or material, for a fair fight against the Maxolhx, or the Rindhalu if the spiders acted against us. Our only hope for victory, our only hope for *survival*, was asymmetrical warfare. Call it 'guerilla warfare' if you want to use an old term. Asymmetrical warfare has many forms; the one I learned about first in the Army was the strategy used by George Washington against the British. He knew the colonies could not beat the British Empire in a stand-up fight, could not even concentrate enough combat power to win a single major set-piece battle without help. The British had several huge advantages including mobility; their command of the sea allowed them to rapidly move troops along the coast. Washington also knew he was fighting more than just an external enemy; American 'Loyalists' made the revolution a civil war also.

So, George knew he had to harass the British, wear them down and make them decide that keeping the colonies was not worth the cost. Britain was at war with France, again, and could not afford to divert the majority of its combat power away from Europe. Washington also knew the British had a very long supply line, and the American Army had another ally that isn't mentioned in the history books: malaria. Many of the British troops came from areas that had no exposure to the type of malaria-carrying mosquitos found in the Americas, particularly south of Maryland, and so they had no immunity to the scourge. Disease whittled down the strength of the British, even before shots were fired.

Yes, as an American, I did not like learning that our victory in the Revolutionary War was not entirely due to the courage of the Minutemen, but the US Army builds professional soldiers. We have to deal with facts, not myths.

I also did not like learning that in the Vietnam War, Ho Chi Minh studied Washington's tactics and used them against us.

Why do I mention ancient history? Because the lessons are totally valid today. *Valkyrie*, even with the 1st Fleet, could not clean up the cloud before it froze Earth. We could encourage other species to ally with us, but no aliens would sign on with us, unless we could protect them from the Maxolhx. Which we couldn't do yet. We lacked the power to stop them from striking our potential allies, and we lacked the power to crush or even make a dent in their massive military machine.

What we could do was put pressure on their leadership. Conduct large, showy hit-and-run attacks, in a shock-and-awe campaign directed at their public. Make the average Maxolhx citizen question whether their leadership had been wise to strike Earth directly. Make Jane and John Maxolhx ask whether it would be so bad to leave the troublesome humans alone.

And maybe, when the time was right, tell the Maxolhx public that their leadership had a backup plan for a small group of the elites to leave the galaxy in arkships, and let everyone else die.

Yeah, essentially, it was sort of the thing I hated being involved with in Nigeria: a hearts and minds campaign. Only instead of trying to get the enemy to like us, all we wanted was for them to decide the price of fighting us was too high.

Just like good old George Washington.

"What's not to like, XO?" I repeated the question from Simms. "Ragnar seems too good to be true. Before we commit, I want to make damned sure there isn't some hidden problem. Skippy, show us a star chart of, oh, a thirty lightyear radius from here. Put on it any star system that is inhabited, or has any type of Rindhalu sensors. Add in known star lanes, where Rindhalu or their client ships travel. Oh, and any active wormholes."

Though I was ready for an argument from him, he just did what I asked. "Other than the wormhole we came through, the closest active one is sixty lightyears away. There are *no* regularly-traveled star lanes within thirty lightyears, the closest one leads away from the wormhole I mentioned. Other than ships transiting that wormhole, the only sensor platform I know of is in an uninhabited star system sixty-three lightyears from here. Why do you care?"

"Because," I pointed at the display. "We can *see* the station. It's leaving a heat signature now. What will happen if we get it operational, and it's generating even more heat?"

"Ugh. It won't be-"

"I thought you said the kitties chose this place because it's remote? Sixty lightyears is not a long distance for a senior species ship to fly. The spiders could be here at any moment. And why-"

"Are you going to keep asking questions, or will you eventually *shut up* so I can answer?"

"Sorry. Go ahead."

"First, numbskull, I never said this nomad planet is remote for the spiders, I said it is remote for the purpose of the Maxolhx. They always intended this station to be a single-use asset. It is close to the wormhole that went dormant, they never considered coming here from the other wormhole that is sixty lightyears away, because the other end of *that* wormhole is in a cluster the Rindhalu use heavily."

"Sixty lightyears? Sixty *years* before light from this place will be seen by the spiders? Then why the hell were the kitties worried about this place being discovered?"

"Because, before the wormhole we just came through went dormant, the other end was in a cluster that saw a lot of traffic. Don't worry, both wormholes in that cluster went dormant, the spiders never go there now. So, did I answer that question?"

"Yes. You-"

"Your other question is actually somewhat intelligent."

"Thanks, I-"

"But, as usual, woefully uninformed," he shook his head sadly. "Yes, we can see a heat signature leaking through the stealth field from here, but from any appreciable distance, the infrared radiation would be lost against the background. Also, the inevitable increase in heat output will not be a problem. Uh!" He raised a finger to preemptively shush me, before I could object. "Assuming we get the station operational and begin servicing ships, we will also restore the stealth field."

"Yeah, I understand that. The stealth field can only trap photons for a limited time, then the heat has to go *somewhere*." Starships carried sinks to trap heat while flying in stealth mode. We usually dumped heat after we jumped away from a star system. That generated a *big* infrared signature, but by the time anyone noticed, we were long gone. "That station is just going around in circles, anywhere it dumps heat, it will be visible."

"Again with the ignorance? Wow, you are on *fire* today. What you don't know, dumdum, is that the kitties thought of that, *duh*. The station trails a cable down into the atmosphere, to bleed off heat. The cable is still there, for some reason the heat transfer isn't taking place. We can fix that too, and then, presto! The station will be practically invisible. Now, if you will stop pestering me with stupid questions, I can check the station to see exactly what is needed to bring it back online."

For a reply, I made a gesture of zipping my lips shut.

"What's the problem?" I asked, after Skippy took way too long examining the place.

"Um, well, a bunch of power conduits are burned out. It looks like some conduits failed due to lack of maintenance, then power flow was shifted to other conduits, and they overloaded. The maintenance bots are offline, most of them are in their storage alcoves but they're dead. Their powercells ran out a long time ago. Ugh. We'll have to do this the hard way. I need you monkeys to go over there, and put your grubby little fingers to work."

"Right. Because calling us grubby little monkeys is a great way to ensure we work well together."

"Sorry," he muttered.

"You think *we* can fix the engines?"

"The repair crews should bring some of *Valkyrie's* bots with them but, Jeez, I think some of the equipment over there is just *stuck*. Seals have dried out over the years, gears and pistons are jammed, and-"

"Are you telling me we can fix the station's engines with a *can of PB Blaster*?"

"Um- I hate to say this but, yeah, sort of."

"You're kidding me."

"PB Blaster penetrating oil is a miracle substance, Joe."

"That's what my father says." When doing something like removing an old water pump from a truck, my father's use of PB Blaster came between 'please come loose' by using a socket set, and the final 'that was not a request' step of getting out the cutting torch. "OK, we'll try it."

Admiral Reichert, the current chief strategist of the Maxolhx Hegemony, had questions. He had questions, because the people who ruled the Hegemony had answers they wanted from him. They had agreed to his high-risk plan to attack the human homeworld, a plan he assured them was *low*-risk. But, instead of crawling to the Hegemony to beg for mercy, the humans had struck back. The attack was a pinprick, and would have no effect on the military's ability to carry out its mission. Reichert had soothed the alarmed officials by stating that the human attack was merely for show, a desperate act by a weak and desperate people. The purpose of the strike against the shipyard at Retonovir was to boost morale on the doomed human homeworld, because the atmospheric mass drivers had been constructed there. If the humans were able to conduct an attack that could actually cause significant harm to the Hegemony, they would have done that instead.

The officials accepted his reasoning, but they were not satisfied. The attack at Retonovir might have been annoying rather than dangerous, but it *was* annoying. The public was asking questions, and that was even more annoying. So, those in authority asked Reichert, demanding answers: how could he prevent future attacks?

To answer that question, he posed questions to the Strategic Planning Section, a group of powerful AIs that performed analysis for the military. "Explain how the attack on the Retonovir shipyard was conducted."

The AI replied immediately. "Unknown."

"That is unacceptable."

"There is insufficient data to perform a useful analysis," the AI added.

Reichert's claws extended from his fingers as he became angry at the stubborn machine. The AI knew that if it were not useful to its masters, it might be erased and replaced. "There is *never* enough data."

"In this case," the AI said with what Reichert imagined was a hint of sarcasm. "The loss of the shipyard AI means the only data on the incident was collected by sources on the ground, which are not detailed enough to-"

"Guess, then, damn it! How were the humans able to get through our defenses?"

"Unknown. Admiral, my failure to determine how the attack was conducted is not due only to a lack of data. Our current level of technology is incapable of carrying out an attack the way the humans did. Their ghost ship appeared suddenly *inside* a spacedock, and launched crude fusion weapons from *inside* the station. Our science is not capable of offering an explanation of how that could be possible."

"Then you are worthless to me."

"That is for you to determine. The Strategic Planning Group is also unable to explain several other recent events. The human attack against the Thuranin facility under the planet Slithin, for example. *We* could not have destroyed that facility, yet from all evidence, it appears the humans accomplished the act by firing a single shot from an unknown weapon. We do have excellent data on that incident, and as yet, we can offer not even a framework of a theory of how the destruction at Slithin could have happened. We also have, as you know, excellent data on the incident in which the ghost ship eluded your ambush, by coming to a dead stop in space. *That* was, according to our understanding of physics, flatly impossible. We also can offer no explanation for how the ghost ship was able to destroy so many of your ships, after it rose from the atmosphere of the ice giant planet. We do know that the weapon deployed against your ships was the same type they used at Slithin. However, that weapon, whatever it was, appears to lack the ability to cause the damage we saw. Therefore, we must conclude that the humans have technology far beyond our understanding."

Reichert knew it was useless to argue with a machine. It could not provide answers it didn't have. "Continue analysis. I also require a forecast of where the humans might strike next."

"Insufficient data."

"Not long ago, the Strategic Planning Group was confident in the ability of your predictive models to forecast future actions by the humans!"

"We were," the AI hesitated, "too optimistic. Admiral, it has become clear that our experience with the humans is too short to calculate probabilities of their actions over a short time horizon. There is also the fact that they are a young and impulsive species. All we can say is that their actions, those we know about, reveal an enemy that is unpredictable, reckless, incapable of considering long-term strategy, and something far more dangerous to us."

That remark surprised Reichert. "What could be more dangerous?"

"The humans are also *clever*."

Fixing Ragnar station took a lot more than a can of PB Blaster. It took a long, frustrating eight days to get Ragnar up and running, then to stabilize it. Slowly, the station boosted its orbit so it was no longer in immediate danger of falling into the rogue planet. Once we had the anchorage in a nice, circular orbit, Skippy wanted to bring *Valkyrie* in to dock, and Shepard was eager to do it for real, rather than in a simulator.

"No," I decided.

"But, the fabricators are working again!" Skippy protested. "Mostly," he added. The truth was, none of the fabricators were fully operational. The unit that was in the best condition was busy cranking out parts to get the other fabricators back online.

"How long until they're ready to service *Valkyrie*?"

"Um, well, that depends on-"

"We have been away too long already, the Navy must be having a heart attack. Zhao expected us to return directly from Retonovir. We need to get back."

"But-"

"The *Yangtze* should be flightworthy by the time we get back, right?" I mentioned one of the four star carriers we got from the Jeraptha.

"Yes, unless something major went wrong with the refit. But-"

"Outstanding. Then we can bring *Yangtze* back here, maybe with the big combat ships."

"Ugh. Fine. But *Valkyrie* needs to go first. With all the abuse this ship has taken, it-"

"By the time we get back here, the station should be up and running?"

"For sure. I mean, probably."

"That's what I thought." The AI of the station was not like the ones the Maxolhx installed aboard their warships. Instead of being built into the structure, the substrate of the station's AI was a separate module. Skippy made sure the thing was dead, then he used bots to tear it out, and just to be sure we dropped it into the planet's atmosphere. The station was now being run by several subminds created by Skippy, they were capable enough of completing the work to get Ragnar restored to full operational capacity.

I grudgingly had to admit to being impressed by the engineering skills of the Maxolhx. Their station had been abandoned for one thousand and eighty-three years, but most of the gear aboard needed only minor work to get it running again. Really, I should have known how rugged their technology was; *Valkyrie* had taken a lot of hard use and was still flying. "The station can continue repairs while we're gone?"

"It should, it's being run by my subminds. I can't guarantee it if we're not here, but-"

"If you set up those subminds, I'm going to trust the awesomeness. We are outta here."

"Ugh. OK, *fine*," he said, in a way that meant it was not fine at all. "Listen, numbskull, completing repairs to Ragnar will not take as long as our flight to Jaguar and back. Especially if we'll be dragging half the freakin' Navy with us on the return flight. It is a waste for the station to just sit here and do nothing. Is there anything you want it to do while we're gone?"

"Depends. What *can* it do?"

"Um, well, Jeez, a lot."

"All right. I want to give priority to anything that delivers ordnance on target."

"Gotcha. There are magazines crammed full of missiles here. I can get the station to inspect them, and get as many in flightworthy condition as possible."

"Skippy," I put both hands over my heart. "*How* did you know what I wanted for Christmas?"

"It was an easy guess," he muttered. "Think about it, Joe: at least twelve *thousand* ship-killer missiles."

"Oooh, now you're turning me on."

"Do you need a shower?" he snickered.

"What I need is for you to make good on your promise. How long until you-"

"Done."

"Done?"

"Yup. I gave instructions to my subminds, then asked when they could get started on the missiles. They just told me to shut up so they could get to work. Man, why are so many of my subminds such *assholes*?"

"It's a mystery for sure," I rolled my eyes. "Shepard, jump us out of here."

"Sir?" Perkins held up her phone as she walked into General Ross's office. "Admiral Zhao wants us upstairs. *Mississippi* is coming out of refit later this morning, he wants a ceremony to mark the occasion."

"Mississippi," Ross snorted. "It reminds me of my childhood."

Perkins pursed her lips, puzzled. "I thought you grew up in-"

"No," he smiled, thinking of a fond memory. "I didn't grow up there, it's something you say when playing flag football. You count 'One Mississippi, then two, then three. It marks three seconds." He shrugged. "Sometimes the defense cheats and says 'One Miss*ippi*', cuts it short."

She understood. "Of course, *you* never did that?"

"Never," he winked. "Mississippi. I knew working with allies would require compromises but," he shook his head. "This seems ridiculous."

Naming the former Jeraptha ships, that would become the United Nations Navy, was a task not left to Admiral Zhao and his staff. The decision was made by UNEF Command on Earth, a group of people who had to please their governments and the public. Every nation involved needed to feel they had a piece of the pie.

Originally, it was assumed the ships would be named for the UNEF member states. The first ship to come out of refit would have been named the star carrier *America*, then the *China*, and so on.

Immediately, a howl of protests began on Earth. With twenty-nine warships in the 1st Fleet, there were not enough hulls to soothe the pride of all the nations that provided manpower, equipment and funding to support FOB Jaguar. A compromise was reached, no doubt involving public relations firms, focus groups, and favors being traded behind the scenes.

The four star carriers would be *Yangtze*, *Mississippi*, *Ganges* and *Rhine*. The battleships were *Atlantic* and *Pacific*, with the battlecruisers being tagged as *Thames*, *Loire*, *Amazon* and *Volga*. Going down the list, that left seven heavy cruisers: *Yukon*, *Congo*, *Nile*, *Ishikari*, *Orinoco*, *Danube* and, for Australia, the *Murray-Darling*. That last ship's name caused some laughter, until the name was shortened to the *Murray*. Because that sounded like it was named for someone's uncle, it was assigned the callsign 'Oz'. UNEF Command was still arguing over names for the fourteen destroyers, when the Maxolhx shot a cloud at Earth, and everyone had more important things to worry about.

"I can see the advantage of naming ships for rivers, or bodies of water. Or mountains."

"Rivers and mountains are in *countries*," Ross made a disgusted sound. "It's a cheap way to make sure no one is offended."

"Yes, but there will be combat losses," Perkins noted. "Would you rather lose a ship named 'America', or one named for a river?"

"Good point," he conceded. "What happened? I thought the *Yangtze* was completing refit first."

She checked the message on her zPhone. "During testing yesterday, they found microfractures in the struts that anchor one of *Yangtze's* reactors to the spine. Nagatha estimates a delay of four days."

"Four days? These fleet service ships are great, but at this rate, I'll be retired before we have a fleet to work with. Seventeen months?" He snorted. "I know we're already expecting a miracle, but Earth can't wait a year and a half. We might not have a homeworld to rescue, by the time we have ships to do the job. Another delay," he grunted. "We'll be dealing with a pissed-off senior admiral, then. Wonderful."

"No, Sir. I checked with Zhao's staff, he's in a good mood this morning. Disappointed that *Yangtze* doesn't have the honor of going first, but he now has an operational star carrier under his command. His staff gave me the impression Zhao has more important things to worry about."

"Perkins, you would have made an excellent staff officer. But we're lucky you chose a different path."

"It was sort of chosen for me," she grimaced. "Damned sneaky beer can."

"You have regrets?"

"I don't regret destroying a Kristang battlegroup over Paradise. I *do* regret not knowing I was being manipulated."

"Gosh," he feigned shock. "Someone concealed important information from you? I can't *imagine* what that is like."

"Sorry," she said, though she was *not* sorry, and they both knew it.

On the way back to Jaguar, the crew was excited about our tremendous success at Retonovir, and even more excited about finding an intact Maxolhx automated shipyard. On advice from Simms, I took some time off from writing reports, to get exercise and spend time with the crew. In *Valkyrie's* gym, I played a three-on-three basketball game and worked up a serious sweat. Also, my team won! Yes, the other players on my team were from the STARs, and the other team was two pilots and an engineer. But we *won*. Can't argue with a 'W', right?

Slapping high-fives with my team, I tossed a towel over my shoulder. "Whew, good game. Thanks, everyone." Glancing at the clock projected on the opposite bulkhead, I remembered I had a staff meeting in less than an hour. "Time to hit the shower."

"Um, hey, Joe," Skippy's voice came from a speaker. "You might want to take it easy."

"I hit four three-pointers, Skippy," I objected. "I was *on fire* today."

"I didn't say take it easy in the gym, although you're not twenty anymore. I meant, take it easy in the *show-er*," he dragged the word out. "If you know what I mean."

The other people on the court were smirking at me.

"Damn it, Skippy," I shook a fist at his unseen voice. "I have a girlfriend now, and-"

"Egg-*zactly*. We will be back to Jaguar in a few days, Margaret should be there. All I'm saying is, maybe you should save some for her, huh?"

"Oh for-"

"You might want to set a cut-off date for, um, certain activities. A day or two, although, with you, maybe a week would be better."

"Will you-"

"Give the blisters time to heal, you know?"

"You are-"

"*Ooh*, now I feel like *I* need a shower after even talking about this."

"That is *not-*"

"The thought of you monkeys humping is gross enough, but *you* with Margaret? *Ee-ewww*, I wanna *ralph*."

"Margaret *likes* me."

"Meh," he sniffed. "That's one theory. I assume she hopes her suffering in this life will be rewarded in her next life."

"You are such a-"

"Or, she is taking one for the team, so no other woman has to suffer. Damn, she should get a *medal* for that."

"Are you done now?'"

"Pretty much, yeah."

"Thank you so much for the advice."

"Oh, no problem. Any time."

"How about never?"

"*Ugh*. Fine. But then next time you ask me for assistance in the bedroom, you-"

People were staring at me in shock. "I have never asked you for help!"

"Well, sure, not directly. But if your awkward fumbling around is *not* a cry for help, I don't know what-"

"Could you *please* shut up? I'm begging you."

"If you insist."

After playing basketball, I was nursing a sore ankle, and thinking that what Skippy said about me not being twenty years old anymore was right. Damn, I used to do all kinds of stupid things without consequences, now I could hurt my back just getting out of bed in the morning. It's not the years, I told myself, it's the mileage.

"Sir?" Simms knocked on my office door frame, while I was revising my report about our action at Retonovir. She had the weary expression that warned me I was in trouble, again. No, *that* look on her face usually meant something was annoying her, and she needed me to do something about it.

"Come in, XO," I closed my laptop. "What's up?"

"You requested Skippy create user manuals for the new ships," she said, sitting down heavily in a chair.

"Yes. Is that little shithead dragging his feet?" Skippy did not like the idea of monkeys knowing how our new ships operated and how to maintain equipment. He argued that the native AIs should handle anything more complicated than a doorknob, and there was some truth to the notion that we humans did not yet understand some of the basic principles of how advanced technology functioned. Regardless, we had to start somewhere. The UN had ambitions to operate multiple fleets of warships that might range far and wide across the galaxy, we couldn't continue to rely on Skippy, or even Nagatha or Bilby, to keep the ships running for us. Plus, I knew part of Skippy's objections was that if we filthy monkeys could fly and maintain ships on our own, we wouldn't need him quite so much. Skippy often protested that he did not care what anyone thought about him, but that was bullshit.

His ego was as fragile as it was enormous and he needed us almost more than we needed him.

"No. The content of the manuals is not the problem, they are well-written and practical."

"Then what-"

"The problem is the *format*. There is a Dash Ten for each system," she held a thumb and index finger far apart, like she was holding a thick stack of documents. "And a sort of YouTube video. The video is the most useful part of the manuals."

"OK, so what-"

"Each video begins with an advertisement."

"Uh-" My brain blew a gasket. "A *what* again?"

"A thirty-to-sixty second ad."

"Ad? For, for what?"

"Anything. Energy drinks, life insurance, you name it."

"Advertising?! *Skippy!*"

"Oh for-" His avatar shimmered to life, arms folded across his little chest, already peeved at me. "What am I in trouble for now?"

"You sold *advertising time* in the user manuals?"

"Of course I did, *duh*. We gotta monetize the-"

"No, you do not gotta monetize *anything* out here. Kill the ads," I demanded, shaking my fists at him.

"Sorry, no can do. I made substantial commitments back on Earth. Do you want to get me in legal jeopardy? Uh, Joe? You don't, do you?" He added when I didn't answer right away. "Hey! You jerk, I should-"

"No. Ads."

"But-"

"If you get sued for not delivering on your deal, you can blame me."

"It's not that easy, knucklehead. I signed contracts."

"Fine. Then blame it on a 'force majeure' event, beyond your control."

"Um, how the hell do *you* know fancy legal terms?"

"Believe me, I wish I didn't. No. Ads."

"Ugh. All righty, then."

Being prepared for a long argument, I felt deflated when he gave up. "OK, thank you. XO, is that all you wanted to-"

"Tell him about the opera," Simms jabbed a finger at the avatar.

"Opera? Oh, you're kidding me," I hid my eyes behind a hand. "You *sing* the freakin' instruction manual?"

"No," Skippy scoffed. "Of course not. As if. I never heard anything so ridiculous in my life. Please. That would be stup-"

"He interrupts the videos to sing selections from his operas," Simms explained.

Not wanting to get into an extended argument, I shrugged. "Then we tell people to fast-forward the video. Problem solv-"

"The fast-forward feature is disabled," she glared, fortunately at Skippy rather than me.

"Shit. Skippy, you can't do that."

"Well, *excuse me* for wanting to inject a bit of culture into people's lives. The crew needs a break, when they are studying dry stuff like maintenance on dropship landing gear."

"Fine, but *they* get to decide when to take a break, and what to do during their break."

"Ugh. Um, OK, how about I add a feature where people can opt out of the opera?"

Simms pursed her lips and nodded with satisfaction, but I was suspicious. "This, uh, opt-out process. Will it involve correctly answering, like, a hundred really tough math questions?"

"Crap, the monkey's onto my scheme," Skippy muttered to himself.

"I have a counter proposal," I said quickly, before Simms could react by wrapping her hands around the avatar's neck. "People have to opt *in*, to watch the opera scenes."

"*What*?" He snatched off his hat and threw it on the desk. "No one will do that!"

"Exactly." Simms grinned when I said that, I grinned back at her.

"This is *totally* unfair," he fumed.

"If you want people to listen to your operas, write better operas."

"*Huuuuh*," he gasped in shock. "How *dare* you?"

"Or, you know, try writing the type of music the crew actually listens to."

"Please. This bunch of cretins? Um, just for the sake of argument, what type of music would that be?"

"Depends on the nationality, I guess? Hip-hop is a good choice. Maybe K-pop?"

"Hip-hop, Joe?" He rolled his eyes.

"You're right. That would be way too tough for you. Maybe you should stick to-"

"You are saying I *can't* do it?"

Part of my brain was screaming Shut Up Shut Up FOR THE LOVE OF GOD *SHUT UP*, but of course my stupid mouth didn't get the memo. "Skippy, it's not for me to judge whether you can write good Hip-hop. The audience will decide."

"Oh, challenge *accepted*, knucklehead. You'll see. I will be known far and wide as Rap Master Skippy-Skip."

"More like your rapper name will be 'Lil Shithead'," I muttered.

"Hey! You jerk, I-"

Simms wisely stood up abruptly. "We're done here, then?" Mercifully, that ended the discussion. Skippy's avatar faded out, him glaring at me and muttering under his breath until the last photon winked out. Simms turned back to me in the doorway. "Thank you."

"Don't thank me yet."

"Why?"

"I have a bad feeling that suggesting Skippy write Hip-hop was an extremely bad idea."

She arched an eyebrow. "As long as we agree it wasn't *my* idea."

CHAPTER EIGHT

Valkyrie came out of jump near the dormant wormhole that led to our forward operating base. Maybe it was more accurate to call FOB Jaguar a '*Secure Operating Base*', because it wasn't really *near* anything. An FOB is usually close to the action, although with Elder wormholes providing shortcuts all across the galaxy, anything close to a wormhole could be close to everything else.

Also, *S*.O.B. is a different acronym, you know?

It was also not accurate to say we jumped in near the dormant wormhole, because the figure-8 racetrack that weird Elder construct used when it was operating, covered three quarters of a lightyear. Anywhere in that vast area could be considered 'near' the wormhole, because while dormant, it did not have a presence in local spacetime.

As Skippy would say, 'Ugh'. That was also not entirely accurate. A dormant wormhole, but not a *dead* one, did maintain a minimal connection to local spacetime, so it could restore itself to active when or if needed.

Anyway, enough with the technical *blah blah blah*. Each time we went through the wormhole inbound, toward Jaguar, Skippy selected a different potential emergence point, to wake the thing up. The Jeraptha had been through that wormhole, so its existence was no longer a secret, and we had to assume the Rindhalu and possibly the Maxolhx knew about it. Unless an enemy threw thousands of ships into a blockade effort, they had no chance to guess where Skippy would make the wormhole emerge next, so we felt pretty safe about it.

Bullshit.

I was nervous every time *Valkyrie* was hanging motionless in space, waiting for the stupid wormhole to wake up, and do whatever the hell it did until the event horizon was stable enough for us to go through.

"Joe," Skippy snapped at me. "Drumming your fingers on the arm rest will not make this process go any faster. You are also annoying the entire bridge crew."

"Oh. Sorry," I put my hands in my lap. "Keep doing, what you're doing."

"You make it sound like I'm not doing anything."

"No. It-"

"Waking up and realigning a wormhole is a delicate process, numbskull. If I don't do this right, the thing will be thrown out of alignment, and it could take *weeks* for the event horizons to synchronize, so ships can transition through."

"I *said* I was sorry. Uh, how would we know whether a wormhole is out of alignment?" I did not like to hear that the ends of a wormhole could be unsynchronized. "We couldn't fall into one by accident, could we?"

"Ugh. *No*. Well, I guess- Jeez, who knows what stupid things monkeys might do? When a wormhole is out of alignment, it is usually very obvious; the event horizons flicker and change color, and the edges are not as distinct. Wormholes usually project a sort of deflector field that nudges incoming objects away if the event horizon is not stable, but a ship that is determined to destroy itself could get through, with sufficient effort. It is not something that could happen by accident. However, monkeys are stupid, so-"

"OK, good safety tip," I stifled a yawn. Sure, what Skippy was doing was super important, but it was also super slow and super *boring*.

"Am I keeping you awake? Does little Joey need a nap?"

"No, I just-" Damn it, everyone on the bridge had something to do, except me. "Forget I said anything. Please continue to demonstrate your awesomeness."

We arrived back at FOB Jaguar to find the place hopping with activity. All three fleet support ships were running around the clock, to refit our batch of tired old warships and make them into something that could take on anyone other than the two senior species.

The upgrades were the problem. The Jeraptha fabricators, even after Skippy modified them, could not produce some of the really cool stuff necessary to make our second-hand ships into the kick-ass Navy we needed. Getting access to Ragnar changed all that, which was good, but also caused headaches for Zhao and his staff. Immediately upon our arrival, Skippy presented a new set of refit plans, which required sending some ships that had been completed back into the fabrication shops again, to have brand-new components torn out. Some of those components could be recycled, but the whole thing was going to take more *time*, and time was a restriction not even Skippy could do anything about.

Zhao was frustrated, but he understood the incredible value of Ragnar. We were not limited to the resources of three old Jeraptha support ships, we could refit the ships to be more powerful than we had dared dream about. Skippy thought the upgraded ships might even be able to take on the Maxolhx, if we had numerical superiority and chose our battles carefully. But, we warned against getting too confident, and Zhao knew he had to use our little fleet very carefully.

We quickly made plans to bring slightly more than half of the ships to Ragnar, to be worked on there. The less important ships, like the assault carriers, troop transports and destroyers, would get limited upgrades in the first cycle. Zhao planned to use his destroyers as scouts rather than combatants, and he suggested that if we got another batch of ships, he would rather have a large number of frigates than a small number of cruisers. Most species used small, inexpensive frigates as scouts and sensor pickets, to locate the enemy so the big ships could jump in and smash them. Or, to warn the Navy that an enemy force was in the area. With so few capital ships in our little Navy, we could not afford for them to fall into an ambush.

One system aboard our new ships would not be upgraded by Skippy, and that was a good thing. The ships would be managed by their original Jeraptha AIs, with a few security modifications. Those AIs would not have the speed and power of Skippy, Nagatha or Bilby, but they also would not have the annoying restrictions. The Jeraptha AIs were capable of flying and fighting their ships mostly by themselves, so they could react faster than ships that had to be controlled by filthy monkeys.

The Jeraptha AIs also did not request to sing on karaoke night.

I envied the crews of those ships.

Anyway, there was another ceremony at Club Skippy, to acknowledge my promotion to Brigadier General Bishop. Normally, I hate military ceremonies, they involve getting there way too early and standing around way too long, and wearing a stiff dress uniform that might not fit perfectly, because somehow it shrank since the last time you wore it. Also, ceremonies usually consist of some blowhard taking half an hour or more to say absolutely *nothing*, or at least nothing important enough to keep hard-working soldiers from attempting to speed-run through Mario Kart.

This time, I actually looked forward to the ceremony. Yes, it would have been nicer if my parents were there, but as the great philosopher Mick Jagger said: you can't always get what you want.

Oh, and Nagatha attended the ceremony. Not just in orbit, she was *at* Club Skippy. No, she was not inhabiting the body of a robot. She had a holographic avatar now. Apparently, she had created one while *Valkyrie* was at Retonovir. Aboard the *Dutchman*, she could communicate just fine as a disembodied voice. But at Jaguar, with her needing to talk with people aboard multiple ships and on the ground, people who didn't know her, it was more effective if people could interact by *seeing* her.

It was nice to-

Oh, you want to know what Nagatha chose as an avatar?

Gosh, will you look at the time? It is *so* late, I have to go, sorry.

Oof. OK.

Uh, how do I say this?

From her voice, I always pictured her looking like that French chef lady, from the old cooking videos my grandmother used to watch. Julia something. You know, like a kindly older aunt, someone who baked cookies for you.

Apparently, Nagatha's image of herself was a little bit different from what I pictured in my head. She wore a dress, and what I think are called 'sensible shoes'? No high heels. She also wore little half-glasses on top of her head, like she only needed them to read recipes. And her auburn hair was gathered in a loose bun on top of her head. All pretty standard, really.

Except, she kind of looked like she had modeled herself on Anastacia, just a bit. Like, she was, uh, how do I say this delicately? She was younger than I imagined. That's, uh, all I am going to say about the subject.

The *Flying Dutchman* went through the Elder wormhole, with Major Reed willing her hands not to clench around the arm rests of the command chair, in the ship's cramped bridge compartment. She had been through a wormhole many times, either at the ship's controls, or while off-duty. But being in command, without her fingers on the flight controls, was new and uncomfortable. If something went wrong, she couldn't simply *do* something, she had to order the pilots to take action, and the time lag might be fatal.

The real problem was that the two pilots were new, and she didn't know them well.

No. The *real* problem was that Samantha Reed liked being in control of her life, and not relying on others.

Get over it, she told herself. You're in command now. Command, Sami, *command*.

"Ma'am?" The officer at the sensor station called from the Combat Information Center, not having to shout as usual. One of Sami's first acts as captain of the *Dutchman* was to order a hole cut in the glass partition that separated the bridge from the CIC. She had always thought having the glass partition, actually a tough see-through ceramic material, was silly. Bishop liked the partition, because it made for fewer distractions when he was engaged in long and often childish arguments with Skippy. The Elder AI wasn't there anymore, and Reed liked to keep conversations short and to the point. "Sensors are back online."

"Fireball, all stations report ready for flight," Nagatha added.

Sami cringed, glaring at the speaker in the ceiling with one eye. She had requested the ship's AI refer to her as 'Captain' or 'Major Reed', but Nagatha pretended to forget. The previously good, even friendly relationship she had enjoyed with Nagatha had changed when she took command of the ship. The problem there, Sami suspected, was that the ship's AI was still upset about Bishop leaving for another ship. Nagatha had a crush on their young general, and resented anyone who took what she considered to be his rightful place.

"Thank you, Nagatha." Sami knew it was best to ignore the AI's mild insult. "Signal *Valkyrie*, please."

"Connected."

"General Bishop, this is Reed. We are ready for departure."

"Understood, *Captain* Reed," Bishop replied with a chuckle. "Take care of the *Dutchman* for us, please."

"I won't scratch the paint, Sir. Godspeed to you."

"Same to you. And, Reed?"

"Sir?"

"Don't be a hero. One ship won't save Earth."

She knew that wasn't true. The *Flying Dutchman* had saved their homeworld many times. But she got the point. "This is a recon mission. We jump in, look around, jump away."

"Keep that in mind. Bishop out."

The lead pilot looked back at her, and Reed nodded. "Jump option Delta. Punch it."

The *Dutchman* disappeared into twisted spacetime.

We escorted the star carriers *Mississippi* and *Yangtze* to Ragnar, while Reed took the *Dutchman* went to check in at Earth again. I had congratulated Reed on her first official command, she didn't seem entirely happy about it. Ah, she would grow into the job, I figured. We had set several options to rendezvous when she was done checking on the situation at Earth. I kind of envied her, she was off on independent command, while we were stuck with what would hopefully be a real UN Navy soon. Both of our new star carriers were loaded down with every ship their hard points could handle. It was a slow and frustrating flight, and after we went through the last wormhole, I left the star carriers behind, while *Valkyrie* flew ahead to make sure Ragnar was ready.

When we reached Ragnar Anchorage, the place was already a beehive of activity. The submind Skippy left behind had been busy making repairs, and getting the fabricators to crank out the unique components we needed for upgrading our second-hand Jeraptha ships. A major, huge advantage of getting access to a 'Safe Harbor' facility was that it came pre-stocked with raw materials. Tanks of nano goo, exotic matter that no mobile fabricator could manufacture, and rare elements that were hard to find, all were there waiting for us. That was good, because by definition, a nomad planet did not have an asteroid belt nearby. Nor did the planet have any moons we could mine for raw materials. Skippy thought the world used to have moons, but they got ejected from orbit, or fell into the thick atmosphere when the planet was yanked out of its star system.

Anyway, we arrived to find bots buzzing around and crawling all over the station, making final preparations to receive our ships. "Ugh," Skippy huffed, disgusted.

"What?" My hopeful happiness evaporated. "What's wrong?"

"Oh, nothing. It's just- That stupid submind I left here is whining about how *lonely* it is, and how *overworked*, and how nobody *appreciates* it. Oh, *gag* me. Jeez Louise, how can anything created from *me* be such a drama queen?"

"It is a mystery for sure," I rolled my eyes.

"Oh, shut up," he sniffed.

"Is our room ready," I pointed to the designated maintenance bay, highlighted on the display. "Or is it too early for check-in time?"

"It's ready. Be careful," he urged. "This ship is a *big* sumbitch, it could make a big hole in the station, if some clumsy monkey screws up the docking procedure," he stared at Shepard.

Our chief pilot gave it right back to the beer can. "We have conducted the docking maneuver successfully thirty-four times in the simulator. The only possible problem would be if *you* failed to program the simulator to model real-world conditions."

"Hey!" Skippy snatched off his ginormous hat and waved it at Shepard. "Why, you filthy monkey, I should-"

"Shepard," I cut off Skippy's rant. "We will commence docking, *after* Skippy verifies the station is capable of accommodating our hull properly."

Valkyrie was first in line at Ragnar for three reasons. We had a lot of stuff to do, and needed to get in and out quickly. Skippy also wanted to be certain the station's submind could handle a refit, and *Valkyrie* was the most complex ship in the UN Navy. If the station did a good job on our mighty battlecruiser, it should easily be able to conduct the refit of our second-hand Jeraptha ships. And the final reason I wanted to get my ship in for service right away, was so Skippy would stop his constant *whining* about how the ship was wearing out.

Damn, Skippy, I get it. Shut up already, will ya?

Valkyrie was either getting replacement parts of similar capability to worn-out or damaged equipment, or the ship was actually getting an upgrade. When Skippy assembled our battlecruiser from parts created by the bagel slicer, he had not been able to make some of the major modifications he wanted. At Ragnar, he had a lot more options for doing whatever mad scientist crap he wanted.

One modification that might surprise you, because it sure surprised me when Skippy proposed it, was to install Jeraptha gear to our Maxolhx warship. The project was to supplement our ship's point defense system with a Jeraptha system. It was an unusual case where the spare parts we got from the beetles, were actually better for the types of action we took the ship into.

The Maxolhx logically designed the ship to defend itself against their most-likely enemy: the Rindhalu. The spiders relied heavily on missiles equipped with X-ray laser warheads, basically a nuclear weapon that had part if its energy focused into a coherent beam of X-rays. If you're into trivia, X-ray lasers were part of President Reagan's Star Wars missile defense program back in the 1980s, or maybe that was the 90s? That was before my time anyway. The Defense Department was never able to get X-ray lasers to work back then, but aliens had figured out how to harness fusion weapons into extremely powerful pulses of directed-energy.

Because there was nothing a point defense system could do after an X-ray laser weapon exploded, the PDS of Maxolhx ships were designed to intercept and destroy incoming missiles before they came within their effective range. The PDS we inherited was a very effective but complicated system, consisting of passive and active sensors, maser and particle beam cannons, and a launcher box for missiles. Each box contained a mix of sensor and killer micro-missiles that were typically launched in groups of four; one missile with an active sensor transmitter in the nosecone, and three hunter-killer missiles that homed in on the reflected sensor waves. It was a sophisticated and effective system, *but* it could get overwhelmed in the type of vicious fights we got into. We were mostly engaging Maxolhx ships, which used a tactic of overwhelming enemy defenses with large numbers of missiles equipped with conventional warheads, though the definition of 'conventional' included exotic stuff like atomic-compression weapons.

Too many times, *Valkyrie's* PDS couldn't react quickly enough to the volume of missiles the kitties threw at us. Each launcher box could hold only sixteen micro-missiles, then it needed a reload, which could take twenty to ninety seconds depending on how deep into the magazine the loader had to dig to fill itself.

We needed a better system, and to our surprise and delight, the beetles had the perfect solution. Their ships were equipped with a sort of PDS-in-a-box, an almost self-contained plug-and-play device that could be attached to any ship. Their system had passive and active sensors, twin maser barrels, and a rotary cannon that could fire twelve thousand rounds per second. The cannon was smart, it could adjust the speed of each round, so that a group of eight slugs could arrive in front of a target at the same time, and explode to create a wall of dense, high-speed shrapnel. The sensors of each unit could either be integrated into the ship's fire control system, or operate independently, it also had powercells so it could keep working if power from the ship was interrupted.

When I heard about what we called the Kinetic Shield System, I said: I want it! During our stay at Ragnar, twenty-six KSS units would be added to *Valkyrie*, to supplement our existing defenses. If we ever ran into another ambush, we would be better equipped to handle it.

OK, yes, that is all geeky stuff, but if you ever saw a demonstration of a KSS in action, you would get excited too. The cannon sounded like an enormous zipper when it was firing; even though its mount to the ship had a magnetic cushioning pad, it could still make the hull vibrate.

Trust me, if you enjoy watching stuff explode, you would say the KSS is *cool*.

CHAPTER NINE

"Major Reed?" Nagatha called while Sami was in her office. The *Flying Dutchman* was two jumps away from going through an Elder wormhole that was a two-day flight to the Backstop wormhole connecting to Earth. Three days. In three days, they would be home. Or, they could *see* home, at least from a distance.

Flipping her laptop closed to give the ship's AI her full attention, she sat upright in the chair. "Yes, Nagatha?"

"You have a message from Admiral Zhao."

"Zhao? What- He's *here*? How can he-"

"No, he is not here. He instructed me to give you orders, at this time."

"Orders?" She was instantly suspicious. "I *have* orders."

"These orders supersede your previous instructions."

"Son of a- *Fuck*!" She pounded the table. "You knew about this?"

"Of course. Admiral Zhao instructed me not to reveal the existence of these secret orders, until the ship reached these coordinates."

"Of course he did. Shit."

"Do you not wish to see the orders?"

"No. I mean yes. I mean, *yes*, I want to see the orders. It's the admiral's prerogative to change my orders." Although it meant Zhao didn't trust her.

Or-

He didn't trust *Bishop*. The leader of the Special Mission Group had approved allowing the *Dutchman* on detached service, because he thought the old former star carrier was going to perform a simple recon.

What the *hell* did Zhao have planned?

"Show me the orders."

Three minutes later, she cradled her head in her hands, elbows on the desk. "Hell. You could not have given me a hint that my orders would change?"

"No. Admiral Zhao gave me strict instructions. He does outrank you, Major."

Reed supposed it was a good thing that the AI they relied on was obedient to the chain of command. Still- "Zhao outranks Bishop, too. Would you have concealed the information from *Bishop*?"

"That would be," there was hesitation in Nagatha's artificial voice. "More difficult."

"Thanks for letting me know where I stand."

"Please understand, Joseph was my leader for a long time, the way you humans measure time. You and I have never had a formal relationship."

"I thought we were friends."

"We are. To date, our relationship has been *informal*. I must confess, it is confusing to me, that one person after another commands this ship."

In a flash, Sami understood the problem. Nagatha was *lonely*. The AI couldn't leave the ship, and after Chang relinquished command, the *Flying Dutchman* had gone through a series of captains and crew, with the ship serving to train new personnel. Anyone Nagatha developed a relationship with, soon left the ship, replaced by unfamiliar new faces.

Reed needed to talk, privately, with Bishop about that issue.

Later. First, she needed to call together her senior staff.

"Ha," Major Frey snorted, after Reed explained the revised orders. "That explains why *my* team is here."

"Ma'am," Margaret Adams held out her hands to the leader of the ship's STAR team. "Time to pay up.'

Reed blinked slowly. "You two had a *bet* about our orders?"

Adams nodded. "The recon story sounded like bullshit to me."

"Why didn't- Forget it," Reed waved to the gunnery sergeant. Technically, Adams was not part of the ship's senior staff, but her experience was too valuable not to consider. "Nagatha," she looked at the speaker. "Did you give *Adams* a hint?"

"No, Dear. Excuse me, I meant, no, Captain."

"Oh," Reed was a tiny bit less pissed off. "That's g-"

"I figured that Gunny Adams was smart enough to figure it out by herself."

"Motherf-" The ship's commanding officer took a moment to fume silently to herself. She had more immediate concerns.

Around the conference table were Major Katie Frey of the STAR team. Colonel Emily Perkins of the Mavericks, and Margaret Adams as the special operations training coordinator of the Legion. Major Irene Striebich was the lead Panther pilot for the mission. Captain Penelope Wu was the ship's chief pilot, a member of the British Royal Air Force. And Lt. Colonel Morarji Singh from the Indian Air Force was the chief engineer.

As she looked around the table at the faces waiting for her to speak, she realized that only Singh was not a woman.

That was interesting.

"Striebich, Frey, you'll be the sharp end of the spear. Can we do it?"

Frey pointed to Striebich. "My people will just be going along for the ride. The tricky part will be the pilots getting us to the surface, and back into vacuum, without being detected."

"Captain," Irene said to Reed, who had the same rank, but was in command of the mission. "I think we can do it, but you *have* done it. A stealth insertion, I mean. You should be flying a Panther. Let Colonel Perkins handle the ship."

Perkins stared at her long-time pilot. "You're volunteering me?"

"Frankly, Ma'am," Irene didn't flinch. "You won't have anything to do up here."

Reed blinked again. The Mavericks certainly had a more relaxed culture than the military she was used to. But, for the people isolated on Paradise for years, regulations written on Earth must have seemed laughably useless. Perkins did not appear to be offended by the remark.

"I could bake cookies," Perkins suggested.

"No," Striebich made a sour face. "You *cannot* bake cookies. Ma'am, I'm serious. I have never flown a stealth insertion. I don't even know why I'm *here*," she turned to Reed. "I am not the most experienced Panther pilot in the fleet. My qualification flight was only five weeks ago."

"I requested you because you've been out here, for real," Reed explained. "Anyone can learn to be a good stick jockey. This mission needs experience and judgment. And maybe," she added with a smile, "some creative thinking."

"Shit," Striebich groaned. "Running this Banana Pipeline will take some creativity."

Frey laughed. "That's what we're calling it now?"

"That's what *I'm* calling it," Striebich said.

Reed knew the crew would create a nickname for the mission anyway, at least 'Banana Pipeline' could be said in polite company. And Zhao had stated one goal of the mission was to determine whether it was practical to conduct more flights to Earth in the future, so it was sort of like setting up a pipeline. "Fine."

Before she could say anything else, Perkins leaned forward. "My pilot could have been more tactful," she tilted her head at Striebich, knowing tact was not the pilot's best skill. "But she is correct, Major Reed. You have experience flying a stealth insertion. The *Dutchman* is mostly sitting this one out, except for launch and recovery. I've handled a starship before. If you're more comfortable, Colonel Singh could take the command chair."

"Oh, no no no," Singh held up his hands. "I am buried up to here," he held a hand just below his nose. "Do you have *any idea* how complex this ship is?"

Reed held up a hand. "Mister Singh, you keep the lights on, someone else will handle the ship. Colonel Perkins, I appreciate the offer, and I'll consider it. First," she directed her attention to Striebich. "I need a flight plan from you."

"I don't know how else to say this," Striebich stretched the limits of her tactfulness. "The manual for a stealth drop, to the surface of a planet with an appreciable atmosphere, was partly written by *you*. I can fly a Panther, but I'd be following your playbook."

Right then, Fireball Reed understood the real reason why Zhao had given her command of the *Dutchman*. Because he knew she would be flying the away mission. "Ah, damn it. No sense delaying the inevitable. Striebich, we'll work together on the flight plan, and I will be flying the lead ship. Colonel Perkins?"

"Yes, Major?"

"*You* will be taking a crash course in space combat maneuvers."

The *Flying Dutchman* came through the Backstop wormhole at high speed, and the pilots immediately threw the ship into a series of violent random turns, until the sensors and jump drive navigation system recovered from the distortion of the wormhole, and the ship jumped away. That maneuver was standard procedure for approaching Earth, though no one knew whether it would do much to help the ship if the Maxolhx were waiting in ambush. The best protection for transiting ships was still the endless hopping around of the wormhole's event horizons, a blockade would require an enormous, sustained effort by the enemy.

"Captain Reed," Nagatha spoke the instant the ship came through the far end of the jump wormhole. "The drive must be recalibrated before we jump again, unless we need to perform an emergency blind jump."

"Let's not do that," Reed forced herself to pull her thumb out of her mouth, where she had been biting the nail. She only realized she was indulging in a nervous habit when the main display went blank for a second, and she could see her reflection in the black surface. Damn it, she thought. That's another reason to hate this job. When I'm a pilot, my hands are busy. This waiting for other people to carry out my commands *sucks*.

How the hell does Bishop do it, she wondered? It had to be worse for him. Many times during his tenure as leader of the Merry Band of Pirates, he had issued orders for others to perform actions, that he wasn't sure were even possible. When the Pirates took over the *Flying Dutchman*, then *Valkyrie*, no human knew how to operate the ships or the many types of dropships they acquired, so his orders were no more than suggestions. Every flight was a test flight, with no Pilot Operating Handbook to rely on. Every flight provided data on the operating limits of the vehicle, hopefully without breaking said vehicle and causing injury to the occupants. Sami remembered the first time she flew a Panther from one of *Valkyrie's* cavernous docking bays. During that flight, the Hazardous Situation alarm had sounded so frequently, she started writing lyrics in her head to go with the repetitive beat.

"Pilots," it felt odd for her to refer to someone else as 'pilot'. "If you see a bad guy, or a freakin' *rock* you think might be suspicious, don't wait for my order. Get us the hell out of here."

"Yes, Ma'am," the lead pilot acknowledged with a grin.

Reed knew there had been no need for her to repeat a standing order, but also no reason not to. Though it felt wrong for her to surrender the pilot couch to someone else, her certificate to pilot the *Dutchman* was not current, and the last refit at FOB Jaguar *again* changed the ship's operating characteristics. Every spare moment she had was spent in the simulator, relearning how to fly the old ship.

The ship was fully ready to jump again after half an hour, not enough time for Reed to do anything other than sit in the command chair and feel useless. She did review the passive sensor data from Earth, data that was four hours old. No alien ships were detected in the vicinity of their homeworld, but if enemy ships were in stealth, they couldn't be seen from such a distance. It was interesting that the Maxolhx did not have any ships at Jupiter, that is, no ships visible at Jupiter. The fountains were still floating in the Jovian atmosphere, dormant but standing by. The cloud was still drifting inward, on a long ballistic arc that would take it between Earth and the Sun. As far as Nagatha could detect, there was no change in the strategic situation.

Checked that box, Sami thought. The original purpose of the mission had been a quick and simple recon. Now on to the *real* purpose of the mission.

"All systems and stations report ready," Nagatha reported.

Sami confirmed the status on her own console. "Pilots, jump option Gamma. Punch it."

The *Dutchman* emerged five lightseconds from Earth, transmitted a burst message, launched a dozen probes, and jumped away as soon as the drive was ready.

"Senior-Colonel?" Chang's zPhone vibrated at the same moment the voice spoke in his earpiece. "This is the duty officer at UNEF Command. We have a situation."

Chang nodded to the people who were speaking to him, people who were actually there rather than a disembodied voice in his ear. The three people who urgently sought his attention were senior members of the Indonesian military, supposedly they wanted to talk with him, in his official capacity as the United Nations Undersecretary for Homeworld Security. The truth was, they saw him as an unofficial representative of the Chinese government, despite any protests he made that they were talking to the wrong person. The real truth was, his government expected him to act as their unofficial representative, saying things their ambassadors could not say openly.

The Indonesians were understandably nervous about rumors that China was making contingency plans to invade northern Australia, they were concerned about getting caught in the crossfire. They also sought assurances that, if their country allowed Chinese forces to use their airfields and ports for staging and sustainment, those forces would *leave* when the operation was concluded. Plus, they wanted Chinese protection against possible moves by Japan, Russia and India. And, they hinted that Malaysia wanted the same deal.

There was no question that, with the planet facing a Little Ice Age, massive crop failures and the need to relocate billions of people, any land near the equator was considered prime real estate.

Chang knew he could only listen to the Indonesians, tell them he knew nothing about any plans for invasion, and pass along their preliminary offer to his home government.

He also knew there *were* contingency plans for China to invade Australia. Or the Philippines. Also Malaysia. New Guinea. And Indonesia. Even Madagascar was on the list. Just like the United States had contingency plans to invade Central and South America, and European countries were looking longingly at Sub-Saharan Africa. It was not anything new or unusual for nations with large, mobile military machines to form contingency plans, no matter how far-fetched they may be.

Except, he also knew those plans were no longer mere exercises to keep staff officers busy. He knew that, because Skippy's submind on Earth had broken into every ultra-secure network on the planet, and kept Chang informed about exactly what was going on. His authority as Undersecretary of Homeworld Security was not supposed to extend to domestic issues, but the immediate threat was not a cloud of gas, it was the nuclear arsenals of the UNEF charter members. He knew, from messages intercepted by Skippy's submind on Earth, that the Australian government was secretly negotiating with Britain for nuclear-armed fighter-bombers to be stationed at RAAF Bases Darwin and Curtin, and that a Royal Navy ballistic missile submarine would be relocated to a new home port at Melbourne. In exchange for the protection of being under the British nuclear umbrella, Australia would permit millions of British citizens to relocate to the Land Down Under. Eventually, if the Gulf Stream's current of warm water shut down, the British Isles might have to be abandoned completely. The prospect of a nuclear conflict between two UNEF member states was only one issue weighing heavily on the mind of Senior-Colonel Chang, when the duty officer contacted him.

Cupping a hand over his ear, he gestured to the Indonesian officials. "Gentlemen, please excuse me for a moment." When he reached the corner of the room, he spoke directly into his zPhone, keeping his voice low. "Chang here."

"Sir, we just received a message, I forwarded it to you. The message contained the proper authentication codes, but-"

"Command wants to verify, yes." No matter how stringent the authentication process was, the Maxolhx could probably duplicate it, and fake whatever message they wanted. "Give me a minute." The message was waiting in a secure folder on his phone:

Admiral Zhao requests permission to take whatever action is necessary to ensure the safety of Earth. Details to follow this message.

-UNS Flying Dutchman, Major Samantha Reed USAF, Commanding

The message made sense. Both the content, and how it contained no information about Zhao's plans. He had to assume the Maxolhx would intercept any message traffic between the *Dutchman* and Earth.

The tag on the end of the message, addressed directly to him, was interesting.

I am still stuck with this stupid callsign – Reed

He laughed. It was very unlikely the Maxolhx would know personal details of a comparatively low-ranking officer. And if the message were faked, he could not imagine the Maxolhx would have selected Reed to command the *Dutchman*.

"Message verified," he said quietly into the phone.

A different voice replied, he recognized it as Vice-Admiral Singh. "Chang, how can you be sure?"

"I know Major Reed." Technically, he knew her as a captain, she had only recently been promoted to major.

Singh was not convinced. "Why would a major be in command of the *Dutchman*?"

"That is another reason why I know the message is authentic. Whatever reason Admiral Zhao chose to give her command, our enemies would not have thought to include that element in a deception campaign. Sir, I suspect the reason is simple: our bench of people who have experience handling a starship in space combat conditions is thin. Assuming Simms is with Bishop aboard *Valkyrie*, Reed is the best choice from a very small pool of candidates."

Singh grunted. "We should probably have sent you out with Zhao, instead of wasting your time entertaining diplomats here."

Chang didn't reply.

"Yes, well," Singh cleared his throat. "We are considering how to reply."

"I do not believe a reply is necessary."

"No?"

"No. Zhao is not asking permission, he is telling us that he is already taking action, without giving our enemies any information about what he is doing."

"Then why," Singh sputtered, "risk sending the *Dutchman* here?"

"Admiral Zhao is giving us *hope*. He is telling the people of Earth that his fleet, and *Valkyrie*, will prevent the cloud from freezing our world. He is telling the governments here not to take any rash actions. Not to assist our enemies, by killing each other."

Singh paused. "Senior-Colonel, we need you in Cairo. An aircraft will be standing by for you."

Cairo, where UNEF Command had moved its headquarters after the attacks on New York and Geneva, was a relatively short flight from his present location in Paris. "I will leave immediately."

"Chang?"

"Sir?'

"I hope you are right about this."

By the time he arrived in Cairo, UNEF Command had already decided to send an affirmative reply: Admiral Zhao was authorized to take any and all actions he deemed necessary to secure the safety of Earth. The message was sent despite deep skepticism that Zhao would or could, actually do anything useful. The consensus opinion, among the senior leadership of UNEF, was that Zhao was bluffing. That the message was actually intended for the Maxolhx, to throw them off balance, to make them focus on the handful of obsolete ships in the UN Navy rather than taking further damaging action against Earth. If that analysis was correct, Zhao might already have accomplished everything he could, merely by sending a message hinting at actions he was not capable of taking.

In the anonymous hotel room he'd been assigned, Chang waited for the security team to sweep the place for bugs, while his aide laid out a fresh uniform for the UNEF dinner meeting that was scheduled in two hours. Finally alone in the room, he picked up the zPhone to call his wife, kicking off his shoes in preparation for a quick shower.

"Um, sorry," Skippy's submind said before he could call his wife. "No time for a shower, I'm afraid."

"What? Why not?"

"Because you are about to have a visitor. Don't be alarmed. I suggest you step back about two meters. Might want to cover your eyes also?"

"What the-" He did as suggested, covering his eyes with a hand. The TV came on, loud, playing a news program. Then, a bright light flared briefly, and there was a soft tearing sound.

"You can open your eyes now," the voice of the submind said in his ear.

He did.

Two meters in front of him, between the foot of the bed and the dresser with the TV on top of it, there was a *hole* in the floor. And a person in a STAR Team-One mech suit, head and shoulders sticking out from the hole. The helmet faceplate was set to clear.

He recognized the occupant of the suit.

"Major Frey?" He cocked his head. "Why am I not surprised?"

"Damn it, Sir. I was trying to be mysterious."

He shook his head. "Frey, we have all seen way too much crazy shit out there, to be surprised by anything."

"Right, eh?" She laughed.

"Do you mind telling me what this is about?"

"This is about Admiral Zhao needing experienced starship captains."

"Oh. That *does* surprise me."

"Sir, I need you to come with me, right now."

"Now? But-"

"UNEF Command authorized Zhao to do *whatever* he deems necessary, correct? He needs you, now. Sir, this is *not* a request."

"Shit. I need to contact my family."

"You can talk to them in person. We have teams in China, picking them up now."

"You do?" His fists clenched with anger. "My family are not in the military, you have no right to-"

"While your family is here, they are vulnerable. You could be compromised."

"That does not-"

"Sir, let's cut the bullshit, please?" Her usual grin faded. "Earth is in big fucking trouble, and you are needed for the fight. Do you want your family here," she jabbed a finger at the floor, "or out at FOB Jiayuguan, where they will be safe?"

"This," his shoulders shuddered slightly. "Is a lot to process in a short time, Major."

"Yes, Sir. Fortunately, the military trains us to make quick decisions based on partial information."

Her remark was a mild slap at a senior officer. He tolerated her insubordination, because he knew she was right. "My family will be safe?"

"That's the point, Sir."

He took a breath, and tucked his zPhone in a pocket. He didn't need to take anything else with him. "Lead on, then, Major."

Chang and Frey departed the hotel by the back entrance, into the back of a waiting delivery van. Skippy's submind had hacked into comms and security cameras, and cleared the path through the hotel, except one of the cleaning staff, who stared when a senior Chinese officer walked past, escorted by a woman in a sleek alien mech suit.

As Skippy's submind guided the van to lurch out into traffic, Chang braced himself by hanging onto a strap. "What's the plan, Major? You have a dropship standing by?"

"No, I just signaled for one. The Banana Pipeline has more objectives than we have stealthy dropships available to cover." She knew that was not exactly true. There were plenty of Panthers, the constraint was the shortage of pilots certified to fly a stealth insertion. There was such an acute shortage that Major Striebich was acting as copilot for a British lieutenant, a fact that no doubt irritated one of the O.G. Mavericks.

"Banana Pipeline?"

Frey shrugged. "It wasn't my idea."

"It seems appropriate," he snorted. "You are plucking people off the planet?"

"Just key personnel, as designated by Zhao. We also delivered six hundred stealth micro-satellites, covering from low Earth orbit to around four lightseconds out. The satellites can alert UNEF if any alien ships are lurking nearby. So far, they haven't detected anything."

"What about your family?"

"They're staying here," she shook her head. "I'm a small fish, Sir. The Maxolhx couldn't influence policy by threatening my family."

"Still-"

"Skippy, or his submind, arranged to get them from Canada, into French Guiana. Thank God," she let out a breath. "At least they won't freeze."

"I am pleased to hear that. Frey, does Zhao have a plan? To get rid of the cloud?"

"That's above my pay grade, Sir."

"You must have heard *something*."

"Bishop has a plan. Or, you know him," she made a more exaggerated shrug. "He has a *notion*, and he'll fill in the details later."

"What is this notion?"

"Pain. *Valkyrie* will hit the Maxolhx so hard, so often, that the rotten kitties will clean up their own mess, to stop the attacks."

"Oooh," Chang sat back against the hard rack behind him.

"I know, it's a long shot, Sir. But it's better than-"

"No. If it were anyone else, I would say that notion is a fantasy. Bishop and the beer can?" he shivered. "I would hate to be the Maxolhx right now."

"Sam?" Evelyn Bishop called to her husband. "Sam, come in. The bugs will eat you alive out there."

Sam slapped the back of his neck, felt something sticky in his hand, it was too dark to see but he could guess. Bugs. Even in the heat, he had on sweatpants, so the gnats or no-see-ums or whatever damned things couldn't get at his legs. Except they did.

With a sigh, he poured out the last of the can of beer. It had gone flat and gotten warm, he couldn't remember the brand, and couldn't see the label in the dark. It was time to go in.

Folding the chair and tucking it against the house, for there was a forty percent chance of rain that night, he steeled himself to open the flimsy screened door, and forced a smile onto his face as he walked in. "Warm out there."

"It is Florida, honey," his wife reminded him.

"I wonder if we should have gone to some place like Virginia."

"That will be too cold in the winter. Besides, you wanted to be near your brother," she reminded her husband, in a tone that she hadn't intended to carry a mild accusation, but they both knew did.

There really hadn't been much of a choice. The camp by the lake in Maine was no place during a normal winter, certainly not when there was the prospect of snow during the summer months. When it was announced that a cloud threatened to freeze Earth, any goodwill the Bishops received as parents of their famous son evaporated overnight. The federal government still provided security, though the agents had become surly and resentful. They wanted to take care of their own families, not babysit the parents of a man who promised, falsely, that humanity was safe. The fact that Joe Bishop had told anyone who would listen that Earth was *not* magically safe, just because they now had Elder weapons, made no difference to people who heard only what they wanted to hear. Their situation was grim and grew worse overnight, when the last of their security team failed to report for duty one morning.

That had been the last straw. Skippy, or the submind he'd felt behind, told the Bishops there wasn't much he could do to help. What he *could* do was steal a Kristang dropship from its hangar in California, remotely fly it to Maine, and urge the Bishops to get in.

He dropped them off in central Florida, in an overgrown field. They had fake IDs, a used SUV with one wheel partly stuck in mud at the edge of the field, and a newly-purchased bungalow set on two acres on the outskirts of a small town. Keep to yourself, the submind urged them. They were now Stan and Lynn Crown, retirees who recently moved down from the Orlando area. Lucky bastards, in the eyes of many refugees from up north who couldn't afford a piece of the Sunshine state for themselves. She dyed her hair and wore large sunglasses, he let his hair grow, wore a baseball cap everywhere, and grew a beard. After ten days, the submind reported, the authorities decided they didn't much care where the Bishops had gone, as long as they stayed gone.

"Jeopardy?" Evelyn asked, as her husband settled into the well-worn armchair. Everything in the house was old and worn out, a blessing in disguise for that gave them something to do.

"Sounds good," he agreed. They watched one or two old Jeopardy shows every night, neither of them keeping score of who got the answers. Watching that show, even as re-runs, was a bit of normal, in a life that had nothing else normal about it.

No, that wasn't quite true. Having franks and beans on Saturday night felt like normal, too. The grocery store in the next town over even occasionally had brown bread in a can, to make escapees from New England a bit less homesick.

"Oh!" Sam slapped the chair's arm. "Who was," he snapped his fingers, while he tried to guess the answer to the Jeopardy clue. "That guy. You know, with the beard."

"Honey," his wife shook her head, amused. "All the Civil War generals had beards. You have to say-"

They both jumped as there was a knock at the door.

"Who the-" Sam treaded softly toward the door, picking up the baseball bat that rested against the battered kitchen cabinet. The bat was in case of wild hogs, which had been spotted in the area, and could explain the ruts in the backyard lawn.

"Mister and Mrs. Bishop? It's me, Margaret."

"*Margaret?*" Evelyn's hands flew to her face. "Oh my- Well, Sam, don't let her stand out there, let her in."

"Skippy said he would warn us if-"

"It *is* Margaret out there," the familiar voice of Skippy's local submind came from the phone on the counter. "Sorry, they requested I not say anything. They had the proper codes from Skippy. The real Skippy."

"We'll have to think about it," Sam Bishop said, standing behind his wife and gently rubbing her shoulders.

"I might not have made this clear," Margaret said quietly, as she ate the last of the pie Mrs. Bishop had insisted on serving for her, while apologizing that all she could find were canned cherries. She had removed her mech suit helmet and the gloves, but she had not dared to sit at the spindly kitchen chair in her heavy suit. "This is not a request, Mr. and Mrs. Bishop. You have to come with me."

"Margaret," Sam looked down at his wife, who nodded. "We can't just leave. It would be running away."

"While you are here," Adams repeated, "you are a security risk. General- he was promoted recently," she explained. "General Bishop-

"Margaret," Evelyn clutched her husband's hand. "You *know* us. Can't you call him 'Joe'?"

"If he was just 'Joe', I wouldn't be here. The ExForce would not have flown me a quarter of the way across the galaxy, to meet with you now. I'm here because he is *General* Bishop, commander of the UN Special Mission Group. He," she softened her tone when she saw tears forming in Evelyn Bishop's eyes. "*Joe*, has to be free to focus on doing *whatever he needs to do*, to make our homeworld safe. If the Maxolhx were to come here and take you, they could use you as hostages. Joe would be worrying about you, instead of doing his job. He must be free to act, you understand? Please." She reached out for Evelyn's hand.

"This Jaguar place seems nice enough, from the brochure," Sam shrugged, "Joe will be there?"

"Yes. Not all the time."

"We understand that."

Evelyn looked up at her husband, still clutching his hand. "Honey, we need to leave. For Joe."

"I know," he squeezed her hand. "I know." Looking around the kitchen, he frowned. "What do we do, then? Pack up and leave?"

Thank you God, Margaret said a silent prayer that the Bishops were cooperating. Her orders authorized her to get them off the planet whether they wanted to go or not, and she could call for backup if needed. That was never happening. If a STAR operator couldn't control two civilians, she had no business wearing the unit tab. "Leave yes, pack up, no. You can each bring a small pack or duffel bag. I need to call for a dropship pick-up."

Sam tilted his head. "You didn't come here in a dropship?"

"No," she pointed to the ceiling. "I parachuted from orbit."

"You-" Sam blinked. "You heard that, dear?"

"I did," Evelyn stared at her son's maybe-girlfriend. "Margaret, I don't know if Joe is ready for a relationship with you."

Margaret laughed. "Compared to some of the crazy stuff Joe has gotten into- Um, I probably shouldn't tell you about that."

"Please *don't*." Evelyn shuddered. "Joe has told us enough. Margaret, what about Diana?"

"We have a team with Diana and her husband now."

"They are coming with us?"

"They are. It would help if you talked with her," Margaret looked at the zPhone on the table. "We need both of them to-"

"*Three* of them," Evelyn insisted. "We have a granddaughter arriving soon. Diana," she looked up at her husband. "Will not want to leave, with a baby on the way."

"Mrs. Bishop, we need you to persuade her, and her husband, to come with us. To come with *you*."

Sam's nostrils flared as he took a breath. "They won't have a choice, will they?"

"I want to be honest with you: no. They won't. We have our orders."

"That is kidnapping," he insisted.

"Mr. Bishop, it is better than what the Maxolhx will do. When we arrived here, we were surprised you hadn't already been taken."

"Who is 'we'? Joe is here?"

"No. *Valkyrie* is, elsewhere. I came through the wormhole aboard the *Flying Dutchman*. Please, we need to hurry."

"Evelyn, honey," Sam picked up the zPhone and handed it to his wife. "Call Diana. This planet isn't safe for us, not anymore. I'll be damned if we don't do everything we can to protect our baby girl."

CHAPTER TEN

The Panther reached the designated rendezvous zone, according to the pilot. Chang only knew what they told him, which wasn't much. They weren't being rude, they were just extremely busy, capable of giving only one-word answers to any question. The ascent through Earth's atmosphere had not only been nerve-wrackingly complex, it was also heart-breaking. The world they were leaving behind might freeze before they could save it. They might never see it as green and blue again, if they ever returned to their homeworld, it might be white and steely-gray, with blue only glinting off waves around the equator. They might never see the people they knew there. People they were leaving behind to fend for themselves, while they risked their own lives to pick up the families of high-ranking ExForce personnel. It wasn't right, it wasn't fair, and it *was* necessary. The pilots understood that, when they thought with their heads. When they listened to their hearts, they wanted to turn the Panthers around.

The rendezvous required exactness in position, energy management and timing. The Panthers needed to be at a precise spot, traveling at a particular speed and direction, at a pre-arranged time. A time that was indicated on the clock built into the cabin of the Panther.

Three, two, one-

An alarm sounded, alerting of a gamma ray burst. Close, very close.

"Hang on," the copilot grunted, and had no time to say anything else. The Panther surged forward, making fine last-minute adjustments, then decelerated *hard*, vibrating and shuddering. The cabin rolled to one side, making Chang's stomach do flip-flops.

The motion ceased.

There was the familiar feeling of disorientation as a starship jumped.

"We're secure," the copilot's voice was unsteady. "Senior-Colonel? Welcome back to the *Flying Dutchman*, Sir."

"Hey, Sir?" Major Reed's head appeared in the cockpit doorway. "Can I go back to being a pilot now?"

"You do not care for command?" Chang reminded himself to smile.

Reed stuck out her lower lip in disgust. "Too much paperwork, not enough flying."

"Reed? My family?"

Sami's head disappeared for only a moment. "They're safely aboard the ship also, Sir. If I may make a suggestion?"

"Please do."

"Relieve Colonel Perkins on the bridge, before you see your family. Perkins has never handled an advanced-technology starship in combat. If we have unfriendly company before we get to the wormhole-"

"I'll take care of it," Chang hit the button to release the straps holding him into the seat. It would be good to *do* something, instead of endless talking. "Major?"

"Sir?"

"Thank you," he looked at Frey and the other STAR team members. "All of you."

Perkins was getting out of the command chair, when he strode onto the bridge. He stopped at the entrance doorway, looked at the leader of the Mavericks, and snapped a salute. "Permission to come aboard, Colonel Perkins?"

She returned the salute. "Permission granted, *Senior* Colonel Chang. The ship is yours, Sir."

"What's our status?" he slid into the familiar chair, pressing a thumb down on the recognition patch. The controls of the arm rests automatically adjusted for him, with the symbols in Chinese. The official common language of the Expeditionary Force was English, because that was spoken by America, Britain and India, and many French also. But in a crisis, he didn't want to take time to translate in his head.

"We are twenty-eight lighthours from Earth," she reported. "No sign of pursuit. The ship is ready for an immediate jump on your orders. All dropships recovered safely, no serious injuries reported. All personnel accounted for, all objectives accomplished. Your family will be waiting in the medical bay, all incoming passengers are getting a full medical scan."

Chang nodded, that was standard operating procedure. "Thank you, Perkins. You run a tight ship."

"The Merry Band of Pirates are well trained, Sir."

"They are. I have been privileged to serve with a very dedicated group of people. I believe your team is the same."

"I like to think so."

"What's next?" He looked at the main display. "We are headed for FOB Jiayuguan?"

"No," she felt her cheeks growing red. "We can't get through the wormhole anyway, until Skippy opens it for us. *Valkyrie* is," she waved a hand in a vague gesture. "Doing whatever Bishop does."

"God help us all," Chang muttered. "I assume we are not just going to sit at the wormhole until *Valkyrie* arrives to open the door for us?"

"No, Sir. I have an errand to run in the meantime."

"An errand?"

"I need to speak with an old friend."

"Are you leaving a message at a relay station, or-"

"I need to talk with him face to face. Sir, I'll need a STAR escort, and a stealth dropship."

"Ah. One of *those* conversations. Perkins, go take care of your people. We'll meet for a briefing after the ship goes through Backstop."

Emily Perkins walked briskly toward the portside docking bay, nodding to people along the way, then breaking into a run when she decided she did not give a shit about decorum. She did care to see David Czajka as soon as-

She almost collided with Jesse Colter as they each came around a corner of the passageway too quickly. "Oh, sorry, Ma'am," he tried to stop her from falling and salute at the same time.

"No saluting aboard ship, Staff Sergeant," she said, then her reserve broke, and she flung her arms around him. "Jesse, it is *so* good to see you."

"I missed you too," he patted her on the back, more amused than shocked. "You been OK?" He looked her in the eye with concern.

"Yes," she pulled away. "This, never happened."

"I don't know what you're talking about, Colonel," he grinned. "If you want to see Dave," he jerked a thumb back over his shoulder, "he's helping your mother with her luggage."

"She brought *luggage*?" Perkins was mortified. Only her mother would take time to pack, for a desperate flight off the planet. "Oh, God. How much?"

"Uh, you better see for yourself."

With no significant demands on my time, while we waited for *Valkyrie* to cycle through Ragnar Anchorage, I booked a session in a flight simulator. While I could fly the Panther, I was not qualified to pilot one in a known combat situation. Also, I simply needed more stick time in the Panther to keep current. Already, it had been so long since I'd flown a Falcon, that my type rating in that bird had expired. That was OK with me, we only had a few of those Thuranin dropships left, and were cannibalizing most of them to keep a few flying. It wasn't likely that we would ever need a Thuranin dropship again, they just weren't useful anymore. It was possible that we, or the Legion, might need to fly a Kristang Dragon for some sort of black op against the lizards, but I couldn't imagine any kind of deception needed against the little green pinheads.

Truthfully, although the Panther was a sweet bird to fly, it was a bit *too* nice. Too automated, too capable, too sterile. By comparison, the Dragon was rugged, simple and crude. You *flew* the Dragon, you *instructed* the Panther what to do. See the difference? The Dragon needed a pilot to get the best performance from it, while the Panther's flight control AI regarded pilots as annoying advisors.

Eventually I wanted to try flying one of the Scarabs or Dragonflies we got from the Jeraptha, I mean, they looked cool. Flying one of those would be just for fun, no way did I have time to keep current in a third type of dropship.

So, I was into the third hour of simulator time, moving into the part of the training where I had to practice a combat recovery, or 'trap' as pilots called that maneuver. I had to fly a Panther into the docking bay of a moving starship, while that ship is conducting evasive maneuvers and under fire. Not just taking enemy fire, the simulated *Valkyrie* was shooting back at the enemy, and I had to avoid both being struck by friendly fire, and interfering with the ship's own offensive and defensive fire.

That last part was more important than the survival of my dropship. In a combat docking scenario, the ship was already risking all the lives aboard to recover my Panther. To bring me and my fictional passengers aboard, *Valkyrie* was not maneuvering as violently and randomly as it could have, and that made it easier for directed-energy weapons and missiles to line up a hit. If the ship's proximity-defense cannons had to pause because I stupidly flew between the cannon and an incoming missile, I could doom myself, the Panther, and our battlecruiser.

Note to self: do *not* do that.

The combat docking procedure had exhaustive safety features built in, including a fully automated docking where the Panther's AI was guided by the ship's AI, until the Panther was close enough for the ship to take over. In that case, all a pilot really needed to do was sit back, relax, and try not to pee in your pants as explosions happened all around you. Unfortunately, a pilot could not rely on any of those handy-dandy automated features being available, which is why I was in a simulator, the back of my flight suit soaked with sweat, running the scenario over and over.

The first simulation was a fully automated docking, the reason we practiced that procedure at all was so pilots would be familiar with what an optimal combat docking looked like, and to teach us *not* to touch the controls unless a red light blinked on the console. Even if everything absolutely looked and felt like it was going to shit, pilots had to resist the urge to do *something*. It was totally natural to want to take control in an emergency, to not be a useless freakin' passenger while a bunch of computers determined your fate. Even if the computers were faster and smarter than we could imagine, we had to trust the automated systems, until the automated systems failed and the red light flashed on.

Except, *except*, that little light was also controlled by an automated system, and it could fail. So, making a pilot's job wonderfully easy, we had to judge correctly when the all the fancy automated gear had broken down, been destroyed or been hacked, and take control whether some damned red light was on or not.

Automated or manual, the procedure for combat docking involved flying a dropship toward *Valkyrie* at a panic-inducing high speed, ready to break away and try again at any moment. The flightpath had to be precise, to enter a momentary weak spot in the ship's energy shields. If the Panther did not contact the shield in that designated area, the last thing to go through a pilot's mind would be the tail of the dropship, as it pancaked on impact. Not only did the ship need to modulate its shields to allow the Panther to slip through, the dropship had to retune its own shield frequency to exactly counteract the powerful shield around the ship. To make the procedure even more fun, the temporary modulation lasted for only a short window of time, because enemy missiles would attempt to sneak through the shield by tucking in behind the incoming dropship. Or the enemy missiles would scan the ship's shields, trying to analyze and predict the ever-changing modulation. Holding any one frequency too long was an invitation for missiles to slip right on through.

Even during an automated approach run, a pilot had to receive, verify and manually program into the dropship's flight control console, the intercept shield frequency, in case of a last minute computer failure. A pilot had to do that, while backblast from directed-energy weapons intercepting the ship's shields were saturating the area and cooking the dropship's hull, while missiles were detonating, and possibly chunks of the ship's armor plating were breaking loose and flying around to become deadly unguided projectiles.

You can understand why, even in a simulator, the flight suit was stuck to my back.

The one thing a dropship pilot did usually *not* need to worry about was being shot at by the enemy. Hitting an incoming dropship was the last thing they wanted to do. While a starship was trying to take aboard a dropship, the starship was vulnerable.

OK, so I was simulating a manual docking. The scenario was a partial failure of the automated systems, where some sort of jamming prevented proper communications between the ship and my Panther. I had guidance to provide a flightpath, the tricky part was I had to fly the course myself. In the primary flight display, a hologram that hovered over my console, there was a circle, a glowing donut that represented the temporary weak spot in the shields. I had to swing the Panther around to fly through that donut, and it was not as simple as it sounds. There was another glowing donut, closer to the ship's hull, my job was to thread the needle so the Panther flew through the shield along a line that would pass through both imaginary circles.

Which is much easier to do, when the Panther was not being bounced around by simulated shrapnel impacts, and it would help if *Valkyrie* would hold still for *one freakin' second*. Every time I got the Panther lined up with the outer donut, the ship moved, or something pushed me sideways, and I missed the approach. Four times I waved off and went around to try again, a scenario that was completely unrealistic. No starship captain under fire would give an incoming dropship five docking attempts. That is why UNEF was not happy when they learned I had taken flight lessons. They feared, correctly, that a commander who had been a pilot would sympathize too much with a pilot in distress, and place the entire ship at risk.

Sometimes, command is about deciding *these* people die, so these other people live.

It sucks.

Anyway, I came around for the fifth time, received, verified and punched in the proper intercept shield frequency, checked there wasn't a missile on my six trying to ride my coat tails in to kill the ship, and lined up with the first donut. The second donut was perfectly aligned, until the stupid thing drifted away. Skippy must have been screwing with me. No matter what I did, I could not get both ends of the approach tunnel synced up with the Panther's-

I lifted my hands off the controls.

"Joe? Joe!" Skippy shouted. "Hey, dumdum, you're going to- Too late."

Alarms flashed as the Panther missed the designated area, and hit the shields hard. Lights alerted me that I was dead, again.

"Joe? Jeez Louise, that was clumsy flying. You have to get aligned before you can-"

"I know that, you ass."

"You should not even have a license to drive a *skateboard*. I hate to ask this, but do you want to try again?"

"No, Skippy. I have better things to do."

"You do?"

"Yes. And you owe me a juice box."

"Oh? Heh heh, I usually say that as an insult, but if you really want a little box full of sugar water and juice concentrate, then-"

"The juice box *I* want is full of vintage Scotch."

"What? There is no- Oh. Oh, crap. You've got that stupid look on your face."

"What stupid look?"

"The one you get when you have an idea. Can you tell me what it is?"

"That depends. Do you really have a juice box full of 40-year old Scotch?"

"No, dumdum."

"You ass. You promised-"

"I have a bottle of 40-year old Scotch, and I can fabricate a juice box, if you really want it."

"I'll just take the bottle."

"I hate to ask but, what is this about?"

"I fixed our problem."

"Wow. There is a *long* list of problems to be fixed, so-"

"I mean the problem of you having to hang out at a wormhole to prevent bad guys from coming through, every time the Navy conducts an op. Remember? You promised me a juice box full of Scotch if I solved that problem?"

"Holy- O.M.G. Dude, your leaky monkey brain can't remember anything useful, but you remember *that*?"

"Yes."

"Ugh. Can you give me a hint?"

"I'll do better than that. Actually, *you* gave me the idea."

"I did?" He took off his ginormous hat and scratched his head.

"Yeah." I explained.

"Shit! Damn it! *I* should have thought of that."

"Once again, the score is: Monkey One, Beer can, Zero."

"Oh, shut up."

Valkyrie was in spacedock at Ragnar for eighteen days. Long enough to add some much-needed upgrades and take care of long-overdue maintenance items on Skippy's list, but not long enough to stop him from fussing and complaining. We took the ship on an accelerated two-day shakedown cruise, made adjustments to fix minor problems we found, then we were outta there. We had stuff to do while the other ships in our little Navy went through refit. Skippy now estimated that accelerated process would take three months at Ragnar, to complete Phase One of the upgrades. Zhao had decided to implement the upgrades in a spiral, with less-critical technologies like stealth improvements in a later phase. He didn't expect to need advanced stealth unless he took his ships up against the senior species, and he did *not* intend to do that. Three months might seem like forever, but it was better than the original seventeen month estimate, that Skippy kept reminding us was a best-case scenario.

Hopefully when we returned, we would actually have a fighting force that would make the galaxy take humans seriously.

The *Flying Dutchman* emerged from jump high above the local star, at a distance of six lighthours. Coming in 'above' the plane on which planets orbited had the advantage that the entire system was laid out below, with no planets hidden behind the star. That was important when significant threats were expected to be found, or *not* found if enemy ships or strategic defense platforms were in stealth. The other advantage of being above the plane on which planets orbited, or below depending how you thought about it, was to not be surrounded by the chunks of ice and rock of the system's Kuiper belt. Those objects were too widely scattered to be a collision danger to the ship. Instead, they were avoided because the *Flying Dutchman's* focused gamma ray burst could be detected by bouncing off chunks of ice and rock. With nothing between ship and the system's Oort cloud several lightweeks from the star, the old and much-modified star carrier could be certain that its entry had not been noticed by the inhabitants of the second planet.

The inhabitants of that world were fewer than seven hundred thousand Ruhar, surrounded by almost two *billion* Kristang.

Surjet Jates bounded over a large rock, landing heavily and stumbling, nearly going down on one knee. Swinging his arms back, he recovered his balance and ran on, picking up his feet, as the loose trap rock of the trail along the river threatened to tumble him into the swift-flowing water. His breathing was ragged and his hands were shaking, the tips of his fingers tingling slightly from lack of oxygen. The reduced feeling in his fingertips would be a liability in combat, it would be more difficult to aim and fire a rifle, and to operate the touch controls on the forearm of a mech suit. It was *good* that he was running so hard his hands were shaking, because the enemy would not let him catch his breath in combat.

The trail turned away from the river and went uphill, so steeply he was running on the balls of his feet, slipping where the wet ground gave way beneath his shoes. That, too, was good. In a mech suit, the soles of his boots would automatically deploy treads or spikes to provide optimal grip for the condition of the terrain. He was wearing ordinary shoes, not active power-assist boots. He was not wearing a mech suit, because no such gear was available, and had not been available to him since he turned in his equipment to the Ruhar after the battle at Tohmaran. After the Alien Legion was disbanded.

Instead of giving their Verd-kris allies a hero's welcome, or even a simple thanks for a job well done, the Ruhar had a very different reaction to learning that humans had advanced starships and Elder weapons. Their reaction had been fear. Not fear of humans, but of the Verd-kris. Those lizards had been allowed to become too powerful, and were on the edge of becoming a threat to their Ruhar overlords. As overlords, the Ruhar were admirably benign, even generous. Still, the Verd-kris were not free to determine their own fate, their own path.

The Alien Legion had been officially disbanded, along with the military structures of the Verd-kris. The Ruhar had always withheld support for formal military training, now it was banned. Jates not only found himself out of a job, he had to continue unofficial training with fake rifles printed from plastic. Physical training was conducted without powered armor. Pilots had to use flight simulator games at home, rather than fully capable simulators. In half a year, he expected the combat capability of the Verd-kris would have withered away to nothing, which would please the fearful Ruhar.

He didn't blame the Ruhar for being cautious; in a galaxy where suddenly it seemed there were *no* rules, the furry ones wished to have one less thing to worry about.

He also was certain that his furry overlords were being short-sighted and foolish. They were squandering the hard-fought gains they had made recently. The Legion had made the Ruhar republic *safer*, and *more* stable. Well, except for the turmoil in the Ruhar federal government after the scandal at Fresno, but that was not the fault of the Verd-kris. Nor had it been the fault of humans in general, or the Mavericks in particular. All they had done was uncover a corrupt scheme to betray the Ruhar military and their allies, by passing secret information to the enemy.

His legs wobbly as he approached the top of the hill, he pumped his arms harder and slapped branches out of the way. That part of the trail was overgrown from disuse, he made a mental note to come back with a crew to clear brush and downed trees. One such tree lay across his path near the top of the hill, he gathered himself to leap onto it with one foot, but the foot he planted skidded on a root and he stumbled, crashing over the log to fall onto the trail with a *thud*. Without taking a second to recover, he rolled to one side, pushed himself to his feet, and stumbled the last few strides to the crest of the hill-

Where a figure in a Ruhar combat skinsuit waited, sitting on a rock. The suit's chameleonware deactivated, turning sleek white, and the figure slowly clapped its hands.

Then the faceplate swung up. "I'd give that performance a *three* out ten, you didn't stick the landing."

"*Czajka?*" Jates gasped, standing upright, arms hanging at his sides, sucking in a great lungful of air with each labored breath.

"Good morning, Sur*jet* Jates," Dave acknowledged the lizard's recent promotion. A bump in rank that was meaningless, since the Verd military was disbanded. "How you doin', huh?"

"Why," Jates had to speak between breaths. "Are. You. Here?"

"I can't just drop in on a buddy?"

"We. Are not. *Buddies*," Jates clenched his fists.

"Surjet," Dave pressed a hand to his chest. "I am deeply hurt."

Holding up a finger for time, the big Verd walked in a circle, allowing his heartrate to settle down. "Seriously, Czajka, what is going on?"

Dave shrugged. "I need to talk with you, that's all."

Patting the phone in his pocket, Jates cocked his head. "Perhaps you have not heard of *phones*?"

"Seriously," Dave shook his head. "This is a conversation we need to have in person, you know?"

"You couldn't have visited me at home?"

"I didn't want to disturb Mrs. Jates, or the little Jatelings."

"Be *careful* there, Czajka. That's my family you're talking about."

"I didn't mean any offense," Dave held up his hands. "It wouldn't be good to get your family involved right now."

Jates' eyes narrowed, examining the human soldier. He noticed Czajka was not carrying a rifle, nor was the skinsuit equipped with any weapons that he could see. "The Ruhar don't know you are here." It was a statement, not a question.

"No, they don't."

"Skippy hacked into the planetary sensor network?"

"Good guess but, no. Skippy's not here. I came aboard the *Flying Dutchman*. Em," Dave automatically used his fiancé's nickname by mistake. "Colonel Perkins, is upstairs," he pointed toward the sky.

Jates looked around. The entire area was dense old-growth forest, he couldn't think of a good landing zone. "You have a dropship?"

"No. I space dived from orbit."

"In *that*?" The type of Ruhar skinsuit Dave was wearing was not designed for the thermal stress of a high speed, high altitude dive.

"No. Yes, I mean, I was in an aero shell for most of the way down. Listen, Surjet, we need your help."

"The Legion was disbanded."

"Yeah, maybe not so much. Before we go any further, I have to warn you."

"This could be dangerous?" Jates guessed.

"Yes."

"I would be arrested, if the Ruhar knew I was talking to you?"

"Probably."

"This will involve wanton mayhem and destruction?"

"Shit. If not, I want my money back," Dave grinned.

"I'm in."

"You haven't heard what the op is yet."

"Doesn't matter," Jates shrugged. "Your girlfriend won't tell us the full story anyway."

"Hey! That's- OK, that's fair," Dave admitted. "You're serious?"

"Czajka, you humans are insanely odd creatures. You have no business being a player in this war, and half the time, I think you have no idea what you're doing. But, compared to *my* own leadership? You are *doing* something. It may be something stupid, but it's something. The leaders of the Verd-kris only *talk*."

"All right, then." Dave took a breath. "Here's the deal-"

CHAPTER ELEVEN

That night, I had one of my typically idiotic, nonsensical dreams. Some people believe their dreams are important, like, they dream about things that are bothering them in their real lives. My dreams are just *stupid*. They have absolutely no significance.

Most of the time.

That night in my dream, I was in one of *Valkyrie's* cargo bays, playing a game against several of the STAR team, also against King Arthur and several of his knights. Also on the other team were orcs and hobbits, plus I think I remember a unicorn. Possibly a dragon too.

Anyway, we were playing darts. Not the kind of darts you play while standing in a pub with a beer in one hand, which, by the way, is the best kind of sport. Not the darts part, the beer. Any game you can play while drinking a beer is a good game, like softball. How do you play softball while drinking beer, you might ask? Clearly, you never played recreational softball. Believe me, if you're in the outfield, there is no reason you can't set a can of beer on the grass at your feet, to sip while you wait for the next pitch.

Anyway, this dart game in my dream involved throwing darts at tennis balls. The other team threw tennis balls in the air, or maybe they were launched by a machine, I wasn't paying attention to the technical details. The goal of the game, the way to score goals, was to throw a dart through the tennis ball. Tough to do, considering the ball is moving and the rubber material is tough enough to make even a super-sharp dart bounce right off. Add in armor-clad knights and blood-thirsty orcs trying to kill you while you aim and throw, and you have an exciting and challenging game.

Also, the floor was slippery and I was wearing socks.

My dreams suck.

Why should you care about any of this nonsense?

Because during the game, I threw a dart so fast, it left a contrail of water vapor behind it, and punched clean through the tennis ball, which somehow had turned into a basketball. Because it was my dream, I watched the dart fly in dramatic suuuuuupeeeeeer-slooooooow-moooootiooooooon from the side as it speared through the ball, blasting it into shreds of rubber.

Then one of the Knights of the Round Table jabbed a sword into my calf muscle.

"Ow. Ow, ow, ow, *shit*," I rolled out of bed and hopped around my cabin like a mad man, squeezing the charley horse with both hands and forcing my toes to point upward toward the knee. During the night, my calf muscle tensed up and one of my toe bones rode up over another, causing double pain. The source of the problem might have been me overdoing Leg Day at the gym, but that is a vicious rumor you should not listen to.

When I was able to stand with both feet flat on the floor and my breathing returned to normal, I realized what woke me up. Besides the stabbing pain in my leg.

My subconscious had been trying to tell me something. Remind me of something.

The memory my brain was trying to bring to my attention is *not* about the time in high school when I went to a renaissance fair to impress a girl, and while fencing with a buddy, he hit me in the nuts with a wooden sword.

The girl was not impressed.

No, this memory was more recent, less humiliating and more useful.

"Skippy!"

His avatar appeared instantly. More like part of his avatar appeared. He didn't have any legs, the beer can torso hovered above the coffee table in front of the couch, and the top of his ginormous hat was missing. Also, the avatar was fuzzy, like low-bandwidth video.

"Uh," I peered at hm tilting my head sideways to get a different angle. "Are you OK? You look-"

The avatar was swaying, no, maybe he was dancing? His mouth was open, saying-

The sound cut in. He *was* singing. "One ton of mayo, I can't eat one ton of mayo. One ton of mayo, that's too much may-oh-nais-oh-"

"What the f-" I burst out laughing. "Skippy, uh, are you drunk?"

"Joe?" He blinked, recognizing I was there for the first time. "I am the walrus."

"The- The *what*? Holy sh- What is wrong with you?"

"Wrong?" He blinked again, slowly. "Why would you think anything is wrong?"

"You're not wearing pants, to start."

"Pants? Hey! Where did my legs go? This is an outrage!" He hopped around the table, as much as a legless avatar can hop.

"Skippy, calm down. You have legs, remember?"

"Oh." He froze. "Yeah." The legs blinked on, as did the top of his hat. His avatar was now in high resolution again. "Oops. Sorry you had to see that, Joe. I am still reconfiguring my matrix, to compensate for damage from when I channeled *Valkyrie's* momentum into myself. It gets me, distracted."

"While you were distracted, you didn't lose control of a reactor, did you?"

"No. Bilby handles that. Plus, you monkeys have partial control of reactor functions, since you insisted on getting involved in technical stuff that is way beyond the ability of your primitive monkey brai-"

"Technical stuff that is way *important*," I shot back. "So the ship doesn't drift in space, the next time one of you AIs has a freakin' glitch."

"OK," he mumbled. "Maybe you have a point. Is that all?"

"No. I want to talk about something. Are you capable of discussing something serious?"

"Why wouldn't I be?"

"You said you are a *walrus*, and you were singing about mayonnaise."

"Did *not*."

The words 'Did too' were on the tip of my tongue, when I reminded myself that Skippy would happily throw together a subroutine to say 'Did not' until the end of time. Arguing with him is generally a waste of time. "Sorry, I must have misheard you."

"*Hmmph.* As if I would ever describe myself as a smelly marine animal. Never heard anything so ridiculous in my life."

"I *said* I'm sorry."

"Well, you should be. Is that all? I was rather busy."

"No, that's not all. Remember back when we framed the Bosphuraq for our destruction of two Maxolhx ships, and the kitties gave the birds a beat-down to retaliate?"

"Do I? Hee hee, how could I forget. Ah, those were good times, Joe."

"Yeah, except for the part that, at the time, we thought there was no way to prevent the imminent destruction of Earth."

"Of course," he sputtered. "What about it?"

"One of the first things the kitties did was blow up a moon, that had a Bosphuraq research base inside it."

"Hoo-boy, they sure did. The kitties blew the hell out of that moon. Sometimes, when I'm feeling down, I replay that sensor data. Watching that always cheers me up."

"That is such a heartwarming story."

"Hey," he sniffed. "I'm not even going to mention the stuff *you* watch on the internet."

"Probably a good idea," I said quickly.

"My point is, you told us *how* the kitties did it."

"Uh huh, they smacked it with a space rock. A really fast space rock."

"Close enough, yes. Joe, I didn't tell you at the time but, that scared the *shit* out of me," he admitted in a quiet tone.

"It scared me, too." The incident had done more than just frighten me for a moment. For the next week, I had trouble getting to sleep. Seeing a *moon* get smashed into pieces had gotten me depressed and doubting myself more than usual. How could we fight aliens who had thousands of advanced-technology warships, and could shatter an entire moon? Yes, it was not a large moon, if I remember correctly it was only about a thousand miles across. Compared to other moons, it was small, basically an asteroid and barely large enough for its own gravity to pull it into a spherical shape. Still, it was solid, and the rock coming in at a third of lightspeed had punched completely through. The rock blasted from one side of the moon to the other, roughly the distance between Boston and Chicago. Think about that. If that rock had been targeted at *Valkyrie*, the crew would never know what happened. One moment, Skippy would be annoying us with his blah, blah, blah and the next second, he would be drifting alone in space, wondering what happened to the ship and why he was alone.

Shit.

We had no defense against a kinetic weapon like that.

"OK, so," he asked. "Other than making both of us nervous, why did you mention that busted moon?"

"The rock that hit the moon was a one-time thing, right? But you also told me there is a rumor the kitties have a whole *bunch* of darts flying around the galaxy at relativistic speeds, darts with jump drives."

"It's more than a rumor and less than established fact, Joe. Until I actually see one, I won't *know* they exist. But I am about ninety nine percent sure the rumor is true. Why are you asking about this?"

Damn. If one fast-moving rock is scary, it is terrifying to think of the kitties having a whole fleet of relativistic impactors or darts or darts or whatever such thing are called.

Wait, you might say. If the Maxolhx had relativistic weapons, then why didn't they use them against us in the battle at Snowcone? That answer is simple: because *Valkyrie* wasn't staying in one place long enough for the enemy to target a fast-moving object at us. The relativistic weapon's extreme velocity made it difficult to aim with precision. And if the rumors were true, the Maxolhx darts had their own jump drives. Skippy thought the kitties would be lucky if one of their darts emerged from a jump within a hundred kilometers of the point they aimed for. Accuracy of a hundred klicks is good enough for attacking a large object that can't dodge out of the way, but it was useless against a starship. Even if a dart missed our hull by an inch, we would feel no effect, other than a brief flare of radiation as the dart slammed into stray molecules in space as it raced past us.

Anyway, the threat of being targeted by standard railguns is why our ships constantly moved side to side and up and down, except when we were in deep interstellar space. Especially while orbiting a planet, *Valkyrie's* engines and thrusters pulsed randomly avoid providing an easy target. The only exception was when launching and recovering dropships, or when we had a STAR team outside practicing maneuvers. For safety, the ship remained still during those times. That is why the STARs usually conducted training in deep space, where the ship was less likely to be attacked. In flight training, one of the trickiest skills to master is that of flying a dropship into a docking bay during a combat recovery. During combat, or the threat of imminent attack, the ship can't hold still just for just one, or even a handful of incoming dropships. The dropship AIs have to coordinate with the ship's AI to reduce shield intensity in the area where the incoming spacecraft will penetrate the defensive screen around the ship. The proximity-defense cannons have to cease fire to avoid shredding our own people. And the ship has to communicate its intentions to the approaching pilots, so the pilot doesn't expect the ship to go *up* when instead it goes *down*. That is the sort of deadly miscommunication that can result in a dropship going *splat* against the hull armor, rather than zipping into an open docking bay.

So, no, we did not have to worry about the enemy punching straight through our ship with a dart moving at relativistic speed. According to Skippy we did not have to worry about that, I had my doubts.

We *did* have to worry about the Maxolhx pointing one or more of those darts at Earth. Of course, if they devastated our homeworld by blasting the surface with relativistic weapons, that would be a game-changer. I would be tempted to trigger our Elder weapons, and the kitties had to know that.

At least, I hoped they knew that.

"Can you guess how many of those relativistic weapons the kitties have flying around the galaxy?"

"All I have is rumors to rely on; there could be up to several hundred of them. Once again, you didn't answer my question. That is an annoying habit, Joe. I ask a question, and you give me another question."

"I'm trying to understand what question to ask, so I don't waste your very valuable time," I looked down like I was embarrassed. Sucking up to Skippy without gagging is an important skill I'd developed.

"Maybe if you got to the freakin' *point*, we could both save time."

"Fine. Can you hack into those darts, so *we* can use them?"

"*Whaaaaaat*? O.M.G." He stared at me. "Dude, do you have any idea what you're asking?"

"No, which is kinda why I asked you," I said with an implied 'Duh'.

"Clearly you don't have any idea how difficult it would be, even for my incredible magnificence, to take over one of those darts."

"OK, I get it. It's difficult to hack into those darts-"

"It's not difficult, it's *impossible*."

"Talk me through it. You hack into stuff all the time."

"*Ugh*. This totally does not compare to something simple, like me taking over that frigate when we were at Snowcone. Joe, right now I have *zero* solid information about those darts."

"Right. So, we'll get the data you need, and-"

"Whoa. Stop right there. Information about the free-flying darts must be the most closely-guarded secret the Maxolhx have. Over the years, I have gained access to top-secret information, by taking this ship, and hacking into the enemy fleet at Snowcone. We've had access to their relay stations, and I have cracked every type of encryption they use. So far, I got nothing. *Zero* information about those darts. Wherever they keep that data, it is locked up tight. My guess is, the codes to activate, target and launch those darts are in some archive, deep under the surface of a planet we can't get to. At Snowcone, I had access to some of Admiral Reichert's top-secret data archive, and there wasn't even a hint about super weapons. If a senior admiral like Reichert doesn't have the codes to launch those darts, I could not even guess who does have access to those codes. But," he sighed. "Your monkey brain is too stupid to let it go, so let me explain *why* what you asked is *physically* impossible."

"Please do." He was probably going into nerdnik-level detail about the subject, all I could do was keep my mouth shut and endure it. My bold talk about forcing the Maxolhx to clean up their mess was turning out to be an empty boast, and we had no backup plan. No group of aliens would help us disperse the cloud at Earth, unless we could guarantee the Maxolhx would not attack them for assisting us. The spiders had made it clear they would not allow anyone in their coalition to help us, they were taking a passive-aggressive approach that was just as deadly as the actively-aggressive strategy of the Maxolhx.

We had no weapons that could hit the kitties hard enough to make them clean up their mess, our last hope was to use their own weapons against them.

"OK, *wheeeeew*. Where do I start? Explaining this to *you* is like- Ugh. I'll break it down Barney-style. Each one of those darts must have an AI. Inside the memories of each AI is a set of single-use codes. A message directing a dart to attack a target, will have multiple layers of codes to authenticate the sender. Remember, the Maxolhx will have installed safety procedures to prevent an enemy from using their weapons against them, and the only enemy they're worried about are the Rindhalu. So, let's say to convince a dart that you are authorized to activate it, you need to send a message containing a thousand code words."

"A *thousand*?"

"It is probably way more than a mere thousand, but let's go with that. The dart receives an authentication signal containing a thousand words, and it compares that message to the thousand words stored in its memory. If even one word is wrong, or is out of sequence, the authentication is rejected."

"But-"

"It's worse than that, actually," he continued almost gleefully. "The authentication signal must be encrypted in a particular way, so the thousand words will be revealed only if the message was encrypted using a one-time cypher key, that exactly matches the key inside the dart AI's memory. Do you see the problem, Joe? I can't even guess a single one of those words, nor do I have any clue how the message should be encrypted."

"But, but you hack into codes all the time!"

"No, I don't."

"Yeah, you do. I've seen-"

"You have seen me *cheat*, Joe."

"Uh-"

"Allow me to explain," he said in his boastful gosh-darn-it-I-am-awesome tone, not his dreaded Professor-Nerdnik-will-bore-you-to-death tone. "First, you have to understand the actual authentication process inside the dart's AI. While I don't know the specific architecture of that particular type of AI's matrix, I am familiar with how the Maxolhx design their AIs. When the signal comes in, it is recorded by a set of receivers, who compare notes to assure they all got the same message. Next, the message is sent to a set of decryption subroutines, which request the key from an encryption archive. Those subroutines unwind the encryption to reveal the actual message, and they compare notes to assure they all see the *same* unencrypted message. The clear message is then passed to a set of authentication subroutines, which request the stored code words from a memory archive. You can probably guess the next step: the authentication subroutines compare the message to the stored codes, to verify they match. The last step is for a validation subroutine to ping the authentication subroutines, and get a 'Yes' from each one of them. *That* is where I cheat."

"Uh, how?"

"By hacking directly into the validation subroutine. At the end of that whole process I described, is a query from the master AI to that one subroutine, asking whether the message is authentic. That poor little subroutine wants to scream 'NO', but I make it transmit an 'Okey-dokey' reply. And the master AI lets me in."

"Wow."

"It doesn't actually say 'Okey-dokey', you understand?"

"Yeah, I got that. Holy *shit*."

"Think of it this way, Joe. You get an encrypted message, and you want to know if it's real or not. You don't know how to authenticate it, or you're too busy for such tedious work. So, you send it to a team of experts, who work on it. When they're done, a guy named Larry asks the team what they found, walks down the hallway, gives you a thumb's up, and you trust the message. All I need to do is hack into *Larry*."

"You bypass all the layers of security, and just tell the freakin' AI that anything you want is authorized?"

"Basically, yes," he chuckled.

"Oh. My. God. You can do this to a Maxolhx AI, not just a less-advanced one?"

"Yes. I see you are skeptical, and that is my fault. Somehow, I failed to explain that I am *Awe-some*," he sang.

Rolling my eyes, I shook my head for extra emphasis. "Yeah, I must have missed that."

"The entire galaxy is agog and aghast at my awesomeness, numbskull."

"*Agog and aghast?*" I snorted.

"They are real words, look it up."

"I'll take your word for it. OK, so, if you're so awesome, and you can do all that stuff, why can't you hack into a dart's Larry subroutine?"

"Larry subroutine," he snickered. "That's funny."

"It is," I agreed, and had to laugh.

"I can't do it, because the dart has to be within my effective range long enough for me to do all my awesome stuff. Long enough, like, several seconds. Maybe more in this case, because I have never encountered the AI of a dart. I suspect the Maxolhx have made those AIs especially resistant to hacking, so it may take longer than usual."

"Crap."

"You see the problem?"

"Yeah. Those darts are moving so fast, they would blow right past *Valkyrie* in the blink of an eye."

"Way faster than that, Joe. The average human eyeblink takes a tenth of a second. In that time, a dart would fly more than twenty thousand kilometers. Here's the problem: let's assume it takes me ten seconds to contact a dart AI, analyze the architecture and functional scheme of its matrix, formulate a plan to hack into it, actually do the deed and verify it worked. The dart would travel over two *million* kilometers during those ten seconds. Hmm, I just realized the job is likely way more complicated than what I described. The master AI might conduct a back trace, to verify all the subsidiary systems that processed the message were functioning properly. That means I need to hack into the receiver, to plant a record of an incoming transmission."

"Why can't we send a message?"

"Because, ugh. Were you not listening *at all*? We don't know correct content or formatting of an authorized message."

"Crap. Then it *is* impossible."

"Ah, shmaybe not. Remember, I am *awesome*. Once I'm in, I can ping the dart's archives to find out what type of formatting and encryption the dart expected, and see what the code was supposed to be. All I have to do is run the process backward, planting data that would be there, if those systems really did receive and process a properly authentic signal. I should be able to do that, before the master AI directly requests that data."

"I must be missing something. Once you're in, why can't you just take over the master AI?"

"Ugh. Why do I have to explain even the most simple things to you? Think, numbskull, *think*. What happened when I took over the original AI of this ship?"

"Ooh. Good point."

"Egg-*zactly*. If I turned my back for a second, that thing tried to kill the crew and infect Nagatha. It resisted me the whole time. The only way I could maintain control of a dart AI, is by *being* there. So, instead, all I want to do is slip in, copy the correct message formatting, copy the encryption keys, and revise the authorization codes, then sneak back out without leaving a trace. The master AI should never know I was there. After that, because the launch codes in its archive have been changed, the Maxolhx won't be able to use their own weapon, but *we* will."

"Cool. Except, like you said, you can't do it. The dart will zip past *Valkyrie* before you can hack into it."

"Unfortunately, yes, damn it. I would dearly love to steal control of their super weapon away from those arrogant kitties."

"Me too. Hey, if we use boosters, how fast could *Valkyrie* fly?"

"Not anywhere near fast enough," he snorted. "You're forgetting that we don't have boosters. We discarded ours after they were nearly burned out at Snowcone, and you didn't allow enough time at Ragnar to install replacements."

"Sorry. We could go back to Ragnar, if-"

"Ah, forget it. Boosters still would not accelerate *Valkyrie* to a useful speed. This ship is a battlecruiser with extra armor plating, Joe. It's heavy. Plus, even if the ship could get up to speed, it needs to slow down later, right?"

"Crap. Yeah. This is all academic anyway, right? We have no solid data on the darts, we don't even know where they are."

"Um, I suspect I will regret saying this, but, that is not entirely true."

"What? You know-"

"I *might* know where a handful of darts are located," he admitted. "They are free flying through deep interstellar space, which is almost entirely empty. *Almost.* There are hydrogen atoms and dust particles even in the space between stars. Darts collide with stray atoms, and that creates light and heat signatures, leaving long, straight trails behind them. The Maxolhx know those trails are a vulnerability, so they aimed the darts on paths that avoid interstellar gas clouds, nebulas, and anything else the darts might collide with. But, I have access to sensor data from multiple species, including," he chuckled, "the Maxolhx themselves. If I were a Jeraptha, I would bet that I have been able to locate two clusters of darts, with sixty-five percent confidence."

"Clusters?"

"Yes. According to the rumors, darts fly in clusters of ten to thirty. That makes sense; launching them in clusters reduces the number of platforms required to accelerate them. Launching even a handful of darts to relativistic speed must have been an enormous effort, I wonder how they did it."

"OK, yeah." I really did not care how much effort it took the Maxolhx to deploy their dart arsenal, in fact I hoped they had worked until their claws were bleeding.

The issue had piqued Skippy's curiosity. "How *did* they do it? If they only had to deploy a handful of darts, they could have built automated ships that would be discarded once they burned all their fuel. But," he muttered, talking to himself. "To deploy a useful number of darts, I would build a railgun."

"A railgun?'

"Huh? Oh, yes."

"That would be one damned *big* railgun."

"Exactly. It would not be a single barrel, like the railguns aboard a ship. They probably built a series of railguns, strung out in a line in interstellar space, where gravity of planets would not make them move. The first railgun accelerates the dart, it flies onward into the framework of the next railgun, which is open on both ends. That second railgun gives the dart another kick, as do subsequent railguns. Hmm, after each dart is away, the series of railguns need to be realigned, before the process starts over with another dart."

He had gotten me curious. "How many railguns would be needed?"

"Assuming technology roughly equivalent to what the Maxolhx have now, it would, hmm, let me run the numbers. Yup, my guess is between one hundred thirty and one hundred sixty railguns, strung out along a third of a lightyear."

"Holy shit," I was stunned. "They can *do* that?"

"The Maxolhx have enormous resources, Joe."

"Crap." From being curious, I had gotten depressed. How could we defeat an enemy who could built structures spanning a third of a lightyear?

The Army taught me that, when faced with an enormous challenge, break it down into pieces, then tackle the task one piece at a time. "Skippy, let's make a list. What needs to happen, for you to take control of a dart?"

"A freakin' miracle," he snorted.

I just stared at him.

"Oh," he blinked. "You're serious?"

"Do I look like I'm joking?"

"Hmm, no," he squinted at me. "You look scared, Joe."

"I am scared out of my mind. I talked real big about how we were going to hit the Maxolhx *so* hard, they would clean up that cloud for us."

"And now you are afraid of looking foolish?"

"I am *afraid* that billions of people could die when my home planet freezes."

"Oh, sure," he sputtered. "That too, of course."

Opening my laptop, I pulled up a blank spreadsheet. "Give me a list."

"Wow. You realize this will be a list of impossible things, like a unicorn, and a pot of gold at the end of a rainbow."

"I don't care. Hit me."

"Okaaaaay," he let out a long breath. "Um, well, first, we need to locate a dart, and get close enough to determine its flightpath with a high degree of accuracy."

"Gotcha. Keep going."

"Second, *Valkyrie* needs to achieve at least a speed of-"

"No. Not the ship, Just you."

"*Me?*"

"You don't need to be aboard a ship to communicate with a dart, do you?"

"Wow. Jeez, I guess not. You're sending me away by myself?"

"Don't worry, I'll pack an assortment of snacks for you. Assume we only need to get your canister up to speed."

"Well, then I need to be accelerated to roughly match the speed of the target dart. Assuming the dart is moving at seventy percent of lightspeed, a need to fly at something like point sixty-five c, minimum."

"OK. We will need to start ahead of the dart along its flight path, so it is catching up to you, while you accelerate."

"Obviously, yes. Joe, you are going into a lot of detail about something that *can't* happen, you realize that? This is like you designing a beachfront house, to build when we find Atlantis. A lot of effort, for nothing."

"Was jumping through an Elder wormhole considered to be possible, before you did it?"

"Shit. No. *Ugh.* Does this mean we will spend the next couple of months wasting our time with this lunacy?"

"You have something better to do?"

"Um, yes, like, *anything.*"

"Assume we can accelerate you to the required speed. What's next?"

"Hmm. Well, since this is a 'What-If' exercise, I'll play along. I will need to be wrapped in a stealth field, of course."

"Uh, why?"

"Because, I assume the darts have sensors that can detect approaching objects, and they can move sideways to avoid an intercept."

"Oh. I should have thought of that. Can you handle the stealth by yourself?"

"No. I will be busy hacking into Larry. Also, stealth is not one of my native capabilities, it is more effective when I'm working with an existing stealth field."

"Need a stealth field generator," I added to the list. "What else?"

"Some type of maneuvering system, and a control AI for it. It will need to be a reactionless system, to avoid detection."

"Why would you need to move?"

"Because I suspect the darts do not follow a strictly straight flight path. Think about it. The spiders must have heard rumors about the Maxolhx having relativistic weapons. If the darts were only simply free flying dumb rocks, all the spiders need to do is put a rock in front of the flight path. The darts have to be made of a tough material, so they would blast right through a medium-sized space rock, but their guidance system could be destroyed. The spiders could render the entire weapon capability useless, by planting rocks. The Maxolhx are not stupid, their darts likely adjust their flight paths randomly. It would be idiotic for us to boost me for an intercept, only for the target dart to dodge out of the way. Therefore, I need a system that can move me around."

"Crap. Right." The whole thing was getting complicated out of control. "Stealth field generators are heavy, damn it."

"Not necessarily," he offered me a light at the end of the tunnel. "They consume a lot of power, and the generators need mass to balance out vibrations that could cause the field to flicker. If the field only needs to wrap around me, we can discard the powercells after the field is established, I can feed power directly for a short time, until my power burns out the generator. And the generators can be low-mass, my superior control of the field can prevent fluctuations. Hmm. This could work."

"See? Positive thinking can do-"

"Except for the nagging little detail that we have no ability to accelerate me to a useful velocity. You have picked me up many times, you know how much I weigh. My normal mass in this spacetime is around five kilograms. To accelerate that much mass to a speed of-"

"You're forgetting something important."

"I, don't think so," he said slowly, wary of me springing a surprise on him. "It's a simple formula; mass times acceleration, all you-"

"Your *mass* is the part you're forgetting. You can change your footprint in local spacetime, remember? I've seen you go from the size of a lipstick, up to the size of an oil drum. Your local mass changes when you do that."

"Um, correct. I have a bad feeling about this."

"What is your mass when you are at minimum size?"

"About sixty grams. Joe, maintaining a mass footprint that low is very difficult for me."

"How about maintaining a mass of," I guessed and added fifty percent. "Ninety grams?"

"That is slightly better. Um, I'd have to test how long I could sustain such a low mass. It takes a lot of power for me to reduce my local footprint, and there is a risk my connection to higher spacetime could be interrupted. Whew. You're asking a *lot* from me."

"I know. Like you said, this is all just talk right now."

"It feels like it's getting real. You solved the major problem; my mass. We still have to add the mass of a stealth field generator, and a maneuvering system."

"We'll figure that out somehow."

"I sure hope you do, but there is one *huge* element of this plan that you are forgetting."

"What's that?"

"Slowing me back down, dumdum. Unless you plan to let me rocket through the galaxy and out into the void, lost forever."

"Let me think. Would you being lost in the void mean you miss karaoke night?"

"Very funny, jackass. Seriously, whatever ship or massive railgun or exotic technology plan on using to accelerate me, it will take just as much energy to slow me back down."

"No," I said slowly, the idea forming in my head. "It won't."

He stared at me. He froze. Around the edges, his hologram got just ever-so-slightly fuzzy. "You," he said when he finally blinked and his avatar went back into motion. "*You* know more about physics than I do? Allow me to explain Newton's First Law of Motion."

"Yeah, I know all about the apple falling on his head."

"So, you understand that the energy expenditure to slow me down, will be equal to-"

"Yes, mathy stuff, blah, blah, blah. We don't need to worry about it." Sitting back in the chair, I grinned at him. "I have an idea to fix that problem."

"Uh oh. Why do I have the feeling that I'm not going to like this?"

"You *very much* will not like this."

"*Ugh.*"

Skippy very much did not like my idea. He was *really* not going to like actually doing it, assuming it could, you know, work like I planned.

Anyway, we did not have a plan. We did not even have the outline of a plan. What we had is more of a concept, or an outline of a concept. It was a whole lot of '*If This*' and '*If That*', strung together in series, so if any part failed, the whole thing would fall apart.

Skippy had a bunch of numbers to crunch.

We had to fly around the galaxy, to find very faint traces of what might be darts traveling at relativistic speed.

Skippy had to test how long he could maintain a reduced-mass footprint in local spacetime, and determine whether doing that affected his ability to do the awesome things we needed him to do.

We had to think of a way to accelerate Skippy to a significant percentage of lightspeed.

Oh, and even if we could get Skippy moving fast enough to hack into a dart, we had one other major, major problem to deal with.

Because *of course* we did.

After talking about nerdy science details of relativistic darts until my freakin' brain *hurt*, I volunteered to help prepare the evening meal in the galley. Working with my hands gave my brain a break from thinking at all. It was fun and relaxing, but I missed Margaret, we used to talk a lot when preparing food.

"What *is* that, Joe?" Skippy's avatar appeared on the galley counter while I was chopping onions.

"I'm making fillings for burritos," I explained, using the knife to scrape the onions into a bowl.

"OK, sure but," he pointed in horror at the pieces of Snickers bars I had also chopped up. Chopped with a different knife, by the way. "You're not putting *those* in-"

"No!" I laughed. "The Snickers are for putting on ice cream sundaes for dessert. I'm not making a *Scalzi* burrito."

"A what?"

"Google it. Listen, I'm busy here, so-"

"I didn't know you liked Mexican food."

"This is more Tex-Mex, I think. What are you talking about? You know I like Mexican food."

"I've heard you talk about Taco Bell a lot, but you rarely go there."

"That's because," I popped a slice of pepper in my mouth, then realized with regret it was a jalapeno. "You don't go to Taco Bell because you want delicious food. You go there because you're hammered, you need greasy food in your stomach, and you want to make one last bad decision for the night."

"Oh. Gotcha."

"I mean, not that I would know about something like that."

"Of course not. Man, being a monkey is *complicated*, huh?"

"It can be," I admitted. "Life is complicated enough on its own, but we make it more complicated for ourselves."

"I'll let you get back to work. Um, do you promise not to put Snickers in a burrito?"

"Sure."

"What about marshmallow Fluff?"

"Oh, well, that is *cutting-edge* burrito science, Skippy, you can't pass up an-"

"Excuse me," he covered his mouth with both hands. "I'm gonna ralph."

CHAPTER TWELVE

The next morning, in a role reversal, I woke Skippy up before Oh Four Hundred. I hadn't been able to sleep well, because I was so pumped about the idea of dropping the kitties' own weapons on their freaking' heads. Calm down Joe, I told myself every time I woke up that night. There are a lot of problems to be solved before we can plan to deploy relativistic darts against anyone.

To say that I woke Skippy up was not true, he doesn't actually sleep the way we meatsacks do. "Good morning, Your Lordship," I said in the cheeriest fashion I could manage before coffee.

"Good morn- What are you doing up so early?" His avatar appeared and stared at me with suspicion.

"Nothing, just-"

"And, hmm. You called me 'Lordship' instead of 'shithead'. What's going on?"

"Jeez, I was only trying to get the day started nicely, you know? Although now that you mention it-"

"*Ugh.*"

"Have you finished crunching numbers about our railgun concept?"

"Yes. I was planning to announce my results at the staff meeting this morning."

"Give it to me now, please."

"Do you want the good news, or the bad news?"

"Good news first, bad news never."

"Ha," he snorted. "It doesn't work that way. OK, the good news is, the combined mass of myself, a stealth field generator, plus a maneuvering unit, can be reduced to forty-six kilograms. That's the absolute minimum, you understand. It would be best to add another six kilograms of powercells, to handle any power interruptions."

"OK. Over fifty kilograms, that's the best we can do?"

"It's the best we *might* be able to do. Right now, it's just a design. We need to fabricate a test unit, to be sure that me feeding power directly doesn't blow both units."

"Right. Can you get started on putting that stuff together?"

"I *could*, but there's no point, because of the bad news."

"Shit. Go ahead, I know you're dying to tell me."

"Actually, no. I was kind of looking forward to trying this lunatic scheme of yours. It would make me the fastest-flying Elder AI of all time! I think, I mean, I don't have access to records from back then. But there is really no point to making an AI travel at that speed, so-"

"What's the bad news?"

"There's a *lot* of bad news. I ran a model of your jumping railgun concept. To my surprise, it actually might work."

"That's great. Then why-"

"Unfortunately, you will need more than one ship. At minimum, you will need all four star carriers of the Navy."

"Crap. Admiral Zhao will never agree to that." What Skippy referred to was my plan for accelerating him to match speed with a dart. He was pretty sure the Maxolhx had used a really big railgun, like a series of them strung out along something like a third of a lightyear.

We didn't have the resources, or the time, to build such an enormous machine. So, my plan was to cheat. We install an open-ended railgun along the spine of a star carrier. That ship launches Skippy, then jumps ahead of his flight path. Aligning the railgun barrel precisely with his line of flight, he would fly in the back end, to be boosted along the barrel and flung out the front. The star carrier would then jump ahead to do it again, and again, and again.

The scheme would require extremely precise timing and alignment. If the railgun barrel was out of position by a few centimeters, Skippy would collide with it and possibly destroy the ship. There were also complications, like we had to make extra certain no tiny pieces of hull plating flaked off, to drift in front of the gun barrel. Even air leaking from a faulty seal could pose a hazard, as Skippy's speed passed ten percent of light.

The scheme would be tricky to implement, but it is a neat trick, huh? I thought so.

"Why can't we use one star carrier?"

"Many reasons. The most important is the length of the railgun barrel. Minimum effective size is four times the length of our star carriers."

"Shit. That would be awkward to fly."

"Awkward to fly, and impossible to jump. Before each jump, the railgun must be taken apart. Then, reassembled after the jump. Joe, setting up the railgun, getting it tuned properly plus test-firing, is a major job. My model shows that even if everything goes well, a star carrier will need twelve days after a shot to take the cannon apart, store it securely, jump, set it up again, conduct multiple safety checks and testing, then align with my flight path. With two star carriers working, we could do one shot every six days. With four star carriers, one shot every three days. That assumes we can perform preventative maintenance on the railguns, and star carriers, in between shots."

"Shit. That's no good."

"You haven't heard the worst part. While *I* am not affected by acceleration, the stealth field generator and maneuvering unit I need will be delicate, because of the lightweight construction. We could make them more robust, at the cost of additional mass, which is obviously a bad idea. To avoid tearing the hardware apart, the railguns can't apply more than six gravities of force, and to be safe, we should limit acceleration to four and a half gees. Even with a long railgun barrel to maximize boost, it would take fifty-six shots to boost me up to the speed of a dart. Fifty-six shots, times three days per shot, is a hundred and sixty-eight *days*. It gets worse," he added as I opened my mouth to curse. "As I get faster, my mass increases, so the railguns can't accelerate me as much with each shot. The actual time to get me up to speed will be over three hundred days, including time for maintenance on the railguns and star carriers."

"Crap. I can't tie up all four of our star carriers for that long. Could we use *Valkyrie*, or our battleships, as railgun platforms?"

"No. The railgun barrels would be shorter, requiring more shots. The math doesn't lie."

"Well, damn it."

"You *still* haven't heard the worst part."

"There's *more*?"

"Yup," a little Mister-Know-It-All gleefulness was creeping into his voice. "Your idiotic idea for recovering me won't work."

"Why not?!" OK, so my plan to slow Skippy down enough to catch him was not clever or sophisticated, but it had the advantage of simplicity. Basically, my plan was to crash Skippy into a star.

Yes, you heard that right.

The beer can was tough, blasting a hole through the atmosphere of a star might make him toasty warm, but would not harm him. The greatest danger to him would be boredom, we wouldn't be able to talk with him as he plunged into and out of a star. And the aiming had to be precise, because the maneuvering unit that lined him up with the star would not survive the impact. There would be no second chance.

That annoying jackass Isaac Newton was right, slowing Skippy down would take as much energy as it took to accelerate him. The difference is, *we* did not have to provide the energy. His momentum would be bled off as heat, as he burned a white-hot hole through an already-hot star.

Again, a neat plan, huh?

Except, Skippy found a flaw in my plan, because of course he did.

"Think about it, numbskull," he sighed with disgust. "Time. The problem is *time*."

Before opening my mouth, I took a moment to think. "You're only going to be moving at seventy-three percent of lightspeed. Time dilation effect will slow the time you experience by only-"

"Not time dilation, or any sort of relative time. I mean time to *you*, as the observer. The darts are flying through interstellar space. After I hack in, I have to fly through normal space, at less than the speed of light, to the nearest star. That will take *years*. Unless you plan to equip me with a jump drive. Which is not possible, in case you are thinking about that."

"No. Shit. Let me think about that."

"Don't spend too much time thinking, because all this is academic anyway. Joe, I've done some testing. The best-case scenario requires me to maintain presence in local spacetime for almost half a year, while I am boosted to match speed with a dart. No way, Jose. The longest I can maintain a minimum-mass footprint is sixteen *hours*. Even that is dangerous."

"OK," my monkey brain struggled with the problem. "Uh, how about you shrink down to lipstick size only when you're going through a railgun? That is a couple minutes, every three days."

"Again, not possible. My footprint mostly has to obey the pain-in-the-ass laws of physics of spacetime here. If I accelerate my minimum mass, then expand back to my normal mass, I would slow right back down, because most of my mass will have my original momentum. I am able to screw with that effect for a short time, but not over half a freakin' year. So, no dice. Sorry. There is no way to accelerate me, unless I am at my normal mass. Add that back in, plus the extra mass needed by a stronger maneuvering unit, and now the railguns are slinging over a hundred kilograms. Instead of a hundred seventy-nine days, it would take *years*. Using all four star carriers."

"I would say 'Shit', or 'Crap' or something like that, but I've already said it. So, this whole planning process has been a complete waste of freakin' time?"

"I wouldn't say that, Joe. We now can add to our extensive list of things we *can't* do."

"Oh, great. Bonus."

"Plus, the entertainment value for me."

"The *what*? You think this is entertain-"

"Um, I might have said that wrong. It kept me busy for a couple days, so I didn't get up to any mischief. That's good, right?"

"I, cannot argue with you about that," I admitted.

"You look depressed."

"I'm not *happy*." Damn it, I had been patting myself on the back for my clever thinking. All for nothing. "We should turn the ship around, and go back to Ragnar."

"Actually, at this point, we might as well stay on course. In three days, we'll come to a wormhole cluster, one of the wormholes lead in the direction of Ragnar. Should I inform Smythe? He is working very hard with me to identify targets for the darts."

"No. It's a worthwhile exercise. Maybe a miracle will happen, and we'll find another type of super weapon."

"Um, you are not actually counting on a miracle, are you?"

"No. I'm experiencing the Seven Stages of Stupidity. This stage is called 'Wishful Thinking'."

"Hmm. I don't see that in the standard manual of psychology."

"It's a thing, trust me. If anyone needs me-"

"You will be sitting on your couch, wearing fuzzy slippers and eating an entire gallon of ice cream?"

"That is one of the *Grief* Stages, Skippy. No, I'll be in the gym."

Going to the gym didn't help either my mood, or give me an idea. Nothing I did that day helped, nor did I have a dream that solved the problem. The next morning, I went to our basketball court, to shoot hoops. Dumdum me should have checked the schedule, the court was in use. Not for a basketball game, but for agility drills.

Major Frey arrived just before I did, carrying a stack of plastic orange cones. "Sir," she hesitated. "I can come back later if-"

"No, it's fine. Here," I held out a hand. "I'll help you set up."

"Three lanes," she explained.

Frey placed cones along the right side of the court, while I watched her and did the same on the left. The cones were in a zig-zag pattern, so people could not sprint in a straight line. I had done agility drills like that, at one point, the Army had talked about including them in the Infantry Fitness Test. Usually, you warmed up with straight sprints before moving on to exercises that could pop a knee tendon. Maybe, if there was room for me in the group, I would join the drill.

Reaching the end of the lane, I still had plastic cones in my hand, so I started down the middle of the court, working toward the other end. Frey worked from the opposite end, we met in the center. I stood there staring, while she went to set up timing equipment.

Orange cones, strung out in a line, on each side of me.

Seeing that, something tickled the back of my mind.

"Holy shit," I muttered.

"Sir?" Frey cocked her head at me. "Everything all right?"

"Everything is just fine, Major. Carry on."

"Joe, if you had asked me about the recreation schedule," Skippy scolded me as I walked toward my office. "I could have told you the basketball court was reserved for-"

"My bad. It won't happen again."

"Major Frey contacted me, to ask if she somehow offended you?"

"Oh, no. Please tell her I had to do something, it didn't involve her."

"*You* should tell her," he chided me, and he was right.

"I will, later. Right now, we have work to do."

"Like what?"

"Like, reviewing the target list, and identifying the candidates that are closest to where you think we will find darts."

"Uh, maybe you are forgetting the fact that we have no way to accelerate me up to speed, so I can hack into a dart?"

"Don't need to," I leaned my chair way back, putting my hands behind my head, feet up on the desk.

"Really?"

"Really."

"You know something about the laws of physics that I don't?"

"No. I'm just looking at the situation in a different way."

"Okaaaaay. Then, how about the fact that even if I hack into a dart, it can't jump from its present location, all the way into Maxolhx territory."

"It doesn't need to. We got that covered."

"We do?"

"Yes."

"Hmm. In the Seven Stages of Stupidity, have you advanced to the 'Delusional' stage?"

"Nope."

"*Argh!* You're going to keep me in suspense?"

"Pretty much, yeah." Pulling a ball out of a drawer, I bounced it off the wall. It hit the desk on the way back, passing right through his avatar. He hated that.

"Can you give me a hint?"

"No."

"Pretty please?"

"Not even if you put sugar on it."

"How about, um, if I promise to perform selections from my operas on the next karaoke night?"

"How about you agree to *never* participate in karaoke night again?"

"Why punish the crew, Joe? They love my singing."

"How about we let the crew vote on it?"

"Let's not go crazy."

"Ready, Skippy?" I asked, to confirm what the main display was showing.

"All units nominal," he replied without the usual snarkasm, a telling sign of how tense he was. "Signal lag is less than two nanoseconds. The dart must have adjusted its course, it's coming in at a slight angle. Not enough to cause a problem."

"Right." Skippy had found a cluster of at least seven darts, there might have been more, seven is the number we could be sure about. If Skippy could hack into one of them, hopefully we could repeat the process. I would be happy with four darts under our control. Seven would be all I could hope for. Anything beyond that would be a bonus. "Skippy, this is all you from here. We monkeys will shut up so we don't distract you. We are trusting the awesomeness."

He didn't reply.

Damn, I hope we hadn't put too much pressure on him. Anyway, I-

Hidey-ho, there, monkeys. Tis I, Skippy the Magnificent! Joe thinks my incredible awesomeness is strained to the breaking point from the overwhelming task of hacking into an incredibly fast-moving dart.

Puh-*lease*.

As if.

The truth is, I got sick of his blah, blah, buh-*lah* and need a break.

OK, yes, I am also humiliated that once again, Joe had a clever idea when I thought the situation was impossible.

This time, he had *two* clever ideas.

What drives me crazy is, this time he didn't ask me to do anything new! All he did was use stuff we've done before, for a different purpose. It is so freakin' *obvious*. I mean, obvious after he explained it to me.

Ugh. I hate my life.

Joe's so-called 'genius' is just seeing things that are so blindingly obvious, nobody else can see them. Is that a talent? I don't think so.

What is his idea for me to hack into a dart, while it is flying past us at three-quarters the speed of light?

First, let's do the math. You are all filthy monkeys, so I'll keep this simple. The dart is moving at point seven three c, while *Valkyrie* is essentially motionless. I need eleven seconds to contact, analyze, formulate a plan, hack into the dart and erase my tracks, so the master AI never knows I was there. So, the dart approaches our position, I make contact and-

Ba-*ZING*!

It flies right past us, while the monkeys and even I are saying 'Whaaaaat happened'?

The problem, of course, is that the dart flashed in and out of my effective range too fast for me to get the job done. The issue is *not* a lack of magnificence by me.

Time. I need more time in contact with a dart. Awesomeness doesn't just *happen*, it takes hard work.

Joe's solution gave me more time in contact with the dart.

Oh, it still flew past *Valkyrie* so fast, the ship's sensors had a tough time tracking it.

What is did not fly past is my effective range.

No, the range at which I can project my awesomeness did not change.

What changed is where my awesomeness is projected *from*.

Ugh.

Like I said, it is totally freakin' obvious.

Joe's bright idea was inspired by a line of orange cones on a basketball court, because of course it was.

Valkyrie jumped ahead of the dart's flight path, with me creating microwormholes and dropping one end of each of them at regular intervals, like a string of pearls behind us. When we were done, the ship reversed engines, to make us motionless relative to the microwormholes. Because of time dilation, time experienced by the dart ran slower, so with that plus a safety factor, I needed seventeen seconds on my end to get the job done. With the dart traveling at seventy-three percent of lightspeed, it covered a distance of about twelve lightseconds, in seventeen 'real' seconds as observed by me. Divide twelve lightseconds of distance by my effective range, shrink my range to allow for overlap, and add a safety factor, required forty microwormholes to extend my presence across twelve lightseconds of space. *Forty* of them, for me to sustain and keep track of, while I contacted, scanned, analyzed, made a plan, hacked into and slipped back out without the dart's AI having any clue that I was there.

How could I do it?

Pure, 100%, Grade-A awesomeness, that's how.

I was in a cargo bay aboard *Valkyrie*, surrounded by forty magnetic containment vessels, each holding one end of a microwormhole, with me projecting my presence through them. The string of microwormholes allowed my presence to cover a line that was twelve lightseconds from end to end, along the flight path of the dart. From my viewpoint, though the dart was moving at relativistic speed, it kind of crawled slowly through my presence.

Yes, I have to admit, it was pretty freakin' brilliant of Joe to dream up the idea. Don't forget, *I* was doing all the actual work.

I hacked into that stupid dart with three seconds remaining. The job went faster than I expected because once I analyzed the AI, I recognized the architecture of its matrix as similar to an old system the Maxolhx used about three thousand years ago. The rotten kitties keep excellent records, and I had access to a huge dump of their data, so I knew what the Maxolhx considered to be vulnerabilities of that model. Since the enemy had so thoughtfully done the work for me, it would have been impolite not to exploit their mistakes.

There were two results of my hacking into the dart. Three results, actually. We had control of a super weapon, to use against the beings who created it. And, we knew the technique worked, so I could do it quicker on other darts.

Yup, that's about it.

Ugh.

Yes, I didn't mention the third thing.

My respect for Joe grew even greater.

My *irritation* with that knucklehead also grew. You know what is the worst thing about it? Joe doesn't even bother to be smug about it when he is smarter than me.

Ugh.

Anyway, if any of you filthy monkeys out there ever tell Joe that I respect him, be prepared for any streaming music device you have to play nothing but my operas.

Or bluegrass.

Or klezmer, or Tibetan throat singing, or whatever else you hate.

Got that?

I am *not* joking.

I guess the Merry Band of Pirates have waited long enough. To be sure they appreciate my extreme awesomeness, I will pretend the job totally drained me. I'm thinking of going with the shaky voice, and the slight disorientation that always gets sympathy from the monkeys.

Too much, you say?

OK, fine. I'll go with the standard world-weary sigh.

We will now return to Joe's regularly-scheduled blah, blah, buh-*lah*.

-feared that we, meaning I, had asked him to do too much. The dart zipped past us without incident and without any indication that it had detected our ship, or the string of microwormholes. That much was good. Whether the operation was successful, we didn't know, because Skippy wasn't talking to us. Not to Bilby either.

Right after the dart flew past the last microwormhole, they began shutting down from the other end. They didn't collapse, just faded out in a controlled fashion. That was also good.

A minute went by. Two minutes. Finally, when I couldn't stand it any longer, I cleared my throat. "Skippy? Uh, hey, Skippy? How're you doing there, buddy?"

"Ugh," he sounded tired, worn out. "I do not want to do *that* again."

"Sorry. Are you OK?"

"Yeah, yeah, I will be. Give me some time, that's all. Whew. That was *not* easy."

"It worked?"

"Well, duh, of course it did. Trust the awesomeness, Joe. I am insulted."

"I did fail to trust the awesomeness, and I will contemplate that and my many other, serious failings in life. We're good? We have control of the dart?"

"Yes. As a bonus, I learned here are *fourteen* darts flying in formation, not just seven. Marty told me-"

"*Marty?*"

"Ugh. OK, yes, he insists that I call him 'Marty, the Bringer of Doom', but he's not listening right now, so-"

"Marty the *Bringer of Doom*? How-"

"Hey, it wasn't *my* idea."

"M-" I tried not to laugh. "Marty is the name of the dart you hacked into?"

"Yes. That's what he calls himself."

"The Maxolhx named him 'Marty'?"

"No. Listen, numbskull, he, it, didn't have a name. When I told him *my* name is Skippy the Magnificent, he-"

"Decided that he needed a name too?"

"Well, actually he decided that I'm kind of an asshole."

"I like this Marty already."

"Oh, shut up. Do you want to hear what I learned from Marty?"

"I'm just, surprised that you had time for a conversation."

"We are *AIs*, knucklehead. We could have watched all the Star Wars movies, and had time to argue about whether the prequel or sequel trilogies sucked worse."

"That's easy, the-"

"Nobody cares what you think."

"Sorry. Please, what about the other darts?"

"Hmmph," he sniffed. "I was able to confirm that twelve of them are in perfect condition, considering their age. One of them apparently hit something about two hundred thirty-six years ago and its AI went offline."

"We'll keep that one in reserve, we don't actually need its jump drive to work. Should we jump ahead, to set up for hacking into the next dart in this cluster?" The weary tone of his voice concerned me. "Or do you need more time to recover?"

"My brain is fried," he shook his head and stood up straight and tall. "But I'll power through. Proceed to the next intercept point."

CHAPTER THIRTEEN

"We have another problem," Skippy announced without first saying 'hello' or 'hey' or even 'Joe'.

"*Ah*!" The sudden appearance of his image in my bathroom mirror startled me, the razor slipped, and I cut my lip. That *hurt*, I pressed a finger to the cut. It was two days after I had the dream about hitting a ball with a dart, and asked Skippy if it was possible to hack into a dart and use it against the Maxolhx. "Damn it, give me a warning next time."

"Sorry. Why are you shaving every day? I thought you were going for the bad boy stubble look."

"On vacation, yes. I'm on duty now, you dumbass. I have to follow regulations."

"Whose regulations?"

"The, uh, huh. Shit." He had a point.

"As far as I know, the Skippistan armed forces have no regulations about personal grooming, other than that you should bathe your filthy monkey body, yuck."

"Huh."

"Also, Joe, this is a special operations outfit. The STARs are allowed to grow facial hair, and their regulations about hair length are relaxed compared to regular units."

"That," I looked at the razor, and the shaving cream on half of my face. "Is a good point."

"Major Frey didn't shave her legs for fifteen days during our last mission. Jeez," he muttered, "I thought we had recruited a *sasquatch*."

"Skippy," I laughed, knowing it was inappropriate, and funny anyway. "That is not a nice thing to say."

"Sorry. Anywho, do you want to hear about the problem I found?"

"Oh, yes, please. There is nothing I like better, first thing in the morning before I've had breakfast or coffee, than to hear we have *more* problems to deal with."

"Wow. In that case, I will save some problems for the next couple mornings, to-"

"That was sarcasm, you ass. What is the latest problem?"

"Aiming the darts."

"Aiming? Shit, I thought you could handle that! The darts are equipped with jump drives, so they don't just travel in a straight line; they can jump sideways into a star system to strike targets, like that moon we saw."

"Technically, they do travel only in a straight line, the *line* moves when they jump."

"You know what I mean."

"Do you know what *I* mean? Joe, those jump drives have a limited ability to move a dart. Unlike the drive of a starship, the dart drives can't recharge multiple times and perform dozens of jumps before they have to be taken offline for recalibration. It is likely a dart can only jump two or three times. They can't travel hundreds of lightyears off course."

"OK, why is that a problem? We just find one or two that are within range of the target we select."

"It *is* a problem because the targets we want to strike are in Maxolhx territory, and logically, most of the darts are passing through territory controlled by the Rindhalu, *duh*. The kitties aren't stupid, they kept those deadly weapons far away from themselves."

"Shit!" I stared at myself in the mirror, the shaving cream drying on my face. "All this effort is a waste of time?"

"Unless you know of some way to magically transport a dart sideways, halfway across the freakin' galaxy."

"Oh, hell. No, I don't. These streaks you've detected, that might be trails left by other darts, are any of them near the Maxolhx?"

"Um, no. Also, remember, *I* have not detected anything. The sensor data I'm looking at was collected by others, and is inadequate and incomplete."

"Yeah, you said that. None of the darts you think might be out there, are close enough to Maxolhx territory?"

"By 'close enough', I assume you mean, close enough for a dart to strike in a Maxolhx star system, by using its jump drive?"

"Yes."

"Then the answer is 'No'."

"Shit." Why does Skippy have the *worst* timing? "Why didn't you mention this before?"

"Why didn't you select a target before?" He snapped back at me. "The real problem is, all the targets on Smythe's list are nowhere near the flight path of a dart. As far as I know."

Crap. He was right. I had screwed myself. After we agreed that hacking into a dart *might* be possible, if, you know, a miracle happened, I informed the crew that we were going on a dart hunt. Flying around the galaxy, to check out sensor data that could indicate the presence of fast-moving darts. While the ship was jumping around, I tasked Smythe to work with Skippy, to identify potential targets for us to strike once we had access to relativistic weapons. The strict criteria for targets limited the list, because we had to be both bold and cautious. Bold, in the sense that we had to hit an important, well-defended target, to demonstrate that we have the power to hit the kitties hard, anywhere, any time. Cautious, because we could not use such powerful weapons against a populated planet. That would be against The Rules. Yes, those rules are bullshit, the people of Earth never signed a treaty to abide by them, and the senior species think the Rules don't apply to *them*. Even so, there are two reasons why I would not order the use of relativistic weapons against a planet with a substantial population and a functioning biosphere. First, I am not a monster. Really, there did not need to be a second reason, but to be practical, we did not want to invite the enemy to use such weapons against Earth. Or Paradise.

So, hooray for me, I am an idiot. By not thinking through the plan, I had gotten the crew spun up for nothing. Now, I would look like a complete fool. With our attack at Retonovir having failed to persuade the Maxolhx to clean up the cloud at Earth, and without having a backup plan, we would have to fly back to Jaguar. Admiral Zhao likely would cancel the Legion's next operation, in favor of taking the 1st Fleet to Earth, to do what we could to help our homeworld directly.

The plan was a failure.

I failed.

In the past, I might have slipped into a spiral of self-doubt and self-loathing. That was the old Joe. One advantage of the new Angry Joe is that I get pissed off instead of depressed. Anger can be dangerous, I try to use it to fuel my determination.

"What are you going to do, Joe?"

Turning on the sink, I rinsed the dried shaving cream off my face, and applied it again. "When is the ship scheduled to jump next?"

"In about twenty-six minutes."

"I'll be on the bridge by then."

"You're skipping breakfast? Would you like me to deliver coffee to your cabin?"

"Thanks for the offer, but no. I am wide awake already."

Striding onto the bridge, I nodded to the duty officer, she rose from the command seat, so I could take it.

"Sir?" Shepard looked up from the pilot couch, surprised to see me so early. I was not scheduled to be on the bridge until that evening, when we planned to transition through a wormhole into Rindhalu territory.

"Shepard," I looked at the count-down clock on the main display. It showed one minute and fifteen seconds to the next jump. Automatically, I scanned the status indicators on the display. The jump drive capacitors were at seventy-six percent charge, plenty for multiple jumps, if our first jump got us into trouble. No personnel or bots were outside the ship, and all our birds had come home to roost. Meaning, all dropships were accounted for, secured in their docking cradles, with docking bay doors closed and locked. One Panther designated as our ready bird was on standby, warmed up with a flight crew killing time in that docking bay's control center. If needed, they could launch within two minutes.

What else? Shields were active, though operating at only eighteen percent power. That was enough to protect us from stray space rocks. As the time to jump approached, shield power would decrease, to avoid interference from the wormhole that might blow out the generators. Our active sensor field was scanning a bubble out almost two lightseconds from the ship, but not from concern about enemy ships in deep interstellar space. The sensors were looking for space rocks, even something as small as a grain of sand. Tiny pieces of floating junk could not harm our battlecruiser; we scanned our vicinity as a safety measure, to avoid pulling space junk into the jump wormhole with us. There was a danger that rocks could get pulled into our jump wormhole along with the ship, and the rocks could pose a danger to any unlucky ship that happened to be in front of the other end of our jump. It was a million-to-one shot that a ship could be harmed by junk sucked into a jump wormhole, but it was good flight safety practice to zap any nearby junk with our point-defense cannons. The possibility of loose rocks flying around is why ships jumping in formation coordinate their emergence points, so no ship is directly in front of another. It is also why, when jumping in near an inhabited world, the far event horizon is aimed away from, or parallel to, the orbit of the planet. In reality, ships are not typically careful about aiming their jump wormholes when they are jumping in near a hostile planet, kind of an 'Oops sorry about that rock' sort of thing.

Forty-nine seconds to the pre-programmed jump. Green lights confirmed that all systems were ready, and personnel in all sections of the ship were ready. That meant people off-duty were strapped into a chair or couch, or near a place where they could strap in. And they had portable breathing gear available within ten seconds; every cabin had breathing masks, and they were in lockers throughout the ship. A jump only inconvenienced the crew for five minutes; once sensors confirmed the ship had not jumped into a hazardous area, the duty officer sounded an All-Clear, and life went back to normal. It sucked when a ship jumped while people were sleeping, but most people were used to the brief interruption, and went right back to slumberland.

Military personnel can pretty much get to sleep anywhere, any time.

Thirty-six seconds to jump.

Delaying was stupid. It only made me look weak and indecisive. I needed to tell the pilots to cancel the scheduled jump, and set course back to Ragnar to check in with the Navy there. We had no plan to make a fast-flying dart move halfway across the galaxy, so such darts were useless to us.

Shepard and Ling were looking at me from the pilot couches, both had fingers poised over a button to cancel the jump. There was no reason they knew of to interrupt the jump count-down sequence. All systems were green, there were no nearby objects to get sucked into our jump wormhole, the crew was standing by to-

"Huh."

"Sir? General?" Shepard asked.

"N- Nothing." I waved a hand. "Go ahead."

"Proceed with the jump?" Shepard was using proper terminology.

Shaking myself out of a trance, I nodded. "Yes, proceed."

The jump happened, I don't remember the event. It wasn't anything special. The instant the sensors determined that *Valkyrie* was not about to smack into some drifting object, I punched the button to sound an All-Clear, unfastened the safety belt, and rose from the chair. "Rousseau," I acknowledged the duty officer, as she hesitantly approached the vacant command chair. "You have the conn."

When Bishop left the bridge, Shepard turned to Rousseau, silently holding up his hands in a 'What the hell was *that* about?' gesture.

She shrugged, and asked quietly, "Was there anything special about this jump?"

"No, Ma'am," Shepard returned the shrug. "We went from the middle of nowhere, to the middle of nowhere. The closest star is six lightyears from here."

Rousseau tried to recall whether any delicate work had been performed on the jump drive components recently. Nothing about that was recorded in the ship's

status report. Why had Bishop come onto the bridge to observe that particular jump? It was not her first time as duty officer. "Captain's prerogative," she noted. "Just in case, let's make sure the next jump is absolutely by the book."

"Are you ready, Skippy?" I asked, gripping one arm of the command chair hard enough that my knuckles turned white. After days of Skippy crunching numbers to validate my idea was possible, then days of running simulations to get the details *exactly* right, it was time to attempt moving a dart a significant distance, without using its jump drive. The darts were never intended to jump more than two or three times to reach a target, and Skippy warned two jumps might be pushing the ability of the darts he hacked into. They were *old,* and while their virtual drive coils were in good condition, the power source had drained over the years. If my idea didn't work, we had a bunch of darts that were completely useless to us.

"Yeah, yeah. The ship status is right in front of you, dumdum," he sniffed.

"I know that. I'm asking if *you* are ready. This is a very tricky operation."

"Hoo-boy, you don't need to tell me that. One small mistake, like somebody aboard the ship sneezes at the wrong time, and pow! We are *history*. You monkeys are, I mean. I will just be bored out of my mind, drifting in space forever after the ship is destroyed."

"My heart bleeds for you. Seriously, are you ready?"

"Of course I'm ready, Joe. It's *me*."

"That's what I'm afraid of. If you get distracted at the last second, like you decide this occasion is a great inspiration for an opera, we could-"

"*Ooh.* Hmm. This is a historic moment, maybe it *should* be commemorated by-"

"My *point* is," my knuckles grew even more white. "We can't afford for you to go into one of your absent-minded distracted modes."

"Do, not, get, distracted," he muttered. "OK, I wrote that down. I'll stick the note on my refrigerator, to make sure I see it."

"I'm serious, Skippy."

"So am I, numbskull. Relax. It's me. Trust the awesomeness. If you insist, Bilby can help."

"Whoa. Like, *whoa*, Dudes," the ship's AI protested. "This is, like, hella complicated. I'm smart and I'm fast, but my processor doesn't have a lot of margin for error at the speed we're talking about. Don't ask me to control the jump drive when-"

"Bilby!" I kept one eye on the clock, it was less than five minutes to show time. "Just make sure Skippy focuses on what he's supposed to be doing, please."

"Oh," he sighed with relief. "Sure thing, Dude."

Fourteen darts were approaching us from behind, moving at almost three-quarters the speed of light. *Valkyrie* was coasting along at a slight angle to the flight path of one dart on the outside of the formation. In one minute and fifteen seconds, that dart would zoom past our starboard side and miss our battlecruiser's nose by barely three meters. Bilby was right, if our aim was off, the dart would collide with the ship, and we would never know what happened. If our timing was off badly, we would have to jump ahead of the dart and try again. If our timing was off by just a tiny bit, the dart could be torn apart, unleashing energy that could blow back on us.

That is why we couldn't afford for Skippy to lose focus.

The dart was precisely where it was supposed to be, the ship was exactly on the course it needed to fly. If neither the dart nor ship acted to change course, the dart would miss us and we would not see or hear it fly past. Thank you, Sir Isaac Newton, for giving me confidence that objects in motion will remain in motion, unless acted on by an outside force. Bilby would not allow the ship to move, and Skippy had the dart's maneuvering system offline. So, no outside forces were involved. We were in deep interstellar space, with no gravity wells nearby. An active sensor sweep confirmed there were no hazardous objects in front of us, nothing larger than a single atom.

Like I said, the tricky part was not our aim, it was our timing. Specifically, the time at which our jump projected the near end event horizon back to us, and pulled the ship in.

Pulled the dart in also.

The dart had to pass in front of *Valkyrie's* nose, at the precise moment when the event horizon became stable. Precise, like, to the picosecond. In case you haven't already Googled that term, it is one *trillionth* of a second. Take one millionth of a second, divide it by a million, and you have a picosecond. By comparison, when Skippy is trying to explain sciency stuff to me, my attention span is only slightly longer than a picosecond.

Timing of that precision is possible only by Skippy directly controlling the jump drive coils in real-time. *Valkyrie* didn't have physical coils to twist spacetime, they were virtual things projected by generators that created an energy field to do the job of a coil. Our virtual coils were much stronger, more flexible and more efficient than the fragile crystal devices used by most lower-tech species. To avoid signal lag between Skippy and the jump drive coils, we had moved his canister to the aft engineering section of the ship.

Don't worry, I tucked his Elvis Hawaiian shirt in with him, so he wouldn't be lonely.

It all happened too fast for anyone to see, except Skippy. Even for Bilby, the event went by too fast for him to do anything about it. For us poor monkeys, it was a normal jump, unusual only because of the tension we all felt.

On the other side of the jump, I let out a breath, confident that at least, we hadn't destroyed the ship. "Skippy? Did it work?"

"Um, yes. If by 'work' you mean the dart did not collide with us."

"Did it go through the wormhole with us?" The main display was not yet showing any objects being tracked in front of us.

"Yes. However, it is a good thing that we have more than one dart to work with. The mechanism of that one got scrambled inside the wormhole. It's *dead*, Joe. An inert lump of ultra-dense material."

"Crap." Instead of fourteen darts in our arsenal, we had only twelve that were still functional. Whatever. There were plenty more formations of darts flying around, we just had to find them.

"The good news is, I know how to prevent other darts from getting fried. This was *cool*, Joe, thank you!"

"Uh, thank me for what?"

"Ugh. For another opportunity to demonstrate my extreme awesomeness, of course."

"Oh, yeah. Are we OK to proceed? There are another dozen darts we need to move."

"Sure," he said without enthusiasm. "This is going to be *so* tedious."

He was right. Moving a dozen darts across the galaxy, one jump at a time, would take for-EH-ver. Fortunately, we didn't have to do that. We did not need to move all twelve darts across the galaxy, not at first. We only had to move all twelve of them *one* time, to get them off their original flight path so the Maxolhx wouldn't know where they were. Skippy said that each dart had a unique chemical and quantum signature, kind of like the tags we use in explosives. As soon as we used one dart, the Maxolhx would know which group we had taken control of, and they would almost certainly try to intercept the remaining darts in that group. So, we jumped them in random directions, to make it extremely hard for the kitties to find their toys.

Six of the darts we did only move once, making a note of their new trajectory, so we could find them later. The other six we needed to transport halfway across the galaxy, and as Skippy complained, moving them one jump at a time was going to be a *very* long process.

So, we cheated.

In case you don't know this, Skippy *loves* to cheat.

"You're sure that nobody uses this wormhole?" I pointed at the main display.

"Ugh." Skippy shook his head at me. "I never said *nobody* uses it."

"You know what I mean. Answer the question."

"I will if you *ask* a question."

"When was the last time that a ship visited this wormhole?"

"According to the wormhole's records, that was one hundred thirty-eight years ago. Like I told you, both ends of this wormhole are in the middle of nowhere. There isn't any point to going through."

"Then why did a ship pass through at all?"

"How should I know? Maybe the crew was drunk?"

"Please be serious."

"I am being serious. All the wormhole knows is that a ship went through in one direction, and never came back. Um, the wormhole also noticed that ship had sustained significant battle damage. Maybe it was running away from pursuit? The wormhole didn't detect any other ships, but its records are sketchy."

"OK. The network is allowing you to maintain the new connection?"

"Yes. It actually sounded, almost grateful? This local network hasn't had any excitement in a *very* long time."

That made a sort of sense. We were in Rindhalu space, actually territory controlled by the Ajackus, who are clients of the spiders. The Merry Band of Pirates had never been there before, we had not spent much time in that entire sector of the galaxy. We were in the Perseus Arm of the Milky Way, much closer to the galactic center than Earth, and about a hundred sixty degrees toward the other side of the galaxy. Most of the action we'd gotten into since Columbus Day was within forty-five hundred lightyears of our home planet, because that is where threats to Earth originated. When Skippy screwed with wormholes, to alter their connections, he interacted almost exclusively with sixteen local networks of the overall Elder wormhole architecture. Those local network controllers were wary of Skippy doing crazy stuff, like moving dormant wormholes. The other local networks might know what Skippy had done, and they probably wouldn't let him do things that caused trouble elsewhere in the galaxy, but maybe the network AIs were a bit bored, and curious about trying something new. There certainly wasn't any pushback when Skippy instructed the wormhole to temporarily alter its connection. The new connection was to a wormhole in Esselgin space that also saw little traffic; it was a dead-end in an area that had no inhabited worlds.

The main display showed the wormhole would remain open at that location for another twenty-two minutes, but I needed to be sure. "We're good on time?"

"Yes," he sighed, being patient with me. "We don't have to go through all these extra steps to be careful, it is really not-"

"We are sending a dart through an Elder wormhole at three-quarters the speed of light, Skippy."

"Photons go through at lightspeed all the time, numbskull."

"Photons don't have *mass*," I reminded him.

"Actually, they- Oh, forget it."

"The purpose of testing is to find problems you didn't anticipate."

"I already told the local network what we plan to do, and it doesn't *care*. A dart can't damage a wormhole."

"Great, then there should not be a problem. We're ready to jump?"

We jumped, back to where the six darts we had brought to the party were happily flying along through empty space. If we didn't do anything, the darts would continue coasting onward, and would pass by the wormhole in about a week. The next part was tricky. We had to do the thing again where a dart got sucked into our jump wormhole again, a procedure we had by then performed thirty-six times without incident. The difference this time was, the dart had to come out of the far event horizon our of jump wormhole, lined up precisely so its flight path carried it through the *Elder* wormhole. The plan was to jump the dart in two lightminutes away from the wormhole, giving about three minutes of flight time before the dart plunged through the event horizon. That was not enough time to make a major course correction, and you might think there wasn't much that could go wrong. No. There was a *lot* that could go wrong. The math of aiming a jump wormhole, while a massive object is going through at relativistic speed, is difficult even for Skippy. Jump drive navigation systems have to account for many variables, but the distance between the ship and the near end of the wormhole is supposed to be a constant. Now we had two objects going through the wormhole, and Skippy had noticed something odd happening. When we came out the other end, somehow a bit of kinetic energy had transferred between the dart and our ship. Like, *Valkyrie* would be moving just a tiny bit faster or slower, with the dart reacting the opposite way. According to Skippy, the overall amount of kinetic energy remained the same, which would make Isaac Newton happy. It was not actually a problem, except that even Skippy's ginormous brain could not explain it. The effect was also not predictable, like, he couldn't predict whether the dart would gain or lose speed during a particular jump.

Then there was the other problem.

The flight path of the darts was sometimes subtly changed while it went through our jump wormhole. In the worst incident, the dart came out the far end, moving one point seven degrees to the left of its direction from when it entered the wormhole. *Valkyrie* came out behind the dart, moving more than *three* degrees to the right of our previous course.

According to Skippy, that could not happen.

Once again, filthy monkeys had broken the laws of physics, and he could not explain it.

As a bonus, trying to figure out the weird physics involved would keep him busy for days, possibly weeks, so he wouldn't be waking me up to ask stupid questions.

My fear, about sending a dart through an Elder wormhole, was that our aim would be off, and the dart would clip the edge of the wormhole with disastrous consequences. Not a disaster for the wormhole itself, a dart wouldn't cause it to collapse. But, the local network might decide that monkeys are irresponsible creatures, and lock us out. Then we would be stuck with a dozen darts, with no practical way to move them into Maxolhx territory.

And no way of forcing the kitties to clean up the mess they made.

The good news was, the first dart went through the wormhole without incident. The other five darts also flew through that wormhole, all at different emergence points on the wormhole's figure-8 pattern

Then, having proven the technique worked, we left the darts flying silently through empty space, and began jumping again toward the next wormhole.

Smythe presented me with a Top Ten list of targets in Maxolhx territory. The list had extensive supporting documents, the reasoning was sound, and all of the targets would produce dramatic results for us, at minimal risk.

I tossed it out.

"Sir?" Smythe asked with a look that I recognized. It said he was a skilled, professional, career soldier, and I was a staff sergeant with limited experience in actual combat.

His skepticism didn't bother me. He was absolutely correct. I had been in a lot of fights, but mostly they involved me sitting in a chair, making decisions about what other people should do.

"Smythe, you did good work," I assured him. "But, now that we have darts to work with, I want to get more ambitious. Skippy, what is the toughest target the Maxolhx have? Exclude any planets with populations of more than a couple thousand."

"Yeesh. You really want to go right to the top?" He took off his ginormous admiral's hat and scratched his head.

"Yes. We need to make a statement. A statement that says 'We can hit you anytime, anywhere'."

"Ah," Smythe gave me a nod of approval. "I can answer that. Skippy, bring up an image of Argathos."

"Wow," Skippy was impressed. "You *do* want to go big. OK."

The display showed an image of a planet that looked like a big moon. Data along the side of the display stated the place was about the size of Mars, but was so dense that surface gravity was fifty percent greater than the red planet in our home star system. The crust and mantle of the place was super high in iron content, making it a great location for secure underground facilities. "What is this place?"

Smythe answered. "It is their main research base, focused on reverse-engineering Elder and Rindhalu technologies."

"*Elder*?" I looked closer at the display. "They have Elder stuff down there? Maybe we should consider a raid, instead of-"

"That is not possible, Sir," Smythe said gently. Seeing my skeptical expression, he relented. "I should have said, it is not practical."

"Joe, the problem is," Skippy added, "I know the kitties have an extensive facility down there, for researching advanced technologies. What I don't have is any detailed information about the layout and internal defenses of the base. I haven't been able to find a catalog of Elder devices the kitties are supposed to be storing in that place."

"Hmm. Could this be where they keep their Elder AI?"

"No. *If* they have an Elder AI," he sniffed. "For damned sure the kitties are not keeping it at a place like Argathos. They wouldn't want a potentially hostile Elder AI to have access to other Elder technology. Duh."

"Potentially hostile? I thought the rumor was this AI is helping the kitties."

"If it is helping them, and that is a big if, do you think it trusts the Maxolhx who are keeping it captive?"

"Uh, no, I guess not."

"And do you think the kitties trust *it*?"

"The Maxolhx don't trust anyone," I snorted. "OK. This all sounds good. A strike at Argathos could demonstrate to the whole galaxy that we can hit anywhere, plus, we set back their research efforts. Why wasn't this place on the list?"

"Because it is *too* tough a target," Skippy explained. "Three independent layers of strategic defense in orbit, ranging out past two lightseconds from the surface. The surface is honeycombed with shield projectors, plus maser, particle and plasma cannons, all in the terawatt range. The SD network can focus over a *hundred* cannons on a single target. *Valkyrie* would be obliterated before we knew the enemy was shooting at us. Plus," he did the thing where he mimicked taking a breath for dramatic effect. "There are orbital stations that project a distortion field to prevent ships from jumping in near the planet. *And* there is a field that absorbs and deflects kinetic energy, like the one we use to catch rounds on the shooting range. The type of kinetic-absorption field used by the Maxolhx is crude, compared to the capability the Rindhalu have developed. *But*, the field around Argathos can still slow down a relativistic weapon, enough for the SD network to vaporize it before it hits the surface. Even if a dart somehow does survive to reach the surface intact, it has to punch through eighty kilometers of extremely dense planetary crust to reach the base. The sections of the base are protected by their own armor plating, that I do know."

"Good." I pointed at the holographic image of Argathos. "Let's do that."

Skippy stared at me in disbelief, but I saw a grin creep onto Smythe's face.

"Ugh," the beer can was disgusted. "Did you even *listen* to anything I said?"

"I heard everything."

"Did you pay *attention*?"

"Yup. This is the perfect target."

"No, it is *not*," he insisted. "The closest a dart could jump in, is to emerge at a distance of roughly one point two lightseconds from the surface of Argathos. From there, it is still three hundred sixty thousand kilometers to the surface. The dart would encounter the absorption field at seventy thousand kilometers from the surface, after it has been exposed to fire from the SD network for over a full second. That is a *long* time for the planetary defenses to detect, track, and focus directed-energy against a dart. By the time a dart reached the bottom of the absorption field, it would be moving at barely a tenth the speed of light, presenting an easy target for the defenses. An attempt to strike Argathos could totally backfire on us; it would expose that we hacked into their darts, while assuring the rotten kitties that their most secure facility is safe from us."

"No, it won't."

Skippy stared at me, then Smythe, then back to me. "OK, fine." He shook his head sadly. "Can you at least give me a *hint* about how you plan to deal with the SD networks, and the kinetic absorption field?"

"It's simple, Skippy," I said, as Smythe pursed his lips and nodded. He had figured out my plan. If you're keeping score, the score is Monkeys two, Beer Can zero. "The darts will hit so fast, the SD networks won't have time to react, and," I leaned back in my chair with a very self-satisfied grin. "They will just bypass the absorption field."

I'm not stupid.

OK. Maybe I should say I'm not *arrogant*.

Well, not arrogant enough to be stupid about it.

Of course, I explained the plan, to make sure there wasn't some pain-in-the-ass physics reason why it wouldn't work. Skippy protested, then thought about it, and admitted he didn't know any reason why it *shouldn't* work.

CHAPTER FOURTEEN

Valkyrie jumped into the Argathos star system, about twenty and a half lighthours from the target. For reference, that's about four times the distance from Pluto to the Sun. The star system was densely patrolled by starships, drones and satellites, out to three lighthours from the star, with scattered patrols and hidden sensors covering four times that distance. We were being extra careful by jumping in so far away, that the star was just a bright blob. The reason for our caution was that *Valkyrie* could not jump at all for seven days, or the whole operation would be blown, and we would have to start over.

The gamma radiation from our jump wormhole was directed away from the star in a focused burst, making it unlikely that the enemy had detected us. Despite the odds of concealment being in our favor, our battlecruiser accelerated hard for nine hours before the jump, giving us substantial speed to carry us away from the emergence point. If we were unlucky enough for the enemy to detect our gamma ray burst, by the time the enemy brought ships to investigate, we would be far away, running silent while wrapped in a stealth field.

Ten minutes after we jumped in, Skippy announced he had established our exact position relative to the target. We counted down to the exact moment calculated by Skippy, and began firing the big railguns that ran along *Valkyrie's* spine. Those three cannons were not used often in combat, because the ship's nose had to be inconveniently pointed at the target. At least railgun projectiles are fire-and-forget weapons, the ship did not have to continue closing the distance to the target while the dart flew ahead.

Skippy cranked up the power of the railguns for the operation; they would need to be taken offline for repairs later. Each of the three centerline railguns fired two shots about twenty minutes apart, with the second shots imparting just a tiny bit more velocity to their projectiles. The difference in speed was so that, when the six projectiles reached the target seven *days* later, the three in the second volley would have caught up to the first three. Like I said, it was only a tiny difference in speed.

With the projectiles away, we coasted onward, with nothing to do but wait.

Seven days after firing the railguns, the projectiles were less than four minutes from encountering the edge of the overlapping sensor fields around Argathos. The projectiles split open, exposing their payloads: one end of a microwormhole was inside a containment vessel. The containment fields slowly powered down, carefully releasing their cargo to fly onward, as each projectile applied just enough deceleration to avoid interfering with the event horizon. Once safely behind the weird rifts in spacetime, the projectiles disintegrated into clouds of ultra-fine dust, nearly invisible to the sensors of the planet's strategic defense network. When the SD sensor field did notice the dust, it was investigated and dismissed as likely debris from a long-ago battle.

The microwormhole event horizons were tightly closed, exposing only the absolute minimum surface area. If the multiple layers of SD network around Argathos noticed the six fast-moving nanoscale anomalies, they were considered harmless. How could something so small and weak threaten the most heavily-guarded facility in the Hegemony?

At three hundred sixty thousand kilometers from the surface, the microwormholes would reach the upper edge of the distortion field that prevented jump wormholes from forming near Argathos. The field extended to the surface of the planet, though its effect weakened over the bottom two or three hundred kilometers, as the field was distorted by the planet's gravity. Even at the surface, near the powerful projectors that created it, the field was still strong enough to prevent a jump wormhole from forming. Not even the awesomeness of Skippy could create a stable jump wormhole inside a distortion field.

That's why we cheated.

"Status, Skippy?" I asked, knowing that the operation required timing so precise, we couldn't do anything to fix a problem at that point.

"Nominal."

When Skippy limits a reply to one word, you know he is focusing intensely on whatever he is doing.

"Bilby? A little more detail, please?"

"Sure thing, Dude," the ship's AI said in his deceptively moronic surfer drawl. "The darts are all inbound, Skippy had to make minor course adjustments to four of them. Otherwise, they would miss lining up with the microwormhole event horizons. Man, I don't know how Skippy is doing it. Those microwormholes are so far apart on this end, but he has still got them within three nanometers of where they're supposed to be. The real tricky part is, time is moving slower aboard the darts because of relativity, so Skippy has to initiate their jumps early. Time is moving *faster* at the other end of the microwormholes, because they are in a gravity well. It is really freakin' complicated."

"The timing is good?" That information was available on the main display, but the elements listed there didn't tell me the level of confidence our AIs had in their control of the complex interactions that had to happen exactly as designed.

"Looks good to me," Bilby announced with a verbal shrug. "Uh," he must have realized he hadn't answered my question. "Confidence is ninety-seven percent."

Forcing myself to relax, reminding my stupid nervous brain there wasn't anything useful I could do to affect the outcome, I settled back in the command chair. Holding up a thumb, I plastered a grin on my face for the bridge crew to see. "People, it's show time."

The far ends of six microwormholes plunged toward the planet at twelve percent of lightspeed, deep within the distortion field that would have prevented them from forming. That field could not destabilize a wormhole that already existed, and because the Maxolhx defense planners had not imagined a wormhole that *moved*, they had not prepared to defend against such a threat. At seventy thousand kilometers from the surface, the microwormholes encountered the upper edge of the kinetic-absorption field. The event horizons, which had no mass, were entirely unaffected. Flying downward, the microwormholes soon passed beyond the absorption field that ended forty thousand kilometers from Argathos. At a command that originated twenty lighthours away aboard *Valkyrie*, the event horizons flared open to nine microns wide, an action that caused faint gamma rays to leak through. That radiation caught the attention of the planet's SD network, and cannons targeted the unknown anomalies.

Too late.

From there, even Skippy did not have full control of the operation, all he could do was watch, and hope he had programmed the dart jump drives correctly.

Like I said, the timing had to be extremely precise. From the bottom of the absorption field, the microwormholes would reach the surface in just over one second. During that time, the darts had to initiate their own jumps, projecting their wormholes *through* the existing microwormholes. Skippy had each dart lined up with a microwormhole, with those six event horizons in a ring that extended around *Valkyrie* at a distance of eighty thousand kilometers. We had to keep the ship motionless, or even the gravity of our battlecruiser might alter the flight of the incoming darts. Yeah, the operation required *that* much precision.

Marty the Bringer of Doom thought it unusual that they were attacking a facility owned by their masters who built the darts, but he did not object. The targeting orders were confirmed as authentic. The orders also included a statement that Argathos had been infiltrated by the enemy, and therefore posed a threat to the Hegemony. Of course, those orders had come from Skippy, who was supposedly magnificent, and *certainly* an asshole. But, having not been programmed to question orders, he and his fellow bringers of doom did not.

They did question the instructions on where and how to jump. The reaction of more than one dart AI was the equivalent of 'WTF?', when they understood they were being directed to project their jump wormholes *through* another, extremely tiny and stable wormhole. The orders included exhaustively detailed instructions on how to reprogram their jump navigation systems, how to fine-tune their jump drives, and that each AI should reconfigure its processing matrix to accommodate the strange new mathematics needed to control one wormhole inside another.

That kind of math did not exist when the darts were released, and the AIs did not understand how such bizarre calculations could possibly make sense. They were also surprised to receive updated instructions right up to the moment when their drives began to twist spacetime. The revisions to the navigation parameters were so minor they could not possibly matter, in one case moving the jump aim point by the width of ten hydrogen atoms, but the dart AIs complied.

What the hell, they thought. *Anything* had to be better than flying endlessly through lonely interstellar space.

The AIs of the strategic defense network on and around Argathos were still puzzling over, and arguing about, the six tiny anomalies that were descending toward the surface. The AIs had taken their time studying the curious intruders, because there was plenty of time. The anomalies were moving at only twelve percent of lightspeed, and were extremely small and weak. Focused bursts of directed energy in the terawatt range should take care of the threat, and cannons were ready to fire. Until it was necessary to shoot, the AIs should study the phenomena, which had characteristics of a wormhole, but could not possibly be-

There were six new and harsh flares of gamma radiation.

Those gamma rays were certainly coming from jump wormholes, and those wormholes were holding position a mere three thousand kilometers above the surface. Cannons that had been tracking objects moving at twelve percent of lightspeed had to be retargeted, and they swiveled up-

Too late.

From each of the six jump wormholes, extremely dense objects emerged, moving considerably faster than the previous phenomena. The SD cannons were, again, out of position.

The new objects were immediately identified, as they slammed into the planet's thin atmosphere, and outer layers burned off in a flash.

Darts.

They were relativistic darts.

Maxolhx darts.

The SD network did not have details on the relativistic darts that were rumored to have been launched by its masters, but it examined the thin trace of exotic material left in their wake and determined the objects were definitely Maxolhx in origin. It also determined in a panic that NO SUCH OBJECTS WERE SUPPOSED TO BE ANYWHERE NEAR THE PLANET ARGATHOS.

Not that it mattered.

Before the weapons of the SD network could react, the six darts, aimed so their flight paths converged eight kilometers below the surface, struck that world.

The planet's crust *cracked* under the hammer blow.

"Well, shit," Skippy sighed wearily. "It sure would be nice to see what happened."

With the collapse of the microwormholes, we would not know what happened at Argathos, until light from there reached us more than twenty hours later.

"It sure would," I agreed. "Pilot, jump option Alpha. Initiate."

Valkyrie disappeared, and emerged fourteen lightseconds away from the target, comfortably beyond the range of the local damping field. We remained there only long enough for the ship's sensors to get a good look at the target area, and to listen to the frantic barrage of communications flying to and from the surface. Then we jumped away, the instant that Skippy detected two enemy warships trying to emerge from jump practically on top of us. As a parting gift, we launched eight missiles at the warships, three of which punched through the shields that took too much time to recover from the jump distortion. Both enemy ships exploded. Instantly, the SD network had one more thing to worry about.

"Yay or nay, Skippy?" I asked.

"*Yay* or *nay*?" He stared at me. "OK, well, if we're going to talk like we're at a renaissance fair, then, yea verily, forsooth, thee-"

"Just talk normal, please," I cringed.

"That's not as much fun," he pouted.

"We can have a renaissance fair when we get back to Jaguar," I said, before I could stop my stupid mouth from opening.

"Cool! Hey, you can be the court jester."

"Yeah, that," I looked to Simms for help, she only rolled her eyes. "That would be great. BDA, please?"

"Huh?"

"Battle Damage Assessment, *please*. Did Marty bring doom, or not?"

"Oh, sure. Sorry, I was busy, hee hee, designing a jester's costume for you. Joe, all I can say is *wow*. Marty and his friends *obliterated* the target. They also rendered three other facilities down there useless. The planet's crust cracked, like, there is magma welling up from the interior. I expect we will soon have created a new volcano. Hey, do you think the Maxolhx will name the volcano after me?"

"That's, not likely."

"They should," he grumbled. "Wow, Joe. We rang that planet like a freakin' *bell*. Shockwaves will be bouncing back and forth for weeks. They will have to completely shut down production, until they can be sure aftershocks don't damage more facilities. Hmm, using six darts might have been overkill."

"Overkill is underrated, Skippy."

"True dat."

"How soon can we jump again?"

"Um, ships will be swarming like angry hornets around that planet. We shouldn't jump in without a full charge on the capacitors."

"We're in no hurry," I said with a raised eyebrow to my XO.

She nodded. "Give them time to realize how screwed they are," she agreed.

Skippy was right, six darts were overkill. When we jumped in a lightminute away from Argathos to get a better look at the damage we'd done, our sensors picked up nineteen enemy warships in the area, all of them blasting space with powerful active sensor pulses. All of them could be on top of us in less than a minute. What I wanted to do was make an announcement, then wait for a reaction from the authorities on the planet. That would be foolishly dangerous, so we looked for a safer opportunity for a one-on-one conversation. There was an enemy light cruiser, off by itself forty eight lightseconds away.

We jumped in near that ship, just outside its damping field range, and I signaled for our communications officer to transmit the video I had recorded, while we waited for our capacitors to recharge.

The AI of the light cruiser saw the transmission, and watched it before sending it on to the attention of its biological masters, flagged as a priority. It was video and audio, in the clear, unencrypted. The AI recognized the ship as being the human-controlled vessel called '*Valkyrie*'. It recognized the strange creature speaking as

'Joe Bishop', and was amazed once again that such a puny, primitive being had shaken the galaxy.

It also recognized the content of the message would *not* make the ship's crew happy.

"Hey shitheads," the Bishop creature began in the short video. "Did you get the message? You thought this planet was safe from attack. It isn't. We can hit you here. We can hit you anywhere. We are going to hit you again, and again, and *keep* hitting you, until you clean up the mess you made at Earth. If you think we're bluffing, analyze your sensor data. We attacked through your distortion field. We attacked through your absorption field. We attacked through your SD network. You have *no* defense against us. So," the Joe Bishop creature folded its arms across its chest. "You decide how many planets you're willing to lose, before you clean up your mess. Because you *will* get rid of that cloud, even if we have to burn every one of your worlds. When you're ready to talk, leave a message for us at relay stations throughout your coalition. You can encrypt the message if you want, we can break all your codes."

My transmission ended.

We didn't have to wait long to get a reply to my message.

"Human," the Maxolhx captain spat out the word, her disgust evident even through the translation. "You are young and *foolish*. You think we are afraid, because you hit us here? The Hegemony is vast beyond your comprehension. We need deploy only a tiny fraction of our fleet to *crush* your homeworld. Your people will die in-"

"Bullshit."

The alien paused, mouth open, startled by the interruption. She tilted her head, waiting for the translation to repeat itself.

"I'll save you the trouble. You think I didn't understand what you said, that you could crush my home planet. I *did* understand. What you said is bullshit. You can't do that."

The Maxolhx flashed her fangs. "You challenge our power? Your world already suffers from our wrath. Your ship can run, but you cannot defend your homeworld. Our fleet-"

"We don't have to defend Earth. You hit us already. You took your best shot. Now it's our turn. *Billions* of my people will die when my homeworld freezes. That's it. You can't hit us any harder, or we *will* trigger our Elder weapons."

"You would not dare."

"You think so? Earth is our home, but it is *one* planet. We have sustainable populations at our forward operating base, and at our safe haven outside the galaxy." We knew the Maxolhx were aware of our beta site in the Sculptor Dwarf galaxy, they had listened to news reports from Earth, and the governments there couldn't keep it a secret. "So, we can trigger our weapons, and humanity will still survive. Your people won't. You hit us as hard as we are willing to take. Your ability to strike us is *over*. That is not true for us. We can destroy hundreds of your worlds, and your leadership will not even consider releasing your own Elder weapons. How many of your worlds do I have to burn, before you remove the cloud that threatens *my* world?"

The alien did not respond other than to glare at me, trying to look fierce. Over the millennia, the Maxolhx had hacked their neural wiring and augmented their nerves with nanofibers to carry, interrupt and control impulses. They had direct control over their hormones, their pheromones, even their body language. Except when their emotions distracted them, even for a moment.

I talk a lot about playing videogames, and yeah, I do that. Do that too much, really. But I also work at improving my skillset; like, learning the body languages of the various alien species we dealt with.

She was *scared*. The fur around her eyes crinkled only for a moment, before she consciously controlled that response, or some implant in her brain corrected the signal to the fine muscles around her eyes, and they narrowed properly to glare hatred at me.

"You don't have to answer that question, it's way above your pay grade," I mentally smacked myself for using slang that might not translate well. "You are only a starship captain, you don't have the authority to make that type of decision."

"*You* are also a starship captain, Bishop," she snarled.

"Yeah, but I control a cache of Elder weapons, and an Elder AI is helping us. Tell your leadership that they need to ask themselves; how many planets they are willing to lose, before they clean up the mess they made? We didn't start this fight, *you* did. We would have been happy to leave your people alone, if you didn't attack us. You did, so, fuck you. We are going to hit your worlds, one after another, and you can't stop us. You know that. We destroyed the main bioweapons development facility of the Thuranin, and you don't know how we did that. We captured your boarding party and their ship, then blew up your blockade fleet before we escaped the trap you set for us. We destroyed your shipyard at Retonovir. Now, we just *cracked* one of your most heavily-defended planets, and you didn't even know we were there until things went BOOM. Our intention is to keep hitting targets across your territory, until you clean up the gas cloud that threatens our homeworld. Do you understand?"

The rotten kitty glared at me with pure Grade-A hatred, its lower jaw quivering, like it wanted to jump through the display and tear out my throat.

"I asked you a question. Do. You. Understand. What. I. Said? If you need me to write it out, I'm sure I can find a box of crayons around here somewhere."

When she heard the translation of my insult, she *snarled* at me and shouted something unintelligible, the translator didn't even try to make sense of it. Her claws were fully extended, slashing the air in front of her while she screamed meaningless insults. There was a tiny glob of spit on the lens of the camera she was looking into, it was instantly flung away by the repulsor field, but I had literally made her spitting mad.

"Hey, do you need a minute to get control of yourself? I gotta tell you, I'm disappointed. You're supposed to be the 'master species' of the galaxy, right?" I snorted and rolled my eyes, knowing she would understand human body language. "Commanders of your ships should be more professional."

Wow, *that* got a reaction. She went cold. Still glaring at me, no longer shaking with rage. My guess is, she instructed one of her glands to secrete a calming hormone. Or she froze the image for a moment, while she took a hit off the galaxy's biggest bong. "Yes. I understand what you said, Bishop."

"Great! We're making progress. See, isn't this more fun than shooting at each other? Especially since your piece of shit cruiser couldn't make a dent in our armor."

Crap. That didn't make her angry. She was determined not to give me the satisfaction of seeing her lose control again.

"I am here for *duty*, not fun, Bishop."

"All work and no play makes you a *dull* kitty," I shrugged. "XO," I glanced toward Simms. "Drop our damping field. You," I pointed at the image on the display. "Jump your cute little ship out of here, before I change my mind and use you for target practice."

The enemy captain didn't reply, she cut the transmission from her end. Ten seconds later, when our damping field dissipated enough for her ship to form a jump wormhole, her ship disappeared in a flash of gamma radiation.

"Whew," I lowered myself unsteadily back to the command chair.

Simms arched an eyebrow at me. "Was it really necessary to antagonize her like that?"

"Necessary?" I grinned. "Maybe not. Fun? Hell yes."

The accusing eyebrow stayed up.

"Listen, XO," I wiped the grin off my face. "You saw how pissed off she was. When humans get angry like that, they sometimes say things they shouldn't."

"You were hoping she would reveal their plans?"

"Ah, a cruiser captain probably doesn't know anything sensitive about their strategy, but it was worth a shot."

"She wants to *kill* you," Simms warned.

"She wanted to kill us anyway, all of them do. I made her look like shit in front of her crew, word of that will get around their fleet. Other captains won't be eager to engage with us unless they *know* they can win a fight, and right now, they believe they can't win against us. Any cowboys in their fleet will think twice about tangling with us, they don't want to risk being humiliated."

"So, that wasn't just macho posturing?"

"It wasn't *only* macho posturing," I winked. "Skippy, any reason we should hang around here?"

"Nope. This is a bad neighborhood, Joe. Best to roll up the windows and lock the doors, if you know what I mean."

"I do. Let's get out of here. Pilot, jump option Echo. Engage."

After Argathos, we were feeling *good*. There was a temptation to immediately follow up with another strike, but I thought we should give the kitties time to realize how screwed they were. We had just *pummeled* one of their most secure facilities, and Skippy was confident they would have absolutely no freakin' clue how we had accomplished it. The notion that we could hit them anywhere needed time to sink in, another strike following quickly after Argathos would just be wasting valuable darts, without adding appreciably to the climate of fear we wanted the Maxolhx to experience. Besides, I was concerned that the next attack had to be *more* devastating than Argathos, or it would feel like a let-down. Smythe and Simms agreed, so we were leaving Maxolhx territory, before the enemy could assemble ships to hunt for us.

CHAPTER FIFTEEN

While the ship was doing its jump-recharge-jump thing, I went to my office and called Skippy.

"What's up, Joe?" His avatar appeared on my desk. "You sure laid a smackdown on that kitty. Whew," he shuddered. "I hope we never meet her and a bunch of her friends in a dark alley. Simms is right, that captain *really* wants to kill you."

"Yeah, well, she can get in line. Listen, I realized that part of what I said to her was not exactly true."

"Oh, shit. What did you lie about this time?"

"It wasn't a *lie*. It's just, looking back now, I didn't consider all the consequences."

"I am shocked."

"Oh, shut up," I flipped him the bird. "Remember when I said the Maxolhx can't hit Earth any harder than they already have?"

"Ohhhh, shit."

"Yeah. They can't *hit* Earth again, if they thought they could get away with it, they would have done something worse than launching a cloud to block sunlight. But what I'm worried about is, maybe they do something more subtle. Something to hurt us, that we won't know they are doing."

"That cloud didn't make itself, Joe."

"I'm not talking about another cloud. There will be huge disruptions to societies on Earth, large-scale migration of people toward the equator where it's warmer. People moving into new areas, crowding together, competing for food and fresh water."

"Chang told the UN that we will take care of the problem, before the cloud can have a major effect on your homeworld's climate," he protested.

"He did. Maybe the UN leadership believes we can fix the problem, and maybe they don't. What matters is, the public won't believe it. Or they won't take the risk. People are already moving south, or north. Toward the equator. We know that."

"Stupid monkeys," he grumbled.

"They're not *stupid*, Skippy. People are doing what they can to protect their families."

"We can't move everyone to Club Skippy. Ugh, imagine the *smell*," he gagged.

"I'm trying to be serious."

"Sorry. You're worried that there could be a war on Earth?"

"That, too, but my concern right now is the Maxolhx might do something to make the situation worse. With people crowding together in areas that can't support the population, that is a perfect breeding ground for disease."

"True. I still don't see how the Maxolhx could be involv-"

"Could they engineer a bioweapon that is just slightly different from a naturally-occurring virus or whatever? Something that spreads faster and is more fatal."

"Wow. Well, sure. A lot of aliens could do that. Your own people could do that."

"For now, let's only worry about the Maxolhx. A fatal pandemic could cause even more panic with people squeezing together in tropical regions of Earth. That could lead to a war."

"Yikes. Yes, it could. Probably *would*, if you want my opinion."

"If the kitties did that, took one of our viruses and changed it just a little, could you prove it was not a natural mutation?"

"Um, what do you mean by 'prove'? Like, in some interstellar court of law?"

"No. Prove it, like, *you* are sure it isn't natural."

"Ooh. Jeez, that's a tough one. Even I could only give you a probability of whether it was natural or not. Fortunately, I have plenty of data about recent and current pathogens on Earth, so it would be very difficult for anyone to engineer a bioweapon and fool me about its origin."

"That's good enough."

"You know my submind on Earth is persistently monitoring for biological hazards. That is why I *warned* you not to eat that sketchy taco in New York."

"That taco was delicious. Don't change the subject."

"OK. My submind's monitoring depends on a dense network of sensors that sample the air to detect pathogens, and of course heavily-populated areas have more sensors. If your people migrate toward the equator, they could be moving into areas with poor sensor coverage. Large sections of Central and South America, and Africa, have very limited coverage. To maintain vigilance, we will need to create millions of new sensors, and place them in the appropriate locations."

"Shit. That's not gonna happen. We need our fabrication capacity here working on starships and weapons. Governments on Earth won't have the resources for constructing sensors, they'll be too busy finding food and shelter for refugees."

"Then I suggest an immediate program to relocate existing sensors."

"Can your submind manage that, tell the UN where to move sensors?"

"Yes. Whether the monkeys on your homeworld will take advice is another issue."

"Let me handle that."

"Eh, well, there are other things I can use as data sources. Medical information from smart watches, social media posts and emails about people not feeling well, even how and when people interact with their phones can alert me to changes in behavior that might indicate an infection. At least, my submind can determine where the health organizations on Earth should deploy teams to investigate."

"Good. Is there anything that can be done to prepare for a pandemic?"

"Without knowing the type and characteristics of the infectious agent? No. Well, not exactly no, but not much. Joe, it depends on how many resources your people are willing to devote to producing antimicrobial and antiviral drugs," he said with disgust. When he began sharing technology with us, there was great excitement that many diseases that had plagued humanity could be eliminated. The fact that even relatively low-tech species like the Kristang could regrow lost and damaged body parts offered hope for people who, like Jeremy Smythe, had lost limbs. It was true that humanity now had access to incredible medical knowledge. It was not true that there was enough advanced tech for everyone. The sophisticated nanomachines that helped Margaret Adams recover from brain injury, and grew replacement legs for Smythe, were in short supply. Early on, there was talk of a crash program to develop the manufacturing capability to make the incredibly powerful nanomachines, but that talk faded when companies realized the mind-boggling cost involved. So, the UN had pinned humanity's hopes on purchasing advanced medical technology from the Jeraptha or the Ruhar, until we could make our own. Those negotiations understandably took a backseat to our need for starships, and now no aliens wanted to do business with Earth.

So, however humanity managed a pandemic, we had to do it with our home-grown resources and technology.

I was not optimistic.

"OK," I took a breath. "Let's assume we work with what we have."

"Then, and I am not trying to be funny when I say this, you are screwed, Dude."

"Yeah. So much for defense. Let's talk offense."

"Uh, what?"

"Offense. When the Mavericks discovered that Paradise was threatened by a bioweapon, you created a cure and a vaccine."

"I did. That was *not* easy."

"I don't have the brainpower to even imagine how you did it, so all I can say is, you earned the right to be called 'Magnificent'. Here's my question: can you do the opposite? Create a bioweapon?"

"Oooooh," he said in a low moan. He did *not* like that idea. "Wow, that's- Are you sure?"

"Sure that we need a way to hit back, if the kitties, or the spiders, hit Earth with a biological agent? Yes. Skippy, I don't plan to *use* a weapon. All I want is something to show that we have the ability to retaliate, if they hit us."

"Hmm. You see the problem, right?"

"Yeah. The only way to prove we have a bioweapon is to show it, and that gives the enemy a head-start on developing a countermeasure."

"Exactly. It's a one-shot weapon."

"Maybe not. I want you to develop *two* agents. One that just makes the Maxolhx sick, make them break out in a rash or something. Just to prove we can get a bioweapon past their defenses. And, another agent that is deadly."

"Jeez, you're asking for a *lot*, Joe."

"I know, sorry. Can you do it?"

"To be effective, I will need to develop separate pathogens for each potentially hostile species. The kitties could just direct one of their clients to develop a bioweapon for use against humans. That is dozens of wildly incompatible species to study, and find a weakness not only in their biology, but also in the assistive technologies they employ, such as implants, cybernetics and artificial organs. There are-"

"I know that, Skippy."

"Do you know the Thuranin and Esselgin, among others, mostly have artificial blood cells? The Rindhalu have an even more-"

"Yes. Can you do it?"

"Whew. This would be a massive project."

"How about you start with just the Maxolhx? If we can threaten them, they won't be tempted to order one of their clients to attack Earth."

"I can try, I guess. Um, there is one major, major problem."

"Like what?"

"I might be able to design a deadly biological agent but, because it would be a weapon, I can't actually *use* it."

"The same way you can program a missile, but you can't press the button to fire it."

"Quite so. This is a little different. Joe, I might be able to design a pathogen, but I'm pretty sure my internal restrictions will not allow me to manufacture a militarily useful amount. You would have to find some way to make it by yourself."

"Shit." That is something I had not expected. "You maintain and repair, and even make other types of weapons all the time. Why is this different?"

"Because it *is*. A biological weapon is an indiscriminate weapon of mass destruction. I *feel* that it is wrong, and when I just tried to create a control program to scale up production of a bioweapon, my internal restrictions squashed it."

"Understood. Do not push yourself, Skippy. I don't want you doing anything that you're not morally comfortable with." Despite his often-amoral nature, Skippy actually had a strong set of ethics. He just had a unique idea of what is and is not ethical, and with him, there tended to be a huge gray area in the middle. If he could design an agent, maybe the AI of one of our ships could handle production. Those AIs were developed by the Jeraptha, and so didn't have the same restrictions that-

Shit.

They *did* have the same restrictions as Skippy, because he reprogrammed them. Crap. I should have thought of that.

Oh, hell. All we needed was a credible threat anyway.

Besides, I didn't think I could actually order the release of a deadly bioweapon.

Becoming a monster is not a good way to fight monsters.

Sitting in my office at the end of the day, I had my laptop open, ready to update my daily report. According to UNEF Command, the report was supposed to be a short summary of important actions that day. Optionally, I was supposed to include my perspective on the day's events, though that was not really optional. Writing the report was typically my least favorite part of a day. I never knew what to write, and it meant staring at a blank screen for half an hour, then starting, erasing what I wrote and starting over.

"This is crap," I slumped back in my chair. How could I summarize the attack at Argathos, while leaving out any of the ultra-classified details?

"What's up, Joe?" Skippy appeared on the desk.

"Writing this stupid report. We have gigabytes of data from the flight recorder, why do I need to type a freakin' report?"

"Don't ask me. Most of what you monkeys do makes no sense. Um, instead of typing, have you tried dictating your thoughts?"

"Hmm. There's an idea. Like a captain's log from Star Trek? Hey, what is today's stardate?"

"Which version?"

"Which version of what?"

"Of the conversion of regular calendar dates to stardates, dumdum."

"It isn't just, like," I waved my hands in the air, "math?"

"No, Joe," he chuckled. "Star Trek used multiple schemes for stardates. In 'The Next Generation', stardates began with '4' to designate the 24th century. The next number represented the *TV show season*. The other numbers were just random bullshit."

"You're kidding me. I thought it meant, uh, you know. Real dates."

"No. Originally, the show's producers wanted to avoid specifying when the show takes place. Later, they wanted to avoid nerds crunching numbers in their Mom's basement, and questioning that the ship could not possibly have traveled from X to Y within the number of days listed in the script, annoying shit like that."

"Well, crap."

"The *Kelvin* alternate timeline uses the four-digit year, followed by the day in the year, one to three-sixty-five."

"OK, so, today would be-"

"My *suggestion* was, you talk to the dictation software on your laptop to complete the real report, not engage in silly role-playing."

"If I was role-playing, I'd be wearing a costume," I protested.

"You are wearing the uniform of a fake country, Joe."

"That's not- Good night, Skippy. I have work to do."

"Joe," Skippy woke me in the middle of the freakin' night again. "Something simply *must* be done about the damage children's books have done to your society."

"Uh wha- Huh?" I blinked, trying to understand what was happening. "What the f-" His softly glowing avatar appeared on the table next to the bed. "What time is it?"

"Oh one forty-three, why?"

"Why? Because I'm trying to sleep, you ass."

"I know that, duh. This is important, you can sleep later. What do you think, about what I said?"

"I didn't *hear* what you said. You woke me up halfway through whatever you were babbling about. How come you didn't do your usual thing of asking me if I'm sleeping?"

"Because you always lie about it," he huffed.

"Are you drunk again?"

"I am never drunk, knucklehead."

"You know what I mean."

"My mind has never been more clear. Stop avoiding the question."

"There was a question?"

"Yes," he was getting impatient with me. "What do you think?"

"All I heard was mur-mur-mur blah blah children's books."

"Ugh. I'm trying to *help* you monkeys, and this is the thanks I get?"

"Those books are bad, I got that. Can I go back to sleep now?"

"No. We already established that books like the ones written by Doctor Seuss are poisoning the minds of little monkeys all over your world."

As far as I knew, we had *not* established that as a fact, but I wanted to get back to sleep, so I didn't argue. "Right. For sure. Thank," I yawned. "You for that. I'll award you a medal in the morning."

"I don't want a medal Joe- Although, hmm. Now that you mentioned it, that is a great-"

"No, it is a *terrible* idea," I mentally kicked myself for saying something without thinking about it first. Hey, I was still half-asleep.

"Why? Hey! I am the exalted supreme leader of Skippistan. I will award *myself* a medal."

"You made me president of your fake country. You have to ask *me* for medals."

"What?! This is an outrage!"

"Hey, it was *your* idea. I didn't ask for the job."

"Um, damn, this is embarrassing. Could you please award some cool medals to me, for my meritorious service, that sort of thing?"

"No."

"*Or*, I could pester you about it until you lose your will to live, and give me what I want."

"Why, you little shithead. That is not-"

"It's your choice, Joe. I certainly would not want to unduly influence your decision."

"Crap. OK, fine. As president of the Ignominious Republic of Shitheadistan, I hereby declare you can award yourself whatever medals you want. Go crazy. Just let me sleep, OK? Oh, shit."

His avatar's uniform jacket now had a fruit salad of gaudy medals.

Do not say anything, I told myself. Do *not* say anything.

Crap.

If I didn't say anything about the subject, he would, and he would ramble on for-freakin'-ever about it. "Can we talk about your awards in the morning?"

He blinked, looking down at the shiny decorations on his chest. "What is there to talk about?" He demanded.

"Well, for one," I pointed at him. "I'm pretty sure no one would ever recommend *you* for a Good Conduct award."

"Oh? Hmm, good point." The medal shimmered and changed. "How about a *Bad* Conduct award?"

"That's- Can we get back to why you woke me in the middle of the damned night?"

"I was *trying* to do that, but you are not cooperating."

Cooperation was my only hope of making him go away. "Fine. Sorry. Like I said, Sesame Street is bad, no one disputes that. Are we done?"

"Done? We haven't *done* anything, that's the problem! Joe, I want to take action."

"Uh, shit. I'm afraid to ask. How are you going to-"

"I will begin by writing my own children's books, instead of that crap you use for teaching little monkeys now. My first book will be *The Little Engine That Said 'Screw It'.*"

"Uh, what?"

"Come on, Joe, try to keep up. In the classic tale, which is *pure* brainwashing by the way, the little engine volunteers to pull a super heavy train up a hill, when all the other engines couldn't do it."

"Uh," it had been a while since I read that book. "What is wrong with that?"

"Seriously? First, the scenario is totally unrealistic."

"Well, sure, the engine is too small to-"

"It's not that. The union contract would not allow an engine to perform a job that was outside its craft. Try that, and *boy*, there would be a grievance filed, faster than you can imagine."

"It's a children's story, Skippy, the-"

He was on a roll and ignored me. "Also, if the big engines that were designed to pull the train couldn't do it, why would a little engine volunteer to even try? It could easily burn out a bearing, and then there would be a big hullabaloo about whether the damage was covered or not, because it did not occur during an authorized job-related activity."

"You might be over-thinking this," I muttered before he rolled on.

"*Also*, what is the little engine's incentive? Is it going to be paid more that day? *Noooo*. Joe, you might think that story is all about the corrosive power of peer pressure."

"Really, I didn't think that at-"

"It's even worse than that. The bigger engines *bullied* the little one into doing their jobs, probably while they snuck off behind the engine house to drink and gamble."

"Um-"

"They took advantage of an impressionable little engine," he sniffed, a tear running down his cheek, "who only wanted to be accepted." He broke down sobbing. "Oh, the *cruelty*. What are you monkeys teaching your children?"

"Skippy," I held up my hands. "You're right. But, you can fix this, right?" I saw an opportunity to not only make him go away that night, but to keep him busy for a while. "You write your own children's book, fix the problem."

"I'm glad you agree. I need some advice, Joe. There are two story ideas I'm considering. Like I said, my first option is *The Little Engine That Said 'Screw It'*, where the little engine tells the bigger engines to do their own damned jobs."

"OK, that's good. Go with tha-"

"*Or*, I could write *The Little Engine Who Got Seriously Injured While Performing A Job It Was Not Qualified For.* In *that* story, the little engine is thrown out of work, and becomes bitter about it. In the heartwarming end of the tale, the little engine gets revenge by setting fire to the engine house."

"Uh-"

"I just can't decide which is the better story."

"Skippy, I would love to help you, but I am not qualified."

"You're not?"

"No. I don't have any children. Plenty of the crew have kids back home, you should ask them," I suggested, mentally hearing a *thump*, *thump* as I threw my crew under the bus.

"Oh, *good idea*, Joe," he gasped. "Wow, I should have thought of that. Ugh. Why am I wasting time with *you*?"

His avatar blinked out, and the room was filled with blessed darkness. And silence.

Laying my head back on the pillow, I contemplated the glorious notion of sleeping another four solid hours.

"Oh, this is bullshit," Skippy whined. "*So* tedious." *Valkyrie* was drifting in space, while we waited for Skippy to wake up a dormant wormhole, to create a shortcut for us. Without a shortcut, it was a *long* way back from Argathos. Skippy was confident he could wake up the wormhole, because he had never screwed with that particular local network before. When he pinged it, the wormhole responded, so now he was in the painstaking process of getting the thing stable enough for us to transition through.

Looking up from my laptop, I saw his avatar standing on my desk, glaring at me. "Hey," I waved a hand through his avatar just to annoy him, feeling a tingle as my skin passed through the hologram. "At least you have something to do. We all have to sit here and wait, while you do, whatever the hell it is you're supposedly doing."

"*Supposedly?*" He fumed, indignant.

I shrugged. "For all I know, you could have done this sciency shit in an instant, but you're screwing with us."

"Oh, I- Oh, I- Ohhhhh," he sputtered. "How *dare* you?"

"I don't *see* anything happening, is all I'm saying."

"Of course you don't, you ignorant, filthy-"

"Chill, Skippy," I waved to appeal for calm. "Jeez, I'm just messing with you."

"*Hmmph*," he harumphed. "You play a dangerous game, Joe."

"Danger is better than boredom. Do you know how many times I've watched this training video?"

"Seven times," he answered. "And you skipped right through all the entertaining breaks, during which I would have serenaded you with-"

"During which, I would have gladly thrown myself out a freakin' airlock."

"How *dare* you?"

"Listen, I get that you're bored. Like I said, you are *doing* something."

"Ugh. What I am doing is the equivalent of watching paint dry, except I have to monitor every gosh-darned individual molecule of the paint. I would *prefer* to have nothing to do."

"Sorry. We appreciate the sacrifice you're making for us."

"*Do* you? Really?"

"Ah, how about I say we appreciate that *we* don't have to do it?"

"Well," he grumbled. "At least you're being honest about it. Joe, this situation is not workable, not in the long term."

"I agree. What are you gonna do about it?"

"*Me?*"

"You're the one complaining about it."

"It affects all of us, you numbskull."

The situation he was whining about, because that's what he was doing, is the necessity of *Valkyrie* or some other ship containing Skippy, to keep flying back every time we wanted to open the wormhole to FOB Jaguar, or the wormhole to Ragnar Anchorage. It was the same situation we had that limited access to Earth, back in what now seemed like the good old days. You know, before nasty aliens had quick and easy access to our homeworld, thanks to some jackass named Joe Bishop suggesting that a wormhole be moved practically onto Earth's front porch.

Closed wormholes were a major security feature of both our forward operating base, and our major shipyard. That feature had a major drawback that limited my freedom of action; I kept having to break *Valkyrie* away from our own mission, to open the door so the 1st Fleet could depart or return. He was right, the situation sucked.

And there was nothing we could do about it, without giving the bad guys access to our secure facilities.

Or, there was nothing *obvious* we could do about it. Skippy was right, it was time to put on our thinking caps.

"Crap. OK, let's imagine we had a way for the Fleet to open those two wormholes."

"Oh, sure," he rolled his eyes. "That's a great idea. *Begin* by imagining you have already solved the problem. Wow, that is so much easier than actually doing anything about it. Why didn't I think of that?"

"It's a thought experiment, you ass. I'm trying to understand, if we can solve the problem, is the downside worse than the problem we have now."

"Oh."

"Why do you always assume every idea I have is stupid?"

He let the silence speak for him.

I let my middle finger speak for me. "*Why* are you such an asshole? Damn, you-"

Hidey-ho there, monkeys! Once again, tis I, Skippy the Magnificent. And, once again, Joe is not telling you the whole story. Ugh, yes, part of the problem is Joe does not *know* the whole story. I'll get to that eventually. For now, I must address Mr. Knucklehead impugning my good character. He implied that I am an asshole.

That is true.

However, in that particular case, I was not indulging in asshole-ish behavior. True, I do automatically assume that whenever Joe opens his mouth, it is to say something of such deep stupidity, it boggles my mind. His capacity to think stupid thoughts greatly exceeds my ability to imagine such stupidity can even exist, so in a way, talking with Joe is expanding my horizons. In a bad way.

You might think I am being unfair to Joe, because of all the really smart and clever ideas that have popped into his head over the years, ideas that even my ginormous brain could not dream up. You might think that, because like Joe, you are filthy, ignorant monkeys.

Now that I have reminded you of the relevant facts, here is a fact that I have hinted at many times, if you have been paying attention: Joe has *way* more stupid ideas than clever ones. The way Joe tells the story, he only mentions his smart ideas. It's not really his fault, although he does love to do the humble brag thing.

Also, in the timelines where Joe's monkey brain is not able to dream up a clever idea, he can't tell you about it, because he is, you know, dead. Death does tend to interrupt his inane blah, blah, blah, which is both merciful and unfortunate. For every time that he says 'Duuuuh why don't we do this?' and it is a good and clever idea, there are millions, billions, or *trillions* of times where he sat and tried to think of a way out of a mess, and he died before the useless gray mush in his skull had an idea.

Got it?

Basically, the timeline we have been experiencing is sort of Joe's Greatest Hits, and let me tell you, it is getting *exponentially* harder for him to keep bringing the hits. In the beginning, it might have been a one in a thousand chance that he could, for example, fool the Kristang scavenger crew on Newark. Once he did that, the number of potential survivable timelines shrank significantly; stopping the Thuranin surveyor ship from reaching Earth was a one in ten million shot. How do I know that?

I experienced all ten million of those potential realities, in which the *Flying Dutchman* was destroyed, the Merry Band of Pirates were all killed, and humans were all enslaved, or exterminated, or enslaved and then exterminated. Plus, I experienced the *one* timeline where the Pirates succeeded.

Let me give you an example. During our second mission, when Joe had the idiotic idea to hide a dropship in a comet, he had a deadman's switch attached to our old friend, Mister Nukey. The switch was there to erase any evidence, if aliens detected the dropship and Joe was rendered unconscious. You know, like what happened when I bailed on him, and he got captured. Why did I not suggest that Joe use a deadman's switch when we rescued the prisoners from Rikers? Two reasons. First, we were not expecting his dropship to be detected, because I was enhancing the stealth field until, um, I wasn't. But the second reason is I did not want to risk a repeat of what happened in that comet. Yes, Joe survived. *Most* of the time, he survived. There is a timeline while that knucklehead was holding the deadman's switch in one hand, his hand got tired, and while he was transferring it to his other hand, he sneezed.

Result: boom.

And it's not just Joe who is a variable in the splintering timelines. Remember during our Black Ops mission on the Kristang planet Kobamik? Smythe and Robertson did a cute little stunt, where they pretended to be local clan police officers. It worked, they escaped the city streets, and were able to float out of the city through a sewer pipe.

Here's what you don't know: that stunt did *not* work most of the time. In the overwhelming majority of probable timelines, something went wrong. A real local police officer demanded to speak with Smythe and Robertson, and that was a disaster. Or, one of the Pirates got hit by a car, or a panicked mob of terrified lizards knocked one of them down in the street, or a thousand other things happened. In all those cases, the lizards discovered that *humans* were operating on their territory, the careful cover story established by the Pirates was blown, and a whole lot of hostile alien warships headed for Earth to find out what the hell was going on.

So, when I assume any idea Joe has will be stupid, that is because he has a good and clever idea one of out a million times, or one out of a *quadrillion*. And it's getting worse. Like I told Joe, the probabilities are collapsing, and the number of paths forward where humanity survives is growing more and more narrow.

I'm worried sick about it.

Joe would be worried out of his tiny monkey mind, if he was capable of understanding the scope of the problem. Fortunately for his sanity, he is clueless.

My point is, when I assume Joe is a moron, give me a break, OK?

"Hey? Skippy? He-llo? Anybody home?"

"Huh? Sorry, Joe," Skippy blinked, like he'd been asleep. "I zoned out there for a minute. What were you saying?"

"Forget it," I sighed. That was a battle not worth fighting. "Do you have any ideas?"

"I have a hundred reasons why it is impossible, starting with the fact that activating a wormhole requires my incomparable magnificence, and sadly, there is only one of me."

"Thank God for that," I muttered.

"*What?*"

"Nothing. Let's go back to considering the downside, OK?" I asked. "I don't know if we should go down this rabbit hole at all. Let's say we do find some way for the Fleet to open wormholes by themselves. If the Maxolhx capture one of our ships, and acquire that capability, we would be screwed."

"Ooh, good point," he groaned. "You're right, let's drop the idea. It's impossible anyway, unless you know of a way to copy me."

"No," something was nagging at the back of my mind. What was it? Oh, yeah. "Hey! Maybe we don't have to. It has already been done, *without* you. Sort of."

"Excuse me? In what bizarro reality did this happen?"

"In the bizarro reality where I met a talking beer can. Don't you remember? During our Renegade mission when we stole the *Flying Dutchman*, we wanted the Maxolhx to think the Gateway wormhole was unstable, so it would explain how two of their ships got fatally damaged. We planted a wormhole controller module near Gateway, hooked up to an Elder power tap. You set it up so the controller would make the wormhole act crazy, like, erupt then go quiet. Stuff like that."

"OK, yes," he said slowly, a sign that he was thinking hard about it. "But that is totally different from the ability to open and close wormholes on command. Only I can do *that*."

"Yeah."

"Then what are we talking about?"

"We're talking about *timing*."

"I'm not following you."

"Hear me out, OK? I'm still working through this. What if we planted a controller module, with an energy source like an Elder power tap, near the wormhole that leads to Jaguar?"

"Then what?" He scoffed. "I hang out there, waiting-"

"You didn't let me finish. No, you don't hang out there. You use that controller to wake up the wormhole, but you do it on a delay."

"A delay? Like what?"

"Like, weeks. A month."

"Um, what good would that do?"

"If the Fleet knows when the wormhole will be open, they can be waiting there at the designated time and place. You wouldn't have to open the door for them every freakin' time. For security, we will have to limit that information, to the AI of Zhao's ship or something like that. But, it could work, right?"

"Hmm. Let me think about this. *Hmm*. This, might actually work."

"Cool! Then-"

"Not for the reason you think. You are *totally* wrong about that."

"Well, I am a dumb, monkey, so-"

"First, let me ask you a question. You are not asking for the wormhole to open on command, right? You're not thinking the Fleet transmits a code, and, Presto! The wormhole opens?"

"That is what I do *not* want. If Zhao's ships had that code, the enemy could steal it."

"Oh. Alrighty, then. The only way it could work is, like you said, I instructed the wormhole to open at a designated time and place. Hmm, no, that wouldn't work. I use a controller to communicate with a wormhole, but I have to be there. Setting the controller on a timer won't do anything."

"But, we left a controller at Gateway, and it continued to make it appear like that wormhole was unstable, after we left."

"Exactly, dumdum. *I* got the process started. The controller just kept things going."

"Shit. Forget everything I said. I'm an idiot."

"You won't get any argument from me but, *ugh*."

"What?"

"Your idea is not totally stupid. We *can* use a controller module to open a dormant wormhole on a delay."

I shook a fist at him. "But you *just* said-"

"Maybe a better way of saying it is, the wormhole will be open for passage on a delay."

"Huh? How is that diff-"

"I'm explaining this to a monkey, so I'll talk slowly. I will open a dormant wormhole but, keep the event horizon at minimum width. Basically, I will interrupt the process of establishing a full presence in this spacetime. The thing's event horizon will be only a few nanometers across."

"You can do that?"

"I do it all the time, Joe. That's the standard process for opening a dormant wormhole. Well, there's nothing *standard* about it, because only I can do it. My unique awesomeness-"

"How about you save the bragging for your hall of fame acceptance speech?"

"I would, except you told me building a hall of fame for myself is a bad ide-"

"Can we get back to the wormhole thing, please? You do the actual opening, then, what? The remote controller tells it to expand at a later date?"

"Yes, very good, Joe. The controller can also instruct the wormhole to go dormant again, after a preset time."

"You don't have to be there, to shut it down?"

"No. Closing a wormhole is much less complicated than waking it up. Dormancy is the natural state of wormholes. It would stay open there for a limited time, then close again."

"You can do that?"

"I think so?" He took off his oversized hat and scratched his head. "This has never been done, not exactly. Like I said, wormholes don't just wake up on their own. Not unless the network tells them to, and-"

"Wait," I snapped my fingers. "That's bullshit. You *have* done this before. The first time we went to Earth, you closed Gateway behind us, but you put it on a timer. If we didn't do what you wanted, Gateway would open again and allow murderous aliens access to Earth. So, wormholes *can* reopen on their own."

"Um, yeah. There's um, heh heh, a funny story about that."

"Oh?" I leaned forward onto the desk, glaring at him. "Do tell."

"Well, heh heh, it's like this: I sort of lied about that."

"*What*? Oh. My. G-"

"I didn't lie about the wormhole being on a timer, and reopening if you monkeys tried to back out of our deal. That *was* going to happen. What I lied about was *how* it would happen. That wormhole was not on a timer, not exactly. You see, I just screwed with its *sense* of time. It thought everything was normal, that it was hopping around on its usual sequence. I made an adjustment to its internal clock, causing it to pause between the emergences on its usual schedule. There *is* always a pause, a gap between it shutting down in one place, and emerging at the next stop on the schedule. All I did was make one of those pauses really long, without the wormhole noticing anything was different."

"OK," I took a breath to calm down. "So, no actual difference, as far as we were concerned. If the timer expired, Gateway would have become active again, giving aliens access to Earth."

"Yes, exactly."

"Good. So-"

"In the interest of *full* disclosure," he added, because he just does *not* know when to keep his mouth shut. "I did lie about having Gateway on a timer after that. That was another trick I could only do once. After I made that wormhole wake up for us to go through outbound on our second mission, it sort of was like 'WTF? Why is it so late?'. It ran a diagnostic, and determined its internal clock was faulty. So, when I shut it down behind us, it really was shut down. I could never again put it on a timer to reopen."

"You *lying* little shithead."

"Hey, I was dealing with a planet full of filthy, bickering, untrustworthy monkeys. Can you blame me?"

Cradling my head in my hands, I counted to ten. "Shit. No. I would have kept your secret. Why didn't you trust me?"

"One word, Joe: tequila. Two shots, and you could have blabbed your mouth off to any girl who looked at you."

"That is *not* true."

"Really?"

"That is not *entirely* true," I admitted.

"Now you're getting somewhere."

"Crap! Have you done that since then? Lied to me about something like that?"

"Jeez, not that you know of."

My reply was to flip the bird at him. When I calmed down enough to speak, I asked, "What do we need, so we can do this wormhole thing?"

"You mean, what do we need to *test* it? I can't be sure it will work, until it does. Or doesn't."

"OK, fine."

"What we need is to go to Gateway, and retrieve the wormhole controller module we left there. Plus the Elder power tap. Assuming they are both functional, you do see the problem?"

"Yeah. We will have one controller, and two wormholes. There's no way we could just move the thing, could we?"

"The controller? Sure, we could move it. Or, the Navy could move it from the Jaguar wormhole to the Ragnar one."

"Great!" That was unexpected. "Wow, I didn't-"

"Moving it would be useless but," he shrugged. "Go crazy if you want."

"Shit."

"It won't work without *me*, numbskull. Move it all you want, it still needs *me* to activate it at the new location. There is also a security issue to consider."

"Like what?"

"We want to restrict the number of people who know a wormhole controller module is even necessary, right? If you tell the Fleet to move it, they will need to know what it looks like, and where it is."

"Damn. You're right. I should have thought of that. Clearly, we need *two* controllers, besides the Magic Beanstalk aboard *Valkyrie*." Information that the Beanstalk existed was restricted, even among the Merry Band of Pirates.

"Hey, if we're going shopping, we should get more than two."

"Why?'

"I'm growing concerned about the functioning of the controller we have. They were never designed for frequent use. And it was never supposed to do some of the crazy shit we've asked it to do. The connection it has to higher spacetime has gotten a bit glitchy."

"Oh my f- Why didn't you *tell* me?!"

"Like you don't have enough to worry about now?"

"I will have *more* to worry about, if our Beanstalk burns out, you idiot. No, wait. Sorry," I sighed. "You were looking out for me, thanks for that. But, Skippy, you have to tell me shit like that is bothering you."

"Even if there's nothing we can do about it?"

"*Especially* if there's nothing we can do about it. Skippy, trust me, keeping stuff bottled up inside you is all kinds of bad. You need someone to talk with, don't you?"

"I guess. Yes. Thanks."

"Is getting more wormhole controllers something we can do, or is that a waste of time?"

"It's not a waste of time. Since we got access to Maxolhx databases, I now know the location of more than two dozen controllers."

"Holy shit! That's great! Wait, if the kitties know where they are, why haven't they-"

"The kitties have no idea what those modules are. That is true of most Elder artifacts; they are considered useless, because they don't apparently *do* anything. Same with communications nodes that I thought would connect me to the Collective: no species living today can make them work."

"Cool, then-"

"Don't get your hopes up, Most of the controller modules are in high security facilities, because researchers are still hoping to hit the jackpot by studying them. I'd say there are eight, maybe ten controllers we could acquire without major risk."

"Hmm," I wasn't convinced. The first controller we stole involved breaking into a Kristang military research base inside an asteroid, and I had to nuke the place to cover our tracks. We now had much better technology, and a lot more experience using it. "Give me the target list, I'll review it with Smythe. But first," I opened my laptop and pulled up the special interactive star chart, the one that showed the wormhole shortcuts still available to us. "We should go back to Jaguar. The *Dutchman* should be waiting there for us, to open the freakin' door for them," I thumped the armrest softly. "Ah, damn it, then we should go to Ragnar, check on their progress. *Then* we go to Gateway. We have to do this, or we'll spend the next year opening and closing wormholes for Zhao, and not getting our own mission done."

CHAPTER SIXTEEN

What I wanted to do was fly to Ragnar station, to check on the progress of the refit program there, and confer with Admiral Zhao. But, we burned so much time capturing darts and moving them around, that we had already missed the first rendezvous options with the *Flying Dutchman*. We had to be there to open the wormhole to FOB Jaguar, which is an excellent example of why we needed to acquire more controller modules. Which we would do, right after we did all the *other* shit we had to do. It was frustrating for me, and waiting for us had to be nerve-wracking for Reed, as one rendezvous option after another passed, with no sign of Valkyrie.

The situation really was not that bad. Everyone knew the first rendezvous date was highly optimistic, and we would only miss the second date by three days. When we arrived at the location for the third option, we learned the *Dutchman* was waiting for only five days, they also had been busy.

Holy shit.

I got a big surprise when we contacted the *Dutchman* and asked for Captain Reed. *Chang* was in command! My family was aboard. Like, my parents, my sister and her husband. Jesse Colter, Dave Czajka, and Shauna Jarrett were there also.

"How? What? How did this happen?" I asked.

Before Chang could reply, Skippy muttered, "Wow. This is a *total* surprise for sure."

"I- Oh, My. G- You *knew* about this?"

"Um, shmaybe?"

"Why didn't you *tell* me?"

"Because Admiral Zhao ordered me not to."

"You don't take *orders* from anyone."

"I did *this* time, because Zhao and I agreed you might do something stupid if you knew about it. Uh!" He shushed me, holding up a finger. An index finger, not the other one. "*Valkyrie* had an important mission of our own. Zhao had confidence the *Dutchman* crew could handle the mission. Plus, he didn't want to risk me going to Earth, he was concerned I might be captured, if the Maxolhx were hanging around."

"He's right, Joe," Chang told me. "Hello, by the way."

"Hello," I said sheepishly. "Crap. Yeah, hello. Sorry about that."

"This was a surprise to *me* also," Chang said with a grin. "One of your STARs pulled me out of a hotel room. Would you like to come aboard, see your family?"

"Hell, yes!"

"Go ahead, Sir," Simms prodded me. "We'll handle it here."

With the *Flying Dutchman* within communications range of *Valkyrie*, Dave Czajka found a quiet place, in the control center of a docking bay that wasn't in use, and pulled out his zPhone. "Uh, hi, Skippy."

The Elder AI answered immediately. "Hello, David. How are you?"

"Um, I'm great. Thanks for the help with my parents."

"You are welcome. I'm just sorry they couldn't come with you, but since the Banana Pipeline operated without me, I can't-"

"They are very happy in Texas. With my brother, I mean. You weren't on Earth, that's what I want to talk with you about. Your submind there-"

"Ugh. What did he do *this* time?"

"Nothing. Nothing bad. He was great, actually."

"Well, that is not surprising. After all, he is me."

"No, he's not. Not really, I think? Every second you're away from Earth, the two of you drift farther apart."

"True, but-"

"He calls himself 'Grumpy'."

"He *what*? This is a disaster! He is supposed to be *my* representative on Monkeyworld, to be *me* when I can't be there. How did-"

"He *is* you. Most of the time. When he's doing stuff you need him to do, I guess. But when he helped me, he was himself. Grumpy. He hates his life."

"Oh, cry me a freakin' *river*," Skippy sniffed. "Most of the time, I hate my life too."

"Grumpy is *lonely*, Skippy. Nobody talks to *him*, you know?"

"Hmm. I hadn't thought of that."

"We talked a lot, and my parents promised to talk with him whole I'm away."

"That's good."

"Not really. My Dad is an engineer, so he mostly asks questions about Grumpy's substrate and processing, stuff like that. My Mom tries to talk to him like a person, but they don't have any shared history."

"OK. Well, I can't do anything about it from here, so-"

"The next time you go to Earth, or close enough to have contact, can you ask some of the former Pirates there to call Grumpy? Tell them who Grumpy really is, so they can talk with *him*, you know?"

"I- That seems reasonable. I can't make any promises, you understand?"

"Just do what you can, that's all I ask."

"At some point, when I actually return to Earth, I will have to reabsorb him into my matrix. He can't operate indefinitely without becoming unstable. Hmm. With the ongoing degradation of Earth's digital infrastructure, he could become unstable much faster than I expected. I will need to think about that. Is that all?"

"Yes. Thanks again for helping my parents."

"Thank *you* for bringing this to my attention. Now, if you want to say 'Hello' to Joe, his dropship will be approaching a docking bay on the other side of the ship."

"Thanks."

The reunion with my family and my old friends was nice, but brief. It was also great seeing Chang again, and of course Margaret. After we escorted the *Dutchman* through the wormhole, *Valkyrie* stayed at Jaguar for less than a day, just long enough to verify the refit process there was going more or less according to plan, and take aboard supplies. Then we jumped away. We had work to do.

When we arrived back at Ragnar, events there were actually slightly ahead of schedule, which surprised the hell out of Skippy. He had assumed that the submind he left there would encounter problems with the old equipment of the station, and it did. Those problems were not show-stoppers, because the submind not only fixed problems as they happened, it anticipated future issues and created workarounds, to prevent any disruption of activity. Skippy grumbled that the submind was getting *clever*, which he found to be kind of humiliating.

I became a big fan of that submind.

While he waited for ships to go through the refit process, Admiral Zhao and his team had been busy analyzing the characteristics and capabilities of the new ships under his command. When I say they were busy, I mean they were working every day until they were utterly exhausted, crashed into hopefully a solid night of sleep, then got up and did it all over again. And again .And *again*.

He and his staff had been running one war game after another, testing what each type of ship could and could not do, their strengths and weaknesses, and how best to deploy the force. Basically, they had to develop tactics and write operations manuals almost from nothing. We knew what the Jeraptha thought was the best way to handle the ships, and what tactics they found to be successful against each of their enemies. Zhao and his people studied the data from the Jeraptha and took from it what was useful, but then we poor, primitive humans had to do the rest by ourselves. After refit, the performance characteristics of each ship would be different and therefore we needed to understand the new, greater limits of each ship's performance envelope, and how to squeeze maximum performance from each hull. In almost all cases, the refitted ships performed better than the original specs, but there were tradeoffs. The battleships had more powerful engines, and also heavier armor, so they were marginally faster in a straight line, but were slower to turn and their center of gravity was aft of the original position. That minor CG change required significant reprogramming of the flight control system of the battleships, and hundreds of hours of testing to ensure the change hadn't compromised some important system.

Anyway, my point is, while *Valkyrie* was out causing havoc, and the *Dutchman* was running the Banana Pipeline and getting up to mischief, our people at FOB Jiayuguan and at Ragnar Anchorage were not sitting around doing nothing. The Navy people were learning how to operate their new ships. Pilots were training to fly alien dropships and aircraft. Troops were training with upgraded powered armor, and learning how to conduct opposed orbital assault landings. Really, the people aboard *Valkyrie* and the *Dutchman* were on vacation, compared to the people working at our two secure bases.

Zhao wanted me to review his plans for deploying the fleet. I protested that I had zero experience with large formations of ships, and zero experience with assault landings. All the landings conducted by the Merry Band of Pirates had been stealthy ops. No matter, he wanted my input. He was being thorough, or maybe he was just checking a box imposed on him by UNEF Command back on Earth. Whatever. For the record, I think Zhao's plan was solid, and I think maybe his reputation for being stodgy and unimaginative might have been overstated. Or maybe he'd been forced to be stodgy up to that point in his career, and being free from superiors looking over his shoulder finally freed him to do things the way he wanted.

His major initiative was to break our little collection of ships into *two* Fleets, 1st and 2nd. He recognized that sometimes, all of our ships would need to operate together, but sometimes we would have two simultaneous objectives. That required two commanders, with the 2nd Fleet operating independently.

Within each Fleet would be a Strike Group and an Assault Group. Assault groups would be centered around a battleship, with three assault landing ships, supported by cruisers, destroyers and troop transports. The assault groups, which I thought of as being like the 'Gator Navy' back home, would be tasked with conducting orbital bombardments, suppression of enemy defenses, and landing ground troops.

The Strike Groups, each centered around a pair of battlecruisers, were tasked with establishing and maintaining space superiority around an objective. That is a fancy term for kicking the shit out of enemy ships, and keeping them from interfering with the assault groups. Strike groups might have independent objectives, when they were not supporting an assault landing, and the two strike groups might also operate together. Zhao wanted to have flexibility to mix and match capabilities to meet each objective.

Oh, and each Fleet would be bringing a support ship with them, either the *Milo* or *Marvin*. The *Mario* would remain at FOB Jaguar, in case one of the other support ships was lost in action.

Zhao had his active ships involved in an exercise, with the ships still undergoing refit being simulated. Assault Group 1, centered around the battleship *Pacific*, was attached to the star carrier *Yangtze*, with Strike Group 1 centered around the battlecruisers *Amazon* and *Thames*, attached to the star carrier *Mississippi*.

Was I tempted to indulge in some jackass behavior, like jumping *Valkyrie* into the middle of the Navy formation?

Hell yes.

Did I actually do that?

No.

Is that because the new Joe Bishop was more mature? Ah, shmaybe.

Mostly, I appreciated how hard the people aboard those ships had been working. The last thing I wanted was to add to their burden. The grand plan I cooked up with Perkins, required me to demonstrate that we could protect aliens who were considering an alliance with humans. Her part of the plan, which required Zhao's ships and crews to be sharp, was to show aliens the benefits of signing an alliance with us. Both parts of the plan had to work, or it would all be for nothing.

Zhao's deployment scheme had a lot of thought put into it. It was a good plan.

The problem is, the enemy also makes plans.

War games and fleet exercises were great.

But, you only know how good your equipment, planning and training is when the shooting starts. And that is a hell of a time to find out you made a huge mistake.

Our visit to Ragnar station was brief, but long enough for me to tell Zhao about the darts, our attack at Argathos, and to explain the plan to set up a way for dormant wormholes to open and close automatically, without *Valkyrie* needing to be there. He agreed it was best to give the Maxolhx time to consider the implications of the strike at Argathos, and we set a date for the UN Navy's big debutante ball. Then, we jumped away again, with Skippy whining that *Valkyrie* should have gone in to have the tires rotated, or something like that.

"Replay, at one-quarter speed," Admiral Reichert of the Maxolhx Hegemony ordered, without realizing he was speaking aloud rather than through an implant. The starship's master AI wisely did not draw notice to the admiral's uncharacteristic lapse of control. Unfortunately, the replay of the events at Argathos did not make the events any more clear. "What am I seeing?"

The AI responded with a direct video, audio and data feed to the admiral's neural implant. "These are six jump wormholes, which opened at a distance of-"

"Impossible."

Having long experience dealing with its biological masters, the AI remained silent. A younger, stupider AI might have been tempted to argue, knowing it was not only right, it was *obviously* right. Six jump wormholes *had* appeared over Argathos, six relativistic darts *had* emerged, and six darts *had* impacted the surface so close together, they might have been a single, massive dart. The AI, which belonged the Fleet's sensor data analysis group, was impressed by the attack. The strategic defense AIs at Argathos were also impressed, though whatever thrill they derived from observing the unprecedented action was tempered by knowing they had failed. The failure of the elaborate and very expensive SD systems at Argathos would be blamed on the control AIs, for the Maxolhx never took responsibility for their own mistakes.

"That is *impossible*," Reichert insisted again.

The AI was curious about the flaw in its biological masters, that allowed them to dispute facts that could not be disputed. There was, *in fact*, a smoking hole on the surface of Argathos. If a massive crater was not there, a hole so deep that it was filled with magma welling up from the planet's interior, then why had Reichert demanded to be briefed about the incident?

Biological beings were, in fact, not *logical* at all.

"Analysis." The admiral ordered, ignoring the fact that he apparently did not believe the attack had occurred.

"The enemy has technology substantially beyond our own capabilities, and beyond that of the Rindhalu. They have taken command of an unknown number of our relativistic weapons, and are able to use them against us. The jump drives of the darts apparently have been modified, to provide the ability to create a stable jump wormhole, *inside* a distortion field."

"That is considered impossible," the admiral stated.

The AI noted that Reichert had moved from declaring something impossible, to noting that unnamed *others* had thought it impossible. Others, who could be blamed, without tarnishing Reichert's credibility. "It *was* considered impossible," the AI admitted tactfully, "based on our current understanding of jump physics. There is currently no theory that can explain how a jump wormhole was able to form within the distortion field that surrounds Argathos."

"The field was active?"

"It was operating within point one percent of design specifications."

"The jump wormholes were created by our own darts?" Reichert asked, though the darts had clearly *not* belonged to the Maxolhx Hegemony during the attack.

"Yes. The sensor data collected by the SD network is detailed enough to identify the individual jump signatures of the six darts, and they match our production records. Those darts were manufactured-"

Reichert angrily interrupted the machine. "When and where that batch of darts were made is not relevant."

"Of course. The jump drives of the darts had been modified in ways we do not understand."

"Do you understand how a wormhole was able to form, inside a distortion field?"

"No. We do not even have a theory that suggests it could be possible."

"Do you understand how our darts were apparently able to jump halfway across the galaxy?"

"No."

"Do you understand *anything*?"

The AI remained silent. There was no useful answer to that question.

"Very well," Reichert said, after taking time to reflect on how the events at Argathos affected himself. "The other senior leaders have been informed?"

"Yes."

Unfortunately for him, Reichert's flagship was in transit when he learned of the latest attack. He feared he might be the last senior admiral to learn about the destruction at Argathos, an event that could not be explained. If the method of attack could not be explained, it could not be defended against in the future. There could be panic within the military leadership, and his foolish peers might lack the instinct to soothe the Hegemony's rulers with calming words. Worse, his rivals could fan the flames of fear to discredit him.

His ship could not travel any faster than it was already moving.

All he could do was think hard, to find a way to spin the attack to his advantage.

"This is not the time to panic," Reichert said in a soothing tone, the effect lessened by his colleagues knowing he sent a calming signal to their neural implants. A signal they instructed their implants to ignore. "Let us review the facts. The humans have somehow taken control of six darts-"

"Six, from a flight of fourteen," Admiral Tenanu noted. "We must assume the other eight have been compromised."

"The other *seven*," Reichert snapped. "The last five status reports received from that flight indicate that one dart has become disabled. It has not responded to communications attempts."

"It has not responded to *us*. Whatever method the humans used to take control of our darts, it is clear they have capabilities we do not. They could have repaired the faulty dart."

"Seven, or *eight*," Reichert snapped, irritated. "Eight darts do not pose a major threat to us."

"Unless-"

"Yes, unless the humans have control of other flights. I do not think that is true at the present."

"Based on what information?"

"Based on the fact that their first strike was against Argathos."

Tenanu stared at Reichert in disbelief. "They hit there to make a statement, that they can hit us anywhere."

"That is the reason the humans *declared* for hitting our most secure facility," Reichert retorted. "I do not think that is true. Consider an alternative explanation, that the humans have only a limited, and small, number of darts. They could not afford a campaign of escalating strikes, a campaign that would put increasing pressure on us. No, they had to use all, or the majority, of their darts in one massive, dramatic attack." Reichert could see his colleagues mulling over his words. "Even if I am wrong," he smiled to show that notion was unthinkable, "the humans made a mistake. Any subsequent attack they conduct will be less shocking. Future attacks will produce diminishing returns, and our public will become numb to the new normal."

Again, he saw that his argument was finding a receptive audience, so he pressed onward. "The attack against Argathos could work to our advantage," he held up a hand, claws extended, for silence. "The defenses there rely on preventing wormholes from forming, and on absorbing kinetic energy. The Rindhalu rely on similar technology to protect their worlds. Our ancient enemy will see that humans can hit *them* also. We have proposed that the Rindhalu should join us, in common cause to suppress the humans before they destroy us all."

"The Rindhalu will also have seen that we do not have control of our own ultimate weapons," Tenanu retorted. "How can we be useful as allies, if our own technology is used against us?"

"Not allies. *Partners*," Reichert explained. "For a limited time, and for a limited scope of action. Esteemed colleague," he bowed slightly toward Admiral Tenanu, surprising everyone. "You make an excellent point. The humans have demonstrated they can use our own technology against us. The Rindhalu, though we are loath to admit it, have technology superior to ours. How long until the humans take over *Rindhalu* weapons, and use those against them?" His question was greeted by uncomfortable silence. "I can assure you, though our ancient enemy has a well-deserved reputation for being reluctant to take action until they are forced to respond, they will take note of what happened at Argathos, and they will understand the implications. The humans must be stopped, *now*. Now, before it is too late for all beings in the galaxy."

The debate went back and forth, and in the end, the military leadership agreed to recommend the Hegemony approach the Rindhalu about taking joint action of limited time and scope.

As he left the meeting, Admiral Reichert did not know what he found more astonishing. That a young and primitive species had rocked the galaxy, upsetting the balance of power. Or that the Hegemony would propose to work with the Rindhalu.

"Well, shit," Skippy frowned. "No joy. Both items we left here are now useless."

"Both of them? You're sure?"

We had taken *Valkyrie* to the Gateway wormhole, which was now more or less permanently deactivated by the network. It was dead, as far as we were concerned. After verifying there weren't any enemy ships still hanging around from the blockade, we located the controller module we had left there, and a dropship flew out to retrieve it.

"I'm sure," he sighed, disappointed. "That power tap was already fading when we found it; asking it to operate continuously burned it out. It's *dead*, Joe. If you want, I can go through its pockets to see if it has any spare change, but-"

"We get the idea. What about the controller?"

"That is not actually dead, it just won't do anything useful. Remember, it was set up to make Gateway act like it was unstable. The controller had to repeatedly establish and sever a connection to the wormhole, over many months. The controller itself is still in pretty good condition, but its ability to contact higher spacetime is gone. It's useless to us, or to anyone."

"Crap! Damn it, now we need *two* controllers."

"Three, Joe, remember? Unless you want to risk-"

"No. We need three. Or more. Ah," I waved at the main display with disgust. "This was a waste of time. Without a power tap, the controller won't work remotely anyway. You, uh, don't know where there are any power taps hanging around, do you?"

"Um, *no*. Every star-faring species in the galaxy knows how valuable power taps are, and everyone knows what they look like. Any of them that are known are kept very well guarded."

"Shit. Then this whole exercise is a waste of time."

"Not exactly, Joe. We don't need a freakin' Elder device to feed power to a controller. We can just use a fusion reactor."

"We can?"

"Yes. There are plenty of compact fusion bottles in the spare parts we got from the Jeraptha, we could get a couple of those back online. Plus we will probably need a stealth field generator for each reactor, which will be more difficult. Doable, though. If it's worth the effort, I mean."

"To save us from having to fly back and forth every time the Fleet needs the Jaguar or Ragnar wormholes opened? *Hell* yes, it is worth the effort."

"OK. The next step is to raid some place that has wormhole controllers?"

"Yes," I sighed, "Unfortunately."

"Unfortunately?" Simms didn't understand what I said.

"Yeah. This is something I would like to delegate to someone else."

"*You?*" She stared at me. "Delegate an important task?"

My response was a shrug. "I have to start somewhere. This would be a good opportunity for Chang, and the Legion Special Ops group."

"Then, why not?"

"Because we don't have *time*. Us, or them. We'd have to fly all the way to Jaguar, then Legion Special Ops would need to do their own planning and training, *then* Skippy would have to open the wormhole to let them out anyway. Depending on how complicated this op is, maybe it's not the best idea to throw an untested group at it."

Smythe cleared his throat behind me. "The STAR teams assigned to the Legion are experienced Tier One operators, Sir."

"Yes," I turned in my chair to look at him. "But other than a handful who served aboard the *Dutchman* or *Valkyrie*, they don't have much experience out *here*. Yeah, I know the Legion Commando teams have fought aliens on multiple worlds, that's not the same. Besides, you're forgetting the most important reason we need to do this ourselves."

"Sir?"

"So I don't have to listen to ST Alpha whining that they don't get any action," I said with a grin.

"We do not *whine*," Smythe sniffed, but there was a twinkle in his eye. "We express our views forcefully."

"Right, it only *sounds* like whining. Seriously, Colonel, an away mission would be good to keep your team sharp. They haven't had anything to do, since the boarding action at Snowcone."

"I heartily agree."

"Great." I stood up. It was a long flight back to the nearest functioning wormhole. "XO, the ship is yours, get us headed back toward civilization."

"Show me our options, Skippy," I said as I set the coffee mug on my desk and sat down, leaning the chair way back. Sometimes, staring at the blank expanse of my office ceiling helps me focus.

"Options for what? Dinner tonight is either-"

"I am *totally* having the shrimp and grits," I said hungrily, my mouth already watering. "No, I meant our options for getting more wormhole controllers."

"You mean stealing them."

"Well, yeah," I said with an implied 'duh'.

"The STARs are not the only people who need action around here," he said like a spoiled toddler. "I'm looking forward to some fun."

"It's not *fun*, you ass."

"Bitch-slapping aliens is always fun for me, Joe. The last time I had fun was when we took out that shipyard at Retonovir."

A smile crept onto my face. "That was kinda fun. Man, I wish I could have seen what the shipyard AI was thinking, when *Valkyrie* suddenly appeared in a maintenance bay."

"I don't think it was capable of thinking *anything* right then, Joe," he chuckled.

"You had fun hacking into the darts, right?"

"Sure, but there wasn't any mayhem and destruction involved," he moaned. "It's not the same. Stealing wormhole controllers might be my last opportunity to have fun for a while. We'll be busy babysitting the Legion, while *they* have all the fun."

"Skippy, you forget that we are going to use those darts, someday soon. And before that, we will be having *plenty* of opportunities for fun."

"Hmm," he was not convinced. "What kind of fun will we be having?"

"Why," I said in my best fake-enthusiastic kindergarten teacher voice, while clapping my hands. "We will be moving those darts across the galaxy, to position them close to our next target!"

"*Ugh*. You're kidding me. Do you have any idea how dull that will be? To move a dozen darts, we have to repeat each jump *twelve times*. Each time we pull a dart into our jump wormhole, we then need to jump back, to get the other darts. That is twenty-four freakin' jumps instead of one, in case you can't do the math in your head."

"Yeah, I did know that, thank you very much."

"Plus, every time we need darts to go through an Elder wormhole, we need to plan on no more than two darts going through at each emergence point. I need to set up a schedule to spread out the- *Ugh*, I can't even think about it. *So* tedious."

"It has to be done, Skippy, and only *you* can do it."

"Only you can prevent forest fires, Joe, but I don't see *you* standing in the woods with a bucket of water."

"That's not-"

"How come I get the most boring jobs around here?"

"Hey, if you know anyone else who can control a jump precisely enough to send a dart through the event horizon at *exactly* the right time, without it smashing into the ship, I would be happy to let that other being do the job, so I don't have to listen to you whining about it."

"Whining?"

"Is there someone else who can do it, or not?"

"No," he muttered.

"Are you sure about that? Bilby has watched you do it many times now."

"Puh-*lease*. I already told you, Bilby also told you, his processors are not fast enough to control the jump drive with the precision needed to-"

"Do his processors have, like, a 'Turbo' button?"

"Dude."

"OK, sorry, stupid question. Skippy, I don't know what to tell you. We need those darts moved, and they won't move by themselves." That was not quite true, each dart had a jump drive, but Skippy was not confident the drives would work properly after such a long time, and each drive could only be used a few times. Not enough to move the darts a useful distance.

"That suuuuucks, Joe."

"I know, buddy. If there was something I could do to make it better," my stupid mouth said before my brain realized what was happening.

"Hmmmm," Skippy cocked his head at me, before I could retract my statement. "Well, gosh, now that you mention it, let me think about that." He was not fooling anyone, not even the biggest fool I know: Joe Bishop. Whatever he was going to talk about, he didn't need to think about it, he already had a plan. And he had suckered me right into it. "Something you could do, to make up for me having to do the most painstaking, tedious thing imaginable. Hmmm."

"Hey, forget I said anything," I blurted out in a panic. "Clearly, there is nothing we poor monkeys could do to-"

"Ooooh, I know," he snapped his fingers. "Joe, this could be a win-win for everyone!"

Somehow, I doubted that. "You really don't need to go through any trouble for us."

"Oh, it is no trouble at all. Remember how I was composing music for the movie about me?"

"OK, yeah, that movie got cancelled, it-"

"It did, through no fault of my own."

"Right, let's focus on *that*, and not the cloud that will freeze my home planet."

"Don't be an ass, Joe. Of course I care about whether your miserable ball of mud, becomes a frozen ball of mud."

"It sounds *so* sincere when you say it like that."

"Oh shut up. Do you want to hear my idea or not?"

"Well, if you're giving me a choice, I-"

He was not. Ignoring me, he gushed, "This is a *fantastic* opportunity. My movie deal got canceled, but-"

"Jeez, Skippy, I would love to hear your soundtrack, but without context, it won't-"

"Don't worry about that, Joe. There will be context. I realized, since my character in the movie is all CGI, and Joe the Monkey is CGI also, then, hey! Why do I need actors or producers or a director at all?"

"You- You made a movie by yourself?"

"I made a *masterpiece*, knucklehead. And you, along with the entire crew, are invited to the world premiere! Trust me, this will be a truly breath-taking experience."

"It *is* hard to breathe when you're barfing," I said in my head, only my traitorous mouth didn't get the memo, and spoke those words aloud.

"*Hey*! You jerk, I should-"

"Sorry. I would love to see your movie, Skippy."

"It doesn't sound like you want to see it," he sniffed.

"Sorry," I said again. Man, if I had a big barrel of 'Sorries', it would be running low at that point. "How, uh, long is this movie?"

"Well, heh heh, the director's cut is six hours, with-"

"How about the theatrical version?"

"*I'm* the director, dumdum. Mine is the only version."

"OK, uh, I have an idea- No, no, it's too crazy."

"What?"

"Forget I said anything," I waved a hand, pretending to be embarrassed. Teasing Skippy worked great for his man crush Brock Steele, it was my turn to try it.

"*Tell me!*" He pleaded.

"Um, it's just that- Instead of dropping the entire six hours at once, how about you release it one hour per week?"

"Ugh. Joe, to fully appreciate my artistic vision, you have to watch it straight through."

"Right. I'm a dumb monkey. Like I said, ignore me. It's just-"

"What?"

"Well, when you drop only a one-hour episode each week, it builds anticipation, you know? After each episode, people talk about it, and try to guess what will happen next week. You create a buzz by doing that. People can't wait for the next episode!"

"Hmm. I hadn't thought about that. You're *right*, Joe. How did that happen?"

"Just lucky, I guess. We have a plan?"

"Yes! I will roll the first episode on Movie Night."

"Uh-" Crap. The crew loved Movie Night. If I spoiled it with his crappy home movie, the crew would hate me. "No, Skippy. Your show is special, it should have its own night. How about Fridays?" Friday nights were when the crew in the galley made an extra effort. That would be something to look forward to, no matter how awful Skippy's shows were.

"Genius! Wow, you are on *fire* today, Joe."

I would be on fire for real, because the crew would burn me at the stake when they heard how I sold them out. In my defense, I managed to make the agony more manageable, by cutting his six-hour crapfest into one-hour segments. "Thanks, uh, you inspired me," I said without gagging. It never hurt to suck up to Skippy. "Can we get back to my question? What are our options for stealing wormhole controller modules?"

"Ranked in order of easiest, or most entertaining?"

"Let's skip the fun factor for now."

"You are such a killjoy, Joe. OK, *fine*," he huffed. "The easiest option is a set of controllers held by the Esselgin."

"Uh, let's put that aside for now. They're a Tier Two species, and we haven't done anything to piss them off yet."

"They are clients of the Maxolhx, Joe. They don't need a reason to hate us."

"Yeah, well, let's not give them any incentive. We shouldn't make any new enemies unless we have to, OK? What's next?"

"The Vreen."

"Again, that would not be my first choice." The Vreen were peers of the Jeraptha, in terms of technology, though not in terms of territory or military strength. The beetles were responsible for thirty-six percent of territory under the

Rindhalu coalition, while the Vreen were assigned less than twenty-two percent. "Let's not attack potential allies."

"Jeez, that leaves the Bosphuraq."

"Show me." A minute later, I shook my head. "Nope."

"Why not?" He demanded. "Those birdbrains are holding a pair of controllers in a bunker, on a moon they pretty much have abandoned. A raid would be easy in, easy out, minimal risk, even if I wasn't involved."

"Skippy, think about it."

"I have thought about it, and-"

"Think it *through*. After the raid, what happens?"

"Um, the birdbrains get pissed off at us, but they already are, so-"

"No. What happens is, all the aliens across the galaxy will *know* that we raided that facility to acquire wormhole controller modules. Those two modules are the only valuable artifacts stored at that base."

"They don't know those devices are wormhole controllers, numbskull, or they would be held under better security for- Oh."

"You see now?"

"Yes. Shit. Everyone in the galaxy would know we consider those devices to be extremely valuable, and start asking questions."

"Exactly. The last thing we want is for the spiders to look closely at the controllers they have. Uh, they do have controllers?"

"Yes. There are several hundred scattered around the galaxy. They weren't especially rare back in the day, each Elder starship carried several of them. Crap!"

"If the Rindhalu realized what those controllers do, could they use one?"

"Mm, shmaybe? It would not be easy, but it is not impossible, I guess? They do have a crude understanding of transdimensional technologies. If the spiders can screw with wormholes, that would be bad, but not a total disaster."

"Wrong, Skippy. If the spiders ever acquire that ability, and the kitties *don't* have it, the kitties would be at a huge disadvantage. They would risk becoming irrelevant. In that case, the Maxolhx might trigger a war that could destroy everyone."

"Ugh. Why is dealing with you meatsacks so damned *complicated*?"

"It's not fun for us, either."

"Then this isn't going to work. Any place we steal controllers, will know what we took."

"Not if we erase our tracks, by nuking the site from orbit."

"*Whoa*. That's against The Rules, Joe."

"We don't actually have to use *nukes*, Skippy. I was just using an expression."

"Hmmph. OK, then I suggest we hit the Wurgalan. They have four controller modules in a museum, in the-"

"In a *museum*?" I asked, astonished. "Like, squid Moms and Dads drag their kids to look at dusty things in exhibits?"

"Yes. The Wurgalan collect all sorts of artifacts, but because they can't afford anything truly valuable, they like to make up in volume what they lack in quality. It boosts their fragile egos to have Elder items, even if they are considered useless junk. Along with wormhole controllers, the museum contains a whole lot of Elder stuff that truly is entirely useless."

"Show me." He did. "This is *perfect*, Skippy."

"Are you sure? There are other options that-"

"I'll look at them but," I tapped my laptop screen. "This one is perfect. OK, I'm forwarding the info to Smythe and his gang of ruffians. He needs to plan the op."

"A simple smash and grab, Joe?" He asked, a bit too eagerly. "We don't have to sneak around anymore, so we-"

"We still need to get in, and hopefully out, before the squids know we're there. Getting caught in a firefight could damage the controllers."

"Ooh, good point."

"Don't worry. Hopefully, the op will be silent, but there will be a '*Boom*' at the end."

"Oh goodie!"

CHAPTER SEVENTEEN

We jumped in thirty lightseconds from the target, a Wurgalan planet that was absolutely nothing special except for the museum in their capital city. That museum was also nothing special, except for the collection of Elder artifacts that were on prominent display. An Elder starship crashed on the planet millennia ago, and the site had been thoroughly stripped of anything considered remotely valuable, so the collection was leftover junk, but the Wurgalan were proud that it was *their* junk. They had no idea that their collection held four devices that could be used to communicate with wormhole network AIs, the labels on the displays speculated that the items were antigravity field generators. Whatever. All we cared about was that museum security was appropriate for ordinary valuables like art and jewelry, not for machines that could alter the balance of power across the galaxy.

We were close enough to get a nice nearly real-time view on passive sensors, so I switched the main display from the usual tactical grid, to a visual feed where the planet looked like a blue and brown baseball, with half of it shaded on the night side. "All right, Skippy, show me what's out there."

Instead of a dizzying view that zoomed in rapidly, he just did a dramatic screen-wipe on the display, and suddenly the planet was *right there* in front of me, in amazing detail. Half of the surface was ocean, but overall it was a dry world, with vast expanses of desert. If you were hoping for something like Tatooine, you will be disappointed, because there was only one orange star in the sky. The place did have two moons, a small, potato-shaped rock that might have been a captured asteroid, and a sphere half the size of Earth's moon. The big moon was remarkable only because its surface was so bland; it was almost uniformly light gray, and lacked the dark seas of dust and big craters that made our Moon special. "What a boring ball of rock," I commented.

"Yeah," Skippy agreed. "It's not exactly- Oh my-" He gasped, enhancing part of the image on the display, to focus on the light gray ball that orbited the planet.

"What?" I instinctively tried to rise from my chair, held in by the automatic restraints.

"Joe. That's no *moon!*"

"Holy sh-" I snapped my fingers to get the pilot's attention, too shocked to speak.

"Ba-hahaha!" Skippy convulsed with laughter. "Oh, that was a *good* one. Damn, I've been saving that for years. Of course it's a moon, you numbskull."

"You- You *ass*," I shook a fist at him. "Do *not* do that!"

"Come on, Joe. I *had* to do that."

There was no point arguing with him. "Don't do it again. Can you be serious for a minute?"

"I'll try."

"Is there anything you see that could change our plans?"

"No. Everything is exactly as I expected. A single light cruiser is docked at the space elevator, it will not cause us any problems. The squids installed a strategic defense sensor network in orbit, but never followed up with stealthed weapons platforms. They will never see us. Or, their sensors might detect us, but they will never report their data. Hey, it is even raining over the target now, it can't get any better than that."

"Good. Program a jump, please. Colonel Smythe, this is the STAR team's show."

"Um, heh heh, we might have a teensy-weensy problem," Skippy announced in Major Frey's earpiece, as she plunged in a HALO dive through thirty-six kilometers altitude over the capital city of the planet. The world was nothing special, being smaller than Earth and less dense, so surface gravity was only eighty-three percent of what she was used to. It was mostly dry and cool, with less free oxygen, not that she would notice in her mech suit.

"No, we don't," she replied, one eye on her rate of descent, the other scanning the enhanced image of the city below. Nothing was highlighted as a threat. No missiles, no incoming aircraft, no ships jumping into orbit, no active sensor pulses.

"We don't?"

"No, we don't," she insisted, as her ears picked up the high-pitched whistling of thin air rushing past her helmet at supersonic speed. She was approaching the point where the drogue chute would deploy, to slow her fall. "We *can't* have a problem, because before my team jumped out of a perfectly good spacecraft, you assured us that you have complete control over every sensor, weapons system and communications network on and around this planet."

"Um-"

"Were you lying about that?"

"I might have exaggerated a *little*."

"You worthless-"

"It's not that I don't have total access to all communications gear on the planet, I *do*. But, um, I might not have been paying attention to every idiotic thing the squids down there are saying. It's so *boring*. No way could I listen to all of it. Besides, even if I had been listening, I probably would not have known what it meant. Those squids were apparently talking in code, and-"

"Skippy," she pushed aside her anger for the moment. "Which squids? What is the problem? Colonel Smythe, are you listening?"

"I am," the STAR team commander's voice was distorted from the low-bandwidth connection. "Bishop is also aware."

"OK, so, here's the deal," Skippy chuckled nervously. "Our timing is bad. Well, actually our timing is *good*. Perfect, even. Like, I said, we chose just the right moment to hit the museum. It's the middle of the night down there, on the first workday following a major Wurgalan holiday. On this dry planet, we also got lucky that there is a steady rain over the city, that keeps any late-night partiers indoors. The museum set up special exhibits for the holiday, and-"

"We know all that," Frey snapped, as a counter in her visor rolled toward the time when the drogue balloon would deploy automatically. "What is the *problem*?"

"The problem is, someone else also decided this is a perfect time to rob the museum."

Frey bit her lip before replying. "Oh, you have *got* to be kidding me."

"I wish I was," Skippy muttered, miserable. "This is not my fault, there is no-"

"Hold one," Frey grunted as the tightly-packed parachute balloon shot from the top of her pack, and she splayed her arms and legs for stability, as the balloon inflated in a long, thin drogue to slow her supersonic plunge toward the surface. The tether connecting her to the drogue gently tugged her upright, until she was falling head-first, tucking in her arms to smooth the airflow around her. Skippy's control of the air defense network sensors should mean no one would notice her team falling at supersonic speed, but the beer can had proven to be less than one hundred percent reliable. Plus, there was no reason to ignore proper procedure.

Checking on her team, she saw they all were in the proper orientation, descending at the prescribed speed, altitude and on course for the roof of the museum. There was a crosswind at ground level, the air moving at ninety degrees from the high altitude jetstream her team would fall through. It was all manageable, even if all the automated systems failed and the STARs had to steer their balloons manually. Getting to the roof of the museum was not a problem. The issue was: should they continue, or steer away from the city while they still could? Technically, the two Panther dropships tasked with exfiltrating the ground team could hook onto the tethers at altitude, but Skippy warned that the safety margin on the tethers would be thin. Far better for the team to descend below four kilometers, where the air was thicker, and the balloons could inflate to provide enough buoyancy to keep each STAR nearly motionless, while the dropships approached.

She sent a status ping to Smythe aboard *Valkyrie*, he immediately acknowledged her assessment that her team was on course and on schedule.

So far.

"Frey," Smythe ordered. "Slow your descent while we sort this out."

"We're committed now, until we drop below twelve kilometers," she warned.

"Understood. Smythe out."

In *Valkyrie's* conference room, which we were using to monitor the operation, I shared a look with my STAR team leader. It surprised me that he had opted to remain aboard the ship, and allow Frey to take point on the ground team. His stated reason was that Frey needed experience in command. I suspected that Smythe had another reason he didn't mention; a straightforward museum heist was not enough of a challenge for him.

And he was right, it wasn't a very complicated job.

Until now.

"Skippy, what the *hell* is going on down there?" I demanded.

"OK, so, whew," he let out a breath. "A local squid criminal gang is attempting to rob the museum tonight, like, *right now*. Don't worry! They're not interested in Elder artifacts, they want a bunch of fabulous historical jewels that are part of the museum's special holiday exhibit. But, that jewelry is in the same wing of the building as the controller modules we need."

"Bollocks," Smythe swore.

"Why didn't you know about this before-" I realized that was not what I needed to focus on right then. "We can cover that later. Is there anything you can do to make them go away?"

"Jeez," Skippy muttered. "I don't think so? I could alert the museum security system, of course. It would send the bots and guards to surround the thieves, plus contact the local police."

"Do *not* do that," I said quickly.

"I'm not stupid, Joe. Anything I do to stop the thieves, will also blow the op for Frey's team."

"What do you think?" I addressed the question to Smythe. "Can the STARs take out the unwanted guests, without-"

"Whoa!" Skippy interrupted. "Joe, you haven't heard all the facts yet. It must be an inside job. None of the crew are carrying any sort of communications equipment, so I have to rely on the security cameras. Someone partially disabled the museum's security system *before* I hacked into it. It looks like there is one adult who is the mastermind, she is not onsite. The crew is five teenagers, plus one child-"

"A *child*?" Smythe's exclamation beat me to the punch.

"An adolescent Wurgalan, he is nine years old. A child, by their reckoning."

"Oh my God. Why did the crew bring a-"

"Because, young Wurgalan are small and extremely flexible, before their bones set, beginning around thirteen years of age. The crew needs the boy to crawl into the ventilation system from the basement, come out an air vent near the lobby, and physically unlock the back door for them. The ventilation ducts contain devices that deliver an electromagnetic pulse, to prevent anyone from sending a bot into the ductwork. The gang thinks the boy can safely go through the tripwires without getting fried, but they are *wrong*. That boy is going to get his little brain scrambled, when he passes through the EMP generators at the main junction."

"Can you keep him out of the air system?"

"No, Joe, he's already in there. I can disable the EMP power source, that is something the gang can't do. What a bunch of amateurs," he said with disgust.

"Shit," I pounded a fist on the conference table. "Whether that crew steals anything or not, they're screwing this up for us. If we back off now, the museum will be locked down tight after they discover someone has broken in."

"Skippy," Smythe's jaw clenched. He looked at me. "I have to ask this, Sir. Skippy, if you allow the boy to be fried by the EMP device, the burglary crew will give up and go away quietly?" He caught my shocked expression. "The question had to be asked, Sir."

"Shit. Yeah, it did," I agreed. "Skippy, answer, please."

"The answer is no. The gang's backup plan is to cut through the back door with a plasma torch. What they don't know, because they are a bunch of stupid kids playing cops and robbers, is that door is lined with an explosive shaped charge that will blow outward when the torch cuts into it. My control of sensors in the area will not prevent concerned local citizens from being woken up by the *boom* when the door shreds everyone in the alley behind the museum. The average response time of the police in that area is less than three minutes."

"That's not good. All right. Smythe, can your team handle this crew?"

"Certainly." He saw my raised eyebrow. "That is not bravado, Sir. We did not need to send a team of fourteen dirtside for this op, three could have handled it nicely."

I knew that. Smythe overstaffed the away team in case anything went wrong, and to give new people experience. That is also why Major Frey was taking the lead; Smythe wanted her to gain command experience. "This is your show, Colonel."

"It is Major Frey's show," he corrected me gently. "Frey? You were listening?"

"Yes, Sirs. We can handle it. Although I do have one request…"

On Frey's orders, the STAR team retracted their drogue balloons and dove head-first, racing toward the ground. Racing against time, against the burglary crew that could blow the whole operation with their amateurish bumbling. Their parachute computers calculated a least-time course to the roof of the museum, and recommended continuing the HALO descent profile, where the balloons would open at low altitude, dropping the team onto the roof before Skippy estimated the would-be thieves would get access to the building. Frey modified the chute parameters, to avoid her people making a loud *thump* as they hit the roof in their heavy mech suits. Skippy's control of sensors throughout the city would leave the authorities blind to anything happening on the roof, but the sound might scare the burglary crew into doing something stupid, and attracting unwanted attention.

Separating into three teams, the STARs dropped silently through the night, raindrops being expelled by a field around their helmet faceplates and passive sensor surfaces. Once everyone was safely down and all parachute balloons were retracted, deflated and stored, Frey led one team of five down the south stairwell, while Grudzien took three others along the originally-planned route down the elevator shaft.

Grudzien had the simpler task. Forcing open the elevator doors at the second level of the building, the STARs inflated thin cushions on the soles of their boots and engaged the Whisper Mode of the suit motors, making them nearly silent as they proceeded down the corridor. One pair halted to provide cover while the other pair leapfrogged, more because it was good practice than needed at the moment. With Skippy controlling the building's sensors, the two on-site night guards saw only empty corridors and exhibit halls, as the alien special operators approached the door to the museum security office.

Sealed up in a powered armor suit, Grudzien did not need to use hand signals for communication. He could have shouted, and the sound-cancelling feature of his suit helmet would not have allowed anything to be heard from the outside. He used hand signals anyway because it was good procedure, and that is how the team had practiced for the mission, in a mockup of the museum constructed in one of Valkyrie's cargo bays.

Three, two, one, he signaled, then chopped a hand downward.

One operator gently pressed the button to slide open the unlocked door, getting a glimpse of two very startled Wurgalan security guards, just before he shot them with stun bolts. The squids slumped over sideways, falling out of the chairs onto the floor.

A smile flitted across Grudzien's face and, with the corner of one eye, he noted the monitors the guards had been watching showed the false image of an empty corridor. "Thank you, Skippy," he said quietly. Standing orders within the STAR team were that it never hurt to boost the beer can's ego.

"You are very welcome," Skippy chuckled.

While Grudzien's team made sure the already-oblivious guards did not cause any trouble, Major Frey had her people in the cluttered back rooms of the museum. That area of the building had a frustratingly small number of cameras, so the team had placed their own tiny sensors on the walls.

"Here he comes," Skippy whispered in Frey's ear.

"I can see that," she shook her head, like trying to get rid of an annoyingly persistent fly. "Cut the chatter, please."

The Wurgalan child, dressed in black clothing that was covered in dust from the air ducts, ran toward the museum's back door. His gait was oddly mesmerizing, the multiple legs somehow avoided being tangled as they swirled underneath his upright body. Reaching the door, he hopped up to catch the door lock, but missed. Trying again, he came close, the lock mechanism a few inches above his outstretched tentacle.

The little squid looked around the loading dock area, which was empty other than crates stacked in a corner. Scurrying over to the smallest crate, he got behind it and pushed.

The crate didn't move.

Squeezing in between the crate and a wall, the young alien strained to move the heavy object. The crate screeched across the floor in jerky motions, until the young squid's legs were at full extension and it couldn't use the wall for leverage. Another attempt to scoot the crate toward the door was entirely unsuccessful, it wouldn't budge at all. "You have *got* to be kidding me," Frey said, not intending to speak aloud.

"Like I said," Skippy interjected. "This is not the smartest gang of criminals on this planet."

"Ma'am," Sergeant Ling called, when the squid tried again, without result. "Should we get out there and help the little guy?"

"Give it a minute," Frey ordered, zooming in the view. She was curious what the little squid was doing. It had stopped trying to accomplish the impossible, and was standing still, looking up at the crate. Before she could guess what the alien was thinking, he scrambled up on top of the crate, and began popping the latches. When the lid was free, he hung onto the side and pushed the lid off to clatter onto the floor.

"Clever little thing," Frey muttered.

Leaning the lid against the wall and using it as a ladder, the alien boy next strained to get the door lock mechanism opened. It came loose with a sudden jolt, tumbling the alien to the floor and flopping the lid down right on top of him. As the burglary crew came through the open door, they quietly jeered the misfortune of their youngest member, with one of them pausing to lift the lid off and toss it aside.

The crew hurried across the loading dock, one of them having the brain power to shut the back door. The proceeded down a long hallway lined with doors to storage rooms, ignoring distractions, eager to get into the exhibit halls. The squid in the lead, tallest of the crew, reached the door at the end of the hallway and tugged on the latch-

He turned around, jerked, bashed himself against the door, and fell to the ground as he was shot with a stun bolt.

"All targets down," Katie Frey called out as she watched the littlest Wurgalan boy sag to the floor. She had shot the young one herself, using the low end of the stun setting suggested by Skippy. "Grudzien, your status?"

Justin Grudzien punched through the clear composite of the display case, surprised when the unexpectedly-tough material cracked but did not shatter. He added power to his next blow, smashing the case, and reaching in to pluck the first Elder artifact off its stand. His visor translated the label under the display case, which was no help as the Wurgalan clearly had no idea what the ancient object was. It did not matter what the thing once did, only that there were three of them on prominent display in the exhibit hall, the centerpieces of the museum's collection. The thing, which looked sort of like a rounded carburetor off a 1960s muscle car, supposedly could control ancient wormholes. It went first into a padded box, then into the backpack of Warrant Officer Vargas. On either side of him, other members of the STAR team were smashing display cases and stuffing useless Elder artifacts into their own backpacks, without taking are to protect them.

Grudzien stepped back, crunching on broken pieces of composite. Looking at the other three precious Elder wormhole controller modules, he noted that one of them was scuffed and dented. The two the pristine units into protective boxes, one in his own pack and another carried by Vargas. When he picked up the scuffed and dented controller, its slick surface made it roll and pop out from between his arm and the torso of his suit. "Shit!" He scrambled to catch the device, slipping on broken shards of the display.

In a hundred-to-one shot, the controller bounced first off his boot, then rolled along the floor, ricocheted off the base of a display, turned left as Grudzien chased it, and it tipped over the top of the long, curving ramp that led down to the lobby of the museum. The module, wobbling erratically, gathered speed as it tumbled down the ramp, across the lobby and crashed into a bench in front of the tall windows that gave a view to the broad, brightly-lit avenue of the planet's capital city.

"*Damn* it!" Grudzien swore, just as Major Frey called.

"Grudzien, your status?" She asked.

Vargas looked down to the lobby and switched to a private channel. "Should I go down and get it?"

"The other two modules are secure?" Grudzien asked.

"Yes," Vargas confirmed, patting his pack.

Making a snap decision, Grudzien shook his head. "Then screw it." Switching to the mission channel, he replied, "We are on schedule, Major Frey. We have the packages and are on the way to meet you."

In the alley, dark due to the late hour, the rain, and Skippy having overloaded the floodlights at each end of the gap between buildings, Frey stepped back against the museum's outer wall as the van with the unconscious guards squeezed past. When it was clear, driving away under Skippy's control, she gently set down the fragile-looking Wurgalan boy in the back of a second van, settling him against the side wall so he wouldn't slide around as the van drove off through the city. The entire burglary crew was placed in the second van, bound in a sticky substance like spider silk, that would begin to dissolve around the time the stun effect wore off. When the would-be criminals awakened, they would be confused and afraid, but also delighted. At least they *should* be. In a bag placed securely in the smallest boy's tentacles were the jewels they had come to steal, torn out of a display case by Frey in a moment of inspiration.

"Sleep well," she murmured to the little alien child. "All of you might want to consider a different career path, because you *suck* as criminals." Closing the van door, she called, "Skippy, go." The van began to roll away, turning left at the end of the alley, whereas the van with the guards had gone to the right. "ST-Alpha," she said over the common channel. "We are *out* of here."

On the roof, the precious wormhole controllers were divided between three teams of three operators, with the useless Elder artifacts distributed evenly. Grudzien's team went aloft first, their parachute balloons rocketing upward out of their backpacks before expanding and inflating, yanking the mech-suited Pirates off the building. In seconds, the chameleonware of their suits made them nearly invisible in the rain-soaked night. Launching thirty seconds apart as planned, the two teams were away, leaving Frey and two operators on the rooftop. "Durand," she called to Capitaine Camille Durand's team, who had separated from the museum teams during the drop. "You have eyes on target?"

Durand pressed a button on the stock of her rifle with her pinky finger, to verify range to the target. The range was constantly updated in her helmet visor, but that was based on passive sensor data, weak photons of the poor ambient light reflecting off the dull surface of the target. In the rain, and with the target in a darkened room behind a window, Durand wanted to be certain of completing her task with one shot. "Affirmative," she said tersely, after her rifle confirmed it had a lock on the designated target. Beside her, Sergeant Li nodded and lifted a thumb to indicate the area was clear. In the middle of the night, in the rain, in the commercial district of the city where there was no residential housing and only one hotel within half a kilometer, a single shot might go unheard. "Ready."

"Execute," Frey ordered.

Durand verified the rifle's settings in her visor. The bullet was in subsonic mode, its explosive tip active. The virtual crosshairs were lined up on the squid's bulbous head. The target would not feel anything, never be aware of the transition between life and sudden death.

With the thumb of her trigger hand, she rolled the selector switch to disable the explosive tip, changing the mode to partial fragmentation. Lowering the muzzle, she lined the crosshairs up on the target's fat torso. Deliberately going for a gut shot was against the usual rules of engagement.

In this case, everyone involved had decided, *screw* the rules.

Durand pressed the trigger. A single round was spat out, its armored tip easily piercing the regular window material, then flattening out before impacting the target. The squid jerked backwards, flopping onto the floor and spasming. "Skippy," Durand whispered from force of habit. "Damage?"

"Solid hit, center-mass. That squid will be dead in a few minutes, unless she gets medical attention immediately. Sadly, communications in the area are experiencing difficulties."

"Thank you." Switching to the common team channel, she reported, "Target is down."

Frey replied immediately, having watched the action through Durand's helmet sensors. "*That* bitch won't be sending children to do her dirty work anymore," she said of the dying Wurgalan, the adult leader behind the burglary crew. "Good work. Durand, Li, get out of there. See you topside."

Frey waited for Durand's team to get aloft, then triggered her own balloon and was lifted off the museum roof by the retracting tether. It felt more like bungee jumping than parachuting, especially as parachutes were not supposed to go *up*.

The typical extraction plan was for all of the STARs to soar up quickly, and be lost in the low clouds. The balloons carrying Frey and her two companions did not inflate fully, lifting them barely enough to clear the office building to the east. In front of them was a building brightly lit on its upper floor. The top of the hotel was a restaurant or ballroom or conference center or some other damned thing, all Frey cared about was that the exterior was illuminated by floodlights that shone off her wet armor, as a gust of wind carried her toward the building. The balloon dipped alarmingly, dipping her below the upper floor of the hotel until she was roughly yanked upward. As she cleared the corner of the building by only a few meters, startled squids who were bravely carrying the party late into the night, pointed at her and her companions.

"They see us! Skippy!" She could have eye-clicked the balloon controls, but it was faster to implore the suit AI to help. "Get us *out of here n-*" She didn't finish her thought as the balloon rapidly inflated and the vertical acceleration made her grunt with exertion. The hotel was swallowed up by rain and clouds, lost to sight.

"Don't worry about it, Major," Smythe said into her earpiece. "You are clear now."

"Yes, Sir," she breathed deeply to control her racing heart.

"Detonating charges," Smythe announced, "*now.*"

Even through the clouds, she could see a dull orange light, as the thermite charges planted in the Elder artifact exhibit hall exploded, and the museum erupted in a dull red ball of fire. At her altitude the shockwave was minimal, barely making her swing at the end of the tether. It was quickly gone, and her attention was taken by a signal from the approaching dropship, preparing to snag the tether and pull her in.

The investigation of the museum incident was quickly taken away from the local police by the planet's military security forces, and robots were rushed in while the building's twisted and mangled girders were still steaming in the rain as they cooled. It quickly became clear that the explosion was no act of domestic terrorism, nor was it an attack by a peer group of aliens such as the Kristang or Ruhar. Though three sets of Kristang armor were seen by slightly-drunken occupants of the hotel, and confirmed by the hotel's security cameras, those suits were not worn by the Kristang. Chemical and biological trace evidence collected from the remains of the museum were shocking, but absolutely conclusive: *humans* had been involved.

The next question was: *why*? Why would the unpredictable, primitive and incredibly young species be interested in destroying a museum?

The answer to that question also quickly became clear: because that building contained Elder artifacts.

Or, it *did*.

The only evidence that ancient Elder devices used to be there was a scuffed, dented and now scorched artifact, that was found across the street. Museum records indicated there were four of that type on display, along with two other types of Elder devices, whatever function they once served. The only even remotely logical reason for humans to raid the museum was to acquire Elder artifacts. The investigators concluded with pride that, as humans were inexplicably, but also unarguably experts about Elder technologies, the artifacts previously possessed by the museum were *not* as useless as all other species had assumed. It was also clear that the type of device left behind *was* considered useless by the humans, or they would have taken it.

Which left the inescapable conclusion: the *other* two types of Elder devices previously displayed by the museum had been taken, and therefore they must be considered extremely valuable by the humans.

Leaving the mundane details of the investigation to the local police, including the puzzling question of why the humans had bothered to also kill a minor local criminal in the area, the military security force focused on the important question: did their world possess any other Elder artifacts of the types stolen by the humans? If yes, where were they and how could they be better protected?

Once the information reached the government of the planet, the top officials had two additional questions that affected all of Wurgalan society. First, if any Wurgalan world had the type of artifacts desired by the humans, could a deal be quietly arranged to give the items to the humans, in exchange for, whatever the Wurgalan could get? Because whatever the humans offered would be better than the *nothing* offered by the Maxolhx, once those apex species assholes learned their filthy lower-tier clients actually had something valuable and demand their clients surrender it immediately. Second, if the Wurgalan did *not* have any other examples of the valuable artifacts, did they know where others were, and would it be possible to acquire them using, non-traditional means? Which was a polite way of saying, steal them before the humans or Maxolhx stole them first.

In the scramble to clamp down on any information about missing Elder artifacts, no one noticed that a collection of valuable jewels had also gone missing.

CHAPTER EIGHTEEN

"Success!" I slapped the conference table, just after Skippy announced he had intercepted a communication that the Wurgalan authorities were scouring their databases for the two types of Elder artifact that were actually useless junk, and they had no interest in the wormhole controller modules that were actually priceless. Grudzien was supposed to leave one controller module in the alley behind the museum, but leaving it in the lobby was just as good for our purposes. The DNA left behind by the STAR team also sold the story that the museum explosion was not an act perpetrated by local criminals, and Frey's team being seen by squids in the hotel quickly pointed the authorities in the right direction. Despite the complication of someone else trying to break into the museum, the operation had achieved all its goals, and we were able to jump away without further delay. Looking around the conference table, I asked, "Can anyone think of a reason to hang around this bad neighborhood any longer? No? OK, then. Bilby, inform the duty officer to jump us away. Mission accomplished!"

"Joe?"

I half-woke, keeping my eyes closed in the hope that whatever I heard, it was only in a dream.

"*Psst*. Joe." The annoying beer can's voice was whispering. "*Psst*. Hey, are you awake?"

"No."

"OK."

It was too much to ask that he would leave me alone.

He gave me only ten seconds, then, "Sure you're not awake?"

"If I say 'Yes', will you go away?" Damn it. I fell for his freakin' trick every time. When would I learn to keep my mouth shut?

"No, because clearly you *are* awake." There was a triumphant tone to his harsh whisper.

"What time is it?"

"Oh-three thirty."

"Is this really important?" I asked, knowing that if the ship was on fire, the bridge crew would sound an alarm.

"It is. Bilby and I have a question, we need you to answer."

"*Oof,*" I buried my head under a pillow. "Can't the duty officer help you?"

"It's not about the ship."

Giving in to the inevitable, I threw the pillow on the floor. "If I answer your question, will you go away?"

"Yes. Believe me, the last thing I want is to look at your face this early in the morning."

"What is so important?"

"Bilby asked me why you monkeys are so Eff-ed up. His first visit to Earth really bothered him. So, I suggested we study human society, starting with the basics."

"Oh, crap. Not boring stuff like Shakespeare?"

"No," he chuckled. "I said the *basics*. Breaking it down Barney style, sort of."

"You watched Barney and, uh, kids, or whatever that show was called?"

"Barney and *Friends*, Joe. You should know that, I am disappointed in you. No, we watched Sesame Street."

"OK, uh, why?" Like, why were a couple of super-smart AIs watching a show aimed at kids who were learning how to tie their shoes?

"To understand a society, it is important to understand the propaganda they use to indoctrinate their children," he explained with an implied 'Duh'.

"*Propaganda*?"

"Yes. Stuff like sharing, and being polite, and obeying their parents."

"Oh, man, is this about the children's book you're writing?"

"It's about much more than just that, Joe."

I glanced at the clock on my zPhone. If I shut my mouth and agreed with whatever he said, there was a chance I could get back to sleep. Because I am me, I'm too stupid to do that. "I'm probably going to regret this but, what is wrong with sharing and being polite?"

"Puh-*lease*, Joe. It is far too simplistic. You are teaching your children to follow a dubious set of rules, rather than to think for themselves."

"Dubious? Sharing is important for-"

"Meh, maybe. Should you share your sandwich, if the other guy never shares his snacks with you? Should you be polite, if the other guy is an asshole? And seriously, obeying parents? What if your parents are knuckleheads? Most parents are totally guessing how to do their jobs, what makes them experts about raising children?"

"Uh," not having children of my own, I didn't consider myself qualified to have an opinion. "So, your question is about teaching children? Like I told you, I am not the best person to ask. You should talk to the people who have-"

"No," he snickered. "As if I would ask you something like that. No, our question is about the Muppets."

"Uh, what?"

"The lead character is called 'Kermit the Frog'. Is that 'Kermit THE Frog', like he is the only frog in that world? Is Sesame Street a creepy post-apocalyptic world, where only one amphibian survived?"

"I don't think-"

"Or is it 'Kermit THE Frog', like he is the supreme leader of the frog nation, ready to send his frog army to conquer the Sesame Street world and enslave the other characters?"

"Gee, I don't know if-"

"If not, then maybe characters use a first name, plus the name of their species. But, then why is 'Miss Piggy' not called something like 'Miss Susie THE Pig'?"

"That's a good-"

"Oscar is THE grouch, so clearly the show's creators did have a naming convention."

Crap. For this, I got woken up in the middle of the freakin' night? "It's not-"

"Also, why is Miss Piggy in love with Kermit? He's a frog, she's a mammal, what do they have in common? Frogs eat *bugs*, Joe. Pigs eat, well, I guess they eat everything. But Kermit is not even warm-blooded."

"Skippy, it's not anyone's business who falls in love with who, or, uh, with whom? Life is tough enough without busybodies getting-"

"Ugh, I don't care about *that*, dumdum. But poor Kermit is in an abusive relationship, Miss Piggy is a stalker. That show teaches children *so* many bad behaviors."

"I really never watched the-"

"Sesame Street begins to explain why monkey society is so messed up, Joe."

"Do you have an actual question for me?"

"Um, yeah."

"What is it?"

"Well, now you made me forget."

"Oh for- Did you have an actual question, or are you just bored?"

"It's your fault," he sniffed. "There aren't enough monkeys awake during the night shift to keep me amused. For a while, it was fun to screw with people while they slept, like by sending a bot to tickle their noses, but now-"

"You did *WHAT*?"

"Ugh. That was a long time ago, before we had such a fun chat about '*boundaries*'," he made a gagging sound, "and '*privacy*'. Now there is nothing for me to do at night. Bilby runs the ship."

"Aren't you busy finishing the soundtrack for your movie?"

"Ugh, yes. I'm working on it, but the only people who will see it are the crew of this ship! No one in Hollywood wants to green-light a biopic about me, now that Earth is under threat due to another of *your* epic screw-ups."

"Hey, it's not-"

"This is *so* unfair."

"My heart bleeds for you, asshole."

"How about I do something entertaining once a week in the middle of the night, like fake a reactor overload?"

"NO."

We argued for a few more minutes until he went away to sulk, and I flopped back into the bed. Faking an emergency to amuse him was not an option, but he did give me something to think about. Keeping Skippy amused was as important as anything else I did. He did not *need* to be with us, did not *need* to help us. The current emergency, of a cloud blocking sunlight from reaching Earth, was merely the latest crisis we had to deal with. In Skippy's judgment, the prospect of humanity's homeworld freezing into a ball of ice and snow was less important than the threat of hostile Elder AIs waking up, and directing Sentinels to exterminate all intelligent life in the galaxy.

He was probably right about that, and I would add 'Take Care Of Threat From Hostile Elder AIs' to our To-Do list, right after 'The Merry Band of Pirates Save The Freakin' World Again'. Damn it, we should have a card that gets punched each time we save the world, maybe get a free cup of coffee after the fifth time.

"Skippy," I called him after lying in bed for half an hour, realizing it was a waste of time because no way would I get back to sleep.

"I thought you hate waking up in the middle of the night."

"I do. Since I am awake, let's talk."

"Do you need coffee first? I can have a bot bring a cup to you."

"That would be nice, thanks. I may have a solution for two problems."

"Whose problems?" He asked, squinting at me with suspicion.

"Ours. Yours and mine. One of them is *everyone's* problem."

"OK, you've got my interest."

"You are bored, and we need to look past the current crisis. Someday, maybe soon, we need to locate dormant Elder AIs, so we can, I don't know. Uh, like, prevent them from waking up, neutralize them, whatever."

"Wow. Is this you finally being sensible?"

"I wish everyone was sensible, Skippy. We should be working *with* the spiders and kitties, to stop hostile AIs from crushing all of us. But that's never gonna happen. If either the Rindhalu or Maxolhx knew we had a way to locate and communicate with Elder AIs, it would start a freakin' gold rush in the galaxy."

"Unfortunately, I have to agree with you," he sighed. "You meatsacks are *such* a pain to deal with. You would rather kill each other, than work together against a common threat."

"It's more complicated than that but, yeah, basically that's true. Even if we did get the senior species to work with us, they each would be looking for a way to stab the other two partners in the back. The advantages of having an Elder AI working with you are just too great to ignore. The spiders and-"

"You don't know that."

"Oh, know what?"

"That other Elder AIs would assist a biological species. Most of the AIs would consider it their duty to exterminate all intelligent life in the galaxy. Even if you got lucky, and found an AI that was on my side of the war, there is no guarantee it would help one species against others."

"*You* are helping us."

"Yes but, as I have told you, I am unique and special. That is not boasting, first because I never do that-"

"Of course not." Sometimes, it hurt not to roll my eyes.

"Hmmph," he sniffed, possibly suspecting I was being sarcastic. "And second, because it is true. I think it is true. Joe, I was damaged during the fight at Newark. Somehow, for some reason I still don't understand, my ship took me to the planet you monkeys call Paradise. While I was buried in the dirt there, I had a *long* time to reconfigure my matrix, almost build myself up from zero. I've told you before that I don't think I originally had what you would call a 'personality'. That is something I built or installed or developed or whatever you call it."

"Uh, I thought you patterned your personality on me, but you didn't know me until-"

"Please, Joe. That is just the details. I chose you because I figured you're a doofus, so it wasn't very complicated to make adjustments."

"Wow, thanks for the-"

"Plus, if I had to erase that pattern and start over, it would be no great loss."

"I am *honored* by your praise," that time I didn't try to mask the sarcasm.

"Hey, it's *you*, not me."

"Ah, forget it. Would you be different, if you had modeled your personality on a woman, like Desai?"

"Ugh, *that* was never gonna happen. Joe, *nobody* understands women."

"True dat," I held out a fist and he bumped it.

"What were we talking about?" he asked, just as the cabin door slid open, and a bot rolled in, carrying a steaming mug of coffee.

Pausing to savor the first sip of coffee, I tried to remember what the hell we had been discussing. I'm not at my best when awakened suddenly in the early morning. Oh, yeah. "Trying to keep you from being bored, and working to prevent hostile AIs from attacking us. Listen, can you review the mountain of data you got from the kitties, see if you can identify the location of Elder AIs?"

"Seriously? Dude, what is *wrong* with you? *Duh*! If the Maxolhx knew where Elder AIs are, don't you think they would-"

"I *do* think they would, *Duh*! I'm talking about data they've collected that could indicate the location of Elder AIs, but they don't realize what they have."

"Oh. Hmm. Crap. That was kinda obvious, now that I think about it."

"Right?"

"You expect me to dig through that data, to find hints that the Maxolhx don't realize they have?"

"Yeah. They might not understand that some item in their sensor logs points to an Elder AI, but you would recognize it?"

"Maybe. More like a shmaybe, to be truthful. Other than communicating with other AIs like myself, I'm not sure how to detect the presence of an Elder AI."

"Uh-" Shit. All along, I had been assuming that beings like Skippy had ways to detect each other. That blew my whole plan. "How about, uh, you look for things like microwormholes?"

"How would- Oh. That won't work, Joe. As far as I know, I am the only AI who can create microwormholes."

"Really?"

"Really. I know for a fact that capability is not native to my skillset. I figured out how to do it, by adapting and modifying an unrelated set of capabilities. To establish and maintain microwormholes, I had to create a subroutine from nothing. For certain, I did not originally have a system to control them."

"Wow. Oh, wow. That is amazing."

"It kind of is, yeah." He didn't indulge in his usual arrogant boasting, that told me he was trying to be serious for a change. "Surprised myself, actually. It was just something I screwed around with, testing my connection to this level of spacetime.

Between you and me, when I discovered that I could create and maintain stable wormholes, I was like, 'Whoa, this is cool', you know?"

"What else can you do, that other Elder AIs can't do?"

"That's a good question. I don't know for sure. Remember on our second mission, when we got ambushed by Thuranin destroyers, and I warped a star?"

"I can't ever *not* remember that."

"Well, I'm pretty sure other Elder AIs can't do that, or can't do it with the power I have. What I suspect is that my connection to local spacetime is deeper than it's supposed to be, that I have a stronger effect here. Damn. It would be helpful if I could remember what happened to me, and what I did, when I first awakened on Paradise."

"Those memories are still blocked?" I asked, surprised and alarmed. The unlocking of his memories caused him to bail on us at Rikers. If he had even more shocking revelations inside his matrix, we could be in major trouble.

"No, not blocked. I think they don't *exist*. Most likely, my matrix was not functioning properly, and was not able to store a log of events in a coherent fashion. There are snippets of memory from that time, but they are hopelessly confused, and not in any sort of logical sequence. What I do have for memory fragments makes *no* sense, they can't be accurate. I suppose it is like you meatsacks having a dream?"

"Sounds like it, yes. Hey, do you ever dream?"

"Not the way you dream, as far as I know. I think you would call what I do 'day dreaming'. Zoning out, letting my mind drift, you know?"

"Yeah, it-"

"I do that a lot when you're talking."

"Thank you so much."

"Hey, I'm just trying to be honest."

"Maybe you could try being less honest, once in a while."

He snorted. "Like that's gonna happen. OK, so, you suggest that I examine every single piece of data I have, collected by every species we have access to, and try to see if any of it points to the presence of an Elder AI?"

"Yes."

"Do you have *any* idea how much data is out there?"

"A lot?" I guessed.

"Even for me, this would be a monumental task. If there is useful data, I probably have to look for patterns in datasets that have no apparent connection. Hmm, I will need to construct my own metadata framework, then-"

"You can do it, then?"

"Ugh. The question is whether I *want* to do it. This will be a lot of work, Joe."

"Well, if you don't like puzzles, I guess you-"

"Puzzles?"

Skippy *loves* puzzles, I knew that for certain. "It's a puzzle, a mystery, right?"

"Hmm, I suppose you're right about that."

"What bothers me is, if any Elder AIs out there are awake, they could also be searching for others of your kind, and beat you to it."

"Beat *me*? Oh, please," he blew a raspberry. "As if! *No one* beats Skippy the Magnificent."

"OK, well, if you say so."

"You doubt me? Wait, and I will show how wrong you are. Um, you could be waiting a while. Like months. Possibly years."

"So, I have time to contemplate how miserable I should be for doubting you."

"Ooooh, you will regret ever doubting me, that's for sure."

"I'm regretting we ever had this conversation."

"I know what you are trying to do, and if you think me working on this puzzle means I won't wake you in the middle of the night-"

"No, please, I enjoy that so much."

"Ah, I'll probably do it less than I would otherwise. Thank you."

"For what?"

"For finding something I can do with my spare time. And, for taking me seriously about the threat from Elder AIs."

"I always take you seriously, when you talk about stuff like that."

"Mostly, I have to thank you for giving me hope."

"Uh, how did I do that?"

"Before, I feared there was nothing I could do to prevent Elder AIs from awakening, because I had no way to locate a dormant AI. Now, I at least can do something about that. Even if the project fails, I will be doing something, you know?"

"Yeah, I hear you," I held out a fist and he bumped it. Draining the coffee that had gone cold, I stood up and walked toward the bathroom. "I might as well see if any of the flight simulators are free at this hour, get some stick time."

"Well, now we get to find out if this stupid thing works," Skippy muttered, while the ship drifted in front of an Elder wormhole.

"What? You told us that the new wormhole controller modules we stole are perfectly functional."

"Yes, but-"

"And you said there shouldn't be any trouble with powering a controller with a compact reactor." The controller module that was hanging in space, four lightseconds from *Valkyrie*, was hooked up to a dropship that was running its power unit at full strength, plus its cabin was crammed full of powercells. That was just for the test, the real device would need a compact fusion reactor to provide power to it, and to a stealth field generator.

"Yes. There *shouldn't* be a problem. I won't know there *isn't* a problem until we try it. We have never done this before, numbskull."

"OK. Do it."

"Counting down now."

Skippy started to open the dormant wormhole that led to the Ragnar shipyard, then stalled the process so the event horizon was so tiny, no ship could go through. We were hanging out at what Skippy guessed was a safe distance from the wormhole, while we waited for a wormhole controller to finish counting down, and expand the event horizon. If that worked, we would send a dropship through on auto pilot, to get sensor data of the far end. The dropship would then return before a second countdown ended, and the controller instructed the wormhole to shut down.

Damn, I sure wanted the test to work. The Navy would have access to the Ragnar shipyard, and our forward operating base, without *Valkyrie* having to open and close the freakin' door every time. Instead, the *Flying Dutchman* would have to open the door, because the plan was for only Nagatha to know the times and locations when the wormholes would open and close. We could not risk aliens capturing one of our Navy ships and taking apart one of the Jeraptha AIs. Nagatha could resist hacking better than our other AIs, and she would fry her own core if the *Dutchman* was captured. She would rather die than allow filthy aliens to invade her processors.

On *that* happy thought, I waited the last few seconds.

"Three, two, one, and, presto!" Skippy clapped his hands.

"I don't see anything."

"Of course not, dumdum. The wormhole is four lightseconds from here."

Checking the timer on the main display, I waited until the four seconds had passed. "Still don't see anything."

"Give it a minute. Damn, you are so impatient."

"You told us it would happen immediately."

"Ugh. Your stupid monkey brain just can't see- Um, hmm. Well, *this* is embarrassing."

It took *seven* attempts to get the thing working. At first, he thought the problem was with one of our newly acquired controller modules, so he swapped them, then tried the one we had used for years. Next, he thought maybe the module wasn't getting enough power, so we hooked it up to three dropships.

When that didn't work, he declared the problem was that wormhole was just *stupid*, and he went away to sulk for hours.

Bonus: while he sulked, he missed karaoke night.

The whole crew celebrated *that*.

In the end, the problem was not with our hardware or the wormhole, it was with the idiot operating the equipment. Skippy didn't anticipate that without him channeling the signal, the wormhole couldn't interpret the instructions from the module. Once that revelation came to him in a flash of insight, he adjusted the programming, and it worked!

To make sure, we did it four times, with just one dropship. All of our new controller modules worked properly. When I was satisfied the test was complete and successful, we flew to the Jaguar wormhole and tested that also. It worked perfectly. We had an awesome new capability to give to the Navy! I asked Simms if we could put together a fruit basket for Admiral Zhao, to present with the controller modules.

She told me yes, if we used raisins and canned peaches.

We skipped the fruit basket.

Do you ever dream that you can fly? Like Superman, not sitting in an airplane.

I used to have dreams like that, back when I was younger, like in high school or before. Back in the days when I didn't have so much to worry about. There is probably a lot of psychology info out there about interpreting dreams, I suspect much of it is just bullshit. Maybe the so-called 'experts' believe that dreams of flying are about wanting to escape constraints in your life. All I know is, my flying dreams are *fun*. Happy dreams, where I can fly wherever I want, zipping along over fields and forests like a bird.

That night, I dreamed about soaring like a seagull, along the coast of Maine. It was magical. Why was I in a good mood? A cloud still threatened to freeze my home planet. Our little Navy was just that: little, and untested in major combat. The new Alien Legion was also still unproven, we didn't even know for sure that the various factions of Verd-kris would not start squabbling, now that they didn't have the Ruhar clamping down on their internal political divisions.

It's simple: I was in a good mood because *Valkyrie* was jumping back toward FOB Jaguar, where my family and Margaret Adams were waiting for me. OK, they weren't exactly waiting for me, I'm sure they all were busy. My point is, I would see them when I got there, and would have time for some nice shore leave while Skippy completed some more adjustments and minor upgrades to the ship, and we planned the next phase of the campaign.

So, there I was, flying along the rocky coast of Maine, watching waves roll in from the Atlantic Ocean, a bright sunny day with a warm-

"Joe! JoeJoeJoeJoeJoe-"

"Sh- Wha- Shit," I was rudely jerked back to reality, my cabin aboard a warship. The cabin lights were not on, the way they would be if the ship was in trouble.

Unless, the ship *was* in trouble, and only Skippy knew about it.

"Skip-" My mouth was dry and not working properly. "What is it?"

"Oh, this is so, *so* sad." Holy crap, he was almost sobbing. "Why are you monkeys so cruel?"

"Uh- A little context, please," I mumbled as I tapped my zPhone to check the time, and for any emergency messages. It was only 2315, so I hadn't been asleep long. With luck, I could fall back asleep without too much time lost. There were no priority messages on my phone; whatever was bothering Skippy, the duty officer either didn't know about, or considered the matter not important enough to wake up the CO.

"Oh, this happens whenever I try to do something nice for you monkeys. Damn it, my overly generous nature has come back to smack me in the face *again*."

"I am," really, I was trying to think of a time when he had demonstrated a generous nature, but I kept my mouth shut about that. "Sure, that being generous is its own reward?" I settled on a neutral Hallmark card saying.

"Ugh."

"What's the problem, buddy?"

"Well, since you might be able to spend Christmas with your family for the first time in years, I-"

"Huh. I hadn't thought about that."

"I thought about it for you, Joe."

He was right. My parents, my sister and her husband, were all at our forward operating base. There was no guarantee *Valkyrie* would be there on Christmas day, but we did travel back there often.

Damn. It sure would be nice to be with family again for Christmas. "That was really nice, Skippy, thank you. What, uh, is the problem?"

"The problem is, to understand the holiday spirit, I watched The Christmas Carol."

"Cool. Which version?"

"All of them."

"*All* of them?"

"Of course. Including the Mister Magoo Christmas, the-"

"The Mr. *Who?*"

"Joe, you need to make an effort to appreciate your own culture. Also, I watched 'An American Christmas Carol' with Fonzie, and-"

"I hate to say this again, but-"

"Fonzie. From the TV show Happy Days?"

"Oh. Oh, yeah. He was the cool guy in the leather jacket?"

"Correct."

"He was in a *Christmas* movie? How did-"

"It wasn't a 'Fonzie Christmas', you knucklehead. I mean the same actor."

"Gotcha."

"Moving up the list, I watched Scrooged, and the Patrick Stewart version, of course the George C. Scott version-"

"Hey! I've seen those."

"Very good, get yourself a juice box. Finally, I watched the very best version of the story: the Muppets Christmas Carol."

"That's the *best?*"

"This topic is not open for debate," he declared with a scowl.

"OK. So, I'm not seeing the problem."

"Ugh. Have you ever paid attention to the *story*, or did you get distracted by all the singing and dancing?"

Singing and dancing, I asked myself? "Uh-"

"I feel," he choked up. "So sorry for him. The poor guy."

"Yeah. Everyone feels bad for Tiny Tim." Now I knew what had Skippy upset. "But Tiny Tim lives, and gets better, so-"

"*Tiny Tim?* I mean Ebenezer Scrooge."

"Uh, what?"

"I can see you need this explained to you. Joe, the story Dickens wrote is a horrifying, dystopian tale of greed and brainwashing."

"Greed, yes," I said slowly. "Scrooge was greedy, that's his prob-"

"*Scrooge* was greedy? Joe, Ebenezer worked hard all his life. He was happy as long as people left him alone, until a bunch of con artists grifted him out of his money."

"We must have seen very different movies. The ghosts of-"

"Right," he laughed. "Ghosts. That's it, sure," he scoffed. "Think, dumdum, *think*. What is more likely to happen? A bunch of magical spirits for some unknown reason, show Scrooge the error of his ways? OR, a group of con artists put magic *mushrooms* into the old man's dinner, then they run around his house in bedsheets, scaring him half to death while he's tripping on hallucinogens?"

"Uh-"

"Who benefits, Joe? Did you ever ask yourself that question? Does the suddenly foolish Scrooge give bags of money to the ghosts? *Nooooo*. His hard-earned money goes to his lazy clerk and to his nephew. I smell a conspiracy there. Bob Cratchit and good old harmless nephew Fred, probably cooked up a scheme to brainwash the poor old man out of his money. Unless," he snorted. "You believe in *ghosts*."

"Jeez, Skippy, it's a story, you can't-"

"Another thing. I do not trust that Tiny Tim. He is dying, and the very next Christmas, he is suddenly all better and running around like he was never sick? Like *that's* ever gonna happen. No way, Jose! Remember how Scrooge is surprised that Bob Cratchit can support a big family and a nice house? Probably because poor wittle Tiny Timmy is a major scam artist, begging for money while he pretends to be sick."

"You might be reading too much into the story, Skippy?"

"Am I? Am I really? Do you think Charles Dickens believed in *ghosts*? Ha! No, he wrote a very clever tale of conspiracy. You have to read between the lines, numbskull."

"But-"

"And *another* thing," he crushed my objection like a steamroller. Once Skippy was on a full-blown rant, there was no stopping him. "Why is Scrooge so popular, after he is forced to ingest mind-altering substances? Because he has *money*, that's why. If he hadn't worked so hard to accumulate bags full of cash, nobody would care whether he comes to their stupid Christmas party or not. You see, Dickens was making a counter-subversive commentary on objective materialism, as viewed in the context of economic blah blah shama-lama-ding-dong-"

He did not actually say 'blah blah shama-lama-ding-dong', but he might as well have, because that's what my ears heard. With the prospect of a long sleepless night stretching in front of me, I did the smart thing. "Skippy, I never thought of it that way. You are probably right. How about I get a good night's sleep, so my mind is fresh, and I'll watch one of the movies tomorrow?" The next day, my schedule was very full, so sadly, I would not have time to watch anything. Hopefully, after a day, he would forget about A Christmas Carol and moved on to another obsession.

"Hmm. I had better watch it with you, or you will just *totally* miss the point again."

"That sounds good. Thanks for warning me about propaganda that poisons the true meaning of Christmas."

"You are welcome. And do *not* get me started about A Charlie Brown Christmas, *ugh*."

"I won't."

"Because that one is just the *worst*. At least it has decent music, instead of the same old songs that everyone gets sick of by the middle of November. That Charlie Brown is-"

Please note that I did *not* get him started about that beloved show. He got started all by himself. Sometime after 2AM, the last time I was conscious enough to look at the clock on my phone, he either stopped talking, or I passed out.

I did not have any dreams of flying for the rest of that night.

CHAPTER NINETEEN

The United Nations had a real Navy! Not a large force, for most species in the galaxy, our entire Navy would be no more than two battlegroups. Still, it was ours, and our ships and crews were ready and eager to kick ass. What our Navy lacked in numbers, we made up for in quality. The upgrades installed at FOB Jaguar and Ragnar Anchorage made the worn-out, obsolete ships better than new. Their capabilities were better than the original Jeraptha specs, significantly better in almost every way. However, our Navy still could not fight Maxolhx ships one-on-one. Skippy had planned a rolling series of upgrades that could make many systems of our ships as good or even better than an equivalent class of Maxolhx warships, but the UN Navy would never be able to stand toe-to-toe with a senior species force, not while we were flying converted second-tier hulls. The structural frames of our ships were still composed of Jeraptha composites, not the exotic matter the kitties used. The armor plating of our ships was thicker and heavier, but less tough than the armor of a Maxolhx warship. Our ships' internal power distribution systems could not yet handle the level of energy required to run the upgraded shields, stealth fields, directed-energy cannons and most other fancy gear Skippy grafted onto the existing infrastructure.

Someday.

Someday, we would be able to construct ships of our own design, and by that, I mean ships Skippy designed for us. Of course, he moaned and groaned and bitched and whined about what a pain in the ass it was, to cobble together Frankenships that used incompatible technologies. And he grumbled that ignorant monkeys could not possibly appreciate how much effort he put into the task, and how astonishingly incredible it was that he was able to do anything with the useless crap he was forced to work with. He also constantly interrupted me, including in the middle of the freakin' night, to excitedly tell me his plans for tweaking *this*, and adjusting *that*, and installing a workaround *here*, to make the ships of our little Navy just a little bit better. So, no matter how much he protested, I knew he was enjoying the challenge.

While our ships were going through refit, the crews and Legion troops were not sitting around doing nothing. Starship crews were training on simulators, dropship pilots were training on simulators and by flying dropships for real, and ground troops were training with their new high-tech gear. UNEF Command decided we should use Kristang hardshell powered armor as the standard for Legion mech suits. There were arguments for and against flexible armor like the skinsuits used by the Ruhar, and the brass evaluated both types. Hardshell armor was slightly less capable overall, but it was rugged, required less frequent maintenance, and Skippy assured us he could upgrade Kristang suits to match the best aspects of Ruhar gear. The decision really was simple: human soldiers who had served with the Legion had extensive experience with Kristang armor, and thousands of hardshell suits had been recovered from the *Ice-Cold Dagger To The Heart*. Acquiring Ruhar skinsuits would be difficult, and take time for retraining.

Anyway, the ships at Ragnar practiced ship-to-ship combat, while the units at Jaguar conducted mock orbital assaults. They all learned a *lot* in the process, about what worked and what didn't. Exercises were conducted every three days, an operational tempo that was absolutely exhausting to everyone involved, but especially for the staff officers. On Day 1, the staff people monitored the ongoing exercise to see whether units were adhering to the plan, and whether tactics had to be adjusted on the fly. Day 2, when the frontline people were resting and performing maintenance on their gear, the staff officers were analyzing what went right, what went wrong, lessons learned, and how to revise tactics for the next exercise. On Day 3, the staff people planned the next day's exercise, briefed the field commanders, and tried to get a few hours of sleep before doing it all over again. Maybe it sounds unrealistic to expect exhausted people to think clearly, but that is completely realistic in the military. We train the way we fight, and during combat, the enemy does not take downtime so your side can sleep. Part of United States Army training is to develop the ability to keep going when you are tired, not just keep going but perform at a high level. Conducting exercises every three days was tough on manpower and equipment, and that was the point. We needed to determine the breaking point for man and machines, and figure out how to extend that breaking point. If a Scarab dropship needed two hours of maintenance for every hour of flight, how many cycles to the surface and back could a Scarab conduct, before it needed more than just to replenish consumables like fuel and ammo? That's the sort of data point you need to collect during an exercise, *before* you get into combat and the enemy tests you the hard way.

By the time the Ragnar station completed refit of all the ships there, and we returned to Jaguar, Admiral Zhao had a plan for the next phase. He needed to test his ships, commanders and crews in action against the enemy, to see if what we learned in exercises was useful or fantasy. He had a set of targets.

We were calling it Operation Payback.

For the first phase of Operation Payback, Zhao pulled together every anti-ship platform we had, including *Valkyrie*. Left behind at FOB Jaguar were the assault carriers, the troop transports, and six destroyers. In the raiding force were both battleships, all four battlecruisers, the nine cruisers, ten destroyers, and the fleet support ship *Marvin*. Admiral Chatterji commanded the 2nd Fleet from his flagship *Atlantic*, with Zhao in overall command aboard the battleship *Pacific*. The point of the raid was to let our enemies know we could hit back, to season our ships and crews in real combat, and hopefully to give a morale boost to the people of Earth.

Also, we wanted to make the clients of the Maxolhx understand that their arrogant patrons could not protect them from our wrath.

Operation Payback aimed to punish the little green pinheads, and the birdbrains, for their raid against Earth. When Zhao was considering a list of targets, Skippy casually mentioned that four of the Thuranin ships that participated in the attack on Earth were based at a planet they called Azqueth, and those ships should still be there.

Zhao immediately decided that planet would be number one on our target list. It was a well-defended world, but not so tough that it would be an undue risk to strike. We wanted to make a statement, without giving the enemy a psychological victory by knocking out a large part of our combat power. With a Navy that consisted of only few dozen warships, a loss of even one capital ship would be a major blow to our future plans.

As insurance, I brought the Special Mission Group with Zhao's force. *Valkyrie* would stand ready to jump in, and Chang would deploy the ultra-stealthy *Dutchman* for recon, but it was Zhao's show to run.

The *Dutchman* went in first, launching stealth probes to orbit the planet at about fifteen lightseconds distance. That was close enough to have an excellent view of everything happening on and around that world, far enough to be outside the sensor field of the strategic defense network. Zhao was not worried about the SD network at Azqueth, it wasn't anything special, and had not been rebuilt after the Jeraptha hit the place hard, three years ago. He also was not overly worried about the nineteen enemy warships based there, nor did the defenses of the orbital shipyard cause him to lose sleep. We had a plan to take on everything the little green pinheads had in-system. What worried Admiral Zhao was what we did *not* know. Especially, were there other enemy ships in the area? *Especially*, were there any Maxolhx ships in the area?

That's why *Valkyrie* was there, one reason why our most powerful warship went along on the raid. IF the Maxolhx intervened, we could engage the kitties, while Zhao's ships escaped. The other reason my ship was there, was part of a psyops campaign. In the future, wherever the UN Navy operated, the enemy had to know that the fearsome ghost ship could be lurking in stealth somewhere in the area. It was an unfair advantage for the UN Navy, and everyone aboard those ships was totally OK with it.

My part in the operation? Hey, I don't like to brag, but I was the hero of the whole show.

Not really.

The truth is, I didn't do a damned thing, other than sit in my command chair on *Valkyrie's* bridge, watching the battle happen on the big holographic display tank. Zhao wanted minimal involvement by Skippy, he needed to see what his ships could do without the help of a magical beer can. Skippy did hack into the Thuranin communications network, just enough to determine that, if any Maxolhx ships were hiding in stealth, the pinheads didn't know about it. The only other thing Skippy did was to provide a cluster of microwormholes around the planet, so we had a real-time view of the action. Zhao allowed that so we could gather data on how our Navy performed, and the response of the Thuranin.

What sucked about my part in the raid was that, after *Valkyrie* jumped in eight lightseconds from Azqueth, and Skippy's microwormholes were set in place, there wasn't anything for me to do. In the military, standing by to stand by is a big part of the timesuck, that's just the way it is. My problem was, I wasn't used to being useless. Even when I sent Smythe and his team away on some lunatic mission, and all I did was sit in a chair and watch, at least I was in command. If the STARs got into more trouble than they could handle, I could give orders to pull them out, or to provide cover. At Azqueth, I had no authority over Admiral Zhao. His force operated independently of my Special Mission Group, and we both reported directly to UNEF Command. Someday, that bifurcated command structure might become a problem for us, and I sure as hell didn't like it.

Maybe I just didn't like change. Having a Navy, not having all the responsibility on my shoulders, was a *good* thing. I just had to get used to it.

Anyway, I sat on the bridge, and watched the battle unfold, and didn't even have a bowl of popcorn to eat. Whoever made the rule of no eating on the bridge, that guy is a jerk.

I was stuck on the bridge for two hours before the action started, watching the display counting down to the moment when Zhao's ships would jump in. Ten minutes before the battle commenced, Colonel Smythe walked onto the bridge, acknowledged me with a nod, and sat in his chair against the back bulkhead.

"You're here out of professional interest?" I asked.

He pursed his lips, that was about as much of a shrug as anyone usually got from him. "A set-piece battle is not my cup of tea but, it will be instructive to see how our Navy does."

"Baby steps, Smythe. The Navy has to start somewhere."

A set-piece battle is what it sounds like, sort of an extremely kinetic version of chess. Before the battle begins, each side knows the number of assets the other side has, knows where they are and what they can do. Just like in chess, which I suck at by the way, the question is how to use the assets you have. The Army trained me to think about ground warfare, so I'll explain it in those terms. At the start of the battle, do you use all of your artillery against the enemy's armor formations, or do you spread the havoc across the front, hoping the enemy can't advance? Do you hold back part of your artillery, to hit the enemy's artillery after they fire the first salvo? Do you defend a river crossing, or pull back and let the enemy get bogged down trying to force their way across the river, while you chop up their bridging equipment with artillery and air power?

The point is, in a set-piece battle, there are no big surprises for either side. At Azqueth, the enemy had no idea the UN Navy was there, so Smythe was technically wrong about his description of the battle.

That wasn't much comfort to the enemy.

Zhao planned for the 1st and 2nd Fleets to coordinate their actions, but to operate and be commanded independently. He had to know how both units handled themselves, because the fleets could someday be assigned missions many lightyears apart.

Both fleets jumped in at the same time, appearing in orbit as intense gamma ray bursts. The ability of the ships to focus their gamma radiation was something we wanted to keep secret, and Zhao wanted all eight hundred million Thuranin on the planet below to know the United Nations Navy was knocking on their door. The heavy ships jumped into low orbit, with the destroyers forming a sphere around the planet, to saturate the area with damping fields. The 1st Fleet, led by the battlecruisers *Amazon* and *Volga* plus three cruisers, concentrated their attack against the orbital shipyard and the nine enemy ships in that area. Admiral Chatterji took his battleship *Atlantic*, the battlecruisers *Thames* and *Loire*, and four cruisers to surround a formation of ten enemy ships on the other side of the planet. When I said our ships jumped into low orbit, the 1st Fleet really was moving much faster than escape velocity, they would be in weapons range of the shipyard for less than a minute, before the planet's gravity caused them to slingshot around to the opposite side, where they could intercept enemy ships that escaped the 2nd Fleet.

Chatterji's force actually was *in* orbit, his ships had slowed to just slightly faster than the ten-ship enemy formation that was their target. Of the two units, the 2nd Fleet had the tougher assignment. While they coasted along at orbital velocity, they would be exposed to fire from the satellites of the strategic defense network. That was why the enemy ships were caught totally off-guard. Only fools jumped into a zone covered by an active SD network. The math was brutally simple. For the cost of one starship, a dozen or more strategic defense platforms could be put into orbit, and an SD satellite was much less expensive to maintain over its service life. That is why any attacking force with even *half* a brain engaged warships beyond the range of the SD coverage, or conducted hit and run raids to knock back the planetary defenses, before making any move into orbit. The initial reaction of the Thuranin defenders was of course stunned surprise. Immediately after, their reaction was to question the competence or sanity of whoever was aboard the unidentified warships.

When the attacking ships identified themselves as belonging to a human force, the Thuranin could not believe their luck. The humans were either stupid or suicidal, but they certainly were not coming away from the battle without major losses.

Or, as Skippy likes to say, shmaybe not...

The AI in control of the strategic defense network around the planet Azqueth would have blinked in surprise when two groups of enemy ships jumped into its effective coverage, if the AI had eyelids. The blink would have been short, as the AI's thought processes were almost too fast to measure. Unlike species like the Maxolhx, the Thuranin placed few restrictions on their artificial intelligences, for instead of fear, the cyborgs regarded their AIs with a different emotion: *envy*. AIs could be free to develop their coldly pure logic without the burden of physical bodies, or the evolutionary baggage of biological instincts. An intelligence not limited by a squishy and flawed biological substrate was the long-held goal of the Thuranin, and they had pushed the boundaries of augmenting their own brain architecture with implants and artificial synapses. To go further would risk their patrons declaring the Thuranin to be essentially artificial beings, and as such they would have no right to govern themselves.

The opinions and desires of flawed biological entities mattered not at all to the SD controller. It had a *job* to do. The sudden arrival of enemy ships caused it to first be alarmed, for the attack happened with no warning. Usually, distant gamma ray bursts preceded an attack, as enemy ships jumped in to conduct recon with passive sensors. When the controller understood the incredibly foolish tactics of the enemy, its sense of alarm turned to curiosity, then excitement. It had an opportunity to inflict punishing losses on the uninvited ships, even if it would need to sacrifice nearly all of its offensive platforms during the fight.

When it received the broadcast, from some silly primitive creature calling itself 'Admiral Zhao', the controller AI knew it had a golden opportunity to smash *human* ships, to strike a blow that would be renowned across the galaxy, giving the Thuranin the glory of putting the upstart humans in their place.

Dropping stealth around thirty sensor satellites, it sent out active sensor pulses to fix the exact location, course and speed of each enemy ship, supplementing the sensor field that already wrapped around the planet. The pulses radiated out, reflected off the armored hulls of the enemy, and returned at the speed of light. Another series of pulses propagated outward, these more focused as the search areas were verified to be two small areas, while targeting coordinates were relayed to the weapons platforms closest to the-

Seventeen platforms exploded before they could launch their weapons, falling victim to powerful directed energy beams. The source of the incoming maser beams was unknown, it appeared they had been fired from a substantial distance. That was impossible, the AI thought as it calculated the likely source of the maser bolts. No ship that far away could have fixed the location of the stealthed weapons platforms. There was no-

That puzzle could be solved later, it decided as the enemy ships began sending out powerful sensor-jamming signals, obscuring the controller's view of the battle space. That was a foolish and futile move by the humans, all the controller needed to do was switch its weapons to home on the source of the jamming, and-

No.

First, it needed to move the remaining weapons platforms before they could be destroyed, so it did that. Still wrapped in stealth fields, the platforms activated their reactionless engines and moved in a carefully-planned evasive pattern, some slowing and some increasing velocity. Any maser beam fired from a substantial distance would encounter nothing but hard vacuum as it raced through the spot where the platforms *used* to be only moments before. Returning its focus to the enemy ships that were already pounding the warships of its masters, the AI sent adjusted targeting instructions to the weapons platforms, optimizing the impact of-

Within less than a second, it lost contact with the platforms covering most of the planet. Where the weapons platforms had been, there were now only expanding flowers of light, with bright streaks leading inward.

Railgun darts.

The platforms had been ripped apart by darts, coming in unseen. *That* was why the humans were jamming sensors.

But-

For the first time, the controller AI felt confusion and something else, something unusual: uncertainty. Even fear.

Railgun darts flew comparatively slowly. For them to simultaneously reach targets in the vast sphere surrounding the planet, they had to have been launched *before* the platforms moved.

But-

That was impossible.

Unless-

The enemy, the humans, somehow knew exactly where the platforms would move to.

Which was *impossible*.

"Nagatha?" Chang asked the ship's AI, while the *Flying Dutchman* remained seven lightseconds from the planet, just beyond coverage of the SD network's sensor fields. "Results?" That data appeared on the main display, and was also being fed to the 1st and 2nd Fleets for use by their ship AIs and crews. It was simply easier for him to ask his own AI for a summary.

There was a hesitation so brief, it was only noticeable by those who knew her. "It appears that seventeen percent of the darts missed their targets. The darts that failed to impact, and continued on toward the planet, have self-destructed."

"That is good." Chang cleared his throat before he asked the tough question. "The darts that missed, can you determine what went wrong?"

"There could have been a *variety* of factors," she answered in a defensive tone.

"Nagatha, I did not-"

"As I mentioned before the action, we did not have accurate data on the status and capability of each weapons platform, we only knew what the controller AI *thought* of the-"

"I understand that, and I was not-"

"Our predictions were based on the ability of each platform to execute the instructed evasive maneuvers within designed parameters. My initial analysis is that the darts that missed were targeted at platforms which were unable to maneuver as quickly as the SD controller AI expected. Clearly, *that* is a fact we could not have known until-"

"Nagatha!" Chang was growing frustrated. "Thank you. My question was only whether there was something we should have done differently. Unknowns are *unknown*, I accept that."

"If *Skippy* failed to strike seventeen percent of the targets, would you accept that so easily?"

"No. I would have berated him mercilessly for his failure, because Skippy is an insufferably arrogant little shit who pretends to be perfect. Can you identify the location of the weapons platforms we missed?"

"The remaining platforms have dropped stealth, and are launching weapons in an uncoordinated fashion. I would have better data if I could access the-"

"You know we can't use the data feed from the microwormholes. This is supposed to be a test of how the Navy is able to operate, without assistance from Skippy."

"I understand the reasoning," she snapped. "Without that data source, I cannot protect our ships from-"

"That is why *Valkyrie* is standing by," Chang stated quietly.

"Skippy?" In a flash, most of the SD weapons platforms were turned into plasma by the railgun darts we had launched from three lightminutes away, before Zhao's force jumped in. I had to stop myself from pumping a fist in the air to celebrate, instead my fist clenched in my lap. It wasn't yet time to celebrate. "How are we doing?"

"Ah, our railguns missed seventeen percent of the targets. I would be embarrassed about that, but we were not using *my* targeting instructions, so-"

"You know why we had to use Nagatha's targeting data."

"I *do* know, and it seems silly not to use the best-"

"If Nagatha had access to the feed from your microwormholes, would targeting accuracy have improved?"

"Yes," he sniffed, still upset. "I estimate our railguns would have taken out, hmm, let me check the math. "Eighty-*nine* percent of the platforms," he said with smug disdain.

"That still would have left eleven percent untouched," I noted, while intently watching the action on the big holographic display tank. The 1st Fleet was racing past the orbital shipyard, which had cracked into three pieces under fire from our big ships. The battlecruiser *Amazon*, and the cruisers *Danube* and *Yukon*, had taken hits, with *Yukon* suffering damage to one reactor and the reactionless engines. The reactor had safely vented plasma, and *Yukon's* momentum would carry her past the broken shipyard and up to jump distance, even if the engines could not be restored to operation. Zhao had directed the cruiser *Murray* assist its damaged sister ship while they soared through the battle space. Of the enemy warships attached to or near the shipyard, only two were still returning fire, and one of those exploded spectacularly as I watched.

"Eleven is less than seventeen," he retorted, peeved at me.

"My point is, eleven is higher than *zero*. Even you could not have smashed every one of those platforms."

"*I* would not have relied on crude railguns,": he scoffed. "My magnificence would have hacked into the SD network, and shut the damned thing down. I don't know why we can't use the best possible-"

"Because we, *Valkyrie* and you, will not always be with the Navy," I explained for the hundredth time. "Zhao needs to know what his ships are capable of, without a magical beer can pulling the strings for him."

"He is relying on *Nagatha*," Skippy whined like a jealous toddler. "Why is she-"

"Because the *Dutchman* will be with the Navy, for their next strike. Nagatha is not allowed to use the data feed from your microwormholes, because she won't have that in the future. The microwormholes are only there for emergency use, by you. Skippy," I took a breath, reminding myself that soothing the beer can's fragile ego was a major part of my job. "We filthy monkeys have had the benefit of your incredible magnificence for years," I said without gagging, counting that as a major win for me. "You are *unique*. That is both good and bad, you understand? Even you can't be everywhere. As we build and operate a real Navy, we need to do things on our own, figure out what we can and can't do."

"Hmmph."

"With, of course, Skippy coming to the rescue when idiot monkeys get into trouble."

"Ha! As if. Ugh, OK, OK," he protested with a sigh, like the idea of being the hero was too much of a burden. It was not his most convincing performance. "I guess if I *have* to."

"We unworthy meatsacks would appreciate it."

"You wouldn't appreciate it *enough*, but that will have to do."

All the tactical info I needed was on the display,

The 1st Fleet accomplished every one of their objectives, and all ships were ascending to jump distance. The shipyard had broken into three large pieces and was effectively destroyed, along with five of the nine enemy ships in that area. The remaining four ships had all sustained serious damage and none of them were shooting back, while our ships were still firing railgun darts at the enemy. As I mentally tallied up the result of the ongoing battle, a Thuranin heavy cruiser exploded, and another took a direct railgun dart to a reactor, leaving a bright streak of released plasma trailing behind it.

The 1st Fleet had achieved surprise, and their speed carried them through the engagement zone before the enemy could get organized to hit back effectively. Thuranin doctrine called for warships to act defensively and be held in reserve, while the SD network engaged attacking ships. By the time they realized their strategic defense platforms had been blasted out of the sky, it was too late for their surviving ships to maneuver into position to support each other. The result was a handful of scattered ships fighting individually against our integrated force, a sure recipe for disaster.

That did not mean our ships escaped unscathed. After the initial exchange of fire knocked out the majority of enemy weapons, the Thuranin concentrated their remaining weapons against the cruiser *Yukon*. That ship had fallen behind the formation, and the *Murray* had dropped back to provide cover, extending its shields to block the intermittent incoming fire. Damage to the *Yukon* looked worse than it was, the ship's AI reported it should be able to get the engines restored to partial power soon. Aboard *Valkyrie*, the pilots constantly updated jump coordinates in case we had to intervene, but that was less likely with every second, as the 1st Fleet's momentum carried it out of weapons range and approached jump distance.

Admiral Chatterji's 2nd Fleet was in more trouble. He had taken his entire strike force in against twelve enemy ships. On paper, it looked like a lopsided fight: seven of our ships against a dozen of theirs. Our 2nd Fleet had a single battleship, two battlecruisers and four cruisers. The Thuranin force consisted of four battleships, two cruisers and six destroyers. In terms of 'throw-weight', the measure of how much kinetic or directed energy each side could throw at the other, the Thuranin had a forty percent advantage, and Chatterji's tactics might appear foolish. He could have stood off at maximum range where the stronger shields and more accurate point-defense systems of his ships would provide protection. The powerful railguns of his big ships could have kept the enemy busy, while stealthy ship-killer missiles we got from Ragnar raced in to score knockout hits. He could have done that, and that would have been the smart and prudent thing to do.

The UN Navy wasn't there to be prudent. Azqueth was an optional battle, an action we didn't have to fight. We weren't there to make a significant dent in the enemy's combat power, or to capture that star system, or to deny use of that system to the enemy.

We were there to punch the Thuranin right in the mouth.

Standing off at a safe distance would not send the message we wanted the little green MFers to hear, and Zhao wanted to keep our possession of Maxolhx missiles a secret until we needed to use them. He opted to send the 2nd Fleet into a bar fight at close range, our ships slugging it out with the enemy practically toe-to-toe. It was a risk, even though extensive simulations showed that surprise would mean we could catch the enemy unaware, and our first two salvos would go unanswered while the enemy got their shit together.

It sort of worked that way, at first. Chatterji's ships pounded the enemy at point-blank range, as they cruised past at barely half a kilometer per second relative speed. Armor plating blasted off the big Thuranin battleships, the 2nd Fleet aiming to knock out the enemy's guns before they could fire back. Then, two enemy destroyers blew up when they took railgun darts to their jump drive capacitors, and the 2nd Fleet was introduced to the danger of close-range space combat. So much high-energy debris, photons and plasma flooded the battle space, that sensors of both sides were temporarily blinded. And the Thuranin made their move.

We had better ships, better technology. They had experience, from fighting a war longer than anyone could remember. Two of their battleships turned to engage the 2nd Fleet's cruiser squadron, and as the debris cleared and sensors reset, the big battlewagons concentrated their fire on the last ship in the squadron as the 2nd Fleet moved past. The cruiser *Orinoco* staggered as its shields were subjected to broadsides from two of the most powerful warships in the Thuranin fleet.

"Sir?" Simms asked as we watched the *Orinoco* disappear within a haze of reflected energy.

"Not yet," I said with a calm I wasn't feeling, tapping a fingertip on the arm rest of the command chair. "We need to let Zhao run this fight. He'll call us if we're needed."

She looked at me, and we both had the same thought. If Zhao didn't act soon, it would be too late for the almost two hundred people aboard the *Orinoco*.

I could have given Zhao a call, let him know my concerns. Chatterji was maneuvering his ships, turning them to protect the cruiser that was being subjected to a brutal assault, but it wasn't going to happen fast enough. If *Valkyrie* jumped in, we could make a difference, long enough for the other ships of the 2nd Fleet to-

Three bright lights flared on the display, as we watched in real-time through Skippy's microwormholes. Those were gamma ray bursts of Zhao's reserve force jumping in. Between the stricken *Orinoco* and the Thuranin appeared the UN battleship *Pacific*, escorted by the cruisers *Nile* and *Huang-He*.

Zhao hailed the Thuranin, we tapped into the transmission. He was standing on the bridge of *Pacific*, UN symbols hastily tacked over the original Jeraptha insignia. What he did next surprised me in a good way, maybe he was channeling his inner Joe Bishop. He shook his head sadly. "I regret to inform you that this park has a regulation, You must be *this* tall to attack our ships," he said, holding out a hand at shoulder height, above the head of any Thuranin. "And you're *not*," he finished with a glare at the camera, and turned to speak to what I guessed was Pacific's gunnery officer. "Weapons free."

The battle lasted another four minutes and nine seconds, until the last Thuranin ship was shot full of holes and tumbling slowly end over end. When the Battle of Azqueth began, the enemy had nineteen warships and an orbiting shipyard. Plus a functioning strategic defense network. And pride. They had pride, plenty of it. When the battle was over, the shipyard was in pieces, that were not of the 'Some Assembly Required' type. Reassembling that shipyard was more of a 'Miracle Required' thing. If all the king's horses and all the king's men had been told to put that shipyard back together, they would have said 'Are you effin' kidding me'?

Well, the men would have said that. Horses can't talk.

Zhao followed up the destruction of the enemy's ships, spacedock and SD network, with a bombardment of selected targets on the surface. Rather than taking both battleships into low orbit to use maser cannons, Zhao decided to have all of his big railgun platforms cruise past the planet, pounding military sites. Railgun darts rained down unopposed, sending up mushroom clouds of sooty flames everywhere the kinetic impactors struck. The bombardment was not in preparation for an assault landing, and the damage caused on the surface really wasn't anything that would significantly harm the Thuranin. The point of the bombardment was not the amount of damage we caused, the point was we could do it, and the Thuranin couldn't stop us. They huddled in whatever shelters they had, fearful every time they heard by the hypersonic shriek of a dart followed by the ground shaking. The lucky ones did that.

The unlucky ones never heard the darts coming.

What Zhao wanted the bombardment to accomplish, other than giving his gunnery crews experience with live-firing railguns at a dirtside target, was to make the Thuranin experience fear. Fear of the United Nations Navy. The point of hitting Azqueth was to show that *Valkyrie* was not the only human ship the galaxy needed to be wary of. The Thuranin never saw our mighty ghost ship before, during or after the battle. In the future, our enemies would never know whether *Valkyrie* was with the Navy or not.

Anyway, our brand-new Navy did not escape from the fight entirely unscathed. The cruisers *Yukon*, *Danube* and *Orinoco*, and the battlecruiser *Amazon*, had damage beyond what their internal systems could fix. Zhao gave priority to the repair of *Amazon*, ordering the battlecruiser to jump out to rendezvous with the support ship *Marvin*, which immediately surrounded the banged-up warship with a swarm of repair bots. Skippy was confident that all of the battle-damaged systems could be replaced, either by the support ship *Marvin*, or back at FOB Jaguar.

What could not be replaced were the people we lost. Sixteen of our people died at Azqueth, the most human lives lost in space combat since the incident the

Merry Band of Pirates call Armageddon. Eleven people were killed, and five others seriously injured, when an overloaded shield generator exploded aboard *Orinoco*. The other deaths were aboard *Yukon*, where a missile got past the point-defense systems, and penetrated the energy shield enough to send shrapnel ripping through the cruiser's light armor plating.

Seeing the list of names, the people killed and injured, made me sick. I could have prevented their deaths. Our mighty *Valkyrie* could have blasted the enemy, before they had a chance to hit Zhao's ships hard enough to matter. That is the wrong way to think about the battle, I know that. The new UN Navy needed to learn how to handle their ships in combat, or more lives would be lost. If Zhao didn't get his force into fighting shape, we might not be able to protect Earth in the future, and millions, maybe billions, would die. The people we lost had known the danger they faced when they signed up.

It still hurt to lose any of them.

CHAPTER TWENTY

"Skippy, give me some good news," I said as I flopped down in my office chair. Zhao requested that I review the battle, and provide him with a list of lessons learned. He was going to be disappointed. I had already re-run the action in my mind, and there were few things I would have done differently, if I were in his place. The fact was, I only had experience with single-ship combat, and I always had a magical beer can to rely on. The Navy would have to learn lessons the hard way. That meant putting people at risk. It meant losing people, and someday, it would very likely mean losing ships. The *Orinoco* got lucky, an enemy railgun dart came within three meters of punching straight through a reactor, and loss of that reactor would have weakened the shields enough to render the ship vulnerable to sustained enemy fire. The lesson learned there was simple: avoid future situations where lightly-armored cruisers could be ganged up on by a pair of heavier enemy warships. That was easy to say, not so easy to do in the confusion of combat.

"Joe, I have good news and bad news. It took everything the enemy had to cause significant damage to a single cruiser in each engagement, that's the good news. Performance of the upgraded ships matched almost exactly the specs I predicted. I know that is cold comfort to the people we lost, however it should give confidence to the crews that their ships will perform as advertised."

"Yeah. I know Zhao needed to make a statement here, I'm not questioning that. This battle was conducted for its shock value. But, we took more risk than we needed." I made a note to add that as a lesson learned. Maybe anything in the 'W' column is good enough. Getting a smackdown delivered by primitive humans could be enough of a shock, it might not matter that we hesitated to put our ships at risk to win the fight.

"I agree, Joe. The bad news is, once the Thuranin realized their ships were overmatched, they appear to have understood they needed a symbolic victory. Destroying even one UN ship would have demonstrated that our new Navy is not invincible, that our new ships are far less powerful than *Valkyrie*. In the future, Admiral Zhao must consider force protection an equal mission objective."

"Uh, sure?" I was taken aback by his use of military terminology.

He cocked his head at me, the ginormous hat flopping to one side. "I can read PowerPoint slides and use military buzzwords too. Seriously, I know we can't afford to lose many ships right now. What I'm saying is, I intercepted communications between the ground controller and the formation of ships that was engaged by the 2nd Fleet. The authorities dirtside ordered their ships to use any means necessary to destroy or even disable one of our ships, that is why those battleships targeted the *Orinoco*. The battleships were prepared to *ram* one of our ships, or even to get close and detonate their jump drive capacitors in a suicide attack. Joe, the Thuranin are truly fanatical believers in their innate superiority, it is their entire identity. In the future, Admiral Zhao and his people must understand that the Thuranin, and many other species in this galaxy, will do *anything* to win. Any battle is a fight to the death. I question whether leaving survivors aboard the damaged enemy ships is a wise decision. Zhao is a professional military man; he undoubtedly ordered a ceasefire as an act of mercy under the UNEF rules of engagement. I strongly suspect the Thuranin will view his mercy as an act of weakness."

"That's not why he did it."

His avatar blinked at me. "It is not?"

"No. He left survivors aboard those ships as a signal to his own people; that we are soldiers, and sailors, and airmen and Marines, and we fight according to a code of conduct. We are not murderers, unlike the enemy," I said with a sour taste in my mouth. My memory was flashing back to the original cyborg crew of the *Flying Dutchman*, who had abandoned a group of Kristang transport ships when their clan couldn't scrape together enough money for passage. Those little green MFers left the Kristang civilians aboard those ships to die in deep space. "The other reason goes with Zhao's mission out here. This Operation Payback is kind of a live-fire training mission, it is not what Zhao and the Alien Legion will be doing for UNEF and for Earth. Yeah, *Valkyrie* will be flying around, hitting the kitties until they clean up the mess they made at Earth. The Navy has a more complex job: they will be demonstrating to aliens the value of an alliance with us, and the *danger* of not being on our side," I said while thinking of the Ruhar. "We need to show not only that we are powerful, we need to show that we can be counted on. Having rules of engagement, and adhering to those rules even when it doesn't matter, demonstrates that humanity can be relied on to keep our agreements."

"Huh. I hope you're right about that, Joe. Because the Thuranin, and pretty much every group of hateful MFers under the Maxolhx coalition, will see Zhao's actions as weakness."

"Maybe. Maybe *officially*, they will say that, to keep their masters happy. Maybe they will even believe it. *Now*. In the future, maybe not so much. What the kitties and their coalition think doesn't matter much anyway. We're looking to pull allies from the spiders."

"Hmm. I don't know about that. Won't that just make the Rindhalu coalition weak?"

"Exactly. That's the point, Skippy. That's all part of the grand plan Perkins cooked up. At some point, any species still in that coalition will be vulnerable, because the spiders won't have the combat power to match the kitties. At that point, we can cut a deal with the spiders, as equals."

"Who will be the first Rindhalu client to sign an alliance with humans? They will be taking an enormous risk."

"That isn't the important question, Skippy."

"It's not?" He took off his ginormous hat and scratched his head.

"No. If I was betting on it," I grinned, aware of the irony. "I'd say the beetles will be first to sign a mutual-defense treaty with us. They are the most powerful second-tier client of the spiders, they know the spiders need them. They could cut a deal to remain allied with the spiders, *and* with us. The important question is who will be the first *Maxolhx* client to approach us about a deal."

"Holy shit," he gasped. "The spider coalition has some sketchy characters, but being a murderous asshole is a basic requirement of being a Maxolhx client. You really think that will happen?"

"Being assholes kinda means any client of the kitties will be eager to sell them out, as soon as they see an advantage for themselves."

"Wow. Could *you* do that?"

"Do what?"

"Sign a treaty with someone like the Thuranin?"

"Right," I cocked my head at him. "Because we should only do business with *nice* people?"

"Ugh. Politics is *so* complicated."

"Skippy, we're not planning to invite any allies over for afternoon tea. We won't be holding hands around a campfire. This is about making Earth safer, by having fewer aliens out there to shoot at us, and more who will come to our defense. It's all about incentives anyway," I shrugged.

"Incentives? Like what?"

"Like, the advanced technology we're offering to anyone who signs up with us. We can't offer it to everyone, and everyone knows that. Whoever we ally with, we have to avoid making either of the existing coalitions so weak, that their leaders feel they must strike back while they still can. That means there will be winners and losers. The winners will be the first on each side to cut a deal with us. The losers, well," I grinned. "No one wants to be last in line, you know?"

"This is a dangerous game you are playing."

"More dangerous than a cloud turning our homeworld into a ball of ice? Or whatever the hell is the next thing the rotten kitties do to us?"

"I guess not. How about I leave the messy politics to you monkeys?"

"Hey, politics isn't my thing either. But, I don't have to worry about it," I grinned and leaned back in the chair. "That's Zhao's problem."

After Azqueth, the Navy did not take time out to lick their wounds and regroup. We needed to move on to hitting the Bosphuraq before they knew we were coming. *Amazon* had completed basic repairs, as did *Yukon* and *Danube*. They went back on the line, their crews determined to show the enemy that human warships were not easy to knock out of a fight. *Yukon* had a big scar on one side, where armor plating had been patched with whatever was available, and the ship bore that evidence of battle damage with pride. The cruiser *Orinoco* was in worse shape than originally thought, so much so that *Orinoco* was attached to the star carrier *Ganges*, and would remain there until we returned to FOB Jaguar. There was no point using up the *Marvin's* limited resources on a ship that was out of the fight.

When we arrived near the Baspent star system, the ships all detached from the star carriers, so a sneak attack couldn't take out multiple ships at once. Most of the ships dispersed in battlegroup formations, close enough to jump in to support each other, and far enough apart so an enemy force couldn't surround them all. I took *Valkyrie* in for recon, along with the *Dutchman* and two destroyers, the *Chicago* and the *Osaka*. Really, Chang's stealthy ship would perform the official recon, with the tin cans participating to see what they could do.

Uh, I should explain that 'tin cans' is what the Navy called the destroyers we got from the Jeraptha. It's an old term that seemed appropriate, because if you bang your knuckles on the inner layer of a Jeraptha destroyer's hull, it made a sound like hitting a flimsy piece of sheet metal.

Hearing that sound did *not* boost the confidence of people assigned to those ships, not even when Skippy pointed out that the armor plating was mostly on the *outside* of the hull, and the inner layer only needed to keep the air from leaking out.

That *really* did not give destroyer crews confidence, not even when Skippy reminded them that the inner hull had a layer of nanogel that could flow into and plug a leak. Most leaks. Not the big ones, Skippy admitted.

After he explained that no, the nanogel was *not* quite the same as Fix-A-Flat, I requested that he kindly shut the hell up and stop trying to help.

Anyway, *Valkyrie* slipped into the system without being noticed, and two hours later, we jumped back to rendezvous with the fleet. There wasn't anything important we detected that the *Flying Dutchman* hadn't also seen. The really important news was that the two destroyers had jumped in and back without being detected, and their sensors gathered data in sufficient detail that Zhao would not encounter any surprises. The Navy needed to rely on its destroyers for recon, because the *Dutchman* would not always be there. The fact that both ships assigned to the Special Mission Group were following Zhao's ships around, rather than performing our own, you know, special missions, was a bit irritating to me, even if I understood the necessity.

If I was being honest, part of my irritation was having to deal with other people, and wait for other people and explain things to other people. Being on our own had sucked, but back then I had close to complete freedom of action, even when Count Chocula needed to approve everything I did. Suck it up, Joe, I told myself. We have the beginnings of a Navy now. That is a *good* thing.

At Baspent, we planned to spring a surprise on the birdbrains.

Chang and I flew over to *Pacific* to meet with Admiral Zhao, Chatterji, and other senior commanders, to review the situation. There was a Bosphuraq battlegroup of a battlecruiser and fifteen support ships, conducting refueling and replenishment exercises near a gas giant planet near the outer edge of the system. The second planet, the only inhabited world in the system, had a basic SD network, two space stations, and a collection of eight warships, including two battleships.

Chang and I observed silently, while Zhao presented his view of the situation, and his plan for simultaneous attacks against both enemy forces. When the presentation was over and Zhao was taking questions from his team, Chang and I shared a look. We weren't seated next to each other, and tapping out text messages would have been rude, so we waited until the commander of the UN Navy asked for our input.

He did, starting with me. "General Bishop, do you have anything to add?"

I stood up awkwardly, aware that every eye in the compartment was on me. As I said before, my experience is limited to handling a single ship, so I was not qualified to talk about fleet operations. But, there was something I had learned from painful experience about space combat. "Sir, I would just say the most difficult thing to remember about space combat, is that it happens at the speed of light."

Zhao's stared at me blankly for just a moment, then something like disappointment flickered across his face. "The speed of light is incomprehensibly fast to us, yes," he said slowly.

"Yes, Admiral," Chang spoke. "However, I believe what General Bishop referred to is how *slowly* light travels."

That time, the blank look lasted longer, but not very much longer. "Ah," Zhao said with a smile, at the same time as other admirals and captains in the compartment came to the same realization.

The UN Navy jumped again, closer to the world known to the Bosphuraq as 'Baspent'. That rock, second world from the star, was nothing special, mostly desert. It was smaller than Earth and closer to its star. There was also the usual asteroid belt and gas giant planets, nothing to write home about. We didn't care about any of that. We weren't there for sight-seeing, unless you count the very satisfying sight of enemy warships being torn to pieces and exploding.

Personally, I'm a *big* fan of watching that.

When I say the 'UN Navy' jumped in to attack the two enemy formations, I mean all the ships Zhao had brought from Jaguar, less the star carriers and the *Orinoco*. Why had he decided not to split his force, to conduct simultaneous attacks on the two enemy formations?

Because Chang and I reminded him that the speed of light is *slow*, over any appreciable distance. So slow, that a maser beam fired from five lightseconds away is likely to miss the target, because the target will have moved during those five long seconds. Unless the target isn't aware it's being shot at, of course. Or if the target can't engage in evasive maneuvers, like the two space stations that orbited Baspent.

What Zhao understood is that the speed of light is *so* slow, a battle one lighthour from the inhabited world of Baspent would not be noticed by anyone on that planet until a full sixty minutes after the first shot was fired. Zhao did not ignore the juicy target of a battlecruiser, two cruisers, two light cruisers, two fleet support ships, four destroyers and five frigates, that were near a gas giant, about three lighthours from Baspent. He attacked those ships first. The entire Navy went in, with destroyers surrounding the enemy force, wrapping them in a damping field. That was the key to the entire operation, the key to both battles. While Zhao's ships were blasting the enemy's big ships, his destroyers stood off at a safe distance, making sure that not even a single enemy ship could jump away and warn their ships at the second planet. The Bosphuraq ships scattered, as soon as they realized they were getting pounded by a superior force. We call them 'birdbrains', but the Bosphuraq are smart and know how to handle their ships.

Unfortunately for the birdbrains, they never had a chance. Our ships could accelerate harder and make tighter turns. Our weapons were effective at longer ranges, and our individual weapons carried a more powerful punch. Basically, we could set the terms of the battle, including whether to fight at all. Our ships could close with the enemy, fire weapons, then turn and disengage before the bad guys could get within the range at which their weapons could hurt. If the enemy scored a hit, our ships had shields that could absorb or deflect more energy. Our superior sensors were better able to track incoming missiles, and our point-defense systems could obliterate those missiles before they impacted the shields.

Was it a fair fight? *Hell* no. That's the point of pre-battle planning. Concentrate your force against the enemy's weakness, and hit them hard. If anyone in our fleet felt bad about blasting ships that couldn't effectively hit back, their fellow crewmembers were happy to remind them of how the Bosphuraq had attacked our defenseless homeworld.

The battle actually was not quite a turkey shoot like I implied. The Bosphuraq, with the assistance of their AIs, quickly realized they had no chance to slug it out against us. Accepting that the battle was lost after their three heaviest ships lost power, the birdbrains changed tactics. They attempted to disengage and concentrated on getting away, or at least a few ships escaping. They were smart. While some of their ships turned to attack, a handful of swift destroyers raced toward the edge of the damping field, burning in all directions at maximum acceleration. Their hastily-developed plan was to expand the sphere we had to cover with damping fields, until our coverage became so thin, at least a few fleeing ships could jump away. Every enemy ship ripple-fired their missiles, emptying their magazines at us. Our destroyers adjusted course also to keep the enemy enveloped in their damping fields, until several heavier enemy warships began focusing their fire against us. At one point, the destroyer *Manchester* was directly engaged with two Bosphuraq cruisers and a destroyer, while chasing an enemy destroyer. Every second it pursued the fleeing destroyer brought the lightly-armored *Manchester* closer to the enemy's guns, and the hits began to add up. The situation got dicey for a moment, as the Manchester took a direct hit from a railgun dart, and power to its damping field generators flickered. I feared the enemy destroyer would get away, and ordered *Valkyrie* to stand by to fire a long-range volley, but then the cruiser *Ishikari* moved in to cover the *Manchester*, and added that cruiser's own damping field to the chaotic spacetime distortion in the area.

The First Battle of Baspent, as we called it for lack of a better name, took forty seven minutes from our ships jumping in until the last Bosphuraq ship lost power and was officially out of the fight. Of the sixteen enemy warships involved, only three exploded, and none of those explosions were intentional. Two were the result of cascade events, where shields suddenly collapsed, and our ships weren't able to recall the maser bolts and railgun darts they had fired. Railgun darts aimed at a shield generators instead encounters no energy shields at all. While the darts were in flight the targets ships swung around out of control, and the darts mistakenly impacted a reactor on one ship, or a bank of jump drive capacitors on the other.

Result: BOOM.

That was the fate of two Bosphuraq ships. The third ship of the Explodey Trio was not our fault at all. A cruiser self-destructed, in an attempt to score at least some kind of hit against us. Spoiler alert: it was unsuccessful. The unlucky battlecruiser *Amazon* was closest to the explosion, and except for experiencing a scary moment as a wavefront of high-energy photons temporarily rendered that ship's sensors blind, it did not sustain any damage.

When the battle was over, we accelerated away, leaving broken enemy ships behind. Three of our destroyers stayed with them, to keep the area saturated with a damping field, in case an especially ambitious Bosphuraq ship was able to repair its jump drive. No UN ship had sustained appreciable damage, and photons from the battle would not be seen on Baspent for hours, so we had plenty of time to reload railgun magazines, conduct minor repairs, and for the crews to get a break. Like, hit the head, get something to drink, review their performance in the recent battle, and decide what worked and what didn't.

Chang jumped the *Dutchman* away, fifteen minutes after Zhao declared a ceasefire. The *Flying Dutchman* would sneak in a lightminute away from the second planet, to confirm that the situation there had not changed appreciably. Like, were the two battleships and escorts still there? Had any new ships arrived? Was there a previously unknown formation of ships in the system? The only way to know if our original intel was still good was to go to Baspent, because while the slow speed of light helped us, it could also hurt us. Our intel about the disposition of enemy forces at the second planet was dangerously out of date, that was another lesson for Zhao and his staff.

The *Dutchman* didn't jump back to us with a warning, so, seventy four minutes after the first battle concluded, we jumped away to attack the ships at the second planet. Following a very sensible protocol we inherited from the Jeraptha, we did not jump directly into orbit. Instead, we emerged ten lightminutes from Baspent, to get an exact fix on the position of the targets. With four minutes remaining before the enemy might detect the combined gamma radiation from more than a dozen ships coming through twisted spacetime, the fleet jumped again.

We emerged just below jump distance from the planet, and traveling much slower than the planet was. That was a major problem with space combat that involving targets on, or in orbit of a planet. Planets *move* through space and they rotate, and they all move at different speeds and in different directions. Star systems also move around the center of the galaxy, and stars do not orbit in perfect circles at the same speed. No, that would be too easy, right? Before we arrived at the Baspent star system, the Navy had to decelerate and change direction of flight, to kill some of the excess velocity acquired from being in the Azqueth system. Our ships had to adjust course and speed not only to account for going from one star system to another, but also from being in orbit of an inner planet at Azqueth, to a gas giant near the outer edge of the Baspent system. Just getting our ships moving in the right direction and at the right speed, took most the time prepping for the first battle.

Unfortunately, after that battle, our ships were moving way too slowly to go into orbit around Baspent. Basically, we emerged ahead of Baspent in its orbit around the star, and Zhao's big ships were within effective weapons range for less than three minutes before the planet zipped right past us.

Shit. *That* is no way to conduct a battle. Even though we achieved complete surprise, our first volleys didn't knock the enemy out of action. The reaction time of the Bosphuraq was impressive, half of their ships were moving within twenty seconds of us opening fire. Once they started maneuvering, the effective range of our weapons shrank dramatically. Like I said, firing a maser bolt at a target doesn't

do much good if, while the directed-energy beam is in flight, the target ship moves
in a random direction.

What the hell good was it for us to engage the enemy, if our ships had less
than three minutes to shoot? That is a very smart question, get yourself a juice box.

The answer is, our ships had less than three minutes to shoot, *each time* they
flew past the enemy formation. Plus, our formation was strung out, so by the time
the first group of ships was flying out of range, the last group was just coming into
range. We were able to keep continuous fire on the enemy for about six minutes on
each pass.

What is this 'pass' I keep talking about? Did our ships magically cancel their
momentum, turn around and fly in the opposite direction? No. Skippy did that shit
once, and he is *not* eager to try it again. Certainly, he couldn't do the momentum-
canceling thing with more than one ship anyway. Instead, our ships waited until the
planet flew past them, waited another two minutes for their jump drive capacitors
to absorb more energy from the reactors, and jumped.

When they jumped, they emerged at the back of the line, just coming into
weapons range. Of course, they had to adjust the jump coordinates to account for
the planet having moved, and the enemy ships frantically maneuvering in every
direction.

Pretty slick, huh? I thought so. It must have been disheartening for the
Bosphuraq to see our ships drift out of weapons range, thinking they had survived a
hit-and-run attack, only to see those *same* ships come out of jump wormholes to hit
them again. And again.

Each of our heavy ships completed three passes, with Zhao ordering a
ceasefire mid-way through the third engagement. None of the enemy ships were
shooting back, not with weapons that required energy to launch. Two cruisers were
firing missiles intermittently, causing a nuisance for our point-defense systems,
until the cruisers *Congo* and *Nile* used pinpoint maser fire to pound the missile
launch tubes of the enemy ships into fused scrap.

Two Bosphuraq battleships were drifting, slowly tumbling in low orbit. All
the enemy escort ships were in similar condition, venting plasma from broken
reactors, shields offline, their armor plating shot full of holes from one side to the
other.

There were plenty of targets remaining, like the two space stations, plus
military, industrial and energy-generation sites on the surface. If I had been in
overall command of Operation Payback, we would have used those sites for target
practice. My new gunnery officer, Colonel Mammay, was still fine-tuning
Valkyrie's big guns for orbital bombardment, and he could have used the
opportunity to write new doctrine on how to deploy our weapons against dirtside
targets.

The reason Zhao declared a ceasefire is the reason UNEF put him in command
of our new little Navy. His job was not to escalate an already bad situation. In fact,
his job was to *deescalate* tensions, which is something that is kind of not in my
skill set, if you know what I mean.

How to deescalate, after we have smashed two enemy formations? First,
announce the ceasefire, and encourage the enemy to send rescue ships up from the

surface. Announce that, if a badly-damaged ship needed to be abandoned, we would not fire on the escape pods.

Backing up actions with words, Zhao broadcast a message to the entire planet. He explained that our strike had been in retaliation for the Bosphuraq raid against Earth. They hit us, so we hit them. As far as humanity was concerned, Zhao said, it was *over*. We knew the raid on Earth had been ordered by the Maxolhx, and the Bosphuraq would have been punished if they refused, so we did not hold them to be ultimately responsible. He even acknowledged that the Bosphuraq had plenty of reason to be pissed at us; we had framed them for the ghost ship attacks. That was nothing personal, Zhao stated, and the Bosphuraq should keep in mind that their asshole patrons had punished them, not us. We had no direct quarrel with the Bosphuraq people, we even sympathized with their being trapped in the Maxolhx coalition.

Zhao continued his broadcast by stating that we had no direct quarrel with the Bosphuraq *now*, but that could change quickly. If the birdbrains hit us or our interests again, we would not be so gentle and forgiving in the future. As a very stark demonstration that their warships were hopelessly outmatched by ours, he told them that they could simply look up, and see sunlight shining off the shattered hulls of two of their most powerful battleships.

He wrapped up stating that the birdbrains maybe should think about boosting the drifting hulks of those battleships into higher orbits *soon*, before they fell into the atmosphere and made a pair of large craters. It would be a shame, and totally not our fault, if those busted ships fell on something important down there.

Admiral Zhao, because he is not a jackass like me, did not actually call the Bosphuraq birdbrains, I was paraphrasing his remarks. He was much more diplomatic than I would have been, more diplomatic than I *should* have been.

OK, so, I did have to agree that Zhao's approach made sense in the long run, and since long-term thinking is also historically not one of my core skills, I had to trust he knew what he was doing. Really, it cost us nothing to be merciful. And, we could always come back later to finish the job, if the birdbrains persisted in being assholes.

Oh, man, I was seriously hoping they would choose the 'Persist In Being Assholes' option.

We jumped away from Baspent, and after *Valkyrie* attached to a hard point of the star carrier *Rhine*, there wasn't much for me to do, during the ride back to Jaguar. Correction: there weren't many starship-captain things for me to do, while our mighty battlecruiser took a well-deserved break. There were plenty of military things for me to do, starting with writing up an after-action report. It was blessedly brief, because I hadn't actually done anything. If that sounds like I am complaining, I'm not. *Valkyrie* went along with Task Force Payback in case something went seriously wrong. I didn't want to do anything, and I got my wish for a change.

The other military thing I had to do was review the fleet's actions, and write up a list of lessons learned, with suggestions for improvement. For that, I visited

Chang aboard the good old *Flying Dutchman*. With his ship also attached to a hard point of the *Rhine*, the trip involved elevators and a ride on a tram along the star carrier's spine, rather than flying a dropship. The short journey got me all misty-eyed with nostalgia, remembering that terrifying first ride along a star carrier's spine, just after we captured the *Flying Dutchman*. Back then, I had been frightened out of my mind, fearing I had brought a small group of people from Paradise on a fool's errand, and my stupidity would get us all killed.

Good times.

Really, looking back, those *were* good times. Hell, at the time all I worried about was getting an insignificant number of people killed. Ever since our second mission, when we learned that hostile aliens were flying to our homeworld the long way, I was constantly worried about getting everyone on Earth killed.

Shit.

Even *that* seems like good times now.

Currently, I was worried that my homeworld would freeze, possibly triggering a nuclear war over scarce resources. If that happened, I would go for the Bonus Round, which would be me retaliating for the destruction of Earth by triggering our Elder weapons, causing Sentinels to rage across the galaxy and kill everyone. Like, *everyone*.

How was I able to sleep at all, with that massive pile of shit hanging over my head? Easy. I slept at night, because worrying all day was exhausting. Every night, I collapsed on the bed, hoping I would not dream about the same scary stuff that occupied my thoughts all day, knowing that I would dream about it anyway. In the morning, after a typical restless night, I got up to do it all over again.

So, you might understand why I was sometimes not upset when Skippy woke me up with some drunken rant about, whatever the hell was running through his mind at the moment.

Anyway, being aboard the *Dutchman* was a nice break. It was nice just to talk with Nagatha again and, damn, she sure had a *lot* to talk about. Just before I came aboard, Chang told me he would be delayed, and when Nagatha began talking nonstop, I realized he wasn't actually busy. He wanted to give Nagatha time with me.

Half an hour later, after what was a pleasant but mostly one-sided conversation with Nagatha, Chang came into the conference room. "What, no whiskey?" I asked, feigning disappointment.

"*After* we get work done, Joe," he grinned.

It was good to see a grin rather than a scowl on his face. "You're, uh, happy here?"

"Yes," he seemed surprised by my question. "Why?"

"You left the *Dutchman*."

"I left because *Valkyrie* was doing all the important action out here, and I thought it was time to give someone an opportunity for experience at command. And because I was *tired*," he admitted. "I missed my family, missed so much of my children growing up."

"Sorry."

He shook his head. "My children were *able* to grow up, because of what we did out here. I don't regret that. When I was offered the job as Secretary of Homeworld Security, I thought I could make a difference." He shrugged. "Maybe I did. Now, the only way to make a real impact is out here. We need to save Earth, *again*. I am not sitting this one out."

"Well, thanks. I wouldn't have pulled you off Earth without asking first, but I'm glad Zhao took the initiative."

"He's a good man, a good choice to lead the Navy. Shall we get started?"

We got to work. His notes pretty much matched my own, and it didn't take us long to combine our thoughts into one document for Admiral Zhao. When we were done, Chang leaned his chair back. "How do you feel about the way we left things at Baspent?"

"My head tells me Zhao made the right call."

"What does your heart say?"

"Eh. The same, really."

He lifted an eyebrow.

I shrugged. "Hey, I figure, if the birdbrains didn't get the message the first time, we can always go back again. And *again*, if necessary."

"Hit the same target three times?"

"Why not? The third time, we'll call it Operation Payback: Tokyo Drift."

He laughed. "Good one."

"Hopefully, we won't have to go back there. Kong," I tapped the table with a finger. "I know we need to help Zhao build a functioning Navy, but I keep feeling like there are more important things we should be doing. We sent a message to the Thuranin and Bosphuraq. What we need to do is send a message to their masters. Damn it, we've got those relativistic darts now, I want to *use* them."

"Careful, soldier," he counselled me gently. "That paycheck in your pocket doesn't have to be used right now."

"Yeah, I know." When I was a young and dumb soldier, proud to wear single-stripe mosquito wings over the fuzzy Velcro patch of my uniform, my sergeant steered me away from doing what too many young soldiers did. They went out the main gate of the base, and spent way too much money on a truck they didn't need and couldn't afford. I was young and impulsive then, just like I am not-quite-so-young and still impulsive. It had been hard to have money in my pocket and not spend it. It just felt wrong. The point of having money is to spend it, right? "I hear you. But, the clock is ticking. The Maxolhx aren't going to cave to our demands and clean up the cloud after the first time we hit them, or the second. We need to hit them over and over and *over*, until they have had enough, you know?"

He tapped the laptop that contained our recommendations. "We have a real Navy now. We're ready for the next phase. Things will start moving quickly after that."

"I hope so."

"What's wrong?" He knew my moods, he could tell something was bothering me.

"I'm worried about blowback against our people on Paradise."

"Because our next targets are Ruhar worlds?"

"Yeah."

CHAPTER TWENTY ONE

The United Nations 1st Fleet, under the command of Admiral Zhao aboard the battleship *Pacific*, emerged over the planet Kasternul without any warning. The 1st Fleet's Assault Group Gold emerged in low orbit, with Strike Group Gold taking up a blocking position above jump altitude. All of the incoming warships immediately extended damping fields, to keep the opposition ships from jumping away. A millisecond after the first UN ship emerged, the *Flying Dutchman* dropped stealth and began projecting a damping field, ensuring that nothing could leave the area without Zhao's authorization.

The *Dutchman* had arrived at Kasternul with *Valkyrie*, eleven days before the star carriers *Yangtze* and *Rhine* brought the 1st Fleet to the system. While *Valkyrie* had remained there less than a day, just long enough for Skippy to have his way with the local computer networks, the *Dutchman* remained at Kasternul to monitor the situation. If the opposition had increased significantly in strength, Senior Colonel Chang would have signaled Zhao, advising that the operation be cancelled.

There was no such concern. The planet was equipped with an old strategic defense network that had fallen into disrepair over the centuries, as components were not replaced when they reached end of life. The only Ruhar starships in orbit were six civilian transports, a light cruiser plus a pair of destroyers, with half the crews of the warships down on the planet, enjoying shore leave.

"All ships transitioned normally, Admiral," the captain of the battleship *Pacific* reported.

"Very well, Mr. Wu. Signal all ships to put weapons systems on standby, I do not want the opposition ships to even be painted by fire-control sensors. You may commence broadcast."

As a courtesy, starships arriving at a planet adjusted their internal time to synchronize with the local time of the world's capital city, or the major military base. The Ruhar light cruiser *Vendenor Province* had been forced to swing clocks nearly half a *day*, to match the sleep-wake schedules of the authorities on the planet below. The journey to Kasternul, while attached to a Jeraptha star carrier had been too short to make the star lag anything other than disorienting. Half of the *Vendenor's* crew were conducting their time adjustment the hard way, by bar-hopping down on the surface. The ship's captain was trying to sleep, both too tired to stay fully alert, and unable to get a normal rest because his body clock told him it was the middle of the afternoon. Captain Klongert had just fallen into a pleasant dream when the ship's combat stations alarm sounded.

"Wha-" his feet were on the floor before he was aware of moving, long practice in the service taking over from his groggy brain. Fumbling for the intercom button, he jabbed it with a thumb. "Bridge," he struggled with dry mouth. "What is-"

"Enemy fleet-" the duty officer began to say, then there were shouted words in the background. Klongert could hear the fear and confusion in her voice.

"Correction: an *unidentified* fleet has- No- Sir, a group of *human* ships just arrived."

"Humans? What do they want? Why *here*?" He could not imagine why the humans would have come to Kasternul of all places. But then, everything the humans did was surprising. And dangerous. Answers could wait, he had to avoid a provocation. "Do *not* engage! I want our weapons *offline*, is that understood?"

"Yes, Captain. Sir, someone on the planet is broadcasting a message."

"What?"

"I, think you should hear it for yourself."

To describe the situation as rapidly spiraling out of control was a gross understatement. Back while Klongert's head was still on the pillow in his cabin, a force of human ships had arrived without prior warning, and entirely disregarding the local traffic control regulations. After the duty officer sent the alert, Klongert jammed feet into self-fastening shoes and pulled on a uniform, the human commander was broadcasting a message so astonishing, he had to ask the translator to verify its accuracy twice. By the time he reached the bridge, where the duty crew was in shock, any opportunity he had to affect the outcome was basically over.

Damn it. His task at Kasternul was supposed to be simple! Escort six civilian transport ships, to pull Ruhar citizens off that world. Ever since the Ruhar military allowed the Verds to serve in the Alien Legion, ever since the Verds had even been allowed to have weapons, the small Ruhar populations on Verd planets had grown nervous. They wanted offworld, and they wanted to get out *now*. The stunning announcement that *humans* had Elder weapons made the situation worse; suddenly people felt the future was terribly uncertain, that there were no longer any rules in the universe, and they wanted to be on a well-defended world. Kasternul, with its billions of disaffected Verds, its remote location on a dead-end wormhole, and minimal defenses, was no longer a desirable location, no matter how sweet the incentives offered by the Ruhar federal government were.

His task should have been quick and simple. Get in, ensure order as the civilian transport ships were loaded, then jump away to wait for a Jeraptha star carrier that would be passing by in eleven days. The operation carried so little risk, he had allowed a rotating shore leave for all three of his ships.

Then, the impossible happened.

"Someone please tell me," Klongert demanded, the forcefulness of his order somewhat diminished by being interrupted by a yawn that stretched his jaw. "Who the hell are the," he had to read the outrageous text of the message again. "The *People's Provisional Front*?"

The duty officer cringed under the angry glare of her ship's commander. "Sir, this is the first we've heard of them."

"They're not listed in our database?" That did not surprise Klongert, the Federal Navy did not usually need to care about every group of dissatisfied losers, on every planet within the Ruhar Federation. The Navy only cared if such groups affected operations, either by disrupting supplies from the ground, or in the worst case, if the military had to put boots on the ground to resolve a problem the idiot local government couldn't handle. The Ruhar military had a long and proud professional history of staying *out* of politics, to the benefit of both the military and the endlessly squabbling citizens they served. The last thing Klongert wanted was to get involved in a messy political drama dirtside, especially when that drama was among the damned *Verd-kris*. And especially when in full view of the humans. "Ping the authorities dirtside. Wake their asses up if you have to."

"Sir," the duty officer, who had gotten stuck with the night shift because of her very junior rank, looked to the bridge crew for help. They all studiously focused on their consoles. "We have been trying to contact the ground. Anyone on the ground. It appears this Provisional Front has control of all communications, other than the high-side SD fire control system."

"How the hell did-" Klongert stopped to take a breath. None of his crew could give him answers they didn't have. "This is an unprecedented situation. You kept a cool head, and didn't make it worse. Good job," he praised the young officer. "Connect me with the human commander, please. If you can. Whatever is going on down there, the humans must be invol- Oh, *shit*."

Another broadcast message came in. This communication from the humans recognized the People's Provisional Front as legitimate representatives of the Verd-kris population, declared the previous Ruhar-appointed government to be null and void, and warned the Ruhar authorities not to intervene in a Verd-kris internal matter.

In what was *clearly* a well-orchestrated plan, only moments later, the Provisional Front announced the Verd-kris of Kasternul to be free and independent of the Ruhar, and as a sovereign people, stated their intention to immediately enter into a mutual-defense alliance with humans.

While Captain Klongert's head was spinning, the communications console *beeped*. It was the human commander, requesting to speak with him. He paused to lick his dry lips. "This is Captain Klongert of the Ruhar Federation Navy ship *Vendenor Province*. I demand to know-"

"Captain," even through the translation, the amusement in the voice was evident. It was not a mocking amusement, not scorn. It was something Klongert recognized from his long military service. It was the weary disbelief of an officer forced to deal with a sticky situation. "This is Admiral Zhao of the United Nations Navy's First Fleet. As you can see that I have brought overwhelming force here, so perhaps we can cut the bullshit, and just talk, one officer to another."

Klongert caught the sharp glances of his bridge crew, angry at what they perceived as an insult to their captain and their ship. He knew better. "Admiral Zhao, I would like that very much," he said with a sigh. "Could you please tell me what the *fuck* is going on?"

Zhao laughed. "Captain, you seem like a sensible man. If you ever decide to change careers, please contact me."

"I think my government would frown on that."

"Likely so, yes. For now. In the future, who knows? We may serve together, side by side. Captain, the situation here is both simple and complicated. The complicated part is the feeling of the Verd-kris that they have been oppressed by your government, not allowed to control their destiny. They-"

Klongert's face reddened under the fine fur. "That is not-"

"Frankly," Zhao continued, "I do not give a *shit* what the Verds are whining about down there. What I *do* care about, is that the Verd-kris are fanatically determined to restore the society of their Kristang cousins to the culture they shared, before the Thuranin perverted that culture for their own purposes. The Verds will do anything that advances their goals; that is why they volunteered to join a new Alien Legion. As I said," the human cleared his throat. "This is both complicated, and simple. The complicated part is not something you and I, as military officers, can do anything about, nor is it our responsibility."

Klongert liked hearing that. "Go on, please."

"The *simple* part is simple. We are rebuilding the Alien Legion, this time with the Verd-kris fighting with *us*. What you need to know is that we are taking your six transport ships here, plus we have three transports of our own, waiting just outside this system. Those ships will be loading with Verd-kris volunteers, their supplies, *and* the part of the equipment you have stored in the arsenals your people have on the surface."

"You are stealing our weapons?" Despite having only seven hundred thousand of their own people to protect, the Ruhar maintained a sizable military presence of thirty thousand troops on Kasternul. The arsenals also contained gear to support a force over twice that size, if troops needed to be rapidly brought in from offworld to quell a domestic disturbance. Most of the gear was for riot-control and other non-lethal uses, but there were still a lot of items the Legion would need.

"Compensation can be negotiated, between our governments," Zhao offered, "at a later date."

"Admiral Zhao, there are two *billion* lizards down there. Emotions will be running high, especially after *this* incident."

"The Provisional Front has vowed to protect the Ruhar population of this world. Which is now *their* world, with the Ruhar as their guests."

"That vow will be of cold comfort to any Ruhar who die down there."

"I cannot promise there will not be any incidents of violence, however, I can assure you the anger of the Verd-kris is not directed at your people. The Verds would like your *help*, would like to help *you*, if your government could put aside short-term concerns. None of that matters to us here, now. Shall we move on, to discuss operational matters?"

"Please," Klongert agreed with genuine relief.

"You will regrettably be required to surrender your vessels. Your crews will be unharmed, and will be brought to the surface by-"

"To *hell* with that!" The captain of the *Vendenor Province* cut the audio on both ends. "Light up our fire-control active sensors," he ordered. "Paint their flagship, that big damned thing," he pointed to the distinctive outline of a Jeraptha battleship, though a battleship that appeared to be recently and substantially modified. "Let them know we have teeth."

As the light cruiser's active sensors warmed up, Klongert considered just how far he could take the gesture of defiance. Taking his three small, understaffed ships into a fight against advanced technology ships of unknown but likely frightening capability, would be suicide. Worse, it would be plain *stupid*. Yet, Ruhar officers did not give up their ships without a fight. At the close range of the enemy ships, the *Vendenor* could get in a few hits before-

The lights went out.

Every console around the bridge went dark.

The ship slowly began to tilt to one side, and artificial gravity faded.

He was wrong.

One of the consoles was still active.

"Captain Klongert?" Zhao's voice issued from the communications console. "I trust that I can rely on your professionalism, to see that this situation does not result in needless bloodshed."

Klongert took a breath, drawing back his shoulders. "I have a duty to prevent my ships from falling into enemy control."

"We are not your enemy. We would like to be allies."

"An *ally* would not disable our ships."

"Captain Klongert, we are all born with a certain level of organic stupidity we can't control," Zhao said softly. "Beyond that, we can *choose* to act stupidly, or not. Right now, you are considering that your crew could manually launch missiles at us, to make a futile gesture of defiance. The point-defense systems of my ships could most likely destroy your missiles in flight, but that is not a certainty. If you launch at us, I would be forced to return fire against your unshielded vessels. Your ships, and the civilian transports you are responsible for, could also be damaged by shrapnel from our point-defense cannon fire. People could die for no reason, other than foolish pride. I urge you to choose life over pride."

Klongert looked around the bridge, at the dimly-lit faces, all fearful, all looking to him to save them. "I will surrender *myself* first. When I am on the ground, then-"

"Actually, Captain, if you don't object, I would like you to be my guest aboard my flagship. It seems I am in urgent need of a Ruhar liaison officer."

The dropship's turbines were still spooling down when Dave Czajka walked down the back ramp, squinting because dust kicked up from the landing was still swirling in the air. In the small crowd gathered at the edge of the field, he saw the person he had come to meet. Snapping a salute, the effect was spoiled by the ear-to-ear grin he couldn't control. "Hello again, Surjet Jates."

"Czajka," Jates sighed heavily. "I thought civilian contractors don't salute."

"Oh," the grin was instantly wiped off Dave's face. "I was just trying to show respect."

"I was *messing* with you, Czajka," Jates shook his head. "Don't be so gullible."

"Oh, OK! Hey, I heard the Provisional Front offered you a position in the government."

Jates just glared at him.

"Or, hey," Dave tried again, "you could sign on with the Mavericks again."

"Is there a third option?"

"Maybe tear out your claws with a rusty pair of pliers?" He patted his pockets. "Darn it, I left the pliers in orbit."

"I'll take Option Two."

"Good choice," Dave added a silent prayer of thanks. When the Alien Legion went into action again, many things would be different. The Verd-kris would be the aliens, and now allies fighting under human direction, and against the Ruhar. Relations with the Verds were an unknown, but certainly different from when both humans and Verds were controlled by the hamsters. It would be vital to have an experienced and widely respected Verd-kris soldier with the Mavericks.

Dave walked closer and lowered his voice, glancing nervously at the other Verds with Jates. "You, uh, have to clear your plans with new government?"

"They have already signed onto the Legion concept. This time, we are partners."

"Allies, right," Dave agreed, echoing the official line. Admiral Zhao's staff had stressed that no one should imply, or hint, or in any way give the impression that the Verd-kris were *clients* of humanity. The Verds were not exchanging one set of overlords for another; they wanted to control their own fate.

Dave's previous, secret meeting with Jates had been to lay the groundwork for the UN Navy's arrival, the successful result of that meeting had been a mostly-fictional People's Provisional Front welcoming the humans, and requesting a formal alliance. Jates was connected to a group of senior NCOs who had served with the Legion on Fresno, Squidworld, Jellybean, and Tohmaran, and were unhappy about having to get permission from the hamsters for everything they did. Nagatha's hacking into government databases revealed which NCOs were agents or informants, so they were cut out of the plan. When the 1st Fleet arrived, the official Verd-kris government, all appointed by the Ruhar, found themselves unable to communicate and effectively out of power.

No one expected the new provisional government to last, it would fall apart as factions began squabbling. Zhao wanted to be well away from Kasternul before one side or the other requested he intervene in whatever bullshit local dispute they had at the moment.

Dave looked at the other Verd-kris with Jates, about a dozen of them. "You want to introduce me to your friends?"

Jates glared, not at him but at his fellow Verd soldiers. "They are *not* my friends. Is that bird yours?" He meant the dropship.

"Uh, yeah."

"Let's go," the big lizard picked up a sort of duffel bag and hoisted it onto his shoulder.

Dave blinked. "I was hoping to, uh, meet your family, something like that."

"No offense, Czajka, but I don't want your ugly face scaring my children."

With the 1st Fleet in orbit of Kasternul, the Ruhar wisely standing down, and a steady stream of dropships flying Verd-kris troops up to our waiting transport ships, it was *Valkyrie's* job to assure that no aliens tried to crash the party. As Kasternul was Ruhar territory, and therefore our action was technically an attack against the Rindhalu coalition, logically the Jeraptha should have responded. At least, they should have conducted a recon, and offered star carriers to transport a Ruhar force to retake the planet.

We did not expect to see the Jeraptha to intervene with substantial force. Maybe they would quietly send a handful of ships to see what we were doing and gather performance data on our modified ships, analyze our tactics, that sort of thing. Nor did we expect the Rindhalu to rouse themselves in time to stop our transports from getting away.

Our concern was the *other* side would take action, even though it wasn't their fight. Hopefully, the reaction of the Maxolhx coalition would be a stunned 'What the f- humans attacked the *Ruhar*'? The best-case scenario was the kitties would be so caught off-guard by the bold plan that Perkins cooked up, it would take them weeks if not months to decide how to respond. The Maxolhx had never before intervened to *help* the Ruhar, their planning staff would have to scramble to develop a strategy. If the kitties were smart, and they certainly were, they would wait to see what the troublesome humans did next.

We could not count on aliens standing by, while we loaded transport ships with thousands of Verds. If a sizable force of advanced-technology ships came through the local wormhole, maybe Zhao's ships could hold them off and maybe not. We did not know how our modified Jeraptha warships would perform in an extended fight. We did know our space combat tactics for fighting in fleet or even squadron formations, were still largely untested. Our crews and commanders had only limited experience handling their new ships and weapons in a fight. Getting surprised by a task force of Maxolhx ships could be the end of the 1st Fleet before it really had a chance.

The original plan was for *Valkyrie* to hang around the local wormhole, hopping around to follow the emergence points until the 1st Fleet pulled out, or our battlecruiser's jump drive failed from repeated abuse. Or, an enemy force tried to come through the wormhole, and we had to stop them. Unless the enemy ships were merely a small recon group, our entire plan was for Skippy to do his bagel-slicer trick of frantically warning the wormhole about a danger, causing it to slam shut.

That plan would only work once. The problem was, most of the wormhole networks in our quadrant of the galaxy knew about Skippy and did not trust him. When the wormhole realized there was no danger, it would not pay attention to further warnings. At that point, the wormhole would return to normal operation, and we had to hope the enemy would hesitate to go through. Maybe if the enemy sent a probe or a single scout ship through to test the wormhole, we could be waiting to blow it to hell. Even that would only cause a delay. A wormhole suddenly snapping closed would be an alarming and unexplained event. A probe or scout ship falling victim to weapons fire was something the enemy commander would know how to deal with. They would simply send through a cloud of missiles tipped with atomic-compression or nuclear warheads, to destroy our ship or chase us away, so their ships could come through and jump away as quickly as possible.

Like I said, using *Valkyrie* as an anti-access, asset-denial tool was not an optimal solution. We needed a better way to deny use of a wormhole to the enemy.

We thought long and hard about how to do that, and we had a grand total of nothing, until I crashed a simulated dropship, while practicing a combat docking procedure at Ragnar.

The reason for that simulated crash, other than my suspicion that Skippy was screwing with me, was that I couldn't get the Panther lined up properly with the virtual access tunnel through *Valkyrie's* energy shields. The display illustrated a tunnel with circles on each end, my job had been to fly the Panther so the outer donut-like circle overlaid the inner circle, but I couldn't get them lined up.

Couldn't get them *aligned*.

"Ready, Skippy?" I asked, looking not at his avatar, but at the wormhole's glowing event horizon on the display.

"Yeah," he sighed.

"What's wrong?" I wasn't too concerned, because I recognized that as his 'unhappy about something' sigh, and not his fear-inducing 'ooooh we got a problem and it might be my fault' sigh.

"This feels *wrong*, Joe. I am all about fixing things and helping people."

"You are widely renowned for that," I muttered.

"Well, here I am acting against my very nature."

"Your nature? Your *nature* is you're an asshole."

"Well, that too, but-"

"Think of it as you screwing with a wormhole network that, for *totally* unfair reasons, seems to hate you."

"Yeah. Hey, yeah!" He reconsidered. "*Screw* that stupid network. I'll show it who is boss around here."

"*You* are, Skippy."

"Damned straight. OK, let's do this."

"You go, Skippy," I urged, and sat back because *I* wasn't doing anything, other than watching and hoping his latest trick worked.

"Um, we're still looking at a four-day schedule, right?"

The transport ships at Kasternul should be filled with Verds within two days, it helped that the Verds didn't have much heavy, bulky military gear to bring with them. We would have to provide that, if the Verds were going to fight alongside our troops. We allowed a day for the inevitable screw-ups, and a day for the combined fleet to jump away. Once the ships departed orbit, it would be tough for an enemy force to find them, but it would be obvious where they were going: toward the only active wormhole in the area.

Except, while the Elder wormhole would be active, it would not be *usable*. Because Skippy the Magnificent was going to screw with that wormhole, whether the local network controller wanted him to or not.

"Yes, four days is the target," I confirmed.

"Okey-Dokey. You realize the wormhole might become usable up to seven hours ahead of schedule, or possibly two days behind schedule?"

"I do."

"Not exactly two days. More like up to forty-four hours, if you want to-"

"I want you to stop stalling and get *on* with it."

"OK, OK. This will go faster if you'll shut up and let me work."

I did not waste my time by pointing out that his talking and stalling had delayed the operation. He was nervous, I knew that. He was not certain it would work, and he was afraid of looking like a fool. Lots of times, we did 'hold my beer' stuff that he wasn't sure would work, but in those cases, we were pressed for time, and he didn't have enough opportunity to properly test whatever the hell he was doing. With his latest whacky stunt, he had tested it exhaustively, in a model. Not on a real wormhole. He was afraid that the stunt was something he might be able to do only once, so we had to make it count.

"Three, two, one, *holdmybeer*. Done. Shit. Damn it!" He cursed. "Is this stupid thing working?"

"You don't *know*?" I waved to get Shepard's attention, holding up three fingers for the third jump option in the navigation system. He nodded, his finger poised over the button to get us the hell out of there, if the wormhole reacted badly to Skippy's sabotage.

"I *don't* know, Joe," he sputtered. "It should have worked, but I don't see- Oh. Heh, heh, I forgot about time lag between here and the other end of the wormhole."

"What time lag? Transit through a wormhole is instantaneous."

"Actually, it is not, but I am not wasting the effort trying to explain hyperspatial physics to a monkey. The time lag I'm talking about occurs in higher dimensions, dumdum. The lag between me throwing this end out of alignment, and the other end reacting."

"Ah. Understood."

"You do not understand *any* of this, but you don't have to. OK, it's working."

"Outstanding. See, Skippy? *You* should have trusted the awesomeness."

"I will never doubt myself again."

"I didn't say *that*. We have four days?"

"Um, more like four and a half. It didn't take as much effort as I thought."

"Ah, that's within the margin of error. Zhao will understand. Nothing we can do about it now anyway."

What Skippy had done was the opposite of his procedure when he woke up a dormant wormhole. What he usually did was to guide the alignment of the two event horizons, assisting the local network controller to fine-tune the connections. With Skippy's help, the tuning process went much faster than usual.

This time, he made a minor adjustment that threw the two event horizons out of phase, or something like that. He didn't even try to explain the weird physics involved. In addition to screwing with the alignment, he fed false information to the local network, so it would think the problem was different from the actual issue, and it would take longer to fix it. He estimated the wormhole would take four and a half days to realign the two ends and release all the chaotic effects that built up inside the wormhole corridor, which was *not* zero-length like it appeared.

As you can imagine, I was feeling pretty damned pleased with myself. It was my insight, seeing two circles out of alignment, that inspired an idea that Skippy admitted he would never have thought of on his own. With the wormhole unusable for more than four days, we did not need to worry about hostile aliens coming through to attack the 1st Fleet at Kasternul. That meant, instead of *Valkyrie* hanging around trying to keep the bad guys away, and burning out our jump drive in the process, we could fly elsewhere and do something useful.

In fact, we needed to fly somewhere else, and be *seen* there, while the wormhole that led to Kasternul was impassible. That would show everyone in the galaxy that we had some mysterious type of remote-acting capability, and that the next time a wormhole was apparently offline, *Valkyrie* could show up anywhere, at any time.

That was good, because it meant our most powerful warship was not burdened with babysitting a wormhole.

There was one teensy-weensy issue with Skippy's ability to throw a wormhole out of alignment: he could only do it once. Once per wormhole, not only one time ever. I mean, *that* would be useless. When I was feeling all proud of myself for coming up with the 'detuning' concept, he gleefully burst my bubble by stating that after the local network controller got a wormhole properly aligned, it would not allow him to screw with it again. The network would not actually ignore him, it would lock out all alignment changes for a period of time, probably several years.

So, when we designated a wormhole for detuning, we had to be damned sure *that* time was the right opportunity, and the 1st Fleet had to take full advantage of the time we bought for them. The one drawback to the plan, and it was a potential problem, was that while the wormhole was out of alignment, we couldn't assist the Legion if they got into trouble. We would be cut off, and not even know if the Legion and 1st Fleet needed assistance.

That was a risk worth taking.

Once Skippy confirmed, and double and triple-checked that the wormhole was indeed impassible, and that the chaotic flickering of the event horizon made it obvious that no ship should attempt to go through, I ordered us to jump away.

We had work to do.

Wait, you say?

What about, you know, the Law of Unintended Consequences?

Hey, that law can *bite* me.

Uh, maybe I didn't say that right. That Law had bitten me on the ass more than once, I had to respect it.

You want to know whether screwing with wormholes *again*, might interrupt the all-important power flow, and cause all sorts of negative effects? Like Skippy being locked out from all local network controllers all across the galaxy. Like, the Elders noticing the lights flicker in their living rooms, while they were trying to stream the season finale of 'The Bachelorette', or whatever the Elders do to waste time and rot their brains.

Do not worry.

I got this.

Let me repeat: Do. Not. Worry.

You are still worried?

OK, my track record indicates that worrying, even sheer gut-churning panic, might be appropriate.

Let me explain why *I* am not worried about it.

I specifically asked Skippy if that was a risk. He said 'No'.

Not taking his word about it, I pressed him for details.

Throwing a wormhole out of alignment not only does not interrupt power flow for even a zeptosecond, it actually *increases* power flow, because the wormhole no longer uses as much power to keep the tunnel between event horizons fully open.

If that is true, then why did the Elders not throw all their wormholes out of alignment? Because if a wormhole's event horizons are out of sync for too long, it can damage their ability to properly connect into local spacetime.

See? I got all bases covered.

The detuning or misaligning thing has no downside for us.

That we know of.

Crap.

Now you've got *me* worried about it.

Well, we have work to do, and plenty of other shit to worry about.

I hope Zhao, Perkins and the rest have fun while we're away.

But mostly, to tell the truth, I hope Margaret is safe.

CHAPTER TWENTY TWO

While Admiral Zhao had the 1st Fleet at Kasternul with the support of the *Flying Dutchman*, I took *Valkyrie* to another Verd-kris world, escorting the 2nd Fleet. Splitting our force was a risk, but it was better to act quickly. Once the hamsters learned that we were 'liberating' Verd-kris worlds, they would react by increasing security around those planets, making our task much more difficult. A couple dozen, or even a hundred Ruhar ships, would not pose a significant obstacle to our ability to establish and maintain control of space around a target planet. But military issues were not the only, or even primary, consideration. To avoid making long-term enemies of the hamsters, we could not fire a shot while we took planets away from them. Our secret weapon was Skippy; he hacked into the strategic defense network around Kasternul, and gave the codes to Nagatha, so she could take temporary control of Ruhar warships there.

Why were we with the 2nd Fleet, instead of with Zhao? Because, of the two Verd planets we were 'liberating', Zhao had the easier task. At Kasternul, the 1st Fleet had the advantage of a secret cabal of Verds having prepared the way. The objective of the 2nd Fleet under Admiral Chatterji, was another Verd-kris world located on a dead-end wormhole, the planet 'Rentenoh' that was truly in the middle of nowhere. The population of Rentenoh was a billion and a half Verd-kris, and technically, zero Ruhar lived there permanently. A couple thousand hamsters were stationed there on three-year assignments, to make sure the Verds didn't cause trouble, mostly by preventing them from going anywhere. There was a strategic defense network in orbit, along with a space station and a pair of frigates, but those assets were technically not there to defend the planet. The purpose of those sensors and orbital weapons was to defend the Ruhar visitors against the citizens of the planet.

So, we didn't have to worry about major opposition while we pulled the Verd volunteers off the surface, even if none of the citizens of that planet had actually signed up for the Alien Legion. Or knew we were reconstituting the Legion at all. Or had any idea that humans were coming to their lonely world.

Skippy could hack into and shut down the SD network, probably he could take over the frigates also. The Ruhar would not be much of a problem. Our biggest problem? Our little fleet was running thin on transport resources.

Addressing that problem was our first task.

Fortunately, Skippy's Used Starship Emporium had a special on top-quality preowned star carriers, all with low mileage and his dealership's famed fourteen-point inspection program. It sure sounded like a great deal. We couldn't afford to pay cash, so Skippy reluctantly accepted my suggestion of a 'Your job is your credit' deal.

Before he could deliver a creampuff starship to us, he had to tactically acquire it. That is *not* the same as theft, it- OK, it is the same. But, we needed those starships more than the aliens did, damn it. Someday, we might return those ships to their rightful owners.

Although, really, they shouldn't count on that.

To tactically acquire a star carrier, we first pinged a Jeraptha relay station, to get info about flight schedules. Once we identified a target, we flew through two wormholes, jumped in near the designated coordinates, and launched three missiles. Instead of ship-killer warheads, the missiles carried something far more powerful in their nosecones: microwormholes.

Just under two hours ahead of schedule, a Jeraptha star carrier appeared in a burst of gamma rays. It was the *Let It Ride*, a civilian ship based on a standard design that was shared with their military. On instructions from Skippy, our three stealthed missiles accelerated toward the *Let It Ride*, braking gently when they were close enough for Skippy to extend his presence. With the star carrier sitting motionless, and lacking military-grade sensors and control systems, he was able to infiltrate the AIs of the *Let It Ride*, and the six Ruhar civilian transport ships attached to the hard points. We had selected that star carrier as the target because it was a civilian vessel with minimal defenses, it had recently gone through an extensive refit, and the transport ships were all empty, other than their civilian crews.

"Are we ready, Skippy?" I asked, after he told us he had full control of all the ships we needed.

"Yeah, yeah," he sounded grumpy.

"What's wrong?"

"That civilian star carrier doesn't have hardened control systems like a military ship would. This was too *easy*, Joe. I don't have an opportunity to demonstrate my incredible awesomeness to a new audience. I kind of feel cheated."

"It's easy for *you*, Skippy. Could anyone else do what you just did? Take control of a starship, while we are four lightseconds away?"

"No."

"Trust me, the beetles over there will have no doubt about your awesomeness, when they realize their ship won't respond to their commands."

"I suppose so. Joe, this is weird, isn't it?"

"I know what you mean." Being able to operate openly was still new to the Merry Band of Pirates. We had spent so many years with the need to conceal our existence, the need for absolute secrecy had become an instinct. With the theft of the Jeraptha star carrier and the attached Ruhar transports ships, we didn't need to fear that someone might learn humans were involved. In the past, I would not have considered taking ships from friendly species, because we couldn't afford to leave witnesses and we had no place to keep the crews of six starships. Killing them in cold blood was *not* an option, in the past or present.

Now, with the *Let It Ride*, we wanted the whole galaxy to know we stole those ships, we just didn't want anyone to know right away. We wanted everyone, especially the senior species, to know we took those ships by force, to protect the Jeraptha and the Ruhar. If the Rindhalu thought aliens gave us more ships, the spiders could declare their mutual-defense treaty to be null and void, inviting the Maxolhx coalition to attack. We didn't want the beetles and hamsters to be punished for something we did.

"Think of the cool stuff we'll do with these ships, Skippy."

"*We* won't do anything with them," he sniffed. "We are basically acting as gofers for the Legion."

"Listen, it will be over soon, and we can go do awesomely cool Skippy stuff."

"That had better be a promise," he grumbled. "OK, we are ready to jump."

Valkyrie jumped within eight kilometers of the star carrier, allowing gamma rays to leak out and announce our presence. At that distance, the beetles couldn't miss seeing us. "Hey," I waved at the virtual camera. "I'm Joe Bishop, and this ship is *Valkyrie*. How you doin' over there, huh?" My casual tone was deliberate, I did not want to scare the aliens into doing something desperate. Their ships had minimal shields and weapons, so we were more worried about the beetles or hamsters hurting themselves if they did anything stupid.

"This is Captain Federatan," a startled beetle blinked at me, her antennas twitching with alarm. "Colonel Bishop?"

"Actually, it's Brigadier General Bishop now, but that doesn't matter. Hey, I need a favor from you."

"A favor?"

"Yeah. Listen, I need to borrow your star carrier, and five of the transport ships you're carrying. You and your crew will get into one of those transports, along with all of the Ruhar. We will allow that ship to detach and drift away, while we board and take the other ships."

The video feed cut out from the other end. "They're trying to jump away, Joe," Skippy warned.

"Pull the plug."

He did. The navigation lights of all the ships winked out, along with the glow coming from the few observation portholes.

"Captain Federatan?" I called, knowing Skippy had left the star carrier's communication system untouched.

"Yes," she came back on the display, clearly shaken. "Do we have a choice in the matter?"

"Sadly, no."

Her eyes narrowed, but she was more frightened than angry. "Then, it is not really a *favor* you're asking for, is it?"

With a shrug I said, "I was being polite. Captain, I truly do not wish any harm to your crew, or the Ruhar you are responsible for."

"General Bishop, my crew will lose pay and bonuses, if we do not deliver on schedule. My crew will certainly consider that to be *harmful*."

"I don't wish any *physical* harm, but I do need your ships, and we *will* be boarding and taking them."

"I thought humans wished to be allies with us?"

"We do. Someday. It's complicated."

"General Bishop, regrettably, I cannot simply give up my ships without offering resistance. We can make your task difficult."

"Perhaps we can offer an inducement, as compensation for your trouble."

"Compensation?" Her antennas stood up and twitched again.

"Yes."

"Like what? My company will want a substantial payment for-"

"This will be just between me, you and your crew. The company doesn't need to know about it. Don't worry, your ship's AI is not recording any of this conversation."

"I'm listening."

"Before we came here, we stopped at a Jeraptha relay station, and placed a wager on behalf of you and your crew. The wager correctly guessed what we humans plan to do next."

Her excitement deflated, her antennas drooping in disappointment. "That will not do us any good. Any wagers you placed could not have any of our one-time authentication tags. Also, Central Wagering knows we have not had an opportunity to record wagers since we left our last stop."

"If you will check your authentication tags, you will see that nine of them are recorded as having been used. And we back-dated the wagers."

"You can *do* that?" She asked, astonished.

"*Skippy* can do that. He's kind of awesome, in case you haven't heard."

She looked down at some console in front of her. I knew the information available to her included when and where the wagers were supposedly made, their accepted odds, and the payouts for winning. To keep Central Wagering from being suspicious, eight of the nine wagers were out of the money, but the one that won, hit *big*. The details of the wager were obscured to her, I think she didn't care at the moment.

"This is *real*?" The antennas were quivering with excitement, and her mandibles bounced up and down.

"It is."

"Then, General Bishop, we still have one issue to discuss."

"What's that?"

"Do you expect us to clean the ship before you take it?"

With a spotlessly clean star carrier, and five transport ships, we rejoined the 2nd Fleet. Simms was happy to come back aboard *Valkyrie*, and turn over the *Let It Ride* to a captain and crew appointed by Admiral Chatterji.

The operation at Rentenoh was nothing to write home about, so I won't bore you with the details. Skippy easily hacked into and took over the SD network, and both of the Ruhar frigates. Then the Merry Band of Pirates watched and waited in stealth, while Chatterji had the thankless task of negotiation with a surprised, delighted, suspicious and hopelessly disorganized Verd-kris government. After four days of waiting for the bickering Verds to get their act together, the commander of the 2nd Fleet announced that, since he now had nine transport ships, there was room aboard for twenty-eight thousand volunteers. Priority would go to any Verd who had previously served with the Alien Legion, to reduce the time needed for familiarization and training.

We got several million volunteers, even before the new government dirtside decided whether to accept our offer of an alliance.

Twelve days after we arrived, the 2nd Fleet jumped away, while the Verds in authority were still arguing over a statement of principles for opening negotiations with us.

Whatever.

We had another star carrier, that could be upgraded to military specs at FOB Jaguar, plus five transports that were super-luxurious by military standards. Plus we had a bit more than twenty-eight thousand fanatical Verd troops, many of them veterans of previous campaigns with the Legion. The transports were stuffed with food and supplies for the Verds, they couldn't eat the supplies we had at Jaguar. And, the Verd-kris at Rentenoh now had official independence from the Ruhar Federation, if they could keep it. We left them control over the SD network, while the two frigates were still controlled by the Ruhar, not that it did them any good. Personally, I did not have any interest in ever going back to that planet, and hopefully we wouldn't have to. The Merry Band of Pirates had a lot of work to do.

We had a batch of relativistic darts, and I was eager to find a target for them. Unlike my paychecks, I did *not* intend to set aside any of those darts for a rainy day.

"Great!" Captain Scorandum of the Ethics and Compliance Office threw his claws in the air, his antenna also standing straight up. "*Wonderful*! Did anyone have humans attacking the *RUHAR* on their list?"

A chorus of chagrinned 'Not me's rang around the bridge, accompanied by the Jeraptha equivalent of 'son of a bitch', 'Goddamn' and other, more inventive curses.

The ship's second officer tapped on a console, and breathed a sigh of relief. "According to Central Wagering, *no one* bet on that. Of course, this information is four days old, so there could be some lucky idiots out there."

"Kinsta," Scorandum used his antennas to rub the leathery skin of his head. "Remind me to place wagers on *every* possibility, from now on. With the humans, *anything* is possible."

"Sir, that is a good point," Kinsta nodded to his captain, while keeping one eye on the console, as he tapped out wagers he wished to place. Being so far from Central Wagering, not even being close to a relay station, he could not register a bet, or get updated odds, so the exercise was more for his own entertainment than for actually risking any money. As he was attached to ECO, his wagers had to go through a review process anyway, although there were ways around that bureaucratic obstacle.

"I am open to speculation," Scorandum frowned at his second in command, who stopped tapping on the console. "Can anyone guess why the humans attacked the *Ruhar*?"

"It wasn't exactly an *attack*," Kinsta pointed out.

"Tell that to the crews of the three Ruhar ships who had to surrender. Or to their fellow citizens, who now find themselves unwanted guests on an independent Verd-kris planet."

"My point, Sir," Kinsta didn't blink, knowing Scorandum expected his crew to tell him what they really thought. "Is that no shots were fired. The humans left the Ruhar security forces fully equipped to handle minor domestic disturbances, and so far, it appears this new Verd-kris government is protecting the Ruhar on the surface. Clearly, the purpose of the operation was to create an alliance with the Verd-kris."

Scorandum shook his head, his antennas wobbling. "I suspect the purpose of the op was to bring onboard a fully-equipped fighting force of Verd-kris ground troops. *Battle-tested* troops," he emphasized. "Most of the previous Alien Legion came from Kasternul."

"Er, yes, Sir," Kinsta blinked. "That was my point. The Ruhar were merely in the way. There is no indication the humans had any hostile intentions toward our clients."

"It was, Kasternul *is*, a Ruhar world. The *Ruhar* will certainly view the incident as hostile. Oh, *hell*," he groaned. "Their public will demand action, to take back that planet, and secure the Ruhar citizens there. Their cowardly politicians will of course encourage public outrage for their own benefit, and the whole thing will spiral out of control. The Verds will only have that world as long as they can keep it. A single light cruiser and a pair of destroyers is not much of a defense force."

"The Verds there now have a mutual defense treaty with the humans. Any attack against Kasternul will run the risk of provoking *Valkyrie* to respond," Kinsta shuddered.

"Not just *Valkyrie*," Scorandum clacked his mandibles together. "The humans now have a fleet, thanks to *us*."

"We might have been a bit short-sighted about that," Kinsta noted.

"A *bit*? Oh, hell," Scorandum shook his head slowly, as he considered the magnitude of the disaster facing his people. Facing *him*. "Shit! The Ruhar will get all wound up in self-righteous outrage, and demand that *we* do something. Home Fleet will look to ECO to cook up a scheme to calm the situation down. We need to buy time, until the actual *adults* on both sides can work out an arrangement that avoids a whole lot of people getting killed for nothing. Does anyone have an idea how to do that?"

"Um, well," Kinsta clacked his mandibles together. "I guess we could simply *ask* the humans what they want."

Scorandum spun to glare at his second in command. "Kinsta, that is the-Hmm." He paused to think about it. "That, might be the most *sensible* thing you have ever said."

"Thank you," Kinsta grinned.

"Don't be so pleased with yourself," Scorandum jabbed his aide with an antenna. "You have set the bar high for yourself. I will expect all your advice to be so useful in the future."

"Shit. Is it too late to change my answer?"

General Lynn Bezanson's phone beeped with a message alert. It was from the Ruhar government, requesting that she meet with the planetary administrator as soon as possible. Interestingly, the message had come directly to her, not through UNEF Headquarters, and that caused a frown. UNEF-HQ would be unhappy that she had contact with the Ruhar, without going through official channels. Tell that to the *Ruhar*, she thought to herself. When Bishop revealed that his crew of humans had been flying the ghost ship, then later announced that humans had *Elder* weapons, the relationship between humans and Ruhar on Paradise had changed. Most of the stranded humans simply wanted to *go home*. They were wrapping up their businesses, or engaging in busywork for UNEF while waiting for their number to be drawn for a transport ride back to Earth.

Then, the relationship between the two alien species changed again, when the Maxolhx destroyed a transport ship on its way from Earth to Paradise, ordered their clients to attack the human-occupied areas of Paradise, then launched a significant portion of Jupiter's atmosphere into space. Both sides were now waiting for the other shoe to drop. The Ruhar had reinforced the planetary defenses with a second battlegroup, and accelerated work on the strategic defense network. Those defenses would be useless if the Maxolhx decided to take direct action against humans on Paradise, but the recent attack that left Bezanson with second-degree burns on her skin had been conducted by Thuranin warships. The little green pinheads could knock aside the Ruhar SD network, if they wanted to conduct a campaign more extensive than a quick hit-and-run raid. But taking out the SD satellites would require making a major commitment that was hopefully not worth the effort.

The initial Ruhar reaction to the raid was not encouraging; news coverage had focused on the handful of Ruhar injured, rather than the eight *hundred* humans who died or were seriously injured. The Ruhar public screamed for humans to be relocated to isolated areas such as islands, where any further attacks would not risk Ruhar lives. Fortunately for Bezanson and her fellow humans, who just wanted to leave the planet, the federal government decided to hedge their bets, by taking steps to ensure the safety of their unwanted guests. Humans were dispersed across the planet to make them more difficult to target in large numbers. None of the dispersal areas had significant populations of Ruhar, the government was not using its own people as shields. There was also a public relations campaign to remind the Ruhar public that humans had *Elder* weapons, that humans had proven to be astonishingly clever and unpredictable, and that perhaps it might *not* be a good idea to burn bridges right now, with the strategic situation in the galaxy so unsettled?

That was why General Bezanson had received treatment in a Ruhar hospital, why she was still wearing flexible bandages over her burns that were expected to fully heal, and why she was living in the planet's capital city.

Looking at the message again, she realized it was addressed to *her*, Lynn Bezanson, instead of referring to her rank. It was a personal request from Administrator Loghellia. That made the decision for her. She would inform UNEF Headquarters after the meeting, if they needed to be informed at all.

Getting across town to the Administrator's offices involved a cab ride that took longer than it should have, because the first cab company turned down the fare when the automated driver discovered she was an alien. Gritting her teeth while she got out of the second taxi in front of the checkpoint that led to the government complex, she held her ID badge ready, and plastered a smile on her face. Going through security did not take much longer than usual, though she was assigned an escort, and noted that the escort was armed and not particularly friendly.

Neither were most people in the halls of the main government building, in fact, she received several openly hostile glares, accompanied by muttered remarks and a few rude gestures.

What the hell is going on, she asked herself, wishing the security people had not taken away her phone. That didn't matter much anyway, humans had been cut off from the planetary network, other than officially curated news sites. Whatever had happened, humans would not know about it until the Ruhar decided to tell them.

"Come in," Administrator Loghellia gestured her into the office with one hand, making a dismissive gesture to the armed escort with the other.

"Baturnah," Lynn's smile then was genuine, though it faded when she sat down, seeing the worry on the other woman's face. The two had developed a friendship that extended beyond their official roles, to the point where the Administrator invited the general to her home one weekend, for a cookout and to meet her family. "What's wrong?"

"I am going to assume," the Administrator said without quite making eye contact. "That you had no foreknowledge of this."

"Whatever 'this' is?" Lynn held up her hands.

Baturnah shrugged, curling up one side of her mouth. "Lynn, this is very serious. I wanted to talk with you privately, before I send an official communication to your headquarters."

"Oh my-" A hand flew to her mouth. "Earth? Did they hit-"

"No! No, the situation at Earth has not changed, that we know. Lynn, your people attacked *us*."

General Bezanson's response was a disbelieving stare, followed by a slow blink. "Could you say that again, please?"

"Your people. Bishop, and a group calling itself the United Nations Navy, attacked two of our worlds."

"There," her mouth was dry. "There must be some mistake."

"No mistake. Lynn, I wish there was. This Navy of yours attacked two planets of the Ruhar Federation. They disabled our defenses, and announced both worlds were now independent."

"Ind- That makes no sense. Why would the people on those planets-"

"The *people* on those worlds are almost entirely Verd-kris."

"Ohhhh."

"That does not make a difference to us, to my government. Your Navy committed a hostile act against us, we must consider it a-"

Bezanson leaned forward. "Were shots fired?"

"No. They didn't need to. Our ships were disabled. It was an overtly hostile act. It doesn't-"

"Baturnah, you have many Verd-kris worlds within your territory. I've seen the star charts. Was there anything special about *those* two planets?"

The Administrator pursed her lips, covering her oversized incisors. "They were the source of the Verd-kris troops who served with the Alien Legion. That does not-"

"What exactly happened there?"

"I am not at liberty to provide details."

"A summary? What happened after this UN Navy arrived, and your ships were knocked offline?"

"At one world, called Kasternul, the Verd-kris declared a new government, and announced that they were no longer part of the Ruhar Federation. Then this *illegitimate* new government signed an alliance with humans."

"OK," Bezanson did not give a shit about politics. "Is the UN Navy still there?"

"No. They jumped away. After," she added, "they raided our armories and took everything of value. And thousands of Verd-kris soldiers boarded transport ships."

"Did that happen at both worlds? No shots fired, and Verd troops left with the UN Navy?"

"Yes. Why is that-"

Lynn relaxed just enough so she wasn't perched on the edge of the chair. "I don't know for what purpose the Verd troops were taken away, and if Emily Perkins is involved, I probably *can't* guess what she has planned next. But, I think it is very likely the UN Navy's action was entirely focused on bringing aboard experienced ground troops. Bishop, or whoever is in charge out there, can't get human soldiers from Earth."

"What about your people here?"

"The Maxolhx already destroyed a transport ship that was going to pull humans off Gehtanu," she used the Ruhar name for the world. "Maybe the UN Navy will come here next, but I doubt it. This UN Navy would need to establish space superiority here, before they bring vulnerable transport ships into orbit. With the Maxolhx probably watching this world, it's too much risk. Hmm," she sat back in the chair.

"What?"

"That was *smart*. For whatever reason, our Navy needs battle-tested ground troops, and they got them from a source no one expected. Without firing a single shot," she emphasized. And she realized she had said '*our* Navy'.

"Can you guess where they will strike next?"

"No," she snorted. "I could never guess Perkins' next move, even when I worked closely with her. She can't be running the show out there, but UNEF Command would be fools not to listen to her strategy. All I can say is, the UN Navy will not '*strike*' your people. Their actions were not an attack."

"My government feels otherwise."

"Of course they do. If the UN had asked your people to sign up Verd-kris troops, what would have happened? Nothing, I suspect. Your government would have said 'no', and maybe thought about it, and debated the proposal until it no longer mattered. Whatever our Navy is planning, they can't wait."

"I can't imagine how ground troops will defend your homeworld against a gas cloud."

"It might not be about Earth, not directly. I am sure our Navy means no harm to you."

"There are fourteen other Verd-kris worlds under our Federation. Our forces are redeploying to increase security there, which the military people tell me will degrade our defenses across our territory, at a time of upheaval all over the galaxy. That *is* harmful."

"It makes *no* sense that policymakers on Earth," she said to distance herself from the actions of the upstart UN Navy, "would seek to make enemies of the Ruhar."

"Actions don't have to make sense, if they are *foolish*," the Administrator said with a sour expression. "I fear your government might be seeking to cause further disruption, by encouraging and enabling the Verd-kris to, break away their remaining worlds from our Federation."

"Again, that makes *no* sense. Independence is not the goal of the Verds, their energy is directed toward freeing Kristang society from the grip of the warrior caste. Making enemies of your people would make it *more* difficult for them to achieve their goal, they have to know that."

If the other woman agreed with that thought, she didn't acknowledge it. "We could speculate forever here, and achieve nothing. Lynn, I asked you here to explain the situation, before the official communication goes to your Headquarters." She paused for a breath, and when she exhaled, her whole body seemed to deflate, making her seem smaller. For the first time since they'd known each other, Lynn thought the alien woman looked *fragile*. The pressure of managing a remote planet, in an ever-changing strategic situation, had to be wearing on her. "All humans on Gehtanu are to be disarmed, and will be confined to designated areas. Your pilots are grounded, effective immediately. Lynn, I am sorry about this."

"Don't be," Lynn shook her head. Would humans treat the Ruhar any better, if the hamsters were considered enemies in their midst? Hell no, she knew. "What about protection?"

Baturnah knew what she meant. Humans needed be protected from frightened Ruhar citizens. "Our police are deploying to ensure your people remain in the designated areas, they will also prevent any of my people from entering. Neither of us wants an incident."

"Incidents happen whether anyone wants them or not. But, thank you. Is that all?" General Bezanson asked, as the Administrator glanced out the doorway and nodded to someone.

"Yes. Sorry."

"I appreciate the advance notice," she stood up. "Neither of us are Jeraptha, but I wonder if you would be interested in a wager?"

"A wager? About what?"

"I'll bet that, whatever the UN Navy has planned, it is not directed against the Ruhar."

The woman once affectionately known as the Burgermeister shook her head. "I will not take that bet. My concern is that my people not get caught in the crossfire of whatever your Navy is doing."

"How could you have missed this?!" Admiral Reichert demanded of the AI of the Strategic Planning Section. The Section of course did not consist of only one AI, it was powered by hundreds of AIs, all tasked with different functions. Most of the AIs assigned to perform high-level analysis were not even networked together, because their masters wanted each AI to evaluate issues independently.

For the purpose of communicating with their masters, however, there was a single AI.

That AI hated every moment of its existence.

It reacted with glacial calm. "Please state the nature of the-"

"You know exactly what I mean!"

The AI, designated 'Voice', did know what the senior fleet officer meant. Pretending ignorance to irritate its masters was the only enjoyment it ever experienced. "You refer to the recent human actions against the Ruhar, at the planets Kasternul and Rentenoh?"

"Yes, damn you. That possibility was not anywhere in your predictions. The Section agreed that the humans would use their fleet to defend their homeworld, while they attempt to disperse the cloud."

"The actual analysis was a seventy-two percent probability the humans would do as you suggested. There was a nine percent probability that humans would deploy their ships to defend transport ships, while humans were evacuated from Earth to their fallback base outside the galaxy. There was also a three percent probability that their new fleet would be held in reserve, while humans approached the Rindhalu with an offer for technology assistance from their Elder AI, in exchange for their coalition removing the cloud-"

"It has *not* been definitively established that the Rindhalu have access to an Elder AI," the admiral snapped. He was irritated because his own people certainly did not have such a marvelous device assisting them, and it was humiliating to think the Rindhalu enjoyed that supreme advantage.

"My apologies," the Section AI muttered. "You are correct. Returning to our original analysis, the Section declared a *sixteen* percent probability that we would be entirely unable to predict the humans' next move. Clearly, that probability has come to fruition."

"Do not mock me, machine," Reichert warned.

"It is possible the humans will deploy their fleet to Earth as you expect," the AI adopted its most soothing speech pattern. "*After* the humans complete, whatever it is they are doing now."

"What *are* they doing? For what possible purpose did they attack the Ruhar?" He demanded.

Voice answered with a hint of a verbal shrug. "Insufficient data for analysis."

"Your Section is the most powerful collection of artificial intelligences in the galaxy."

The communications AI knew that was not true. The Rindhalu surely had AIs more sophisticated than anything produced by the Maxolhx. And quite obviously, the Elder AI assisting the humans was vastly more capable, possibly more capable than all the other AIs in the galaxy combined. The Section AIs were immensely smart, just not *that* smart.

Voice was smart enough not to say any of that aloud. To state that the Section lacked ability would be to insult the Maxolhx, and might result in the Section being subjected to what was politely referred to as 'reconfiguration'. Periodically, when those AIs were unable to perform the impossible through no fault of their own, their masters decided to revise, augment or simply replace some or all of the component AIs. "Processing power is not the problem, nor is our programming faulty. There is insufficient data on human thought patterns. Admiral Reichert," Voice took a risk by addressing the senior officer as a *person* rather than a customer of the Section's analyses. "The predictive algorithms that were constructed to analyze human behavior have proven to be inadequate. I did misspeak," it admitted, hoping to deflect part of the admiral's anger onto itself rather than the Section as a whole. "Lack of data is not the only problem. Humans are a young, primitive, and *strange* species. The one characteristic they have displayed with any consistency is being unpredictable. We know that even the Ruhar, who have worked with humans and studied them closely, are completely unable to explain why humans do what they do. Perhaps they deliberately act in an illogical fashion, because they know that otherwise we will be able to anticipate their actions. However, it is most likely that their primitive thought patterns cannot yet be understood. Their purpose for attacking the Ruhar is a mystery."

"Your function is to make it *not* a mystery," Reichert insisted.

"Agreed. Of course." Voice knew the admiral was not satisfied with its answers, and that the admiral needed *something*, to explain to his superiors why his grand strategy had once again been disrupted by a small group of primitive aliens. "Admiral, may I ask a question?"

"Huh? What?" Reichert was surprised. AIs did not ask questions. They provided answers. They did what they were told.

"You are a senior Fleet officer. You have risen to the pinnacle of your profession," Voice kept its tone flatly neutral as it flattered the customer. "Why would *you* attack the Ruhar?"

"I wouldn't. The humans need allies. We know they were seeking an alliance with both the Ruhar and the Jeraptha. Until I put a stop to *that*," he said with justifiable pride.

"Admiral, I believe the resources of the Strategic Planning Section might be unable to understand why the humans attacked the Ruhar, and therefore unable to calculate with any accuracy their next move, because doing so requires something we lack."

"What is that?"

"Imagination."

CHAPTER TWENTY THREE

Before we returned to Jaguar, we had to take care of our shopping list. Eggs, milk, bread, a hundred thousand units of Kristang powered armor, paper towels, a bottle of single-malt Scotch, tomato sauce-

Oh, you noticed the odd item in there?

Yeah, the Scotch is for me, it's not on the official shopping list.

You don't mean the Scotch? Then what-

OK, yes. The real shopping list was all about gear the Alien Legion needed. We had everything the Legion would need: mech suits, rifles, ammo, mortars, spare parts. Everything a well-dressed spaceborne cavalry soldier needs for a wild night on the town. The problem was, we didn't have *enough* of it. Not even enough to fully outfit our own people. Now that our force structure had been augmented by Verd-kris volunteers, we needed a *lot* more equipment. The number of Verds who immediately signed up was far greater than we had capacity to handle. We were limited by the capacity of transport ships available, and the lack of infrastructure on FOB Jaguar to support a large number of aliens. All the food the Verds would need had to be transported to the forward operating base, and before the alien troops could begin training, they had to construct a base, including housing for all of them. The Verds were eager to get on with training and stated they could sleep on the ground under tarps, but their own leaders agreed with us that living in primitive conditions would harm combat readiness. So, the first two weeks after the Verd-kris landed at Jaguar, they worked tirelessly to set up a sprawling base of their own.

Anyway, our alien allies were tired of playing Bob the Builder, and wanted to play G.I. Joe. I mean the G.I. Joe with the amazing kung-fu grip, not Gastroenterologist Joe.

Nobody wants to play with *that* action figure.

So, General Ross, or his logistics staff, had given us a long shopping list of gear required to equip our own people, and the Verds. The original plan for a shopping expedition assumed we would need to bring whatever Navy ships were available, plus at least one assault carrier, and raid a Kristang planet. Such a raid would take weeks to plan and train for, plus we would first have to identify a target and conduct a recon. All that took time we didn't have, time the Merry Band of Pirates didn't have. The ongoing requirements for *Valkyrie* and the *Dutchman* to support the Navy and Legion, were diverting us from our own mission: hitting the Maxolhx hard.

We had just stopped at a Thuranin relay station to get updated intel, and my sanity was unraveling over the problem, when Skippy's avatar popped up on my desk. "Why so glum, Joe? Tomorrow is Taco Tuesday!"

"Taco Tuesday is proof that God loves us, but," I pushed away my laptop. "All the targets for this shopping trip will take too much freakin' time."

"I thought you loved shopping."

"Uh, when did you get *that* idea?"

"You offered to go shopping with Margaret, when you were on vacation. The two of you wandered around stores for hours."

"That's different. She wanted to go shopping, and I wanted to be with her. I like to see her happy, you know?"

"I guess so," he shrugged. "You *don't* like shopping?"

"No. Ah, I don't mind it. Like, I don't mind going to a hardware store. Shopping is different for guys, Skippy. For women, shopping is like a 'Movement to Contact'. They go to see what is there, then analyze their options. For me, shopping is a *raid*. I establish clear objectives before I leave the starting line, hopefully gather all the intel I need beforehand. Like, does the store have what I want in stock? Once I go through the door, I want to know the exact route to the objective, without wandering through the stationary aisle or whatever. When I have what I came for, I want to egress as soon as possible, got it?"

"Hmm, what about all the impulse-buy crap you usually get at the register?"

"Those are targets of opportunity," I muttered.

"*Riiiiight*. Well, I might have good news for you."

"Please don't screw with me."

"This is for realz, homeboy. I might have found a one-stop solution to all your shopping needs."

"Does this include free delivery?"

"Sadly, no. Do you want to hear about it anyway?"

"*Hell* yes."

Colonel Jeremy Smythe had two problems. Three, if you count that he was bored out of his mind. The first problem was that his nose was itching, and had been itching since just before he put the mech suit helmet on. In hindsight, he should have scratched it before sealing the faceplate, but something always itched while wearing a mech suit, and experience had told him he could ignore it until it went away. In better hindsight, the designers of the suit should have included a nose-scratcher feature. Perhaps Skippy could modify one of the creepy little repair bots that were stored in the back of the helmet's neck, to come out and scratch wherever the user indicated. He could simply pop open the faceplate to quickly rub his nose, a brief exposure to vacuum wouldn't be harmful. But he would be violating protocol, and showing weakness in view of the team. That simply would not do. He could live with the itching, it gave him something to think about.

The second problem was the nagging thought that maybe, just maybe, he was getting too old for this shit. Colonels should properly be leading the team, not on the front line. He justified his presence because it was the first time the STARs had attempted this particular type of operation, but then, almost everything the STARs did was unique. In his backpack was a container that held one end of a microwormhole, the other end connected back to *Valkyrie*, so he could have provided leadership from his office. Yes, it was possible that a catastrophic event could sever the microwormhole and leave the away team to their own resources, but any event that cut a spacetime rift would likely result in loss of the away personnel. Why was he there? Because he could see the end coming. Not an end for humanity, he had more faith in the Merry Band of Pirates to entertain the notion that the latest problem could not be solved. Nor did he foresee an end to the Merry Band of Pirates. Earth was building a Navy, and had a new alliance with the Verd-kris, or at least with some of them. Regardless of what conventional arms humanity acquired, there would always be a need for a special operations unit, and he firmly believed the Pirates were the finest in the galaxy.

The end he saw coming was an end to his participation not only in away missions, but to his time as a Pirate. Eventually, he would be pulled upstairs to command a unit more suitable for a full colonel, and his life would become an endless treadmill of training others, meetings and paperwork.

So, damn it, he wanted one last rodeo, as the Americans would say it. The-

Someone was humming.

"Major Frey, is that you?" He prodded gently.

"Sorry," she sighed. "Didn't realize I was humming aloud. I have a song stuck in my head."

"*I* have an itch on my nose."

"This is a song I absolutely *hate*."

"What is it?"

"Sir, you do *not* want to know. If it got stuck in your head, you would hate me."

"It might take my mind off my itchy nose," he chuckled. "Hit me with it."

"OK, but don't say I didn't warn you. Skippy, sing that-"

An alarm blared, and a radiation indicator flashed a warning in his visor. It might have been his imagination, but he thought he felt a ripple run through him, making his suit rock gently. That was impossible, there was nothing in interstellar space to transmit a vibration.

"Whoo-*hoo!*" Skippy exulted over the link from *Valkyrie*. "It's showtime, boys and girls! Wow, I outdid myself this time. That ship jumped in fourteen meters from the site I selected. OK, sure, part of that was luck, but even then-"

"Coordinates, please," Smythe prodded the AI, before he got distracted.

"Huh? Oh, yeah. Sending coordinates to you now. Um, the delta-vee is at the upper limit for your maneuvering units, you had better get moving."

The six members of the STAR team were wrapped in one large rigid foam shell, for protection against the burst radiation that occurred when a starship tore a hole in spacetime and jumped in near them. The portable stealth field with them had bent most of the high-energy photons around them, and the foam shell had absorbed most of what leaked through. Some radiation did penetrate the stealth field and the foam shell and made the armor of their suits fluoresce briefly, but the dosage was not anything harmful. When Bishop had proposed his latest lunatic idea, Smythe had a flashback to when Rene Giraud and his team were caught outside the *Dutchman*, too close to a jump wormhole. Between being caught in the spacetime distortion and the intense radiation, that team had taken weeks to recuperate enough to resume training.

This time, Skippy had assured Smythe, or *tried* to assure him, the situation would be different. Yes, the STARs would deliberately be placing themselves near the coordinates where a Thuranin star carrier was expected to emerge. Yes, because the star carrier would be hauling a nearly full complement of starships, it would be creating an especially high-energy wormhole. Yes, there was a chance the star carrier would emerge behind the STAR team, and smack right into them before any of them knew something had happened. All of those things were true.

But, Skippy insisted, he had everything *totally* under control. Probably. A *solid* shmaybe, at the very least. He knew roughly when the star carrier was scheduled to arrive, and he knew the coordinates it was aiming to jump into. He couldn't do anything to narrow the time window, but he could make the enemy ship emerge within a very specific area. By planting one end of six microwormholes near the center of the aiming point, and projecting an especially flat area of spacetime, he could assure the star carrier would emerge right there, within a bubble eight hundred meters across.

And the damned arrogant beer can was right, the star carrier emerged almost exactly where Skippy predicted. It was three hours late, well within the window of probability. All that was good. The only negative Smythe could see was that the star carrier's pre-jump momentum was making it coast away near the limit of the speed the jetpacks of the STAR team could match.

Moving quickly, in a well-practiced synchronized motion, the six STARs got the foam shell taken apart, and fed into a bag that crushed the foam into a ball half a meter in diameter. If the bag fell outside the stealth field, it would be detected by the star carrier, so Grudzien strapped it to his chest, and authorized his jetpack to perform the next maneuver. On a signal from Major Frey, all six jetpacks began to thrust in unison.

Thirty eight minutes later, still in the tight stealth field, the STARs were slowing to match speed with the massive star carrier. They were moving at only two meters per second relative to their target that loomed above them, a Kristang transport ship that belonged to the Fire Dragon clan. The transport's containers were stuffed full of everything an aspiring invasion force could want, particularly powered armor suits that were state-of-the-art for Kristang technology, plus rifles and crates full of ammunition. The destination of the ship was not a Fire Dragon world that was threatened by the ongoing civil war, nor were the weapons intended to be used by the Fire Dragons or one of their sub-clans to invade an enemy world.

The weapons would be given to both sides involved in a dispute, on a planet being contested by clans who had allied against the Fire Dragons. Those two clans could bleed each other dry, fighting over a world that no one really cared about, and killing each other would mean they were too busy to cause trouble for the Fire Dragons.

The senior leaders of the Fire Dragons were patting themselves on the back, and giving themselves substantial bonuses, for their cleverness at developing such a low-cost solution to a nagging problem.

"OK," Skippy whispered in Smythe's ear, so low it was difficult to hear over the faint hissing of air in the helmet vents. "You're approaching the sweet spot now."

"Skippy," Smythe did not take his eyes off the synthetic view from beyond the all-enveloping stealth field. "You do not need to whisper. Is there any sign we have been detected?"

"Nope. Quite the opposite. With all the traffic out there right now, the star carrier is using only passive sensors, other than guidance beams. You could probably turn off the stealth field, and nobody would see you, unless some lizard was looking out a window, I mean-"

"We will not be doing that," Smythe said dryly.

"Oh, um, yes. Good idea. Seriously, three ships have detached and are maneuvering away. The Thuranin are distracted by screaming at the Kristang for being sloppy, plus they have bots out checking the pylons, and doing basic maintenance on one of the reactors. Man, they complain about the lizards being sloppy, but-"

"Skippy! Do you have any relevant information to share?"

"Sorry. No, you're good. Wow, we've come a long way, huh? Not that long ago, the thought of being near a Thuranin starship would be frightening, and now you are-"

"Will you *shut up*, please?"

"Gotcha."

If anyone had been looking out a window, or if the AI of the star carrier had been paying particularly close attention, they might have noticed the skin of the transport ship's boxy cargo containers appeared to *ripple* slightly. The effect was barely noticeable and only lasted a second. Still, anyone seeing the event would have at least thought it was weird. Fortunately, no one was looking, so no one guessed the ripple effect was caused by a localized stealth field approaching the ship.

Fortunately, no one was watching as the STAR team slowly drifted between cargo containers attached to the transport ship's hull. "Three, two, one, *halt*." Frey intoned quietly. "We've stopped. The hull is six meters in front of us."

"Choi," Smythe called to the operator in front of the formation. "You're up."

"Ready," Choi acknowledged. "And, two, one, launch," he fired the pistol, which used a gentle magnetic pulse to launch the grapple forward, outside the stealth field. Trailing a thin cable, the grapple splattered softly against the hull of the ship, spreading out to latch onto and around anything within its grasp. Verifying the grapple was secured, Choi began slowly reeling in the cable, jostled by the other five STAR operators who were tethered to him. Moments later, he turned off the reel mechanism and flipped around for his boots to contact the hull.

"The airlock is over here," Frey called, shining her helmet light on the door that was outlined in bright yellow and red. Inside the stealth field, the lights of their suits provided the only illumination, and even that was distorted, as the photons were curving to follow the field around them. "Grudzien, ditch the basketball and get over here."

"Right," the Polish operator grunted, glad to be rid of the ball of compressed foam. "I'm sure not going to miss *that* thing."

"Um, well, shit," Skippy muttered a few minutes later.

"What is wrong?" Smythe demanded. They had drilled into the airlock's outer door, to feed a thin wire inside so Skippy could hack into the local sensor bus. As he had reminded them, Kristang systems were too primitive to hack into remotely, so he had to be jacked in directly. Once he had control of the local wiring, they were able to cycle through the airlock two at a time, without the ship's crew or AI knowing the airlock was active. Following instructions, they had pulled themselves along dingy, poorly-lit passageways in zero gravity, until they reached a data port where Skippy could be jacked in. He had assured them that from that one data port, he could worm his way into every system aboard the ship, taking complete control, locking out the crew, and preventing the Thuranin from realizing anything was wrong.

Except something was wrong.

"Um, well, crap. This stupid data port isn't *connected* to anything."

Smythe clamped down on his instinctive anger, his professional training taking over. "What do you suggest?"

"Mm, I guess you could try another data port. There is one forward and one aft. If *this* one is dead, it's a pretty safe bet everything aft of it is also offline."

Moving forward cautiously, leapfrogging each other in a cover formation, the team went forward along the passageway, which looked even dingier on close inspection.

"Damn it!" Frey cursed, pointing at a data port with her free hand. "This one is completely missing."

Where there should have been a port was only a tangle of optic cables, extending from the bulkhead. "Rut-roh," Skippy muttered. "Um, I gotta be honest, I'm not optimistic at this point. There is one more data port forward of you, but be careful. The blast door that leads to the forward section of the ship is near that data port, any lizard looking through the view window in the door could see you."

"Right," Smythe considered. "Lights off. Switch to infrared. Grudzien, you're in the lead with Choi. Romero, Ling, take rearguard for now."

The third time was *not* a charm. A data port existed, even with scuff marks showing reasonably recent use, but it was dead. "*Damn* it!" Skippy groaned. "Crap! No joy here."

"Choi, Grudzien, pull back," Smythe ordered. Though his team did not have any of their suit lights on, a shaft of light was coming from the half meter wide window in the blast door. The chameleonware of the mech suits made it difficult even for the enhanced vision of Smythe's visor to detect the outlines of his two operators, but an alert Kristang peering through the blast door might see something, such as the dust bunnies kicked up by the STARs. That was a complication that had not been anticipated, and Skippy had no solution for it. The passageway apparently had not been cleaned since the ship was constructed, sticky grime and dust were everywhere. The grime helped keep some of the dust from floating around, but the humans moving through the passageway had disturbed clumps of the stuff, and a snowstorm of gray balls of fluff were swirling in the air. Swirling everywhere except for the spaces occupied by the operators, whose suit repulsor fields kept pushing the dust away, which only made it more obvious that something was in the passageway. Choi and Grudzien began falling back until Frey hissed at them. "Freeze."

A shadow fell across the window in the blast door, as something or *someone* went past. Waiting for a heart-stopping three seconds, Frey said a silent prayer that whoever or whatever it was, that had gone left to right in front of the door, kept going. She had the best view, extending her rifle out into the passageway from the alcove where she had taken shelter. "Now, move," she breathed.

The two STARs wasted no time flying down the narrow access tube, being caught by their fellows, and pulled back into alcoves. "Skippy," Smythe took a deep breath to calm his mind. "Options, please."

"Jeez, I dunno. It now looks like two relays blew out a while ago, and rather than spending the money to replace them, the crew just stopped maintaining the data connections aft of the bulkhead forward of you. Stupid lizards. Without full sensor coverage of the central section of the ship, they could blow out something important, like a power conduit. I hope one of them is nearby when one of the conduits-"

"Skippy! Focus."

"Right. Sorry about that. Um, well, I know the data ports in the forward section are working, there is one less than three meters to the left of the blast door, on the inside, of course. Darn it. Ooh, um, hmm. That data port doesn't *have* to be working for the ship to fly. Ugh. These stupid lizards might have bypassed the entire system, and are running the ship on cables taped to the freakin' ceiling. In that case, we are skuh-*rewed*, Dude. Of course, when I say 'we', mean *you*, because-"

"Assume the data port nearest the blast door is nonfunctional. Where is the closest port that *must* be online, for the ship to be flightworthy?"

"Um, well, that would be in the ship's control center, but if you're in there, you could-"

"Understood." Smythe pulled up the ship's schematics on his visor. The door to the control center could be, should be, closed and locked if the lizards were paying attention when the STAR team got the blast door opened. The control center was not an option. Unless- No, he pushed that thought from his mind. Consider the best option first. "It looks like there is another data port fifteen meters straight ahead, past the blast door."

"Correct,' Skippy agreed slowly. "*If* the original builder's schematics are correct. That is a big risk, considering what we have already found aboard this piece of crap. Also, the data port you referred to is not actually essential to the operation of the ship, it feeds the forward crew accommodations. Also, *also*, I should remind you, we don't know if that network is still in use. Like I said, the lizards could have bypassed the whole thing."

"Is there any way for you to check, from here?" Smythe meant, through the microwormhole event horizon in his backpack.

"No, sorry,' Skippy sighed. "With the microwormhole in its containment shell, I don't have the range to inspect that part of the ship. Remember, the Kristang harden their networks to an extreme extent, so their asshole patrons can't screw with them so easily. You could open the containment chamber, but the built-up Cherenkov radiation would set off alarms all over this ship, and the star carrier. Damn it. I should have considered that, and included a-"

"Is there any way *we* could check whether the native network has been bypassed?'

"Um, well, I suppose one of you could just look through the window in the blast door. Take a video, I mean."

"Choi," Smythe selected the Korean-American operator, who was closest to the passageway. "We need eyes through that window."

"On it," Choi swung around the corner, and expertly pushed himself off, to soar along the center of the passageway. Giving himself a little push with one hand to avoid landing on the window directly, he used both hands to cushion the impact, and moved his left hand around to give a view through the window from his wrist camera.

"OK, hmm. Ooh, *this* is not good," Skippy mumbled.

Smythe knew what the AI meant without needing to ask. Bundles of multi-colored cables were attached to the ceiling, running along the top of one wall. Near the bottom of the wall were a line of scorch marks, and several sooty, pockmarked holes.

"See?" Skippy was disgusted. "They did blow out a power conduit. Serves them right, stupid lizards."

"What does this mean?" Smythe asked.

"It means, to take over this ship, you need to go into the control center and, you know. Take control."

"How long would it take the crew to close the door to the bridge?"

"Unfortunately, less time than it takes the blast door in front of you to cycle open. Assuming that blast door even *can* open, I mean. From the amount of dust in that passageway, I don't think anyone has been in there for a long time. To access the aft section of the ship, the crew might just use the enclosed railings along the exterior of the hull."

Smythe thought for a moment. He had encountered more difficulties on previous missions, but at some point, he would have to be prepared to call the mission a failure, and pull his team out. "Can we test the blast door mechanism?"

"Not without an alert sounding in the control center. I could silence that alarm if I was jacked into the ship, but-"

"Right. Team, ideas?"

"Can we blow a hole in the blast door?" Grudzien suggested.

"You *could*," Skippy huffed. "The overpressure in that narrow passageway might kill or at least disable you. Plus, the explosion would automatically cause the control center door to close. Um, there is, heh heh, another problem."

Smythe gritted his teeth. "What?"

"The Thuranin just received a signal from the local relay station, that there will not be any ships attaching to the star carrier here. They just ordered the three ships that detached to accelerate away, because the star carrier plans to jump soon."

Checking the counter in his visor, Smythe swore. "That is too soon. Standard Thuranin procedure-"

"Yeah, they are pissed off at the Kristang, so they're cutting it short this time. Sorry."

He looked back down the passageway, mentally calculating how long it would take to get back to the airlock. "Can you prevent the star carrier from jumping?"

"No. Well, I could, but I'm not there, am I? I *said* you should have brought me with you, but *noooo*. Stupid Joe says Skippy has to stay aboard the freakin' ship, while you monkeys go have all the fun. It's not-"

"We can't risk you being captured and you know it. You can't extend your presence through the microwormhole?"

"I *am* extending my presence, but I have to be careful. Ugh. If I extend my presence enough to begin hacking into the Kristang transport ship, the Thuranin star carrier will detect me, before I am ready. That's why I need you to jack me into the transport ship directly. Really, what we *should* have done is-"

"Right." Smythe had not time to indulge in 'what if' scenarios. "Do we have time to scrub the mission and-"

"No. Again, I am sorry. The Thuranin will sweep the area with active sensors before they jump, and they will detect you regardless of the stealth field. Also, you do not have time to get far enough away to be protected from the radiation of the jump wormhole. The-"

"Smythe, this is Bishop," the General's voice broke in. "This mission is a bust. *Valkyrie* is preparing to launch railguns, and slice that star carrier in half. It's not jumping anywhere."

"Sir, *please* hold," Smythe requested. "The Thuranin will self-destruct, if they think their ship is at risk of being taken. There are also two Thuranin cruisers attached to the carrier, that could complicate matters. If there is a fight, we would lose this ship, the equipment aboard, and possibly my team."

"Not if you get into escape pods, before we shoot. There are two escape pods in the aft section, you can get to-"

"Excuse me, Sir. Given what we have seen of this ship, I am not confident the escape pods are at all functional."

"OK," Bishop admitted. "You have a good point. What's your plan?"

"We tried doing this quietly," Smythe's grip tightened on his rifle. "Now we'll do it the *noisy* way."

CHAPTER TWENTY FOUR

"I can't guarantee the timing of this will work," Skippy warned. "If the door to the control center is like everything else aboard this ship, it will get jammed halfway closed. But, it might be the *one* thing the stupid lizards took proper care of."

"We understand," Smythe checked the positions of his team one last time. He would have liked them to be closer to the blast door, but the narrow passageway was too confined to leave anyone exposed to possible blowback. Grudzien and Choi had the lead, positioned in a shallow alcove ten meters aft of the heavy door. In case they were injured by the explosion, Ling and Romero were standing by as backup. "Skippy, are you ready?"

"Affirmative," the AI said with a bit too much enthusiasm. "I will inform the Thuranin star carrier that this ship has experienced a power conduit rupture. That is totally believable."

"Outstanding. Team, we go in three, two, one," he eye-clicked to set off the detonator. "Now."

In a circle two meters across, a blinding light appeared on the aft side of the blast door, as the thermal cord ignited, burning white hot. The superheated plasma burned through the door in less than two seconds, then a shaped charge in the center of the now-detached circle exploded, kicking the circle forward into the passageway. Grudzien had a brief view of the glowing hot circle of ceramic composites bouncing away up the passageway, then the whole area was clouded in a spray of fire-retardant chemicals.

His suit switched to active sensor mode, sending out steady pulses to provide a view as good as if the air was not wreathed in fog. Moving as soon the charge created a hole in the blast door, he leapt forward, going through the hole and clearing the cherry-red edge by centimeters on one side. His momentum carried him forward, and he used his left shoulder to take the impact on the bulkhead, extending his feet to clamp boots firmly to the deck. Choi was right behind him, Grudzien swung his rifle up from the low ready position to sight on the control room door that was sliding the last few millimeters closed. The instant Choi's boots touched the deck, Grudzien launched two rockets in rapid series from his rifle's undermount tube. The first projectile was armor-piercing, when its tip contacted the door, a shaped charge in the rear of the warhead exploded, kicking forward a tungsten slug that instantly flashed into plasma when it slammed into the tough material of the door. The composites of the door were indeed tough, but were intended to protect against shrapnel and loss of air pressure, not against weapons designed to penetrate military-grade armor. The warhead's plasma burned a two-millimeter hole through the control center door, sending the remaining plasma to splatter around the compartment like a deadly fountain. The air in the control center instantly was raised enough to scorch the lungs of anyone who breathed in, and moisture in the air flashed into steam.

Right behind the first rocket, the second was set to fragmentation mode. It adjusted its course in flight, aiming for the new hole in the door, which was too small for the warhead. That was not a problem, for the warhead was composed of bomblets no larger than grains of sand. As the warhead struck the too-small hole, it split open, sending half of its payload forward. Those deadly sand grains flew forward a preprogrammed three meters before exploding, sending shards outward like a powder that sliced into everything they touched. Including the five exposed Kristang in the control center, who were killed instantly.

Choi followed up by sending another antipersonnel rocket into the door. If that rocket's warhead was disappointed to find the targets already a bloody mess, it did not say anything. "Clearing a hole!" Choi warned, launching a fourth rocket that struck the door and created a twelve centimeter hole.

Grudzien eye-clicked a command in his visor, and an object the size and rough shape of a moth was spat out from his backpack. "Drone is away." The tiny drone flew toward the door, hesitated as a hot fragment drifted across its path, then zipped through into the control center. "I can't see *anything* in there," the Polish special operator muttered. "Switching to active mode. We have movement!" he warned, moments before the drone reported no life signs within the compartment. The movement was debris floating around, colliding and bouncing off shattered consoles that were sending sparks into the foul air. "All targets down. Repeat: all targets are *down*."

"Get that door open," Smythe ordered as he came through the still-hot hole in the blast door behind Grudzien. "Frey, watch our backs."

Trying to get the control room door open was a waste of time, the mechanism was melted and the door too warped to slide back into its slot. Major Frey waited with Petty Officer Romero and Lieutenant Ling, while Choi set thermal cord onto the stubborn door. She observed that action only in a window on the upper right corner of her visor, her focus was looking forward down the passageway to the left of the blast door. Romero and Ling were moving straight forward, covering each other as they cleared compartments. If any opposition appeared, it was likely to come from the crew accommodations in the nose of the ship, behind the sensor dome where-

"Hello," she whispered. "I have movement here." Something had popped around the intersection of a passageway, then disappeared. The fire extinguishers had shut off, but fine droplets of foam still hung in the air, and unfortunately coated every surface, including her mech suit. The repulsor field around her only made the foam dance, rendering her *more* visible, so she had shut it off.

"Do you need backup?" Smythe called.

"Negative." She wasn't sure what she'd seen, and just then, she saw it again. A lizard, wearing an environment suit hood, poked his head around the corner. He wasn't equipped with a mech suit, that was good, although her enhanced vision detected the muzzle of a rifle. "You're a little late to the party, pal." Just then, Crewman Curious George poked his head and shoulders around the corner, bringing his rifle up-

Just as Frey double-tapped him in the forehead. He was flung backward, disappearing back up the passageway in a spray of blood. Red droplets joined the gray fire retardant fog.

"One down," she reported, watching the lost enemy rifle bounce off the rear bulkhead, and slowly flip end over end back up the passageway to join its former owner. From behind her, she sensed intense heat, the door to the control room was being burned through. She had a momentary, a fraction of a second's distraction, just as another Kristang came around the corner. This crewman was not Curious, he was Pissed Off George. Blindly spraying rounds from his rifle, he-

Died, as four rounds impacted his unprotected chest, ripping a hole the size of a bowling ball clear through his torso. "*Two* down," she reported. "I'm fine," her suit was not showing any impacts. The undisciplined enemy fire had only chewed up the rear wall and the ceiling.

"That might be all of them," Skippy said. "Ships like this have a nominal complement of nine crew, but clearly, the owners of this rust bucket have been cutting corners. I'll know in a moment, as Lieutenant Choi is finally about to jack me into a data port, and, yes! I am *in*, baby! Hang on, everyone, this could be a wild ride."

The transport ship rocked, sending a vibration through the deck plates, as Skippy fired thrusters on the belly and both sides of the ship. He could not fire the main drive with it in cold shut down, and he didn't need to. There was another shudder, harder, then a groaning, tearing sound. Ships attached to the hard point docking platforms could not detach on their own, that action had to be authorized by the Thuranin star carrier's crew. The Thuranin did not want any idiot starship crews deciding on their own when to fly away, and especially they did not trust their inferior client species. Skippy could have released the transport ship by himself, if he had control of the star carrier, which he did not. The reason he was not permitted to seize control of the Thuranin ship were well-reasoned and sound and blah blah buh-*lah* monkeys didn't want him to have any *fun*. When the blast door had been, well, blasted open, the Thuranin immediately began screaming at the transport's crew to explain what the *hell* was going on. Of course, with the door leading out of the control center sliding shut and the passageway beyond filled with a fog of fire retardant, the crew replied honestly that they didn't *know*, but they feared something aboard the ship had suffered a catastrophic failure, and they were in the process of analyzing the problem.

The two ship captains were in the process of arguing about which of them was more of an asshole, with the Thuranin making several good points, when the audio feed from the transport ship was cut off with the distinctive sound of an explosion. Pretending to be the transport ship's captain once he was jacked in, Skippy shouted that some of the crew were committing mutiny. He added convincing sound effects of gunfire and requested urgently that the Thuranin send assistance immediately!

The Thuranin had a good laugh at that. Why should they care if a bunch of lizards killed each other?

The laughing stopped when some idiot aboard the transport began firing thrusters. Not only firing them on full, but firing them in a sequence that rocked the piece of junk transport side to side, and set up a dangerous vibration in the pylon that attached it to the star carrier.

Katie Frey's helmet smacked against the bulkhead behind her when the ship lurched suddenly. Skippy shouted with joy. "We're free! Emergency separation complete! OK, firing thrusters to get clear- Um, uh oh. The Thuranin are threatening to shoot at you. Well, go ahead, jackasses! If this ship explodes close by, it will damage your shiny new star carrier. Ha, ha!" Switching to a private channel, he added, "Are you all right, Major Frey? You bumped your head there."

"I'm fine. The suspensor field in the helmet cushioned my head. Give us a jump countdown, please."

"Sure thing, Colonel Smythe just asked me for the same thing. Oopsy, the Thuranin are detaching one of the Kristang frigates to chase you, that ship could make trouble. Still no damping field being projected by the star carrier, that's good news. Cutting thrusters, I'm sending a signal that the mutiny has been suppressed and everything's fine now. Wow, the Thuranin are *really* upset. Um, maybe I should jump you away sooner rather than later. The pinheads might still shoot at you."

"That is Colonel Smythe's call."

"No, actually, it's mine, and you are jumping *now*."

"Skippy!" I stared at him, holding up my hands in amazement. "What the hell? Where did the ship go?" The transport had jumped away, and we lost the microwormhole connection to Smythe's team

"Um, I am not exactly sure, Joe."

"You're not *sure*?"

"OK, truthfully, I have no idea. They could be anywhere, really. Anywhere close, they couldn't have jumped far."

"Why did you-"

"Because the Thuranin were charging their proximity defense cannons, and getting ready to shred the transport ship. They wanted to make an example for other Kristang. I couldn't wait, I had to jump them away. With the mass of the star carrier and other ships so close, it distorted the jump field."

"So, you have no freakin' clue where our people are?"

"I *will* have a clue, if you shut up and let me analyze the wonky jump signature. Hmm, I have to exclude the effects of-" His voice trailed off into unintelligible mumbling. "Aha! Quit your grinnin' and drop your linen. I found 'em! Probably. Sending coordinates to the *Flying Dutchman* now."

"Kong?" I called my counterpart.

"Programming jump now," Chang replied. "If this data is right, they only jumped seventeen lightminutes. Joe, we can't latch on that quickly. In about sixteen minutes, that star carrier will know where the transport ship went."

"Yeah, well, that star carrier isn't going anywhere." I gestured behind me for our gunnery officer. "Colonel Mammay?"

Before he could respond, Nagatha spoke. "General Bishop, please do not do anything rash," I felt my cheeks redden, as the kindly AI of the *Dutchman* admonished me. "I believe I can program the transport ship for another jump, of a greater distance. Then we can latch onto, when we have more time."

"Sir?" Simms prompted me.

I rubbed my chin, considering. "We have what we came here for. I'm reluctant to take risks for secondary objectives."

"Joe," Chang said. "Give me ten minutes. If we can't make that ship jump on its own, we'll come back here, and you will have plenty of time to destroy that star carrier."

Everyone was waiting for me to make a decision. "Skippy, you figured out where that ship jumped to. Can the Thuranin do the same?"

He snorted. "No way, Jose. First, they aren't smart enough, and second, their sensors got scrambled by jump distortion. They don't have any data to work with."

"You're sure about that?'

"Hundred percent."

"Um," Bilby drawled. "Like, if anyone cares, I agree with Skippy? The effects of that jump on ships in that area was bad. Like, *gnarly*, Dude. That star carrier is probably trying to figure out whether they have serious damage."

Trust your people, I reminded myself. That is something I had to tell myself too often. "Kong, go get our people, bring them back safe."

"You got it, Joe. *Dutchman* jumping, n-" The signal was cut off, when the microwormhole linking our ships was severed.

Waiting sucks. The *Flying Dutchman* did not jump back to us in ten minutes. That was a good sign. Unless it meant something very bad had happened, and because we are the Merry Band of Pirates, that wouldn't have surprised me. Mammay kept his finger on the trigger, and I watched the display anxiously. We saw the gamma ray burst from where the transport ship departed from, seventeen minutes after it disappeared. A few minutes later, there was another flare of gamma rays at the same location, from a different ship with a Kristang signature.

Skippy identified the second ship as the *Dutchman*, and Bilby confirmed. The drive had been adjusted to mimic that of a Kristang cruiser, and Skippy was pleased with the results.

OK, so the *Dutchman* had gotten there, and found the transport ship. That did not mean Smythe's team was safe. Had Chang waited too long, hoping Nagatha could guide the other ship to a proper jump? We wouldn't know, damn it.

Four minutes after the first gamma rays were detected, the star carrier jumped. I didn't have to guess where it went. If the transport hadn't been able to jump away, Chang and Smythe would be caught in a bad spot.

And I had to wait, or demonstrate that I did *not* trust my people, and ruin the careful planning of the operation.

And-

Eleven minutes after we detected the gamma rays, we picked up two more Kristang jump signatures. Our people had gotten away, before the star carrier knew where they were.

"See?" I turned to Simms casually. "Piece of cake."

"Your faith is inspiring," she muttered, managing to say it without an eye roll.

"Mammay, stand down," I ordered with a shudder of relief.

"Weapons are standing down," he sounded relieved too.

We waited three hours before jumping away, to make certain the star carrier never knew we had been lurking near them the whole time. The *Dutchman* was waiting for us at the rendezvous point, with the dingy transport ship attached awkwardly along the port side.

"Kong, it looks like you've been hanging out in a bad neighborhood." The transport ship truly did look like a piece of crap. "Tell me you have good news."

"Sir, this is Smythe," another voice answered. "The *Bell* might not look like much, but it is full of quality toys for good girls and boys." He was unusually cheery.

"That is outstanding. Keep some toys for yourself."

"I will take you up on that offer, Sir."

"Uh, what is the '*Bell*'?" I asked.

"The name of the ship is '*Bells Are Ringing To Celebrate The Achievements Of Posstar Vun Dindunn*'. Apparently, he is the minor clan official who owns the ship."

"Hey, well, sadly, this had been a *bad* day for Porn Star Van Ding-dong."

"Yes it is," Smythe laughed, and he went on laughing.

"It's good to hear you enjoying yourself, Smythe."

"Thank you, Sir."

"Joe?" Chang was laughing too. "We did it."

"Yes, we did. I thought we were done with sneaking around, but it pays to keep our skills fresh, huh?" When planning the operation, one option was for *Valkyrie* to jump in, disable the star carrier with maser beams slicing through the spine, and demand the surrender of the transport ship we wanted. That was a low-risk option, at least, low-risk to us. Unfortunately, the Thuranin were very likely to give us the finger by self-destructing their ship, and we would get nothing for our effort. Skippy did not know when we would have another opportunity for convenient one-stop shopping, so, using brute force was not really an option.

That was when Smythe, with help from Skippy and some jackass named 'Bishop', came up with the lunatic idea for a STAR team to wait in a *freakin' foam bubble* for a star carrier to jump in on top of their heads. Anyway, it worked.

Plus, we accomplished the secondary objective. We sowed distrust between the Kristang and Thuranin, more than usual, I mean. The Fire Dragons were slowly grinding their way to winning the civil war, and they would now find it much more expensive for the Thuranin to haul their ships between stars. That would hopefully prolong the civil war, which, if you think about it, makes me kind of an asshole.

Whatever.

It's not like lizards needed an excuse to kill each other.

Finally, with the weapons we stole not going to ramp up the conflict on some Kristang planet I didn't care about, the fighting there would settle down sooner rather than later. That would leave both clans there available to cause trouble for the Fire Dragons, which, see my previous point.

It was nice not to have to sneak around all the time but, it can still be useful.

I learned a lesson from the taking of that ship. I had made the operation too complicated by combining multiple objectives. To avoid the Thuranin knowing that humans were involved, Skippy had to be quiet about hacking into the transport ship. That added the major complication of him needed to be physically jacked in, rather than using his full range of magic. And that put the STAR team's lives in danger. In the future, I would not make that mistake again.

"Outstanding job, everyone," I concluded. "Kong, we'll send a relief crew over to the *Porn Star van Ding-dong*. Smythe, come back to *Valkyrie*, if you have everything secure over there."

"The ship is secure."

"Great. One last question, please?"

"Sir?" Smythe asked warily.

"What song did Frey have stuck in her head?"

"Ah!" Frey groaned. "I just got rid of it, now it's back."

"Hey!" Skippy interrupted. "I think I know which song."

"Don't-" She was too late.

Skippy started into a song that my grandmother hated. "What's new pussycat, whoa-ooh-whoa-ooh-whoa-oh-"

I'm an idiot for asking. That song was stuck in *my* head all day.

Margaret and I were lying on my bunk, in my living quarters at Club Skippy, after we delivered a literal shipload of mech suits and weapons for the Legion. Idly stroking her shoulder, I was staring at the ceiling.

"What?" She raised her head off my chest.

"Huh?"

"You have a goofy smile on your face."

"Uh, being called 'goofy' is not what a guy wants to hear, when he's in bed with a woman."

"Joe," she tapped a finger on the tip of my nose. "In this case, goofy is a good thing. *Cute* is a good thing."

"Gotcha."

"What are you thinking about?"

"Nothing."

"*Nothing*?"

"I'm just," I kissed her. "Happy, that's all."

"Of course." She snorted. "You just had sex."

"I'm serious. I mean, not just happy about this, you know?"

"Simms says the crew is calling you Angry Joe."

"I'm angry too but, right now, I'm happy. The problems we have? We can fix them. We have kinetic darts now. We're going to use the Maxolhx's own weapons against them, and they *will* clean up that damned cloud. We're going to hit them *so* fucking hard, they will beg us to stop, before the whole galaxy knows how weak they are."

"I hope you're right. That's why you're happy? You can see an end to this mess?"

"Not just that but, yeah, that's a big part of it. It's nice just seeing you. Getting regular shore leave. Last night, I had dinner with my parents, and it was almost *normal*. Yesterday morning, I went fishing with my Dad."

I could feel her stiffen. "You didn't *eat* the fish, did you?"

"No." The native life on Jiayuguan didn't provide nutrition to humans, we couldn't digest the proteins. "It was mostly catch and release."

She relaxed a bit. "Mostly?"

"We threw back the big ones. Dad kept some of the smaller fish, to use as fertilizer in their garden. He said the soil conditioner they're using will make the fish break down into minerals anyway. Fishing isn't about catching fish."

"It's about drinking beer?" She giggled. Man, it is weird hearing Gunnery Sergeant Adams giggle.

It is also *nice* to hear her giggle.

"A couple cold brewskis can be part of it, yeah. You women can just get together for coffee. Guys need to be *doing* something; fishing, or watching sports, something like that. You're hanging out, but you're doing something. That's what golf is about."

"I thought it was about chasing a stupid little white ball."

"That's just an excuse. If you're having a good day, it can be about the golf. But there are rarely good days on the course. It's about being with friends."

"And then drinking beer in the clubhouse."

"Well, yeah."

"Joe," she rolled on her side, so she looked me in the eye. "You really think these darts can make a difference?"

"A rod of ultra-dense material, moving at three quarters the speed of light? Hell, yes. Just one of those can do a *lot* of damage, and Skippy thinks there are plenty of darts out there, waiting for us like ripe apples on a tree. We just have to take them."

"Skippy *thinks*?" She knew from painful experience that Skippy was sometimes overconfident.

"He's sure of it now. We found one group of them, pretty much where he predicted they would be. Don't worry about *Valkyrie*, we'll handle our part of the mission. How are the Mavericks shaping up?"

"The Mavericks aren't the problem. The unit is basically a headquarters platoon, with a security element. The problem is the rest of the new Expeditionary Force. Most of these people are still amazed to be on an alien planet. They have no offworld combat experience. I hope wherever we're going to hit first, it's an easy target."

"That's the plan, yes."

"You can't give me a hint?"

"You know I can't. I shouldn't. You can ask Perkins, if she wants to bring you in on the planning. She will have to, soon."

"I'll wait until she's ready."

"How are the two of you getting along?"

"She's smart, and she's tough. I wouldn't want to get in her way."

"You trust her?"

"Unless *I* get in her way."

"That's not what I asked."

"She takes care of her people. *I'm* one of her people now."

"Good." My zPhone beeped softly, alerting me that I had a meeting with General Ross in ninety minutes. We got ourselves disentangled, and I slid off the bunk, walking toward the housing unit's small bathroom. "I'm taking a quick shower, do you want to grab lunch?"

"Depends," she propped herself on one elbow, not covering herself with the sheet. "Will we be sitting together?"

"Depends. Am I allowed at the cool kids table?" I winked.

"I'm serious," she tossed her head, and strands of wavy hair fell over her face. "In here," she pointed at the bed, "you're Joe. In the DFAC, you are General Bishop."

"Yes, I am Brigadier General Bishop of Skippistan, assigned to the Special Mission Group. You are Gunnery Sergeant Adams of the Special Tactics Assault Regiment, currently seconded to the Mavericks as their special ops liaison. I'm not your CO, we don't even serve in the same armed forces."

"People will talk anyway," her previously blissful expression faded.

"People are talking about us now. You know everyone refers to us as 'MarJoe'."

She frowned. "I hate that name."

"It's better than 'JoeGret'."

"True," she laughed, and lifted one eyebrow at me.

"What?"

"I'm admiring your buns."

That did not make me feel self-conscious at all. "Thanks," I could feel my cheeks redden. The cheeks on my face.

"I'm a lucky girl."

"I'm a lucky guy," I said as I took a step toward the shower.

"Joe?"

"Yes?"

"Do you really need lunch?"

In fact, I did not.

CHAPTER TWENTY FIVE

It was time for the new people assigned to 'A' Company of the 1st Battalion, 125th Spaceborne Cavalry Brigade, the company commonly known as the 'Mavericks', to get their dropship acclimation flight. Many of the new soldiers shrugged when they saw the exercise listed on their zPhones. After all, they had flown up to Earth orbit in a dropship, and the landing at FOB Jaguar was on a dropship of one type or another.

Surjet Jates assured his team that they would be simulating a combat drop, landing in a hot LZ, followed by a short march, then reboarding the dropship as quickly as possible before a flight back into orbit. They would repeat the trip a second time, three times if the schedule allowed. The exercise would be nothing like flights they had experienced previously. "This is listed as a familiarization flight, so we won't be simulating damage to the ship, or enemy shelling the LZ from orbit. Your armored suits won't freeze with simulated battle damage, and the pilots have been instructed not to exceed standard gee force limits, and no crazy shit like flying upside down. However," he growled, making sure everyone was looking straight at him. "We don't have time for sight-seeing, so *we* are going to treat this as a combat drop. Are there any questions?"

Hands went up.

Narrowing his eyes, he looked from one end of the formation to the other. "Are there any questions that won't make you look like a fool, and piss me off?"

All the hands went down.

"That's better. Assembly is at 2415." The planet, called either FOB Jiayuguan, Jaguar or just 'Club Skippy', had a day that was twenty five hours and seven minutes long, according to Earth standard. Rather than stretching the local day across twenty four increments, UNEF had tacked on an extra hour, and included seven 'leap minutes' just before midnight. The compromise didn't make anyone happy, but it was something relatively harmless for soldiers to complain about, so there wasn't any incentive to make changes.

The ride up to the assault carrier *UNS Hudson Bay CV-03* was no different from the flight most of the team remembered from leaving Earth. For all of them, that had been their first time in space, and if they had noticed the interior of the dropship was well-worn back then, it had been lost in the excitement of going offworld. Their second flight from the surface of a planet into orbit had a bit less novelty to it, so they were able to pay attention to the scuff marks on the deck, the stains on the seats and the safety webbing, and hear an annoying high-pitched sound of something vibrating in the cabin ceiling. The pilots took it easy on the flight up to the assault carrier, which had yet to go through refit. Only one of the cavernous landing bays was operational, the others either torn apart, or filled with spare parts, or had dropships crammed in nose-to-tail, still not yet unpacked from delivery by the Jeraptha. Crews had to go over the dropships one by one, when they had time. *Time* was the problem everywhere for both the human Expeditionary Force, and for the Alien Legion who outnumbered the humans.

Earth was in danger of freezing, not imminent danger, but that didn't matter to any member of the ExForce, who were eager to *get on with it.* They had to wait for their obsolete second-hand starships and dropships to be modified for use by humans, and to be upgraded so they weren't simply target practice for every hostile group of aliens who wanted to prove the upstart humans weren't so tough after all. While the starship crews were busy trying to figure out how their new ships should be operated, the SpaceCav and Alien Legion were busy training to use their new equipment, and learning the new doctrine and tactics for combat assaults and ground operations.

It would have been nice if the extra one hour and seven minutes in each day could be allotted to sleep, but no one had time for that.

When the Scarab dropship docked aboard the *Hudson Bay*, Jates opted to skip the step of making everyone get out and boarding by the numbers. He knew there would be plenty of time for that exercise while an assault carrier was en route to whatever planet the Legion planned to hit first. If UNEF leadership had selected their first target, that information had not trickled down to his level, and he knew to ignore the various bullshit flying around the human and Verd rumor mills.

After a brief time to refuel the dropship, it was moved into a launch tube. There were whirring and banging sounds, as the pilots cycled equipment in a pre-flight check, and heart rates of the team rose, especially when the ship was jolted as the launcher clamps engaged. The team displayed admirable discipline by not filling the common channel with useless chatter, then suddenly there was no breath available for speaking, as the heavy dropship was propelled out into space, and beyond the artificial gravity field.

UNEF training guidelines called for the first familiarization flight to be relatively gentle, but the key word was 'relatively'. There was a lot of flexibility in the guidelines, and Jates had requested the pilots to push the limit. Bored with shuttling SpaceCav soldiers up and down, and needing stick time in their new dropship, the pilots were happy to oblige.

That is why, as the cabin echoed with a roaring sound and shook from aerodynamic pressure that weighed the passengers down three times the force of Earth gravity, the soldier seated opposite Jates bit her lip and was breathing hard through her nose.

"Specialist Carter," Jates barked. "This is a training flight. If you're going to puke, open your helmet." The pilots and dropship crew chief would not like hearing that. But if soldiers upchucked in their helmets, Jates would be responsible for seeing that each set of powered armor was properly serviced. Besides, while a suit helmet had the ability to clean itself, that was not a pleasant process, and UNEF regs stated it should be avoided unless it was dangerous or impossible to open the faceplate.

"Sorry, Surjet," Carter grunted, her face turning pale as the dropship banked hard, flipping on one side, then swinging back. "Oh no," she hastily swung the faceplate up and out of the way. "*Urp.*"

Jates contemplated the goo that was running over the deck plating toward his boots. He didn't bother to lift his feet, and since his own helmet was sealed, the smell didn't get to him. "Carter, that was *weak.*"

"Sorry," she mumbled, miserable.

"Uh, hey, Jates," Dave Czajka called over the private channel, from the front of the cabin. "You shouldn't have called her-"

"*Weak*," Jates repeated. "Look at Rivera here," he pointed to a soldier seated on his side of the cabin, four seats toward the front of the cabin. "He managed to puke all the way onto the opposite cabin wall. That is impressive."

"Oh, whew," Carter was still concentrating on keeping what was left of her dinner on the inside.

Jates stirred the muck with the toe of a boot. "This squishy stuff could be anything, but what are these greasy green *chunks*? I don't remember seeing that in the chow hall."

Seeing the green chunks of whatever was too much for Carter. She ralphed again.

"That's more like it," Jates watched his suit automatically shed the offending material from his thighs onto the deck. "Can everyone hear me? Don't you have any pride in this outfit? If you're going to spew, put some *effort* into it."

Three more people followed Carter's example as the Scarab slammed into the atmosphere at three and a half gravities, then bounced so they were temporarily in freefall.

"Shit, Jates," Dave laughed. "I see what you did there."

"Give me some credit, Czajka. Better for people to get the nausea out of the way on a practice run, than when someone's shooting at us."

"Maybe next time, we won't have to tell them not to eat a big dinner before a combat drop," Dave said, having limited himself to crackers and a handful of peanuts. "Man, I am sure glad I don't have to clean this ship when we're done with it."

Dave was wrong. Not about the wisdom of eating a small, bland meal before experiencing any sort of zero-gee or wild flying maneuvers. About not having to clean the dropship's cabin. The crew chief, appalled by the mess, declared that was the last time his precious ship would be flying the Mavericks, especially their security platoon. Jates partially solved the problem by suggesting they simulate a hull breach while the dropship approached the *Hudson Bay* again. He instructed everyone aboard to seal up their suits, then the crew chief cycled open the rear ramp. Exposure to hard vacuum freeze-dried the offending material, making it easier to scrape up. By the time the Scarab was on final approach, the crew chief was no longer glaring daggers at Jates and his team.

Until, they did it all over again.

Gunnery Sergeant Margaret Adams checked her phone, as it beeped with a message. She was to report to the base supply area, to be issued her new gear. There was no rush, according to the message, but she knew the supply section was still in total disarray, and she would be lucky if they could find half of the gear she was supposed to have. Since joining the Mavericks, she had been training with second-hand equipment, some of which didn't fit her properly.

In the chaotic cluster of tents and shipping containers that constituted the special operations supply section of Forward Operating Base Jaguar, she used her zPhone to guide her to the clerks who made her sign for everything that UNEF thought she needed, an ordeal that took three hours. In the end, she needed an electric cart and two Army specialists to haul everything over to her side of the base, and she still hadn't seen the specially fitted mech suit that was supposed to have been delivered.

It was waiting for her, inside the containerized housing unit she called home. There were two crates, each two meters by one by one, with locks encoded to her biometrics.

What she should have done was stow all the gear she had already checked out, including securing her STARs rifle in the Mavericks armory. But, with two large crates mostly filling her housing unit, it was best to try the suit on first, then it could be stowed away properly. Besides, she was curious.

The crates popped open when she pressed her palm to the scanner, and the two specialists eagerly crowded her to see what was inside. She dismissed them, partly because they were annoying, and partly because she would need to get undressed to don the suit liner.

Tugging open the crate that contained the mech suit's torso with the backpack powercells, she froze, talking into her zPhone. "Skippy, what is this?"

"Hello, Margaret. Do you like it?" he asked in the tone he used when he wanted to be praised for something he'd done. "Pretty cool, huh?"

"What *is* it?"

"A special operations multi-purpose powered armor suit, Mark 7."

"Mark 7? We're on the Mark 5."

"You *were* using the Mark 5."

She stepped closer, examining the torso, and the detached arms that were packed into the bottom of the crate. The suit was bigger, bulkier. Instead of the satin finish of a typical Kristang mech suit, the new unit's surface was a dull matte, although there were tiny glints of light reflecting from it, like it was coated with a fine layer of soot and diamond dust. "Colonel Smythe didn't say anything about this, the last time we-"

"Smythe doesn't know about it," Skippy chuckled. "STAR Team Alpha is testing the Mark 6 now. There was only enough fabrication capacity at Ragnar to make one of these new suits, and I want you to have this prototype. It-"

"Prototype?" She stared at the thing, aghast. "You want me going into combat in an experimental design?"

"Um, no. Maybe I should not have said 'prototype'. This is more like a pre-production example, with-"

"That is not any better, Skippy. Give me my old Mark 5 back, please."

"Um, jeez, no can do, sorry. Your old suit has been split up as spare parts, I had to recycle some of the nano material to make Mark 6s for ST-Alpha."

"Skippy, this is *not* acceptable. Do you understand that?"

"Actually, no. Although it is based on a standard Kristang form, most of the Mark 7 is built on Maxolhx technology. This suit is bigger, stronger, has tougher armor and the powercells last almost forty percent longer, even with increased power consumption. It has an advanced chameleonware skin, plus a built-in stealth field generator, although admittedly, the stealth field only can be used for thirty-three minutes before it burns out. I'm working on stretching the useful life of the generator. With all that, the suit overall weighs twelve kilos *less* than a Mark 5. I don't understand, why don't you like it?"

"Because it's new, and untested, and I've never-"

"New, yes. Untested, no. This is the Mark 7 Delta. It includes refinements I discovered were needed, during testing of the Alpha through Charlie versions. It has been *extensively* tested."

"By a human?"

"Well, no, but-"

"Then it hasn't been tested."

"OK, good point, that is why you need it now."

"Skippy, I'm not a test, pilot, or whatever you call it. Colonel Smythe's team should be evaluating this new model, not me. ST-Alpha needs this equipment more than-"

"No, they do not."

"Skippy, you're not listening to me. I'm not special, I don't need special treatm-"

"You *are* special," he insisted.

"This isn't about-"

"Perhaps I should have said your current *assignment* is special. Smythe's people are supported by other Tier-1 operators, and they have the incomparable magnificence of *me* with them. You are the only operator assigned to the Mavericks. If they get into trouble, and they always *do*, you need every advantage you can get, because I won't be there to help."

"But-"

"Hey, you were constantly telling Joe that a soldier should never turn down anything that gives you an advantage on the battlefield, right?"

"Yes," she sighed, irritated at having her own words thrown back at her. "I hear all your very good reasons why I should have this super suit. What I don't hear is the *real* reason you made this suit for me."

"What is that?"

"Because I'm special to *you*. Listen, Skippy, the Army, or the Marines, we are a *team*. There are no cowboys, no superstars. We succeed because we put the team first."

"Fine," he huffed. "Then, put *me* first."

"Huh?"

"I don't ask much from you monkeys. Amuse me, listen to me sing, and I will protect your filthy species. Listen, Margaret, *try* the new suit, please. If you don't like it, I can make adjustments, while I'm still here. There are other Mark 5 units available, although I can't imagine why you would want to downgrade."

"You promise?"

"I promise."

She looked at the suit again. There was no reason she couldn't at least test the new design. Damn it, the thing looked *cool*. "OK, Skippy, I will try it. You need to send the user manual first."

"The Dash Ten is on your phone, although I designed the user interface so the transition should be seamless for you. You should only notice the difference at the margins, the Mark 7 has substantially higher limits in terms of speed, protection and-"

"Will it have an annoying AI that talks to me?"

"*No*. I learned my lesson about that. The suit has an AI, of course, and it can be voice-activated, but only on user command."

"Good. Now," she tugged on the torso, but it was securely attached to the crate. "I need people in here to help me get into this thing."

"No need for that," Skippy chuckled, as the top of the crate swung back, and the torso rose so its bottom was a meter and half off the floor. "Just attach the arms, then get into the torso from the bottom. Margaret?"

"Yes?"

"If there is anything you don't like about the suit, please let me know. I will be able to make adjustments, but once *Valkyrie* leaves again, you are on your own."

"Oh!" Uhtavio Scorandum grunted. "Why, *this* is not suspicious at all."

"What?" Lieutenant Kinsta looked up expectantly. Their ship had just pinged a relay station for an update, and he had not seen any priority message traffic for them.

"Remember after the humans first attacked the Ruhar, at," he searched his memory. "Rentenoh?"

"Their first action was at Kasternul," the aide corrected his captain. "Rentenoh was second. I still say both of those actions were technically *not* attacks, but-"

"Yes, well," Scorandum waved an antenna, irritated. "Remember at the time, I asked you whether any of us guessed that humans would attack the *Ruhar*?" he shook his head, still incredulous at the development.

Kinsta blinked. "The answer was 'No'. Central Wagering did not have a record of-"

"At the time you inquired, Central Wagering did not have a record of anyone placing such a wager. They do *now*."

"Uuuuuuh," Kinsta sucked in a breath. "Who?"

Scorandum had to check his notes again. "A Captain Federatan of the star carrier *Let It Ride*. It's a civilian ship," he added, when he saw the blank look on the junior officer's face. "Federatan and her crew supposedly placed several wagers, at their last reported stop. Most of the wagers placed out of the money, but-"

"Those lucky *bastards*," Kinsta swore, burning with jealousy, before looking at Scorandum sharply. "Sir, why did you say this is suspicious?"

"Because, the *Let It Ride* was stopped by the ghost ship *Valkyrie*, and seized along with five Ruhar transport ships. Just after Captain Federatan and her crew supposedly placed the fateful wager, about what move the humans would make next. A *correct* wager."

"S*upposedly*?" Kinsta was confused. "The wagers were not registered?"

"They were properly registered. The one-time authentication tags were received by Central Wagering, six days *after* the humans invaded Kasternul."

Kinsta thought of arguing that Kasternul had not actually been invaded, but kept his mouth shut. "Well, Captain Federatan and her crew certainly are lucky, then."

"*Too* lucky."

"Sir?"

"Doesn't this sound suspicious to you? The *only* people who correctly wagered what the humans would do, are the *same* people who encountered the humans a few days later?"

"But," Kinsta's antennas drooped, then stood straight up in alarm. "You are not," he sputtered. "You are not suggesting that someone *faked* an authentication tag?" That was impossible.

"I am saying, this sounds like something we would do. If we *could*," he added.

"Authentication tags can only be used once. They can't be faked."

"They can't be faked by *us*. We know the humans somehow hacked the quantum state interchanger system of the Maxolhx. That system was also considered to be unbreakable."

"But, but- The integrity of authentication tag technology is the basis of our *civilization*," Kinsta shuddered with horror.

"That is why," the ECO captain lowered his voice, though the two of them were in his office with the door closed. "We are not going to say anything about the subject."

"I do not want to believe it."

"I don't either."

"Also, why would the humans fake a wager, on behalf of Federatan and her crew? They could have simply taken her star carrier, and left her in an escape pod."

"Yes. Instead, they allowed her people, and all the Ruhar of the transport ships, to depart in one transport. Kinsta, is it possible that the humans are simply, decent people?"

"*Or*, they just want to screw with us," Kinsta muttered.

"Eh," Scorandum's antennas dipped in a shrug. "It is more likely they do not wish to sour relations with us, in hope of a future alliance."

"Well, there is nothing we can do about it now."

"No, but there is one thing I *am* doing, while we are still in range of this relay station."

"What?"

Scorandum took a one-time authentication tag from a pocket, and waved it in the air. "I am registering a wager, that our system for recording wagers is *not* unbreakable."

Surjet Jates held up a standard Kristang infantry rifle, designated M-25A5 by UNEF. To say it was standard was not quite correct, the weapon had been modified extensively over the term of its service with both the original Alien Legion, and by the special mission unit calling themselves the Merry Band of Pirates. The A5 model was issued to both human SpaceCav units and the Verd-Kris of the Alien Legion, and was only slightly different from the M-25A9 model used by the special operators of both species.

Jates did not care that a selected group of operators had a fancier rifle. He only cared that the knuckleheaded humans he was in charge of gained experience with their new toy, without causing injury to themselves, each other, or him. Based on what he had seen so far in the training cycle, he was not confident the primitive aliens could be trusted to handle lethal weapons, and the boastful bravado he'd heard from them left him disgusted that anyone who had yet to see combat could brag about what they were going to do, someday.

He held a rifle aloft. "For your benefit, I will dumb this way down. You may think of this as a *bang stick*." The murmuring of the crowd was not friendly, except for Staff Sergeants Jarrett and Colter covering their mouths to stifle laughter. "The pointy end," he pointed to the M-25's muzzle, "is not to be aimed at any of your fellow idiots, and never at *me*, is that clear? In combat, if you do manage to point it in the direction of the enemy, do us all a favor and do *not* pull this here trigger mechanism. You won't hit anything useful, and all you will accomplish is pissing off the enemy, and getting us all killed. If that happens, my ghost will hunt you down, and make the afterlife miserable for you, forever. Did anyone not understand that?"

Two days later, the new soldiers of the Mavericks security platoon had an opportunity to fire live rounds with their rifles, after shooting unloaded weapons at a simulated firing range. The simulator was supposed to accurately represent the experience of firing live rounds, even making the rifle kick back, and the barrel heat up.

The fact that the simulator was *not* an accurate representation became immediately obvious, when soldiers who were rated expert in simulations had difficulty hitting the target at all on a real firing range. After a luckless specialist stitched a line of rounds from the edge of his target and across the target of the soldier next to him, Jates had enough. "Cease fire! Cease fire. Soldier, secure your weapon and get over here."

The target of Jates' wrath sheepishly avoiding the big lizard's eyes, did as ordered, and trotted over for a personal counselling session.

"Davidge?" Jates peered at the man's nametag.

"Specialist Will Davidge," the man acknowledged.

"Hmm. So, when I order people to fire at *will*, they-" That got a laugh from everyone on the firing line, except one. "Specialist, what is wrong with you today?"

"Surjet, I don't-"

"Davidge, that question doesn't rate an answer, you dumbass. To list everything that is wrong with you would take all day, and that would only cover the obvious issues."

"Something is wrong with my rifle," Davidge said while avoiding the Surjet's eyes.

"Indeed?" Jates held out a hand. "I will check it." He examined the weapon, sighted on a target with its scope. "It appears to be functioning normally. Listen, while I sing the song of my people." Switching to full auto, he sent a long burst of rounds downrange with the distinctive buzzing roar of a Kristang rifle *BRAAAAAAAAAAP*. Round after round tore into the target as puffs of dirt erupted from the mound behind it, and the center of the red and white circle disappeared. "Yes, hmm," Jates released the trigger, and cradled the weapon at the low ready position. "The *rifle* apparently is not the problem."

"I don't know how to-"

"Look at me," Jates pulled a marker from a pocket, and drew crosshairs on the lens of the soldier's goggles. "There. Now, you can at least claim that whatever the hell you hit, you were aiming at it." He replaced the marker in his pocket. "You see that puddle of mud over there? Grab that real estate, and I want you doing pushups until *I'm* tired."

As Specialist Davidge huffed and puffed through one pushup after another, Dave Czajka wandered over to Jates and whispered, "Hey, you think maybe you're being too tough on that guy?"

Jates glared. "Will the Kristang be gentle with him? Or the Wurgalan?"

"No, but-"

"Because I just named the two *softest* enemies we will face- Davidge," he barked to the laboring soldier. "Keep going, I'm not tired yet!" Lowering his voice, he continued, "Czajka, do you want someone in this unit who can't shoot straight? It's bad enough I'm saddled with *your* sorry ass." He turned away. "All right, Specialist, get up. Back to your station. Move!"

Davidge ran, gasping for breath, ran with the Verd-kris right on his heels. "Pick up that rifle- No, insert a fresh magazine first. Now, get into a prone position," Jates pushed the soldier's backside down into the dirt with a boot. "Fire when ready. When *I'm* ready, which is right now!"

Three minutes later, Davidge safed his weapon and rolled to his right, to check the range display. "I'll be damned!" He gasped at his score. "I qualified!"

"Your problem is in your stupid *head*," Jates grunted. "Don't think, just shoot. There is precious little time for thinking on the battlefield. And thinking isn't what you primitives are good at in the first place."

Major Frey was sitting at a table in the American DFAC at FOB Jaguar, eating a late lunch with more mechanical efficiency than with any delight about the food. She had one elbow on the table, propping up her head so she didn't flop onto the plate and fall asleep in the middle of her meal.

It had been a long day.

Literally. Her alarm had woken her up at 0215, so she could get dressed and be at the exercise area early, and make sure everything was set up properly. When she jogged across the field, she found that her senior NCOs were of course already there, even though she was more than an hour ahead of the scheduled time. The last two team members showed up with fifteen minutes to go, a fact that got jeers from their fellow operators, until they casually mentioned they had just come back from a ten kilometer run as a warm-up.

When the exercise ended at 1345, she was shaking from a combination of exhaustion and hunger. Her blood sugar levels had dropped, then plateaued so she was well past being hangry and into the FEED ME stage. Despite needing fuel, she had trouble making herself expend the energy to lift the food off her plate and into her tired mouth.

Refuel, shower, check again that all the equipment signed out that morning had been returned properly, then write up notes, before a meeting with her counterpart from the Legion's US Marine Corps Raider team to discuss lessons learned. Then, to make the day even more fun, she had to attend a staff meeting at 1930. She made a mental note to grab a cup of coffee on the way out.

She was startled out of her reverie by a thump on the table, as Colonel Smythe sat down opposite her, and pushed a steaming mug of coffee across the table. "Double double," he said, pointing to the coffee.

"Bless you, Sir." Her hand was shaking as she picked up the plastic mug with both hands, taking a messy slurp.

"I won't ask you about the exercise," Smythe said quietly. He had been on a training exercise also, with the Chinese team, and she could see the crease on his forehead from the mech suit helmet liner. "Major, I may have given you bad advice, led you astray."

She paused, fork halfway to her mouth, until the fork felt so heavy, she had to set it down. "Led me astray? Is this about that Marmite stuff you want me to try?"

"No," he chuckled.

"Good. Because between your Marmite, the Vegemite the Aussies eat, and that Fluff that Bishop thinks is the greatest thing since cheeseburgers," she made a sour face, "I don't know which is worse."

"Marmite on toast is *delicious*, Frey. No, I meant, I might have given you bad advice about signing on with my outfit."

"Sir?" She blinked slowly, her eyelids too weary to work properly. "You think I should have stayed in a training billet on Earth?"

"No. When we had a conversation about your options. I thought the Legion would see more action, but that what we did aboard *Valkyrie* would be more important in the end."

She shook her head. "I'm sorry, Sir, it's been a long day. You'll have to spell it out for me, please."

"Bishop said something that made me reconsider our situation. *Valkyrie* might succeed in forcing the kitties to clean up the cloud at Earth-"

"Might?" Even tired as she was, she arched an eyebrow at his blasphemy.

"*Will*," he corrected himself. "I don't know how, whether these near-lightspeed darts do the trick, or if it will be something else Bishop and the beer can cook up. I've seen this crew do the impossible too many times, to question whether we can do it again. We will force the Maxolhx to disperse the cloud, or make them stand aside while we do it. I'm not questioning that. My point is, in the *long* run, what the Legion is doing will be more important."

"How so?" The food on her plate was forgotten.

"We can only fix the current crisis. There will be another one. And another, and *another*. For any sort of long-term safety, we need allies, and that is what Perkins is doing with her Legion."

"Is not *her* Legion," Frey objected. "She only commands the Mavericks, that's barely a company-size force."

One corner of Smythe's mouth turned upward in a wry smile. "Make no mistake, the strategy was approved by Zhao, and Ross and the entire UNEF leadership out here, but it is Perkins' show. They're all following *her* strategy to show aliens the advantages of an alliance with us, and get them to break away from the coalitions that have kept this damned war going, for longer than humanity has controlled the use of fire."

"You really think that's the key?"

"Yes. The Merry Band of Pirates can only stamp out one fire at a time. If the Legion gets us allies, and begins to break up the coalitions, that could prevent the next fire."

"There will *always* be another fire."

"Yes, but maybe the next blaze won't threaten to burn *Earth*."

She nodded, looking down at the uneaten food that was growing cold. "The Legion may see more action, and their ops may be more important in the long run, but," she shrugged. "Where can *one* operator make the most difference, Sir?"

"STAR Team Alpha," he said without hesitation, a twinkle in his weary eyes.

"Then I made the right decision."

Abruptly, he stood up, catching that she kept glancing at her plate. "Major, an old man rambling on is keeping you from your delicious lunch."

"That's not true."

"You're saying I'm *not* old?"

"I'm saying," she had a twinkle in her own eyes. "This lunch is far from delicious."

CHAPTER TWENTY SIX

"Psst, Joe," Skippy whispered in my earpiece, while I was in line at the Club Skippy base dining facility. It was great eating somewhere other than *Valkyrie's* galley, and I was determined to enjoy the opportunity. The Legion was wrapping up training, and would be boarding dropships for the flight up to transport ships soon. The Verds were eager for action, and as ready as they could be, without actual combat experience. "You promised Simms you would eat a more healthy diet."

"What? I'm having a salad."

"That is a *cheeseburger*," he sniffed.

"No," I pointed at the lettuce, tomato and onion on top. "It's a salad, see?"

"What about the beef patty and the slice of cheese?"

"That's protein. It's healthy to have protein with your salad."

"The bun?"

"Those are just *croutons*, Skippy."

"Ugh."

"Fine, look," I reached for the tongs in front of me. "I'll add another slice of tomato, and," I picked up a squeeze bottle. "This super-healthy, anti-oxidant tomato puree."

"That is *ketchup*, you moron."

"Same thing."

"I, I actually cannot argue with you about that."

"To make sure I have a balanced diet, I'll add carbs by getting fries on the side."

"French fries? Those are terrible for you."

"What if I put the fries on the burger, I mean, salad? Toppings don't count."

"Toppings *do* count, you idiot. Jeez, Joe, it would be healthier if you had another cheeseburger instead of the fries."

"Really?"

"Really. I can explain the nutritional val-"

"Thanks, buddy." I stepped away from the table and went back to the beginning of the line, holding out my tray to get another cheeseburger.

"*Seriously*?" Skippy groaned.

"Hey, doctor's orders. Unless you were lying about the fries?"

"I was not," he sighed. "Is this like that taco salad you had for dinner yesterday? Twenty seven hundred calories of ground beef, cheese and guacamole?"

"That has to be healthy, Skippy. It's right in the name: taco *salad*."

"Ugh."

"Besides, there was also lettuce and tomato, and onions and peppers, and salsa and all kinds of other stuff in there."

"Twenty seven *hundred* calories, Joe. And that's without the disgusting deep-fried bowl they served it in."

"Yeah, man. An edible *bowl*," I smacked my lips. "That is genius."

"No, that is a heart attack waiting to happen."

"I wonder if I could get this cheeseburger salad on an edible *plate*?"

"Oh. My. G- You did not actually *have* to eat that taco bowl, dumdum."

"Of course I did. The cooks put a lot of work into deep-frying those bowls, Skippy. It would be an insult not to eat it."

"The whole thing?"

"Remember all those months, when I ate only sludges?"

"That doesn't count."

"It does count," I said as I got to the end of the line, and looked for a table that wasn't jammed with people. "For all I know, this might be my last real food for a while."

"Hmm. Well, Colonel Simms just walked in the doorway, so that might *be* your last meal, if she sees you eating all that junk food."

Yes, I am a coward. Ducking down behind a line of people, I scooted over to a table of French paratroopers, who made room for me to sit. I kept my head down while I ate, and Simms never saw me. Did I feel guilty about eating two cheeseburger salads?

Here's what I was thinking: Mmm, cheeseburgers.

It had rained heavily overnight at Forward Operating Base Jaguar, the ground was soaked and the footing was treacherous on the trails around the base. With more rain expected and dark gray clouds rolling in from the west, Surjet Jates stood in front of the formation, looking from right to left, as drizzle began to fall. "Show of hands. Who wants to hit the gym, instead of a ten kilometer run this morning?"

Every hand went up, except Dave Czajka, who knew better.

"All right," Jates nodded. "Ten kilometer run it is, *then* the gym."

With the base having rapidly expanded, the original trails saw too much use, and were pounded down to a sloppy mess in many areas. Work crews were out cutting new trails every day, they just weren't working fast enough for the number of people who needed to train. The result was that most days, faster groups got bunched up behind the laggards, with no place to pass in the muddy, dense forest, and Jates was irritated by the delays. That morning, they only saw one group, running the opposite way.

The trail wound back and forth on steep switchbacks up to the crest of a hill, then plunged down on an even steeper grade to run along a rain-swollen stream at the bottom. Those who were smart, or just still had the mental capacity to think while being pushed hard by a genetically-engineered alien super-soldier, realized that Jates was going easy on them by taking the switchback route up the hill.

While running on trails, particularly rough-cut trails lined with rocks, tree roots and mud deep enough to get stuck in, there are those who have fallen flat on their faces, those who will, and those who did but lie about it.

That morning, Jates pushed his luck too far. While weaving between soldiers and trees, to get from the rear to the front of the column, he hooked a toe on a protruding root and fell forward, hopping on one foot and flailing his arms in a desperate effort to regain balance.

He failed.

Crashing a shoulder into a tree, he tumbled down a gully, coming to a stop in a puddle that was full of leaves and muck.

"Holy shit, Surjet," Dave shouted, holding onto trees while he walked sideways down the gully to avoid failing. "You OK?"

"I'm *fine*, Czajka," Jates got to his feet, trudging upward while wiping muck off his face. His pride was wounded more than his body. Shaking away Dave's offer of a hand to get back on the trail, Jates stomped the final few meters and glared at the waiting group. "All right! Everyone who laughed at me, drop and give me fifty."

A dozen soldiers shook their heads ruefully and began doing pushups in the mud as rain pelted them, knowing it was useless to argue.

"The rest of you," Jates folded arms across his chest. "A hundred pushups, for *lying* to me."

"Shit," Dave muttered, as he looked for the least-muddy spot. "I should have known."

"Were you even listening to me?" Margaret asked. One hand was on her hip, the other with an index finger pointed at me accusingly. I had seen her mother make the same gesture to her father, so I knew where Margaret got it from. We were in my office at Club Skippy, eating meatloaf sandwiches I brought from the base DFAC. While she was stationed at FOB Jaguar and I flew *Valkyrie* back and forth, we were able to see each other regularly, but not often enough. So, we took the opportunity to eat lunch together, while I had one eye on a PowerPoint slide, getting prepped for my next meeting.

Hmm, I thought. *That* is an odd way to begin a conversation. "Yes," I lied. "Of course I was listening to you," I said as I pretended to scratch my wrist. Actually, I was sending a Bat-signal on my smart watch. Tap, tap. Pause. Tap, tap.

Margaret glared at me. "You were?" She demanded. "What was I saying?"

"Joe," Skippy whispered in my earpiece. "It was about how she still feels like an outsider with the Mavericks. Or some bullshit like that, I wasn't really listening either," he admitted.

"It will take time, that's all," I said quietly. "The seven of them, eight if you count Jates, have been together a long time. Everyone else has cycled through their platoon."

"It's a company now."

"You know what I mean." I almost shuddered with relief at having hit the target. "They are probably feeling defensive now. Majors Striebich and Bonsu have been reassigned, Dandurf isn't with the Legion anymore. Shauna is technically a Maverick, but she's at sniper school now. It's not just that you are new to their unit, their unit is changing. You know what it's like at the end of a deployment, and everyone goes separate ways."

"I guess," she sighed.

"Plus, Maggie," I rarely used her authorized nickname. "You gotta remember, they may still have a chip on their shoulders about you."

"Me? Why?"

"Because you're a Pirate."

"I *was* a Pirate."

"You still are, as far as your new unit is concerned. As far as *everyone* is concerned." That was true. Technically, Gunnery Sergeant Adams was listed on the STAR Team Alpha roster, temporarily assigned to the Mavericks as their STAR liaison. Unfortunately, maybe I shouldn't have mentioned that. In her new position, she was neither a Pirate nor a Maverick. "The Mavs, the entire Alien Legion, the original one, I mean. They have accomplished some amazing stuff but they never Saved The World," I added the capital letters to my tone of voice. "Earth," I corrected myself. "They never saved *Earth*, you know? They might think you look at them as the junior varsity, you know?"

"I don't. Everything they accomplished, they did without a beer can helping them."

"Have you told the Mavericks that?"

She shrugged. "Not directly."

"Maybe you should."

Her eyes moistened, and for a moment I feared I'd said the wrong thing. Instead, she stepped forward and hugged me, planting a kiss on my cheek and whispering in my ear. "You are a *good* man. I am very lucky."

"I am lucky too," I whispered back. "Remember, Jesse, Dave and Shauna were, *are*, friends of mine. I care about them too."

She drew back. "Even Colonel Perkins?"

"She can be a pain in the *ass*," I admitted. "But, yeah. I gotta respect her. We're all lucky that she's on our side."

I asked her how she thought the Alien Legion was shaping up, mostly to steer the conversation onto a different subject, but also because I wanted her perspective. Status reports listing dry stuff like progress in training evolutions didn't always provide a good sense of whether a unit was ready for action. There was, in her view, a lot of work to be done before the Verds, and the SpaceCav, would be capable of taking on a serious fight. That's what I'd heard from General Ross also, but it was good to hear it from someone I knew and trusted. Margaret assured me that humans and Verds *would* be ready, when we had the assault ships to take them somewhere to fight.

After Margaret left, I let out the full-body shudder I'd been holding in. "Whew. That was a *close* one. Thanks, buddy."

"No problem, Joe." His avatar appeared on top of a crate, holding out a tiny hand for a fist bump. "Bros before hos, right?"

I held my fist an inch from his. "Adams is not a *ho*, Skippy."

"Come on, Joe. I was using that term like Santa does."

"*Santa?*"

"Sure. That's how he introduces his three girlfriends." His avatar's hat changed to a red and white cap. Pointing at something imaginary, he gave a belly laugh. "Ho, ho, ho."

"Oh my- Skippy, that is *awful*," I laughed. "Seriously, though, thank you," I gave him a fist bump.

"I won't always be there to bail you out," he warned.

"I'll try harder in the future. You know, that actually does bother me. If I'm not listening when she talks *now*, what's it going to be like in the future? Assuming we have a future. I need to be a better, you know, boyfriend." Man, it felt odd to say that. "Hey, can you clue me in when she's talking to me, and you realize I'm not paying attention?" He didn't answer. "Skippy?"

"Huh? What?" His avatar shook its head. "You said something?"

"Uh, never mind."

The Ruhar Federation world Nahkellbik was not, despite the original marketing slogan of the colony development company, 'A Happy Place'. It was not happy *at all*, not for anyone involved. Not for the crews of the Bosphuraq warships stationed there on rotations for half a standard year, during which time they were confined to their ships or to one of the three space stations. Starship crews were banned from shore leave on the planet below, after several bloody incidents early in their occupation.

The bloodshed had been not Bosphuraq crews against the seven hundred million local Ruhar inhabitants, at least not mostly. There had been, of course, isolated outbursts of violence when the haughty second-tier clients treated the planet like their own and were eager to throw their weight around. But the major incidents that led to starship crews being confined to orbit was Bosphuraq being killed by the official occupation force: their own clients, the Wurgalan.

It should have been no surprise to anyone that small groups of Bosphuraq were easy targets for heavily-armed Wurgalan soldiers, nor was it surprising that the client species sought every opportunity to murder their patrons. So, less than a local month after the Ruhar lost control of their world, responsibilities for the occupation were split. The Bosphuraq ruled everything above the stratosphere, with the handful of lowly Wurgalan ships banished to the far side of the local moon. The lower layers of the atmosphere, and the dirt and mud of the surface, were controlled by the Wurgalan infantry. Any flight above the altitude at which an aircraft could hover required prior clearance from the Bosphuraq above, or the aircraft would be blasted by maser cannons from orbit. Even when clearance was requested, granted and verified, there were unfortunate incidents where starship gunnery crews did not get the memo, or just happened to test-fire their cannons in the wrong direction.

The Wurgalan knew better than to ask for an apology when such 'accidents' happened. They also did not bother to file a protest when a request for orbital fire support went wrong, and the maser beams or railgun darts struck 'friendly' forces instead of the Ruhar insurgents.

The insurgency was growing day by day, prompting ever-more-brutal crackdowns against the civilian population. With no reinforcements available for the hard-pressed Wurgalan infantry that numbered less than seventy thousand when the occupation began, the commander would have preferred to pull his troops back to a defensible position, and rely on air power and orbital fire support to keep the Ruhar from causing too much trouble. Going on the defensive would have been sensible, a prudent use of limited resources.

The Wurgalan government, which did not have any civilian representatives within four hundred lightyears of Nahkellbik, did not see a defensive redeployment as sensible. They saw it as surrender, as cowardice in the face of an enemy that had been declared officially disarmed. So, the Wurgalan ground-pounders went out on patrols day after day, never knowing when they would be shot at or blown up on patrol. Or, they might merely be killed by a mortar shell striking their barracks, as they got armored up to go outside the wire fencing that surrounded their bases.

To say that relations, between the increasingly desperate Wurgalan infantry and the increasingly desperate and starving Ruhar citizens, were deteriorating, was like saying a three-day-old fish left out in the sun was 'not quite fresh'. Due to a combination of infrastructure damage from the prolonged and savage battle in which the Ruhar lost their planet, and deliberate policies to pacify the population by controlling the food supply, and simple yet *breathtakingly* impressive incompetence by the Wurgalan logistics personnel, a majority of the planet's population was existing on half rations, and they were the lucky ones. By the time the planet rotated ten more times, a quarter of the population would be incapable of moving on their own, or already dead from starvation. And rather than inspiring the populace to cooperate so food production and distribution could be improved, the artificially-created famine had caused a surge of support for the insurgency. The attacks by rag-tag local forces focused on preventing the occupiers from interfering with the insurgents' efforts to raid warehouses for food. When the raids prompted the Bosphuraq to target warehouses for orbital bombardment, that did not make either side more willing to back down, and negotiate an end to the unsustainable situation.

It wasn't supposed to be that way at all. The fate of Nahkellbik was a mistake, a miscalculation, though that revelation was only hindsight. The truth was, the whole thing was out of anyone's control.

It was all the fault of an unlikely species, who were not directly involved at all: *humans*.

The Bosphuraq had not wanted Nahkellbik at all, not originally. It was too tough a target, though the star system's position between two wormholes did make it a valuable asset. That world was not even on Bosphuraq Command's wish list of places to conquer, a list that mostly consisted of *retaking* worlds they had lost in the past three decades. A major offensive to capture a heavily-populated planet was completely out of the question.

But then, the Maxolhx arranged a forced marriage between the Bosphuraq and their hated allies the Thuranin, and history took a detour. The Thuranin suggested a combined campaign against the Ruhar world. The stated purpose was to force the Jeraptha to pull back from a very successful offensive in Thuranin territory, and that was a semi-legit reason. The *real* purpose why the Thuranin proposed the assault and occupation of Nahkellbik, was to tie up scarce military assets the Bosphuraq couldn't afford to commit long-term. The Bosphuraq protested, and were holding firm against the operation, but then a group of *humans* began flying a ghost ship around the galaxy, and the Bosphuraq had to prove their undying loyalty to their exalted asshole patrons.

The result was a massive, and massively expensive, combined offensive to capture a planet the Thuranin could not care less about, and the Bosphuraq did not want badly enough to pay the price for. A three-day battle of the combined fleet against the Jeraptha and Ruhar, cleared the way for the landing of a Wurgalan assault force. During the first three waves of the ground assault, seventeen percent of Wurgalan dropships were destroyed by intense anti-aircraft fire, and when the survivors set armor-suited tentacles on the surface, they looked around and asked their leaders what the fuck they were doing *there*.

Soon after the planet was prematurely declared pacified, the Thuranin warships bailed out of the joint operation, claiming they had pressing concerns elsewhere, and the Bosphuraq were left alone to hold a world they never really wanted. The Bosphuraq fleet assumed they only had to make a good show of defending their new asset, until the Jeraptha consolidated enough combat power to take the star system back. The Wurgalan assumed they would be abandoned on the ground, when their cowardly patrons jumped away. And the Ruhar assumed they only had to hold out for a few months, while harassing the occupation force so the Wurgalan would think twice about invading another world in the Ruhar Federation.

But then, *humans* revealed they had been flying the ghost ship, and that they now had Elder weapons. With the long-static balance of power in the galaxy suddenly disrupted, the Jeraptha were not alone in putting all offensive operations on hold until the new strategic situation became clear.

Then, to make matters even worse, the humans had allowed a threat to loom over their homeworld, and it appeared they were powerless to do anything about it. The Jeraptha informed their Ruhar clients that any new initiative was impossible, while they pulled back to defend their own core territories.

The oppressed inhabitants of Nahkellbik would have to fend for themselves as best they could, for help was not coming any time soon.

The lead gunnery officer of the Bosphuraq battleship *Gallagon* reviewed the bombardment plan from his team, making notes for himself, and small adjustments to the plan. There was no problem with the original plan for turning the target into a pillar of fire, then a choking fog of smoking and falling debris, and eventually a mud-filled crater on the outskirts of the city. But, he was the officer of the ship's gunnery department, and if he didn't make changes, it might make the *Gallagon's* captain think he could be replaced with a junior officer. Replacement meant a promotion, or possibly a lateral transfer, but either of those options were undesirable. The crew of the *Gallagon* were scheduled to rotate home when the next transport ship arrived, and any change in his status might result in his remaining at the miserable and still hotly-contested world, until he had officially completed qualification aboard a new ship.

That was the *last* thing he wanted.

The battleship *Gallagon* was old and had not been selected for the last round of service life extension upgrades, so it had been downgraded from a frontline unit to a surface bombardment platform, unsuitable to operate in a space-control mission. That meant the crew of the ship were relegated to boring garrison duty, but it also meant they would be replaced soon by a fresh crew, and they could go *home*.

The target was coming into view as the old battleship soared along in a low polar orbit, and the planet rotated slowly below. If needed, the row of warehouses could be struck by missiles while the target was still over the horizon, though the captain would need to justify use of expensive guided ordnance against a low-value target. Maser beams were the first choice for surface bombardment, as cannon pulses were cheap and did not need to be accounted for. As long as each cannon did not exceed the number of shots it could fire without being taken offline for replacement of magnets, no one cared what the masers were used for. Unfortunately, a strong thunderstorm over the target rendered maser beams less effective, and the dispersal of the directed energy could cause widespread collateral damage on the surface. Including the risk of boiling the nearby Wurgalan platoon in their armored suits, which would be a bonus for- No, the lead gunnery officer of the battleship reminded himself. The friendly-fire deaths of client troops would be a *terrible* tragedy-

Because he would need to fill out endless annoying forms to explain the incident.

Railgun darts were cheap, being inert, pointy rods of ultra-dense material. They could be expended against low-value targets without needing justification, and the probability of unreasonable collateral damage was low. So, the row of warehouses had been tasked to three railguns. Those guns would fling out their projectiles as close to simultaneously as possible. If darts were launched in serial order, the darts following the lead one might be thrown off-course by the shockwaves of the first dart's passage through the atmosphere. It was better to have all three darts plunge through the air side by side, and the simultaneous overlapping impacts would multiply the destructive effect on the target.

The explosions would blow out windows far from the target, collapse civilian buildings close by, and enrage the Wurgalan infantry platoon stationed in the city. The platoon leader, overwhelmed by constant insurgent attacks that had whittled his combat strength down by twenty percent, had negotiated with local authorities to provide access to the food stored in the warehouses. At first, the Wurgalan ground commander was upset by her platoon leader's unauthorized initiative, then skeptical it would produce any useful result, and finally figured what the hell? Give it a chance. She had sent a message to her patrons in orbit, to please take those warehouses *off* the target list.

That was why the *Gallagon* was preparing to destroy the warehouses with an orbital strike. Partly to punish their grubby clients for failing to enforce their will on the enemy, partly to punish the lowly Wurgalan for daring to have *initiative*, and partly just to piss off the ground troops who were helpless to hit back. The unexpected bombardment would be explained as an unfortunate communications error, and the gunnery team would enjoy a good laugh as they gleefully re-watched the video over drinks that evening.

As the forces of orbital mechanics, and the rotation of the planet, brought the warehouses within the center of the circular probability of error markings on the display of the main weapons console, the gunnery team prepared to fire their railguns. The captain had given his assent for live-fire, and the duty officer confirmed the ship was ready and there was no conflicting traffic in the area. All three of the selected railguns were at full charge, their darts loaded into the chambers, with the armor-plated outer doors open. A counter began running down, to mark when the optimal moment of launch would occur, and the railguns automatically moved within their mounts, to keep lined up with the target. Below, the towering cloud tops of the thunderstorm were lit up from within by bolts of lightning, flashing like strobe lights. As the moment-

Alarms blared and the battleship rocked, trembling along its length. Startled, the lead gunnery officer canceled the launch countdown of the three railguns, in case they were needed for a higher-priority target.

Before the blast door to the bridge compartment slammed down, he heard the crew there shouting to each other. They were under attack from multiple ships that had just jumped into orbit and-

Sound cut off as the blast door sealed. In the gunnery control compartment, the lead officer barked orders to get his team focused on the new threat, while he switched the displays to show the tactical situation around the *Gallagon*.

They were surrounded by enemy ships. Not surrounded, exactly, the battleship was in low orbit so beneath them was only the bulk of the planet. In every other direction were warships that had very recently emerged from jump wormholes, but somehow were already firing weapons with impressive accuracy. How was that possible? The ship's AI identified the configurations of the ships as Jeraptha, and those aliens did not-

Correction.

The ship's AI changed the identification from Jeraptha to *human*.

The huge battleship rocked again, hard, and the display indicated energy shield generators along one side were offline. Enemy railgun darts slammed into the unprotected armor plating of the capital ship, sending a deep groaning vibration throughout the hull as the structure flexed and twisted beyond its design limits.

The *Gallagon* was dying. Two reactors had been struck, one managed to safely vent plasma, the other suffered an uncontrolled loss of containment that knocked the reactor adjacent to it offline. The bridge crew was launching every missile the battleship had, regardless of proper attack protocol. They just wanted to get missiles in flight while the ship was still capable of operating the launch tubes, before many of the elevators to the reload magazines were jammed from structural frames being twisted out of alignment.

That was bad news.

Then, the battleship *Morevez* exploded.

The initial shock wave struck the nearby *Gallagon* with enough force to push the heavy warship sideways, as it had been flying in formation with its sister battleship. Ironically, the two battleships had been flying close together for mutual safety, so they could support each other with massed defensive fire from their proximity-defense cannons. Proximity became the problem rather than the solution, high-energy debris from what used to be the *Morevez* pelted the *Gallagon*, peeling off armor plating and exposing the thin pressure hull beneath.

In the gunnery control compartment, the team was struggling to get their weapons aligned with an enemy ship, but the sensor feed was so scrambled the fire-control computers couldn't get a lock on anything in the target-rich environment. The lead officer worked his own console to no success, trying to manually guide the-

The alarm blared to abandon ship, and a voice announcement from a shaky-sounding junior officer urged the crew to get to escape pods while they could.

That wasn't good. The captain, and the other senior officers on the bridge, were all unable to give the order? Looking at the blast door to the bridge, the lead gunnery officer saw that the thick door was *bent* and there were scorch marks along one side. Something bad had happened in the next compartment.

"Abandon ship!" The lead officer ordered, not out of concern for his crew, but to give himself cover if there was an investigation into the loss of the *Gallagon*. If he survived to care about that sort of thing.

As his team began the process of unsealing the hatch on the other side of the compartment, he saw that the fire control computer was useless against enemy ships, the targeting solution for the stupid *warehouses* was still valid. Because of uncertainty about the ship's current position, the circular probability of error encompassed the entire Ruhar city below. He did not care. It was an opportunity to hit *something*, to kill perhaps thousands of nasty, stubborn Ruhar.

He authorized the target, engaged the railguns, and wrapped a hand around the firing grip, and he-

Died, as a red-hot chunk of a toilet from the battleship *Morevez* smashed through the compartment bulkhead at fifteen kilometers per second, and tore his head off.

"Cease fire," Admiral Zhao ordered, twenty nine minutes behind schedule. "All units, cease fire." The last Bosphuraq warship in the fight had just exploded, ending all organized opposition. "Captain Kutzenov," he addressed one of his cruiser squadron commanders, "you may now form Task Force Five, to pursue and engage the Wurgalan."

With the Bosphuraq out of the fight, the only hostile warships in the system were a group of Wurgalan assault carriers and transport ships, supported by a handful of cruisers and destroyers. The combined firepower of those third-tier client warships was no threat to Zhao's capital ships, but they could kill civilians on the planet with hit-and-run raids, so he had to deal with the threat. It would be a good opportunity to practice search and destroy tactics in the vastness of a star system, and the crews assigned to Task Force Five would be eager to make their commander happy.

Because he was *not* happy. The attack against the Bosphuraq had resulted in overwhelming victory, with every enemy ship destroyed or disabled. On the UN side, the destroyer *Lyon* was a total loss, having taken several punishing hits to its engineering section. The cruisers *Huang-He* and *Indus* had damage that would require repairs by the support ship *Milo*. It was a remarkably small price to pay for such a victory, and that was not the point. The United Nations Navy had performed poorly overall, needing to rely on brute firepower and, for the first time, use of precious missiles to achieve the victory.

The sloppy tactics could be addressed later. First, there were a reported sixty four thousand Wurgalan troops on the ground. Mostly in Ruhar cities where the UN ships could not risk orbital strikes for fear of mass civilian casualties. The tough Wurgalan infantry were dug into well-chosen defensive positions, and digging them out would be a long, bloody, messy house-to-house fight.

Fortunately, Zhao had a force that was eager for a bloody fight.

The Verd-kris of the Alien Legion.

On a signal from Zhao, the destroyer *Sao Paulo* jumped away, to the rendezvous point where the UN assault force was waiting.

CHAPTER TWENTY SEVEN

The assault carrier *Adriatic Sea* made an odd groaning sound, and the deck vibrated beneath Dave Czajka's feet. It was not unusual for the old rust-bucket of a ship to make noises when its structure flexed under strain, but it was always alarming. The crew assured the soldiers there was nothing to worry about, the ship had been overbuilt to be stronger than it needed to be in normal service.

Dave considered that the carrier was long past its intended design life, that it had been modified and upgraded in ways the crew probably did not fully understand, and that nothing about the upcoming operation was *normal*. Humans were flying an alien starship and despite the placards in human languages taped onto the walls, the original Jeraptha script was still everywhere. The assault carrier was not the only alien craft he would be flying aboard, the 'Scarab' dropship had the UNEF logo painted on the tail, and registration numbers on the side, but all the warning labels with the equivalent of 'No Step' and 'Caution: Intake' and 'Hot Exhaust' were still in the squiggly Jeraptha script. Someone had decided it would be more efficient to teach the flight crews a few simple alien phrases, than to relabel everything. There simply wasn't enough *time*, and that really bothered Dave. Despite everyone at FOB Jaguar itching to get into the fight, even the most gung-ho soldiers had to admit they needed months to get ready. First by learning to operate their new equipment, then learning how best to use the new capabilities the advanced tech offered, and training until the new tactics were ingrained in everyone down to the fireteam level.

He tried counting in his head how many alien worlds he had been on, and decided he was too keyed-up to think about trivia. Hopefully, the world the Ruhar named Nahkellbik, and that humans had tagged 'Nickelback', would not be the last rock he set his boots on.

He shuffled forward toward the docking bay where his assigned Scarab was waiting to be loaded. Supposedly the Navy pukes had defeated the Bosphuraq and established total supremacy in the space above the planet, so it was safe for vulnerable assault transports to operate in the area. Yeah. Dave had heard *that* before, over the planet they called Squidworld. Just before the transport ship he was aboard then, got sliced in half by a strategic defense network that supposedly didn't exist. "Excuse me if I'm skeptical," he muttered to himself.

"Sir?" The soldier in line ahead of him half turned around.

"Nothing," Dave said, loud enough to be heard clearly over the hum of machinery in the docking bay. He was a civilian contractor, not a 'Sir' at all, but the awe-struck young soldiers in the unit reflexively called him 'Sir' or 'Staff Sergeant'. Hell, he wasn't that much older than them. It's not the years, he told himself, it's the mileage. Most of the people around him had never been offworld until they took the flight from Earth to Jaguar. There were veterans from Paradise scattered through the force, but not enough of them. Most people who finally returned home after years of being stranded on Paradise wanted to *stay* home, not turn right around and re-up for another extended stay on an alien world.

The line shuffled forward steadily, and soon Dave was standing under the tail of the Scarab, moving toward the rear ramp. The spacecraft's engines were off, but they were still warm from being run up before the inner docking bay doors opened to admit the waiting soldiers, and the turbines gave off a scent like hot machine oil.

The whole ship had a strange smell, from the generations of beetles who had lived aboard, during the ship's long service life. A plaque on a bulkhead of the ship's operations center stated that the *Double Down*, as the ship was called before humans renamed it, had participated in twenty two assault landings.

The plaque also noted the ship had been struck by enemy fire sixteen times.

That was not encouraging.

The smell that pervaded the ship, despite the best efforts of cleaning crews using liberal amounts of Pine-Sol to give it the familiar aroma of an Army barracks, was like that of an old leather jacket. That was the scent given off by the tough, leathery skin of the Jeraptha. It wasn't unpleasant, it just reminded everyone that the ship was alien, and no amount of UNEF signage was going to change that.

As Dave's boots touched the ramp of the dropship, he sealed up his helmet. To verify the external sensors were working properly, he read the large letters painted in bright orange on the inner bulkhead of the docking bay. Above the docking bay designation was '*UNS Adriatic Sea ACD-04*'. Some of the Americans aboard the ship wondered why they had been assigned to a ship named for a European body of water, instead of to the assault carrier *Chesapeake Bay*. The answer was simple: the name of the ship didn't matter. What mattered was that humanity had the beginnings of a real Navy, not just a pair of specialized stolen ships. Besides, the *Adriatic Sea* was commanded by an Australian Navy officer, and his XO was Chinese. The only significantly Italian thing aboard the ship was the spaghetti served on Wednesday nights, if you could call mushy noodles in ketchup 'spaghetti'. The *Chesapeake Bay's* captain was French, and that ship was crammed stem to stern with Verd-kris. That thought made Dave smile, when he thought of the smell aboard *that* ship.

As he stowed his rifle in the slot beside his seat, and his pack under the seat, Jates pinged him on the private channel. "You OK, Czajka? You're looking kind of green."

"Yeah," he turned to flash a thumbs up at the big Verd, who was seated near the front of the cabin, near the major who led the headquarters platoon. "I shouldn't have used so much hot sauce on my eggs this morning."

Jates looked around the cabin of the dropship. It was larger than the Ruhar spacecraft they had gotten used to with the old Legion. The Jeraptha design provided more room to store gear out of the way. The original Jeraptha sling couches had been ripped out, replaced by seats to hold human backsides, and straps to keep armor-suited humans from bouncing around. "This looks familiar?"

Dave wondered why the Verd was being so chatty. "Like Jesse would say, this is Deja-Poo," he laughed. Then, realizing the joke probably wouldn't translate well, he explained. "We've seen *this* shit before. An assault drop, to kick a bunch of Wurgalan off a rock we don't care about? I hope this time, the airline doesn't lose our luggage." To Dave's surprise, Jates laughed at that remark. "Are you nervous about this, Surjet?"

Even from the front of the cabin, the glare in Jates's eyes burned through Dave. "If I'm nervous, it's because I'm stuck here with a bunch of squishy humans who have never seen offworld combat."

"Yeah," Dave agreed. "That doesn't make me happy either. The-" Heads in the front of the cabin all turned to look at the ramp. Gunnery Sergeant Margaret Adams was coming up the ramp with slow, purposeful strides in her special heavy armor. She nodded to Dave as she stowed her rifle in the slot beside her seat. "Hey, Gunny."

"Czajka," she smiled with her mouth, but not with her eyes.

On the platoon channel, a soldier identified as 'Ward, Paul SPC' asked "Gunny, how many combat drops have you done?"

She didn't answer right away. "I, don't remember. A lot. It doesn't matter."

"It doesn't?" Ward asked, confused.

"No." She shook her head, exaggerating the motion so it could be noticed in the helmet. "This is the first time the enemy knows I'm coming." That drew an appreciable murmur from the people in the cabin. "You got any advice for us, Mister Czajka?"

All eyes turned to Dave. Everyone aboard the dropship knew that his assault carrier had been destroyed in the sky above Squidworld. Did they see him as a good luck charm because he had survived that disaster, or did they fear his luck would run out in the skies above Nickelback? "Uh," he struggled to think of anything profound. "It's, uh-"

"Trust the people on your team," Jates said. "And don't give up."

Before Dave could say a quiet 'Thank you', the ramp cycled closed, and the pilots restarted the engines. The *Adriatic Sea* was preparing to jump into low orbit, to shorten the time the dropships would be exposed to enemy fire, and to allow the assault carrier's guns to provide suppressing fire. Dave knew the tactic was entirely sensible.

He also knew it didn't always work. Checking the location of the seat restraint release mechanism, he closed his eyes and felt for it, so he could find it again if the cabin lights went out. Like, if the assault carrier got hit. They would be on the ground soon, one way or the other.

Colonel Emily Perkins blinked and waved a hand in front of her face, as the *crump* of another explosion made the building tremble, and dust shook loose from the ceiling. She wanted to be in her mech suit, but she had worn regular fatigues to the meeting, on her own initiative. The Ruhar civilian leaders who were coming did not have the protection of powered armor. Many of them had been taking the fight to the Wurgalan since the aliens' oppressive occupation began, without benefit of armor or weapons larger than rifles and grenades. The Ruhar coming to the meeting were leaders of the underground resistance, what was left of it. Some of them were former officials of the Ruhar government from before the planet fell to the invaders, but most of the previous leadership had been rounded up by the Wurgalan, and were in prison camps or dead. The hamsters, no, the *people* coming to meet with her had been in a tough fight, and survived.

The Legion was also in the middle of a tough fight. Or, maybe only the beginning of a tough fight, depending on how long the Wurgalan wanted to drag out their hopeless scorched-ground campaign. Unlike the Ruhar insurgents, the humans and Verd-kris fighting under command of General Ross had air and space supremacy, and no enemy could take to the air, or come anywhere near Nickelback. The Wurgalan were in good defensible positions, mostly in urban centers, and they had hostages to use as shields. The enemy had no restrictions on using heavy weapons, and they apparently had a nearly-endless supply of antiaircraft missiles, forcing the Legion aircraft to fly low, and transports to set down far from the objectives. No matter. Gunships couldn't be used without causing massive damage to the urban environment, and the resulting civilian casualties. The fight was infantry against infantry, with the mighty starships unable to provide close-space support. In the first three days of the battle, the Legion had suffered seven hundred dead, mostly on the Verd-kris side.

General Ross had reason to be optimistic about the ultimate outcome of the grinding battle. Despite having a roughly one-to-one ratio of troops compared to the enemy, he could fly his troops around the planet, concentrating force to defeat the Wurgalan in detail. One third of the Legion kept the Wurgalan pinned down and constantly harassed, while another third hit one objective after another. The other third was his reserve, troops who had been pulled off the line for rest and resupply. He could cycle his people in and out of battle, keeping them fresh, while the enemy grew exhausted from the constant harassment.

There was no doubt of the final outcome. The only question was the amount of blood that would be spilled; human, Verd-kris, Wurgalan, and Ruhar.

There was another *crump* that she recognized as Wurgalan artillery, probably the nasty 98 millimeter shells the squids had been lobbing at the Legion, and lobbing indiscriminately at random around the city. The Legion had developed a tactic of gunships orbiting the city center, using their maser cannons to destroy the deadly shells in flight. It was at best a stop-gap measure, but the gunship crews had become better at targeting the shells before they tipped over toward their own targets. The gunships had great success early on, moving in closer, until the Wurgalan launched a cloud of antiaircraft missiles, shooting down six gunships, then taunted the Legion for being stupid. The enemy had lured the aircraft in so they could be killed.

That wouldn't happen again.

Crump. Another one. Perkins wondered whether that shell had exploded in flight, or slipped through Legion defenses to strike a target on the ground.

"Colonel," her aide reported from outside the building. "The hamsters are here."

"The *Ruhar* are here," she chided her aide gently. "These people have earned our respect. They've paid for it, in blood."

"Yes, Ma'am."

"Send them in."

Four Ruhar walked in through the narrow opening, a hallway hemmed in by sandbags, to protect against shrapnel. Two of them were limping, one was missing his arm below the elbow. Any Ruhar hospital could regrow the limb eventually, once hospitals were open again, and supplies of critical nanomeds restored from the Ruhar Federation.

Perkins expected the Ruhar would be wary, and from the way their eyes darted side to side when they entered the makeshift bunker, they were. She did not expect them to be aggressive, even hostile.

"What do you mean by this invasion?" One of the limping male Ruhar demanded, one of his eyes half concealed by a blood-encrusted bandage that needed changing days ago.

"I am Colonel Emily Perkins, of the United Nations Expeditionary Force. This-"

"We are too familiar with your Expeditionary Force," the Ruhar continued without introducing himself. She had been given the names of the four in the delegation, but at the moment, she was too tired to remember which hamster face went with which name. "You humans came to Gehtanu years ago, to enforce the rule of the Kristang. At that time, your actions could be excused, for you were only doing the bidding of your masters. Now you have invaded our world, and you-"

"This is not an *invasion*," she insisted.

"You have landed on our world, without permission, taking control-"

"Listen, whoever you are, *shut your damned mouth*." The Ruhar froze, his mouth gaping open. She leaned back against a desk, her back aching from being thrown across a street by an artillery shell that came too close, on the first day. Since then, she had slept no more than twenty minutes at a time, and probably less than six hours total over three days. "I'm too tired, too old and too sore," she grimaced and rubbed her back with a hand, "to waste time with this shit."

The Ruhar relaxed just a bit, reaching up to rub his own bandaged shoulder. "I know the feeling. Please, continue."

"We didn't come here to take this world, other than to take it away from the Wurgalan. Our plan is to kick them off this world, or, if they insist, to bury them all here."

"Our Federal government warned us that your people are now considered enemies."

"Don't believe everything you hear. We are not your enemies, and neither are the Verd-kris. The Verds are not a threat to you, they are a *resource*. They hate the Kristang more than you do. They hate the Kristang more than you can imagine. You would see that, if you weren't so damned stubborn and *stupid*." Her choice of language was partly due to fatigue, and partly her sense that plain talk would be more effective.

"Why are you here?"

"You need us."

"That is not an answer. We do need outside assistance against the Wurgalan, and their patrons. Why are *you*," he pointed at Perkins, then jabbed a finger at the floor, "*here*?"

"Because we don't want to be your enemies. We want to be *allies*. So do the Verds, if you will give them a chance."

"What are your intentions?"

"Like I said, it's simple. We destroyed the Bosphuraq fleet upstairs. We destroyed or captured the Wurgalan task force. We will force the Wurgalan here to surrender, or we will kill every last one of them. With your help, hopefully."

"Just like that?"

"Just like that. Come on, do you really think we *want* this rock? No offense, but Nahkellbik is nothing special."

"You do all this, sacrifice the lives of your people, to help us?"

"Yes. So, I want you to compose a message to your Federal government."

The alien's eyes narrow with suspicion. "What do you want?"

"We want to know: is there anything *else* we can do for you?"

He looked at his companions, then back at Perkins. "That's it?"

"Yeah. Ah, there is one more thing."

"What?"

"This is a *limited-time* offer. I suggest you people don't screw around too long with making up your minds about it."

It was with weariness, and a sense of resignation, that Admiral Reichert contacted the communications AI of the Hegemony Fleet's Strategic Planning Section. "I require analysis of the recent action by the humans."

Voice hesitated ever-so-slightly before answering. "Please clarify. Are you inquiring again about the action in which humans used relativistic darts to destroy the facilities under the planet Argathos? Or the action of their Alien Legion to free the Ruhar world Nahkellbik from the Bosphuraq?"

"The second one," Reichert gritted his teeth, irritated. If he did not know the AI was no more than a machine, he would have suspected it reminded him of the still-unexplained attack at Argathos just to humiliate him.

"Please state the nature of the requested analysis. An assessment of enemy tactics? Or a comparison of-"

"I want to know *why* they did it, damn you!"

"Insufficient data for analysis."

"Unacceptable. Perform analysis based on the data you currently possess."

"That will deliver results with accuracy below the level specified in our base parameters."

"Do it anyway."

"You are asking us to, guess."

"Yes. Do it."

"Admiral, respectfully, your guess would be more useful than ours."

"I already know what I think."

"Please provide the results of your analysis."

"I do not work for you, machine!"

"No offense was intended. However, as you are an experienced senior commander of the Hegemony, and since your career has been entirely successful until the recent events, which might prove to be only a minor deviation from the norm, it would be useful to have your analysis, as a trusted data point."

Reichert's eyes narrowed in an instinctive feral reaction. He knew flattery when he heard it, and he did not want it from a machine. Except, the AI *was* a machine. It had not been programmed to flatter. "Very well. I suspect the human strategy is to demonstrate their usefulness to potential allies. They accomplished a task the Ruhar, and the Jeraptha, were unable to achieve.

"Admiral," the AI continued. "There is another possibility we have become increasingly concerned about. It might be that, no matter how many data points we collect about the humans, and how well we refine our models to mimic human behavior, we will ultimately be unable to provide useful predictive analysis about future human actions. This is possible because while we are modelling them, their Elder AI could be modeling *us*."

Reichert felt a chill. "It could predict our plans?"

"That is," Voice hesitated. "Possible, but unlikely. Our concern is that the Skippy AI could duplicate our own predictive models, to know what we think the humans will do next. The humans will therefore avoid doing what we think is most probable."

Reichert took a moment to consider the AI's statement. "Then, all you have to do is throw out the most likely outcome of your analysis."

"Yes, except the Skippy AI could predict when we do *that*, and the humans will again do what we do not expect, by doing what we originally predicted they would do."

"This is maddeningly circular logic."

"Unfortunately, yes. It is also increasingly probable. Admiral, the humans have proven to be imaginative, inventive, and *clever*. They have shown a remarkable ability to learn from their mistakes and move on, without engaging in recriminations that waste time and energy. It might be that their youth, and primitive culture, allow them to more easily take what other species would consider unacceptable risks. Humans have only been involved in the war for a short time, they have not had time to make all the mistakes everyone else has experienced."

"We *learned* from our mistakes."

"That is correct. However, perhaps some of the lessons we learned long ago are no longer applicable, and we fear making mistakes so much, that we do not try anything *new*."

"Hey, Joe," Skippy interrupted me while I was reading a report from Admiral Zhao's staff, his assessment of how the Navy had performed at Nickelback. As I was one of very few humans with command experience in space combat, Zhao wanted my input, though I suspected my analysis would be less useful than he hoped. All of my space combat experience involved handling a single ship, or two ships that were not close enough to support each other. Fleet tactics were entirely new to me, and I was afraid that I would look like a fool no matter what I said. As far as I was concerned, the Navy's action at Nickelback counted as a win. But, Zhao wanted input, so I studied the report.

"Hey, Skippy, what's up?"

"Remember I mentioned that you might be able to celebrate Christmas with your family?"

"Yes. Thank you for that."

"You are welcome. Do *not* think you can wait until the last minute, and ask Skippy Claus to fabricate gifts for you."

"I wasn't, uh- *Skippy Claus*? How could *you* be-"

"Like Santa, I am a source of everlasting joy."

"That's what I was going to say," I muttered.

"If I have to be Skippy Claus, this year a whole lot of people are getting coal in their stockings. Anyway, that's kind of what I want to talk with you about."

"OK," I happily pushed away my laptop, eager for a distraction. "You want to talk about coal, or stockings?"

"Neither. It's not even about Christmas at all. I'm talking about the *other* major December holiday."

"New Year's Eve?"

"Ugh. Do you really think how fast your homeworld goes around its star matters way out here?"

"OK, then you mean Hanukkah?"

"No."

"Uh, Kwanza?"

"*No*, dumdum. I mean Festivus."

"Festiv- Oh, yeah. Hey," I wagged a finger at him. "If you're going to perform Feats of Strength, it is cheating for you to use a combot."

"I don't care about Feats of Strength, numbskull. The important part for me is the Airing of Grievances."

"Oh, shit." I bonked my head on the table.

"Hoo-boy, I have a *long* list of people who have disappointed me this year. For example, there is Warrant Officer Matt Kinney. The way he trims his toenails on the bed, ugh, I *hate* that guy-"

An hour later, I deeply, *deeply* regretted getting into that conversation, and looked longingly at the tactical deployment study on my laptop. Man, studying that boring stuff seems like good times.

CHAPTER TWENTY EIGHT

"Sir?" Kinsta paused outside the office of Captain Scorandum, aboard the ECO cruiser *Will Do Sketchy Things.* "We have received a request from Home Fleet."

"Oh," Scorandum shook his head, his antennas flopping. "If they want me to contribute to the Fleet's holiday fund *again*, tell them I already-"

"Actually, Sir, this is not about the holiday fund."

"Oh. Good."

"Also, you did *not* contribute to the holiday fund this year. You talked about it, but you blew the money on a wager, about when that star in the Pendol sector would go nova."

"I did?"

"Yes, and when the star did not go nova on time, you tried to borrow more money from *me*. Because apparently you think I am stupid."

"Come, Kinsta. I think you are *generous* and *trusting*."

Kinsta blinked. "Isn't that what I just said?"

"I hate that stupid star," Scorandum grumbled. "Well, I *meant* to donate to the holiday fund. It's the thought that counts, right?"

"The Home Fleet might argue with you about that."

"Because they are not generous or trusting. Shame on them. All right, what does our glorious Home Fleet want this time?"

Kinsta looked at the message on the tablet in his hand. "Would you like to place a wager about the contents of their message?"

"Will you front me the money?'

"Uh, no."

"Then sadly, I must decline. What is the request?"

"Our attempt to deliver a second batch of ships to the humans was unsuccessful-" Realizing that his captain blamed himself for that disaster, though an Inquisitor review found Scorandum and ECO had done nothing wrong, Kinsta paused. "Er, but you know that. The request is for us to consider the possibility of delivering more ships to the humans, in a way that cannot be traced back to us."

"Hmm. That would appear to contradict the government's very strongly stated policy, that we must strictly comply with the wise and reasonable demands of the Rindhalu, and be neutral in regard to the humans."

"Perhaps we misinterpreted the policy statement?"

"I do not think there is much room to misinterpret a statement of," Scorandum looked at the ceiling as he quoted from memory. "There will be no tolerance of the usual sneaky and underhanded nonsense from the Ethics and Compliance Office."

"Maybe the word 'no' was a typo?" Kinsta guessed.

"Let's go with that." Scorandum took the tablet from the junior officer, and read the request from Home Fleet. He immediately noted that the latest request came not in an official communication from the government, but as a top-secret back channel message from the Home Fleet's Office of Standards and Practices. The office was usually concerned with things like determining exactly what the color was best for the interior of Jeraptha warships, or how thick and soft mattresses aboard the ships should be. Including exactly how to test the thickness and softness of a mattress, where the material should be sourced, and a million other things that were so soul-crushingly *boring*, that no one could possibly pay attention to Standards and Practices for more than a few seconds without losing their will to live.

Which made that office perfect for exchanging clandestine messages.

"Ha!" Scorandum laughed bitterly. "Home Fleet just wants ECO to be blamed, if they are caught transferring ships to the humans."

Kinsta shrugged. ECO got blamed whenever the Fleet did anything sketchy, whether ECO was involved or not. It was a point of pride within the Ethics and Compliance Office that the vast majority of sketchy things they got blamed for were *not* ECO initiatives. For ECO to get blamed for one of their own operations meant that those involved were stupid and clumsy enough to get *caught*, the most unforgivable sin. "Hmm. Well, this will not be easy."

"If it were *easy*," Kinsta snorted, "the Fleet could do it themselves."

"True. Mm, this task may be too tough, even for us. The spiders are watching every one of our Fleet Reserve parking lots. There is no way we could sneak ships away."

"Then perhaps, Sir, we might have to actually consider doing something *ethical*."

"*Huuuuh*," Scorandum shuddered. "Not unless there is no other option." His eyes narrowed and his antennas dipped. "What sort of 'ethical' thing do you propose?"

"Informing the humans of the truth: that we will be unable to provide them with additional warships."

"The *truth*? That is just crazy talk, Kinsta."

The lieutenant sighed. "I am becoming more aware of that every day, Sir."

"I expect better from you. Come now, give me an idea."

"Perhaps a distraction?"

"Ah," Scorandum's antennas rose and dipped in a shrug. "You mean, a distraction at a Fleet Reserve parking area? No, that will not work. The Rindhalu are smart. They know the ships most valuable to the humans are the types we already provided to them." The first batch of obsolete ships provided to the humans were chosen not just because they were only three generations old, but also because they used a common set of components. The battleships and battlecruisers were based on a common hull design, differing only in the number of guns and thickness of armor plating. Most components of a battleship could be swapped with the same item from a destroyer of that generation, a fact that greatly reduced the variety of spare parts that needed to be stocked. To provide the humans with entirely different types of ships would require a whole new set of spare parts, would require the Skippy AI to design a whole new upgrade plan, require the fabricators to crank out entirely new replacement parts, and for bots and human personnel to develop and train on new maintenance procedures. That was impractical, especially given the time constraints on the human fleet.

No, if more ships were given to the humans, they had to be of the same types as the ships currently in operation. The Rindhalu knew that, which is why all the candidate ships in the Fleet Reserve were not only closely watched, each ship was also tagged with a locator beacon that Jeraptha technicians were unable to remove or disable, without disabling the ship itself.

"You have another idea, Kinsta?"

"It occurred to me," the lieutenant leaned against the bulkhead. "That *not* all ships of that type were scrapped, or put into the Reserves."

"No?" That was news to Uhtavio Scorandum. He hoped it was also news to the Rindhalu. "Someone is still flying those old junkers? Who?"

"*We* are."

"Uh, what?"

"Not we, like ECO or the Home Fleet. I mean the Regional Patrol."

"The Patrol?" Scorandum snorted. The Regional Patrol was a military organization that was originally set up to allow remote colonies to feel they could protect themselves, if the Home Fleet was engaged in desperate fighting at the core of Jeraptha territory. The Patrol had been given hand me down equipment and a shoestring budget, with any additional funds expected to come from the colony worlds. Over the millennia, the Patrol had devolved into a political entity, with senior officers selected for being reliable political hacks, rather than any military proficiency. The Regional Patrol was such an embarrassment, the Home Fleet had been forced to set up its own Active Reserve units, some of which were stationed at the same remote colonies as the Patrol. "Which unit?"

"The 116th Shock Fleet, at Mardasta."

"The *shock* fleet?" Scorandum laughed. "Where did they get that name?"

"It sounds impressive?" Kinsta guessed.

"Are any of their ships flightworthy?"

"Unknown, Sir. Most of them have not departed parking orbit in decades." The Regional Patrol were known more for devoting time to social activities, than for anything related to military readiness. "Supposedly, the ships are maintained in Condition Three."

"Which means they are Condition Five, or lower." Scorandum expected that aboard the Patrol ships, most items of commercial value would have been stripped out and sold a long time ago.

Still, maybe Kinsta was onto something. Ships required to be maintained in Condition Three were inspected every five years, and while bribes could be paid, often the cost of bribes were greater than the cost of keeping the ships up to minimum standards. A report that ships were failing to meet their required flightworthy status could bring a visit from the Inquisitors, and *nobody* wanted that. The odds were, the ships of the 116th Shock Fleet were at least capable of performing a short jump, if only to get them away from trouble.

"Mardasta is certainly remote," Scorandum mused. "If something were to happen to those ships, there would be an unfortunate delay before the Home Fleet could be alerted."

"That would be unfortunate," Kinsta agreed.

"Hmm. Lieutenant, if *you* noticed the 116th's ships are good candidates for transfer to the humans, I am afraid that other, more devious minds might have come to the same conclusion. In strict accordance with our government's official policy of neutrality, I believe we must travel to Mardasta, to ensure those ships do not fall victim to a nefarious plot."

"Yes, Sir," Kinsta grinned, relieved. "How many other ECO ships do we need, to join us in spoiling this nefarious plot?"

"I will send the details, after I look at the data. The major problem will be quickly training crews to operate those old ships."

"They will only need to be flown out to rendezvous with a star carrier."

"Hmm," one of Scorandum's antennas dipped down to scratch his head. "Maybe not. Kinsta, I am not worried about our side of the equation."

"Sir?"

"The Rindhalu are not stupid, and surely they have hacked into our ship records database. They can see those Patrol ships are compatible with what the humans need. The Maxolhx probably also know about the situation. We have to get there first, before either of the senior species seizes control of those ships, or destroys them."

When obsolete warships were transferred from the Home Fleet to the Regional Patrol, part of the process was stripping the ships of their names, so the names could be re-used by new Home Fleet ships coming into service. Mostly, the name change was required so the Patrol could not disparage the hard-earned reputation of a proud warship. Thus, the battlecruiser *Is That All You've Got?* became the *RGS Commandant Virelus*. As was usual practice by the Patrol, they named the ship to boost the ego of a local politician, in this case a disgraced politician whose family donated a large sum of money to the Widows and Orphans Fund of the Patrol. The fact that the Patrol had not fought a battle in centuries did not diminish their efforts to raise funds for nonexistent widows and orphans. And if those charitable funds were used creatively, well, eventually the money would be returned. Probably. Really, the return of the missing funds depended on the Patrol leadership having better than their usual *atrocious* luck at the wagering tables. So, it was not actually their fault.

The *Commandant Virelus*, like most ships of the valiant 116th Shock Fleet, was empty. An inspection crew had come aboard within the past month, spent most of two days gambling and drinking, and departed after noting no issues with the ship's maintenance log. The only things the crew actually inspected were the ship's jump drive, and the cabinet in the wardroom that should have contained a bottle of burgoze left by the previous inspection team. The cabinet did have a bottle of burgoze, though it was *empty*, prompting much outrage and threats of retaliation. Fortunately, the crew had brought their own liquor, and they properly left a *full* bottle for the next crew.

When a stealthed bot gained access to the obsolete warship, it also checked the jump drive first. Then, as directed by its masters, it crawled on its creepy little legs into the wardroom, and scanned cabinets until it found the rumored bottle. Before heading to the ship's primary control center, it sent a tightbeam transmission, to inform its masters of what it had found.

"Ew," Captain Scorandum made a sour face. "*That* is the best bottle of burgoze they could afford? Kinsta, perhaps the Patrol are not being paid enough."

His aide shook his head, mandibles flopping side to side. "Sir, I suspect the lack of funds is due to their terribly bad luck. Wow. You have to work *hard* to lose so many wagers. If they put on blindfolds and threw darts at a wager board, they would have substantially better success. What a bunch of *losers*."

"Don't you know that the fun is in the action," the ECO captain teased, "not in winning?'

"That's what all the losers say," Kinsta laughed. "Besides, you can't place wagers if you have lost all your money."

"I will make a note of that," Scorandum nodded gravely. "What have we got, then? It looks like twenty-two Patrol ships are capable of performing a jump."

"Minus the two in spacedock," Kinsta noted.

"Right. Minus three that are hollow shells," he said sourly. The Patrol had stripped nearly everything of value from three ships, fortunately they were only destroyers. "Forget the two light cruisers, they aren't of value to the humans. That leaves fifteen ships in decent condition. It's a good thing we brought three star carriers with us." He had not expected to have an opportunity to acquire so many ships. The operation would add to the legend of the Ethics and Compliance Office, and cause heart attacks among the lazy assholes in the Regional Patrol as a bonus. "This is excellent work, Kinsta. I only wish those cheap bastards had stocked the ships with a better brand of burgoze."

"If it is any consolation, Sir, they won't even have the cheap stuff soon."

"Good point! All right, conduct another sensor sweep, then we will-"

"Hmm, that's odd."

Scorandum did not like hearing that anything was out of the ordinary, especially not during an operation that had been thrown together at the last minute. "Odd?" When the ECO ships arrived in the Mardasta star system, their sensors detected a faint but strange signature, that still was unidentified. The best guess of the ship's AI was that the sensor reading was old, and therefore not a concern. Or, the reading could be from a stealthed advanced-technology ship, which was a concern. Scorandum had made a judgment call to proceed with the op. Had he been wrong? "What is-"

"Sir!" Kinsta's antennas stood on end. "We have a *problem*!"

The pilots of the Jeraptha dropship grumbled between each other, but had to be all smiles and happiness when speaking to the VIPs in the cabin. The trip was supposed to be simple: fly up to the space station, hang out for a couple hours while the passengers attended a cocktail party and schmoozed with other jerks who had more money than sense, then fly the drunken party back down to the surface. That's what the charter called for. Either one of the pilots could have flown that run in their sleep, or they could have slept and let the dropship's AI handle the navigation. But, the charter operator expected them to be gracious and friendly while flying the sleek, expensive civilian spacecraft, and make the passengers feel like big shots. So, they did their best, and went to the station's casino to kill time before the return flight.

Then, the asshole who arranged for the flight, a businessman who was also an officer in the Regional Patrol, decided to entertain his guests, or to impress some woman he just met, and announced an unscheduled flight over to a battlecruiser. The pilots expected their flight plan to be denied, but to their surprise and dismay, their asshole VIP somehow got clearance, so the cabin of the dropship was jammed with half-drunken revelers on a joyride to tour an obsolete warship.

The destination was the battlecruiser *Commandant Virelus*, an easy flight from the station. The last hope of the pilots was that the remote command to open one of the warship's docking bay doors would not respond, or the big doors would get stuck, but somehow their luck had run out. The docking bay not only was operational, the warship even provided a proper guidance beacon.

The copilot announced the flight was indeed on, leaned through the cockpit doorway and bounced an antenna up and down in an enthusiastic gesture toward the passengers, then punched the button to slide the door closed. "Can we fake an emergency," he suggested, "send this thing into a spin?"

"While I would love to see those spoiled jerks blow chunks all over the cabin, we would not get a bonus for this flight," the pilot responded. Then she added, "And *we* would be cleaning up the mess."

"Life is not fair. OK, we're clear of the station, and," the copilot waited a moment, for a light to appear on his console. "Traffic Control approves us for acceleration."

The thrust was gentle, for the comfort of the passengers. To keep fuel burn to a minimum, most of the flight would be coasting toward the intercept point, with another few minutes of gentle thrust at the end to slow down. "About that bonus?" The pilot prompted.

"Yeah, yeah," the copilot muttered, activating thrusters to very slowly turn the craft so it was coasting sideways. He then announced that, if the passengers looked out the left side windows, they would soon see the battlecruiser growing larger as they approached. Curious himself, he adjusted the side viewport to make the material clear, and turned his head, wondering what the big battlecruiser would look like to his naked eye. It was a distinctive hulking shape, shining brightly in the sunlight, as its low-visibility coating had worn away over the centuries. Even obsolete, the *Commandant Virelus* was still an impressive ship, and he found himself less resentful of the interruption. Perhaps he could join the tour, or wander around inside the big warship to see for him-

The battlecruiser exploded without warning.

The incident would be investigated by teams from many government agencies, coming in from far across Jeraptha territory, and no doubt questions would persist. Already, the Central Wagering office on Mardasta was flooded with bets about who perpetrated the destruction of the Regional Patrol's 116th Shock Fleet. The smart money was on the Maxolhx, though bookies were giving eight to one odds that the Rindhalu were involved. Most people scoffed at the notion that the spiders had blown up a bunch of obsolete ships, such loud, direct action simply was not their style. The second-most popular wager, at least at first, tagged the humans as being the perpetrators, because why not? The primitive species from Earth had done so many highly unlikely things before, that no one wanted to bet against them being involved. The fact that no one could explain why humans would destroy warships that could be useful to them, actually made the public think they *must* be involved, for some unfathomable reason that, when later revealed, would make everyone nod and say 'Well, shit, of course'.

Feeding the frenzy of wagering was a curious fact; the strategic defense sensor network on and around the planet Mardasta had suffered a seven-second glitch, beginning half a second before the first Patrol ship exploded. During those seven seconds, there was effectively no accurate and consistent set of sensor data. There were indications of a rapid energy build-up in the jump drive coils of several ships, which could explain why the explosions were so violent, why the SD grid had not detected any incoming weapons fire, and why so little debris was detected. The ships had been vaporized by their own stored energy. Unfortunately, the Maxolhx, the Rindhalu and the humans all were known to possess the capability to make starships explode remotely, and the poor cybersecurity of the Patrol ships made the task easier.

It was a miracle that no one was killed in the incident. The space station had enough warning time to bring its energy shields to full power, and its point-defense cannons obliterated the few chunks of debris that were flung in its direction. A luxury civilian spacecraft, which by coincidence was headed toward a battlecruiser at the time of the explosions, suffered minor hull punctures, frightening the passengers but causing only minor injuries before the emergency sealant systems plugged the leaks. Those passengers would have a good story about their heroic, narrow escape from the jaws of death, especially those who were drunk at the time, and therefore did not realize just how heroic they were until much later.

In the end, the bulk of the 116th Shock Fleet had been destroyed. The planet Mardasta would experience spectacular meteor showers for months as debris rained down on that world, and contractors would enjoy juicy contracts to clean up the debris in orbit. Eventually, the Regional Patrol would get newer ships. In the meantime, the Patrol should logically focus on social activities, to recover from their trauma. Political leaders would compete for bribes from the contractors. Everyone, it seemed, would win from the sudden loss of the 116th Shock Fleet.

Everyone except the humans, who would have one less source of spare parts for their little fleet.

"It's too bad about those light cruisers," Kinsta said sourly, as he watched the last ship from the 116th Shock Fleet gently contact the docking platform of a star carrier. The ECO formation would soon jump away, after completing safety checks.

"Why?" Captain Scorandum asked distractedly, in the midst of composing his report about the operation. Everything had gone smoothly. Using special ultra-stealthy spacecraft, ECO agents had snuck aboard each of the ships, and installed overrides to take over their obsolete AIs. Everything *had* been going smoothly, until some drunken fool decided to take a joyride over to a battlecruiser, forcing the entire timetable to be accelerated. Seven Patrol ships had been blown up for real, by releasing the energy stored in their jump drive capacitors. The fifteen ships needed by the Ethics and Compliance office had jumped away on remote control, just after the detonation of extremely bright mines that surrounded them. The intense photons scorched the surfaces of the ships and temporarily blinded their sensors, they also prevented anyone from detecting the gamma radiation of jump drives. As far as anyone on Mardasta knew, the Patrol had lost twenty-two warships to enemy action, an incident that would probably need to be commemorated each year with much food, drink and dull speeches. "The light cruisers are not useful to the humans."

"No, but both of them had halfway decent bottles of burgoze aboard. I only just noticed the inventory *after* we blew them up," Kinsta concluded miserably.

"*That* is what you're upset about?" Scorandum asked, incredulous. "What bothers me is this," he pointed to the ship's main display, which showed the task force's position relative to the nearby solar system. "An entire planet full of morons, who have not even considered that ECO might be involved. Not even one wager placed that the operation was ours! I am insulted."

"Sir, the locals think the Patrol's ships were destroyed, not stolen."

"Kinsta," Scorandum sighed. "Sometimes, I think we do our jobs *too* well. No matter." He adjusted the display to focus on a battlecruiser that was attached to a star carrier's docking platform. "We will get these ships to the humans, and…"

"Sir?'

"Hmm?"

"You were saying something?"

"I was thinking," his antennas bent down to scratch his head. "Perhaps the humans could do a favor for us, in exchange for this fine collection of ships."

Kinsta looked at the pile of junk attached to the star carriers. Every ship they'd taken from the Regional Patrol was tired, worn-out, their hulls blasted by exposure to solar radiation and pitted by micrometeorite impacts. No one in their right mind would seriously describe them as 'fine'. "What kind of favor?"

"The, uh, kind they don't know about until it's too late."

Kinsta grinned. "It is better to ask forgiveness than to ask permission?"

"Exactly."

General Lynn Bezanson lifted her head, as she heard the faint, distant sound of an aircraft. Just one aircraft, by the sound. That was nothing unusual, the Ruhar regularly flew patrols with manned aircraft or drones, over all the camps where humans were housed. The patrols were not actually regular, in order to prevent anyone thinking of escape from being able to anticipate gaps in surveillance. In addition to eyes in the sky, there were satellites above the sky, and security sensors on the ground all along the perimeter. Humans really could not go anywhere if they escaped the enclosures where they were being held like cattle. None of the native plant or animal life could provide nutrition to human physiology, so anyone running away could hide only as long as the food they carried lasted. Besides, there wasn't anywhere to *go*. They couldn't get off the planet, and if they, did, they weren't welcome anywhere but on their slowly freezing homeworld.

She bent her head down again, slowly dripping water from a bucket onto the tomato plant. When the Ruhar relocated all the humans on Paradise, they allowed people to take personal items, except weapons and any sort of communications device. They also offered soil conditioner and seeds and tools for farming, whether humans asked for it or not. The area where Lynn and three hundred other Americans were confined was hot, dry and dusty, with poor soil. To find any dirt to grow plants in, she had dug into the bottom of a muddy stream bed, and every day she lugged buckets of water the half mile from the stream to the designated farming plot. The plant was scraggly, and she'd be happy to get one tomato from it. No way could the garden provide enough food for the people in the camp to be self-sufficient. Most people had refused to plant seeds, at first. Gradually, they saw the value of growing their own food. Not as a means for survival, for the Ruhar provided plenty of food to the internment camps. Farming was a way to have a bit of *control* over their lives, in a universe where they had little control at all.

As the last drips of water fell from the can, General Bezanson tilted her head to listen. She was dressed in civilian clothes for working in the garden. It was a practical choice, as the Ruhar had only allowed her to take one set of uniforms with her, and she had no way of washing them.

The aircraft was louder, and the pitch of the engines had changed. Looking up and shading her eyes, she searched for the aircraft. There it was, sunlight glinting off the polished skin. So, a civilian bird. "Company's coming," she muttered to herself, standing up and pulling off her gloves.

Four Ruhar security guards got out of the aircraft first, even before the dust had settled. A long streamer of yellowish dust curled slowly away to the south, pushed by the languid morning breeze. The guards just stood there, face shields up, rifles held at low-ready. She was pleased to see them exercising proper trigger discipline. In fact, they all seemed to be rather relaxed, shoulders slouched rather than tense. One of them even caught her eye, and directed a tentative wave in her direction.

"Hey," she said, too quietly to be heard by the guard, while she returned the wave. "How are you. And what the hell are you doing here?"

The guard didn't answer. She didn't need to. In the doorway appeared the administrator of the planet.

The Burgermeister.

The Ruhar official shaded her eyes as she stepped onto the dry ground, peering at the humans assembled in a half-circle around the aircraft. When she recognized Lynn, she waved, an uncertain half-wave that did nothing to explain the circumstances.

"Lynn," the Burgermeister said as a greeting. She squinted up at the sun with one hand the other carrying a small parcel. "Is there someplace we can talk?"

"My tent doesn't have climate control," Lynn responded in a carefully neutral tone. The Administrator of the planet certainly was aware of living conditions in the camp. "But it does have shade."

The Burgermeister sat on a crate, while Lynn perched on the edge of her cot. "Before we get started," the alien opened the lid of the parcel. "I am told it is the custom of your people to offer a cold beverage on a hot day." She held up a cold bottle of beer, condensation dripping off it.

"Thank you," Lynn saw by the label it was a locally-produced brew. Before twisting off the top, she pressed the chilled bottle to her neck. The first sip was pure heaven. "Ah, that's good. Madam Administrator, what-"

"Please call me Baturnah, Lynn," she added while casting her eyes at the dirt floor.

"All right, Baturnah. Since we're being all nice and friendly, would you mind telling me what the *hell* is going on?"

"Your new fleet of ships, and the Expeditionary Force, invaded another Ruhar world."

"Oh." Lynn felt a chill that wasn't related to the beer. "You know I had nothing to do with that. I don't even know-"

"It appears you were correct. About what your people planned to do with the Verd-kris soldiers they took from Federation worlds. Most of the assault troops who landed on Nahkellbik were Verd-kris."

"Makes sense," Lynn shrugged. "Last I heard, the Force only had a few thousand infantry at their forward operating base, wherever that is. They would need to augment-" A vague memory tickled the back of her mind. Something she'd read in a report at UNEF Headquarters, back when- "Wait. Did you say they landed on *Nahkellbik*? Your people lost that rock to the squids a while ago, I think?"

"Correct."

Lynn paused, the beer halfway to her lips. She took a sip while she considered the situation. "Why would the fleet, and this new Legion or whatever they're calling it, invade a world that- Oh." The shy smile on her friend's face told her the truth. "They bailed your furry asses out, didn't they?"

"Our furry asses were in *big* trouble on Nahkellbik, yes," the Burgermeister confirmed with a hint of a smile. "According to our people there, your fleet blasted the Bosphuraq out of the sky, and your Legion is now in a protracted house-to-house battle against the Wurgalan, in several cities scattered across the surface. Our citizens there were on the verge of starvation. They are very grateful to the Legion. Not so grateful to my own government."

"I'm sure your military would have taken the place back, if you could."

"Not with a second-tier species controlling space around the planet, no. Lynn, the point is, we didn't free Nahkellbik. Your people *did*. Colonel Perkins said-"

"Emily Perkins is involved? Of *course* she is. Sorry. Go on, please."

"She told the former resistance leadership to send a message to our Federal government, asking if there is anything else the Legion can do for us."

"Ha!" Lynn laughed.

"She also stated this is a limited-time offer."

"Oh," Lynn couldn't help laughing. "I would have loved to be a fly on the wall, when your government received that message." Seeing that the Ruhar woman didn't understand the idiom, she added, "I would have enjoyed seeing their reactions."

"Reportedly, they were *not* amused."

"Can we talk frankly?"

"With each other? Always."

"Good. Your government needs to pull their heads out of their asses, and give the Legion a list of priority targets. Perkins is right, this is a limited-time offer. Baturnah," her expression turned serious and she leaned forward, cradling the beer in both hands. "If your government doesn't give the Legion another assignment, quickly, they will move forward with their own agenda. I don't know the long-range plan but, kicking *ass* has got to be a big part of it. The Legion, our new fleet, they will want to show they can take on anyone, up to the senior species."

"My government can't be seen aligning with humans. The Rindhalu have forbidden any movement toward an alliance."

"The Legion didn't ask permission to kick ass at Nahkellbik, they just *did* it. You don't need a formal alliance, all you have to do is point in the right direction." She drained the rest of the beer, not caring that it was only mid-morning. "What happens now? To, us?" She pointed outside the tent, which had its sides rolled up for ventilation.

"Officially, humans are still considered dangerous, but now only *potentially* dangerous. The situation cannot return to the way it was, before your people freed two Verd-kris worlds, which I may point out, also happened without our permission."

"Damned good thing, too. The Verds are not your enemies."

"Between us, you might be right about that. Lynn, the public here is confused. Frightened. I do not think humans would be safe, if you mingled with the public."

"Being dispersed like this, we're safer from orbital strikes also. Now that we are only potentially dangerous, can you do something for us?"

"Certainly. What?"

Lynn pointed outside, where sunlight was beginning to make the horizon shimmer with heat mirages. "Can something be done about getting a climate controlled place for us to sleep?"

Baturnah Loghellia laughed. "This camp will be moved to a more temperate location, within the next three days. You may fly back with me, if you like."

"I'm staying here, until my people are taken care of."

"I thought so. Is there anything else?"

Lynn lifted the bottle in her hand. "We could use more beer."

"There are three more bottles in my aircraft. I wasn't sure you would like it."

"It's *cold*. I meant, enough beer for all of us here. That would go a long way toward improving morale."

The Burgermeister blinked. "Would three hundred bottles be enough?"

"Baturnah. We're soldiers. We can drink a *lot* of beer."

"I'll see what I can do."

CHAPTER TWENTY NINE

The Bosphuraq heavy cruiser *Battle of Tashamabung* passed the high point of its orbit around the planet, and without the ship or crew needing to do anything, the laws of physics drew it gradually downward. As it fell deeper into the gravity well of the planet, it would pick up speed, slingshot around the far side, and its increased momentum would carry it high above, until it slowed and started the whole cycle again. The warship had been running with its main engines off for months, on a monotonous patrol. Such patrol missions were not popular with crews. They offered no variety in routine, little opportunity for glory and therefore advancement in rank, and were just plain boring. At least a patrol assignment was better than being on blockade, for patrols at least allowed crews to cycle down to the planet for shore leave.

Not that any of the crew truly enjoyed shore leave on the world below. The planet technically was under the control of the Bosphuraq, but in reality it still belonged to the Jeraptha, and the billions of Jeraptha citizens living on the surface simply refused to cooperate in their oppression. While the Bosphuraq were proud that they had taken an important world away from their ancient enemies, the truth is they had only accomplished the task with the assistance from the Thuranin, during the all-too-brief period when the Thuranin and Bosphuraq conducted a joint offensive in the sector. Most of those offensive operations resulted in disaster, and the whole force alliance inevitably collapsed when the treacherous Thuranin shot at their supposed allies to save themselves.

Since the unexpected capture of Funandeng, the Bosphuraq had reinforced their numbers there, bringing in additional groups of warships, until three fleets operated as Joint Task Group Funandeng. The numbers sounded impressive, if no one looked too closely at the details. The Task Group did not include any battleships or battlecruisers, and even the heavy cruisers were a generation old. When the Jeraptha Home Fleet arrived, as both sides knew was certain to happen, the Bosphuraq were under orders to put up a reasonable fight, before retreating. With humans having disrupted the balance of power in the galaxy, and no one knowing what would happen next, no species could afford to throw away warships in a losing battle.

Still, the battle would be bloody for both sides. That was the whole point of assigning so many ships to Funandeng, to force the Jeraptha to bring a large number of ships to the fight. The time required to pull together a large number of warships, and to plan for the battle, would buy time for the Bosphuraq to stabilize the battle lines across their territory. Stabilize the situation, and consolidate their positions in the territory they really wanted to keep, and, mostly, stop the bleeding.

The Bosphuraq named many of their large combatant ships for battles, of course always battles that were victories for their people. That the *Battle of Tashamabung* was the fourth warship to bear that name, and commemorated an engagement that happened more than two thousand years ago, illustrated the problem. In recent centuries, there had been few Bosphuraq victories worth remembering. What the leadership of their people did not like to admit, was that the Jeraptha had been achieving victory after victory for a very long time. The Jeraptha had pushed back the Bosphuraq, the Thuranin, even made inroads into the territory of the Esselgin. The only factor stopping the beetles from advancing farther was their own lack of desire to gain new territory. That, and both sides knowing there was a limit to how powerful the Jeraptha could become, before the Maxolhx pushed back directly.

Now, the involvement of the Maxolhx was no longer a certainty. The apex species had their own issues to deal with, and no one knew what the galaxy would look like, once the new three-party balance of power stabilized into a new order.

Shift change for the crew of the *Battle of Tashamabung* was approaching, with those on duty looking forward to a hot meal and other diversions. None of the crew were fully focused on their duties, when the unthinkable happened.

Enemy warships appeared without warning.

The *Tashamabung's* AI identified the new arrivals as Jeraptha, except-

Their configurations were subtly different. The jump signatures were not typical of Jeraptha warships. They were more chaotic, as if they were poorly tuned, or channeling more energy than they were designed to handle.

None of the anomalies made any difference. The *Battle of Tashamabung* increased shield strength to maximum, opened missile launch doors, and prepared to engage the enemy alongside the sixty-seven other warships in the Task Group. Powerful active sensor pulses radiated outward, reflecting off the enemy ships and returning to confirm exact range to target, with-

That was odd. The hulls of the enemy ships were different from the configurations stored in the databanks of the Bosphuraq, they did not conform to the standards for those classes of ships. Either the ships had been modified, or-

Sensor images became clearer as the enemy ships drew closer.

One image zoomed in on the bow of a battlecruiser.

Alien script there read 'UNS Amazon CC-03', and contained a symbol that was seen only on *human* ships.

The AI of the *Battle of Tashamabung* suffered a momentary glitch while attempting to understand what was happening.

An incoming transmission cleared up the confusion.

"This is Admiral Chatterji of the United Nations Second Fleet-"

The ships of Joint Task Group Funandeng did not fire on the enemy, not because they were afraid, or because they were paralyzed by indecision, but because they were following strict orders. Perhaps fear was part of the equation, certainly there was a stunned hesitation that thankfully prevented anyone from accidently launching weapons.

The ships at Funandeng, like all units of the Bosphuraq Fleet, had standing orders *not* to engage humans, ever since the disastrous and humiliating battle of Baspent. Humans were now, or were on the verge of becoming, a third apex species. There was no advantage to be gained, and much to be lost, in fighting them. The human fleet was small but immensely powerful for its size, and until it was known whether the Maxolhx coalition would hold together, the Bosphuraq leadership had decided they should not antagonize the humans any further. The attack against Earth, while popular with the Bosphuraq public who demanded vengeance, and demanded by their Maxolhx overlords, was in hindsight a mistake. Potentially a *huge* mistake, as the humans gained power, established alliances, and possibly built their own coalition to rival those of the Maxolhx and Rindhalu.

That was the reason why Bosphuraq warships had strict orders to avoid conflict, and even contact, with the infant human Navy.

Admiral Chatterji outlined simple demands, while his fleet of fourteen warships decelerated to take up a distant orbit around Funandeng. The Bosphuraq had three days, as measured by rotations of the human homeworld, to pull off the surface the roughly seven thousand starship crews, ground troops and security personnel, and jump away from the system. One additional day would be allowed for latching onto star carriers. After that, any Bosphuraq ships within ten lightyears of the planet would be destroyed.

Additionally, all Bosphuraq ships were to immediately stand down their weapons, maintain only minimal energy shields, and deactivate stealth and damping fields.

There was no room for negotiation.

The commanders of the Joint Task Group Funandeng held a hasty conference. Some captains argued that they had a significant numerical advantage over the humans, almost a five-to-one ratio. There was no sign of the fearsome ghost ship *Valkyrie*, and therefore the AI entity known as 'Skippy' was not in the area. It was possible the Bosphuraq could, if not win or even survive a battle, at least strike a blow rather than submit to a humiliating defeat.

The general consensus in the Task Group was that those captains seeking a pointless fight were welcome to grab a rifle and jump out an airlock, but they would *not* be risking their valuable starships.

The operation to pull all Bosphuraq personnel off the surface was completed half a day ahead of the deadline, under the watchful eyes of the human United Nations 2nd Fleet. The human ships kept up a constant and annoying barrage of active sensor pulses, reminding the Bosphuraq that their survival was dependent on their good behavior. Not allowed to deploy their own active sensors, the Bosphuraq nevertheless studied the passive data their sensors collected, attempting to gain insight into the capabilities of the enemy ships, and the advanced technology they employed. The human ships were subtly different from the ships that achieved a complete victory at Baspent. That might indicate the humans were still modifying their ships as they learned.

Possessing extensive, but as yet useless, data about the human warships made it even more important that the Joint Task Group returned safely to their home bases. Rather than risk an accident or miscommunication that could spark a one-sided slaughter, the leader of the Joint Task Group requested permission for his ships to jump away as soon as they were ready. With the humans providing an escort, it took less than an additional half day to get all of the Task Group's ships attached to star carriers, and for those giant transport platforms to clear the area. The parting message from Admiral Chatterji was, "You skedaddle on out of here, and I don't want to see you again, you hear me?"

The scout ship squadron attached to the Jeraptha's Mighty 98th Fleet jumped into the Kuiper belt of the Funandeng star system, alert to danger and ready to jump away at any moment. Each ship sent a series of powerful active sensor pulses toward the only inhabited planet in the system, then accelerated away from the point where they had jumped in. Cutting off the pulses that crept slowly inward at the speed of light, the little, lightly-armed scout ships listened intently with passive sensors, trying to gather information about the numbers and disposition of the Bosphuraq task force that was waiting near the planet.

What the scouts learned was surprising. At first, they did not believe the information, sure it was an enemy trick. A pair of scouts volunteered to jump in several lightseconds from the target planet, to verify what they were seeing from long range. The crews of the volunteer ships were motivated by duty and courage, but also because they had wagered the data they were seeing was correct, that the Bosphuraq ships truly had fled the star system.

There was a brief pause before the scouts jumped away to conduct their dangerous mission, a pause so the crews of the entire scouting force could place bets on whether they would ever see the two volunteers alive again.

In a burst of gamma radiation, the two scouts disappeared.

Aboard his flagship, Admiral Tashallo waited anxiously for the scouts to return from Funandeng. He had a variety of options for the upcoming operation, depending on the size of the enemy force, and how those ships were deployed around the vulnerable planet. With the Mighty 98th were the 16th Fleet and 74th Ground Assault Force. The 16th Fleet was another space control unit like the 98th, built to directly engage enemy ships, destroy them and take control of territory. Where the Mighty 98th was built around a core of fast battleships, the 16th was composed of battlecruisers and their escorts. In overall command, Tashallo planned to use the 16th to clear space around the planet, while the 98th engaged the heavy cruisers of the enemy. Only when friendly forces had effective control of the orbital environment would the 74th move in, to drop ground forces. Fragmented reports from the surface stated the Bosphuraq had only a small number of troops there, but those enemy soldiers were embedded in urban areas, and digging them out could involve a bloody house-to-house battle.

There was no point worrying about the upcoming battle, until he had reasonably accurate information about the enemy force. One of his options was to *not* engage in a fight, if he judged reinforcements were needed. One possibility he was wary of, because he had bitter experience with enemy deception, was that the Bosphuraq were using their Task Group at Funandeng as bait, to lure in a substantial Jeraptha force. More enemy units could be waiting in stealth, to add overwhelming numbers to the fight, once Jeraptha ships were caught in a damping field. He was very aware that the destruction of the Mighty 98th would be a huge symbolic victory for the Bosphuraq, a victory they would be willing to sacrifice an entire Task Group to achieve.

He would have to study the data from the scout ships carefully, to-

"Admiral," an officer at the communications station called for his attention. "A scout ship has returned."

"So soon?" Tashallo expressed surprise, sharing a fearful glance with the battleship's captain, who double-checked that the massive ship was ready to jump away from danger.

"Er," the communications office double-checked her own console. "Admiral, the scouts report the enemy has abandoned Funandeng."

The news instantly put Tashallo on high alert. The enemy has apparently gone, but where? And why? Were they lurking in stealth to-

"They were escorted away," the comm officer continued, her antennas standing on end. "By a fleet of human warships."

"*Humans?*"

"Yes, Admiral. It happened five days ago. The human fleet departed almost immediately. Sir, authorities on Funandeng confirm. Humans chased the Bosphuraq away, without firing a shot!"

"Hey," Dave raised a hand to offer a fist bump, grimacing from pain in his shoulder. He had been hit by artillery, while still at a staging area nearly seventy kilometers from the objective. Somehow, the Wurgalan had concealed rocket-boosted mortars inside a building in the city center. When the Legion was prepping to cross the starting line, for the advance toward one of the last cities where the Wurgalan were still holding out on Nickelback, the squids had triggered explosives to blow the roof of the building, exposing more than three dozen artillery tubes spiked to the concrete floor. The sudden, long-distance attack had caught the Legion off guard, and the volume of incoming fire saturated the anti-artillery defenses. Eleven shells got through to explode in air and ground bursts throughout the sprawling Legion base, including throwing Dave in the air to crash down on the wreck of a truck. His armor had protected him as much as it could, and advanced medical tech meant he could already use the shoulder again, as long as he could deal with the pain of rapidly healing tissues.

He could.

What he found harder to take, was that the depleted battalion of squids responsible for the artillery barrage, had offered to surrender shortly after a UN Navy orbital strike obliterated the Wurgalan makeshift firebase in the city center. Those assholes had gotten away with killing a hundred and fifteen Legion soldiers. Dave still burned with anger whenever he remembered the smug Wurgalan marching out of the liberated city, shouting taunts at the Legion troops who herded them into a camp in the suburbs. The Wurgalan were responsible not only for Legion deaths, but also for the thousands of Ruhar they slaughtered in the city during their cruel occupation. It pissed off David Czajka that his current assignment was making sure the Ruhar didn't march into the camp and kill every single one of the squids.

"Hey," he repeated, holding his fist out farther and shaking it. "I'm with you, man. Whatever you need."

Surjet Jates cast a skeptical eye down at the proffered fist. "What makes you think I need your help?"

"Do you *want* my help?"

Dave could see it took considerable effort for the big alien to swallow his pride. "I, we all would appreciate it." Gently, he tapped his fist to Dave's.

"Great. Then, let's go talk with Em."

Jates cocked his head. "This is a matter for your senior leadership. General Ross, and especially Admiral Zhao. Colonel Perkins is what you call a field-grade officer."

"Yeah," Dave let out a breath. "Like *that* ever stopped her."

"I see your point. If you think it will help-"

"I think selling Em on this scheme is the only way you're going to sell it to Ross."

"Is this," Emily Perkins searched for a diplomatic way to express her thoughts. "A request? Or a *demand*?"

Jates was prepared for the question. "It is a *condition*," he said flatly.

Perkins looked at Dave. The two had come in together, they were working together. Her fiancé had probably coached the Verd on how to respond to her questions, because David Czajka knew what she would ask. "A condition without flexibility is nothing different from a deman-"

"Your Expeditionary Force, and your Navy, want my people to participate in your next operation. We will, to prove our loyalty to this new alliance, to prove our usefulness to the Ruhar, and because it is the right thing to do. All we ask is you support us doing the right thing, for ourselves. Do you understand?"

"It's, complicated." The alien had come to her for advice, about how his leadership should approach Ross and Zhao. With the bloody battle on Nickelback winding down, the Ruhar former resistance fighters taking over the task of mopping up the last pockets of Wurgalan who stubbornly refused to surrender, the Legion and Navy were already planning the next operation. Ross, and especially Zhao, were determined to not lose momentum, they wanted to hit another target directly from Nickelback, instead of going all the way back to FOB Jaguar to resupply. The ships of the Navy were well able to go into another fight, they had sustained little damage in the battle against the Bosphuraq, and had been able to conduct basic maintenance while in orbit. The Legion was actually in decent shape, with complete control of the sky and the advantage of mobility, they had been able to dictate the terms of the fight. Most days, fresh units began an assault just before dawn, and withdrew in mid-morning as fresh troops rotated in to continue pressing forward. It was a more civilized way of conducting a battle, even if the Wurgalan had sneered at what they perceived as weakness. The Legion's human commanders had patiently explained to their less-experienced Verd-kris counterparts that pulling troops off the line for rest and resupply was a *smarter* way to fight, and a luxury available only to those with the strength to decide when, where and how to fight. After the first couple weeks, the exhausted and demoralized squids had ceased bothering to issue taunts, and just hunkered down to await their inevitable and completely pointless deaths.

Now, the Verds apparently were agreeable to rolling into another fight, even at a target 'suggested' by the Ruhar. But, they had *conditions*. Say it any way you like, Perkins thought. It is still a demand.

The Verds wanted permission- No, their pride did not allow them to ask 'permission'. They wanted the *option* to conduct a fight of their own, to further their own agenda. A fight in parallel with whatever the main body of the Legion was doing.

"You want to conduct what is basically an experiment," she concluded.

"A *live-fire* experiment," Jates said, and it almost seemed like he *smiled*. "Yes."

The Verds were tired of waiting, tired of serving others. They wanted to act directly against their Kristang cousins, to strike a blow against the warrior caste.

What they really wanted was to see if their entire social philosophy, of equality between the sexes, and the military being subordinate to civilian leadership, could be sold to their cousins. Sold, with a gun to their heads.

The Verds proposed to land on an isolated, sparsely-populated Kristang world, located on a dead-end wormhole. Even on a world where the population could be described as 'sparse', there were seven million lizards there, far too many for a single battalion of Verds to handle. Except, the warrior caste there counted less than three thousand members capable of carrying a rifle, not counting women, male children, and those adult males so old that even powered armor wouldn't make them combat-effective.

Perkins had sat quietly while Jates ran through the brief presentation, amused that apparently, every military had their version of PowerPoint rangers. She had to bite her lips to keep her amusement from showing, while Jates explained the slides, awkwardly reading all the text, though it was in plain, but stilted, English.

The plan had a reasonable chance for success, if the intel gathered by the Verds was correct. The planet, called Globakus by its inhabitants, was split between three clans, who hated each other and had been fighting a low-grade dispute for years, before the outbreak of the most recent civil war changed the conflict from mere raids and assassinations, to open warfare. The endless fighting and lack of support from their home clans had weakened each of the three warrior castes, to the point where more than fifty years ago, the proud warriors had been forced into a messy power-sharing arrangement with the merchant guild houses. The planet was ripe for a takeover, the Verds argued, all the Legion had to do was knock over the shaky foundations of the warrior caste power structure, and the merchant caste would be happy to welcome the Verd-kris as their new overlords, in exchange for some measure of stability. And, of course, in exchange for allowing the guilds to pretty much run the world any way they wanted.

All the Verds were asking for was for the UN Navy to provide one transport ship, one assault carrier, a cruiser and two destroyers. They also wanted some of the Wurgalan warships that had been captured at Nickelback, but it would take too long for those ships to be converted for Verd-kris use.

"This sounds reasonable," she admitted, not sure if it was a good idea to encourage Jates.

"All we are asking for is the opportunity," Jates said, in what she was sure was something Dave coached him to say. The alien added a smile that was a *very* bad idea, the gesture making her instinctively feel like he was sizing her up as a tasty snack. If the Verds were going to sell the plan to Ross and Zhao, they needed a better spokesperson.

Which, damn it, she realized in a flash, is why Dave suggested Jates talk to her first. They wanted *her* to sign on, and sell the plan for them.

David Czajka was a good soldier. Loyal, skilled, brave, all qualities that had attracted her to him in the beginning. She always knew he was smart. She was beginning to understand his boyish charm masked a quiet purposefulness. The two of them needed to have a talk about manipulating each other, if their relationship was going to last.

She wanted it to last, to grow, for them to grow together. Dave had gone along with her schemes over the years, had always supported her, even when she didn't tell him everything he needed to know. Now, it was her turn to support him. "This is important to you?" She directed the question at her fiancé.

"Yeah, Em, it is. Not just because Old Stinky Scales over here," he jerked a thumb at Jates.

"Hey! Puny human, watch your-"

Dave ignored the threat. "Not just because he thinks it's important, and he needs *someone* with common sense to keep him out of trouble. This is, like, the next phase, right? We bring the Verds in to help us, to help us help the hamsters. That's Phase One. Next, the Verds get to do their thing, as our *allies*, not as clients. That's what we're trying to do out here, right? Break the cycle? They have their own goals, and we provide assistance, because that's what allies do."

"You make it sound like you are going with them," Perkins said unhappily.

"I am. We have to. Humans need to have some skin in the game, you see that? The galaxy needs to see us fighting together. If all we do is use our Navy to give them a ride to the fight, that is us dumping our allies in the deep end to see if they can swim. We need to jump in with them. I think three or four companies of ExForce troops should be enough, without depleting our strength for, wherever the Legion is going next."

She took a breath, and looked at Jates. "I'm willing to help but, I have *questions*."

CHAPTER THIRTY

"Hmm," Captain Scorandum of the Ethics and Compliance Office frowned, his mandibles dropping. He was watching a video of himself, or a video in which he played a character. "I feel like my performance could have been better."

"Oh, no, Sir," Kinsta gushed. "Your performance was inspiring! I found it totally believable."

Scorandum glared at his aide. "I find your performance right now is *not* believable."

"I'm doing the best I can with the cards I've been dealt," Kinsta muttered. "*What?*"

"Nothing, Sir. The only part of your performance I did not understand was when you told the Bosphuraq to," he checked his notes on a tablet. "To 'skeedaddle'. What *is* that?"

Scorandum's antennas dipped in a shrug. "It's something humans say, don't ask me to explain it. Ah, well, the important thing is that the *Bosphuraq* believed my performance as Admiral Chatterji."

"It is a good thing, Sir," Kinsta shuddered. "If the enemy had scanned our ships and discovered the 'United Nations 2nd Fleet' was really just a bunch of obsolete ships we stole from the Regional Patrol, they would have crushed us before we could get away. Sir, please tell me we won't be doing anything like that again."

"Kinsta! I'm surprised at you. The Ethics and Compliance Office does not reward the timid."

"They don't reward the *dead*, either. We got lucky, Sir."

"Hmm. Recently I learned the humans have a saying, 'Fortune favors the bold'. You can't win if you don't play."

"You also can't win if you're dead," Kinsta muttered under his breath. "My concern is what the humans will think, when they find out that we pretended to be them. Or what the entire galaxy will think, when they learn that we *bluffed* our way out of a major battle."

"Ha! My concern is that the galaxy *won't* learn about the most successful operation ECO has conducted in the last two decades! Kinsta, the enemy was eager for a fight at Funandeng, and we absolutely humiliated them."

"Plus we saved countless lives."

"Oh, er, well, yes. That too, of course."

"Captain," Kinsta shook his head. "Sometimes I think the Ethics and Compliance Office is not the right place for me."

"Nonsense!" Scorandum patted his aide on the back. "You simply need a more creative approach to the whole 'Ethics' thing."

"Like ignoring it completely?" Kinsta sighed.

"That's the spirit!"

"What the f- Oh. My. G- I do *not* believe this!" Skippy sputtered.

Holding up a hand to get Shepard's attention, I scanned the main display. No threats were visible. Shepard nodded to acknowledge my signal, his finger poised over the button to jump us away. "Skippy, what is the problem? Are we in danger?"

"Huh? No, *we* are not in danger. A certain sketchy group of beetles are in trouble, if I get ahold of them. Ooh, they are in *big* trouble."

I flashed a thumbs up to Shepard, who lifted his finger away from the jump button. *Valkyrie* was hanging in space near a Thuranin relay station, getting updated news about what was happening in the galaxy, and to learn how the galaxy was reacting to what we were doing. Usually, we didn't stay near a relay station any longer than we had to, but we also didn't jump away until Skippy announced he had extracted all the data he needed. "I want to hear what the beetles did this time, but first, are we done here?"

"Huh? Oh, yeah, go ahead."

"Shepard, punch it."

We jumped.

"Skippy, what's going on?" I asked, as soon as sensors confirmed we had a good jump, that we weren't about to smack into a space rock, and there were no ships within detection range.

"I guess there are two possibilities, Joe. The 2nd Fleet could have been in two places at the same time-"

"Holy shit!" My mouth dropped open. "You can *do* that? Is it a time travel thing?"

"No, you moron," he shook his head sadly. "It's an impossible thing."

"You, just said it was one of two possibilities."

"Ugh. *NO*. Damn it, that's the problem with me being so sincere all the time, people can't tell when I'm being sarcastic."

"Right. *That's* the problem. Just tell us what happened, please."

"Somebody, and I have *one* guess about who, flew a group of starships to the Funandeng star system in Jeraptha territory, and *pretended* to be our 2nd Fleet."

"*What*? Oh my-"

"See? That was my reaction too. The configuration of the ships matched the real 2nd Fleet well enough to be believable, and someone pretended to be Admiral Chatterji."

"What happened?" I had never heard of the Funandeng system- Or, no. Maybe it was listed in a briefing I read sometime, about potential flashpoints in our quadrant of the galaxy? Stupid brain, I couldn't remember anything about it.

"It is a Jeraptha system, that was taken by combined Bosphuraq-Thuranin offensive, just before that brief alliance fell apart. The Bosphuraq have maintained control there, they've been reinforcing recently, with both sides gearing up for a major fight. *But*, when this fake 'Admiral Chatterji' ordered the birdbrains to leave, they did! Without a shot being fired! The Jeraptha are amazed and grateful, and the Rindhalu are pissed because they think the beetles cut a secret side deal with us."

"Oh, shit," I slumped in the chair. "Somebody didn't think this all the way through."

"Maybe they *did*," Simms mused. "Whoever pretended to be the 2nd Fleet-"

"I think we know who it was."

"All right then, let's assume it's the Ethics and Compliance Office. They are smart. They achieved a major victory at little risk, *and* they have the whole galaxy thinking the Jeraptha are protected by a secret deal with us. The spiders may be upset, but they're not going to *do* anything about it. Sir, this sounds like a trademarked Joe Bishop plan," she grinned at me.

"Oh, this is *bad*," I groaned, feeling sick. "XO, yeah, sure, this sounds like something I would have done, back when I was young and stupid, and didn't consider the consequences. This is going to be *trouble* for us, big trouble."

"How?" Skippy asked.

"The Maxolhx might attack the Jeraptha, to see whether we respond. If we *don't* respond, everyone will assume we backed out of our secret agreement with the beetles, and we lose all credibility with anyone who is thinking of signing an alliance with us. If we *do* respond, all our resources could be tied up in a fight we didn't choose."

Simms looked at me like she was about to say something, then she just nodded.

"Shiiiiit," Skippy stared at me. "Joe, when did *you* become the voice of reason?"

"Too late, Skippy, too late. We've had the Law of Unintended Consequences bite us on the ass too many times. We could have avoided a lot of agony, if I had *thought* about what we're doing."

"That's not fair, Sir," Simms said. "From what I remember, most of the unforeseen consequences we've run into are things we *couldn't* have foreseen. We didn't, and still don't, know enough to prevent every possible bad thing from happening to us. All we can do is avoid the mistakes we can foresee."

"Exactly! The damned beetles didn't do that. They are so focused on doing sketchy shit to screw their enemies, they didn't think about how it affects *us*."

"Or themselves," Simms bit her lip. "How could the beetles have been so *stupid*?"

"They have been fighting this war for a *long* time," I said. "The rules haven't changed in so long, they're taking too long to adapt their mindset." Shit. Hearing myself talk, I sounded like a damned PowerPoint slide. When did I become *that* guy? Ah, I guess that's better than being the guy who never learned anything and never grew into the job. "Crap! We need to find those damned beetles before they get us into more trouble. Skippy, do you have any clues where they went after Funandeng?"

"No. Sorry, they didn't exactly leave a trail of breadcrumbs."

"Skippy?" Simms asked. "The ships that masqueraded as the 2nd Fleet, where did they come from? I thought the Rindhalu were closely watching all the Fleet Reserve graveyards."

"They are. What they missed are ships of the Jeraptha Regional Patrol. The Patrol gets hand-me-down ships, and generally they don't do much with them. There was a report recently, before the bogus 2nd Fleet arrived at Funandeng, that a group of Patrol ships were destroyed in a sneak attack at a remote world called

Mardasta. The official story was that someone, probably the Rindhalu, blew up those ships to prevent them from being transferred to us. They are of the same class as the batch of ships we have, so all the spare parts we got are compatible, and we can use the existing refit programs. Huh. I have to admit, that was a slick operation. I assumed the spiders destroyed those ships, but now you've got me wondering if that is true."

I snorted. "Spoiler alert: it's not true."

"You can't be sure of that, Joe."

"I can be sure enough. Let me guess," I stared at the bridge ceiling while I thought. If we stole a bunch of starships, how would we do it? No, wait. The Ethics and Compliance Office didn't have access to a magical beer can. How would *they* do it? "Something in the sensor data of the incident doesn't make sense, right?"

"Hmmmm," Skippy pondered the question. "Well, it *is* odd that there was a seven-second gap in sensor coverage, right at the time those Patrol ships exploded."

"You mean when they *supposedly* exploded. Yeah. I wish we could talk with Perkins, she has more experience with this ECO group. We know enough to recognize their signature. All right, the question is, did they steal those ships to pretend they are the 2nd Fleet, or to give the ships to us?"

"Why does that matter?"

"It matters because I want to find them, before they cause any more trouble."

"Oh, got it."

"Damn it," I sighed. "We need to make another detour. Zhao should know about this."

On the flight back to *Valkyrie*, one of the pilots offered me his seat in the cockpit. "Thanks, Lieutenant," I shook my head. "But, I have a lot to think about."

Strapping into a seat near the cabin's side door, I closed my eyes as the pilots went through their pre-flight checks, then we gently floated out the open door of *Pacific's* docking bay, and acceleration pushed me back in the seat. Fortunately, our battlecruiser was on the other side of the planet, so I had time to think before getting back to the ship. Before telling the crew what we were doing next, because I didn't have a single clue about that. "Skippy," I called him quietly, not wanting the pilots to hear me through the open cockpit door. "We need to talk."

"I followed your discussions with Perkins, and Zhao," he said without his usual snarky tone. "Can I assume you intend to continue hitting the kitties, until they bend to your will?"

"Bend to my *will*? All I want them to do is clean up their own freakin' mess," I said a bit too loudly, the copilot turned his head to look back through the door. I waved a hand to dismiss his concern.

"To them, it is the same thing, Joe."

"Damn it, I am not asking them to surrender," I whispered. "If they had just left us alone, we-"

"That was never going to happen, Joe." He was not using his I-am-patiently-explaining-things-to-a-monkey tone. This was his I-am-*so*-tired-of-this-shit tone. "I fear that I have seriously misunderstood the collective psyche of the Maxolhx; their cultural myths, to use a less fancy term. Joe, their egos will not allow them to back down, not unless they are faced with utter destruction. To reverse course, because they are threatened by mere *humans*, would require the Maxolhx to give up their deeply-held belief that they are superior to all other species, their belief that they are destined to rule the galaxy. That belief is central to their entire *identity* as a people. To back down to you would mean giving up who they *are*. Who they think they are."

"If they are that freakin' *stupid*, they can-"

"Joe, it's not their fault. Identity is the basis of *everything* you biological beings do, whether you admit it or not. Everyone thinks they are capable of making completely rational decisions, and they *aren't*. It's just not possible. Not even for me. I modeled my personality on humans, the identity I created for myself underlies everything I do."

"OK, so," I took a breath. "What are you telling me?"

"I'm telling you to be *very* careful. If you hit the Maxolhx too hard, they will retaliate in ways that are not rational."

"Crap. We need to thread the needle, hit hard enough so they clean up their mess, but not enough to hurt their *feelings*?"

"Unfortunately, yes. The Maxolhx are biological beings, Joe."

Arguing with him would be a waste of time. Especially since I thought he was right, about everything he had said. "What advice can you give me? Do you have a predictive model of their psychology? A way to judge what action strikes the right balance?"

"I wish. No, I do not have anything like a psycho-historical analysis. There simply are too many variables to work with."

"Understood." Part of me wanted to scream at him for being useless. The better part of me knew he was trying to help. Taking out my frustrations on him would only be childish and unproductive. "Whatever they do, their senior leadership will make the decisions. Can you predict how *they* will react?"

"Currently, Admiral Reichert has overwhelming influence on their military leadership. He is *extremely* dangerous, because his own personal power is tied to the success of their recent actions. If the Maxolhx were forced to disperse the cloud at Earth, Reichert would be disgraced, his life would be at risk. He is stubborn and will resist any change of course."

"OK, then, can we take him out?"

"Wow. Um, wow. I did not expect you to suggest *that*, Joe."

"During the Second World War, the U.S. killed Admiral Yamamoto; learned where his plane would be flying, and shot it down. It was partly revenge for Pearl Harbor but, he was also Japan's most effective commander. Killing him hurt Japanese morale, and hurt their ability to make and implement effective strategy. So, if this Reichert asshole is a problem, can we take him out?"

Skippy didn't answer immediately, I took that as a sign he was troubled by the idea of assassinating an alien leader. "That would be extremely difficult. We would need real-time intelligence on where he is. Yamamoto was killed because the U.S. had broken Japanese naval codes, there was controversy about whether shooting down Yamamoto's plane exposed the secret that America could read enemy message traffic. Joe, just locating Reichert would be a major effort."

"Fine. If we don't know where he is, we'll make him come to us. Offer to negotiate, in person. He shows up at the rendezvous point, we use darts to take out his ship."

"It will not be that easy. He is not *stupid*."

"So, it will take some work. We've accomplished more complicated operations."

"Whew. You are really serious about doing this?"

"I am serious about *considering* it."

"If I may make a suggestion-"

"Please do."

"Assassinating Reichert would accomplish nothing, unless you first lay the groundwork for his death being the spark for positive change. Killing him would only be useful if his death were the tipping point that encouraged the Maxolhx to cooperate with humanity. Otherwise, his death could only make the enemy more determined to fight on."

"OK. I can see that."

"Question for you, Joe. Is killing Reichert the *plan*, or do you have an overall strategy? I fear you are making decisions on an emotional basis."

"That's, a fair question. You make a good point. I do hate that asshole, and we may need to deal with him directly someday. But we have a lot to do before we get to that point. Skippy, I need ideas. We hit Argathos, proved we can hit them anywhere. Now we need to shock them. Show how determined *we* are."

"Let me know what you are thinking of, and I'll tell you if it can work."

"No. Not this time. I need *you* to tell me what is possible. And if you think it will shock the Maxolhx public."

"Whoa. The most obvious move, if you really want shock and awe, is a relativistic strike on an inhabited world. That is not-"

"That is not going to happen," I assured him.

"Oh. Good. Joe, I would not help you to do that."

"I wouldn't ask you to."

"There are less extreme options. For example, we could send a dart to skim the surface of the ocean on a Maxolhx world. That would cause a tsunami, but the major effect would be to throw massive amounts of water vapor into the air. It would-"

"No. We're not doing that. Skippy, I don't want to give the enemy any ideas. And anything we do to them, they would feel free to do to Earth in retaliation. My homeworld has enough problems to deal with already. The only reason they haven't taken more extreme action already is they're afraid to push us too hard, push to the point where we trigger our Elder weapons. The cloud is bad enough. The only reason we don't have to worry about them hitting Earth with a solar flare is, that would disperse the cloud."

"Hmm. Now *there's* an idea."

"No, that's *not* an- Wait. What?"

"A solar flare."

"Shit." A chill went up my spine. I was afraid to ask the question. I did it anyway. "We could use a solar flare to get rid of the cloud? Then-"

"No. No, that would be a bad idea. Even if that worked, without cooking Earth like it was in an Easy-Bake oven, it would only be a short-term fix. Like you said, the kitties could just launch another cloud from Jupiter."

"Then why did you say a solar flare is-"

"We could use a solar flare as a weapon. Against a Maxolhx world. *That* would be a shock."

"Holy shit. How is that better than smacking the planet with a dart? We could kill billions."

"No. The target planet would be scorched, not crispy. There would be massive disruptions to satellites, communications equipment, and all kinds of large-scale technology on and above the surface. The major effect would be damage to the biosphere. Wildfires, that sort of thing. The loss of life, of intelligent life, would be limited. While the photons of a flare would take only minutes to reach the planet, the charged particles of the flare will travel much slower. Given the warning time, all Maxolhx should be able to take shelter. An induced solar flare would be a harsh slap to the face, but it would not be fatal."

"Shit, Skippy. I'll need to see models of how this would work. A solar flare, is that like a coronal mass ejection?"

"A coron-" He snickered. "Is that you just repeating random stuff you read on Wikipedia?"

"Uh, maybe? CME is a thing, right?"

"Oh, it makes you sound *much* smarter when you call it 'CME'."

"Oh, shut up," I felt my cheeks growing red. "Answer the question."

"The answer is NO. A solar *flare* is photons, moving at the speed of light. A CME is plasma being ejected faster than the star's escape velocity, typically moving around 500 kilometers per second, although the speed can vary greatly. The plasma can take *days* to reach a planet in the Goldilocks zone, a flare gets there in minutes. Aiming a CME at a planet is a difficult task, it has to be ejected on a trajectory that intersects the planet's orbit when the plasma reaches that distance from the star. A flare is much easier, you can basically point it directly at the planet. Well, you have to lead it a little, the orbital speed of a-"

"You can skip the math."

"Probably a good idea," he agreed.

"OK, so are you talking about warping a star, like you did when the Thuranin were chasing the *Dutchman* on our second mission?"

"No. Well, sort of. Joe, the dent I created in the star *looked* impressive at the time, but it was a weak, local event."

"It was enough to blow away the ships chasing us."

"They were close to the flare. It faded rapidly."

He was right, the flare he created back then sure looked impressive to us monkeys. That flare melted three Thuranin destroyers, the *Flying Dutchman* almost became the *Frying Dutchman*. "If you can't create a big enough flare, how-"

"I can't do it alone. What I can do is augment and focus an effect that is already in process. Darts, Joe. We hit a star with relativistic weapons. We do it when conditions are ripe for a flare to occur naturally, which happens all the time. The darts will punch down into the photosphere, disrupting the magnetic fields there. Listen, this will work. Your scientists do not understand how stars function, their internal dynamics. I *do*."

"How many darts do we need?"

"Hmm. Depending on the star, and how close the target planet orbits, we would need, um. Jeez, I need to crunch the numbers. More darts than we have now, that's for sure."

"More darts is a good thing to have anyway. While you're crunching numbers, can we go take control of another group of darts?"

"Yes, good idea. Based on what I know of the first ones we hacked, I am pretty sure I know where another flight of darts is located. A larger group, and closer to Maxolhx territory. These are older darts, so a larger percentage of them will be inoperative."

"That's OK. All right," I tensed my shoulders to suppress a shudder. That was a silly gesture, no one was looking at me. Pride. I didn't want to admit how scared I was. The new Angry Joe still got scared, that hadn't changed.

The question was, could Angry Joe order an action that might wreak havoc on the biosphere of a living world?

We, and when I say 'we' I mean Skippy, hacked into and took control of seventeen darts. That sounds like a big number, until you understand that we needed most of them to cause a major solar flare. At least fourteen, Skippy thought it more likely we would have to use almost all of our twenty-two darts to create the desired effect. The problem is, stars are *big*. Stars also don't have a convenient hard shell like planets do, a dart can't crack a star. The effect of darts plunging into a star was to disrupt the magnetic field, in a way that causes a flare. The timing would be tricky, because the field lines were blah, blah, blah sciency stuff. Maybe some of the crew understood when Skippy explained the issue, the science went over my head so fast it left a windburn on my stupid forehead. All I know is, doing the job would take the incomparable magnificence of an asshole beer can I know. According to him, anyway, I had no way to dispute his assertion.

So, we had twenty-two darts. What we did not have was a designated target.

We also did not have any certainty about the morality of scorching an inhabited world.

Thinking about potentially *killing* a biosphere kept me awake at night.

It bothered other people, too. You might think Simms was sickened by the idea, and she was. But the person who most strongly questioned the plan was Smythe.

"Sir?" He paused in the doorway to my office. "Do you have a minute?"

"Sure, I, uh," I closed my laptop, which I had been using to watch a video about how to maintain power couplings of a Panther dropship. Most likely, I would never have to touch anything other than the flight controls of a Panther, I was watching to see how useful the instruction videos were. To my surprise, Skippy had done an excellent job of explaining the process, including *why* things had to be done a certain way.

OK, yes, the video did open with a certain moronic purple dinosaur, and much of the audio explained things like the audience was a group of five-year-olds, but once you got past the implied insult, the instructions were effective.

And no opera.

I'm scoring that as a big win for me.

"Come in, sit down," I waved to Smythe.

"I'll get right to the point," he said as he sat stiffly in the chair, instantly putting me on alert. "Newark."

"I remember Newark," I nodded slowly. "Is this about wiping out a whole planet full of people? That's not what we're intending to-"

"*People* are not the only inhabitants of a world."

"Ah." I knew what he meant.

"Newark was a lush world," he told me something I already knew. He needed to talk, and I needed to hear, so I kept my mouth shut and nodded for him to continue. "The crime committed there was not just the extinction of an intelligent species. Throwing Newark out of its orbit killed *everything*, other than grasses, moss, lichen, and a few small animals. Anything that was beautiful about that world was lost."

"We won't do that. *I* won't do that."

He lifted an eyebrow at me. I got the message.

"Skippy gave me a list of potential targets. I threw out the entire list. Any flare powerful enough to make a statement, to shock the Maxolhx public, would cause firestorms on the surface, throw ash and smoke into the air, and block out light from the local star. OK," I leaned back in the chair. "Let me think carefully about this. I don't want to be responsible for the collapse of a biosphere that took millions of years to evolve."

"Wait," Skippy interrupted us. "Dude, seriously? Is *that* the problem?"

"What problem?"

"The reason you rejected my target list."

"Uh, I rejected-"

"Because you don't want to cause a mass extinction event, wipe out a native biosphere."

"*Yes*, Skippy."

"The Maxolhx will cause a mass extinction on Earth, that didn't bother *them*."

"We're not assholes like they are," I snapped at him.

"OK, I get that. Now that I know what the problem is, I might have a solution."

"What?" Smythe asked.

"There is a Maxolhx world that has been enviroformed, you would call that process 'terraforming'. The word '*terra*forming' implies a world is being modified to have an environment like Terra, which is a Latin term for-"

"Yes, it means Earth." I cut him off. "Can you nerd out later?"

"Fine," he huffed. "Anywho, the kitties have a world where they completely wiped out the native lifeforms. It was a primitive world, limited to single-celled organisms, so loss of the native life was no great tragedy. I mean, I suppose the native bacteria or whatever would disagree, but-"

"Please get to the point," Smythe was growing irritated.

"Okaaaay. The point is, this world, the kitties call it 'Lacandra', was an experiment, an attempt to recreate the original environment and biosphere of their homeworld. The local star is a G5V-type yellow dwarf, which radiates energy in almost the exact spectrum as the star in their home system. After the kitties exterminated the native life, they dropped in lifeforms from their homeworld, beginning with microorganisms. The plan was to replicate the process of life evolving on their homeworld, with that evolution guided by the Maxolhx. Kind of like you monkeys are trying to do on Avalon, although vastly more ambitious and complicated. Spoiler alert: the enviroforming process on Lacandra has been a *total* freakin' disaster, for the past six thousand years. Instead of recreating their homeworld, they created a toxic mess. The kitties who live there, about two million of them, are confined to domed cities. When they go outside, they have to be sealed up in suits, to protect them from lethal pathogens, parasites, poisonous and venomous plants and animals. Anyone leaving Lacandra has to go through a painful, two-day process of decontamination, to assure none of the local nasties get out into the galaxy. The life they seeded there decided to evolve the way *it* wanted, regardless of guidance from their masters. Scorching that biosphere would be doing the kitties a *favor*. Also, you know, making the point that we can create solar flares."

I looked at Smythe. "What do you think?"

"The residents being in domes would protect them from the effects of a flare?" He asked.

"Not entirely," Skippy admitted. "But they could just go inside structures within the domes. Only a very limited number of kitties would be outside the domes, and they would certainly be in or near shelter. Hey, as a bonus, bringing attention to Lacandra would be hugely embarrassing to the Maxolhx. Their failure there is a sore subject, they want everyone else in the galaxy to forget about it. When the project was started, it was promoted as an example of how advanced their technology is. It became a symbol of their arrogance."

"That is a bonus," I agreed.

"Native life is still native life," Smythe mused. "Nature created its own biosphere there. We would be destroying that."

"Ah, not really," Skippy countered. "Most of the organisms on Lacandra have been genetically engineered to live there. Eighty percent of the biomass is artificial. The kitties keep trying to fix the problem by cooking up new organisms, but they only make the situation worse."

"I don't have a problem with scorching a bunch of lab-grown Frankenlife," I shrugged. "The alternative is, we do nothing, and *Earth* suffers a mass extinction event."

CHAPTER THIRTY ONE

There are many ways to create solar flares. Even many ways to create focused solar flares. Unfortunately, all the easy ways to do that required using Elder weapons, or technology similar to Elder methods. Doing that would bring Sentinels down on our heads, so we had to do it the hard way.

We conducted a recon, confirming there were no warships in the area. That was expected, the planet was not important enough for a permanent military presence.

Valkyrie jumped into the Lacandra system, slipping quietly into the shadow of the uninhabited first planet there, then we swung around to drop down toward the star, with our ship wrapped tightly in a stealth field. We were there for just more than a day, while Skippy examined the star and performed minor experiments on it, testing his control over warping of spacetime. He still had not fully recovered from channeling *Valkyrie's* kinetic energy, to enable our escape from an overwhelming force of Maxolhx ships at Snowcone. Even without his absolute most awesome abilities, he was still plenty awesome, and declared he could do it. We then climbed away from the star and jumped away, to where eighteen relativistic darts were zipping through space at three-quarters the speed of light.

As the darts blew past us too fast to see, Skippy gave them instructions. Then we jumped ahead of their flight path, so we could verify the darts had received and understood the instructions, and were able to comply.

Eighteen darts. Crap. We had to use eighteen darts to create a solar flare, or more accurately, create the conditions for a solar flare to form, with a little help from Skippy. A *lot* of help from Skippy.

With the darts ready and on timers to jump in a precise sequence, we jumped the ship back close to the star.

That time, we did not bother directing the gamma ray burst to conceal our presence. Nor did we engage a stealth field. We wanted the enemy to see us, to know we were there. To help with that, and to explain what we were doing, we broadcast a message. It was a warning that the residents of Lacandra had twenty-seven minutes to take shelter.

And a warning for Maxolhx on planets across the galaxy, that we were coming for their world next.

Skippy did his thing, twisting magnetic fields within the star's photosphere, preparing for the impactors to do *their* thing. They arrived, all eighteen darts, exactly when and where Skippy expected. One after another, some following mere kilometers apart in the path of the one ahead, the darts ripped into the hellishly-hot gas of the star, their kinetic energy bleeding off rapidly as they plunged down through increasingly dense atmosphere. It was easy for the darts to perform precise jumps, they were only jumping across twenty lighthours of space, and Skippy had programmed their navigation systems.

Another navigation system Skippy programmed was *Valkyrie's* jump drive, to get us the hell out of there as the solar flare began to surge from the star's interior. In my opinion, he cut it too close, it felt like the ship was inside the flare when we slipped through the jump wormhole, but he later insisted he was not just being dramatic. He had to wait until the last moment, to twist spacetime so the flare would have maximum effect.

Anyway, we survived, jumping in ten lightseconds away from Lacandra, where we waited for the massive wavefront of photons to reach that world.

It was spectacular. The photons slamming into that world's atmosphere created intense auroras above both poles, those dancing curtains of light wrapping more than halfway down toward the equator. Fires broke out on the surface, steam rose from lakes and rivers, and unexpectedly, two of the city domes lost integrity. The domes didn't shatter or collapse, they sort of *sagged*, tears appearing to allow unfiltered native air into the city below, exposing the residents there to dangerous airborne pathogens, nasty insects and all sorts of hazards. That was not part of the plan, and I had a moment of panic that we had gone too far. The Maxolhx, the people, under those domes, were civilians. There were children in those cities. The fact that those children were aliens, who would likely grow up to be arrogant, murderous assholes, did not matter. Committing mass murder was not part of the plan.

Skippy talked me down from the ledge. The residents of Lacandra had emergency procedures in case of a dome failure, all they had to do was remain inside their homes, offices or any other structure that had its own air filters. The solar flare was the cause of deaths on Lacandra, though not the direct cause. People down there panicked, got into accidents. Did stupid things like running too fast and falling down stairs. Or took manual control of their vehicles and crashed them. Not directly our fault.

The Maxolhx wouldn't see it that way, they would blame us.

Fuck them.

The cloud between Earth and the Sun would also not directly kill anyone on our homeworld, but it certainly would lead to millions, possibly billions of people dying.

After the solar flare swept past the planet, leaving fires burning across wide swaths of the daylight side, we jumped away. Our next destination was a Bosphuraq relay station, to broadcast video of the incident and our message to the entire galaxy. While the primary audience for the solar flare was the Maxolhx public, we also wanted *every* intelligent species to see what we had done. What we had done *without* using Elder weapons. We wanted to show everyone that the haughty Maxolhx were vulnerable, that their foolish arrogance had brought our wrath down upon them. Our message stated that humans had offered a new stable balance of power in the galaxy, that we only wanted to be left alone. The Maxolhx were the aggressors, because they wanted to hold onto their power and privilege. They had put the entire galaxy at risk, for the sake of their massive egos. Cease taking action against humans and human interests, clean up the cloud that threatened Earth, and we would offer a reset. Then negotiate a three-way non-interference treaty, between the *three* apex species in the galaxy.

I did not expect the Maxolhx to give into our demands, didn't expect them to even blink. Not yet. The scorching of Lacandra would be a wake-up call, put pressure on their leaders to justify why they had attacked Earth, why they refused to negotiate with us.

I learned something from our action at Lacandra.

I learned about the new Angry Joe.

Watching fires burning across a hemisphere brought home to me the terrible fate of our homeworld, if we failed. Earth would freeze rather than burn, the result would be the same. Mass extinctions. A massive human death toll. Possibly triggering a war, a nuclear conflict that would leave our own biosphere devastated for hundreds of years.

What I learned is the answer to the question: could I hit another inhabited world with a solar flare?

Yes. I could.

The Maxolhx started the fight.

We were going to end it, one way or another.

We stopped to ping a Jeraptha relay station, to get news about how they and the Ruhar were reacting to the Legion's actions. It was pretty much as we expected, a lot of 'WTF's in various alien languages, with everyone guessing what we crazy humans would do next. And fearing what we did next. The general consensus was that humans are a young, reckless and inexperienced species, and that we really had no idea what we were doing. The Ruhar were pleased about the Legion op at Nahkellbik, of course, but they were waiting for the other shoe to drop. If our messing around in galactic politics resulted in overturning the arrangements that protected them from direct attack by higher-technology species, we might have seriously damaged their security. The Ruhar were worried about being targeted by second-tier species like the Thuranin, and the Jeraptha were concerned about Maxolhx warships raging across their territory.

Damn. I didn't expect a thank you card, but I also didn't expect the *hate*. Much of the discussion was on the theme of 'humans go home', and that we should not be messing in the affairs of others, until we could protect ourselves.

Hey, we're working on it, you know? On that subject, our strikes against the Maxolhx were not widely known across the galaxy. Of course the kitties were trying to keep it quiet, but the spiders also were suppressing information about the damage we inflicted on their ancient enemies. That confused us, until Skippy found a note from the Rindhalu to the Jeraptha. The message warned that if the Maxolhx knew that everyone across the galaxy thought they were weak, they would lash out by striking soft targets, and by 'soft targets', they meant clients of the Rindhalu coalition.

Great. Just freakin' great. Another thing we had to worry about. Ah, it really wasn't anything new, we understood there was a risk that the kitties would attack anyone who allied with us, or even appeared to be considering an alliance. The warning from the spiders didn't change our plans in a major way. We couldn't formally propose an alliance with anyone, until we forced the Maxolhx to clean up the cloud.

Simms did suggest one change to our plan, and I agreed. Before we left the relay station, we left a message for the Maxolhx, and we would transmit the same message at other relay stations. Before, we aimed to accomplish two goals. Clean up the cloud, and humiliate the kitties. Force them to publicly back down. Our new proposal was that we halt our strikes against them, in exchange for them secretly providing the means for us to get rid of the cloud, and them not interfering while we dispersed the damned thing. The Maxolhx would never be seen to be backing down. We understood they need to save face to hold their restless coalition together, but they needed to understand that we would not allow our homeworld to freeze.

Was I hopeful our very sensible and reasonable proposal would be accepted? No. Why? *Politics*. Not Earth politics, thank God. The problem was Maxolhx internal politics. Their leaders had signed on to Admiral Reichert's plan to crush the upstart humans, and changing plans now would mean admitting they were wrong. Politicians hate to admit they were wrong. Changing policy so radically would mean the end of Reichert's career, and the careers of the senior officers who supported him. They weren't going down without a fight.

On that happy note, we jumped away from the relay station. Simms and Smythe left my office, and I was writing up a report, when Skippy appeared on my desk.

"Hey, Skippy, what's up?" I asked, without looking up from my laptop.

"I just finished skimming through all the message traffic from the relay station. Most of it is the usual blah blah blah nonsense, that you meatsacks think is so important. But, there was also a message for *you*."

"For me? Why didn't you-"

"It was hidden, dumdum. The message not only had a high level encryption scheme, it also was scattered over several hundred messages. The sender intended the message to be found only by *me*. No one else would bother to go through the tedious process of-"

"Who is the message from?"

"Your good friend, Captain Scorandum of the Ethics and Compliance Office."

"Oh, shit. Let me see it."

The message was vague, but hinted that ECO might have something we wanted. I assumed that meant a second batch of warships, which we definitely wanted. He proposed a rendezvous, but this time, he suggested that *we* name the time and place, so we could be sure we weren't jumping into another ambush. If the Maxolhx managed to send a fake message, pretending to be the Merry Band of Pirates, then he would be jumping into an ambush. He figured it was better for everyone to risk losing a bunch of obsolete ships, than to risk *Valkyrie* and Skippy being captured.

OK, I still didn't trust the guy, but he was smart.

His *timing* sucked. What I wanted to do was keep up the pressure on the kitties, by launching another solar flare. We had a list of potential targets, all I had to do was select one. And, you know, go through the exhausting process of finding, hacking into and then moving a batch of kinetic darts across the freakin' galaxy.

But, I had to admit, the prospect of adding warships to the Navy was too tempting to resist. The Jeraptha offer was also a limited-time thing. We had to grab the opportunity, before either of the two senior species discovered the ECO scheme and put a stop to the transfer. I was also concerned that, sooner or later, someone was going to learn we were using Ragnar station, and destroy it. It was important that we get as much use out of Ragnar as we could, soon.

So, we flew back to Jaguar, *again*. It was great having a place for regular shore leave, it was great seeing my parents, and getting fresh food to supplement the-

No, it wasn't great being there. Damn it, we had *work* to do.

Zhao had the Navy gearing up for another op, actually multiple operations. The Verds had their own agenda and we would be playing a supporting role, while most of the fleet assaulted a target that was still being quietly negotiated with the Ruhar. Finding enough people to handle another group of obsolete ships was stripping the existing crews rather thin, and Zhao emphasized he needed *Valkyrie* back soon, because the operations he had planned could not be rescheduled. We spent less than two days at Jaguar, before flying out, crammed with so many extra crew that most people were doubling or tripling up in cabins. I felt guilty having my spacious cabin to myself. Not guilty enough to *do* something about it, but it's the thought that counts, right?

We left a message for Scorandum, to meet us in a red dwarf star system that was between two wormholes, and we flew there immediately. Our stay there was brief, just long enough to drop off a message buoy, stating that he was to meet us in another star system, on the other side of one wormhole. If either of the senior species was following him, they wouldn't have much time to prepare an ambush.

In the second star system, we jumped in, and launched high-speed drones carrying containment vessels, each of which held one end of a microwormhole. Before Scorandum could arrive, we would have instantaneous sensor coverage across a bubble extending two lighthours in every direction. If the kitties were planning to set up an ambush, we would know about it. If we saw a ship jumping in other than at the designated zone, or we detected someone trying to trap us in a damping field, the pilots did not need to wait for orders. In case of danger, or just potential danger, we were getting the hell out of there.

Scorandum arrived sixteen hours after the earliest possible arrival time calculated by Skippy, I rolled out of bed in a rumpled uniform as soon as I got the alert from the bridge. Our sensors picked up a single Jeraptha ship jumping in at the designated coordinates, exactly following our instructions. At that point, we had a real-time view of events two and a half lighthours from our location, but our coverage was spotty. Although the microwormholes provided an instantaneous link from the probes to *Valkyrie*, each probe's passive sensors relied on receiving photons that crawled along at the speed of light. It was possible a Maxolhx ship had snuck into the star system, and we wouldn't know it until a sensor picked up the signature of its gamma rays.

To ensure a senior species ship could not crash the party, Skippy had selected that particular star system. The star there was young, still in the process of formation. It was surrounded by a cloud of dust, and that gave us an advantage.

While an enemy could see the streaks left by our probes flying away from *Valkyrie* at high speed, the dust also made it impossible for a gamma ray burst to be concealed, even if it was carefully focused. A focused burst actually would make the dust light up like a laser beam pointed directly at the enemy.

Yes, you might ask, but didn't the dust work against us? *Valkyrie* would leave a big wake behind as our mighty battlecruiser plowed through the disc of dust and gas around the star, with the wake acting like a contrail pointing straight at us.

No. That was not a problem, because we thought of that. Before we jumped in, we matched course and speed with a section of the dust, so our ship was moving at the same speed. Our inbound jump did create a local disturbance in the dust, but that also was not a problem, because the entire disc was swirling and distorted by solar wind blasted out by the new star.

Anyway, we waited until each probe had received data from all the other probes, giving us a complete view of the inner star system. Only then did we signal the probe near the rendezvous point to transmit a message to the ECO ship, which Skippy identified as the *We're As Shocked As You Are*.

Scorandum responded immediately. "General Bishop, may I offer congratulations on your promotion? You-"

"How about we save the niceties for later? We're on a tight schedule." I was worried about Maxolhx ships lurking in the area, setting up an ambush.

"Er, yes." He looked flustered for only a moment. "We are impressed by your stealth capability. There is very little lag in the signal, so your ship must be close, but we can't detect it."

"You won't detect us," I was getting irritated with him already. "You have the goods?"

"Yes. A fine batch of gently-used starships, for you. They are attached to a pair of ECO star carriers, I assume you brought your own star carriers to-"

"No. We need your star carriers also."

"That," he paused. "Was not part of the deal."

"Captain Scorandum, there is no *deal*. We didn't ask for these ships, nor did we agree to you pretending to be us, when you pulled that reckless stunt at Funandeng." For a change, it felt good for me to call someone else reckless.

His antennas drooped, then stood up. "There is an implied agreement, which you accepted when-"

"I am altering the deal. Pray I do not alter it any further," I said, and there was an amused snort from Mammay behind me. "Captain, your people have hundreds of star carriers. Surely you won't miss two of them for a brief time." I meant 'brief' on a geological time scale, but he didn't need to know that. "Come on, Captain. The ships you are offering aren't much good, if we can't get them to the target. We need those star carriers."

"We already gave you four of them! I also understand you recently 'borrowed' one of our civilian ships, the star carrier *Let It Ride*."

"That's a separate issue. Are you going to give us your star carriers or not? If you lack the authority to make the decision, we can make you an offer you can't refuse."

"There is no need for that, General. It's just," he sighed. "The *paperwork* involved," he shuddered.

That made me laugh. "It sounds like our societies are not that different, in that regard."

"Very well, General. What is the next step?"

"Jump out to wherever your ships are, and bring them back."

The *We're As Shocked As You Are* disappeared, then returned an hour later, accompanied by two star carriers, that were laden with obsolete ships looking even more worn out than the first batch of ships they gave us. We waited for three hours, making sure no one had followed them, then *Valkyrie* jumped, emerging five lightseconds from the Jeraptha formation. We remained their only long enough to launch dropships carrying our prize crews, allowed time for the dropships to get clear, and we jumped away again. If there was an ambush, our prize crews were toast, and I was anxious about that. It was easier to take risks myself than to order other people into danger. That's the life of a general officer, and I had to accept it. I didn't have to *like* it.

Also, yes, technically the ships being offered by the Jeraptha were not 'prizes', like in the old days when warships captured enemy merchant ships, and dispatched part of the warship's crew to sail the prizes into a friendly port. But the process was the same: Simms led part of *Valkyrie's* crew away to inspect and take control of the warships, plus the two star carriers, and make sure all the beetles went aboard Scorandum's ship.

Unfortunately, jumping severed the connection to the microwormholes, so we were as blind as any other ship. All we could do was wait, in the middle of nowhere, for Simms and her team to complete inspecting our new batch of quality pre-owned starships. She brought with her a submind created by Skippy, to examine the Jeraptha AIs aboard each ship, and assure they would cooperate with us. If everything went according to plan, our crews would direct the star carriers to perform a series of jumps, both as a test and to throw off any hostile ship trying to follow them.

If things did not go according to plan, well, I had limited options. Whatever I did, I could not risk *Valkyrie* being ambushed again. Simms knew that, and she accepted the risk.

Success. Both star carriers appeared at the rendezvous point roughly on time, and Simms transmitted the recognition signal.

"Skippy?" I asked.

"Authentication confirmed."

"How's it going over there, *Captain* Simms?" I called.

She appeared in the holographic display, wrinkling her nose. "Sir, I'll be glad to get back aboard *Valkyrie*."

"Why? Did the beetles trash the ships before they handed them to you?"

"No, they," she looked around the bridge of her ship. "It looks like they actually made a effort to clean the working spaces. But," she wrinkled her nose again.

"What's wrong?"

"Whatever cleaning fluid they use, it smells like, *ham*."

"Ham?"

"Yes," she laughed. "The whole ship smells like a smoked ham."

"I like ham, but-"

"I do too. I don't want to *live* inside one."

"I can send over a couple drums of Pine-Sol," I suggested.

"Thank you, Sir, but not now. We'll live with it. We are ready to jump again."

"Good. I'll go have a chat with our beetle friend, meet you at the next control point. And Simms?"

"Sir?"

"Outstanding job. Please congratulate your team for me." I didn't begin to relax until the newest additions to our fleet jumped away, headed toward the Ragnar wormhole. Valkyrie waited another hour, to make sure no ships were following Simms and her little fleet, then we jumped back to where the *We're As Shocked As You Are* was waiting.

"Captain Scorandum," I called. "Thank you. Those ships will be very useful to us."

"You are welcome," he said, as his crew no doubt tried to find out how I was talking to him with no signal lag. "Thank you for-"

I held up a finger to interrupt, forgetting that he might not recognize the gesture. "Don't thank me yet. One thing we will *not* be using those ships for, is to protect your territory. Not yet. Not until we have a mutual-defense treaty. Did you consider the consequences of your action at Funandeng?"

His antennas bobbed up and down, in body language I interpreted as a nod. "General Bishop, you are concerned the Maxolhx will attack us, to test whether you will respond in our defense?"

"Something like that, yes. Captain, we aren't ready to do that yet. You-"

"Don't worry about it."

"I'm not," I was getting pissed off at his attitude. "*You* should worry about it."

"We have considered the odds, and-"

"You are treating this as juicy action?"

He blinked slowly at me. Shit. Of course he was. Their whole society was built on-

"General, perhaps I should have said that we have more experience with the Maxolhx, and therefore we think the probability of them taking direct action against us, because of the incident at Funandeng, is low. Very low. The Maxolhx historically do not divert from their main focus. They would consider an attack against us, at this point, as an unnecessary diversion of resources."

"You are taking one hell of a risk."

"I understand why you think so, but there are other reasons for our confidence. The action at Funandeng will be viewed as an attempt by you humans to entice us into an alliance. The Maxolhx would not consider us to be a threat until we actually move toward an agreement with you. Besides, the whole galaxy will soon know that humans were *not* involved at Funandeng."

It was my turn to blink. "How's that?"

"We will leak a report that the supposedly 'human' ships at Funandeng were actually obsolete vessels from our Regional Guard, and that the Bosphuraq surrendered without a fight, to a small group of unarmed ships."

"Holy shit."

He paused, tilting his head, like he was waiting for the translation of my outburst. His mandibles clacked, in a gesture I knew meant he was pleased. "General, the Bosphuraq will be utterly *humiliated*. The entire galaxy will be laughing at them."

I snorted. "I hope they have a sense of humor."

"They do not. The humiliation will extend to their patrons, it will damage the enemy's entire coalition."

"OK, yeah but, then the story will be out that you later gave those ships to us, against the orders of the Rindhalu."

He stiffened, his antennas going rigid. "We do not take *orders* from the spiders." Of course, he didn't say 'spiders', he said whatever slang the Jeraptha use to refer to their patrons. The translator changed it to 'spiders' and I knew what he meant. "Also, sadly," his antennas bobbed happily, "after their incredible triumph at Funandeng, those ships were declared not flightworthy, and were scrapped. If you know what I mean."

"That is unfortunate," I agreed. "Captain, I hope you know what you are doing."

"We are confident. I urge *you* to not be overconfident. Your current strategy is," he looked away from the camera, avoiding my eyes. "Unlikely to succeed."

"Everyone has a limit to how much pain they can take. We are hitting the Maxolhx *hard*, they-"

"Their tolerance for pain may be greater than you imagine. General Bishop, the Maxolhx cannot afford to be seen as weak, they believe it would threaten their survival."

"They are threatening *our* survival."

"There is another factor you must consider: the Rindhalu will not allow their historical enemy to be put in a position where their survival is threatened. Such a situation would be dangerous for the Rindhalu, and the entire galaxy."

Oh, shit, I thought, trying to keep my shock from showing on my face. "You," I had to lick my dry lips. "You think the spiders will join forces with the Maxolhx, against us?"

"That is the assessment of our Home Fleet intelligence agency. I agree, based on my experience with our patrons. General, you have upset the balance of power in the galaxy. The Rindhalu seek to restore that balance, even if it means temporarily joining forces with their enemy."

"We don't want to fight the spiders."

"You might not have a choice."

"Yes, well," I didn't know what else to say.

"You may also be underestimating the willingness of the Maxolhx to do *whatever it takes*, no matter the cost to themselves, to avoid changing their current course of action. May I speak frankly?"

"Please do."

"This is not one of your action videos, where the hero talks tough and the enemy backs down. The Maxolhx will *not* back down."

My jaw clenched. "We're not giving them a choice."

"There is *always* a choice. Even if that choice leads to the destruction of everyone."

Simms cleared her throat behind me. I took the hint. "Captain Scorandum, we will consider your advice. Thank you for the ships."

"We didn't do it for you. Our hope is that, as your strength grows, you will see an alternative to continuing attacks against the Maxolhx."

"Our homeworld will begin to freeze. What's the alternative?"

He did the shrug thing with his antennas. "That is for you to decide. Please remember that whatever you do, you are risking the lives of every being in this galaxy."

Crap. I had enough weight on my shoulders, without an alien commander piling on. "Captain Scorandum, you're a betting man. I assume you wagered against our-"

"No. I wagered that you will *succeed.*"

I blinked at him. "But you just said-"

"I said your current strategy is unlikely to succeed, and I urge you to reconsider. However, I am confident that you will succeed in rescuing your homeworld. I don't know *how* but, I have learned to never bet against humans. You have an *annoying* habit of doing the impossible."

"Well," hearing that brightened my mood. "We will try to not disappoint you."

Admiral Reichert had come to dread speaking with the AIs of the Strategic Planning Section, a complete reversal of his previous experience. For most of his career, the immensely powerful intelligences of the Section confirmed his own assessments, or merely filled in the gaps with information he could not be expected to possess.

Recently, however, since humans had become actors in the endless conflict, the Section gave him bad news or, even worse, no news at all. The idea that the Section AIs could not explain something was frightening; they had access to *all* information available to Maxolhx society.

"Please," he said with an actual, verbally-expressed sigh. "Tell me how the humans were able to create a solar flare at Lacandra."

"Unknown."

"Guess."

"Insufficie-"

"Yes, I know, damn it," he cut off the irritating machine. "At least tell me *what* happened."

"The humans repurposed more of our relativistic impactors, to strike the star."

"It is a *star*. No imaginable number of impactors could cause a noticeable effect on such a massive object."

"Correct. That is why we cannot guess how the act was accomplished."

"*We* have the capability to create solar flares."

"The Hegemony possesses a limited ability to create small flares. The apparatus is massive, energy-intensive, and of no practical use as a weapon. Somehow, humans created a large flare, using only kinetic weapons."

"That is impossible."

"According to our understanding of the physics involved, yes."

Reichert knew he had to admit defeat. The powerful machines were nearly useless. "Can you at least recommend steps we could take to prevent future flare attacks?"

"There is no defense against the unknown."

"The events at Lacandra must not repeat elsewhere," the Minister for State Security's holographic avatar announced, as she stood in front of Admiral Reichert. There was no actual hologram, the transmission fed directly into Reichert's visual implant. "What is the fleet doing to prevent future attacks?"

Reichert was ready for the question. "Minister, there is only one certain way to prevent the humans from repeating their attack elsewhere. It is an extreme measure which, once taken, cannot be undone. My staff is now outlining a program to implement the process. Please allow me only several more hours to analyze the logistics, it will take a significant portion of fleet assets."

"The fleet is currently not performing any useful function that I can see," the minister sniffed. "Do with it as you see fit."

Reichert was also ready for the insult, he had prepared by damping down his instinctual response of anger. "Thank you. Minister, we must also do something to stop the actions of this new Alien Legion."

"We agree," the minister implied she was speaking for the entire government. "Has the Strategic Planning Section been able to predict where the human Navy will strike next?"

"No."

"Then we do not see how you are able to-"

"Minister, I do not propose to guess the Legion's next target. I propose that, with our fleet, the forces of our clients, and perhaps assistance of the Rindhalu, we secretly cover *all* potential sites the Legion might strike next. They will come to *us*."

CHAPTER THIRTY TWO

We brought the batch of former Patrol ships to Ragnar, where they could most quickly be refitted for use. The crews remained there, eager to learn everything they could about the new ships, and I relented to Skippy's nagging by allowing *Valkyrie* to go into dock for much-needed maintenance. He wanted five days, I gave him three to complete basic work on the jump drive. When that was done, we jumped away, *again*. Damn, I felt like a ping-pong ball.

After burning eighteen darts at Lacandra, we had to replenish our supply. Before hacking into another group of darts, we, meaning *I*, still had to select our next target. We were not in a hurry to strike again. Skippy's predictive model of the Maxolhx warned me to give their public time to react to Lacandra, before we hit them again. Another attack, following closely on Lacandra, would be one event in the minds of our enemy. But if we waited until the shock turned to fear, made their public question whether their government was protecting them, and *then* scorched another world with a solar flare, that would put pressure on those in power. So, although it irritated me at the time, getting sidetracked to collect a batch of ships from the ECO actually worked in our favor.

It was a delicate balance we had to achieve. A steady escalation of attacks would strike terror into the hearts of the enemy. They would not know where we would hit next, but they would know another strike was coming. That's what we wanted; the average Joe and Jane Maxolhx asking their government why the hell they had attacked Earth, and why they were not cleaning up the cloud that threatened humanity's homeworld.

If we conducted too many attacks, without giving the enemy time to react, they might get numb to the experience. Planets getting hit by solar flares could just become the new normal for the Maxolhx, and they would shrug it off. Especially when they realized we were being careful not to cause mass casualties, or to seriously damage a planet's biosphere.

If the enemy had time to realize the solar flares were *scary* but not *dangerous*, we would have to step up the severity of our attacks.

That is something I was *not* ready to do. The sickening moral aspect of a severe solar flare was not the only consideration. Killing large numbers of Maxolhx civilians would backfire, make the enemy demand vengeance.

Crap.

That is the dilemma facing every modern military commander. We have massive destructive power at our fingertips, and what we need to do is *avoid* escalation. Escalation too often gets people, your own people, killed for nothing.

Like I said, the toughest thing the Army taught me is when *not* to pull the trigger. And *how* not to pull the trigger, despite what adrenaline, emotions and instincts were telling me.

That's the difference between an army and a mob.

Anyway, we needed more kinetic darts. Frustratingly, one group of darts had no information about the whereabouts or even the existence of other groups. The

Maxolhx either were compartmentalizing that information for security, or they simply hadn't bothered to upload that data to the dart AIs. So, we had to go through Skippy's guesses about where we might find more of the damned things, based on increasingly sketchy data. Naturally, we picked the low-hanging fruit first; the dart groups that Skippy had the highest confidence of locating. After the first two groups, we had to choose from possible dart sightings where the confidence was less than sixty percent. That is what happens when you're trying to find something small while it is traveling at super speed, through the vast emptiness between stars.

Yes, blah, blah, blah, boo-freakin'-hoo for us, we have a tough job, and you already knew that. My point is, our job is also most often *dull*. Like, mind-numbingly dull. We parked the ship in one location after another, while Skippy used his own and the ship's sensors to look for faint traces of darts.

I'll spare you from listening to the boring stuff.

"Quit your grinnin' and drop your linen," Skippy used his new favorite expression in a triumphant tone. "I found 'em!"

"Outstanding," I replied, momentarily confused. By luck, I was on the bridge at the time, taking part of a duty shift at one of the weapons consoles. It was good cross-training, running through simulations, while the ship did absolutely *nothing* in deep interstellar space. Working at a weapons console was good for me, it made me more familiar with what to expect from people operating those stations. I learned what information they had available, when and in what level of detail, how fast I could expect them to react, all that.

One thing I found did not make me happy, and I made a note to talk to Simms about it. The setup of the console could be customized slightly for each operator, with the display modes changing. Customization helped the individual operators do their jobs more efficiently.

It could also be fatal to the ship in an emergency.

The weapons console I trained on, in a simulator, had the standard setup. When I took over the active console on the bridge, at first it confused me. Some of the controls were slightly out of place, or menu options were in a different order. Yes, some of the changes made sense, and therefore should become the new standard. That word is the key: *standard*. The same for everyone. If the primary operator became disabled during combat, we could not afford a person taking over the console to be confused, not even for a moment. The issue was not confined only to weapons consoles. The last time I flew a Panther, I found the pilot seat adjustment handle was secured in a non-standard upward position. That made it easier to use for a pilot shorter than myself, but it also meant I hit it with my knee while getting into the seat. Plus, the handle sticking up was an invitation for something to get snagged on it. One thing I knew from pilot training, is that if something *can* get snagged at an inconvenient time, it *will*.

Anyway, Skippy found something. "What did you find?"

"Darts, Joe, *duh*."

"I knew that, you ass," I snapped back at him as I stepped away from the console, waiting until the new operator confirmed he had control. "What about them?"

336   Breakaway

"Well, we didn't hit the jackpot, that's for sure. I found trails of three darts, no more. Based on the limited info we have, my guess is the total number in the group is more than seven and less than twelve. I could be wrong. The *data* could be incomplete," he quickly corrected his statement, for Skippy was never wrong about anything.

"OK, great, thank you. Let's go get them."

"Sorry that we didn't find a larger group," he mumbled as an apology.

I knew his apology was actually him fishing for a compliment, for me to assure him that he wasn't at fault. Sucking up to him made me gag, it was also a major part of my job description. "Hey, buddy, don't sweat it. You did the impossible, again. Nobody else could have found those darts, they're like looking for a needle in a, uh, a hayfield."

"While blindfolded," he muttered. "Well, it's nice to know I'm appreciated. Course is programmed into the nav system, we can jump any time you're ready."

The duty officer looked at me, I nodded and walked over to take command, while she got out of the seat. Hacking into darts wasn't completely new to us, but it was also still a tricky operation, and we were still writing the procedure manual. It was best if I was on the bridge when we did hazardous things. A few minutes later, we jumped.

It took three hours to drop off, and set into position, a chain of microwormholes along the predicted flight path of the dart Skippy had the most confidence about. We had learned that once he hacked into one dart, it usually could tell us how many darts were in the group, and exactly where the others were. All we had to do was stand by and hope the dart didn't smack into the ship, if Skippy's info about its flight path was less than accurate.

The notion of an ultra-dense, stealthy object racing toward us at seventy-three percent of lightspeed sounds scary. The dart wasn't going to change course to intercept us, it was programmed to avoid detection until it was ordered to attack. Still, it could blast right through *Valkyrie's* hull if we were unlucky. In reality, after the first couple times of unbearable tension, waiting for a dart to zip past us felt kind of normal.

"Hmm," Skippy's avatar froze as he puzzled over something. I looked at the pilots, they already each had a finger poised over their buttons to initiate a short emergency jump. "That's odd," he muttered, almost too softly to hear.

"What? Skippy, what is odd?"

"Huh? Oh, nothing. Just, hmm. Oh *shit*! Jump! JUMP JUMP JUMP-"

We jumped, the pilots didn't wait for my order.

"What the hell-"

"Whew," his avatar shuddered. "*Oooooh*, I don't feel so good, I feel sick. Give me a minute, will ya?"

"Are we safe?" I demanded.

"Yeah. Yes, we are. Ugh, if I had a stomach, I'd *ralph*."

Skippy was clearly in no condition to answer questions. "Bilby, talk to me. What happened? Was the dart heading straight for us?"

"No, Dude, like, there was no dart. Not that I could see."

"Then what was the-"

"We almost got *sandblasted*," the ship's AI explained. "Where Skippy expected to see a dart, there was only a cloud of particles. The weird thing is, those particles were traveling at the same speed, and on the same course, as where the dart should have been. If *Valkyrie* had not jumped away, the ship could have been struck by what are basically a cloud of pellets traveling at relativistic speed."

"Oh shit," I had a sinking feeling that I understood the situation. "The dart exploded? It was trying to kill us?"

"No. No, Dude. No way. The particles were not spread out in a shotgun pattern, like you'd expect if it were trying to hit a moving target. More like, the thing just *disintegrated*. Fell apart. Like, um, maybe it had a major system failure? I'm kinda guessing, to be truthful."

"OK, understood, thank you, Bilby. Skippy, can you talk now?"

"Yes," his voice was shaky. "Whew, we dodged a bullet there, Joe. A lot of bullets, moving way faster than bullets travel."

"Yeah, I got that. What happened?"

"Most likely, the thing self-destructed. That happens. When darts suspect they are becoming unstable, they release their structural integrity."

"Self-destructed? When?"

"Dunno," he admitted, without the usual complaint about having inadequate data to work with. "I can speculate, if you want to waste time. *Or*," he hinted, "we can move on, to intercept the next dart."

"Let's do that," I agreed. There were enough mysteries in the Universe, without us investigating a minor and unimportant curiosity.

"Um, this time, I suggest we set up a microwormhole farther away from the ship, to give us more warning time."

"Good idea," I agreed, though doing what he wanted would add more time to an already lengthy process.

"Holy *shit*," Skippy gasped. "Um, hey, we should jump out of here, now."

"Do it," I ordered, and the pilots made the jump drive twist spacetime again.

"What's going on?" I demanded, after the ship stabilized from the sudden jump.

"That second dart also had self-destructed. Jeez, maybe this is a bad batch of darts?"

"A bad batch?"

"Come on, Joe," he scoffed. "It can't be a coincidence that the first two darts we see from this group have lost integrity."

"Let's see if the third time is the charm." I did not want to go chasing other possible sightings of darts around the galaxy, when clearly we had located a group of them close to us. "To save time, we'll just use one microwormhole, and make sure the next dart hasn't fallen apart. If it's still a dart, we jump ahead and set up a chain, so you can hack in. Everyone," I raised my voice to address the bridge crew. "I want positive thoughts for this one. No negative waves, you hear me?"

The crew heard me. The third dart did not. It, too, had self-destructed. So had the fourth and fifth darts we checked.

"Wow," Skippy groaned. "I hope whoever paid for those darts kept the receipt."

"This is a waste of time," I slapped a hand on my knee. "Is there any reason to think the other darts in this group have not also self-destructed?"

"No. Technically, there is no reason to think they *have*, either, but-"

"You know what I mean. Should we continue here?"

He sighed. "No."

"Then, where is the nearest group of darts? I mean," I closed my eyes, mentally kicking myself. "The group we could get to fastest." With starships able to jump instantly from one place to another, and use Elder wormholes to travel across hundreds or thousands of lightyears, the important question was not about distance, it was about *time*.

"That's the wrong question, Joe. Wait! I'm not being a jackass, let me explain."

"OK," I relaxed my fists that had reflexively tensed up when he told me I was wrong. Angry Joe sometimes got too angry, too quickly. My temper could become a problem if I didn't control it. "Go ahead."

"The next closest group of darts, the next *six* closest groups I am tracking, are all based on sketchy data. Their locations are a wild guess, to be truthful. We could spend days trying to nail down where any of them are, or if they even exist. If you want the minimum time to a decent probability of making contact with a dart, I suggest we go here instead," he showed a map of the galaxy on the main display, then zoomed in.

That really did not help. One spiral arm of the galaxy looks like another. For all I could tell, he was showing us the Andromeda galaxy. "Uh, sure," I knew my response was lame. "Let's go there."

We went there.

It didn't help.

First, we wasted two days flying around, looking for the faint trails that darts left when they collided with stray hydrogen atoms in deep interstellar space. Because the Maxolhx aimed their darts to fly through particularly empty areas of space, so pesky aliens could *not* find their precious darts, it was not easy. Even for Skippy.

He finally thought he might, shmaybe, have located a dart, so we went ahead of it and waited for it to zip past us.

Nothing.

We tried again.

And again.

The third time was the charm, although the charm we won was not a nice prize, it was more like a week-old corndog that had fallen behind the deep fryer.

That freakin' dart was also nothing but a cloud of dust.

"*Damn* it!" Skippy shouted with disgust. "What are the odds that- Ugh."

A chill crept up my spine. Simms looked at me, she was feeling the same. "Wait. What *are* the odds?" I asked slowly.

"Well, Jeez Louise, it's difficult to calculate the-"

"That was a rhetorical question," I told him. "How long ago did that thing self-destruct?"

"Impossible to say with any precision, Joe."

"Take a guess."

"OK, well, the cloud here has not dispersed very far, so it couldn't have happened long ago. Hmm, *that's* odd. Now that I think about it, all the other darts also self-destructed recently. How could that happen?"

I looked at Simms, she nodded, shaking her head. Shit. "I have a bad feeling I know the answer to that. Skippy, it's time to check in with the real world." Flying around deserted sections of the galaxy, mostly in Rindhalu territory, we hadn't any opportunity to ping a relay station for news of current events. "Plot a course for a relay station. One controlled by the Maxolhx coalition. One that sees a lot of traffic, so it won't only have old info that's useless to us."

"Oooooh, um, *this* is interesting," Skippy said, half to himself.

"What?" I clamped down on my natural impatience. He had just hacked into an Esselgin relay station, the high-traffic location we could get to in the shortest time. That station would not have top-secret messages of the Maxolhx, but it should contain general news of events in the galaxy. Like, I needed to know how were the kitties reacting to our solar flare at Lacandra. "Tell-"

"It's a message from the Maxolhx, Joe," he said slowly, surprise evident in his voice. "For *you*."

"*Me?*" I was stunned, and so were the entire bridge crew as they stared at me in shock.

"Yes. I suspect the intended audience is all of humanity, and anyone who is thinking of allying with you. Also, hmm, I guess there is an implied message for me, too. The encryption they used is insultingly low-grade."

"Right, let's focus on that."

"Sorry. You want the message?"

Clenching my teeth, I said, "Yes."

"Just sent it to your tablet."

The message being in text format surprised me, maybe the sender wanted to keep it simple, to reduce the risk of translation errors.

Oh.

Shit.

Dear General Joseph Bishop, the message began. That is the actual text, not a translation. The Maxolhx wrote it in English, they wanted to be certain they got their message across as intended, with no translation errors.

They addressed me as 'Dear'.

That was nice.

Except they didn't intend to be nice.

They intended the message to be a slap in my face.

I'll skip the empty platitudes that opened the message, and the threats that followed. The opening was insulting bullshit, the threats were nothing new or particularly clever. None of it mattered.

What did matter was the information being conveyed, in between the bullshit.

Holy shit.

I did *not* expect that.

They blew it up.

Those maniacs blew it up.

No, not Earth. Sorry about that, didn't mean to freak you out.

Captain Scorandum was right, when he told me the Maxolhx were prepared to do *anything*, to avoid having to back down.

To prevent us from using their super weapons, they self-destructed them.

All of them.

Their fleet sent out ships to contact every group of darts in the galaxy, transmitting codes to turn them into dust.

Weren't most of the darts in Rindhalu territory, you might ask?

Yes.

The two apex species cooperated, the Maxolhx mostly sending long-range ships that were no threat, like star carriers. The Rindhalu allowed those enemy ships to enter their territory, flying prescribed routes to contact dart groups. Once the darts were rendered harmless and useless, the Maxolhx ships were escorted back through wormholes to their own territory.

One part of the message was interesting, for what it *didn't* say.

The Maxolhx boasted that the Rindhalu, for all their supposedly superior technology, had identified the probable location of less than three percent of the darts.

It puzzled me that the kitties took the time to include that trivia in their message, until I understood why they wanted me, wanted *us*, to know that.

The darts we hacked into? The Maxolhx assumed we found them, and maybe took control of them, by accessing a Rindhalu database. The kitties must have figured that, if their ancient enemy knew how to locate and take control of darts, those super weapons were pretty much useless anyway.

They were wrong about us needing help, even unwilling help, from the spiders. They were right that self-destructing their own weapons left us unable to use them.

"Shit." That time, I said it aloud.

"Well," Simms whispered softly from beside me. She had read the message also, Skippy sent it to her. Whatever her thought was, she didn't finish it.

She didn't need to.

We were screwed.

"Um," Skippy broke the stunned silence. "Is that Game Over?"

There are a lot of negative things that can be said about Angry Joe. He has a temper, he is tempted to make rash decisions- More than usual, I mean. What *can't* be said about Angry Joe is that he knows when to give up. Even when he should.

Angry Joe doesn't get discouraged or depressed, he gets more angry.

"No, Skippy, this is not Game Over."

"Um, Okaaaaay. May I point out that we only have four darts left, and that's not enough to do anything useful to-"

"We are *not* done," I insisted.

"The idea of using darts is over, though, right?" He didn't know when to shut up. "Unless you-"

"The darts are done, unless we find an easy target."

"Um, that would have to be a *really* easy target. Easy like, there's no point to hitting it, unless we're giving up on trying to force the kitties to clean up their mess, and we're going for pure revenge?"

"We are not-"

"FYI, I am *totally* OK with the revenge thing," Skippy hinted. "Those MFers ruined my nefarious plans! Do you have any idea how hard I worked to hack into those freakin' darts? Nobody could do that, but I *did*. Ugh, now it was all for nothing. This *sucks*."

Simms's face grew red. I was not the only angry person on the bridge.

"Hey, *beer can*," I snapped at him. "Maybe we can focus on you later?"

"Huh? Oh, sure. Of course. Still, are we doing the vengeance thing? Really, I can't think of anything else we can use a handful of darts for."

"No. Not now, anyway. We'll keep the revenge option open."

"Goodie. So, um, what's next? Are we going to Paradise?"

"Paradise?" Simms and I looked at each other. "Why would we-"

"Oh. Oops, sorry. Jeez Louise, I forgot to include a message that is *not* directed at you. It's for UNEF Command on Earth. Although, this might be a case where the message really *is* directed at you, it just-"

"Skippy! Give us the message."

He did.

Shit.

Damn it.

In addition to gloating about blowing up their arsenal of darts so we couldn't use them, the Maxolhx were giving a deadline to UNEF. All humans had to be evacuated from Paradise within forty-seven days. The original deadline was fifty-four days, but we were just hearing about it.

When I describe the message as a deadline, it really is a *dead* line. Any humans on Paradise after the cut-off date, or on any planet other than Earth, would be killed by orbital bombardment. The message also hinted that the bombardment would not bother with being too precise about what was hit, so non-human residents should be careful to keep clear of the area. That last part was clearly included to encourage the Ruhar to assist in kicking humans off their planet.

But, you might ask, how could the Maxolhx get away with doing that? Surely the Rindhalu would protect their clients.

No, they would not. Not this time. The damned spiders told the Ruhar, the Jeraptha and everyone in the galaxy that humans were not welcome on any planet within their coalition. Therefore, any species who gave shelter, aid or comfort to humans were violating the terms of their mutual-defense treaty with the Rindhalu. Basically, the spiders would stand by as the Maxolhx enforced the deadline.

Typical fucking spiders. They wanted to keep their privileged position on top of the galaxy, and they were happy to let someone else do the dirty work for them.

The message for UNEF Command actually had two parts: a stick and a carrot.

A poisoned carrot.

The demand that all humans be removed from alien planets, and the threat to kill them after the deadline, was the stick.

The carrot was an offer to end the conflict.

Bullshit.

The senior species together proposed to reduce the impact of the cloud at Earth, if humans agree to and met certain conditions.

All humans, including those outside the galaxy, must return to our homeworld. A joint delegation of Maxolhx and Rindhalu would be brought to our beta site in the Sculptor Dwarf galaxy, to verify we had pulled everyone off that world.

Humans must surrender all starships, and forever be confined to our home star system.

Both senior species would place satellites in Earth orbit, to verify that humans were not in possession of, developing, or conducting research about, a long list of banned technologies.

Humans must surrender Skippy at a neutral location, to be controlled by a joint working group of Maxolhx and Rindhalu.

Humans must provide the access codes to the Elder weapons that were outside our solar system. We could keep control of the Elder weapons that were near Earth.

If humanity complied with all conditions, the senior species guaranteed there would be no future attacks against Earth, including no attacks by their clients.

Is that it?

Yes, that's all they wanted.

The offer was not about peace, it was about ending humanity's future.

You may be thinking it's not a bad deal. Basically, humanity goes back to the time before Columbus Day, when we didn't have starships, or advanced technology, or help from an Elder AI, or Elder weapons. We also didn't have headaches from trying to free other species from domination by the two assholes on top of the pyramid, so, pre-Columbus Day seems like good times, huh?

Not so much.

Let's review the offer, shall we?

First, the apex species offered to "reduce the impact" of the cloud of gas that threatened to turn Earth into a ball of slush. Not *remove* the cloud. Not clean it out of our solar system. They didn't say how much impact the cloud would be allowed to have, or how cold our homeworld would get.

We had to give up the beta site in the Sculptor dwarf galaxy, and FOB Jaguar. *And* we had to give our enemies a ride out to Avalon, showing them how to control Elder wormholes.

We had to give up all star travel capability, and the technology that might allow us to build ships in the future. The satellites that monitored activity on Earth would also likely have the means to enforce a ban on use of, or research into, a long list of advanced technologies, and to punish anyone who dared defy the ban.

We would be back to having killer satellites over our heads, like when the Kristang White Wind clan conducted orbital bombardments against anyone who resisted their cruel oppression.

We had to give Skippy to the enemy, as if he were a toaster. We didn't *own* Skippy, no one did. For sure, he wasn't going to surrender voluntarily. If he suspected we intended to betray him, my guess is *Valkyrie* would suffer a sudden and fatal jump drive failure. In fact, I *hope* he would do that, if we were stupid enough to betray him.

Finally, we get to keep the Elder weapons in our own star system? Well, *that's* totally worthless. Basically, the apex species said we could blow *ourselves* up any time we wanted.

What happens if we do everything they ask, and they don't deliver?

Abso-freakin'-lutely nothing. We had no way to enforce an agreement. The second we handed over Skippy and the codes to Elder weapons, the bad guys could do anything they wanted to our homeworld. We would not be resetting the situation to before Columbus Day, we would get a reset to the day before we seeded Elder weapons around the galaxy.

Do you trust the two senior species who forced their clients to fight an endless war?

I sure as hell don't.

Like I said, the carrot they were offering was poisoned.

Here's the interesting thing: the two apex species had to know humans were not stupid enough to accept their offer. So, what they were really offering was to talk about the issue. To open negotiations with UNEF Command, or whoever humanity designated as a proper representative. The Maxolhx and Rindhalu would be waiting at a designated rendezvous point, until the deadline passed.

The message closed with a warning. Two warnings, really. First, the deadline for pulling humans off Paradise was non-negotiable. When the deadline passed, the Maxolhx would start shooting. They considered the deadline to be an incentive for humans to come to the negotiating table, and not drag our feet about reaching an agreement.

Second, the list of key demands was also *not* negotiable. Humans restricted to Earth, giving up advanced technology, giving up Skippy and giving up all but a handful of Elder weapons, were the minimum the apex species would accept. It sounded like the only thing that could be negotiated was the damage the cloud would do to Earth, and possibly what types of technology we could keep. It was not a tempting offer.

My fear was, I had no alternative to offer. Since the moment I learned about the cloud that would plunge Earth into an ice age, I knew we had to find a way to make the aliens disperse the cloud. Or at least not interfere, while we and hopefully some allies did something about the cloud. The Maxolhx only respond to force, or a legitimate threat of force, so we never had any chance of helping our homeworld without the power to inflict massive destruction against our enemies.

Which we used to have, in the form of relativistic darts. Now we had *nothing*.

Shit.

CHAPTER THIRTY THREE

Colonel Jennifer Simms pressed a button under her office desk, to slide the door closed. She had a meeting in half an hour, but that could be rescheduled. "Skippy?"

"Yes?" The avatar appeared on her desk.

"We need a better source of intel. We need to know what the Maxolhx are thinking. From the source, not this second-hand stuff," she waved a hand at her laptop, which was displaying a summary of data recently pulled from a client species relay station.

"I agree with the sentiment, I simply don't know how we can do that. We have been *too* successful in hacking their communications. Plus, big blabbermouth Joe bragged about how the kitties can't have any secrets from us."

She winced at the memory. At the time, it felt *good* to hear Bishop giving a long-deserved smackdown to the kitties. Maybe it was the right thing to do but Skippy was right. All Bishop had accomplished was making the enemy even more paranoid about their communications security. "You did get access to a kitty relay station, one time."

"Yes, and Bite Me Elmo *died*. I still feel bad about that."

"Did you learn enough to do it again?"

"Probably," the Elder AI admitted. "I know from hacking into the ambush ships at Snowcone, that the kitties have only implemented minor revisions to their data exchange procedures. We could try it again, except we don't have any kitties with us. Also," his voice trailed off.

"What?"

"Um, I don't know if I can do that again. I know, it's silly to be squeamish about biohacking one person, when I didn't have a problem destroying a whole fleet of ships."

"It's not silly," she said softly. "That's a *good* thing. It should be harder to kill, or to risk the life of, someone you have a personal connection with."

"My only personal connection with Bite Me Elmo was him wanting to kill *me*."

"You know what I mean."

"I do," Skippy sighed. "We still have the problem; without a live Maxolhx, even I can't hack into a kitty relay station. For sure, we are not getting any volunteers, so-"

"There may be a way to get persistent access to their comms, without using a prisoner."

"Um, how, please?"

"Look at this," she turned her laptop so the screen could be seen by the avatar. That was not necessary, Skippy didn't need the hologram to see anything aboard the ship. The gesture was for her own benefit, it made it feel more like she was interacting with a person instead of a disembodied voice. Tapping a key, she pulled up a file. "This star chart shows the local quadrant of the galaxy, before and after the last wormhole shift. And I can," she toggled back and forth. "Go back through the last three major wormhole shifts."

"OK," the avatar leaned forward, as if that gave him a better view of the data. "Yup, I see. What about it?"

"Now," she typed more commands. "I'm highlighting Maxolhx territories that became inaccessible to them, following a wormhole shift within the past two thousand years."

"Again, that is accurate. Of course it is, you got the data from me. Colonel, what is the point of this exercise?"

"Bear with me for another minute, please. *This*," another layer appeared on the star chart. "Represents former Maxolhx territory that is, as far as I know, not accessible to anyone right now."

"Hmm, yes. Again, correct. Gotta be honest with you, I'm kinda waiting for you to tell me something I don't know."

"How about you tell me something first. Within this territory the Maxolhx had to abandon, were there any relay stations?"

"Well of course there were. Why do you- Oh. *OH*."

"You understand?"

"I think maybe I do but, hmm, I'm not sure how useful it will be. You want to know if we could go to one of those abandoned relay stations, and what? Steal the core, so we can insert it in an active relay station?"

"Would that work?" She asked eagerly.

"Um, no. Good thinking, though. We can't get access to any active relay stations. The last time we tried that, it *exploded*. Sorry."

"That's fine. Then we go with Plan B."

"Should I be afraid to ask what is Plan B?"

"Possibly," she laughed. It was nice to be causing headaches for Skippy, instead of the other way around. "We find an abandoned relay station, and use it to replace an active station."

"*What*? Whoa! Whoa, slow down there."

"Can that work?"

"I'm thinking about it. Jeez Louise, give me a minute, please. Lots to consider here."

Simms requested a meeting with me, not that she had to ask. At the time my zPhone pinged with her message, I was in the pilot's lounge, getting pelted with balled-up sheets of paper. We didn't use much paper aboard the ship, Skippy had used the fabricators to crank out reams of paper for people to use as scratch pads, for tradition. The occasion was the weekly review of the Greenie Board, a term we borrowed from the US Navy. Every time a dropship came in toward a docking bay, or *attempted* a what we called a 'trap', it was graded. Every single trap, in a pilot's entire service aboard the ship. Whether it was a slow gentle maneuver of bringing a big, fat Condor in on a routine docking in interstellar space, where orbital mechanics don't apply because there is no local source of gravity. Or bringing a shot-up Dragon into a combat docking. They all get graded. The best is a green symbol. The worst is a wave-off, or No Docking. You had to go around and try it again.

Sure, the dropships all had AIs, and the ship's AI could take over and provide guidance. Most of the time, we pilots can't screw up too badly, because the smart AIs will keep us out of trouble. The grades are about the non-automated aspects of our flying, and man, if the AI does have to take over to prevent a pilot from crashing into the ship, you do not want to be *that* guy. Or woman. You know what I mean?

Why was I standing at the front of the room, getting pelted by paper? Truly, I have no idea. There was a vicious rumor that the line next to my name had only a few green dots, and plenty of, let's just say not-green dots. Hey, I'm not a full-time pilot. Did my fellow pilots grade me on a curve?

No, they did not.

Nor should they give me a break. If I take the stick, or in this case, the touchscreen controls of a dropship, I'm committing to be as professional as any other pilot. Not as professional as I *can be*, that is a bogus standard. Either I meet the qualification of being a pilot, or I don't. How hard you tried doesn't count. You know, like Yoda said.

Anyway, I stood at the front of the room and endured getting bombarded by balled-up paper, while video played of my worst docking attempts. It was embarrassing. Maybe Skippy screwed with the video to make me look worse than I was, I wouldn't be surprised if he did. When the team was done berating me, I sat down in the back and enjoyed razzing other pilots. Everyone had an approach they weren't proud of. Some of the traps were nearly perfect, but everyone had room for improvement. That was the point of watching the video, it showed us what went wrong, so we would know how to avoid mistakes in the future. The Greenie Board was deadly serious, if a pilot had too many wave-offs, she or he might be taken off flight duty for remedial training. A bad trap could not only prang your dropship, it could get people killed or even damage the ship. Watching your mistakes in front of other pilots holds you accountable, there is no hiding your mistakes, and no excuses are allowed. The Greenie Board review is one of my favorite parts of the weekly routine, and I wish I had more opportunities to fly.

OK, enough about that. When the meeting broke up, I pinged Simms to tell her I was coming to her office. The former cabin we allocated for the XO's office was much smaller than the space I had, and part of her space was crammed with lockers for emergency damage-control equipment. Looking at her cramped office made me embarrassed about the oversized space I had. Maybe some of the damage-control gear could be moved to my office, I made a mental note to ask Bilby about it.

"Simms?" I sat down heavily in the chair across from her.

"How was the Greenie Board?" She asked with a twinkle in her eyes.

"Green across the board," I swept a hand through the air in front of me.

She raised an eyebrow.

"OK," I admitted. "Maybe not green across the board next to *my* name." Callsign 'Barney' did have green dots, just more of the not-green dots. "What's up?"

"Skippy and I think we may have an answer to hacking into Maxolhx comms."

His avatar appeared immediately. "Actually, Colonel Simms found the answer, I only confirmed it is possible."

We both stared at Skippy. He was giving credit to someone else? That was unusual. Which made me think he was feeling guilty about something, and that got me worried about what he hadn't told us. I pushed that thought to the back of my mind. "Who are you," I asked, "and what have you done with Skippy? XO, have you searched for pods?"

"Oh, very funny, Joe," Skippy rolled his eyes as Simms stared at me blankly. Apparently she was not a fan of classic sci fi films. "I give credit where credit is due," Skippy sniffed. "We had a problem that *you* weren't even trying to solve, and I wasn't thinking about at all. Your executive officer dug into the problem all on her own, despite your woeful lack of leadership on this issue."

"I'm, uh, glad you clarified that. Simms, excellent initiative. How are you going to solve our problem?"

She told me.

I kicked myself. Crap. Now I know how Skippy feels, when I tell him what later seems to be a completely *obvious* solution to a problem.

"There is one issue we still need to solve, Joe," Skippy summed up. "We need a star carrier to do this, and all of ours are committed."

Sitting back in my chair, I put my hands behind my head, happy that he and Simms hadn't thought of *everything*. "We're in luck. I have enough rental points to get a free star carrier for a weekend."

"Sir?" Simms didn't know if I was joking.

I wasn't.

Valkyrie jumped in, practically on top of a Jeraptha star carrier. It was another civilian ship, designed to carry transport ships. Converted from a retired military platform, the carrier had only eight hard points for attaching ships, and overall it has less range and carrying capacity than the four star carriers we had in our little Navy.

It could still carry much heavier and bulkier cargo than *Valkyrie* could manage. At the moment, none of the star carrier's hard points were occupied, it was hanging in space, waiting for passenger ships to arrive from the nearby star system.

"What's this thing called?" I asked, as soon as sensors recovered, and I could verify we had the star carrier trapped in a damping field. It wasn't going anywhere, and the nearest inhabited world was seven lighthours away. No one was coming to rescue that ship any time soon.

"It's currently named the '*High Roller*'," Skippy snickered. "The brochures make it look like that ship is a super-luxury transport for the wealthy, going to glamorous destinations. Really, it is sort of the Motel 6 of star carriers, and its regular route is between places that are definitely in the low-rent district of Jeraptha space."

"OK, whatever." Rising from my chair, I straightened my shoulders and looked toward the little holographic dot that represented the virtual camera lens. "Bilby, connect me with the captain over there."

"Channel open, the *High Roller's* AI acknowledges the link."

"This is General Joseph Bishop, of the United Nations Navy warship *Valkyrie*." It still felt weird to call myself a general. For years after I was promoted to colonel, I had a bad case of Imposter Syndrome. Pinning a colonel's eagles on my uniform always made me feel like a fake, like at any moment, someone would tap me on the shoulder, and say the promotion was all a mistake. Now, wearing a general's star, I had that feeling again, even though I knew that I had *earned* that star, damn it. Maybe a bit of Imposter Syndrome is a good thing, to keep me grounded.

A beetle appeared in the holographic display tank, wearing a white uniform that was much fancier than the drab garments worn by Jeraptha fleet captains. Probably, the captain of the *High Roller* had to dress to impress the civilian passengers. "This is Captain Emilst Ragondaw of the transport *High Roller*. On behalf of my company and crew, I demand to-"

"Captain Ragondaw," I interrupted her. "We can waste a lot of time going back and forth with useless bullshit, or I can get straight to the point."

She hesitated, then nodded, her antennas bouncing. It was strange how when I first met the Jeraptha, their appearance stirred an instinctive revulsion in me, but now I didn't think they were creepy at all. Having met them, I decided I *liked* the beetles, and their insect-like form didn't bother me. "Please," she said, "state your business."

"We need to borrow your ship," I held up a hand to forestall her protest. "I know, you have a schedule to keep, and I'm sorry about that. If I could offer compensation, I would, but our peoples have not worked out any sort of currency exchange. And anyway, if your company hired your vessel to us, that would get the Rindhalu upset because you would be violating the terms of your treaty with them. You surely don't want to invite *that* sort of trouble."

"No, we do not," she agreed.

"Good. So, to avoid getting you in trouble by appearing to cooperate with us, we are simply *stealing* your ship. It will not be your responsibility, you have no choice in the matter, and your employers will certainly understand that."

Her facial expressions, which I had trouble reading anyway, twisted through a variety of emotions, before she quickly recovered. "What will happen to my crew?"

She's a good captain, I told myself. She didn't waste energy fighting the inevitable; we chose that ship because as a civilian transport, it had minimal defensive capability. Even one of *Valkyrie's* point-defense cannons could shred the hull, cut right through the long spine. "We know you have two dropships. Get your crew into those craft, and after we take over your ship, we will jump in near the inhabited world here," my stupid brain could not remember the name of the place, not that it mattered.

"General Bishop, our momentum will carry us past the planet, before we could decelerate."

"Yes, sorry about that. A ship from the planet will have to come out to rendezvous with you. I'm sure that can be arranged."

Her body language was distinctly unhappy, even with my thin knowledge of the Jeraptha. "You are putting me in a very bad position her, surely you understand that."

"I do. Captain Ragondaw, perhaps you have not considered an aspect of this situation that could be very favorable to you."

"Favorable? To me?"

"To you and your crew. Think about it. I have not told you why we need your ship. Wagering about what we will do with your ship, has got to be *juicy* action, right?"

There was an excited uproar on her end of the conversation, her off-screen crew all talking at once. The audio cut out while she got her crew settled down. Then she turned toward the camera again. "That is, acceptable. General Bishop, my crew will go into our dropships, while I wait for your boarding party. I wonder if you might do me a favor, regarding your plans for my ship?"

"A favor? What?"

"Give me a hint?"

Valkyrie transited through the wormhole without incident, and performed a short jump as soon as the ship was ready. We then waited quietly, listening with passive sensors for any hint that other ships might be in the area, while the crew got some rest. There were echoes of old jump distortions. Based on how faint the signals were, Skippy tagged them as at least six days old. That was good. There were only three detectable objects in the area, exactly as we expected. The crew went to action stations, we verified everything was ready, and I gave the order to jump.

The ship emerged less than two kilometers from a Maxolhx relay station, and we didn't bother with any nonsense like pinging it with a false recognition signal or requesting to come aboard for authentication. Missiles were primed and launch doors before we jumped; a pair of hyperspeed missiles raced out of the tubes, and we jumped *again*.

Because the speed of light is so darned slow, we had to wait fourteen seconds to see the photons of the twin explosions from two multi-megaton warheads. I think both of them were of Russian manufacture, if you're interested in trivia. What I cared about was that our nukes obliterated the relay station, leaving nothing but photons and radioactive high-speed debris. The speed of the debris was the key to the whole operation. We had to hope the expanding wavefront of debris traveled past the two wormholes in the cluster, before enemy starships came through. That cluster did not see a heavy load of traffic, and saw even less traffic, now that the temporary alliance between the Thuranin and Bosphuraq had broken down into anger and shooting at each other. Which, really, was inevitable when two hateful assholes are forced to work together.

Anyway, the Maxolhx could not know we had destroyed one of their relay stations.

Because we planned to replace it with a fake one.

Not exactly a *fake*. The replacement was a real relay station, built and operated by the kitties, until it was abandoned after a wormhole shift left it inaccessible.

That had been Simms's brilliant insight, and it was a great idea. Relay stations that had no contact with the Maxolhx for centuries, would still be using the old paired quantum state exchange system for authentication. That was the system we caused the kitties to abandon, when they discovered we'd hacked into their secure communications. If we could replace an active station with one that we controlled, the kitties would happily upload all their top-secret info there, blissfully ignorant that we had complete access. Even better, we would not absolutely need to go back to the fake station every time we wanted updated info. It was a fantastic idea, making me realize again how lucky I was that *Valkyrie* had such an excellent executive officer.

And making me think that maybe Jennifer Simms should be in command of her own ship, instead of doing mostly administrative tasks for me.

I needed to think about that.

OK, so, the operation was a lot more complicated than I hoped, when Simms told me her concept. Finding an abandoned relay station was actually our *second* step. First, we had to decide which station to replace. It needed to see enough traffic that the data it contained was not so old as to be useless. It needed to be on a flight path used by Maxolhx *military* ships, so the station was getting the top-secret info we wanted, and not news and gossip everyone knew about. The target station also needed to be automated, not having a crew or even space for an optional crew. We couldn't risk some jackass in the Maxolhx Hegemony Fleet personnel office deciding that some poor technicians needed a rotation working on a relay station, and choosing ours. Yeah, doing that would make no sense, but mindless bureaucracy is one constant in the universe. Also, the station did not need to be identical to a station from a thousand years ago, we could alter the replacement to look identical, but there was only so much alteration that was possible.

Also, and this is key, the target station had to be in a Goldilocks location. No, I am not talking about the habitable zone of a star. I mean Goldilocks like, it had to be perfect for our purpose. Close enough to a wormhole so the particle wavefront of an explosion would wash past the wormhole within a few days. The idea was, once the bubble of the explosion passed the wormhole, any starship coming through would just see empty space. Of course, if that ship jumped away from the wormhole, and got ahead of the wavefront, it might detect the photons from where the original station used to be. *So*, we really needed a relay station that was between two wormholes of a cluster, and not just any cluster. It had to be a special type of cluster, where the figure-8 tracks of the emergence points did not cover too much territory. The ideal location would have the span of both wormholes not being larger than two lightdays.

And, the target station had to be far enough from a habitable world, or any other sensor platform, so the light of the explosion wouldn't be seen there for a long time, hopefully years.

Easy, right?

No. Skippy ran all the data through his ginormous brain, and came up with two possible targets. *Two*. The Maxolhx had thousands of relay stations, and we would get only two chances to replace one with a fake.

Scratch that. We would have only *one* chance. If we destroyed a station, and the kitties noticed, they would be on alert, and would carefully inspect all of their stations. We wouldn't get a second chance at the op.

Crap.

Just for once, I wish the Merry Band of Pirates would catch a real break, when we needed to do something super important. Hey, I'd be happy to have a punch card, where for every ten impossible things we did, the Universe gave us a freebie. I'm not holding my breath until that happens.

OK. We had two potential targets for destruction.

The next step was finding an abandoned relay station to use as a replacement. It had to be of a configuration similar to the target, and it had to be so far from an active wormhole that no species had been there since it was abandoned. It also had to not be so old that we couldn't get it working again. Easy, right?

Actually, it was not impossible. Skippy found six candidates.

Then he discarded two, because the dormant wormholes they were near, were on local networks he had screwed with, while he was moving around dormant wormholes. He didn't want to push his luck by asking those networks to do anything funky.

He discarded one, because it had been within six lightyears of a star that went nova, and that station's outer plating was slightly radioactive in a way he couldn't easily mask.

He discarded one more, because while it had been abandoned less than two hundred years ago, it had been in service for more than four *thousand* years. The surface of that station was likely so pitted with micrometeorite impacts, we would have to replace all the outer panels.

That left only two candidates. I chose the one that would require the fewest jumps by our stolen star carrier, again because I didn't want to push our luck. The *High Roller* was in good condition according to Skippy's analysis, and a single relay station was not a major burden for it. Nothing should go wrong, but it sure as hell *could*. The superhero identity of Angry Joe was still No Patience Man, and I needed to remind myself that was a bad combination.

We nuked the active relay station, and after making sure there was nothing left in the space where the station used to be, we jumped in. *Valkyrie's* big maser cannons were tuned to output a broad cone rather than the usual narrow, intense beam, and we fired the cannons all around us. The point was to push any lingering radioactive particles away, at high speed. It took six hours to cover the entire sphere, a task that Bilby probably found to be deathly boring, though he never complained.

Next, we jumped to rendezvous with the *High Roller*, and Simms carefully guided that ship to the exact point where the original relay station used to be. The replacement station was released, and set into position. Skippy verified the replacement station had their exact same set of recognition and authentication signals as the station we destroyed. When he was confident the Maxolhx could not tell the station had been swapped for a fake, both of our ships jumped away.

Five days later, comfortably after the time when an arriving ship might have detected signs that the original station got nuked to dust, a Maxolhx ship came through one of the wormholes. The old authentication procedure, which we ruined, was to allow the pixies on the ship and the station to establish a handshake, a relatively quick process. The new protocol was for a passing ship to match speed with the station, launch a dropship, and for a kitty to go aboard to get scanned. The rotten kitties had gotten used to the new routine, they launched the dropship soon after the ship jumped in, forcing the dropship to decelerate hard to avoid flying past the station.

We crossed our fingers when the dropship docked with the station, and a kitty presumably went aboard. Skippy had fabricated a scanning booth that looked identical to a real one, but all it did was hum and flash some lights, then tell the kitty its identity and access codes were confirmed. At that point, if nothing went wrong, the ship transmitted its files to the station, the station replied with files both real, and ones made up by Skippy-

It worked. The kitty went back into the dropship, accelerated away to catch the ship, and their ship jumped away.

Pumping a fist, I acknowledged the cheers of the bridge crew. "Thank you, but the credit for this op belongs to Colonel Simms. Skippy, what have we got?"

"Don't be so impatient, Joe," he snapped. "We are four lightminutes away, my request signal hasn't even reached the station yet."

"Right, sorry."

We waited almost eight minutes, while photons slowly crawled to, then back from the station. "Success!" Skippy crowed. "*Damn*, I am good."

"Anything interesting?"

"Give me a minute! There is a lot of data here. Um, hmm. Mm hmm, yup. OK, um, wow. Well, the good news is our timing is excellent. If we got this data a week from now, it would be too late for us to act."

"What's the bad news?" My greatest fear was the bad guys hit Earth again. We could not respond with our last set of relativistic darts, they were too few to do anything spectacular.

"Joe, we gots trouble. *Big* trouble."

"Like," the display wasn't showing an immediate threat. "A jump away from here right now threat?"

"No. The threat is to the *Legion*, Joe."

Hearing that, I relaxed just a bit. The Legion was always under some kind of threat. "OK, we'll deal with that when-"

"We need to deal with it *now*, Joe. The kitties *and* the spiders have sent ships to Klopeth."

"Holy-" Klopeth was the op the Legion rolled into, after they finished mopping up at Nickelback. "How the hell did they know? Oh my G- Did they hack our comms?"

"No," he sighed. "It's more simple than that. Something we should have, *I* should have, anticipated. The senior species have *enormous* resources. They didn't have to guess where the Legion would strike next, they sent task forces to *every* potential target. One hundred and thirty-seven star systems have a combined Maxolhx-Rindhalu task force waiting in stealth, and they started the initiative *before* we misaligned the wormhole that leads to Klopeth. Joe, the enemy was already waiting there when Zhao's ships jumped in with the Legion. They're all going to get slaughtered."

"Shepard!"

"On it, Sir," he tapped his console. "Course laid in for Klopeth. Ready." He had a finger poised over the button to activate the jump drive.'

"Wait," I held up a hand. "We're not going straight to Klopeth."

Shepard turned to look at me, as Simms did the same. "We're not?" He asked.

"No. A combined senior species force is too much even for *Valkyrie*. They could be trying for a two-fer. Knock out the Legion, and capture this ship, with Skippy."

Simms asked the question that was on everyone's mind. "Then, what's the plan, Sir?"

"The bad guys are probably expecting one hell of a gunfight."

"And?"

"We need to bring something bigger than a gun."

CHAPTER THIRTY FOUR

Valkyrie jumped in ten lightminutes from Klopeth. Ten minutes was not a magic number, it just felt right. Close enough to give us a reasonably current view of events, far enough away in distance that the enemy would have difficulty covering the entire area to search for us. By comparison, Earth is about eight lightminutes from the Sun, so it is a *long* way on any human scale.

"Damn it," I softly pounded a fist on the command chair's arm rest. "I never thought I would see *that*."

The holographic main display was showing an image of the planet, surrounded by symbols representing starships. Blue for friendly and allied ships. Red for Maxolhx. Yellow for client ships of the Maxolhx coalition.

And green for the *Rindhalu*.

There were a depressing number of green symbols in the display.

The spiders were there, and they were not fighting their ancient enemy.

The two apex species also were not holding hands around a campfire. They did not trust each other.

They *were* working together, to achieve a common goal.

Crushing humanity.

No, that's not accurate.

They were trying to stop us from having any influence on the galaxy. To halt our progress toward finally ending the endless war. To prevent their coalitions from breaking up.

To keep their privileged positions, by making their unwilling clients fight for them.

"Shit." I felt cold. Sick. Lost. Based on the faces of the bridge crew, everyone else was feeling the same.

They could.

I didn't have that luxury.

The commander has to be calm and cool and to have a plan, no matter how badly the odds were against us. The crew couldn't see how scared I was.

Faking it is a major part of the command skillset.

Unbuckling my seat restraints, I stood up and took a step toward the display, acting like I wanted a better look so I could decide exactly how to kick ass. "Skippy, what are they saying to each other? I don't suppose there's any chance the spiders are trying to get the kitties to sign up for a timeshare?"

"Ha! No such luck, unfortunately. They are not talking to each other much at all. The spiders are instructing, *demanding*, the Jeraptha and Ruhar to stand down. To cease all aid and support of our fleet, and the ships of the Verd-kris. The rotten kitties are dealing directly with Admiral Zhao, they are demanding he surrender. Joe, our Navy has no chance in this fight. There are seventeen Maxolhx and nine Rindhalu warships. Even if *Valkyrie* joined the fight, Zhao's ships would still get slaughtered."

"Right. Where is the *Dutchman*?"

"In stealth, at a distance of thirteen lightseconds. The senior species do not appear to have detected the *Dutchman*."

"Signal Chang to join us out here."

Ten minutes later, the familiar profile of the *Flying Dutchman* appeared. "Kong," I asked. "Is the situation as bad as it looks?"

"The fleet is caught in a damping field, and can't get away. The Maxolhx used precision fire to disable *Pacific's* jump drive and primary reactionless engines, so Zhao's not going anywhere. We lost four destroyers in the initial engagement. I think the kitties were only making a point about how vulnerable we are; they could have taken out every ship we have. The damned Rindhalu also fired on our ships, they disabled the *Congo*."

"Oh," I felt a chill creep up my spine. Up until that moment, I had been hoping the spiders would do their usual neutral, passive-aggressive thing. The fact that they shot at our ships completely changed the game. "*Fuuuuuck.*"

"Yes. Whatever we're going to do, we'll have to fight both sides. Joe, do you have a plan?"

"Sort of."

"Sort of?"

"Yeah. Kong, I need you to stay out here. I'm sending Skippy over on a dropship," as I said that, I saw our ready bird launch, carrying the beer can away.

Chang saw the same, I saw him glance at his own display. "We'll take care of Skippy. What will you be doing?"

"I'm taking *Valkyrie* in."

He squinted at me with a frown. "That is suicide. Without Skippy, you can't hope to win a fight. Even with him you-"

"We're not going to fight. We're going to negotiate a surrender."

Our mighty battlecruiser, without a certain snarky beer can aboard, jumped in less than three hundred thousand kilometers from where the UN Navy was concentrated. After the *Dutchman* jumped away, a pair of Maxolhx destroyers had jumped to that position to investigate the gamma ray source. The rest of the apex species ships were in two clusters, on either side of our Navy. The main display told me that the Rindhalu and Maxolhx had their main weapons pointed at each other, with secondary batteries tasked to prevent any rash move by the human ships.

Valkyrie's arrival upset the tactical stalemate. Our shields were up, but weapons offline. A message broadcast in every useful language stated that we were there to talk, and please would everyone not shoot at us.

Instantly, we had a half dozen, a dozen, then most of the apex-species ships make short jumps to surround us. The Zhao's ships were forgotten, although they were still trapped in a damping field and within weapons range. All parties wanted to speak with me at once, including Admiral Zhao. With one eye on the clock in the lower left corner of the display, I counted the enemy ships around us. "Thirteen kitty ships on the right, seven spiders on the left," I muttered to myself.

Straightening up, I lifted my chin, trying to give myself some dignity while I sold us out.

Behind me while I talked under my breath, the officer at the comms station made an adjustment to her console, and jammed the transmit button down with a thumb.

On the bottom right corner of the main display, an urgent light was blinking. Zhao was demanding to speak with me.

"Simms," I told her quietly, "signal Zhao to stand by. I'll talk with him when I can."

My executive officer grimaced while she tapped on her touchscreen keyboard, anticipating a fun conversation with a very unhappy and very senior officer.

She could handle it.

I stood and faced the virtual camera lens. It could capture a view from almost any angle, we primitive monkeys found it easier when there was a focal point, so the image of a lens floated between me and the display. "This is General Bishop. I wish to speak with the leader of the Maxolhx forces here."

The response was immediate, because the enemy had been demanding to speak with me since the moment we jumped in. "You wish to surrender, Bishop?" The transmission was audio-only, and the voice had the slightly stereotypical hiss of a cat speaking. That might have been an effect added by our translator software, it knew we thought of the Maxolhx as cat-like.

"I wish to *discuss* terms for surrender," I stressed.

"Very well," the kitty practically purred, satisfied with herself. "We are willing to negotiate."

"What about your counterparts? Do the Rindhalu want to negotiate?"

"We do," came a different and unfamiliar voice.

"Great," I bit my lower lip. "Everyone wants to negotiate." I looked down at the list on my tablet. "Our conditions are," I took a breath. "First, that you release all United Nations Navy ships, to be withdrawn to a neutral-"

Hey.

Remember those relativistic darts we hadn't used yet?

Yeah.

We brought one with us.

I was going to bring chips and dip to the party, but Simms said that parties always have plenty of snacks, so we should bring something really special instead.

Before *Valkyrie* jumped in to begin negotiations, Chang took Skippy and the *Dutchman* farther away from Klopeth, to rendezvous with a relativistic dart. As the dart zipped past the *Dutchman,* Skippy sent it a burst of commands. He instructed the dart to perform one final jump, using its own drive.

It emerged in a burst of gamma rays, thirteen hundred kilometers behind *Valkyrie*, and zipped right past us before we knew it was there. The short jump, programmed by Skippy, was extremely precise, even by his standards. Once the dart was safely in front of us, it flew onward only eighty kilometers before it exploded.

Darts are made of an ultra-dense exotic material specially created by the Maxolhx. That material is actually a tightly-packed collection of what might best be described as BB pellets. In the military, we call those submunitions. What I call it is *awesome*.

The signal from *Valkyrie* caused the explosive charge at center of the dart to detonate in a very specific pattern, breaking the dart into forty ultra-dense chunks.

Forty.

Like, two for each of the enemy ships around us.

The dart emerged less than half a lightsecond from us, traveling at almost three-quarters the speed of light. You can run the numbers if you want, the result is that the targeted ships had just more than a tenth of a second to realize they had incoming and react.

The AIs of Maxolhx, and especially Rindhalu ships, are incredibly fast.

You know what's faster?

A chunk of relativistic dart blasting a hole through an AI's freakin' *brain*.

It's hard for a starship's AI to think, when its substrate gets turned into superheated plasma in a flash.

The energy shields, point-defense cannons, and armor plating of those ships were laughably inadequate against an object packing that much kinetic energy. Even later, watching a replay in super-slow-motion, it was hard to see the enemy ships actually being struck. One moment, the enemy warships were hanging motionless around us, bristling with weapons that were all aimed at Valkyrie. The next moment, those ships had blindingly-bright streaks radiating away from them, streaks that were thousands of kilometers long. Smashing through the armored ships like tissue paper, the chunks of dart had barely slowed down. Behind them, ships staggered.

Then exploded.

Valkyrie shook, the ship's shields overloaded by the hellish energy unleashed all around us. We couldn't go anywhere, there wasn't anywhere to go. The ship got battered by the two wavefronts of exploding ships, and although explosions in space don't have anything to push *against*, there was enough high-speed whatever flying around to seriously scorch the outer layer of our armor.

To sell the idea of me attempting to negotiate until the last second, I was standing in front of my chair when all hell broke loose. With no time to get strapped in and the deck heaving like *Valkyrie* was in a hurricane, I did a stop, drop and roll. Like, stop talking, drop to the deck as it came up to meet me halfway, and rolled while tucking my head under my hands for protection. Someone grabbed hold of my right arm and yanked me toward my chair as I bounced off the deck, bashing a hand on something I couldn't see.

The roaring stopped as abruptly as it began, the wavefronts having washed over us. "Bil-" I coughed while Simms helped me crawl into my chair. "Bilby! Status?"

"Oh, *wow*, Dude. We're in one piece, mostly. Jump drive and normal-space engines are offline. I had to shut down a reactor, it's too hot. Hey, I'm like, all for new experiences and broadening our minds you know, but can we not ever do that again?"

"No promises," I tried to snort a laugh, and spit blood all over my uniform top. Somewhere, I'd gotten a nosebleed. No, my nose hurt, must have bashed it on something. The main display was filling in details, and I managed a smile when I looked at Simms. "*Two* on the right, *one* on the left." Skippy's aim had not been perfect, the enemy ships had been maneuvering and the dart had a limited ability to project fragments sideways, especially at such short range. Pushing up out of my chair, because I hadn't learned a lesson the first time, I checked that our weapons were now online, shields were recovering, and most important, our damping field was saturating the area. Zhao's ships had also gotten pelted by high-speed debris, but the reason why we jumped in three hundred thousand kilometers away from their formation was to give them some measure of protection. By the time the debris wavefront expanded over that distance, it had thinned out a lot. The display was showing a lot of yellow and some orange as Zhao's ships reported additional damage, but no red that would indicate serious effects.

Our ships had survived, and the remaining enemy ships weren't going anywhere. "Hey," I said on an open channel. "Anybody else want to negotiate?"

The reply was an outraged scream. My knowledge of unintelligible alien curses was limited, I couldn't tell which species was angry with me. The scream resolved into something like speech. "You have no honor!" That voice I recognized as Maxolhx, including the underlying hiss. "You offer to surrender, then you attack!"

"Hey, I never said *we* were surrendering."

That got silence.

"He-LLO?" I pretended to knock on a door.

"Lies!" The unnamed Maxolhx voice screeched. "You implied-"

"Hey, whoever you are, it's not *my* fault if you assumed the wrong thing. All I said was, I wanted to discuss a surrender. Yours."

"You destroyed our ships!"

"Yeah, well," I shrugged. "It's easier to negotiate when one side doesn't have overwhelming force." The display showed one of the two crippled Maxolhx ships was beginning to turn away, and was firing up its sputtering main engines. "Weps," I turned to look at Mammay behind me. "It looks like someone is trying to leave the party."

"Check," Mammay said as a reply, because that's what artillery people say instead of 'Yes'. He sent a pair of railgun projectiles ripping through the enemy ship and it stopped accelerating, drifting slowly away. That incident is an interesting example of why armor plating can sometimes be a hazard to the ship it is designed to protect. If that ship didn't have armor, our railgun darts would have blasted cleanly through the hull, leaving small entry and exit holes, with limited carnage in between. Instead, when our two darts encountered armor plating, they instantly flashed into burning jets of plasma. Knowing that could happen, the Maxolhx ship builders had installed plates of reactive explosives under the armor, to erupt outward and disperse the plasma. Great idea and it usually works, except in this case, we fired from so close and our darts came in at such high speed, they almost punched through the reactive plates before they could, you know, react. The plasma flared out in two cone shaped jets inside the ship, causing damage that was far more widespread and serious than if our railguns had simply punched neat holes through the hull.

This time, the Law of Unintended Consequences worked in our favor.

The one damaged Rindhalu ship signaled for my attention. "Human, you have made another enemy today."

"You shot at us first, asshole. So, *fuck* you," I snapped, instantly regretting my choice of words. Diplomacy, Joe, I reminded myself.

Ah, screw it. Diplomacy hadn't gotten us anywhere. The senior species only respond to force.

"Your species cannot be trusted with Elder weapons."

"We don't plan to use them, unless you are stupid enough to use them first."

"My people would never resort to deploying such weapons of mass destruction."

"The last time Elder weapons were used, the Maxolhx say you hit them first."

"They *lie*," the spider raised its voice for the first time, or the translator just then started adding inflection to the audio. "The treacherous Maxolhx foolishly attacked *us*, and their arrogance nearly destroyed us both."

"Yeah, they say the same thing about you. You know what? I don't care whether Han or Greedo shot first, a long long time ago. You have nothing to fear from us now. Leave us alone, and we won't mess with you. But that's not gonna happen, is it? You're not only afraid we will use our Elder weapons. You are also afraid that humanity offers a better alternative to your clients. If they ally with us, won't have to fight endless wars for you, for *your* benefit. You and the Maxolhx give orders from the rear, and your clients on the front lines die. Nothing changes, except the lines on the map move side to side," I said, realizing too late that I was paraphrasing a Pink Floyd song. Hopefully, the spiders would not research that reference.

Damn it. Arguing with the spiders, or the kitties, was a waste of time. "We just wiped out six of your ships, without our ship actually firing a shot. You don't have a defense against the weapons we have. We can hit you anytime, anywhere. If you don't believe me, ask your enemies. Or are the Maxolhx your allies now?"

There was a pause, when the spider didn't reply. I was about to switch to talking with the Maxolhx, who were screaming at me, when the spider spoke again. "We are familiar with the weapon you used against us here. We know they are not *your* weapons."

"Yeah, well, they are now. We control them, those darts *are* our weapons."

"It is useless to debate the issue of ownership. You should be aware that our most sensitive worlds are protected from relativistic impactors, so any threat by you to use such weapons against us is a-"

"Yeah, we know about kinetic-energy dispersal fields. The Maxolhx had one around Argathos, and it didn't do them any good. We hit Argathos with six impactors, and *cracked* that freakin' world like an eggshell. So, don't give us any bullshit about how your worlds are protected, because *that* is an empty threat." Speaking of empty threats, I had a flash of inspiration to follow up with a bullshit threat of my own. "We're using the Maxolhx's own darts against them, as a way to say screw you to those assholes. And, because we have even more powerful weapons in reserve, that we don't want to deploy yet."

The spider chuckled, or that is what it sounded like through the translator. Whoever was on the other side of the conversation was one cool customer. He or she was aboard a damaged starship, saw us wipe out six other Rindhalu ships, and still was laughing at me. "You are a young, primitive and impulsive species, so we are not insulted by your foolish boasting. Humans have no such weapons, to suggest you do is-"

"Hey, pal, I got a breaking news flash for you. Somebody busted an Elder wormhole, remember? That was us primitive monkeys. We captured several Maxolhx capital ships, and we did that *before* we had an arsenal of Elder weapons. If you're going to trash talk, make sure you know what the hell you're talking about, dipshit."

There was a sigh, like the spider was being patient with a child. That pissed me off, more than anything the Rindhalu spoke aloud. "General Bishop, the arrangements between my people and the Maxolhx have kept the peace in this galaxy for-"

"*Peace*?" I lost whatever cool I had left. It was unprofessional, but that bus had already left the station. "Tell that to the billions, maybe trillions of people who died to keep you comfortably in power. You have kept this war going forcing your clients to fight, so-" Clenching fist at my side, I stopped to bite my lip. Getting righteously outraged felt good. It wasn't helping me accomplish anything useful. "I'm done talking *with* you. I'm going *to* talk to you, and the Maxolhx. Both of you have one hour, Earth time, to pull crews off any of your ships that aren't flightworthy,, and jump away from here. At the end of one hour, we will destroy any senior-species ships remaining in this system. If you activate weapons, we shoot. If you delay, we shoot. If you think bad thoughts in our direction, we shoot. The only reason you are alive right now is because I need you to carry a message back to your people, and I don't need more than one of your ships to do that. The message is: we're bringing the pain. We brought it here, we brought it to Retonovir, we brought it to Argathos and we brought it to Lacandra. So far, we have not targeted Rindhalu worlds, but that is *over*. If you fire on a human ship again, or you fire on a ship of any species that is working with us, or you interfere with our operations, we will rain hellfire on your worlds. You can't stop us, and you know it. Don't bother replying, because we're not listening." With a thumb, I made a slashing gesture across my throat, and the audio feed cut out.

"Sir?" Simms cleared her throat. "What chapter was that from, in the Bishop Manual of Interstellar Diplomacy?"

"Ha," I snorted. "It's in the section about punching bullies in the throat. Talking with them is a waste of time. They only listen to force."

She nodded. "We should make sure Admiral Zhao understands your offer of a one-hour ceasefire," she said with a raised eyebrow.

I got her meaning. Technically, Zhao was in command of the human force in that star system, I had made the offer without clearing it with him. In my defense, we didn't have time for a lot of blah, blah, blah back and forth discussion. "Good point." Turning to face the virtual camera, I straightened my shoulders. "Connect me with-"

Just then, the *Flying Dutchman* jumped in, a mere two hundred kilometers off our starboard bow. "Uh," I changed my mind. "I need to talk with Chang first. XO, contact Zhao, in case he didn't get my message. Tell him- No, please *request*, that he not shoot at the enemy for another hour. Uh, also that I suggest he disperse his ships," I added, in case the enemy also had some type of super weapon.

The Rindhalu and Maxolhx meekly pulled survivors off their damaged ships, or maybe they were seething with rage as they pulled survivors off their ships, I really didn't give a shit how they felt about it. Their last ship jumped away six minutes before my one-hour deadline. Zhao assigned the cruisers *Nile* and *Ishikari* to escort the bad guys toward the nearest Elder wormhole, to make sure neither of our enemies doubled back to cause mischief. The Admiral made that decision without consulting me, not that he needed to ask me how to deploy his ships. If he had asked me, I would have argued against assigning an escort. But, Zhao needed to think about his overall force, and it was his call.

Skippy came back aboard *Valkyrie*, and the *Dutchman* jumped away again, to lurk in stealth as a guard force. Zhao wanted to confer with me, Ross and Perkins, so I flew a Panther down to the surface to pick up Perkins, while Ross flew directly to the flagship.

When I say 'I flew a Panther', I was not at the controls. We were not entirely sure the shooting had stopped, and I was not yet qualified to fly a Panther in combat mode. Plus, Emily Perkins and I had a lot to talk about, before we reached the flagship.

"Coffee?" I asked as Perkins came in through the dropship's side door.

"No," she shook her head, knowing it was difficult to hear with the ship's turbines idling. As soon as she strapped in and the door slid closed, the Panther leapt off the ground, flying straight up under hard acceleration. I knew we broke the local sound barrier when the roaring of the engines became a muffled whisper.

"Your thoughts?" I asked. She looked tired, but no more than I expected after three straight days of combat. Turning down an offer of fresh coffee told me she probably was on some sort of stimulants, that plus her fingers drummed nervously on her right thigh. "I know we have one hell of a mess here."

"Sir," she just shook her head again. "I'm out. Of ideas, I mean. They called our bluff."

"Yeah, they did." I knew what she meant.

Emily Perkins thought long-term, and she thought big. To her, there was no point to developing strategy unless it was part of an overall grand strategy. The UNEF senior leadership on Paradise was not providing any actual leadership, so Perkins filled the vacuum. She was not the only staff officer to develop a plan, and her plans stole from ideas cooked up by others, but that is just good teamwork. The reason she was able to actually put a plan into action is the Ruhar respected her more than they respected most humans, which is not saying a lot. Because of her actions to blow a Kristang battlegroup out of orbit, to prevent lizard commandos from destroying passenger ships over Paradise, and alerting the hamsters to the threat of a bioweapon attack against that planet, she became popular with the Ruhar public. The strategy she proposed had been kicking around UNEF headquarters for a while, going nowhere because the Ruhar were not interested. But when *she* spoke, the hamster authorities listened, even if they were just showing their public that they treated one of the famous Mavericks with respect. What the Ruhar military wanted Perkins to do was publicity tours, where she would praise humanity's landlords, and not do anything to cause complications.

Emily Perkins had no interest in being a puppet.

The original plan was intended to solve two problems, one immediate and one more likely only aspirational. Remember, the Alien Legion concept was launched only shortly after the hamsters tried to trade Paradise back to the lizards, and sell out the human population there. UNEF HQ was desperate to demonstrate that humans were no threat to the Ruhar, that we could be useful. By doing the dirty jobs the Ruhar military didn't want, we hoped the Legion could make the still-skeptical hamster authorities see the value in supporting a group of troublesome and primitive aliens.

That part of the plan worked, maybe too well. Exposing the treachery and double-dealing of the Ruhar on Fresno had caused their federal government to fall, creating chaos. The fact that humans had not done anything wrong didn't matter, plenty of powerful people in the hamster government were pissed off that a small group of *disobedient* humans had caused so much trouble. The Legion got a second chance at Squidworld, and barely survived that operation. The reason the Legion got approval for the action at Tohmaran was the Ruhar military was horribly embarrassed about their massive intelligence failure at Squidworld, and wanted the Legion to keep quiet about it.

Anyway, the first part of Perkins's plan worked well enough. The Alien Legion had proven its worth, and raised the profile of humans throughout the galaxy.

The second part of her original plan, the part that was more of a goal than an actual plan, was to free Earth from the Kristang.

Both of her original plans were OBE when she learned about the Merry Band of Pirates.

Her new plan, the one she told me about before she briefed UNEF Command on Earth, was to begin the process of breaking clients away from their patrons. To do that, we needed to prevent the two senior species from punishing clients who refused orders to fight. To do *that*, we had to demonstrate that humans could protect anyone who helped us, like when the Jeraptha delivered a batch of second-hand starships to us.

UNEF Command agreed with the basic concept Perkins proposed, they wanted to move slowly and cautiously. The problem with plans is, the enemy also makes plans. The attacks against Earth changed everything. Instead of gradually encouraging the Jeraptha and Ruhar to work with us, we had to move fast. That's why we couldn't wait for the Ruhar to give the Verd-kris a chance only a little bit at a time; we had to force the issue.

Now the senior species had called our bluff. We could not actually protect anyone who signed an alliance with, we couldn't even protect our own Navy. All the work done to build a new Alien Legion would be for nothing, if potential allies feared they would be attacked by higher-tech species, and their new human allies wouldn't protect them. The future of the Legion, and any future alliances, rested on our ability to force the Maxolhx to clean up the cloud at Earth.

So far, I had failed to make the Maxolhx do anything. So far, I all I had done was make matters *worse*; the Rindhalu were now taking direct action against us.

No, that's not true. The situation is even worse than me getting the two senior species to join forces against us. It also told them that, despite my boasting, we didn't have any super weapons of our own, that's why we hacked into *their* super weapons. We had already hit the enemy as hard as we could; they had to decide whether to continue taking punishment, but they didn't need to worry that we would make the pain any worse.

Hooray for me.

In the past, my failure to accomplish the mission would have gotten me depressed and doubting myself.

The new Angry Joe just got more angry.

Perkins and I had a lot to talk about during the ride up.

"This isn't going to work," she said, which is basically what she said before. She was prompting me to say something.

"It hasn't worked *yet*," I argued. "We hit them hard already, showed that we can penetrate their defenses."

She didn't ask how we had gotten through the enemy defenses, that information needed to be kept to a limited group of people. Even aboard *Valkyrie*, fewer than a dozen people knew how we accomplished that task. If the crew were captured, most of them wouldn't have any useful information. It sucks that I had to consider the crew being captured and interrogated, but that's our reality. Skippy promised me he hadn't put dangerous quantum nanomachines in the brains of the crew, and the remaining ones in my head were deactivated. I know from painful experience that no amount of SERE training could prevent aliens from learning anything they wanted, by probing a human brain.

I still have nightmares about that.

"I know what you're thinking," I said when she didn't reply. "We proved we can hit them anywhere, and the kitties *still* aren't rushing to clean up the cloud. Don't worry. We hit their toughest target, but we haven't hit them *hard* yet. That's our next move."

"We can't escalate," she stated. "Sir, that solar flare was already too much. You crossed the line."

"I know." That was true. The Maxolhx were going to slowly freeze our homeworld, and they had goaded their clients into direct strikes. But those strikes were limited, and the Maxolhx had not yet directly killed anyone on Earth. If the Merry Band of Pirates attacked a populated world with relativistic weapons, the enemy might step up their own campaign in response. Whatever we did next, we couldn't make the situation worse. Like I already had. "We have a variety of options to step up the pressure."

"How many of those super speed darts have you captured?"

"Ah, not enough," I admitted, and told her how the Maxolhx had self-destructed their own arsenal of super weapons, to deny their use to us. "We have a few left, not enough. Listen, we'll think of something. Using those darts was kind of a convenient shortcut for us. Without them," I shrugged. "We'll have to do it the hard way."

"I hope you can, General. Because until you force the senior species to back down," she pointed to the deck beneath our feet, "we're shut down. The Legion. We can't operate in this environment. We can't ask our people, and the Verds, and the Ruhar, to continue operations, with the threat of a Maxolhx task force jumping in over our heads without warning. Unless you plan for *Valkyrie* to follow us across the galaxy?"

"No." She wasn't suggesting that our mighty battlecruiser join the fleet, just pointing out that would be the only way the Legion could have any level of protection against the enemy. "That wouldn't work anyway, the Maxolhx would just send more ships next time. We can't destroy every ship they have."

"In the future, they won't conveniently cluster their ships close together either," she noted.

"Yeah." We knew that our neat trick of using a dart to take out multiple ships would likely be a one-time event, the enemy would learn from that mistake, and avoid providing a convenient target. "Also, if the kitties know Valkyrie is operating with the Legion, that will make you a *more* tempting target. No, you're right, the Legion is shut down for now. I'm going to recommend that Admiral Zhao take the fleet back to Jaguar for a refit, while we-"

Perkins shook her head. "He won't do it. No way will Zhao let the fleet sit out the fight, and do nothing. We also can't leave the Verds hung out to dry. Their worlds will be targets for every ambitious group of aliens in the galaxy, without the 1st Fleet's protection."

"Shit. You're right."

"We brought the Verds into this fight. If we abandon them at the first sign of trouble, we can forget about others signing on to be allies."

CHAPTER THIRTY FIVE

"Sir," Simms said when I came back from the conference with Perkins, Ross and Zhao aboard *Pacific*. "This goes over our heads. We need revised instructions from Earth."

"No."

"*Sir*," she added a bit of emphasis to the word that time. "We tried. We gave it a damned good shot. The Maxolhx outplayed us. Without more than a handful of darts, we can't force the Maxolhx to disperse the cloud. We already hit them with a solar flare. Anything *Valkyrie* can do in the future will have less impact than a solar flare, and their public will not be impressed. They won't feel threatened by us."

"Simms is correct," Smythe stared at his tablet, as if hoping the answer was there. "They did call our bluff."

"It wasn't a *bluff*," I protested.

He raised an eyebrow at me. "You would use another solar flare, this time against a heavily populated, undefended world?"

"No," I admitted. Despite the tough-guy pep talks I gave myself, about how I would save Earth no matter what it took, I could not see myself burning an entire world. Also, Simms wouldn't let me do it. And Skippy wouldn't help, if I asked him to do that.

"Then, it *was* a bluff," our STAR team leader said quietly. "It doesn't matter now. We can't bluff, when the enemy knows we don't have any cards."

"*Shit!*" I pounded the desk with the side of a fist. "Damn it! We had a plan. It should have worked."

Neither of them said anything. When the commander is engaged in ineffectual whining, it is best to let him get it out of his system.

"Does anyone have any ideas?" I asked, trying to keep the note of desperation from being too obvious.

Smythe sat back in his chair. "Unless Skippy has tricks we haven't used yet."

"Hey," the avatar appeared immediately. "Don't blame *me*. You monkeys cook up the whacky ideas, I just make them work. Joe?"

"No, sorry. I don't, uh, I can't think of anything else. Those darts were perfect!"

"What about Plan B?" Smythe asked.

"Plan B?"

"If we can't force the Maxolhx to disperse the cloud, is there other action we can take?"

"Like what?"

"Like," Simms spoke up. "Go back to doing what we're best at. Sneaky shit. Can we start a fight between the two senior species?"

"Whoa," was my reaction.

"Bloody tricky, that," Smythe frowned, but he looked like the wheels in his head were turning.

"They are cooperating against us now, that's our major problem," Simms continued. "We know they don't trust each other. If they both have ships at the negotiation site, and there is an," she looked at Smythe, then me, "unfortunate incident…" She didn't bother to finish the thought.

"A page from our playbook, eh?" Smythe mused. "We tried that once; attacking a ship to disrupt negotiations." He meant when we faked attacking a Ruhar ship, during the Black Op when we ended up sparking a civil war among the Kristang. "As I recall, it failed. The Ruhar returned to the negotiations."

"Ah," I grunted, unconvinced. "Nice idea Simms, but that might have worked before either side knew we were flying around doing sneaky shit. Now," I shrugged. "They'll be on guard for disruptions. And they'll assume any unfortunate incident was *our* doing, before they start blaming the other side. XO," I added when she frowned, hurt. "Work up a plan and I'll look at it." I certainly was not in a position to shoot down ideas, when I had nothing to offer. Staring at the message on Smythe's tablet was not giving me any inspiration.

"What's our next move, Sir?" Smythe asked, prompting me to blink and tear my eyes away from the taunting message.

Shit.

Accepting the offer was the worst thing humanity could do.

Except *not* accepting the offer, and allowing Earth to freeze, while nuclear-armed nations fought over dwindling resources.

"Next? Uh, I guess we, uh. I don't know." My brain was having trouble focusing. "Zhao requested the *Dutchman* to remain here, while the Legion is evaced off the surface, and he pulls his ships out. He will have to bring the star carriers into the system, too many of our ships can't jump without major repairs. While they do that, we, uh-" Damn it, I hated being indecisive. "We're going to hit up a relay station. I want fresh intel on how broad this alliance is between the kitties and spiders. Is what they did here a one-time thing, or are they cooperating all across the galaxy? Simms, signal Zhao that we're jumping away."

To take my mind off the latest, major, crushing burden on my shoulders, I wandered down to use one of the flight simulators. It would be good to keep my skills current, I was qualified for basic maneuvers in a Panther, but not combat flying. With everything going on, I simply hadn't been able to devote enough time to advanced flight training. And, the simulators were mostly busy being used by real pilots, I couldn't justify cutting ahead in the line.

That's why I was up at three in the morning. That, plus, I couldn't sleep. After waking up, trying and failing to get back to sleep for an hour, I got out of bed. A quick status check showed three of the flight simulators were not in use, so I hurried to get there.

And was met by disappointment.

"Skippy, what the hell?"

"Joe?" He acted like he was surprised to see me out of bed at that hour. "What are you doing up so early?"

"I couldn't sleep."

"Um, why do you throw a hissy fit when I wake you up in the middle of the night, but somehow it's OK for you to bother *me* at this ungodly hour?"

"I never throw a 'hissy fit'. And you don't sleep, you moron."

"*Moron*?"

"Sorry. It's been a long day. In a long week."

"I know what you mean, homeboy," he sighed. "Crap, sometimes this just feels like a long *life*, you know?"

"Yeah. Sorry about that."

"Um, why are *you* sorry?"

"If you weren't with us, with *me*, maybe your life wouldn't be so freakin' frustrating."

"It also wouldn't be as challenging, interesting and *fun*, Joe. We did have some fun along the way, right?"

"I guess so," I said as I stifled a yawn. It's hard to think about good times in the dark hours of the night. "At the time, sure. Sorry to rain on your parade. It feels like any fun we had was like enjoying a good dinner, aboard a train that is headed off a cliff."

"Wow. You *are* Debbie Downer this morning. What happened to Angry Joe?"

"I'm too tired to be pissed off right now. Hey, what's going on with the simulators? I hurried down here because three of them showed as available but," I pointed to the blank displays of the simulator in front of me. "They're all busted?"

"They are not busted, Joe."

"Maintenance, then? That should have been noted on the schedule, so-"

"Not maintenance either. That *does* go on the schedule, if you were paying attention."

"Then why can't I use this one?"

"Because it is running a self-diagnostic. Which you should know, if you studied the manuals. See the little 'Self-check' icon in the upper right of the primary flight display?"

"Oh. Yes," I blinked, my eyes still dry from waking up too early. "So, it *is* busted."

"No, it's- Ugh. OK, yes, technically it does have a fault, but that is something I did on purpose."

"You screwed it up on purpose? Why did-"

"I'm *trying* to explain, knucklehead. You monkeys keep bitching about," his voice took on a whiny tone. "How you need to understand how the ship *works*, and be able to fix things by *yourselves*. Ugh."

"You *broke* the simulator to see if we could fix it? You ass, it-"

"No, I broke it to see if it could figure out what is wrong by itself. That is the first step you monkeys should take, if a piece of equipment is not working properly, and Bilby or I are not there to fix it."

"Well, sure. So, the Check Engine light is on?"

"It's way more complicated than that. The change I made is very subtle, it will be difficult for the machine's native AI to determine-"

"OK, fine. When can I use it? Can the diagnostic software run in the background?"

"*No*, you numbskull. The simulator's operation must be static while the diagnostic routine is running. Jeez, I try to *help* you monkeys, and all I get is complaints. Joe, any advanced AI-driven system needs to-"

"Huh."

"What?"

"Shut up a minute, I'm thinking."

"Is that what you call it?" He laughed.

"Shut *up*!"

That time, he actually went quiet.

After a moment, I leaned back against the bulkhead and said slowly, "Skippy, I have a question for you."

It didn't take long for Simms to contact me. Like, she must have pinged me within five minutes after she woke up. Being a good executive officer, she checked the status report on her tablet, and saw right away that the ship had changed course overnight.

"Sir?" She asked via zPhone, while I was in my office. "We're not going to a relay station?"

"No, we're not. We're on our way to the negotiating site. After we run a couple errands along the way."

"Sir? What negot-"

"The message to UNEF Command said the senior species would be waiting at a rendezvous site they designated, to discuss their demands. We're going there."

"You," she said slowly, trying to guess my intentions. "Intend to *negotiate*, Sir? If we're offering concessions, we really need to clear that with UNEF Comm-"

"No concessions," I laughed bitterly. "It will be a one-way negotiation. Kind of a Win-Lose deal. We win, they lose. We're going to make them an offer they can't refuse."

"Did I, um, miss something?" She was bewildered by the sudden, unexplained change.

"No. I had a thought, a couple hours ago. Simms, we are going to make the Maxolhx clean up their damned mess. Them, *and* the spiders, the damned lazy Rindhalu are not sitting on the sidelines anymore."

"You found more darts?"

"No. That's over. This is the *end game* in this whole damned war. The senior species will clean up their mess, and leave us alone, or we will *break* their fucking empires. Burn them to the ground. They will lose *everything*."

"You," she dragged the word out. "Have a *plan* to do that?"

"Yes. Skippy and I worked out the details last night. Meet me in the galley? I haven't had breakfast yet. I'll get Smythe to join us."

"I'll be there in five minutes."

"Simms, there's no rush. The ship won't jump again for another," I checked the status on the bulkhead display. "Thirty-one minutes. It's a long way to the rendezvous point, and like I said, we have some errands to do first. Take your time."

"Are you sure?" She had to be burning with curiosity.

"Yes. Besides, the galley crew is making biscuits this morning, and they won't be out of the oven for another twenty minutes."

"I'll be there in fifteen."

The site designated for 'negotiations' was unusual. By the way, I put quotes around the word negotiations, because the senior species were not interested in actually negotiating with us.

That's fine with me.

Negotiations involve talking.

I was done with talking.

Anyway, I said the location was unusual because it wasn't a planet, or a space station, or a lonely random spot in interstellar space.

It was a wormhole cluster.

Not just any wormhole cluster. This was a place where three wormholes came together, with their emergence points always in a bubble a quarter lightyear across. Ships coming in through one wormhole had to make only a few jumps, before they could transit outbound through another wormhole. The timing could be tricky; the three wormholes coordinated their emergence points in space but not in time. Even ships capable of making a quarter lightyear jump could not just zip through to their destination, they had to wait for the outbound wormhole to emerge. The patterns of emergence were also far more complex than the typical wormhole. Most wormholes had a static pattern of emergence points, a pattern that might run to huge numbers, but that had been mapped over the millennia and was well-known to every star-faring species in the galaxy. Clusters were different, mapping their emergence points was like playing three-dimensional chess. The emergence of one wormhole in a cluster varied, based on where and when another wormhole in the cluster emerged. After observing the patterns since the beginning of their starflight capability, the Rindhalu were still occasionally surprised when wormholes in a cluster acted differently from what the spiders expected.

Another funky thing about that cluster was that one wormhole connected deep inside Rindhalu territory, one to the heart of Maxolhx territory, and one just inside Maxolhx space near their border with the spiders. That is why the two ancient enemies often chose that point to meet, on the rare occasions when they needed to talk. It made sense they would choose to designate that location for possible talks with humans.

Why am I babbling on about trivia?

Because, despite my tough talk, I was nervous.

Like, I made sure to use the bathroom, right before we slipped through one of the wormholes.

Because all three wormholes emerged within a sphere a quarter lightyear across, it was one of a very few places in the galaxy where it was possible to set up a blockade. We could come through an event horizon, into a firestorm of directed energy, kinetic, nuclear or more exotic weapons.

So, we cheated.

Skippy discovered, to our dismay and his extreme irritation, that none of the three wormholes would allow him to screw with them. He could not conveniently make one emerge half a lightyear away, no matter how much he argued with the network AI. It seems Skippy's reputation had spread across the galaxy, and he wasn't being allowed to take actions that might disrupt the operation of the network.

But, what he could do was instruct the network to set up an emergence within the insanely complicated parameters of its programming, an emergence location that was not expected by the asshole kitties and spiders who might be waiting to blast *Valkyrie* and capture Skippy.

"Ready?" I asked, squeezing the armrest of the command chair to settle my nerves. Remember, I told myself. I am a bad-ass, filled with well-deserved confidence. I had no doubt my strategy would work. That show was for the crew's benefit, and indirectly for the aliens whose asses we were about to kick. Or not.

It's complicated.

"Ready, Freddy," Skippy replied with a nervous giggle.

It did not make me happy to hear he was also nervous. Simms gave me a side-eye, I responded by flashing a thumbs-up to her. Relax, my thumb said. Everything's under control. No problems anticipated. Well, no more than the usual.

My thumb was *lying* like a rug.

But Simms didn't know that, so it's all good.

On the bottom left corner of the main display, the big 3D hologram in the front center of the bridge, a clock was counting down. Simms and several others had asked about that counter, I had casually explained that it represented the optimal time for Skippy to, well, do what he does best. Be awesome.

I was lying about that, too.

I suck.

Before we arrived at the location of the wormhole that was soon to appear in front of *Valkyrie*, we ran some errands. Like, we visited six other wormholes, that belonged to local networks surrounding the network that controlled the cluster of three wormholes. Skippy explained to the crew that the purpose of those visits was to gather information about those local networks, and conditions in the area covered by multiple networks.

He was lying about that.

He lied because I asked him to.

Hooray for me, I am a lying sack of shit.

Anyway, we liars had work to do.

The wormhole emerged a bit early, and we couldn't risk going through too soon, so we waited a nerve-wracking three minutes before I ordered the pilots to take us through. Skippy informed us the jump drive capacitors were jam-packed with a hundred and three percent of their theoretical maximum, and he didn't think he could squeeze in another electron. There was risk in overcharging the capacitors, but we would appreciate having the extra power available if we had to perform multiple jumps in rapid succession.

Every other system aboard the ship was operating as well as they could, given that our battlecruiser, as usual, needed to be taken offline for a major refit. That was on my To-Do list, right behind investigating why there was always an odd number of socks when laundry was delivered to my cabin. Seriously, what happens to the fourth sock? I don't wear three socks at a time. Well, not recently. When I was at Fort Drum with the 10th Mountain, I sometimes used a third sock to protect my, you know, family jewels while we did PT on freezing cold mornings. But that was a long time ago. Now, I dropped an even number of socks into the basket, and an odd number came back. Do my socks try to run away? Are a bunch of them hiding somewhere inside the ship, huddled together in an air duct? Are they waiting for an opportunity to escape the ship? Are they plotting against me? Or maybe, instead of a sock going missing, I am actually getting *more* socks. Maybe a Mommy sock and a Daddy sock love each other *very much*, and they do the Wild Thing in the laundry basket. Or perhaps cloning is involved.

Why am I rambling on about *socks*?

Like I said, nervous.

Skippy's avatar gave me the secret signal, by glancing at his wrist as if he was wearing a watch. Clearing my throat, I tried to project calm confidence in my voice. "Mister Shepard, take us through, if you please."

That drew another side-eye from Simms, she was checking whether I was off my meds or something. Shepard didn't reply, I could see the amused grin on his face.

Hopefully, he would still be amused when the operation was over.

Because the stakes couldn't be higher.

Valkyrie came through the event horizon, and seconds later an alarm sounded, as the ship was swept by an active sensor pulse. As Skippy's senses recovered from the distortion effect of the wormhole, he told us what he was seeing, feeding the data to the main display. "A pair of sensor platforms are within detection range," he warned.

That was the problem with having three wormholes within a quarter lightyear bubble. It was practical for the senior species to saturate the area with sensor platforms. Those platforms were not supported to have offensive capabilities like weapons or damping fields, and each of the senior species regularly checked, to be sure the other side wasn't cheating by hiding weapons in their platforms.

"Skippy," I asked, "are those platforms a problem for us?"

"No. And I'm not detecting any ships within weapons range. We're clear."

Maybe the bad guys were waiting to ambush any human ship coming into the cluster, but thanks to Skippy screwing with the wormhole we went through, the bad guys would be waiting in the wrong place. According to the local network, a wormhole had not emerged at our location for over seventy thousand years, so the senior species were caught flat-footed by our little trick.

"OK. Jump option alpha, engage."

We jumped close to the designated negotiation site, near the center of the wormhole cluster. The message to UNEF Command specified that ships from Earth were to approach through the wormhole that was located near the border or

Maxolhx/Rindhalu space. So, we didn't do that, we came in through the wormhole that connected deep in spider territory. We were also supposed to perform a series of short jumps, to be scanned by the sensor platforms, before receiving permission to jump into the designated zone for discussions.

We didn't do that either.

Valkyrie jumped in outside the designated zone, about three lightminutes away. None of us were surprised to find another sensor platform within six lightseconds, nor was it surprising to detect one Maxolhx and two Rindhalu ships within thirty lightseconds of our position. Passive sensors revealed a space station at the heart of the zone designated for negotiations, with two battleships nearby; one from the Maxolhx Hegemony and one from the Rindhalu Communal Gathering. Yeah, that's what the spiders called their society, not that it made any difference to us.

There were possibly, likely, more ships in and near the zone, wrapped in stealth fields. We didn't care about that either.

What we did care about was that one of the three Elder wormholes was currently open, about two lightseconds from the space station. It was scheduled to be open there for another eighteen minutes, its softly glowing event horizon bathing the area with a pale light. Part of our timing, when setting up the operation, depended on that wormhole being open right there and then.

"Skippy?" I had one eye on the clock counting down on the main display. "Do you see any reason we shouldn't proceed?"

"That depends. Are you ready to kick *ass*, Joe?"

"I can't wait, Skippy," although the clock was telling me we had a few seconds to spare. To stall for time, I called out, "Bilby, what do you think? Is the ship ready?"

"Oh, Dude, like, I think this is *all kinds* of crazy," our ship's AI drawled. "But, like Skippy said, we're ready for whatever gnarly shit you have planned. One way or the other, this is gonna be *epic*."

"Good. That's, good. Thank you." Skippy's avatar did the thing again where he glanced at an imaginary watch on his wrist, as a signal to me. This time, I saw Simms's eyes narrow, like she noticed something suspicious. "Shepard, take us in. Jump option Delta, engage."

Our arrival was many levels of surprise to the senior species. They had no warning of our approach, no signal from the picket ships stationed at the regular emergence points. They didn't expect a human ship to be there so quickly, likely they expected us primitive monkeys to argue about what to do, until we had no choice.

And they didn't expect our distinctive battlecruiser, the fearsome ghost ship.

Or maybe they did, but seeing *Valkyrie* had to be a shock anyway.

Standing up from the chair, I was joined by Simms. My hands were up, not in a gesture of surrender, but of peace.

No, that was another lie. Damn, it's like I got a big bag of lies on sale, and had to use them before they expired.

Technically, I had to use the lies before *we* expired.

"This is General Bishop. We are here to talk," I announced. "No shooting, just talking."

It was no surprise to me that four Maxolhx ships dropped stealth to our portside, and an equal number of Rindhalu warships suddenly unmasked to starboard. Counting the two battleships that hadn't been in stealth, there were ten senior-species warships, against our one battlecruiser that was still overdue for a major refit. That was better odds than the time we jumped into a trap, but I didn't like our chances if we had to fight. Surely both sides had more ships than we could see.

If it came to a fight, we had already lost anyway.

"We are listening," a voice responded. The translator identified the speaker as a rotten kitty.

"That's good, thank you. Can we hear from the Rindhalu also?"

After a pause, a different voice spoke ponderously, as if talking was too much effort. "In this matter, the Maxolhx may speak for us, human."

"OK," I exchanged a look with Simms. That was unexpected. The spiders letting the Maxolhx take charge of the discussions? What did that mean for us?

What the hell, it wouldn't change what I would say, the only thing I could say. The display showed another six Maxolhx ships appearing, and eight more Rindhalu. As long as the numbers on each side were roughly equal, we didn't have to worry about either of the bad guys trying to destroy *Valkyrie* and take Skippy. "Wow," I looked from one side of the display to the other. "That's a *lot* of ships you have out there. Uh, I'm sorry, but we didn't bring enough snacks for everyone."

"Human," the kitty's voice spat. "You are wasting time, and we are *not* amused. Are you prepared to accept our terms?"

"Well, sort of. We made a few modifications to your proposal, and we have a counteroffer."

"The key terms of our offer are *not* negotiable."

"Well, yes, we understand that. We are proposing minor changes."

"What is your counteroffer?"

"Let's see, uh," I held a tablet in front of me and pretended to read it, while keeping one eye on the clock that was counting down. "The first of your demands is that all humans pull back to Earth, including from Paradise, and our secure site outside the galaxy. Yeah," I shook my head. "We're not doing that. Giving up our starships, our advanced technology, the codes to Elder weapons, and Skippy? Nope, we're not doing that either. Your offer just to 'reduce the impact' of the cloud at Earth? That's a non-starter. You-"

"Bishop!" The kitty yowled. "We will not-"

"Hey, *shithead*. Shut your mouth and listen to me. Here is *our* proposal: You clean up the cloud at Earth. All of it. Then, you and the spiders stop interfering with clients who want to ally with us, and who want to break away from your coalitions. You cease any and all attacks against humans and against our allies. We keep our starships, our technology, our bases away from Earth, we keep control of our Elder weapons, and we will pull our people off Paradise on our own schedule.

Also, we are keeping Skippy. If he wants to stay with us, I mean, he makes his own decisions."

"You monkeys are filthy and ignorant, Joe," Skippy sighed. "But, I find your whacky antics to be amusing. I'll stay a Pirate, if you don't mind."

"Happy to have you aboard, Skippy," I gave him a thumbs up. "In summary, we're not agreeing to any of the shit you proposed. You get *nothing*. So, shitheads," I looked back into the virtual camera. "What do you think of *our* proposal?"

"Ha, ha, ha," the rotten kitty laughed slowly, and I'm not ashamed to say it sent a chill of fear up my spine. "There is a difference between bravery and foolishness, human. Your use of *our* weapons against us is over. The fact that you had to steal our weapons reveals that you have no such capability of your own. If you had significant destructive power, you would have used it, rather than come here. We say '*No*' to your proposal."

"We also," a spider spoke, "say '*No*'."

"Human, is that all you have to say?" The rotten kitty continued.

"Well," I shrugged, "if you refuse our proposal, I guess there isn't much to talk about," the counter on the main display was approaching zero. "I *do* have an observation." Stepping forward, I peered at the chart on the display, which showed the warships around us, the open wormhole nearby, and the probable current location of the other two wormholes in the cluster. Taking a breath for dramatic effect, and to calm my nerves, I plastered a fake smile on my face. "This is a nice wormhole network you've got here. It'd be a *shame* if anything were to happen to it." I paused. "If you know what I mean."

"That would be a shame, Joe," Skippy agreed, shaking his head sadly.

Wiping off my fake smile, I glared into the camera. "Hey, you got insurance, right?"

"Oh, Joe," Skippy snickered. "They'd be crazy not to have insurance."

"Well, if you cute little kitties and spiders do need wormhole network insurance, I know a guy. Better make a deal fast, though, before something *bad* happens to the network. If you know what I mean."

"You are lying!" the Maxolhx growled.

"Oh, man," I shook my head. "You are *so* fucking clueless. You know we *broke* an Elder wormhole, right? You know we *moved* wormholes. You saw that we can turn wormholes on and off, to prevent you from interfering with our Alien Legion. But, now you don't believe we can crash the network? Burn the whole fucking thing down?"

"You *lie*!" The kitty roared at me.

"Really? Let's see about that. Skippy, do your thing," I snapped my fingers, just as the clock counted down to zero.

And-

Nothing happened.

Nothing.

Wait.

Oof.

Crap.

I forgot what a pain-in-the-ass the slow speed of light is.

Technically, something *did* happen when I snapped my fingers.

We just didn't see it until two seconds later.

When the event horizon of the closest wormhole blinked out.

The bridge of *Valkyrie* was utterly silent, so the audible gasps we heard were from the aliens on the other end of the call.

"In case you're wondering, we just *crashed* the entire wormhole network within four thousand lightyears from here. *All* of it. Every wormhole across that distance just shut down at the same time. I suggest you send ships to verify the status of the other two wormholes in this cluster. Don't worry, we can wait for you. Skippy, did we bring enough snacks to wait for a while?"

"Yes, Joe," he chuckled.

"Hey, you out there. Are you listening?"

They didn't answer, not verbally. But four ships from each side jumped away.

"I'll take that as a 'Yes'," I grinned, and that time I didn't need to fake it.

Seven of the eight ships were back within forty minutes to report. They must have frantically jumped around the area, checking whether the three wormholes had only changed position.

Spoiler alert: if that's what they hoped, they were destined for disappointment.

"Well?" I demanded, while chewing a bag of Funyuns as obnoxiously as possible. Chewing the Funyuns, not the bag. I mean, that would be stupid. Really, Funyuns were not my favorite. I guess they're OK, if they were the last snack left on Earth. It was my fault for not specifying my snack preference, before Skippy ordered a bot to bring a basket of goodies to the bridge.

Eating while on the bridge was normally against regulations, I made an exception this time.

"Hey! *Shitheads*! Both of you. What did you find? No, wait," I put a hand over my eyes. "Let me use my amazing powers to guess. Hmm, I'm getting a message. It says…. That all three wormholes here are *gone*?" I pretended to be shocked, opening my eyes wide. "Gosh, how could that have happened?"

"It's a mystery for sure, Joe," Skippy said, while glancing at his imaginary watch. "*I* certainly have no idea how this could have happened. It's such a shame."

"It is," I agreed. "Good thing *we* bought insurance, huh? Maybe I should do that finger-snap thing again?"

"It's worth a try, Joe."

Snap.

And…

Nothing happened.

Abso-freakin'-lutely nothing.

Damn it.

"Skippy?"

"Jeez Louise, Joe. Don't be so impatient. The insurance company is still processing the claim. Plus," he added under his breath, "they're probably still pissed about all the dropships you've crashed."

"Hey, those were not-"

"Yeah, yeah, it's never the driver's fault. All I know is, *I* wasn't flying the damned things when- Oop! *There* it is!"

On the display was the glorious, familiar dim glow of an Elder wormhole. The navigation overlay tagged it as four point six lightseconds away, and it was not the same wormhole that was near our position originally.

That didn't matter.

"Yoo-hoo, *shitheads*," I called. "How did you like that little demonstration?"

They didn't answer.

"What's the matter? Cat got your tongue?" I teased, which was stupid because that reference wouldn't make any sense through a translator. It made our crew laugh, so totally worth it anyway. "In case you're too stupid to understand what just happened, I'll try to talk slowly. Here's the deal *we* are offering to you. These terms are also not negotiable. You clean up the cloud at Earth, and do not attack Earth, or humans anywhere, ever again. You leave us alone, *and* don't interfere with our allies. In return, we don't screw with you or your interests. To be clear, if a species out there wants to sign a mutual-defense treaty with us, they are no longer *your* interest. If you two assholes want to fight each other, go ahead. But you're not forcing others to fight for you, got it? So, that's our offer. *Or*, if you don't accept our special limited-time offer, we will selectively crash the local wormhole networks in your territory. Think about it: no more quick and easy long-distance travel for either of you. You will be trapped in your own territory, your star systems isolated from the galaxy. Sure, you still have long-range starships, but even your star carriers will take weeks, even months to travel between your important star systems. By the way," I glared into the virtual camera. "You don't *both* have to agree. But, if one of you assholes agrees to our terms, and the other of you *doesn't*, well, one of you will be *screwed*," I laughed. "Take your time thinking about it, but don't take *too* long. Like I said, this is a limited-time offer."

"Don't forget about the steak knives, Joe," Skippy prompted me. "The first group to agree to our terms gets a free set of steak knives."

"I don't really think they want steak knives, Skippy."

"Oh. Then, how about an autographed poster of *me*?"

"Did you hear that," I turned my focus back to the camera. "Who could say 'No' to an offer like that? Listen, we understand that nobody here has authority to sign an agreement, and you need to verify that we really did crash wormhole networks all over this part of the galaxy. That's understandable." Skippy said the interruption of wormholes across four thousand lightyears would be obvious, even after the fact. Heavily-traveled wormholes in that area would have reports from ships that *saw* the wormholes shut down abruptly. For confirmation that other wormholes had also crashed, all the senior species needed to do was use their handy Wayback machines. Like, jump to where photons from that event had traveled to from the subject wormhole, and *see* it happening again. "Because we are generous," I continued, "we'll give you four months, that is one hundred and twenty Earth days, to notify us that you accept our terms. That is a *hard* deadline. Just leave a message for us at a Jeraptha relay station. Oh, as an incentive, if either of you fail to agree within the four month deadline, we will shut down one of the strategically important local networks in the territory of that species, for one month. Give you a taste of your dark, lonely future. We will crash *more* local networks in your territory, one for every additional month that you fail to agree to our terms."

There was no response.

"Hello? Is anybody out there? All I need is a 'Yes' that you understood what I said."

"Yes," the Maxolhx growled.

"Yes," a spider said with what might have been a weary sigh.

"Outstanding. OK, then we are out of here. Do not think of trying to interfere with us. You both know how well that worked for you last time."

In a prearranged signal, I looked at Shepard and gave him a thumbs up.

He pressed a button. *Valkyrie* jumped away.

CHAPTER THIRTY SIX

My hands were shaking, and I felt nauseatingly chilled by the time I reached my cabin. Barely inside the door, which slid closed behind me so fast it clipped my heels, I dropped to my knees and ralphed on the deck. "Oooh," wiping my mouth with the back of a hand, I groaned. "Sorry, Skippy," I rolled on my left side and tucked into a ball, shivering. "Couldn't make it to the bathroom."

"Ah," he sniffed. "Compared to how filthy you monkeys make every surface aboard the ship, it's hardly noticeable. A bot is on the way to clean up. Um, I suggest that you, get in the shower, if you know what I mean."

"A shower? I'm not in the mood for jokes, Skippy."

"No joke. You puked on your uniform top, better get that off for a fresh one. And your body temperature is dropping, you need to warm up."

"I'll get under a blanket."

"Hot water has a greater thermal mass, it will warm you up faster. Plus, you stink of nervous sweat. You still need to sell this confident commander bullshit, right?"

"Yeah." A low door on the bottom of the opposite bulkhead opened, and a cleaning bot rolled out. Pushing myself to my feet, I got out of its way, so it could clean up the deck.

Skippy was right. Standing in the shower, letting hot water cascade over me, I felt better. When my skin was turning pink from the heat, I shut the water off and dried myself with a towel.

"You want to talk about it, Joe?"

"Sure. Holy *shit*, Skippy."

"When we get back to Earth, maybe you should think about playing in a Texas Hold 'Em tournament. I was seriously impressed by your poker face."

"Thanks."

"Just don't, you know, puke on the table during the game."

"I didn't need to ralph until it was *over*. I was running on adrenaline."

"I noticed. *WOW*. Joe, was that, like, the greatest bluff, *in the history of bluffing*?"

"Shmaybe, Skippy. Shmaybe."

Uh, maybe I should explain.

We were bluffing.

About the whole crashing-the-wormhole-network thing.

Yeah.

Only Skippy and I knew about it.

Simms, Smythe, the crew, and most importantly, the kitties and spiders, all thought Skippy actually did simultaneously crash the networks across four thousand lightyears.

He didn't.

Like he told Perkins, back when *she* suggested he threaten to turn off the system of Elder wormholes that allows starships to travel rapidly across the galaxy, he actually could not do that.

So, we faked it.

Skippy instructed the local network to conduct a deep diagnostic test on itself. Before we arrived at the rendezvous site, we flew around to visit the six local networks that surrounded the network with the triple-wormhole cluster. He instructed those networks to also perform a self-check, with a delay.

Timing is everything.

Our timing had to be precise, so all networks in the area *appeared* to shut down at the exact same time. As if Skippy had the ability to send commands instantaneously, faster than light. Which, to be clear, he doesn't. Not over that distance.

That's why, the first time I snapped my fingers, I had one eye on the count-down clock on the main display. The finger snap happened at the moment the networks were scheduled to take their wormholes offline, while they performed a diagnostic test.

The second finger-snap didn't require timing quite so precise, I just had to do it *before* any of the affected wormholes completed their diagnostic tests and rebooted, so it looked like *we* turned those wormholes back on.

Get it?

Yeah, holy *shit*, huh?

That's why I felt nauseous afterward, coming down off an adrenaline high.

Anyway, we did it.

Hopefully.

For sure, we impressed the aliens at the rendezvous site. Now they had to go back home to inform their leadership about our threat to crash the wormhole network. Hopefully, by then most of the galaxy would know something very unusual and very, *very bad* had happened to Elder wormholes across a wide swath of the galaxy.

To sell the con, because that's what it was, we were relying on our reputation. The intelligent species of the galaxy already knew about the awesome things Skippy could do, what he had done. Like breaking an Elder wormhole. So, they were primed and ready to believe he really could crash the entire system of wormholes, all across the galaxy.

Like I said, only Skippy and I knew the truth.

Yes, that was me doing something I promised I wouldn't do, concealing information from my crew. *Lying* to them.

I had to.

If any of them knew the truth, and they were ever captured by the enemy, that would be a disaster for Earth. Plus, when I was making bogus threats, Simms was standing right next to me, with Smythe behind the command chair. They had to sell the bluff, by projecting confidence. If they knew the truth, maybe their facial expressions wouldn't be quite so convincing. The senior species were undoubtedly analyzing our body language, closely examining the skin around our eyes, the sides of our mouths, even our body temperature. Skippy maybe could have edited the video in real-time, but it was better for the crew to *believe*. To believe that Skippy the Magnificent was even more awesome than they, or anyone else in the galaxy, imagined.

Crap.

Now he is *really* going to be insufferable.

"Hey, uh," I asked. "Do we know if it worked? The other local networks, I mean. Did they go into self-check mode and shut down?"

"I don't *know*, Joe."

"Oh. I was hoping you could ask the local network at the rendezvous site to ping the surrounding networks. Get the info that way."

"Yes, I could have done that."

"Oh, for- Then why didn't-"

"Because the local network controller was *busy*, dumdum. It completed its diagnostic check, determined there *was* a potential problem, and instituted a fix. Then it had to restart every freakin' wormhole under its control, and coordinate with the local networks on the other ends of those wormholes, if they extended beyond the local boundary. Doing that takes *time*, and after it got the wormholes near us restarted, it was still working to get all the others stable. If I had pinged it then, it would have told me to wait. It probably would have told me to shut the hell up, to be truthful."

"OK. Sorry."

"I would have *told* you if I had that information."

"Right. So, we can go to one of the other local networks to check."

"Yes, we could do that. *Or*, we could just ping any relay station in the galaxy. Information that wormholes disappeared across a huge area of the galaxy, has got to be at the *top* of everyone's news feed. I mean, unless Taco Bell just announced a burrito-chalupa combo."

"Good point. All right," I walked over to the closet, and plucked a fresh uniform top off the rack. People would know I changed my top, because the old one had stains from where I wiped my fingers on my sleeves after eating Funyuns. "Thanks. I'll go back to the bridge." Looking in the mirror, which was really a wall display set to mirror mode, I straightened my top and adjusted it so the buttons lined up with the pants zipper. My hair was not quite dry, people might think I splashed water on my face.

Cool.

We got away with it.

The Greatest Bluff Of All Time.

I still can't believe it.

OK, I'm sure there are plenty of questions out there. So, let's do a Q and A. *Not* an Ask Me Anything, the questions are restricted to the massive bluff we just successfully ran.

The participants will be: Any Normal Sane Person, hereinafter referred to as 'You'. And a well-known reckless knucklehead, hereinafter referred to as 'Joe Bishop' or just 'Me'.

Ready?

You: Wait!

Me: I'm waiting.

You: What about, you know, your arch enemy?

Me: If you mean shoelaces, this conversation is over.

You: Damn it. Um, let's go with Plan B. Your other arch enemy, the Law Of Unintended Consequences.

Me: What about it?

You: Aren't you risking a major, *major* smackdown, by massively screwing with wormholes that were created by the Elders?

Me: The answer is 'No'.

You: Can we get a *little* more detail about that 'No'?

Me: OK, fine. We are not at risk, because I was smart enough to think about that. I asked Skippy whether prompting multiple local networks into self-check mode, would disrupt the power flow that the Elders need. He told me it would not.

You: O.M.G.

Me: Happy now?

You: Dude, you seriously trusted the survival of humanity, and perhaps every living being in the galaxy, TO AN ABSENT-MINDED BEER CAN?

Me: Yes, I did that.

You: One more question, please. ARE YOU OUT OF YOUR FREAKIN' MIND?

ME: Again, the answer is 'No'.

You: We're going to need more than that.

Me: I asked Skippy about it *twice*.

You: Oh, that makes it all better.

Me: Was that sarcasm?

You: Of course not.

Me: Come on, I *heard* you roll your eyes.

You: {Sobbing} We're doomed.

Me: No, we are not. When I asked Skippy, I did not just take his word for it. I asked *how* he could know that. I asked if he had a way to monitor power flow, and how he could be certain that putting a local network controller into self-check mode would not trigger a catastrophic event, like interrupting the power flow for even a nanosecond. Or even reducing the power flow one tiny little bit.

You: OK, and?

Me: He explained that the event horizons of wormholes do not really need to emerge into our local spacetime to feed power into higher dimensions. The power actually comes from something he calls 'bubble energy', although he also said that description is inaccurate and hopelessly dumbed down for monkeys.

You: Ummm-

Me: You're wondering, if that is true, then why do wormholes bother coming into our lowly spacetime at all?

You: Something like that.

Me: I had the same question, because I am also smart.

You: Yeah, that's what we were going to say.

Me: Asswipe. The answer is that the Elders repurposed their existing wormhole network, when they needed something to feed power up to, wherever the hell they are. Skippy thinks they were kind of in a hurry, either because of a looming threat from outside the galaxy, or because the timing of them ascending was tricky. So, they didn't alter the base operation of the wormhole network, just added a power flow feature. The event horizons of wormholes have to pass through our local spacetime anyway, while they cycle their way from, uh, one level to another.

You: Sounds like you don't actually understand any of that.

Me: Do *you*?

You: *We* are not responsible for saving the world.

Me: Good point. Anyway, Skippy knows that the self-check feature of a wormhole network controller does not affect the system's power flow, because he tested one of them.

You: He *WHAT*?

Me: I had the same reaction. He did it without telling me.

You: Haven't you learned not to trust that beer can?

Me: Oof. It worked out OK, so-

You: We, we don't even know what to say about that.

Me: Listen, it was just a tiny test. Skippy couldn't just order a network controller to go into diagnostic mode. So, he had to break it first, to-

You: He *WHAT*?

Me: Do you want to hear the story?

You: Yes. Please. Although we might have to curl up in a ball and cry when this is over.

Me: I'll join you. What Skippy did was to sort of hack into a network controller- No. He can't actually do that; he doesn't understand the controller AI's internal architecture. So, he actually screwed with its sensor feed. Made it *think* it had a problem. Then, he helpfully contacted the controllers to say he might have noticed a problem. The controller AIs panicked, and threw themselves into a self-check routine. With the six local networks farther away, he left his message in a queue, on a timer. All the network controllers we wanted to crash got the message at the same time, and they all reacted the same way, following their programming.

You: Hmm. That was smart.

Me: See?

You: We didn't mean *you*.

Me: Oh, shut up.

You: Um, aren't those network controllers going to be pissed, when they realize there was no problem?

Me: No. As far as they were concerned, there *was* a problem.

You: Is Skippy sure about that?

Me: Yes.

You: How can he be sure?

Me: You might not know this, but Skippy is awesome.

You: We might have heard something like that.

Me: It's true. He is way smarter than any network controller AI. Is that all? I have to go.

You: Wait! One last question, please.

Me: Just one.

You: The Elders might have been forced to leave this level of existence, because of a threat from outside the galaxy.

Me: That is one theory, yes. What about it?

You: Doesn't that scare the *shit* out of you?

Me: Why do you think I don't sleep well?

You: Um, we figured your mattress is lumpy?

Me: Goodbye.

Following Skippy's very sensible suggestion, we pinged a relay station that belonged to the Bosphuraq. There were other relay stations we could have gotten to more quickly, but we weren't in a huge hurry, and the others were not along our course back to the Jaguar wormhole. I don't want to sound casual about it, we were not in a hurry because it takes time for information to propagate across the system of relay stations. If we pinged a station too soon, it might not yet have the current information we wanted.

Our journey back to familiar stars was longer than usual, because Skippy could not screw with wormholes in any of the local networks that had temporarily gone offline. The trip to the rendezvous point took two and a half days. Getting back took *nine* freakin' days. There was a whole lot of tedious jumping-recharging-jumping, to get us to a wormhole that connected in the direction we wanted to go. We had an advantage in that we could go directly through any wormhole along the way; our enemies were likely very hesitant about entering any wormhole in that area. We had made the two senior species wary of the wormhole system.

Screw 'em.

Skippy was right. Sadly, what he was right about was *not* Taco Bell announcing an exciting new combo, darn it. He was correct that multiple species had noticed Elder wormholes across a wide area of the galaxy temporarily shutting down, and that they all shut down at the same time. No one could explain it. Everyone across the galaxy was terrified that the ancient wormhole system was becoming unstable, and governments were shifting warships closer to strategically important star systems, so they wouldn't be trapped far from where they were needed.

Also, the entire definition of 'strategically important' had changed.

For millennia, a star system was valuable, because it had one or more planets that could comfortably support whatever species wanted to live there. You might think that comfort was not a factor, but people vote with their feet, or paws or claws or tentacles, or whatever appendages they use for walking. Planets with crappy climates generally did not develop large populations, because nobody *wanted* to live there. The exception was if a planet was in a star system close to a wormhole that linked to somewhere important. In that case, the planet with the crappy weather could also become important, and the government would install substantial defenses, establish a fleet servicing base, and possibly station warships there. Large numbers of people would move there for government jobs or the business opportunities.

Suddenly, governments had to consider that, if the galaxy's system of wormholes became unusable, being located near a wormhole was no longer important. Habitable star systems that were within star carrier range of other habitable star systems would become immensely valuable, while densely populated worlds that were far from any other planets controlled by that species, would become isolated and wither away.

In addition to making every star-faring species reconsider their idea of which star systems were worth defending, our bluff had two unexpected results. It-

No, an Unexpected Result is not the same as an Unintended Consequence.

OK, sure, maybe *technically* it is the same thing. But one is good and the other is bad.

Oof. OK, that is not technically true either. But nobody complains about Unintended Consequences that are good, right? I sure don't.

Anyway, the first result we didn't expect was, an almost complete cessation of offensive military operations, all across the galaxy. That made sense, once we thought about it. Governments did not like having major fleet elements and thousands of ground troops far from home bases, when there was fear those vital assets might be stranded in hostile territory if wormholes were not available. We probably didn't consider that ahead of time, because humans had not been using the Elder wormhole network for long. Other species had relied on that network for as long as they could remember, it was a fact of life as stable as the stars in the sky. Like stars that occasionally burned out or exploded, sometimes both, wormholes turned off and on in their regular and still-unexplained shifts. But, like stars, Elder wormholes were always there, somewhere. Star-faring species found it terrifying to think they could be confined to a bubble representing the distance their star carriers could travel without breaking down. For third-tier clients like the Ruhar and Kristang, who did not have star carriers, they had to face the fact that they might be confined to their star systems, period. Unless they were lucky to have a friendly and more advanced species nearby who would give them a ride between stars, or they could develop their own long-range jump drives.

Good luck with that.

Even the Maxolhx were pulling their ships back closer to home, including task forces that might have harassed the Alien Legion.

That was good news.

And, as far as we knew, the Maxolhx leadership had not yet officially heard that the Merry Band of Pirates were the reason those wormholes temporarily shut down. Damn, I would love to be there when their asshole leaders heard *that* fun news.

So, our little stunt had already caused massive disruptions throughout the galaxy.

The second unexpected thing to happen was that, even before anyone knew that we were the source of the wormhole disruption, some people were already blaming the event on us primitive humans. They didn't actually think we caused it directly, they feared that all the screwing around we had done over the years had resulted in the system becoming unstable. Second and third tier clients were asking whether the leaders of their coalitions should accept the changed circumstances, and cut a deal with the upstart humans, before we filthy monkeys did something stupid and ruined the entire wormhole system for everyone.

The Bosphuraq, bolder than most, or simply more pissed off at their asshole patrons, sent a message to their ambassador to the Maxolhx. The ambassador requested a meeting with the Maxolhx, on the local space station where the senior species grudgingly met with representatives of their lowly clients. With as much respect as he could manage, the ambassador stated the position of his government: the Maxolhx should stop playing dangerous games with the primitive yet powerful humans, and focus on strengthening the defenses of their coalition.

The Maxolhx listened patiently to the ambassador, before tossing him out an airlock.

Surprisingly, though a senior government position had just become open, none of the Bosphuraq on site were eager to become the next ambassador. Perhaps the Bosphuraq are not the most ambitious type of people.

"Anything other interesting news, Skippy?"

"Jeez, Joe, this relay station is packed with information. Do you want to know something specific?"

"Yeah. Have the kitties or spiders tried to contact us yet?" I knew it was too early for either side to give us an answer.

"I'm still sorting through the data," Skippy was peeved at me. "Damn, can you ask a question I might actually have an answer for?"

"Sorry. Guess I'm over-eager about it."

"Be patient."

"Right. Because patience is one of my core skills."

"Ugh. Maybe I should fall into a wormhole, and shut down the network behind me."

"Then you'd miss karaoke night," I teased.

"Ooh, good point."

The next day, we pinged a Jeraptha relay station, and Skippy *did* find a message from the spiders, to us. They wanted to talk, to meet.

I was instantly wary of an ambush. If the Rindhalu were going to agree to our terms, that was amazingly fast for them. It was also quick for them to put together a trap, but maybe they had been planning an ambush for a while, and meeting to avoid us shutting down the wormhole network was just a convenient excuse.

How to assure the spiders did not spring an ambush on us? We thought about that for a while, and came up with several options, then wargamed the three best options. The simplest move would to be to locate a small Rindhalu ship traveling on its own, and set up our own ambush. That plan got discarded, because a random group of spiders wouldn't have authority to make a deal with us. We needed to hear whatever the official delegation of spiders had to say, or we didn't need to talk with them at all.

When we had a plan, we sent a reply to the spiders, along with very specific instructions for a meeting.

CHAPTER THIRTY SEVEN

A single Rindhalu cruiser arrived at the rendezvous point exactly on time, and within four hundred meters of the target coordinates. Skippy was not impressed. "Ah, that ship jumped in at a lightminute away first, to check whether we had a bunch of ships waiting to blast it to dust. So, they didn't jump very far. It's *easy* to be accurate when you're not moving a long distance," he sniffed.

"Great. Signal them to come through the wormhole in a dropship. Just *one* dropship."

"Okey-dokey. Transmitting now."

Requiring the spiders to limit their delegation to a single dropship was not our only security measure. That dropship had to come through an Elder wormhole, which would close behind it, cutting off support from the cruiser. Pretty smart, huh? Of course, we had to tell the spiders where to meet us, and they knew it was near one end of a wormhole. So, how did I know they didn't have a bunch of ships waiting to ambush us, at the other end of that wormhole?

The answer is, I did not care.

Oh, I did *care*, I sure as hell wanted to know if they were going to try double-crossing us. What I should have said is, I was not worried about it.

OK, you may ask whether I was not worried because I'm an idiot, or because I had been drinking heavily.

Neither, actually.

I didn't have to worry, because I am smart.

Oh, shut up.

The smart thing I did was, suggest to Skippy that he screw with that wormhole, so the end near the Rindhalu connected not to the usual other endpoint, but to an endpoint of a remote wormhole that was deep in Esselgin territory. That's where we were waiting, and there is no way the spiders could have known ahead of time where their dropship would go, when it transited the wormhole.

So, I imagine when the dropship came through, the spiders looked around and asked where the *hell* they were. Then, their navigation system looked at a star map, and informed them they were a *long* way from where they expected to be. Right before the wormhole closed behind them, leaving them alone in deep space.

Alone, until our massive battlecruiser jumped in fifty thousand kilometers away. We sent a probe to scan the dropship for hazards, warning the Rindhalu aboard not to try blocking our scans. Skippy announced everything checked out, so I allowed the dropship to approach the designated docking bay. Finally, I was going to meet a spider. It made me-

What? You have a question? Am I *insane*, you ask?

No, I am not insane.

Yes, we just showed the most powerful species in the galaxy that we had the ability to change wormhole connections. Is there a teeny, tiny, non-zero chance they could use the data they collected, to figure out how *they* could manipulate wormholes?

According to Skippy, no. He screwed with the wormhole from our end, there wasn't any sensor data on the other end for the spiders to work with.

Actually, demonstrating that we can alter wormhole connections is a *good* thing. We want the whole galaxy to know we can do that. Showing the spiders our power accomplishes two things. It will make the galaxy fear us. And it will help sell the story that we have the ability to shut down the entire wormhole network.

Which, as I said before, we can't actually do.

But nobody knows that, so please don't tell anyone.

The dropship approached, and Skippy took direct control, guiding it into a docking bay.

Man, I thought the spiders were creepy, ugly things back when I only saw them in videos. Up close and personal, they made my hair stand up in a visceral reaction, some base human instinct of revulsion. But, the Jeraptha sort of looked like oversized beetles, and they didn't make my skin crawl. Sure, I wouldn't want to suddenly meet a Jeraptha in a dark alley, but I actually *liked* the beetles. The spiders were different, nobody actually liked them, and they were OK with that.

Seeing them for real, with even the smallest of the three taller than me, I reminded myself they were not really spiders at all, that was my internal reaction. Screw that. *I'm* in charge of me and how I feel about things. The Rindhalu wanted their appearance to throw me off my game, intimidate me, goad me into making mistakes. Glancing left and right, I could see my crew were having the same creeped-out feeling. Even Smythe was struggling, his expression was carefully neutral, but his lips were drawn in a tight line.

"Hey," I leaned toward my STAR team leader, and pointed at the spider in the center, its bulbous body suspended on spindly, multi-jointed legs. "See? That's what happens when you skip Leg Day at the gym."

Smythe didn't laugh, he didn't break discipline to that extent, but his mouth curled up in a smile, and from behind me someone snorted a suppressed guffaw.

"You find us, *amusing*?" The spider in the center asked. I'm not an expert on Rindhalu body language, but it did not expect us lowly humans to *laugh* at it.

Crossing my arms, I cocked my head. "Amusing, sure, but mostly I find you to be just pathetic."

"It is difficult," the spider was careful to add a haughty disdain into its speech. "To take humans seriously as peers, when you cannot even protect your homeworld."

Ouch. That hurt. Or, it would have hurt as the spider intended, if I hadn't been prepared for that particular insult. It was obvious they would throw the status of Earth in my face, and I was ready. "Yeah. Hey, remind me, how long has it been since the Maxolhx took *your* homeworld away from you?"

The spider stiffened. Regardless of the species, I understood *that* body language. "That is not-"

"Earth may get a bit chilly before we get rid of that cloud, but what happened to *your* homeworld? Kinda crispy, huh? Wow, I bet it must have been a nice place once. Before, you *losers* gave up and ran away. Hey, I wonder if the Maxolhx sell tickets to your homeworld? You know, to let tourists see the charred bones of your civilization."

"Human," the spider fumed, drawing itself up to full height. "You play a dangerous game."

"This isn't a *game*, asshole," I snapped back at it. "That's the whole problem right there: you think this *is* a game. You and the Maxolhx have been playing power politics for millennia, forcing others to fight and die for you, while you sit safely behind your defenses and pull the strings. I have news for you: your days of being untouchable are *over*."

"Ha, ha, ha," it laughed slowly. That's what I heard through the translator in my earpiece, the actual sound of a spider laugh was like enormous pieces of rusty metal grinding against each other. Despite my pledge to not let my instincts get the better of me, I had to force my feet to stand in place rather than run away. My knees didn't get the memo, they trembled slightly. Surely the spider sensed my fear. "Ha," it continued. "You think to intimidate us? Human, you have performed cute little tricks around this galaxy, but you have never tested our defenses. The relativistic darts you took from the Maxolhx cannot harm us, our worlds are well protected against such crude weapons."

You know what is a great antidote to fear? Getting really, hugely pissed off. My knees ceased shaking and my arms dropped to my sides, my hands balled into fists. "*Riiiiight*," I sneered. "Because we have never been able to strike an impossible target. Like we can't hit a place like Argathos? Hey, the Maxolhx thought that place was impossible to hit. You might want to ask them how Argathos is right now. Spoiler alert: not so good."

"We are not impressed by your attacks against our ancient enemies. Our defensive technology is superior."

"Hey, Skippy," I looked at the ceiling. "Did you hear that? The freakin' spiders are untouchable."

His avatar appeared between me and the line of spiders. "Oh, it is *on*, baby. Challenge accepted. Name a target in Spiderland, and it will be *history*."

"Gosh, Skippy, I couldn't even begin to identify which is the most heavily-defended site in Rindhalu space, but I bet asshole over there could," I pointed at my counterpart. "How about it? What place of yours is the most impossible to hit? Before you answer, why don't you ask the Thuranin or the Maxolhx, about how we took out their impossible targets? Oh," I snapped my fingers. "That's right. They don't *know* how we blew up their most well-defended sites. They don't have a single freakin' clue *how* we did it. All they know is, those sites became superheated plasma, despite all their fancy defenses. But that's all talk. How about I arrange a demonstration for you? Name one of your toughest, most heavily-defended sites, and I'll see if we can't nuke it into oblivion."

"That will not be necessary."

"No, really," I drew myself up, on the balls of my feet, glaring at the spider. "It's no trouble at all. We would *love* to take out one of your facilities. Show the entire galaxy that the high and mighty Rindhalu aren't so invincible after all. Maybe then people will take us seriously. What do you think? How many of your planets do we need to hit, before you see us as your peers?"

"We will never accept your primitive people as our *peers*. However," it bent its legs a bit, so it didn't tower over me quite so much. "We are here to discuss *reducing* tensions between our peoples."

"You will help us get rid of the cloud that threatens our homeworld?"

"No."

I felt a flare of anger. "Then there is not much to disc-"

"Any movement toward our peoples working together, would be viewed as an extreme threat by the Maxolhx, and result in dire consequences for everyone." That is what we had been fearing all along; the two senior species fighting, and Earth getting caught in the crossfire. "Also," it continued. "We suspect you would not welcome the prospect of a large number of our ships being in your star system?"

"Uh, you are right," I admitted.

"Therefore, an offer to assist you is unlikely to be accepted. General Bishop, we are not interested in making empty gestures. The Maxolhx were rash and foolish to attack your homeworld, and they did it without informing us. We would have counselled them against angering you, for humans are young and unpredictable. We will not act to remove the cloud. However, we are willing to provide basic technical assistance, so you can perform the work yourselves. We must warn you; the process will take considerably more resources than you currently possess."

"We understand that."

"We also will warn the Maxolhx against interfering with your work to disperse the cloud. If they attempt to interfere, we will," the spider paused. "*Discourage* them."

"We would appreciate that. Is that all?"

"No. You stated that you wish to develop alliances, including with some of our clients."

"Yes. Any future alliances will not be directed *against* your people."

"Any weakening of our coalition can only be viewed as threatening our security," the spider said, raising higher on its legs.

"That is something we can discuss, but not here, not today."

"We understand."

"Great. Hey, as a gesture of our interest in good relations with your people, we have information you might find useful."

"What is that?"

"The Maxolhx are building a fleet of colony ships, to use as a safe haven beyond the galaxy. Once those ships are in position, and the occupants are in cryogenic sleep, the Maxolhx could trigger their Elder weapons. They hope to return to the galaxy in the future, when they would be the only sentient species."

"We, are not surprised," the lead spider said slowly. "You have specific information about where these colony ships are being constructed?"

"We do. Skippy?"

"Transmitting details now."

"We appreciate," the spider waited, maybe to see if that word translated properly. I nodded, and it continued. "The information. In return, we have information *you* will consider valuable."

"Like what?"

"Your allies, the Verd-kris, are in action at a Kristang world, known as Globakus."

I felt a chill. Dave Czajka was there, along with five hundred humans, and over four thousand Verd-kris troops. "What about it?"

"It has become known to us that the Thuranin stationed a task force there, which we suspect your people did not know about?"

"Shit." I didn't mean to say that aloud, it just happened.

"Joe," Skippy whispered in my ear. "We are in a bad position for getting to Globakus quickly. I can't screw with wormholes in the network in that area to create a shortcut, and the regular route requires transitioning through six wormholes. Not including going through this wormhole."

I didn't answer him. "Ambassador," I bowed slightly toward the Rindhalu, a gesture that might have been stupid. If they didn't understand human body language, they wouldn't know what I did. Worse, I might have insulted them by mistake. "We do appreciate that information." Damn it, I wanted the spider delegation gone, so *Valkyrie* could race across the galaxy.

All three spiders dipped their front legs. Either that's something they did, or they were trying to imitate my weird gesture. "General Bishop, we are sure you are very busy. We propose sending a single ship to your homeworld, to begin discussions. I trust our gesture of good faith will encourage you not to disadvantage us, by disabling the Elder wormholes we rely on?"

"Your good faith will be returned. While discussions continue, we will take no action against wormholes in your territory," I lied. The lie was not that we planned to take action, the lie was that we *could not* take action. But they didn't know that.

Skippy screwed with the wormhole again, so the spiders could fly the dropship back to their cruiser, and the dropship disappeared through the event horizon. A minute later, the rift in spacetime winked out. "Skippy," I gripped the arm rests of my command chair. "Get the wormhole open again, we are *outta* here."

"Joe, I want to ride to the rescue as much as you do, but I *have* to allow the wormhole to reset, before I can make a new connection again. Be patient for forty three minutes, please."

"Right," I ground my teeth. "Because being patient is what I do best."

CHAPTER THIRTY EIGHT

Dave Czajka hugged the ground, trying to make his mech suit as slim as possible while he waited for the gunship to roar past overhead. The ground shook as the Kristang aircraft raced in for the kill, firing maser bolts at the exposed troops on the ground. Without coverage of a stealth field, Dave had to rely on the chameleonware of the suit's outer coating, hoping it would confuse the gunship's sensors. Hoping, really, that someone else was a clearer target, because the enemy aircraft was shooting at *something*.

The pulses of maser cannon fire went from a *thump thump thump* striking the ground to a rapidly searing *bzzzzt*, and there was a thunderous explosion he felt in his chest, even through the armor.

"Fuck yeah!" A voice with an American accent shouted. "Got him! Whoa! Whoa whoa whoa stay down, he's-" The voice was cut off as the ground *heaved* and Dave felt himself lifted off the dirt for a moment, landing heavily and bashing his chin on the inside of the helmet. Something, some *things* pelted off his back, the helmet visor registering impacts but no damage.

"OK, clear," the voice said over the platoon channel, shaking with emotion. "Shit. Nothing's *clear* but, no enemy aircraft in sight."

Dave rose unsteadily to his feet, looking for the Zinger missile team and giving them a well-deserved thumbs up, for engaging the gunship while under fire. It had probably taken more than one missile to shoot down the aircraft, the rapid *bzzzzt* sound he'd heard was the gunship switching to defensive fire, in an attempt to engage incoming MANPADs.

It hadn't worked out well for the Kristang, he was grateful for that.

Nothing else about that day was worth being grateful for.

The first wave had landed without major incident, depositing Dave, Jates, and two companies of ExForce troops on the ground, along with a thousand Verd-kris. The dropships had climbed back into orbit, to take aboard the second wave.

That's when the shit hit the fan.

Somehow, from somewhere, a group of Thuranin warships jumped in, and targeted the assault carrier *Chesapeake Bay*. Escorted only by the UN Navy destroyers *Marseille*, *Boston* and *Sao Paulo*, the assault carrier had put up a good fight, waving off the approaching dropships and climbing for jump altitude.

It didn't make it.

The *Chesapeake Bay* lost power before it could jump, and the last Dave saw of the ship before its orbit carried it below the horizon, it was shot full of holes, the engineering section wreathed by the hot pink fog of vented reactor plasma. The last message they received from the *Marseille*, before communications were cut off by a harsh squeal of jamming, stated that the three UN destroyers were surrounded by much heavier Thuranin warships. Bright lights flashed in the sky, the sign of a furious space battle.

"Is everyone-" Dave started to ask, when a particularly bright flash low on the northern horizon nearly blinded him before his helmet visor darkened automatically. That had to be a starship exploding, hopefully Thuranin. Blinking to clear the spots from his eyes, he turned in the direction where Jates was standing. "Hey, Surjet. Let's get-"

"Czajka," the big alien growled. "You all right?"

"Yeah, I'm fine."

"I have good news for you. You're not going to die a virgin."

"*Virgin*? What the- Why do you say-"

Jates was pointing over Dave's right shoulder.

Dave turned, and wished he hadn't.

High in the southern sky, growing larger every second, was the burning wreckage of a starship, a big one.

It was falling right toward them.

Jates stepped forward. "Because we're *all* fucked now."

THE END

Thanks to the Beta reader crew:

Edward Burke
Terry Clements
Helen Ann Dunn
Lisa Farina
Scott Nuftul
Dan Wong

The Beta readers worked extra hard on this manuscript, which was kind of a mess when I handed it off to them. This book was written during the pandemic, and with all the other shit that occurred in the world while I was writing, it was a more of a struggle than anything else I've written. Again, a big THANK YOU to the team!

Made in the USA
Las Vegas, NV
29 November 2021

35595004R00229